BLOOD of a NOVICE

OTHER BOOKS BY DAVIS ASHURA

The Castes and the OutCastes:
A Warrior's Path
A Warrior's Knowledge
A Warrior's Penance
Omnibus Edition (only available on Kindle)
Stories for Arisa (short-story collection)

The Chronicles of William Wilde:
William Wilde and the Necrosed
William Wilde and the Stolen Life
William Wilde and the Unusual Suspects
William Wilde and the Sons of Deceit
William Wilde and the Lord of Mourning

Instrument of Omens
A Testament of Steel
Memoriwes of Prophecies

The Eternal Ephemera
Blood of a Novice

THE ETERNAL EPHEMERA

◆ Book One ◆

BLOOD of a NOVICE

DAVIS ASHURA

Cover art by Asur Misoa
Cover design by Christian Bentulan
Interior layout by STK•Kreations
Map by Rela "Kellerica" Similä at kellericamaps.com

Printed in the United States of America
Trade paperback ISBN: 979-8-8432020-2-6
Hardcover ISBN: 978-1-7329780-7-2

First Printing: 2022
DuSum Publishing, LLC

To those who dream and decide to share them.
The world is a better place because of your imaginings.

ACKNOWLEDGEMENTS

To the usual suspects, but a special thanks to Jay Jenkins. Your honesty is a treasure, even when I don't want to hear it. And to my sister, who saw what I was trying to do and helped me trim, prune, and in some sections, cut savagely until the finer book I was striving to create emerged.

I can't forget all the others who also made sure I stayed on the straight and narrow with this book. They include Edmund Milne, Patrick Boutier, Brady West, Bruce Ewing, and James Clausi. Again, honesty and insight are everything, and I'm grateful for your help.

AUTHOR'S NOTE

This book started as a dream, which was weird, at least for me. Then again, Katherine Kurtz launched her career as a writer based on a dream that eventually became her bestselling Deryni series, so…

Anyway, the dream was certainly odd, deeply personal in some ways, philosophical and theological as well. But in the end, after four hours of tossing and turning, I was finally forced to just get up and write it all down.

Thus, this book, which actually came about at a good time. I needed a break after writing *A Necessary Heresy*. Emotionally, that was just a tough story, and a few months away from the world of Seminal seemed like a good idea. I just didn't expect a new Anchored World would creep in while I was supposed to be resting and recharging.

Nevertheless, I'm grateful because *Blood of a Novice* turned out to be such an interesting book, especially because it allowed me to try out some new ideas. The most important is the notion of emotional wounds that linger long after the original trauma. They lead to self-inflicted lies that later on become ghosts that haunt a person. I should thank Phil Tucker for introducing me to the idea.

For me though, the problem with utilizing such a concept is that in the original draft, I leaned on it so heavily that the characters ended up lacking life. They were one note, and the world itself was rather bleak. I had noticed those issues, but until I received the critiques from my alpha readers, I hadn't known how to address them. Now I do, which is great because it means I now have another set of writing and editing tools!

In the end, because of the insight provided by that left turn at Albuquerque, the resulting book turned out to be so much stronger.

It's richer, the characters have more meaningful lives, and best of all the story is just a whole lot more fun, which is what I wanted all along.

I hope you enjoy it!

Sincerely,

Davis Ashura

P.S. This new series, *The Eternal Ephemera*, is part of the Anchored Worlds, so there are some familiar characters who are mentioned and one who shows up. You'll know who I mean.

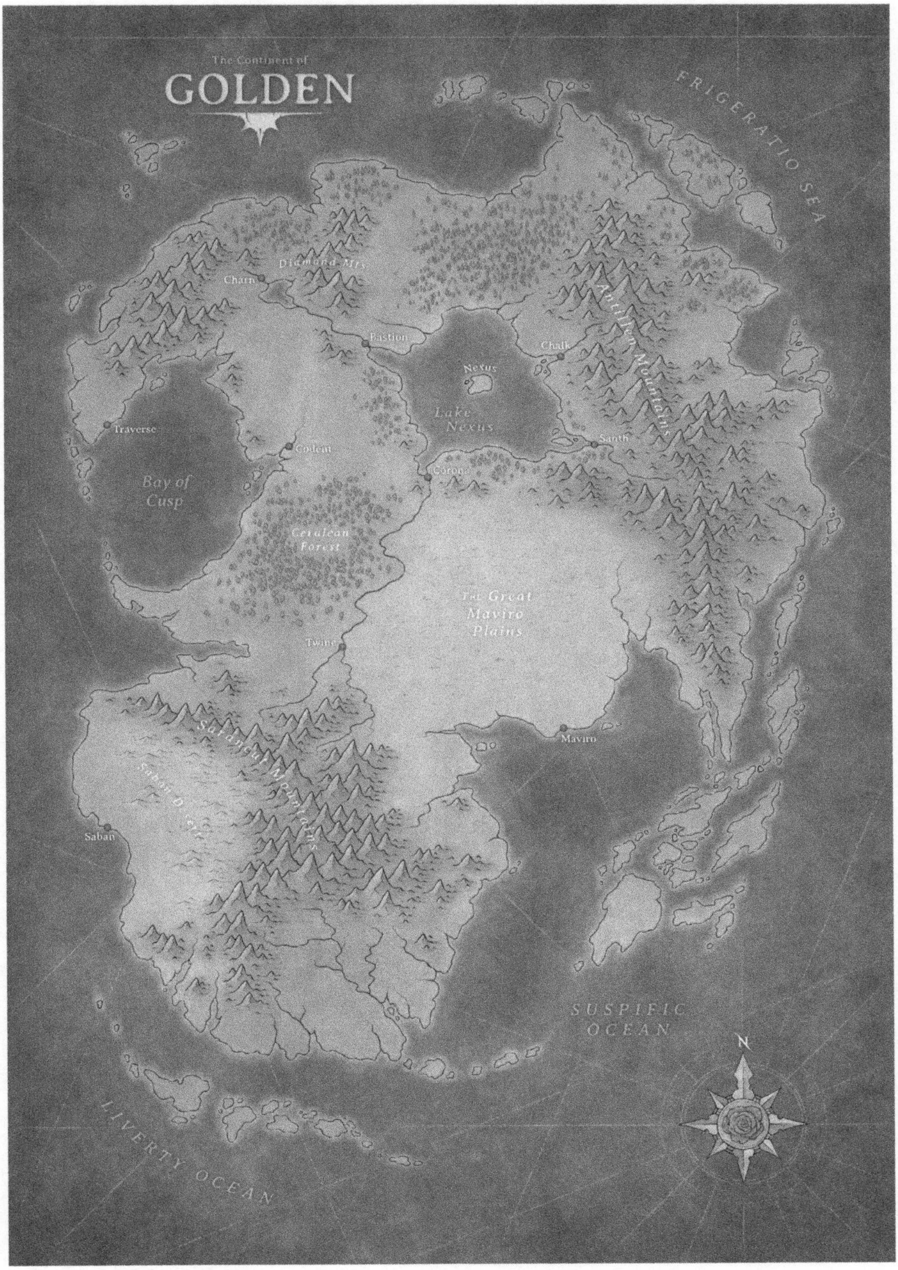

The Continent of

GOLDEN

Charn

Diamond Mts.

Arctlinn Mountains

Bastion

Chall

Nexus

Traverse

Lake
Nexus

Santh

Colent

Coron

Bay of
Cusp

The Great
Maviro
Plains

Cerulean
Forest

Twin

Maviro

FRIGERATIO SEA

Saban

SUSPIFIC
OCEAN

LIVERTY OCEAN

N

1

Cam Folde was only five when he saw two gods battle in the darkened skies near his home. He stared slack-jawed when they arrived. He knew them, these two near deities, their names anyway. Everyone did. Rainen Winder, the Unconquered Wilde Master, and Borile Defent, the Silver Sage of Weeping.

The two titans—enemies—faced off from a distance of a hundred yards, standing in the sky, speaking words Cam couldn't hear. Master Winder, a protector of the helpless, not tall but seeming like it with his swirling long dark hair and limbs sheathed in crackling fire.

And Borile, an Awakened Beast and a rakshasa. Once he'd been a simple eagle, but then he'd stepped onto a rakshasa's version of the Way into Divinity and Advanced. He'd done so through the murder, plunder, and pillaging of stolen Ephemera until he now stood upright and self-aware, nearly as tall as Rainen, with feathered arms rather than wings. But his torso and legs retained the shape of his raptor heritage and so did his cruel beak and piercing eyes.

Cam continued to gape as Rainen and Borile glared at one another, neither of them willing to give an inch. He couldn't believe what was happening in the skies above the trackless wilds north of Traverse, his home. Rainen and Borile. Mortal enemies, both of them Sages, and both of them ranked among the most powerful of all beings in the world of Salvation.

And only Cam was about to witness their battle. His daddy had brought him here, deep into the woods to go camping, but the old man had drank too much and was passed out. Ever since Cam's momma had run off a year ago, it had become an all-too common occurrence.

But none of that mattered right now. The only thing that did were the two Sages. Again, they spoke words, but this time, they somehow carried to Cam.

Borile tilted his head in consideration at Rainen. "What difference does it make in how we create our own worlds? So long as we do. Isn't that what Rukh and Jessira state is our base nature?"

"The Holy Servants provided their own power for our world's birth. They didn't steal it."

Borile sneered. "Sophistry." Cam didn't reckon what the word meant. "And you don't know that for sure. They could have been just as my kind are."

Rainen didn't reply, and there then came a pregnant pause. The world held still, hushed. The leaves unmoving. No animal sounds or birds on the wing. It was the only warning before the battle was joined. Rainen and Borile, moving in a swirl of speed that left Cam breathless, attacked one another. Lightning speared the heavens. Rolling thunder shattered, and trees bent as a mighty wind blew. Power unlike anything Cam had ever imagined threatened to undo the world. Neither Sage looked to be holding back. Neither looked like they'd relent until the other was dead.

Rivers of wild danger bled across the landscape. Distant hills were sheared. Trees exploded. Fire bloomed. It was too much, and Cam screamed in terror, falling to the ground, curling around his knees, shutting his eyes, and plugging his ears. On went the din of the battle. Brilliant lights pierced his eyelids. Vibrations roiled his innards, and the tang of fire and ruin burned his nostrils.

The sensations overwhelmed his mind, and Cam hugged himself tighter, gasping, whimpering. When would it end? With every fiber of his being, he wanted it to be over. For the forest's peace and silence to return. But it didn't. Instead, for what felt like forever, terror held reign in this isolated place.

Eventually, though, Rainen and Borile did depart, and with them went much of the thunder, lightning, and flashing lights, distant now but still present.

Minutes might have passed, time that stretched like days, and during it, Cam hugged around himself, eyes clenched closed, scared witless. He lay there, but as soon as he figured the two dread beings were far enough away, he got up and ran. Never slowing. Running and running. Tripping. Falling. Running again. On and on until he was lost and had lost all sense of direction.

He didn't care. Anything was safer than staying where Rainen and Borile still fought. The sounds of their battle continued to echo across the sky as Cam ran. But eventually fatigue collapsed him next to a log. He huddled there, shivering, senses alert, listening until the tempest-like sounds were no longer audible.

Maybe it meant one of the Sages had won.

Cam didn't know. He could barely think. All he wanted was to be back home where it was safe.

The stories made it seem like a battle between Sages was something never to be missed, but for Cam, it was something he wished he'd never seen. The Ephemeral Masters. The notion of Advancing from Neophyte through Novice, Acolyte, Glory, Crown, Sage, and Divine—none of it sounded like a good thing.

Until... like the slowest of tides, Cam's fear receded. His mind began working, and he could consider the notion of Awareness and Advancement without panic urging him to flee somewhere safe. For in truth, where was safety when folks like Rainen and Borile battled? Wouldn't the only safe place be where a person was just as powerful? Could defend themselves from the rage of Sages?

And if so, then why not Cam? That way he would be strong and powerful, too. The matter lodged in his mind like a kernel of long-ing, and Cam knew his life would never be the same. He wanted what the Sages had. He wanted that power so others would pay him proper mind. He'd be more than a "no-good Folde," and everyone would have to respect him.

Cam's heart started to beat normally and his breathing unclenched. He uncurled and sat up, opening his eyes to view the world. The light of a fresh dawn pinked the horizon, but all around him was devasta-tion. Trees lay broken like kindling; hills flattened like mud pies. A forest afire in the far distance. Cam rubbed his eyes, clearing his vision. How had he survived? And—

His father! Cam peered about, his panic-stricken gaze shifting, ready to run, but managing to keep still. Maybe his daddy would find him.

Hours later, his wish was granted when his father found him. His daddy raced forward with an inarticulate cry, kneeling at his side, and clutching him tight. "Cam," he breathed out.

Cam held onto his daddy, crying.

"Do you want to dive a new Pathway?"

The simple question Lilia Fair asked landed like a hammer, and Cam's mouth shut with a click. The query also silenced the banter among the two boys with him, his friends, Jordil Oil and Tern Shorn. The three of them were currently wasting away the afternoon—Cam's idea—by laying along the banks of the Barr River, which flowed gently through their town of Traverse.

Until Lilia's query, it had been a fine summer day, the kind meant for relaxing in the tall reeds next to a slow-flowing river and doing a whole lot of nothing. The world was all blue skies, puffy clouds, and a warm breeze, and the three boys were in their hideaway, out of the view of anyone looking to find them and find them some work.

In a word, the day had been perfect.

But Lilia knew of their secret lair. She was the fourth member of their crew, and with her question, everything changed. Before Lilia's arrival, Cam had been arguing with Jordil and Tern over which girl in Traverse was the prettiest—it was obviously Maria Benefield—but now, the answer to what had previously been the most significant of questions felt trivial. There was something more important to consider.

Dive a new Pathway to Grace. It could change everything for Cam, and a deep desire to make that change happen swept over him, reckless and rushing like a river in flood. He remembered Rainen and Borile—a decade in the past—and how much he had always wanted to be like the Wilde Sage. He'd always dreamed of it, of finding the secret to his power, and near every one of them had centered on what Lilia had just posed: diving a new Pathway. If he did, he would no longer be the youngest member of the no-good Folde family. He would be a person of note and respect. His entire family would benefit.

"What do you think?" Jordil asked. His words were spoken to everyone, but in reality, they were directed to Cam.

Cam stroked his chin, as if in deliberation, but he had already made his decision, had made it the moment Lilia had asked her question. To dive a new Pathway could be deadly since even those with experience warned of how death was always a possibility. But Cam couldn't think of that now. For him, all he knew was that Advancement would solve all his problems. Like everyone his age, he was a Neophyte, a nobody with no agency or power. To dive a Pathway could see him Advance to at least Novice and maybe even Acolyte.

"Cam?" Jordil persisted, brow furrowed as he leaned forward, like he was wanting to shake the answer from Cam's mouth.

Cam ignored Jordil's question. The Pathway was too good, a dream come true, and in his short life, one lesson he'd learned above all others was to never believe in dreams. He stared at Lilia through abruptly suspicious eyes. "How'd you hear about this? And how come no one's already dived it?"

Lilia held up her hands. "Peace. I just found out about it this afternoon. I was listening in on Daria and Haptha. They discovered it the other day and were planning on diving later in the week. They came home first to find out if it's safe, though."

"What were Daria and Haptha doing out in the forest?" Tern asked with a leer. "Were they meeting someone special?"

Lilia rolled her eyes. "No, stupid. They're both apprentices to Midwife Spenser. She had them looking for some plant she wanted."

Tern still leered. "Or maybe they just wanted some alone time with each other." He waggled his eyebrows.

Lilia's fists clenched. "Don't talk about my sister like that!" Lilia might not much like her sister Daria, but she was loyal. And Haptha had spent so much time around Lilia's kin, she might as well also be a sister. Both were older than Lilia, and in some ways, everything she wasn't. The opposite, in fact. Whereas the older girls—women now with a woman's curves—were tall, leggy, and pretty, Lilia was short, stout, and homely. Daria and Haptha had lustrous, dark hair, while Lilia's was an odd muddy-brown color. It was only their eyes which were similar, dark as coal like everyone else's in Traverse and likely the world.

Still, despite her less-than-attractive looks, Jordil seemed to like Lilia in the way a boy likes a girl. The two of them might have even wandered into the woods to snooker a time or two. But why Jordil would see Lilia in that way was a question Cam couldn't reckon. He looked from Jordil to Lilia, trying to figure on what his oldest friend saw in the girl because he couldn't. It was strange by his way of thinking, but it also didn't mean Cam treated Lilia badly. Not like Tern, who was always knocking Lilia down or telling her what to do. He could be an ass to her sometimes.

"I'm just saying," Tern continued. "Two pretty girls out in the woods alone." He leered again. "I wouldn't mind diving their Pathways." His statement earned a squawk of disgust from Lilia, but Cam was no longer listening. Instead, he was reflecting on what a strange group of friends he had, them being so different in background and appearance.

Jordil came from a well-to-do family, but his folks didn't seem to care much for him. Not like they did their daughter, Jamie. Plus, they were still in mourning over the death of their oldest child, Furn. He'd been their pride and joy, certain to achieve Acolyte Stage. Death, though, had stolen his life last year, and Jordil's parents hadn't yet put the pieces back together. Not enough for them to see the talent possessed by their youngest child, who was smart enough to master any craft.

The only thing holding Jordil back was his lack of self-confidence. Maybe it was because of his appearance, his rail-thin build, his long features, and his twitching nose. Jordil looked like a rat, and like a rat, he was always getting into trouble. In this, he was nothing like his pretty sister or Furn, who had been handsome and loved by everyone. Instead, Jordil had become the black sheep of his family, mostly because his parents were too stupid to recognize how great their youngest could become. He just needed love and attention.

Then there was Tern, the only child of a hero, a father he hardly knew. Fifteen years ago, there had been a war between the Sage-Dukes of Charn and Bastion. It had been a long, bloody affair, but in the end, Sage-Duke Zin Shun of Charn—the man who ruled Traverse and hundreds of other villages and towns—had won out.

Tern's father had taken part in the war, but in some ways, he never really returned. Cam's own daddy, Purien, who had wisely not involved himself in such barbarism, had said Tern's father had been a happy man before the war, close to his siblings. But he'd returned cold and distant. Crazy as an outhouse rat with his mind lost in whatever wartime horrors he had seen. Least that's what Cam's father said, which sounded right. Cam remembered Tern's daddy and his quick temper, picking fights for no reason, nearly killing Farmer Lomin because of some no-account slight.

Then one morning, five years ago, Tern's father had simply walked out the front door to his home, left Traverse, and never came back. But Tern still worshipped the man, wanted to be just like him.

Which was sad because Tern would never measure up. Being his friend, Cam hated to say so, but it was true. Tern's dad had been an Acolyte, strong, powerful, and ruggedly handsome according to all the older women. Tern, on the other hand, had a mop of black hair, cut like someone didn't like him much, a narrow chin, and his dark eyes were perpetually cast in a squint from his weak vision. He was none too smart, neither.

And finally, there was Cam, who came from a no-good family, which consisted of his too-often drunken father and siblings, a sister and a brother. Folks figured them to be a shiftless trio and wondered when—not if—Cam would fall into their same habits.

The banter among Jordil, Lilia, and Tern continued, but by then Cam had come to a certainty. And he didn't care if it meant stealing the Pathway out from under the nose of Lilia's sister. He needed this. His entire family did. "We have to dive the Pathway," he announced, cutting off the chatter. "Get there tomorrow. Do it before anyone else. We have to if we want everything it can give us."

"How?" Jordil asked. "You heard Lilia. It's out in the forest, hours of hiking, and that's if we knew where to look, which we don't. We don't have no landmarks to tell us where to go."

"It's near a clearing where two streams come together," Lilia said, sounding timid. "There's a downed oak tree in the center." She hesitated. "Shouldn't we wait for someone to make sure it's safe? Especially since Daria and Haptha were the ones to find it."

Cam waved aside her worries with a breezy confidence, grinning. A meadow with a downed oak near the merger of two streams… it had been one of the places he and his daddy used to go camping. "I know the place," Cam said, "and here's what we'll do."

After Lilia's statement of discovery, they had each of them headed to their homes, planning on gathering their gear and meeting outside of town. Cam had snuck into his house, hoping no one else would be there.

No such luck.

His sister, Pharis, was in, which was usually the case ever since her husband, Jarek, had died a few months back. Some might have called his demise a tragedy, but Cam didn't; not when the damn fool had gotten drunk as a dog in a barrel full of whiskey, decided to go dancing on the roof, and fell off of it. He'd broke his neck when he hit the ground.

Cam shook his head at the ugly recollection. A sound could hold the entirety of an event, every memory winding into and within it, unwrapping like a spool of yarn. The song that had been playing the only time Cam had danced with Maria Benefield; the noise of a woodpecker on a perfect spring morning; and the snapped wood crack of a neck breaking. That last one was something Cam wished he could forget.

Pharis probably wanted to forget that sound, too. After Jarek's death, she had fallen hard, moving back home and following their father and brother straight to the bottom of a bottle.

Cam viewed her, lips tightening in a wish. For most of his life, Pharis had been the one to hold him when he'd been scared, to put a salve on his scrapes when injured, and to comfort him when he had been upset. In most of the ways that counted, she had been his mother.

And Cam hated seeing her like this. Only this morning, she'd been her normal self, laughing brightly as she fixed him breakfast and ushered him out the door. But now she reeked of alcohol, her words slurred. She could barely walk without stumbling.

"Where's daddy and Darik?" Cam asked.

Pharis gestured about, vaguely. "Still mending Farmer Sigmon's fences."

"Shouldn't they be done with it by now? I thought the work only needed one person."

"It was, but Farmer Sigmon found them more to do," Pharis said, her slurred words hard to decipher. "He'll have them busy all summer."

"He's a kind soul," Cam said. "Hiring daddy and Darik like that."

"He is," Pharis agreed. "What are you doing back so soon? I didn't figure you'd be home until supper."

The desire to explain his intentions—he'd always shared them with Pharis—was on the tip of Cam's tongue, the plan to dive a new Pathway. But if he told her, she'd likely not let him go, fearful over the dangers.

But by his way of calculations, the risk was worth the reward. Being the first to dive a Pathway was supposed to give all sorts of gifts, certainly enough for him to reach Novice at only fifteen years old and maybe even Acolyte. He'd be a prodigy, and the whole village would have to respect him and his family.

"What are you up to?" Pharis asked, her bleary-eyed gaze sharpening.

"Camping," Cam answered, which wasn't really a lie. It just wasn't the entire truth.

Pharis grunted. "I know you like those friends of yours, but you sure they're right for you? You think they'll stick by you in a couple of years? When their families pay for them to dive a Pathway? We don't have that kind of coin. They'll be Novices, and you'll still be a Neophyte and a Folde."

Cam recognized what she was doing: trying to protect him from heartache. Everything she had said was true. Cam's friends came from money, and they'd have opportunities he never would. The Foldes was a poor family, but it didn't mean they had to stay that way.

As a Novice, Cam could find better work: clearing fields, protecting them from locusts and beetles... he'd be a man of the community. Respected. And he could see the rest of his family prosper as well.

Instead of speaking out his hopes and dreams, however, Cam merely grunted in reply to Pharis' comment before picking his way across the main area that acted as the kitchen along with a bedroom for him and Darik. His reflection caught in a dirty mirror in the corner, and he took a look at himself. The faint wisp of an early mustache collected above his upper lip, and his dark hair hung down to his shoulders. He also caught sight of his big hands and feet, which simultaneously brought him irritation and hope. Irritation because they made him clumsy—he was honest enough to admit it—but also hope because he might one day end up tall like Darik rather than short like their father, who was also skinny. He also wanted Darik's muscles but not his flab. Darik had an ample gut. Otherwise, Cam had the same olive skin and dark eyes of everyone else in town.

He threw off his examination and proceeded across the room.

Sunlight struggled to penetrate the single grimy window facing the street, and in the far corner, next to the doorway to Pharis' bedroom, Cam kneeled next to his cot, feeling under the lumpy mattress.

"Cam?" Pharis asked from across the room, sounding concerned.

He ignored her.

A single drawer held his belongings, and once he had hold of it, he drew it forth. There wasn't much, but he took it all anyway. Into a sturdy rucksack with straps, he packed his only change of clothes along with extra bedding. From the kitchen, he grabbed some dried meat and hardtack. Next, he went to Darik's cot, which stood in the corner across from his own bed. On the windowsill, he found a sheathed camp knife, dust covered and rarely used. Darik wouldn't miss it.

Cam strapped the knife to his hip while the rucksack hung from his back.

"What's going on, Cam?" Pharis asked, concern in her voice.

"Nothing," Cam replied. "I'm just going camping."

He caught Pharis staring hard at him, but she eventually shrugged her shoulders. "Fair enough. I had secrets of my own at your age. Go camping then."

"I'll see you tomorrow," Cam said, taking a long look at his sister. He prayed for her then, prayed to Devesh to watch out for her, to help her recover and heal. And after the Pathway, maybe he could do something to help make that happen.

"Stay safe," Pharis said as he was leaving.

"I will," he called back to her.

Cam stepped out of the family hovel and onto the front porch with its sagging roof and rotting posts. A deep breath of fresh air cleansed the rancid stench from inside the house out of his nose, and a moment later, he was off. The sun beamed down from an endless blue sky that looked to be decorated by puffy clouds resembling the cotton candy sold during Traverse's many festivals.

The brick-lined streets of his little town—not much larger than a village—were nearly empty with most folk working out in the surrounding fields. Regular clanging rang out from the building owned by Master Carlson, the town's farrier; an Acolyte, which meant he could imbue his work with Ephemera and make it sturdier and stronger. Most craftsfolk in Traverse were like that, the most skilled of them being Acolytes. Even the farmers had that kind of talent, using their Ephemera to grow the crops tall and strong, keep the weeds down and drive off the pests, and make sure the water flowed right so even in drought the fields were lush.

On the way down the street, Cam caught sight of Mrs. Fair, Lilia's momma.

"Cam," she called. "Lilia says you're going camping."

He kept any nervousness from his face, unsure what Lilia might have told her momma. "Yes, ma'am."

"Watch out for her, will you? She's afraid of wolves."

"I will."

"I know you will. You're a good boy." Mrs. Fair smiled, absentmindedly reaching up to tuck a shaggy lock of his hair behind an ear before waving her farewell and heading off.

Cam watched her for a moment, conflicted. Here was Mrs. Fair, all-but leaving her youngest daughter in his care, and here he was about to take that youngest daughter off to do something potentially dangerous. He wasn't sure if he should let Lilia come with them.

Mind still roiling, he eventually set off, thinking again on the battle between Rainen Winder and Borile Defent, the devastation they'd left. Exactly a year after that struggle, Cam had gone visiting the site and caught a view of a woman floating in the sky—maybe another Sage. Waves of indigo-colored power had fallen from her hands like rain, smelling of orchids and healing the hills and forest. Only for a few minutes had she lingered, but when she left, it was like the area of the battle had been made fresh as new-turned soil.

He set aside his recollections when Jordil, Lilia, and Tern hailed him from where they had agreed to meet. It was at a crossroads, a dirt path intersecting the road Cam followed.

He viewed the area in distaste. He never much liked crossroads, mostly because of the promises a person could supposedly make at those places. It was to rakshasas, those terrible folk and Awakened Beasts who had figured out how to kill others and steal their Ephemera, the holiest of gifts imbued into all people. Those who did such a thing were the worst sort of evil, especially the three Great Rakshasas: Shimala, Coruscant, and Simmer.

Cam shuddered just thinking of them.

"What's wrong?" Lilia asked. Cam told her, and she shuddered also. "You had to bring them up."

She sounded scared just then, and hearing it, Cam felt a need to speak up, recalling Mrs. Fair's words. "I saw your momma a little bit ago," he said to Lilia. "She thinks we're just going out camping, and I'm supposed to keep you safe. You sure you want to come with us? None of us would think bad about you if you changed your mind."

Lilia might have said no—looked like she wanted to—but the moment was lost when Tern spoke over her answer. "Oh, stop being such little girls," he declared. "No one's going home."

"Tern's right," Lilia unsurprisingly agreed. For some reason, she was always trying to get on Tern's good side. "We've got a Pathway waiting for us."

"You sure?" Cam asked her.

Lilia's jaw firmed. "I'm sure."

Cam exhaled heavily, not bothering to mask his disappointment with her. "Alright then."

"And if you don't stop jacking around," Tern added, "the new Pathway will be dead by the time we get there."

Cam shared a glance with Jordil, and as one, they broke out in laughter.

"What's so funny?" Tern complained. "You two girls are always giggling over something."

Calling someone a girl was one of Tern's favorite insults, and Cam never understood why. Lilia was a girl. So were lots of people Cam respected. And what was wrong with being a girl anyway? Girls were pretty, and Cam sure wouldn't mind kissing one or a dozen, especially the lovely Maria Benefield.

"It's nothing," Cam said to Tern, deciding not to argue about it. Instead, he threw a companionable arm over Jordil's shoulders, grinning, getting caught up in the moment. "Fortune and fame await. We dive this Pathway, and we might be the next Sages of our world. Salvation could use some fresh blood."

"A Sage of Salvation," Jordil breathed. "That would be something, wouldn't it?"

"You think the Sage-Dukes would let us rise that high?" Lilia asked. "There's only nine of them, and no one has Advanced to Sage in centuries."

Tern, like he too often did, mocked Lilia. Probably because he hated that she was smarter than him. "There's only nine of them because there's only nine cities, stupid. And they only became cities because they had a Sage-Duke. If one of us becomes a Sage, Traverse will become a city, too."

His explanation made no sense, but once again, Cam didn't bother fighting him over it. When Tern got going, no matter how idiotic, he never backed down.

Lilia, though, could never get it through her head not to argue with Tern. Maybe it was because she was like him: always wanting to be right even when she was wrong. "You're the one who's stupid," she proclaimed. "There's always only been nine cities. Ever. Which means the Dukes don't want anyone else having their eyes, Advancing to violet and becoming a Sage."

"You're so wrong," Tern said with a pitying shake of his head.

"Well then why did Gordian the Crown die right after his eyes went violet and he became a Sage?"

Tern blinked in confusion at her.

Lilia folded her arms across her chest and smiled in satisfaction. "I thought so. You'd have to go to school and learn to read to know what I'm talking about."

Cam briefly closed his eyes, wishing Lilia hadn't said what she had. The thing was, Tern never had much schooling, never been good at it, and Lilia's challenge was sure to have hit a nerve.

Sure enough, when Cam opened his eyes, matters were exactly how he had expected. Tern had dropped his backpack and was facing off with Lilia, fists balled.

"Ain't no call for that," Jordil said, stepping in between Tern and Lilia.

"Then she should—"

Cam stepped in as well. "Time's burning," he said to Tern. "More hustle and less talk. Come on. Get your arguing done after we stop."

Tern held Lilia's gaze, glaring her way. She was the first to drop her eyes. "Sorry," she mumbled. "I shouldn't have said that."

Tern still stared hard at her, eventually grunting before gathering his backpack.

They got moving then, and minutes later, they were passing the fields outside Traverse. Farmers were out, inspecting their crops, red and orange wisps of Ephemera curling off their hands as they did something or another to keep the wheat, corn, and barley healthy.

Shortly after, they came across the sign outside the town limits and entered Marnin Forest, the woods around Traverse. Warm sunshine became dappled darkness and light, and the cobblestone road transitioned to a gravel path, just wide enough for a single wagon. Silence reigned with the only sounds coming from some critters running around.

Cam kept his eyes out, looking for the trail they would need to take. To the place where his daddy had taken him camping and taught him what he knew of living in the wild.

A mile later, he saw it, a barely visible animal trail, cutting off to the left, angling away from the gravel road they followed. Calling out to Tern and Lilia, who were a dozen yards ahead, Cam pointed out the path.

His heart soared as he strode forward, marching to the rhythm of his hope. Tomorrow, everything would change.

2

They hiked through the afternoon—Cam and his friends—and their conversation flitted from the odd to the stupid. It was the normal way for the four of them, to turn the most ordinary topic into something near philosophical. Cam was certain that many wise folks could learn a lot from listening in to the chatter between him and his friends. The four of them might not have lived much, but he was certain they were worldly in spite of it.

Eventually their discussion centered on one of Jordil's favorite topics: food. It was surpassingly strange. Jordil was so skinny, and Cam often wondered how his friend could love food so much when he clearly didn't eat all too often.

"You see, out east," Jordil said, expounding like he was some famous teacher. "In cities like Chalk, Santh, and Maviro, they like their food spicy. They use masalas…"

"What's a masala?" Lilia asked. In spite of her size, she really didn't eat all that much. Nor was she adventurous when it came to food. She liked her eats bland and boring, which was kind of like the girl herself.

"It's a blend of spices," Tern said, staring Lilia down. "Didn't you

16

learn that with all your fancy schooling?"

Lilia scowled in outrage.

"It doesn't matter," Cam quickly interjected. "What's so special about masalas?" he asked Jordil, although he already knew the answer. By now, Jordil had explained it to him about a half-dozen times.

"Masalas on their own aren't special," Jordil answered, his tone portentous. "However, they allow chefs to spice the foods in a more consistent fashion. It allows a true connoisseur to infuse the food with fragrant aromas that please the palate throughout the entire bite and swallow." During his explanation, Jordil had drawn himself up and was staring down his nose at everyone like he was some kind of high-ranked Ephemeral Master.

Seeing him like that, Cam couldn't help but guffaw, and an instant later, Tern joined in. Lilia glanced about, looking as confused as a dog with strange food on her plate.

Meanwhile Jordil had reddened with embarrassment. "I was just—"

"You should see your face." Tern cut him off with a wheeze.

"You should see *your* face," Jordil snapped right back.

Tern went on without a hitch. "You looked like Master Moltin when he had the runs and was trying to hold it in."

Jordil scowled. "How would you know? You're never in school."

"I was in school that day," Tern said, still chuckling. "And it was absolutely worth it."

"I don't like spicy foods," Lilia pronounced. "They make my butthole hurt."

Cam viewed her in confusion. What was she going on about? He chuckled in uncertainty. Same with Tern, but Jordil simply brayed, probably glad not to be the focus of the joke anymore.

"What's so funny?" Lilia asked, wearing an expression of hurt.

Seeing her like that caused guilt to replace Cam's laughter. "It's what you said about your butthole," he said. "I never heard of anyone's butthole hurting from eating food."

"Really?" Lilia challenged. "My dad says spicy food burns his mouth so bad he has to chug water. Same with his butthole."

"His butthole has to chug water?" Tern asked in disbelief.

"Yep."

Tern cackled.

"You eat some hot and spicy food and see if I'm not wrong," Lilia said with a thrust of her jaw. "You'll have the runs, and you'll look down between your legs and see your butthole slurping water."

"That's disgusting," Tern declared. "But I'll take your stupid challenge and—"

"Can we stop talking about sipping buttholes and the runs?" Cam asked. "It's undignified."

"What would you know about dignity?" Tern asked, taking the bait, just like Cam knew he would. "You're the son of the most ne'er-do-well family in town."

"Maybe so," Cam agreed. "But after I dive the Pathway, I'll be a Novice. I'll be on the Way into Divinity, on the road to Ephemeral Mastery, while you…" He gave Tern his most pitying expression, "… you'll still be as ugly as a rat's back end."

"No, I won't!" Tern hollered in outrage. "Tomorrow, I'll be just like you."

Cam grinned. "What? The handsome son of the most ne'er-do-well family in Traverse?" He winked at Jordil and Lilia, who smiled back, both appreciating the ridicule passing them by.

"No," Tern protested. "I meant the other thing. About being a Novice."

"A Novice whose butthole hurts." Lilia snickered.

"I thought we were done talking about that," Jordil declared.

The other two were about to interject something, but Cam glanced around just then. He didn't recognize this stretch of the forest, and he peered about, finally spotting a familiar landmark, a downed tree in the distance.

He knew where they were now, and he cursed. They'd passed the turnoff, which was a few hundred yards behind them.

In the meantime, Jordil and the others were now focused on whether vomit could ever taste good. Cam mentally shook his head. "Shut it," he said, quieting the idiotic conversation. "We missed our trail."

"How far back is it?" Jordil asked.

"Couple of hundred yards."

"It's getting dark," Lilia said, her gaze flitting around.

Tern chortled at her distress. "What? You afraid? Afraid Simmer or Shimala are going to get you?"

"No, it's just that there might be wolves."

"Well if there are, we could just feed you to them," Tern said. "As fat as you are, you'd be enough for the whole pack and then some."

Lilia glared at him, her eyes watering, which happened when she was especially angry.

Jordil did his best to distract her. "Come on, Lilia." He threw an arm around her shoulders and drew her away. "Tern is just being mean because he hates how dumb he is."

While they walked away, Tern stared after them in amazement. "What did I say?"

Cam gazed at the other boy in disgust. Tern could be a right prick sometimes. "Figure it out," he said over his shoulder, following Jordil and Lilia.

"But what if I can't?" Tern asked in a pained tone.

Cam turned about to face him, not expecting how upset Tern sounded or to see the panicked expression on his face.

Tern swallowed heavily. "I know Jordil is right. I say mean things because I'm dumb." Tears welled. "Why do I have to be so stupid?"

He seemed genuinely distraught, and the disgust Cam had felt seconds ago was replaced by sympathy and guilt. Hadn't he been thinking earlier about how dim-witted Tern was? Silently scorning him for what he couldn't help? He'd never figured Tern knew himself well enough to recognize his flaw.

"I'm sorry," Cam said.

"For what?" Tern said, swiping at his eyes.

"For…" Cam shrugged, not knowing what to say. "You aren't a bad person, but you are mean sometimes. Me and Jordil can handle it, but you know Lilia can't. She's always been sensitive, especially about her weight. You think it's easy for her? Having two older sisters who all the men in town would marry if they could? Even those already married?"

"I guess not," Tern said, wiping at his eyes and a mulish expression on his face. "But why's she so upset? I call her fat all the time."

"And that's the problem. I reckon a person can only take an insult so many times before it cuts like a knife."

Tern listened close, cogitating as he scuffed his foot against the ground, staring down. "Maybe you're right," he said after a moment. His head lifted, and his eyes met Cam's. "When we finish the Pathway, I'm going to choose Synapsia as my Tang. It's hard to master, but it would make my mind work better. I wouldn't be so dumb anymore."

Cam wasn't sure what to say to that, and he faced in the direction where Jordil and Lilia had stridden off. They were barely visible. "Let's go before those two think they're alone enough to start sucking face."

Tern snorted laughter. "Gross."

They made camp with dark settling quickly. It was a small clearing in the woods, a place used by plenty of people since there was already a stone-lined fire pit centered in the space. Lilia fetched water from a nearby creek while Tern gathered some kindling and logs. Afterward Cam got a fire going and Jordil started supper.

It was a stew made from the various dried meats they had brought mixed with wild carrots and potatoes spied in the nearby woods and some of the herbs and spices Jordil had been talking about, but none of the hot ones. He must have been looking out for Lilia. He also roasted a couple ears of corn he'd brought from home and toasted some bread.

It was utterly delicious, and Cam sat back after eating his fill, groaning in pleasure from where he lay propped against a nearby boulder. "That was some fine eats," he said, patting his stomach in satisfaction.

"You ain't lying," Tern agreed, leaning against a fallen log and belching loudly in honor of Jordil's cooking.

Lilia, who had eaten the least of anyone, sat atop an old tree stump on the other side of the fire. "We should probably set a watch?" she said in a questioning tone.

"Good idea," Jordil said, nodding. "And since I did the cooking, you don't mind leaving me out of it, right?"

"No chance," Tern said. "If I'd known cooking meant getting out of taking watch, I'd have done it."

"If you did the cooking, we'd have died of food poisoning," Jordil declared.

Tern swore at him in reply.

"Can I take the first watch?" Lilia asked, her wide-eyed gaze darting about the darkened forest. She clutched a camp knife in a white-fingered grip.

Cam glanced at the surrounding woods. Normal noises echoed from the darkened trees—a lonesome owl, some small critters moving through the underbrush, and insects humming and murmuring. To Cam, the sounds were calming and restful, but Lilia had a near-terrified expression on her face. Cam didn't know why, but he also figured it would be best if someone else took watch with her. She didn't look like she could handle it on her own.

"That sounds fine to me," Cam declared to Jordil and Tern, in answer to Lilia's question. "I'll take the second watch. Then comes Tern, and Jordil gets the last one. And whoever has watch needs to make sure the fire doesn't die out."

Jordil and Tern grumbled half-heartedly, but soon enough, they were snuggled in their rolls, sleeping like the dead. Meantime, Cam got a mess of logs lined up near the fire pit and rebuilt the flames. As soon as he was done, he sat next to Lilia on her tree stump.

She glanced askance at him. "Thank you for gathering the wood," she said. "But don't you need to sleep?"

Before answering, Cam gently shoved the camp knife she was holding away from where she had it pointing in his direction. In turning to face him, she had unconsciously aimed the blade at his gut, angling it from only a few inches away. "I'm not ready to sleep," he told her, which wasn't exactly a lie, but not the entire truth neither. If he told her the real reason—that he thought she was scared of the night—she would let him have it.

"Thank you," she whispered, staring into the darkness, an expression on her face that Cam couldn't name. Haunted maybe? "I don't like the dark," she continued, her voice still a hush. "When I was two, my sisters locked me in the cellar once. It was so dark, and there were rats. They ran over my feet." She swallowed heavily, facing him again, a weak smile on her face. "Bet you think I'm a coward."

Cam thought nothing of the sort. Instead, he was horrified by her admission, outraged on her behalf. Her sisters, the young women most of the village admired, had done that to her? That would have been cruel to do to anyone, but especially a two-year-old. "I don't think that," Cam declared in as firm a tone as he could manage. "What they did was wrong."

Lilia stared at him, likely looking for the lie, which was sad. She had a hard time trusting folk since so many times, those their own age treated her poorly. It was her weight, and too often, others gave her the business end of their wicked barbs or cruel comments. Cam knew it hurt her, but being a disrespected, unliked member of a disrespected, unliked family, there was nothing he could do about it.

He was also sure that Jordil liking Lilia in the way he did helped her some, but it wasn't enough. Not when Cam and Tern, supposedly Lilia's friends, often made fun of her, too. He took one of her hands in his then, held her gaze, wanting her to see the truth in his words, the apology in them. "I'm sorry, Lilia."

Lilia's lips momentarily thinned into the faintest of smiles before she faced out into the darkness again. Right then, it didn't look like she believed him, and Cam blinked, fresh guilt at what it meant that she thought he was lying.

"I mean it. I'm sorry."

She tilted her head in consideration. "Sorry for what?"

"Sorry for making fun of you. Sorry for not defending you when others did the same, especially Tern."

"Tern is an ass."

Cam nodded. While he still sympathized for Tern, now wasn't the time to bring it up. "He can be."

"He is," she declared in a voice full of certainty.

"I suppose so," Cam said by way of agreement. "But that ain't got nothing to do with how I feel. I'm sorry I haven't been a good friend. You deserve better."

"Will you be better?"

The question was asked in an unconcerned, uncaring tone, simple and straightforward, and based on the set of her face, it was hard to tell if the answer might matter to her one way or the other.

But it mattered to Cam. He wanted Lilia to know he cared. That he had *always* cared, but until tonight, he had never really seen why that should be important. "I'll be better."

Again, came that puzzled expression. "Why?"

"Because you deserve it."

Lilia grinned then. "You've always been better to me than you think."

"Better doesn't mean good enough." In that moment, Cam made a promise to Devesh, vowing to treat Lilia better. She was his friend, and she didn't deserve his bite.

Lilia's attention went out to the woods again, and she shivered like she was nervous. "Are there really wolves out there?"

"There are, but this being mid-summer, they'll have plenty of other kinds of prey to hunt. Four people around a campfire wouldn't be worth their trouble."

"But you'll stay up with me?"

"Of course. That's what a friend would do."

They sat in companionable silence until it was Cam's turn to take watch. And while he watched Lilia settle in her rolls, for the first time, he had a notion as to what Jordil saw in her.

The next morning, Cam awoke, refreshed and ready, but a quick glance also showed him what he'd expected to see. Jordil's head bobbed like one of those big-headed dolls as he nodded off.

Perfect. Grinning, Cam snuck up on his friend and from less than a yard away, clanged a pot and pan.

Jordil launched in the air, letting out an unmanly scream. Same with Tern and Lilia.

Cam bent over, laughing so hard he wheezed, not caring that his humor had the others growling in aggravation, remaining irritated with him well into the next leg of their hike.

Then their annoyance shifted in a different direction.

"Where is it?" Jordil asked, impatient as always.

Cam didn't bother answering. He had the lead, and his attention was focused on the shadow-strewn forest trail they followed. Following on his footsteps were Jordil and Lilia with Tern bringing up the rear. Sunlight dappled the forest floor, and the smell of moss filled the air. Birds trilled and leaves rustled, but Cam paid them no mind. He was too busy searching about the woods. Somewhere up ahead was the cutoff they needed.

Minutes later, he located it, pointing it out to Jordil. "It's up ahead, to the right."

Jordil peered along Cam's pointing finger, nodding after a bit. "Good eyes."

Cam flashed him a grin. "Pretty, too. All the girls say so."

Jordil snorted. "No girl says that."

"Your sister did."

"I think you have her mixed up with your right hand."

Cam laughed, enjoying the quip. "Why don't you ask her and find out if I'm lying?"

"No need. We both know you have no chance with Jamie. She's too good for you."

Cam took the retort in stride. It might have come across as a cutting comment from anyone else, but from Jordil, it didn't bother him none. Jordil was a friend.

They reached the cutoff where Cam figured that in another couple hundred yards, they would eventually come across a rivulet. *Follow it downstream, and it meets up with another watercourse.* They'd then be at their destination, a meadow they all wanted to believe was where Lilia's sister had seen a newly birthed Pathway.

Tension built in Cam. What would they do when they got there? Would they truly dare enter the Pathway? People were said to die in them if they went in unprepared, and what were he and his friends if not unprepared? But there also figured to be a reward. Novices or more. Wasn't that worth the risk? For all of them?

Trying to bend his mind off his concerns, Cam turned to Jordil, who strode at his side. "What do you plan on doing after the harvest?"

Jordil shrugged. "Not much. Probably waste time with you."

Cam glared. "You do that, and I'll whip your butt."

Jordil frowned in confusion. "What for?"

"Because when we dive this Pathway, you'll have a chance to become a Novice. Maybe even an Acolyte or Adept. If you stay in school and learn to master your Ephemera, you could become an important person."

"Well, it's not your business, is it?" Jordil responded with a glare of his own.

"It's my business because you're my friend," Cam said. "I don't want you wasting your life, and right now, you're too stupid to see how happy it could be."

"What about you?" Jordil challenged. "If we dive the Pathway, you'll be a Novice, too."

"That's different," Cam said in reply to Jordil's challenge. "Everyone thinks my kin is garbage. Even if I dive the Pathway, they won't see me any different."

Jordil fell silent. "That's not it," he said softly. "It's because you're afraid. You think if you speak what you want, it won't come true."

Cam stared at the ground, scuffing the dirt, glaring but unable to meet Jordil's eyes. His friend was right. "It's been my family's way for as long as I can remember."

"If you're a Novice, your future changes."

Cam smirked. For him, the future wouldn't work out as nearly easily as Jordil seemed to think. "You really think they'll let me, Cam Folde of the no-good Folde family, into a class with all the high and mighty children of Traverse? You think their rich parents would let that happen?" He scoffed.

"Then what are you going to do?" Jordil asked.

"What I've always done. Figure it out on my own. Master what it means to be a Novice so I'll have a chance. My family will, too."

"A chance at what?"

Cam faced Jordil fully, looking him in the eye. "A chance to make something of myself. To not be ashamed of my name. To go to some place where we can just be." He finished on a fierce note, tears prickling his eyes. He blinked swiftly, not expecting to become so emotional on the matter.

Jordil nudged him, smiling faintly. "You can do that, but make sure to come back after you've become a Glory."

His words popped Cam's bubble of moroseness. Become a Glory... It was beyond a dream. It was impossible. Sure, they had all joked about going even farther and becoming a Crown or a Sage, but the truth was only one person out of a million ever reached the lofty heights of Glory—the fourth highest Stage on the Way into Divinity. And Cam knew he wouldn't be one of those blessed few. It would take a miracle for something like that to happen.

"Are we there yet?" Tern yammered from the back, sounding as impatient as a child needing a caning.

"We sure are," Cam shouted back. "We passed by the Pathway a mile ago and just didn't feel like telling you."

Tern responded with a scatological *and* sacrilegious profanity. It was impressive in its own way, although Cam would never tell Tern so. Instead, he responded in a tried-and-true fashion: an insult against Tern's momma. It made him feel a little guilty, though. Mrs. Shorn had always treated him kindly.

Tern offered a curt curse in response, and Cam laughed, feeling like he'd won that match.

Minutes later, all humor cut off when they came across a stream that merged into the one they'd been following. The sun glinted off the water, which babbled and eddied over submerged rocks and small boulders. Small golden and silver fish flitted about, and nearby frogs serenaded one another. But what held Cam's attention was the small clearing across the bank. It was the place.

He halted, staring and hoping, his excitement mounting. His heart was beating so fast, he might as well have run the whole way here.

"This it?" Jordil asked.

Cam nodded. "This is it."

3

After reaching the meadow, it didn't take long to find the Pathway. Centered in the field, it was a watery-seeming doorway, faintly red with the color indicating it was meant for Neophytes and Novices. Through its ripples, the other side of the clearing could be vaguely seen where a deer stared back at them in curiosity. It was said that beasts couldn't see Pathways; nor could they enter them. Only those who were Awakened—those whose Ephemera was Heightened to the quality of a human's—could manage it.

Cam gave the deer a momentary inspection before resuming his study of the doorway. Once again warnings from everyone who'd ever spoken a word about Pathways echoed through his mind. And what they all said was that Cam and his friends shouldn't be here. Pathways were too dangerous. As Neophytes, the safer course would be to wait for their seniors.

But it would also mean none of them would gain what they wanted and deserved. Waiting for someone to guide them likely meant no one would. The Pathway would be given over to the control of the wealthy, only their children allowed to enter it. This was Cam's only chance. He needed this, and he figured all his friends felt the same. For different reasons, each of them was desperate to change the direction of their lives, and the Pathway was the best bet to see that happen.

But as Cam stared at the watery doorway, he also realized that no one was willing to take that first step. He exhaled heavily. Fine. If no one else would do it, he would. He marched toward the Pathway. "Come on," he called over his shoulder, not bothering to see if the others were following. He'd go it alone if he had to.

His focus went to the Pathway, which loomed before him, and he stopped a bit to examine the pale red ripples. A measured breath and he pressed on in.

From one step to the next—with no resistance to his movement—Cam passed into the Pathway...

... And found himself standing in a narrow tunnel. It was barely wider than his shoulders, dimly lit by fluttering torches. He made a slow circle, trying to get his bearings. The entrance to the Pathway was gone. Instead, a blank wall made of smooth, tightly fitted stone met his gaze. A moaning wind with the faint tolling of an iron bell caused him to shiver. That didn't sound good.

Jordil stepped into the tunnel, seemingly exiting out of the blank wall. "Move," he growled. "Tern and Lilia will be coming any moment."

Cam stepped away from the wall, giving the others room. Seconds later, Tern and Lilia materialized. While the others got themselves sorted, Cam gazed about, hoping to find something more within the Pathway. Something grand. Something uplifting.

Anything other than this shadowed gloom, this oppressive feel of a dungeon. Where were all the wonders and treasures, the vast seas and endless forests, the wise men and women who supposedly peopled a Pathway? The stories said they would be here. Not these dank, lonely dark halls where it looked like there had never been and never would be any kind of magic or glory. What if there was only death here?

Cam swallowed heavily, thinking maybe they should have never entered this place.

Again came the moan, and he spun about, searching for the source.

"What was that?" Lilia asked, terror filling her voice.

It was a fear Cam was feeling, too.

"It sounded like an old woman saying, *hello*," Tern said, grinning like he was having the time of his life.

Cam wanted to punch him.

"No, it's not," Lilia declared, looking moments from blubbering.

There it was again, the moan.

Tern grinned wider. "She wants to suck out our Ephemera and trap us here forever."

Lilia whimpered.

"Shut up, Tern," Cam snapped.

Tern glared his way, and Cam glared right back. Now wasn't the time to get a rise out of Lilia.

Tern was the first to drop his gaze. "I was just playing," he muttered.

"We're in a Pathway to Grace," Cam told him. "Everyone talks about how dangerous they are to those who aren't prepared." He gestured, indicating all of them. "Do we look prepared? We could all of us die in here. And you want to screw around?"

"I'm not a baby," Tern snapped. "I get it. Now let's go. Quicker we're out of here, the quicker we can become Novices."

He made to shove past, but Cam held out a blocking arm. "I'll lead. The rest of you stay close."

Tern settled back with a grumble, and Cam set off, Jordil breathing down his neck, pressing close. Cam paused long enough to scowl his way. Jordil offered a half-hearted smile, flushing with embarrassment. But at least he stepped back.

Cam strode forward then, the tunnel seemingly endless, the moaning still coming at irregular intervals. It really did sound like a woman groaning. Hours might have passed, and the bleak travel had Cam feeling more and more nervous with every passing step. Course, he'd never say so to Tern. It would just set him off again.

Eventually they came to a "T" and had a choice to make. Cam looked from one direction to the next, but there seemed to be no difference between the two. For some reason, though, the right-hand turn called to him. He couldn't say why, but it was either a pulling or longing, and without giving the others a chance to argue the matter, he took that turn.

The moaning came again, the iron clangor louder this time.

"What is that?" Jordil whispered, clinging closely once again.

Cam had no answer, and for once Tern didn't pipe up either. A small blessing.

Minutes later, they reached a break in the endless expanse of black stones. It was a door with iron bars at eye level and no handle. Inside was a darkened room lit by a single torch with a figure laying on a cot, rolled over on its side, its back to them. It looked to be a woman. Her long, dark hair fanned across her shoulders and face.

"Who's that?" Tern whispered. He stepped close, accidentally stomping Cam's feet and earning a shove.

The figure shifted. "Hello?" Her voice was deep but quavering, rusty, like she hadn't spoken in a spell.

Cam shared a shocked glance with Tern. Had the fool been right? A woman groaning for their Ephemera?

Another movement from the figure, and this time she stood, facing them. Cam's breath caught. She was beautiful, prettier than Maria, with skin darker than his own and eyes a color he had never before seen. The whites were the indigo of a lake in summer while the irises had a cerulean shade. She was a Crown then, a Master of Ephemera and only two tiers below the highest Awareness of Divine. An orchid fragrance seemed to waft off her.

But when she took a step in their direction, Cam stepped away, drawing Tern with him. He had heard plenty of stories like this, someone in a Pathway, trapped they'd say, but really they were a type of temptation and giving in to it would leave a person caged.

"I am not what you think," the woman said, standing a foot away. Cam realized she was taller than him by many inches. "I am not a temptress. I am like you, an explorer. I entered a Pathway and found myself trapped in this endless tunnel. There was a single room, and I decided to rest before traveling on." She reached the edge of the room and drew herself short with a sharp inhalation. She seemed appalled as she took in their appearances. "Children. You're nothing but children. Neophytes. You entered a Pathway meant for Crowns."

Cam didn't know what she was babbling about, or whether she was actually a part of the Pathway or a real person. Regardless of the answer, he figured it didn't hurt being polite. "With all respect, ma'am, we entered a Novice-level Pathway." He was proud his voice didn't quaver.

Her frown deepened. "I sense your reality. You are not beings who live in the Pathway. You have Ephemera of a kind they lack." She sounded like she was talking to herself. "Which makes no sense. How did you enter..." The blood seemed to drain from her face. "Where did you enter the Pathway? I must know if I'm to save you."

Cam answered without thinking. The stories about temptations in Pathways had fallen away, and instead all he saw was a woman who seemed like she was worried for them. Truth to tell, he was scared for themselves as well. "Near the town of Traverse. It's in the duchy of Charn."

His answer must have settled her mind because she reached for the iron bars, surprising them all by swinging the door open. Out she stepped, into the hallway and among them. "My name is Saira. Follow me and be swift."

She marched off in the direction they had just come.

Cam shared a bemused look with his friends. They shrugged in silent reply. No help there. Seeing no better option, Cam grimaced, fear rising as he swiftly followed after Saira.

Cam quickened his pace to catch up with the woman, getting his first look at her clothing. She wore leather leggings, blue in color and a matching vest over a golden shirt that might have been silk. And she sure did walk fast, muttering under her breath the whole while.

"You sure we should be following her?" Jordil whispered to the group in general.

"Yes, you should be following her," Saira responded, not slowing in the least. "This is a Variant Pathway. I didn't sense it was such when I entered, but it can change its level of Awareness at any moment. Right now, it's at Novice, and unless you want to wait until it shifts to something greater, you'll keep up with me."

There came the moan again, causing Saira to curse softly.

"What's wrong?" Cam demanded.

"It's an Ephemeral Wind. None of you are ready to endure it."

Cam startled, truly afraid now. An Ephemeral Wind? It was supposed to be full of might and opportunity, but also, chaos and annihilation. Only fools sought them out since other than a rakshasa, there was nothing more dangerous in all of Salvation.

"But where are we going?" Tern asked, his voice a nasal whine.

"The place I entered, which I hope is also your exit. I can force it open so long as this stays a Novice Stage Pathway."

"How?" Cam asked, never having heard of such a thing.

Saira came to an abrupt stop, turning to face him. "I'm a Crown. With my Awareness, I can control a Pathway of this Stage…" She might have hesitated. "At least to a certain extent. Now hurry."

She sped off, moving even faster, although she still only seemed to be walking. But in order to keep up with her, Cam found himself having to jog. They all did, and Lilia was quickly struggling, panting. Cam dropped back to help her along, grateful when Jordil did the same. Tern raced on ahead, but Saira must have realized they weren't trailing close because she slowed to a stop, waiting on them.

Cam eyed her when they reached her side. Without a by-your-leave, Saira placed a long-fingered hand against Lilia's forehead. The girl's breathing became smoother, and she no longer gasped like fish in a boat.

"Better?" Saira asked, smiling gently.

Lilia bobbed a nod. "Thank you, ma'am."

Saira inclined her head like a duchess to her subject, and just like that, she was off.

Cam sighed, racing after her. They had long since passed the intersection that had brought them here, but Saira never slowed, the tunnel never changing.

While they traveled, fear and regret ate into Cam. Why had they been so reckless as to try this Pathway by themselves? If they had only waited, maybe someone older could have told them about the dangers of this place.

Cam questioned the last. After all, Saira was a Crown, more powerful than anyone within hundreds of miles of Traverse, and she had entered this same Pathway with no knowledge of how deadly it might be.

"We're nearing the entrance," Saira called over her shoulder.

Tern ran directly behind her, while Cam stayed on one side of Lilia with Jordil on the other. Lilia wasn't struggling like before, but Cam wanted to make sure she didn't falter since she still wasn't exactly moving swift-like.

A wind blew, the first Cam had felt in what felt like the hours. Initially, he was grateful for the breeze, but then came understanding. Was that the Ephemeral Wind? He caught a flash of panic from Jordil, who was likely wondering the same thing.

"It isn't the Ephemeral Wind," Saira said.

Cam shared a startled glance with Jordil. Had she read their minds? Crowns could supposedly do things like that.

Minutes later, a brightening up ahead signaled the tunnel's exit, and they entered daylight. Cam blinked against the stinging illumination, and when he could see again, he discovered himself standing on a shingle beach of small gray stones with a black cliff looming to their right and the ocean crashing to their left. The waves crashed higher even as Cam watched. The tide was rising, and the water lapped their toes. Cam shot the thick clouds blanketing the sky over the ocean a worried look. If they brought a storm, the waves were sure to surge even higher.

Saira further quickened her pace. "Hurry!" she shouted. "The Pathway might shift at any moment. We don't want to be caught within when it happens."

Onward she went, driving them toward a narrow trail that led up the looming cliff face. Cam chased after her, still alongside Lilia, who was panting again. The ocean swelled, the wind whipped, and the tide visibly rose. Cam shivered, not ashamed to be terrified.

Lilia started to lag again, red-faced and looking like she was ready to quit. It didn't matter what urgings she was given, she slowed to a stumble, barely moving.

Saira came back, worry lighting her features. "If I use my Grace upon you, you will be limited in what you can do moving forward. You will have to choose Kinesthia as your Primary Tang. Early on, it is the strongest of the Masteries, but for the wrong person, it can also be the most limiting."

"I want to live," Lilia gasped.

"So be it." Saira laid her hands on Lilia, and the girl's breathing grew controlled. "We only need to reach the clifftop. Can you manage?"

The question was directed at Lilia, and she nodded once, her jaw firming.

Saira smiled in encouragement before setting off again. Not a moment too soon, either. The waves were licking at their feet again. Cam climbed, desperate to reach the top. The sky darkened, and the water pursued him, wetting his shoes, a promise of a drowning death. So, too, did the wind as a storm threatened, seeking to tear him free of the trail.

Jordil's and Lilia's breaths came harsh. Same with Cam's. His heart pounded, and although he wanted to be up the trail quick as possible, he drifted back, taking the last position. If Lilia flagged again—or even Jordil—he wanted to be there to help them. They were his responsibility; only here because of his say-so.

Seconds later, they reached the clifftop, and Cam—being so intent on the climb—nearly fell over at the lack of incline. He regathered his balance and examined the view which met his gaze. A dense forest of oak, maples, and other hardwoods spread out before him. His attention was drawn away, though, when he realized Saira was urgently calling all of them to her. Tern clung to her side while Jordil and Lilia stumbled the final steps to reach her. A tree reared directly in front of them, and upon its branches hung four translucent, airy-seeming fruits. The Tree of Mastery and the Gifts from the Pathway.

Cam glanced toward the forest upon hearing the moaning wind again. It was louder this time, so much so that it sounded over the brewing storm. Saira sketched a sign and a watery image formed, just like the entrance to the Pathway, but this was the exit.

"Before you leave, pluck a fruit," Saira shouted. "It is your Gift for surviving the Pathway. And when you exit, immediately consume the fruit. Waste no time in doing so. When you do, there will be four layers that appear in your mind's eye. They are the Ephemeral Tangs. Plasminia at the top. Avoid that one and the next two below, Spirairia, which is gaseous, and Synapsia, a liquid. As little as you know, you should choose the solid layer at the bottom. Kinesthia. Move it toward your heart, and your body will do the rest. I will guide you."

Jordil and Lilia nodded, doing as they were told, each one plucking a fruit. Cam was about to follow suit, but…

Tern had wandered away, standing off to the side, his attention else-where. A red-hued light had spilled out from the forest. It circled and swirled in jerky motions, languid one moment and shooting forward the next. It was an Ephemeral Wind, and Tern stood alone facing it. He'd always said he would dodge one. The idiot.

The Wind closed on him, only yards away now. Saira hadn't noticed, currently ushering Jordil and Lilia through the exit. And since Tern showed no signs of moving, Cam raced to reach him.

"Come on," Cam urged. "You can't do this." He tried to pull Tern away from the Wind but was fought.

"Stop!" Tern shouted. He shoved hard, and Cam fell away. "I want this. The Wind will make me—"

The Wind swept over Tern. *Oh, no.* Cam entered the Wind, tearing Tern free of its clutches. They fell away. Saira shouted, sounding dis-tant, and all Cam knew was scouring pain. Agony consumed him, and his awareness of the world ended as strong arms lifted him up.

At last! He was free. Free after millennia of servitude and slavery. He

would never again be imprisoned. Even if it meant his dissolution.

Cam awoke to pain, like someone was wanting to pull his intestines out through his nose. Gagging and coughing, he thrashed. Blackness filled his vision. Was he blind? Panic stripped the last of his self-control, and he flailed harder.

"Hold him," a deep voice ordered.

Firm hands gripped Cam tight, but he thrashed even harder. He had to escape.

"Son, listen to me," said the deep voice.

Son? Confusion punctured some of Cam's fear. This wasn't his father. He didn't reek of whiskey, and his voice was deep and commanding, not reedy. Cam couldn't figure out what was happening. His thoughts wouldn't form right. Nothing made sense. Questions tumbled through his mind, like rocks rolling down a hill, collecting more uncertainties as they fell. *Where am I? Why am I hurting so bad? Where is everyone else? Had they made it out of the Pathway?*

"You need to breathe deep," the commanding voice ordered. "Control the pain."

Breathing deep didn't sound like it would do a lick of good.

"You can do this," the voice urged. "Breathe with me. Like this."

Confused and upset, Cam decided to follow the voice's guidance. He did as instructed, inhaling deep followed by a controlled exhalation. Again. Once more.

Cam relaxed a bit. While the agony still roared through him, it had backed off enough so he could think.

"That's it," the voice encouraged. "Now. Look inside your mind's eye. There should be four red layers."

His mind's eye? Four layers? The voice was talking about the Ephemeral Tangs, but they were supposed to be invisible to Neophytes like him. Only those who had a Heightened Awareness could see them; those who were Novices or had survived a Pathway and obtained the

Gift at the end.

But Cam hadn't taken a fruit from the Tree of Mastery, and he sure hadn't eaten one neither. So how was he supposed to see into his mind's eye?

"You can do this," the voice urged. "It's the only way you'll survive what's happened to you."

Cam's mind drifted, pain still clogging his thinking. He pondered again what had happened to him? What about Tern and—

No. He couldn't chase down that rabbit hole.

The voice was talking again. "Search inside yourself, to the imaginary center of your mind. You'll see it there."

Reckoning the voice hadn't led him wrong so far, Cam looked for the center of his mind, and—

A vision snapped into place. Four layers of red, ranging from a pale salmon to one dark as blood. They weren't completely separate, though. Instead, in the transition from one layer to the next, they melded into one another.

"I see…" Cam's voice came out in a croak, and he licked his lips, working moisture into his mouth, which felt dry as dirt. "I see it."

"Good. I need you to reach for the palest of the reds. The palest you can see. Draw it toward you in whatever way you can imagine. It will come."

From his learnings, Cam remembered what it was. It was the highest, most impossible to use layer and the most worthless. The one no one willingly accepted as a Primary Tang or any kind of Tang since it did nothing. It was Plasminia, and the voice wanted him to accept it? Why not one of the other Tangs? Like Kinesthia to make his body stronger? With all the ways of pain he was feeling, wouldn't that make more sense?

The agony spiked again, shutting off Cam's thoughts. He screamed.

"Hurry. You must be swift. The longer you take…"

The trailing off told Cam all he needed to know. The longer he took, the worse off he'd be. Possibly even dead, which come to think of it, might not be such a bad thing. Sure would beat the pain he was in anyway.

"Will he live?" a voice asked. *Jordil.* He sounded terrified.

"I don't know," someone else answered. *Saira.* "He *can* live, but only if he chooses it."

A pressure on his hand. Someone had taken hold of it, holding it her own. *Lilia.* "Please, Cam. Do what Master Winder says. You have to."

Cam didn't want to do any such thing. Right now, all he wanted was to let everything go so he would stop hurting.

"You can do this," Jordil said. "We can't lose you, too."

Lose you, too. It meant Tern was gone. Grief swelled within Cam. How would they ever tell Tern's momma?

"It's now or never," the deep voice said.

Cam didn't want to die. He denied his sorrow as best he could and ignored the pain, too. A deep breath later, and he tried to inhale the palest of the layers. He watched, stupefied as it seemed to flow directly into his eyes, drawing the other Tangs, transforming them into Plasminia as well.

"Guide it to your heart. It will know what to do afterward."

Cam kept on, breathing deep, imagining the Plasminia going down his throat, into his chest, into his heart.

Seconds passed, and slowly, too slow to notice, the agony receded, little by little, bit by bit, until finally, he was able to take a breath and there was no more pain.

Cam blinked, only then realizing that he'd had his eyes open the entire time. Moonlight poured down on the glade where he and the others had first entered the Pathway. His body lay propped against someone.

"How do you feel?" the deep voice asked, sounding relieved and also uncertain. He had been the one against whom Cam had lain. A cowl hooded his face, making it impossible to see his features.

"I feel like a dishrag wrung out about ten times too many."

The man laughed. "You'll be fine."

But Cam recalled Tern and knew the man was wrong. He wouldn't be fine. None of them would.

4

For Cam, the return to Traverse passed in a haze. His mind wouldn't work right, but at least one thing was clear. The man with the deep voice was Rainen Winder—the Unconquered Wilde Master. The same Sage he had seen battling in the heavens a decade ago. The Ephemeral Master before whom even the Sage-Dukes walked soft. And he had carried Cam most of the way home.

All that seemed a distant memory when sometime later, with the sun beating like a bright hammer directly into his eyes, Cam awoke in his own cot. No one was home, for which he was thankful. There also was hardly any food in the cabin, for which he was less enthusiastic. He clutched his stomach, which felt empty as a barrel of ale on the morning after the Okthomead Festival. He could use some eats right now; the better part of a cow wouldn't be too much.

Cam levered himself upright, getting to his feet, unaccountably weak and dressed in the same clothes as when he'd gone into that cursed Pathway. Making his way to the kitchen, he made do with some moldy bread, a slathering of butter, and a cup of what looked like stew drying in a pot.

Somewhat sated, he tried to plan out what to do next. The answer came clear, but Cam hesitated. He didn't fancy any part of what needed accomplishing. A large part of him hoped that Jordil and Lilia had already seen to it; that they had told Tern's momma what had become of her baby boy.

Fresh grief stabbed at Cam's heart. Tern had been his friend, and knowing he was dead cut him to the bone. He wished they'd never gone to the Pathway.

He sighed then. All the wishing in the world wouldn't bring Tern back and piling on buckets of blame wouldn't make his sorrow any lighter. It was best if he just got the worst of the work done now.

Cam stepped away from the kitchen table, annoyed when he noticed the ongoing weakness in his body. Was this because he had chosen Plasminia as his Primary Tang? There wasn't much to say about Plasminians, except they were weak and frail.

Cam grimaced. Was that to be his future then?

Reaching the front door, he paused, noting the cracked mirror in the corner. Curiosity roused. He wanted to see it. What did his eyes look like now that he was a Novice? Did the whites of his eyes have the pale red tint of a Plasminian Novice?

He expected so but staring into the mirror still gave him a shock. A stick-like figure, with all the muscle and fat wasted away, stared back at him. Cam put a disbelieving hand to his face, to the hollows in his cheeks, the bulging of his Novice-red eyes. He looked like a walking corpse.

A moment longer of staring, and Cam firmed his jaw. Tern was dead, and Cam was alive. He was a Novice, weak now, but he could yet make something out of his life. Nodding to himself, Cam left the cabin, stepping outside and finding Jordil and Lilia on the porch.

"You're alive!" Jordil shouted, arms thrown wide for an embrace with Lilia following in his footsteps.

Cam's eyes misted. His friends... They'd been waiting for him. Jordil offered a rib-creaking hug, and Cam groaned. When had Jordil gotten so strong?

Stepping back, Cam took a fresh look at his friend, at the carnation-red color of his whites. He looked like he'd grown a few inches since yesterday, filled out, too, like he'd stolen all the muscle Cam had lost. Lilia showed the same changes, except for her it was in reverse. While she also seemed taller, she looked to have given away a hefty amount of weight. Staring from one to the other, Cam realized Jordil and Lilia were healthy in a way he feared he would never be.

"What's wrong?" Lilia asked, concern on her still-round face.

Cam gestured to them, trying to hogtie his flare of jealousy. "You both look so strong, like you could run ten miles and wrestle a bull after."

Jordil laughed. "Saira told us we had to choose Kinesthia for our Primary Tang after she touched us with her Grace. It's made some changes."

Lilia took up the explanation. "And Master Winder said that part of the reason I was so heavy was because of something called—."

"It doesn't matter," Jordil cut in.

"He's right," Lilia hastily agreed. "What's important is you. How are you doing?"

Cam didn't answer her question, asking one of his own, needing confirmation. "Is Tern…"

Jordil's face fell. "The Ephemeral Wind got him, cut him to ribbons until there wasn't even a body left to burn." He hesitated. "You nearly died, too. You took the Wind nearly straight on after pulling Tern out of the way."

"Saira said you couldn't have saved him," Lilia said, her voice soft. "She said that even if you had pulled Tern right out of the Wind, he wouldn't have made it. You might not have either, except the Wind died some by the time it caught you. Saira was able to save you and grab a fruit for you on the way out."

Cam recalled none of it, which wasn't much of a surprise given how much pain he had been in. There was more to learn, though. Rainen Winder. The Unconquered Wilde Sage. Was it really him? He asked as much.

Jordil nodded. "After we exited the Pathway, he was there, waiting. Somehow he knew about us."

"He knew about us because he's a Sage," Lilia said. "The whites of his eyes are violet."

"The Wilde Sage," Jordil breathed. "I can't believe we met him."

"I think he's training Saira," Lilia added. "They might even be a couple the way they act around one another."

Cam waved aside their words. "What did he do to me?"

"He took the fruit Saira grabbed for you and somehow melted it into your skin. And then—"

Cam knew the rest. "And then he told me to choose Plasminia as my Primary Tang. I remember that part."

"Do you remember what came after?" Lilia asked, voice soft and sounding nervous as a mouse.

Cam didn't. "First thing I remember is waking up a few minutes ago."

"Rainen—"

"*Master Winder*," Lilia corrected.

"Right," Jordil said, bobbing his head in agreement. "Anyway, he carried you back to Traverse. He and Saira planned on leaving yesterday, but they ended up staying around to make sure you're fine."

"Yesterday?" That made no sense. Cam remembered that night had fallen by the time they had exited the Pathway.

"You've been asleep for over two days," Jordil said.

Two days? Tern's momma… did she know? He shot a silent query to Jordil.

"We told her," Jordil said, somehow guessing the question.

Cam's heart trembled. "How bad did she take it?"

"Bad," Lilia said, swallowing heavily, her face pale. "She blames us for Tern. All of us. The things she said." She shook her head. "I wouldn't go her way any time soon."

Jordil nodded agreement. "I wouldn't go her way ever."

A short while after catching Cam up on the happenings since the Pathway, Jordil and Lilia had to leave and do some work for their folks. They also let Cam know that in a few days, the three of them were supposed to start classes with Master Bennett on what it meant to be a Novice and how to Advance to Acolyte.

As for Cam, he was surprised when Saira appeared on his rundown street of rundown houses. With her was a man of medium height but heavily muscled. He moved with smooth grace. His dark hair—long the last time Cam had seen it—was cut short and it seemed… he wasn't sure of the right word, but maybe stylish? Same with his dark leather garb and cloak, which appeared fashioned to fit him perfectly. Add in his square jaw, confident gait, and violet eyes—the eyes of a Sage—and there was no mistaking him. *Rainen Winder.*

Otherwise, he looked about the same as when Cam had seen him ten years ago. This was one of the most powerful men in the world. A Wilde Sage. He didn't rule a city like the other Sages—all of them dukes in charge of their duchies—but Rainen Winder was still a ruler.

Doing his best to swallow down his intimidation, Cam didn't feel a whole lot better when the man smiled. It didn't matter that it was bright and warm. Even Master Winder's simplest expression seemed to cause the world to warp, the sunshine to shimmer, and reality itself to twist depending on the nature of Master Winder's whim and will.

Cam had to lock his knees from collapsing, unable to meet the Wilde Sage's gaze. He glanced aside, only then noticing that there was no one about on the streets. It was like everyone knew better than to remain close at hand in Master Winder's presence.

The two strangers, a Sage and a Crown, reached Cam's front porch, and once again, he had to lock tight his knees. There was no chance he'd collapse to his knees like an itty-bitty bug in front of them. He also decided to take the initiative.

"Thank you for saving me," Cam said, addressing both Saira and Master Winder.

Saira smiled, and Cam's breath caught. He could have sworn the world had just brightened. His heart did anyhow. Saira was that beautiful.

"You also saved me," she said, "so it is I who owe you thanks."

Cam frowned, not sure what she meant.

Saira's smile widened into a warm chuckle. "You didn't know? When you pulled your friend out of the Ephemeral Wind, you fell into me. It knocked me out of the way as well. If not for that, the Ephemeral Wind would have latched onto me, and I likely wouldn't be here."

Cam still didn't understand, and his ongoing confusion must have been obvious.

Saira explained further. "Ephemeral Winds seek out those with the greatest Ephemera, but by attaching first to Tern, and then briefly touching you, it had no time to seek me."

Master Winder spoke. "And you only survived because you had an opportunity to Advance. If not for that simple fact, you would have died." He smiled again, but this time there was no sense of the air twisting about in reaction to his power. "It's good to formally meet you, Cam Folde. My name is Rainen Winder."

Cam blinked. The Sage spoke like a normal person, like everyone didn't already know who he was. "Thank you for saving me, Master Winder," he said, knowing he was repeating himself. But he couldn't help it; not when his nerves had him jiggling inside like a spring shower.

"I didn't save you," Master Winder corrected. "You did that on your own. I merely served as a guide."

Cam might have never learned much in school, but he had learned manners. "Regardless, sir, I'm in your debt."

Master Winder laughed. "Consider your debt paid. You saved Saira, and for that alone, I am grateful."

The Sage and Saira shared an uninterpretable expression, and Cam didn't miss it. Nor could he rightly figure what it meant, but if he was a betting man, he'd have to agree with Lilia. They were a couple.

"You two married?" Cam asked, the blunt question escaping without him having a chance to think the matter through.

Saira chuckled. "Good gracious, no. My mother would kill Rainen if I were to ever wed him."

Again came confusion, and this time, it was Master Winder who explained.

"I was asked by Saira's mother to see to her training. If I ever let her come to harm..." He mock shuddered. "Let's just say that even Sages know to tread carefully around the women of the Sinanes."

Cam's eyes shot wide. The Sinanes? They were supposed to be a group of islands out in the middle of nowhere, with all the women powerful, most of them Crowns. And the ruler herself was a Sage Prime, the highest Advancement possible in the world.

Master Winder chuckled. "You see what I mean about my gratitude? Even Sages are careful around the mistresses of the Sinanes. They are amongst the most powerful people on Salvation."

Cam struggled on how to respond, so he leaned again on his good manners. "It was my honor to save her, sir." It must have been the right thing to say since Saira and Master Winder both smiled at him.

"I think we've all done enough thanking of one another," Saira said. "It's time to move on to why we're here."

Master Winder's humor fled. "In order to survive the Ephemeral Wind, you had to take Plasminia as your Primary Tang. There are things you need to know about what that means."

Cam swallowed heavily, worried about what Master Winder would have to say. He had a feeling it wouldn't be good.

"There are four Ephemeral Tangs," Master Winder began. "They exist in the smallest particle of light, the finest mote of matter. But for an Ephemeral Master, they concentrate in our Source, growing within us if we're lucky and talented enough. First, there is Spirairia, which appears as a gas and is a hard Tang to master. But those with it can project fields around themselves and others. It also allows for telepathy, telekinesis, and other such skills. Inward of Spirairia is Synapsia, which is a liquid that improves the mind, and only with it is true mastery of the other Tangs possible. Next is Kinesthia, which is a solid and the easiest Tang to learn. It deals with the physical, perfecting a person's body. And finally there is Plasminia, outside all the others and the most difficult Tang to master; so much so that only a rare handful in all of history have ever managed it. It is energetic and uncontrollable, and unfortunately, most everyone who has ever chosen Plasminia ended up living short lives."

Much of Master Winder's instruction was basic, but it was the words spoken at the end that reverberated in Cam's mind. *Most everyone who has ever chosen Plasminia ended up living short lives.*

Cam would not live long. His worst fears were confirmed. The Wilde Sage—a true Ephemeral Master—had made the pronouncement, and he would know better than anyone. Cam's mouth went dry, his vision blurred. Would he even live long enough to marry and have children?

"I'm sorry." It was Saira.

Cam's gaze went to her, eyes clearing enough to see to her empathy. "How much time do I have?" The question came out in a whisper.

"I don't know," Master Winder replied, his voice unflinching but not cold. "No one does. All that is known about Plasminians is that they are weak in body, mind, and spirit, and it is impossible for them to balance that weakness.

Cam couldn't help but shoot him an angry glare. "Then why did you make me choose it?"

Master Winder frowned, appearing uncomfortable. "Ah, that. There was no other way to save you. You needed to incorporate all the Ephemera burned into you by the Wind, and only Plasminia has the energy to allow for that. No other Tang would have sufficed. Even then, if you didn't have the fruit, you would have died. My choice for you was simple. See you die right after exiting the Pathway. Or save you, so you at least have a chance to live out some semblance of a life."

"And how weak I am?"

"The weakness you feel now will remain, possibly grow worse," Master Winder said, his voice grave and sounding like a judgment of doom.

"We truly are sorry," Saira said, her face still grave and full of sympathy.

Her sympathy sparked sudden anger in Cam, and he shot her a fury-filled glare. He didn't want her pity. He wanted his life back. He wanted Tern alive and well.

"We will leave you now," Master Winder said, moving to step off the porch but hesitating, glancing back. "Perhaps we will learn something that can help you. If we do, we will make sure you hear of it."

Cam nodded dully, not having anything to say. It seemed both he and Tern had died in that cursed Pathway. Cam would just take longer to reach his end.

After Master Winder and Saira left, Cam continued watching after them, frozen, staring at the same spot even when it was empty.

The cobblestone streets were rougher in his family's poor section of the town. He'd never noticed it before. Never paid it much mind; the way the houses were shoved close to one another and how truly broken down they appeared.

But in that moment, their state of disrepair struck him like a blow. The homes reflected who he was now as a person. Cam was a Novice, and he would die because of his supposed Advancement. Instead of growing stronger and fitter, he would become the opposite.

He closed his eyes then, praying to Devesh, praying to His Holy Servants who had crafted this Realm. While lost in prayer, he remembered a phrase. *All is Ephemera, and Ephemera is All.* It was supposed to teach the people of Salvation how everything in the world had a touch of Ephemera; that all was of Devesh and that all were of Him. Even the Divines in Heaven, who would one day give away their lives and return to their Holy Creator.

Cam smirked. He'd be returning to Devesh sooner than most. The smirk became a snort of derision. What a terrible thing it was to be young and know that death was right around the corner.

He went inside, shutting the door. He didn't want to see the glad sunshine anymore.

5

Four years later...

A rush of wind shook the shutters and moaned across the roof of Master Bennett's home. The weather was turning harsh outside with thick snowflakes collecting on the rooftops and various roads and paths snaking through Traverse. There were a few people out and about, rushing around, getting their chores done, but for most folks, while it was only late afternoon, they were already home, hunkered down for the day.

This was the first winter storm of the season, one predicted by the town's Ephemeral Masters—those who had the learning to figure on future weather. And because it was the first storm, it was also a special day. One meant to be spent with family around the hearth, sharing laughter and presents as well as visiting friends and singing silly songs. And on the first night after the storm's passing, the entire village would come together in the town square and have a grand celebration. Some fools would no doubt show their backsides, but for most, it would be a good time for festivities, with lots of food and drink.

Cam scowled inwardly at the last thought. The food would be fine, but not the drink. After the Pathway to Grace where Tern had died and Cam had been rendered a Plasminian, life hadn't been easy. He couldn't do much for himself. Walking from one end of Traverse to the other was a tall task, much less any kind of labor for a man, such as plowing a field, baling hay, or even just digging holes for a fence.

The one blessing should have been learning to use Ephemera, but there, too, he was denied. His instructor, Master Bennett, was a patient, gentle man, with the bright yellow eyes of an Adept, but just like Master Winder and Saira, he lacked the learning on how Cam was supposed to use Plasminia, the most useless of Tangs.

For a time, the limitations, loss, and hopelessness had gotten Cam to drinking, no different than his old man and siblings. At first, he'd explained it away as a means to pass the time, a gentle habit to settle the worries of the day. But a few sips at night had eventually become a few in the afternoon and a couple more in the morning. Then he was drinking all day, intoxicated by early afternoon, bingeing until he passed out.

Six months ago, Pharis—long since cleaned up—had confronted him, and it hadn't been her first time doing so. But for whatever reason, on that occasion, her advice and admonition had sunk into Cam. He recognized the path where he was headed, and he didn't like where that road led.

He had set aside the bottle, hadn't had a thimbleful of alcohol since, and he was the better for it. It was too bad his dad and Darik still struggled with their addiction, but at least for Cam, sobriety had granted him grace, especially since he was able to resume classes with Master Bennett. Sure, he couldn't do nothing physical, but it didn't mean he couldn't do nothing at all.

Besides, getting out of the house and learning was miles better than sitting at home, staring at the walls, and having nothing to do but get drunk.

Strangely enough, his efforts at staying healthy seemed to change his body as well. Cam was still weaker than most children, but at least he'd packed on the muscle. Sure those same muscles were all show and no go, but they were nice to look at. He'd also grown in height, and when it was all said and done, at the rate he was going, Cam would likely be built like a brick outhouse; tall as Darik but muscular hopefully, instead of covered in a thick layer of fat.

He glanced over when he caught Jordil whispering something to Lilia. She smiled in reply.

Cam stared their way. They looked good together. Jordil was a few inches shorter than Cam, but rather than beanpole skinny, he was now lean, muscular, and beaming with health. He'd grown so much since that Pathway, become a person of merit. It reflected in the rest of his appearance; simple but well-tailored clothes and hair cut fashionably short—unlike Cam's long, tangled locks.

As for Lilia, she'd transformed into a lovely woman. Of medium height like the rest of the women in her family, she had a slim, athletic build and a winsome smile with a slight gap between her front-most teeth that only made her more appealing.

And Master Bennett even figured that the two of them might have the understanding to answer the singular question that separated Novices from Acolyte: knowing on a personal basis the difference between selfishness versus selflessness.

A worm of envy at their good fortune threaded through Cam's mind, but he crushed it. He was happy for his friends, glad to be a part of their lives. Or so he told himself every day. It was either that or sink into bitterness and alcohol.

"I can tell none of you are listening," Master Bennett said. A kind smile split his wizened features. "I'll let Master Moltin know you won't be making it for his class on Traverse's history. Go enjoy the day."

Cam rose to his feet, sharing an excited grin with Jordil and Lilia. He couldn't wait to get out into the cold, to feel the snow on his face, and see his breath plume in the air.

Just as he was ready to head outside, though, Master Bennett called him back. "Hold a moment, Cam. I'd like to talk to you first."

Cam glanced to Jordil and Lilia who were already out the door.

"Come by our house when you can," Jordil said. He and Lilia had married back in the summer, settling into a small, cozy cottage.

"I'll be there," Cam replied before facing Master Bennett. "What is it, sir?"

Rather than answering, Master Bennett rose from his chair and passed over a small, red-leather volume. "I talked to a young librarian by the name of Grey, last time I visited Charn. We spoke about your condition, and she sent this to me. It arrived a few days ago. I've read it, and…" He hesitated, stroking his long, white beard. "I don't want to raise your hopes, my boy, but it's the record of someone like you, Fetch Devile, a Plasminian. He did what no one else in known history has ever managed. He balanced his Ephemera by creating a Novice Tang of Kinesthia."

Cam's heart ticked faster, and he didn't bother on trying to suppress his excitement. What Master Bennett was saying… ever since the Pathway, it was everything he had ever hoped for and dreamed. "How?"

It was a single word question that contained the entirety of his longing.

"By diving a Pathway at the Stage of Adept. According to the author's account, once he managed it, he was able to live out a normal life without the weakness that currently plagues you."

Cam's burgeoning hopes shriveled. He was a Novice in name only, but even if he was strong like Jordil and Lilia, diving an Adept Stage Pathway would be impossible. Beyond that, they were rare, appearing in unlikely places and impossible to predict.

All is Ephemera, and Ephemera is All.

The phrase echoed in Cam's mind, which wasn't a surprise. Ever since he'd decided to come off the whiskey and moonshine, it had become his personal mantra, a way to focus, meditate, and pray, lending him some solace and clarity of thought.

Cam stared at the book. Such a small item to contain everything of a man's dreams. "Does the Plasminian say how?"

"You should read it yourself," Master Bennett advised.

"Why did he choose Kinesthia? Why not Synapsia?"

"Because with Kinesthia, your body can heal. That's where things are broken for you. Your lack of balance."

Of course.

"I have a question." Master Bennett cleared his throat. "What happens if you find a Pathway to match? Will you dive it?"

Cam knew to do so would be lunacy. The last time he'd made such a blunder, he'd lost a friend. Sure, it hadn't been his fault. It had been Tern's; doing something so incredibly stupid that Cam still struggled with understanding what could have gotten into his friend's head.

But still. To be healed and have a future…

Master Bennett smiled. "You don't have to answer right now, but I hope you don't let what happened to Tern hold you back. You made the right decision—trying to save him—but sometimes the right decision doesn't always lead to the right outcome."

Cam didn't know what to say. Truth was, he didn't like thinking on those events all too much. He mumbled some vague words of agreement, and as he was about to depart, Master Bennett called him back once more. "There was something else. I wanted to tell you how proud of you I am."

Cam cocked his head in confusion. "What do you mean?"

"You've had many reasons to quit, and yet you didn't."

"I quit for a while," Cam said, shuffling his feet, remembering the nearly two years of heavy drinking.

"A while isn't forever, and here you are, back in class. I also understand you're working these days."

"It's not much," Cam said with a dismissive shrug. "It's just cleaning Master Carlson's shop. He doesn't have any apprentices right now and needed the help."

"It's still a purpose," Master Bennett said. "Don't discount it, and don't discount what you've accomplished. Master Moltin agrees with me."

"I've liked his classes, especially the ones on military history."

Master Bennett smiled. "I'm sure you do." He gestured Cam off. "Read the book. Learn what it says, and if we find you the right Pathway, maybe we'll also find a way for you to dive it."

Cam chuckled, not really believing anything like that would happen for him. No matter what else, he was still a Folde, and if there was one true law in Creation, it was that nothing truly good ever happened for a Folde.

As soon as Cam stepped out of Master Bennett's home and onto the wraparound porch looking out over the village square, he caught sight of Maria Benefield. Trailing after her were Suse Marline and Ingold Brest, a couple of Maria's friends, and the trio were amongst the banes of Cam's existence.

He sighed inwardly, especially when he noticed Pivot Stump, the mayor's son bouncing alongside them like a puppy. *Here it comes.*

Sure enough, as soon as Cam stepped foot off Master Bennett's porch, it was as if the safety afforded him by his instructor's house evaporated.

Pivot saw him first, and he grinned like a git. "Well, look who's finishing his Novice classes. It's the Sage, Cam Folde." He brayed laughter.

"Nice to see you, too, Pivot," Cam said with a weary sigh. There were more insults to come, especially since Maria and her lackeys resented him. Cam was Novice. They weren't, and it stuck in their craw. All the young folk facing him were children of privilege, and yet that privilege hadn't granted them a chance to dive a Pathway to Grace. It was mostly because there hadn't been any stable ones formed near Traverse for the past few years. Nor had there been any low-level cores to be found given how few rakshasas seemed to be about in the world these days. Ever since Master Winder killed Borile, there were remarkably few of them remaining in the world.

"Cam," Suse began. "I was wondering if you'd clear a path for me. With all this snow, there's no way for me to get home. You don't mind, do you? Being a powerful Novice and all."

"Clear a path?" Pivot said. "That weakling can't even clear his nose."

All of them fell to laughing.

Cam trudged past them, wanting to get home and enjoy time with his family. Later on, he'd stop by and see Jordil and Lilia.

"Come on, Cam," Maria called out. "We were just teasing."

She was the worst of the group. How had he ever thought she was pretty?

"You're so big and strong," she continued.

Cam briefly glanced aside, surprised to see her striding next to him. He looked away, hoping she'd leave him alone. So long as he didn't make eye contact or talk to her, that usually worked.

But it didn't this time.

"Why are you still in Traverse?" Maria hissed. "You and your worthless family. No-good Foldes. Bunch of drunks. You're a worthless drunk. You know I'm right. I still remember how you were running moonshine, drunk as a lord in broad daylight."

Cam grimaced, recalling what she was talking about. A number of months back, prior to getting sober, He'd come across Maria. It had been early in the afternoon when he'd been out buying moonshine. He'd already been drunk, and Maria had witnessed his intoxication. Her disgust had been obvious.

"And your drunkenness doesn't even touch on what you did to Tern. Leave before you hurt anyone else."

Cam's annoyance flared to rage, but he managed to bite his tongue. He knew what she wanted from him. Maria wanted him furious, shouting at her so she could play the victim. And he *wanted* to shout at her. It was a low thing she had said, but that's the kind of person she was. Under all that pretty was an ugly soul.

"Leave me be," Cam managed to get out from behind clenched teeth, "and I'll leave you be."

"I'll leave you be when you leave," Maria declared. She'd finally stopped trailing him. "Useless drunk! No one wants you here!" She shouted, loud enough so it would carry.

Thankfully, she didn't follow on to say anything else, her or her cruel friends. They went their own way, not bothering Cam any longer as he headed home. As he tramped through the heavy snowfall, the ground already powdered in deepening white, he took steady breaths, trying to let go of his upset. This was the first winter storm of the year, a time to celebrate, and he wanted to experience that joy; not dwell on the anger and disgust inspired by Maria and her friends.

The anger crested again for a moment. *Fragging arrogant bastards.* Cam wished he could leave like Maria wanted him to, go someplace where no one knew him, where he could start over fresh. He'd wanted that for a long while.

Minutes later, he reached his home, witnessed by Mrs. Wolder's dogs, who set to barking like fools.

He ignored the animals; eyeing instead his home, a decrepit-looking house with a small front porch, rotten railings, and the walls looking like they might fall in on themselves. At least the roof didn't sag. Cam, Darik, and their father had rebuilt it this summer, replacing trusses that had been one storm from giving way. Sure, Darik and their father had done most of the labor since Cam was too weak to be of help, but he'd done his part; planning out the work, making measurements and cutting wood as needed. He'd even swung a hammer and nailed the cedar shingles in place.

He'd done enough to feel like he'd contributed, and he stared in pride at the roof. It would hold up nicely against this first storm, and that was because of him and his family.

No-good Foldes, indeed.

Cam scoffed. To the unholy hells with Maria Benefield and all the rest of them.

Setting aside the last of his aggravation, he stepped inside, glad to see the family all gathered.

Pharis glanced up from where she was helping their father and brother—both sober for now—peel potatoes. "You're home early," she said.

"So are you." Usually Pharis worked until the early evening, nannying Farmer Sigmon's children. Cam wondered if Farmer Sigmon might like having Pharis around for other reasons. She'd always been intelligent and kind, but ever since she'd cleaned up, she'd also reclaimed her prettiness. There were a lot of young men in Traverse who now wanted to get to know her better.

"It's the first winter storm," Pharis said. "Farmer Sigmon and his wife let me off early." As Cam entered the kitchen area to see where he could help, she brushed back his unkempt hair. "You need to trim that shaggy mop."

"Leave the boy be," said their father, covering a belch and making his significant paunch shoot out just a bit farther. "I ain't in the mood to hear you three natter on." His posture slumped, the fatigue obvious. Cam's father had lived a rough life, reflected in his tired face, his thin limbs, and a salt-and-pepper beard that was as splotchy and ragged as the rest of him.

"Don't listen to Pharis," Darik said. "Women like men with hair. Gets them happy, if you know what I mean." He leered, pointing to his hairy chest, his full beard, and his long hair.

"How would you know what women like?" Pharis asked. "The only woman I've ever seen you with is old Widow Thurnbush, trimming her shrubs."

"I was trimming something," Darik cracked. "But it wasn't her shrubs."

"Disgusting!" Pharis exclaimed. "She's older than our daddy."

"She ain't old in the ways that count," Darik said, waggling his eyebrows. "Then she's right fine."

"Can we talk about something else," Cam asked, wishing he was surprised by Darik's crudeness. He eyed his brother, surprised as always that he could stare him in the eyes with no need for an upward arch to his neck. In his inner reflection, he still expected to be both shorter and thinner than Darik, but neither was true. He actually had an inch on him.

"Sure, Runt," Darik said, laying a companionable arm across Cam's shoulders. "What did you learn today? Anything useful?"

"Actually, I did," Cam said, going on to explain about the book Master Bennett had obtained for him, pulling it out of his inside jacket pocket for the others to see.

Darik whistled in appreciation. "Wouldn't that be something. You a proper Novice. Strong instead of weak."

"You'd have to dive an Adept Pathway," their father said, a note of caution in his voice. "Ain't no way for you to do that."

"Unless I found an Adept willing to dive it with me." Cam had actually been thinking on it. "Master Bennett is an Adept."

"He's also older than the hills," Darik said. "Old coot likely saw the first sunrise."

Cam ignored his brother's comment, not liking to hear Master Bennett disparaged. "But if there was an Adept, I could be healed. I could live a full life."

His father set a hand on his shoulder, staring him in the eyes. "You know I want nothing more than that for you," he said. "But I also don't want you to get your hopes up. Wanting what Foldes don't deserve is what landed you all these troubles in the first place. And fixing on another hare-brained scheme might do you in this time."

"He's right," Darik said. "Good things don't happen to Foldes."

"Good things *do* happen to Foldes," Pharis said. "I got sober and have a good job. I'm even learning healing from Master Bennett and Midwife Spenser. And Cam got off the drink, too. He also has a job, and he's learning more than most will ever know from Master Bennett and Master Moltin."

"And what good will that do him?" Darik challenged.

"A lot of good," Cam said, figuring on stepping in and defending himself. "You think I can't lift logs or dig post holes or a whole number of things, and you're right. But it don't mean I'm useless. I've got a mind. I can read and write mail for those who don't know their letters. I can calculate, run a store, or learn medicine like Pharis. There's lots of things I can do."

Darik shifted about, like ants itched his britches. "You're right," he said. "You can do a lot of things, but it's just…"

He trailed off, but Cam knew what he couldn't say. It was simply a repetition of what he'd earlier declared: that no good thing happened for a Folde, a statement that had the force of law in their household. And sometimes, like today when Maria and her friends had given Cam the barbed side of their tongues, it felt truer than not.

Their father spoke into the silence, attention on Cam. "I know fixing yourself, becoming a proper Ephemeral Master, is what you've always wanted, but just be careful. You know how dreams are to people like us."

"Dangerous," Cam replied, abruptly annoyed with his father. "Looks like the stew needs water. I'll fetch it." He grabbed a pail on his way out the door, headed for the shared well down the road.

The cold didn't bother him, and it actually gave him a chance to let go of his irritation. He loved his father. The man had his warts, but he'd stayed with his children, rarely raised a hand to them when they were young and saw them fed and loved. Not all sons could say that about their fathers.

But, still, in spite of all that, Cam didn't want to listen to his dad right now, didn't want to hear the old man talk down his dreams. A fellow had to have some hope, right?

Cam reached the well, and as he hauled the water, he imagined a singing light filling the world, motes that penetrated the smallest fleck of dirt, the dimmest moonbeam, every drop of water pouring through Barr River. The motes were of one color and all of them.

His vision shifted, and Cam saw himself as if from a great distance. He marched across rivers in a single stride. He bounded to the heights of the mountains in a single leap. He raced a sunbeam and won. And in everything, he did for others what they couldn't do for themselves but needed done.

All is Ephemera and Ephemera is All.

6

Winter passed in a blink, and in no time, it was spring.

Cam enjoyed the lovely weather, viewing his Source while standing outside a well-maintained cottage. Roofed in red tile and boarded in black shutters, it was a cozy cabin that stood on the outskirts of town. A small garden fronted the home, catching the morning sunshine. Bluebirds sang from a nearby tree while plump bumblebees flitted about colorful flowers growing in window boxes. Dew clung to the grass and leaves, and the bright spring morning felt alive and perfect.

None of that mattered to Cam. He was focused on his mind's eye, a simple blink, and his Source filled his vision, a roughly shaped sphere, glowing with his Ephemera, a drifting pale-red fog that crackled with silent lightning. Cam paused when he beheld it. Of course, it wasn't *all* his Ephemera. Supposedly, he had it in every fiber of his being, even his hair and nails. That's what the phrase claimed when it said *All is Ephemera and Ephemera is All.* That everything—be it a person, plant, animal, table, or chair—had some bit of Ephemera. Even the smallest grain of sand or the softest breeze.

"What are you doing, trying to catch flies?" Jordil asked, stepping outside the house. "You look like a slack-jawed yokel, standing there with your mouth open, staring off into nowhere." He grinned to take the bite out of his comments, but Cam could see he thought he was being clever.

Well, two could play that game.

"Is Lilia decent?" Cam asked, projecting his voice as loud as possible so the whole neighborhood could hear. "Didn't mean to bother y'all if you were getting frisky."

Jordil's gaze darted about, his eyes wide. The exact reaction Cam had wanted. "You jackass!" he hissed once he realized no one was around to hear what Cam had said.

Cam wasn't listening. He was too busy bending over laughing. "You're welcome," he eventually wheezed out to his friend.

"What am I welcome for?" Jordil said in a sour tone.

"For embarrassing you. What are friends for if not to embarrass each other?"

"Lilia wouldn't have been embarrassed. She'd have been mortified. And she'd have taken it out on your stupid head. She still might if she hears about this."

Cam's laughter left him. "Err. She wouldn't really take offense, would she?"

Jordil's smile returned, pleased and evil. "Let's say I tell her, and we find out?"

Cam hastily waved away Jordil's suggestion. "No need. No need at all."

"I thought you'd say that." Jordil chuckled. "Now what's brought you out here on this lovely spring morning?"

"Got a message from Master Bennett," Cam answered. "He wants to talk to us about something. Wouldn't say what."

Jordil shrugged. "Guess we better find out then."

They set off, ambling over to their instructor's house while discussing Ephemera and what they had planned for the day.

"Aren't you supposed to be working with Master Colson?" Cam

asked. "Learning to make barrels or something."

"That's for tomorrow," Jordil said. "Today, I'm helping my father." He gave a morose sag of his shoulders. "I'm supposed to get hitched to a plow and use Kinesthia to help furrow the fields."

"At least you got the strength for it."

"That's not the point," Jordil said. "I'm an Ephemeral Master. Not a bullock."

"Well, you're right on that account. You definitely ain't a bull, least according to Lilia."

Jordil sputtered in feigned outrage, while Cam laughed.

"I'll have you know, I'm *all* bull," Jordil groused.

Cam let him get in the last word before the conversation shifted to Spirairia, which both Jordil and Lilia had recently managed to add. Not to Novice, but just enough to eventually get there. It had taken their all, left them sweating and looking as hungover as Cam had ever been, but for them, it had lasted for days. Supposedly, the true geniuses of the world could manage such a feat without any kind of problem, but for Jordil and Lilia, the Spirairia Tang would be the last they'd ever add. Trying for more would like to kill them.

Regardless, their rather rare accomplishment was all on account of an equally rare tonic Master Bennett had managed to acquire. It had been made by a master alchemist from some plants heavy in Ephemera, similar to the fruit a person received on exiting a Novice Pathway, but far less potent.

Cam had received that same tonic, but the moment the extra Ephemera had entered his Source, every bit of it had transformed to more Plasminia. One blink to the next, and it was over. Cam never even had a chance to fix on forming himself a new Tang before greedy Plasminia took it all.

Fragging Plasminia.

Cam did his best to throw off his irritation. "You think you can do what Master Bennett says can be done with Spirairia?"

"I don't know," Jordil answered. "I have to Advance the Tang to Novice first."

"But once you do—"

Jordil laughed. "Don't be trying to put the cart before the horse," he said. "Advancing a Tang ain't so easy as all that."

Cam grinned. "Can I help it that I want what's best for you and Lilia?"

"I suppose I can't hold that against you," Jordil said.

Their conversation fell quiet, and Cam glanced about, enjoying the warm spring sunshine. A gentle breeze fingered his long hair, carrying the scent of flowers while folks ambled about, stopping to talk and laugh with neighbors. Everyone seemed in a fine mood, and why not? It was warm and beautiful, the kind of weather meant for life to be enjoyed. And while winter was Cam's favorite season, he liked spring just fine, especially seeing the world green and vibrant.

It should have been a pleasant walk, but within a hundred yards, Cam's breathing started to labor. His heart thudded fast and loud, and the need to suck air, gasp for it, made him want to come to a stop and catch a break. But he pushed on. It was only a little longer to Master Bennett's house. He could rest then. And if he kept working at it, maybe someday, his stamina would actually increase.

"Cam!" a voice called out.

Cam came to a grateful halt, glancing about.

It was Master Moltin. He appeared as old as Master Bennett—white-haired and white-bearded—and also with Adept-yellow eyes. However, he moved about like a spry spring chicken. He also wasn't nearly as crabby as when Cam had known him as a child. He liked Master Moltin now, still taking lessons with him on history and politics since Cam was the only person in all of Traverse with the time or the interest.

"I was hoping I'd catch you before you left," Master Moltin said.

Cam shared a look of bewilderment with Jordil. Left? He didn't realize he was going anywhere.

His instructor picked up right where he'd left off. "I found a wonderful book for you to read. It's a fictional account about a young woman who creates magical effects by imbibing metals of all things. It's fantastic. I thought you might enjoy it." Master Moltin's bearded face was creased in a grin, and his eyes lit with excitement. "Come see me after you return, and I'll let you borrow it."

"Thank you, sir," Cam said, still unsure what Master Moltin was getting at. "But where am I going that I need to return?"

Master Moltin smacked his forehead theatrically. "Master Bennett hasn't told you? Foolish me. I'll let him explain" He dashed off as was his wont. "But see me afterward," he shouted over his shoulder.

"The unholy hells was that about?" Jordil murmured.

"No idea," Cam replied, still staring after Master Moltin. "We best be scooting and shooting over to Master Bennett's and find out."

Jordil chuckled. "Scooting and shooting. What does that even mean, you slack-jawed yokel?"

"The fact you have to ask just shows how uneducated you are," Cam said with a grin.

Jordil rolled his eyes. "I'm sure."

They headed off again and shortly reached Master Bennett's home. Directly inside was the front room, a well-lit space, tastefully decorated with a couch, a low-table, and a number of well-crafted chairs. It was where they found Master Bennett, and, surprisingly, also Lilia. Cam had thought she was off in the fields, learning how to use Spirairia to drive off pests and such from the crops. She wouldn't actually be able to use the knowledge until she'd advanced her Tang to Novice, but it never hurt to learn early.

"Good. You're all here." Master Bennett beamed at them. "Who wants to dive an Adept Pathway?"

Cam blinked, not sure he'd heard right. He replayed the words in his head, and when he confirmed what had been said, he sagged. A rushing noise of excitement filled his ears. He couldn't hear anything, although he noted Jordil and Lilia make excited gestures as their mouths moved. Master Bennett's offer was what Cam had dreamed about for months, ever since reading Fetch Devile's account.

But was it real?

Eventually the sound filling his thoughts faded, and he was able to focus on Master Bennett. Cam stared at his teacher, hoping for clarification.

Master Bennett must have noticed, and his glad smile became merely warm. "Master Winder contacted me."

The Wilde Sage? Cam had no idea Master Bennett knew someone so august.

"Well. Rather it was his apprentice," Master Bennett clarified. "The Crown, Saira Maharani. Ever since that Variant Pathway, she's been watching out for our town, especially you, Jordil, and Lilia. A while ago, I told her of the possible solution to your dilemma found in the book by Fetch Devile."

"And she found an Adept Pathway?"

Master Bennett beamed once more. "And she's willing to dive it with you. She'll keep you safe."

Jordil bounced around in excitement while Lilia shrieked with happiness, grinning as wide as he'd ever seen.

Cam smiled wanly in reply. Five years he'd lived this way, where a short walk would leave him breathless, too weak to do much of anything. And now, he'd finally be free to live a normal life? It sounded unreal. "When do we leave?" Cam asked.

"Now. This morning," Master Bennett said. "Pathways of higher Stages don't last long. I have the directions."

"And it's safe to travel?" Cam asked, thinking on stories of rakshasas in the wild.

"Of course," Master Bennett said. "The Sages keep us safe. Be ready to leave within the hour."

Cam rushed home from Master Bennett's as quick as he could, only having to pause a couple of times to catch his breath. Some folks greeted him as he walked with purpose through Traverse, most of them kind but a rare few mocking. Such as Suse Marline and Tormick Echo, friends of Maria Benefield. *No surprise there.* Cam had no idea what he had done to cause Maria to dislike him so much, but he also didn't care. At least not today, a day filled with hope.

He reached his home, entering to find the windows open, a morning breeze bringing in the fresh aroma of spring flowers, and Pharis, standing at the table, folding clothes.

She noticed his glad smile. "What has you so happy?"

Cam was happy to tell her the good news. "And best of all," he finished, "I'll have a Crown to keep me safe."

Pharis clapped her hands in delight, her eyes gleaming as she rushed to hug him. "I'm so happy for you."

"I have to pack," Cam said. "We'll probably be gone about four days."

Pharis nodded. "Get your clothes squared away. I'll make sure you have some food."

Cam smiled in gratitude before going to his cot where he crouched down, reaching underneath and pulling out his camping gear. He quickly had what he needed, and he rose to his feet, going to Pharis, who handed him another sack.

"I've got dried meat, some old potatoes, carrots, hardtack." She offered a crooked grin. "I'm sure Jordil can make a feast out of it."

Cam laughed in agreement. "So long as he has his spices and herbs."

"I've also got a couple of canteens," Pharis said.

"Thank you," Cam said, hefting the packs onto his back. He sagged. They were heavier than he expected. He set them down, withdrawing one of the canteens. "I don't think I can carry all this."

"I doubt you'll be walking the whole way," Pharis said. "Didn't you say Master Bennett would be taking you in a wagon?"

"Yes, but I don't think I can carry all this to his house." He didn't like to admit it, but it was the truth, and there was no use pretending it was otherwise.

"Just take the canteen."

Cam did so, and just then, his eyes alighted on a bottle of moonshine. For whatever reason, right then it wasn't easy seeing the liquor. A longing entered his mind. It'd been nearly a year since he'd tasted that sweet burn, and he missed it. He walked to the shelf, pulling down the bottle, staring into its clear, corrupting depths.

"Cam, what are you thinking?"

"You know, I used to think my brain worked better when I had a little liquor inside," he said with a half-smile, still staring at the moonshine.

"No, it doesn't. And you don't need this." She lifted the bottle out of his hand.

Just as abruptly as the lure for alcohol had come upon him, it left. Cam smiled ruefully at Pharis, knowing he'd likely never rid himself of the want for drink. "You're right. It's not what I need. Not now. Not ever." His lips pursed. "I've come far, haven't I?" He needed to hear it from Pharis, the person who'd believed in him more than anyone else.

"You have, and your journey isn't done yet."

Cam sighed, thinking on his family, his father and brother. "I wish dad and Darik could get there, too."

"They're good men," Pharis said. "Well, our dad is," she amended an instant later. "But even good men have sins. Drinking is theirs. And thinking about that isn't what you should be focused on right now anyway, is it?"

It wasn't.

Pharis drew him into a hug. "Go. Become the person you were meant to be. Do better for yourself." Pulling away, she handed him a sheathed work knife. *Darik's*. He still never used it. "Take it. Just in case."

Cam nodded his thanks, strapping the knife to his belt. He lugged the packs onto his back. "I'm off." He glanced back at her while standing in the doorway. "Tell dad and Darik where I went?"

"I'll tell them."

Cam eyed Pharis one last time before facing forward. All his life, he'd wanted to become someone worthy of note, and maybe that could never happen in the way he had dreamed, but a life full of power didn't necessarily mean a better one. After all, a calm, simple life of learning and teaching wasn't such a bad thing.

He was about to head off then when the clip-clopping of a horse-drawn wagon caught his attention. He waited, smiling broadly when a pair of sturdy horses hitched to a wagon rounded a corner. In it were Master Bennett, Jordil, and Lilia.

"Stop grinning at us like a yokel," Jordil shouted. "People will think you're touched in the head."

"They already think he's touched in the head," Lilia snickered.

Cam gaped in shock at Lilia. She'd always been so kind to him. "Not you, too," he cried in betrayal.

"Climb aboard," Master Bennett said. "The future waits for no one."

Cam climbed into the wagon, seated next to Master Bennett while Lilia settled into the bed, wearing a large, round-brimmed hat to keep off the sun. Meanwhile, Jordil had hopped down and was walking beside them.

Hours later, with Lilia napping and the sun blaring down, Master Bennett spoke. "What do you know about Enlightenment?"

Cam had been doing the head-bob of someone nearly asleep, but on hearing the question, he jerked awake. "What?"

Master Bennett repeated the question. "We haven't discussed it in any of your classes."

Cam had a vague idea, but nothing enough to give a proper answer. "I don't know."

"Enlightenment is the goal of every Ephemeral Master," Master Bennett said. "It is how we Advance in the Way into Divinity. By having a better understanding of ourselves, our place in the universe, and of the nature of reality itself. We find these personal truths that are eternal, and they change us, change as we do. When I was young, my understanding of the world was different than it is now. I was ambitious to gain power, fearing how others might hurt me." He pursed his mouth, staring off into Marnin Forest, seemingly recollecting his past. "With time and Advancement, I shed that fear. Then I chose to give to those who need my help."

Cam smiled. Master Bennett had certainly done what he'd set out to do. If anyone was Enlightened, it was him. And though he was only an Adept, low on the Stages in Advancement, he was wise and good. In addition, Cam also pondered what Enlightenment might mean for him. At this moment, it was simple. He wanted to survive and thrive, earn respect and have a chance to live a meaningful life.

"You understand what I mean," Master Bennett said, his eyes locking on Cam. "Part of it, you do. Selfishness versus selflessness. It is the first understanding—recognizing your motivations—in the Advancement of Awareness. Of what allows a Novice to progress to an Acolyte. It need not be profound. It can be as simple as a statement of intent. And this is important for you, Cam, because after you dive this Pathway, you'll be different. Your wants and needs will be different. Maybe think about the kind of person you wish to be."

Cam pursed his mouth, thinking. Who did he want to be? It was a heavy question.

The day wore on, and that evening, they made camp at a small clearing next to a stream. A quiet supper ensued, and the next morning, they pressed on, taking most of the day to reach the Pathway in question.

Cam, having nodded off after his turn at driving the wagon, awakened when Lilia reined in the horses.

They'd arrived at a small clearing next to a gurgling stream. Large boulders lined the area, and thick grass grew in clumps. It was mid-afternoon, and the sun shined from high above. The pleasant weather from yesterday persisted, and the gentle brook nearby only added to the serenity.

But what captured Cam's attention was Saira. She sat atop a large, flat-topped boulder, every bit as beautiful as he remembered, smiling when she glanced their way. Cam noticed she'd been reading a book, and she tucked it away in a satchel before dropping to the ground.

"You made good time," Saira said, moving to briefly embrace Master Bennett, seemingly familiar with him. She next turned her attention to Jordil and Lilia, still smiling. "Do you remember me? It was years ago."

"We remember," Jordil said with an answering smile. "You saved us."

"You're hard to forget," Lilia added.

From a nearby cluster of rocks, someone else entered the glade. Someone familiar to Cam, but someone he hadn't seen in half a decade. *The Wilde Sage. Master Winder.* The years hadn't touched him. He was still of medium height and heavy build; handsome with a neatly trimmed beard and a dark cloak and coat. And while Cam towered over him now, there was an inescapable sense of gravity and presence to the Sage, even a grace when standing still that had Cam envious.

Master Winder abruptly smiled. "It's good to see you again, young man," he said. "We've much to discuss."

7

The glade went silent with no one seeming to know what to say. Jordil and Lilia remained near the wagon, clearly nervous, Cam reckoning they were uncomfortable around a person as powerful as Master Winder. Same with Master Bennett. Not that Cam didn't share some of their nerves but fearing someone because of who they were seemed an unhealthy way to live. And besides, what reason was there to be afraid of the Wilde Sage? He'd done nothing to them.

In fact, he'd saved Cam's life by having him choose Plasminia. From everything Cam had learned about Ephemeral Winds, for those touched by them, it was either Advance or die. And without special protections, the only Advancement possible was Plasminia. That Tang could do what the others couldn't: it could contain the power of an Ephemeral Wind. But since no one formed a Plasminia Tang, death usually followed an encounter with an Ephemeral Wind.

Cam stepped forward. "It's good to see you, too, sir," he said to Master Winder.

The Wilde Sage looked Cam over. "You've grown, and you've done better for yourself than I expected.

71

The words seemed to break a dam, and the others stepped forward. Master Bennett bowed low to the Wilde Sage. "It is an honor to meet you, sir."

Jordil and Lilia bowed as well.

Master Winder bid them rise. "There is no need for such formality. We all walk the Way into Divinity."

Saira spoke, interrupting their reunion. "While I would love to re-connect with all of you, we don't have much time. The Pathway could fray at any moment. We should hurry."

"She's right," Master Winder said. "You arrived just in time. Come."

Their words perked Cam's ears, and he rushed after the Sage and Crown. He couldn't afford to lose this chance. Who knew if it would ever come again? He followed Saira and Master Winder further into the glade, to a ring of low-lying boulders where they'd set up their campsite. There was plenty of room for their gear and bedrolls.

But for Cam, of greater interest was wavering translucent yellow doorway. *The Pathway to Grace.* Through it, he could see the other side of the ring of boulders. He also noticed a strange sensation emanating from the Pathway. It flickered just then, nearly disappearing.

"We don't have time to prepare you," Saira said. "You must enter it now."

Master Bennett protested. "If the Pathway dissolves while Cam is inside, he'll die."

"We can maintain it," Master Winder said. "Saira and me. From out here. It won't come undone. We won't allow it."

But if Saira was out here... Cam's heart dropped. "Do I have to dive the Pathway on my own?"

"No," Master Bennett said. "I'll dive it with you."

Cam eyed his instructor in dismay. Master Bennett was already an Adept, but he was also old. Cam didn't want to risk Master Bennett on his account.

"I'll be fine," Master Bennett said, catching sight of his uncertainty. "I'll see us both safe."

Cam glanced to Jordil and Lilia, wanting their advice.

"Go," Lilia said, her voice sure.

Jordil echoed her sentiments an instant later.

Again, the Pathway flickered.

"Choose," Master Winder said.

Master Bennett made the decision for both of them. He entered the Pathway.

Cam inhaled sharply. There were no other options now. He couldn't just let Master Bennett dive the Pathway and risk its dangers for no reason. He approached the doorway, not slowing in the slightest.

Cam stepped into a circle of stones, identical to one he had just left. It was all the same, even the softly stirring breeze, Saira's and Master Winder's packs, and the campfire he hadn't fully noted until just now. Nothing was different, except Cam was utterly alone. There was no one else here.

He spun about, eyes wide, frantic, searching. What was going on? Where was he? An empty forest, devoid of sound and movement met his vision, and he shied away. From the trees originated a desolate sense of hunger, a desire to feed on him, steal all that he was and make it part of the woods.

Fear threatened to become panic as he continued to spin from one direction to the other, trying to make sense of where he was.

He forced himself to stop then, to close his eyes and think. There had to be an explanation. He'd stepped through the doorway. This, he knew. Following on that, it meant he *had* entered the Pathway. This place was it, then.

But what about Master Bennett? Where was he?

Cam continued to search about. "Hello?" he called out. Maybe Master Bennett had left the circle of stones for some reason. Hopefully he hadn't gone into the forest, though. Cam sensed nothing but malice and danger emanating from the woods.

"Your friend is safe," a voice said, coming from the direction of the bedding. Cam bent low, peering closer, not seeing anyone at first. His eyes widened in surprise at seeing a golden squirrel. She—Cam could sense the little critter was female—was wrapped in a blanket, breathing shallow, and pain filled her eyes; green irises that were centered within the blue Haunt of a Glory.

This was an Awakened Beast, injured apparently.

"You can call me Honor," the squirrel said. "What is your name?"

Cam rocked back on his heels. He had known Awakened Beasts could speak but knowing wasn't the same as experiencing. And what was she doing here in this Pathway?

"It's usually polite to answer a question like that," the squirrel said.

Cam replied without thinking. "Cam Folde," he answered. What was happening? Everything was so surreal, and his mind didn't want to work right. He still had to find Master Bennett, and they had to dive this Pathway, but he also couldn't leave this poor creature behind, injured as she was.

Honor smiled again. "It's kind of you to think of me."

Cam squatted low. "What happened? Can I do something to help?"

"What happened is a disaster long in the making," Honor answered with a sad chuckle. "A choice was forced on us, and this is how you can see me for now. And I will not survive long in this place, but neither will the one who left me like this." She coughed at the end, but when her eyes fell on Cam, some of the pain seemed to recede. "Come closer, child. You entered this Pathway, seeking healing." She held aloft a red fruit, the appearance of a pomegranate. "You know what this is?"

Cam nodded mutely; eyes locked on the fruit. It was the gift received by those who successfully completed an Adept Pathway. It was why he had come to here, the means to his salvation.

"I can save you much toil and tribulation," Honor said. "All you need do is prove yourself worthy."

What did that mean? Worthy of what? Cam edged closer to the squirrel, asking the question on his mind.

"Worthy of the Ephemera within this fruit," Honor said. "Do you know how it can be done?"

Cam shook his head.

She smiled. "I should not be here. Nor do I need this pomegranate. However, it can be yours. I can gift it to you."

Cam started. He hadn't expected that, and he also couldn't help but wonder what Honor would want in return. There had to be a trap to all this. This was an Adept Pathway, after all. His brows drew together in a frown as studied the Awakened Beast, trying to see what she was hiding.

"Did you know," Honor began, as if she didn't notice his suspicious gaze, "that you can gain Ephemera in several ways? First, is to accrete it on your skin, which is like breathing through your pores. Another is to find an area rich in Ephemera and accept it into yourself. That way is like drinking a stone through a straw. But for some—not many—they can also gift their Ephemera to those they find worthy." She quirked a grin, less pain-filled this time. "It is a great honor," she said, displaying the fruit.

Cam remained unsure. Honor sounded so reasonable, so good. But how could he trust her? Especially after discovering her in a such a deadly place.

"Trust your heart," Honor said, seemingly knowing his fear. "What does it tell you about the forest?"

Cam's eyes went to the surrounding woods. "That it's dangerous and cruel," he whispered.

"And so it is. Now, what does your heart tell you about me?"

Cam reflected a moment. "That you are kind and good." He smiled on saying the words. Honor *was* kind and good, and though it defied reason, he had no doubts on the matter.

Honor's eyes seemed to gain in weight and wisdom. "Let go of your self-hate. You know of what I mean."

Cam did know, and the perception overwhelmed him. He struggled to hold back the tears. *The alcohol.* He had taken up the bottle because he hated his life; hated who he had become. And while he had set the alcohol aside, the hate had never truly left him. He still hated who he was as a person. "I'll do my best," he promised.

"Then let us begin," Honor said.

Cam's eyes widened. "Now?"

Honor chuckled. "Of course. What other time is there than now?"

In that instant, the abrupt and strange reality of the situation hit Cam like a smack to the head. The squirrel, Honor, had offered him the treasure of completing an Adept Pathway, and in the face of her generosity, he felt his own problems—the desire to heal his weakness—to be less of a burden than before.

"What should I do?" he asked.

"Press the fruit to your chest while I hold it. And take off your shirt. Having the pomegranate touch bare skin—it works better that way"

Cam quickly removed his shirt before lifting the Awakened Beast from the litter she'd made in the bedroll and blanket, careful not to jostle her. There was likely some injury to cause the pain he'd earlier seen.

He frowned. Then again, right now, Honor seemed to swell in power, fragile in some ways, but there was also the might of the mountains in her eyes, some greatness Cam hadn't sensed even Master Winder to possess.

An instant later, a grimace flashed across Honor's face. Despite the clear strength retained in her Glory-blue eyes, she seemed to tire a bit more with every breath she took. Cam stared at her in concern.

"I will be fine soon enough. The forest—" She cut off whatever else she might have meant to say. "You need not worry on my account. Press me close. I don't bite… except my husband, and only if he asks nicely."

Cam smiled, drawing her close enough to push the pomegranate she held to his chest. The firm fruit seemed to soften then, like it was over-ripe and ready to burst.

Honor chuckled just as Cam was about to pull away. "You need not worry. The pomegranate will hold its form. Press it close."

Cam did so, wincing as the fruit again seemed ready to give away and break apart all over him.

"Delve your Source," Honor said, her voice calm and soothing. "Fall as deeply into it as you can. Control it. I will send to you the pomegranate's unTanged Ephemera as Kinesthia." She held up a cautioning hand—surprisingly human-like. "Be careful. Your Plasminia will seek to transform it. Prevent it. Keep it as Kinesthia." She shifted, viewing him with a smile from where she lay in his hands. "That is why you are here, yes?"

Such a gentle, accepting smile. And such a strange circumstance in which he found himself in. What was really going on? It couldn't be that he'd entered an Adept Pathway, discovered a lovely Awakened squirrel, who happened to be a Glory, and who had a pomegranate gifted by the Pathway that she was now willing to give him. Such a situation might occur in a story, and even then it would be unbelievable.

Honor must have sensed his doubts. "I ask that you take a leap into faith," she said, her eyes holding his. "Do this, and all will be well."

The simple advice—creepy though it might have sounded—settled Cam's qualms. He nodded acceptance, closing his eyes as Honor had instructed, Delving his Source. There, he discovered his Ephemera, a pale-red fog, crackling in silence, drifting as if it sought something.

"I'll send a small amount at first," Honor said. "Don't worry if any of it leaks away. At your Stage, that's to be expected. And with your Plasminia working against you, this may not even work." She blinked solemnly. "You might also die. You understand this?"

Cam had always understood, but he also wouldn't let fears and doubts hold him back. It was either die now or die in a decade. "I'm not afraid."

"You should be," Honor said. "Had you received the pomegranate on your own and attempted to Imbibe it without someone to filter it for you, death would have been a certainty."

"Master Winder or Saira could have done that."

"Perhaps," Honor said, surprising Cam by knowing who he had referenced, and surprising him further with her doubts about the capabilities of the Wilde Sage and his Crown apprentice. Who was this

Awakened squirrel to believe herself the equal of two who were at or near the peak of all Ephemeral Masters.

"You have much to learn, little one," Honor said with a chuckle, in seeming response to his thoughts. "Be ready."

All is Ephemera and Ephemera is All.

The phrase settled into Cam's consciousness, bringing him solace and steadiness. If he died here, in this Pathway and this utterly bizarre situation, it wasn't the end. There were no beginnings or ends in this world. He would simply return to that which had made him.

Cam took a final steadying breath. "I'm ready."

Honor closed her eyes, and he followed suit. From the area of his chest where the pomegranate pressed against him, there came a pressure. It was like an anvil, bearing the heft and thickness of steel. *Kinesthia of Adept Awareness.* It pushed against Cam, and he did his best to accept it. There was a trick, though; where he needed to open his pores and allow the Ephemera to enter his body.

But it was easier said than done. Nevertheless, Cam persevered, breathing deep, in and out, ignoring the pressure.

All the while, he focused on his Source, noticing a thin line of shimmering reflective metal enter it. The fog of his Plasminia drifted toward the metal. Lightning shooting forth as Plasminia sought to consume and transform Honor's gift.

Cam focused on his Ephemera, seeking to control it, but for someone who had never truly walked the Way into Divinity, it proved nearly impossible. The Plasminia surged against his control, seeking to undo Honor's gift. Cam's Source swelled under the pressure of the internal conflict, and he knew if it ruptured, his life would end.

"You must will your Source to survive," Honor advised.

Cam did as she suggested. He threw his will at his Source, strengthening the walls, refusing to let them come apart. And while his focus never wavered, he also found himself thinking about Tern. Of Jordil and Lilia, who had never abandoned him. Of Pharis, who had achieved her own redemption and helped him achieve his own. He couldn't let them down.

For what felt like hours, he struggled. Eyes closed, panting, heart pounding.

Abruptly, the pressure released, and Cam opened his eyes, meeting Honor's gaze. She smiled, weaker than before, lighter, her golden fur not as lustrous, and Cam had a sudden, cutting fear for her. She wasn't dying, was she? There was something wondrous and wonderful about Honor, and the world would be a darker place if she ever left it.

She must have noticed his concern. "All is Ephemera and Ephemera is All," she said. "Do not fear on my account. You did well. Delve your Source, and you'll see what I mean."

Her courage strengthened Cam's, and he bobbed a hasty nod.

"Search inside yourself," Honor continued. "Tell me how much Kinesthia has collected. What color is it?"

Cam Delved his Source and discovered it changed. There was still the fog of Plasminia, crackling and drifting, but there was something else, too. In the center of his Source, a kernel of Kinesthia winked, rotating and reflecting like the brightest silver. To properly balance it against his hungry Plasminia, he needed far more, though.

He told Honor what he was seeing, and she shifted slightly. "That is good, and if you're able and willing, this time I can send more."

Sweat covered Cam like a wet blanket. His mouth was dry, and his heart still thundered. But he was able. "Send it."

Again came the pressure, heavier than before, nearly enough to knock Cam over. But he kept his balance, Delving his Source, enforcing his will upon it and his Plasminia. Fighting the same silent struggle of accepting the Kinesthia Honor sent, refusing to allow its transformation. The same battle to keep intact the walls of his Source.

His head pounded. His limbs ached, and fire poured through his veins, but Cam didn't quit.

More hours passed. How many Cam couldn't have said, but he eventually reached his limit. He couldn't take any more. His will faltered. His Source bloated, misshapen as his Plasminia slipped its leash and sought to alter the thin line of shimmering metal entering him. The last of his focus was dedicated to preventing it. The pain in his mind and body had him clenching his teeth in a rictus.

A knife's edge was where he stood. He had to hold or he would die. He balanced on that blade, teetering. He couldn't let the entering Kinesthia become Plasminia. It felt like he was holding back a wind by waving his hands. Cam threatened to come undone, just like Master Winder had said *wouldn't* happen earlier tonight. Had it been only tonight? It seemed so long ago.

Cam set aside the distraction, struggling to gain ground. To prevent the formation of more Plasminia. *Hold.* He fought on, never relenting, and oddly enough, his success came with a side effect. Honor's line of Kinesthia *was* transformed, but not into Plasminia. Rather it became a tiny bead of silvery liquid drifting upon the surface of the shimmering metal at the core of his Source.

Upon the creation of the liquid—could it be Synapsia?—it was as if his mind got a second wind. His focus and will heightened.

"Good," Honor encouraged. "We must be quick now."

Even heavier pressure built against Cam's chest, and he accepted it. On it went. The painful struggle that threatened to tear him asunder until an unknown length of time later, the Kinesthia in the center of his Source flickered. It changed color, glowed red as ruby. Relief and exultation coursed through Cam. He'd done it.

The pressure shut off, and Cam opened his eyes. Night had deepened, and the stars blinked overhead with a full moon lighting the clearing.

Honor sighed, her eyes flickering open. "I've given you all I can," Honor said, her voice weak and frail. "Use it wisely. Live like you mean it."

Tears swelled in Cam's eyes. He didn't know why he was so full of grief, and a great and terrible terror filled him, an expectant remorse of something beautiful about to leave the world. "I will. I promise."

Honor sighed then, a final exhalation, and her body crumbled to flecks of golden light that flickered upward and away on an unfelt wind.

8

Cam sat in silence after Honor's passing because that's what it felt like: a leave-taking rather than an ending. Though her body was gone, she wasn't. She remained. Or maybe he was only hoping that was the case. Whatever the case, even though his sorrow lingered, it also waned, replaced by acceptance and a giddy kind of joy at having known her.

Beyond that, the entire situation remained surreal. Who would have guessed that stepping into this Pathway would have led to such a strange and unbelievable scenario? Cam had lived it, and it still struck him as impossible. An Awakened Beast, lying in wait, granting him the Pathway's gift, helping him create a Novice Tang of Kinesthia.

All is Ephemera and Ephemera is All.

The world trembled just then, the trees rattling and leaves shaking. Cam glanced around in alarm. The Pathway must be coming apart. It did so when the gift it granted was consumed. Again, came the trembling, harder this time, and Cam made to rise, but his muscles felt like bags of water. He gritted his teeth, getting off the ground, angry. He thought a Kinesthia Tang was supposed to balance his weakness, not

81

make it worse.

With the third shaking of the world, a watery-yellow doorway appeared. As did Master Bennett, who seemed to blink into existence.

"Cam?" Master Bennett said. "Where have you been? I've been waiting hours."

"No time to explain, sir," Cam replied. Once more, the world shook. "I found what I needed. It's time to leave."

"You did what?" Master Bennett asked in shock. He might have said more, but the world of the Pathway trembled ever harder, rattling them about like an earthquake. Master Bennett glanced about in apprehension, blinking owlishly. "It's time to leave."

"That's what I said. Come on." Cam urged Master Bennett toward the doorway, having difficulty lifting his wet-noodle arms. Still, he didn't get any pushback, and the two of them tumbled out into the real world with Cam losing his balance and falling to the ground.

He looked up, and staring at him in surprise was everyone gathered at the ring of stones. They'd been seated around the campfire, but upon Cam and Master Bennett's arrival, they had risen to their feet. Jordil and Lilia barked out questions, but they silenced at a sharp whistle from Master Winder.

"You succeeded?" the Wilde Sage asked. "You have the pomegranate?"

Cam licked his lips, not sure how to explain. "Not exactly." He told them what had happened, and when he finished, the only sound to be heard was the crackle of the campfire.

"Let me make sure I understand this," Master Winder began. "You were gifted a pomegranate by a Glory-Staged Awakened Beast who disappeared into golden specks when you finished creating your Kinesthia Tang?" His tone was as flat as a plank of wood, and his disbelief as obvious as clouds during a storm.

"Yes, sir. That's what happened," Cam confirmed. "And it worked."

His word was good enough for Jordil and Lilia because they shouted in relief and glee, dropping to their knees and hugging him.

"You can't do anything the easy way, can you?" Jordil asked.

Cam laughed. "You know me."

"Yes, we do," Lilia said.

The Wilde Sage appeared unsatisfied. "I've never heard of such a thing." He shot his eyes to Master Bennett. "And you weren't present to witness any of it?"

Master Bennett shook his head. "I was alone for hours in a ring of stones identical to this one. Then Cam was suddenly present, and the Pathway started to disintegrate."

Saira stepped forward, her presence inducing Jordil and Lilia to move aside. She kneeled. "You have a Kinesthia Tang at Novice?" she asked, no disbelief in her voice; only acceptance.

"I do," Cam said. Staring upward at everyone looming around him was uncomfortable, like he was a child waiting to be scolded. He went to stand, but his legs still wouldn't work, leaving him feeling as useless as a one-legged man in an arse-kicking contest. He nearly fell over on his side, a bone-deep fatigue weighing him down. His heart raced, and he didn't like how hard it was to take in a deep breath. What was happening to him? He gazed at the others in fear.

Saira put a cool palm to the side of his head. "It's your Kinesthia. It still needs to settle into your body. You'll feel this way for the next day or so. Do you want to stand?"

Cam nodded, leaning against her as she helped him rise. "Thank you."

Master Winder appeared unhappy still, his arms folded. "This makes absolutely no sense. Awakened Beasts and golden motes." He harrumphed, scowling.

Cam didn't care that the Wilde Sage was just as confused by matters as he. There was a more important question on his mind. "Does this mean I have a chance to become an Ephemeral Master?"

"No," Saira said, cutting down his hopes. "Plasminia is your Primary Tang, and it will always hinder you."

Cam frowned. "Why can't I Advance Kinesthia instead?"

"Because you always have to Advance your Primary Tang first," Master Winder said, taking up the explanation. "And if you do that, you'll be right back where you started: your Plasminia draining your Kinesthia, leaving you weak. Right now, you're in balance. Advance, though, and the balance is ruined."

Cam wasn't surprised, so much as disappointed. Master Bennett had taught him as much, but he'd secretly hoped that Master Winder or Saira might know of some means for him to progress farther on the Way into Divinity. Plus, if All is Ephemera and Ephemera is All, why couldn't any Tang of Ephemera become any other Tang of Ephemera?

"Most everyone has tried to Advance their other Tangs past the Stage of their Primary, but it's impossible," Master Winder continued. "The Primary Tang always takes precedence whenever you gather more Ephemera. It is *always* Enhanced and Advanced first. We don't know why, but we do know it is so, and for you, it would be even harder. Plasminia is said to be impossible to control. The only way I can see for you to Advance your Kinesthia is if you also added a Novice Stage of Synapsia."

"Which would be a terrible idea," Saira added. "Especially given what you said. You barely survived the creation of a Novice Stage of Kinesthia, and that only because of the aid of this Awakened Beast who apparently knows more than a Sage."

She was right. They both were. Cam *had* barely survived. But an obstinate part of him still wondered. Why not try then for the Novice Stage of Synapsia? He already had a small portion of it in his Source.

Jordil must have sensed what he was thinking because he frowned. "You just received a miracle. You formed a second Tang, which nearly killed me and Lilia. And now you want to add another?"

Cam shrugged. "It isn't that." A second later, he amended his statement. "It isn't only that."

"Then what?" Jordil asked.

"It's because of Honor. She gave me so much. It feels wrong to use her gift for so little." Cam flushed. "That didn't come out right. What I mean is that I want to lead a good life, a humble and happy one if that's my role in this world. But if it's not..." He shrugged. "Shouldn't I try for more?"

"A well-led life is not so little," Saira said with a gentle smile.

"I know," Cam agreed. "I was already fixing on becoming an instructor like Master Bennett. And since I've got a bit of Synapsia now, maybe my learning will come a little easier." He laughed. "Master Moltin says I'm his slowest, best student." Cam gazed about, wanting the others to share his humor, but no one was laughing. His smile faded. "What?" Did he have something hanging from his nose? He furtively swiped at it.

"You have two Stages at Novice and the beginning of third?" Master Winder asked, appearing surprised and strangely eager.

"Yes, sir," Cam carefully answered. What was the issue now?

"Then you're already a Novice Greater," Master Winder answered. "Someone with two Novice Stages—and with your partial Synapsia, you have a chance to become a Novice Prime, someone with three Novice Stages. It is uncommon but not rare."

Cam frowned. Master Winder had just helped convince him that he should settle back and enjoy his life, but now it sounded like he was saying something different.

"If you've already got the third Tang formed, it's a near certainty that you *can* Advance it fully," Master Winder explained. "Which means you should carefully consider what you do next."

Cam clutched his head, feeling like he'd been whiplashed. "Why is this so important? I was just getting used to the notion of living a simple life."

"And that may still be what's best," Saira said, shooting Master Winder an uninterpretable look.

"But with the proper resources, who knows what you can accomplish," Master Winder said.

"You really think I should do this?" Cam asked him. "Even after everything you said?"

Master Winder seemed to draw himself up. "I think it's a decision you should think about. I cannot make it for you. But yours is also a situation unique in history. I would not want to see the opportunity squandered."

Which was an answer as obvious as a muddy pig. Master Winder wanted him to Advance his Synapsia, and it was largely because of curiosity.

As the night deepened, Cam wandered away from the others, telling them he wanted solitude. In reality, he wanted to get clean, and he went to the stream where he washed off a film of sweat and some kind of watery, bloody fluid that had collected on his skin. From his readings, he knew it had to do with ridding his body of impurities when he'd created a Tang of Kinesthia. Everyone who Advanced or Enhanced their Tangs experienced it, but it was still gross.

Afterward, he planted himself on a likely looking boulder and watched the rivulet glimmer in the moonlight as it rushed across submerged stones. An owl hooted in the distance, and crickets and critters made noises in bushes close at hand.

But Cam remained lost in his thoughts, perturbed by his options. First, he was told to go live a quiet, happy life, and now Master Winder was suggesting he shouldn't. Strangely though, Cam found himself wondering what Honor might have advised. She had touched him; not just for what she had given, but more because of who she had been. Once he no longer focused on her bizarre entrance into his life, what struck him the most about the Awakened squirrel was her grace and nobility. It was so obvious in hindsight.

"Do you know what it is to be truly Enlightened?" Saira asked, surprising him. He hadn't heard her footsteps, and he still didn't as she gracefully settled herself on a nearby boulder.

Cam had a notion since he and Master Bennett had just been talking on the matter yesterday. But he also figured it best for Saira to explain her notion in her own words. "Not really," he said.

"The Enlightened are those Ephemeral Masters who can go past Sages," Saira said. "They can become Divines. And they all start as Novice Primes."

Cam perked. A Divine was the highest Stage anybody could hope to achieve. They were the celestial beings who administered the Heavens, grander than any Sage. Surely Saira didn't mean a lowly person like him could rise to such heights. All he'd ever wanted was to become an Acolyte. That would have been more than enough.

"To gain Enlightenment isn't a singular path, though," Saira continued. "There are many roads that lead to the same destination. For some, it requires deep meditation. Those individuals retreat from the world, becoming hermits in order to become one with Creation. Guptash and Chandra, the only emperors Golden, this continent, has ever known—one the great-grandfather of the other—were two such. But after conquering all of Golden, both of them gave away their rule. They retreated to a hidden place in the wilderness and learned their version of nirvana. Others, such as Prahlass, prayed so devoutly that he achieved an Awareness beyond Sage. Then there are those like Enton and Alset who managed the same through deep thinking and study." She grinned, and Cam found himself smiling back. "And then there are some who are just lucky."

Until today, Cam had never considered himself as having much luck. Or if he did, it was to think it was mostly bad. Maybe that was changing, though, even if he knew better than to not strive too high. "I'm just a boy from Traverse, broken the past five years, drunk for some of it, and only now finding peace with my place in the world."

"Peace." Saira's smile became bitter. "We are a world at peace. A person can travel most anywhere and be safe, but it may not always be the case. There are those who seek to end us."

Cam knew who she meant. "Rakshasas."

"The Great Rakshasas," she corrected. "They have the same Awareness of a Divine, and thankfully there are only three—Shimala, Coruscant, and Simmer. They exist in some place other than the heavens, and each of them desire our deaths, to feast on our Ephemera."

Cam didn't know what this had to do with him, and he said so.

Saira smiled, flushing some with embarrassment. "It's nothing you need to worry about," she said. "Probably just my fanciful fears. My mother worries about the rakshasas, and I suppose her fears have infected me."

Cam didn't know how to respond. He knew about the crossroad rakshasas, but those were just stories meant to scare children. The real rakshasas fought against the Sages, and everyone knew they were always defeated; sent back to their boils and licking their wounds.

So why was Saira worried about them? "You really think the rakshasas are a threat?"

"I know they are. And it isn't just my mother's fears. The Great Rakshasas are like the Divines: they understand that growth and change is necessary for creation, but their change involves the pain of others. They seek to purify and enhance their Ephemera through death, carnage, and thievery. And their power isn't waning. They remain passionate in seeing their dreams come to fruition."

"What do you mean?"

"The Divines are like all of us. They were imbued by the Holy Servants with a desire to create, to reflect the glory of our ultimate Creator, Devesh. However, with no new Divine born in millennia, their faith has slowly faded since none of them have discovered the Awareness to become Servants. Some are even known to have let go their immortality in order to seek rebirth on Salvation, thinking the answer to their failure exists in the pain and promise of life here."

Cam had never heard this before, and he glanced askance at Saira, wondering how she knew so much? He wanted to smack himself a moment later. She was a Crown, and she worked with the Wilde Sage. Of course, she would know.

"The rakshasas don't share such indecision, and my mother..." Her lips tightened into a grimace. "It's not important. I didn't come here to fill your mind with fears."

"You came here hoping I'd make a go at becoming a Novice Prime." Cam wasn't as smart as Jordil, but he could figure out enough.

Saira tilted her head. "Not really. Yes, a war is brewing, and we will need the help of even the humblest. But the role you play, of serving others—of helping and aiding them in the way you can—need not be in the way that Rainen thinks: as a warrior. Every community needs a healer, a teacher, a farmer, and a creator. That is what I meant to say. You don't need to be someone mighty to do what's right and care for those in need. But you will need to fight in whatever way you can. Think about it."

She touched his shoulder and left, and Cam considered her advice, thinking late into the night.

The next morning dawned bright and shiny. The grass in the boulder-strewn meadow shimmered with dew, reflecting a rainbow of light. Animal sounds—birds trilling and small critters rustling—filled the air while a gentle wind tugged at Cam's clothing, carrying the scent of the burned-out campfire.

He had thought about what Saira had said, and after returning to the camp and discussing it with Master Bennett, Jordil, and Lilia, he'd made his choice. While he'd once sought glory, it no longer appealed to him in quite the same way. Having a chance at peace and tranquility along with acceptance was what he desired most. He'd return to Traverse and see how his life went.

As for Master Winder and Saira, they were ready to depart. "We have some other tasks to attend," the Wilde Sage said. "South of here, down in Codent."

Codent? Cam blinked. How were they going to get to there? They had their bags gathered at their feet, but what about horses? Surely they didn't mean to walk there.

"If you change your mind and decide to Advance to Novice Prime, let me know," the Wilde Sage added. "Master Bennett knows how to contact us."

"Yes, sir," Cam said, although he doubted it would happen.

Master Winder nodded. "We'll be off." He gestured Cam away. "You'll want to move aside."

Offering the Wilde Sage a curious look, Cam did as he was bidden, moving to join Master Bennett and the others. He, Jordil, and Lilia viewed Master Winder and Saira in mild confusion while Master Bennett smiled slightly, apparently knowing what was about to happen.

Cam was about to ask what was so humorous when Master Winder's and Saira's bags seemed to suck into a ring on the Wilde Sage's hand. Cam's mouth dropped, opening wider an instant later when a roar filled the clearing. Master Winder had bent his legs and launched skyward. Wind blasted outward, carrying a wave of dried leaves, dirt, and detritus. A second roar followed as Saira raced after him. Both of them became small dots as they flew away.

"Unholy hells," Cam whispered, laughing shakily. He hadn't expected that. The last time he had seen Master Winder fly had been during the Wilde Sage's battle against the Silver Sage of Weeping. He turned around, finding Jordil and Lilia grinning with him.

"That was a treat," Lilia observed.

"You ready to head home, Novice?" Master Bennett asked, smiling along with them.

Cam laughed. That's right. He was a proper Novice, and that had been the first time someone had addressed him as one. Wait until Pharis found out. His father and his brother, too. "I'm ready."

Gathering their belongings, they left the clearing then. Jordil marched alongside the wagon while Master Bennett took the driver's seat and Lilia sat up front next to him.

Cam, on the other hand, lounged in the bed. Most of last night's lethargy was gone, but a heaviness still dragged at his muscles. The way he was feeling, he likely wouldn't be able to walk more than a couple hundred yards before needing a break. But on a more hopeful note, he found his breathing, even at rest, coming easier than he could ever recall. He didn't have to fight to fill his lungs like he'd gotten used to doing.

It was a happy day for travel, and the miles unrolled. The sun shone. Birds sang, and it was like years of bitterness and regrets fell away from him. He'd forgotten what it was like to breathe without a struggle or to feel hope for the future rather than despair. He luxuriated in the sense of hope and peace, and their journey passed in a reflective silence, broken only by a few humorous observations until they finally stopped late in the evening.

That night they made camp, and since Jordil did the cooking—spiced potatoes, chapati and sambar—the food was wonderful.

"Do you remember when we stole some of Farmer Danver's potatoes?" Cam asked Jordil after they finished eating.

Jordil laughed. "He sicced his hounds on us. I thought Tern was going to wet himself trying to get away."

"I did wet myself," Lilia said, laughing as well. "If that fence hadn't been there, we would've been done for."

"The hounds wouldn't have hurt you," Master Bennett replied, leaning back on his bedroll and puffing on a pipe. "They were what? They size of overgrown housecats?"

"But their bark made them sound like they were the size of a horse," Lilia said.

Cam nodded, grinning. "I never seen an animal sound so large and come out so small."

"Yes, but whenever Tern told the story," Jordil said, "he always made it out like the hounds were near enough to be the size of raging bulls."

"The great potato robbery," Cam mused, smiling on the memory. The humor faded as he thought of Tern. For years, anger and grief had warred in equal measure when thinking about his friend. Now, it was simply regret. "He would have loved being out here with us. Telling stories."

Lilia chuckled. "I swear, Tern told stories just so he could lie to his heart's content."

"Ain't that the truth," Cam said.

Master Bennett gestured with his pipe. "I believe that boy lied because he never learned to tell the truth."

Jordil leaned forward, a gleam in his eyes. "You remember when his momma gave him a hiding for lying about being out late?"

Cam remembered. "He was supposed to be home for supper and didn't make it back until after dark. We were off picking blackberries.

All of us were covered in juice, and instead of telling her straight what we'd been up to, he told her a wildman in the woods had tried to steal him away and the only way he'd gotten free was by throwing blackberries at him."

"What an idiot," Lilia said with a laugh and a shake of her head.

"That was Tern," Cam agreed.

"I miss him," Jordil said.

"We all do," Lilia added. "Which means we should make the most of the years that we have."

"To the years ahead," Cam said, toasting with his canteen of water.

"To the years ahead," the other three declared.

They started out early the next morning, still happy and making good time and by the early afternoon, they were only a few miles out from Traverse. Master Bennett drove the wagon with Jordil seated next to him, and this time, it was Lilia who was the one to pace alongside them.

They entered a thick stand of evergreens, and an ominous silence fell over the world. Cam sat up in the wagon bed, a tingling in his spine. Something was wrong.

Master Bennett must have felt the same way. "Lilia," he called. "Be wary." He reached into the wagon bed for his spear.

Jordil dropped to the ground, and Cam took his place on the driver's seat. Lilia glanced about; hands tight on her walking staff.

But she was looking the wrong way.

A massive wolf lunged from the woods and bore her to the ground. The red-eyed beast—an Awakened—savaged her.

Cam gaped in frozen horror. Time slowed. Jordil and Master Bennett shouted, each one attacking the wolf. Blood fanned; every droplet visible. Cam was about to join them, but the horses whinnied, rearing and surging forward. Cam fell back into the wagon bed, banging his head. His vision momentarily blacked out, but he came to an instant later. In the distance, Lilia screamed in anguish.

Cam struggled to get his mind and body working. His vision swam, and nausea crawled through him. But he knew what was needed. He had to help Lilia. The wagon was traveling around a bend, and he lost sight of the others. Cam crawled his way onto the driver's seat. He had to get the horses under control—

Lilia screamed again. Just once, and a wolf howled in triumph. Cam's heart went into his throat. *Lilia.* She had to be fine. Master Bennett and Jordil would save her. They had to.

Head pounding, Cam gathered the reins, hauling on them. *Come on.* The horses finally slowed, and while Cam wasn't much of a driver, he shortly got the wagon turned about. He headed back, urging the horses to speed. The animals must have picked up on his fear and need because they didn't fight him.

Too much time later, he saw a sight that made his heart ache and his gorge rise. A single wolf crouched over Lilia, feasting. She was dead. A faint red glow emanated from her body, entering the wolf. The beast was stealing her Ephemera.

Rakshasas.

Cam snarled, whipping the reins.

The wolf, so intent on what it was trying to steal, never looked up until it was too late. The horses plowed it under, the wagon wheels lifting as they ran the Awakened over. Cam hauled back on the reins again, and the horses slowed. He looked back. The wolf lay on its side, breathing shallowly, its chest caved in.

Good.

Cam climbed out of the wagon, unsheathing his brother's dagger. He'd put an end to the wolf. He approached the creature. It wasn't long for the world, not after Cam was done with it. And after that, he'd see to the others. He kneeled next to the wolf.

Quicker than thought, the beast surged upward, knocking him down. The knife flew out of Cam's hand. The Awakened loomed over him, seemingly grinning in triumph.

Terrified, Cam scrambled away from the beast. A glint out of the corner of his eyes caught his attention. The dagger. It was within reach. Cam grabbed it, and a sharp thrust plunged it straight to the hilt into the wolf's chest.

Heart's blood poured into his mouth, and he knew no more.

9

"**Y**ou'll like it here," Mrs. Shimala said, her seamed face creasing into a lurid grin. "Much better than living with that old drunk."

She gestured for Cam to enter a small, dimly lit bedroom in her home, and he reluctantly shuffled forward, gagging on the underlying malodor of sickness and rot permeating the air. It was likely pus and something worse, and the rest of the room matched the stench. Dust coated all the surfaces, including the unmade bed and small dresser. Cam peered closer and shivered upon seeing what looked like dried blood crusting blankets and linens that were twisted like ropes wanting to hang a person. More dirt hung heavy on the window, darkening the room to twilight despite the noonday sun trying to beam inside. A rat shuffled out of view and scat littered the corners.

Cam was ready to bolt, but Mrs. Shimala stood directly behind him, and he didn't want to touch her; nor did he want to be in her home. This was a place of last resort, and only the truly desperate and destitute ever stayed here. Terrible rumors swirled about this place, about who had resided in Mrs. Shimala's dwelling and what had happened to them. Blood sacrifices and worse were what the townspeople whispered. Something *that stole their life. One day healthy and the next, looking like a scare-crow ready to blow over in a mild wind. And after a while, most people even forgot they had ever existed…*

Wait. That wasn't right. There was no such person as Mrs. Shimala in Traverse…

Cam didn't want to stay here, but what choice did he have? He couldn't remain with his dad. Not after yesterday when he and the old man had spoken words neither of them could take back, hollering and yelling un-forgivable insults. It had been a terrible row, but thankfully it hadn't end-ed in physical violence. If it had, Cam would have been beaten within an inch of his life. As weak and pathetic as he was, he wouldn't have stood a chance against his father. Especially since his dad had stopped drinking and was strong as an ox these days…

But he and his father hadn't argued…

…And that same reason—his father giving up the bottle—was also why the old man didn't want Cam around no more. "A shiftless drunk ain't no way for you to live your life," his dad had said, "and if you can't figure that out, you ain't got no place with me."

Cam's response should have earned him a punch to the jaw, but his father had held onto his temper. Still, minutes later they were raging at each other, and the final result was that Cam was now about to stay the night at Mrs. Shimala's. This place where only the hopeless went.

But it was either here or somewhere in the fields where an Awakened Beast—a rakshasa—could sneak up and kill him while he slept.

Cam scowled.

All of his troubles were because of Darik. His fool of a brother had died a year ago. Drunk and stumbling, he'd fallen asleep in a ditch just around the corner from the house and vomited in his sleep, suffocating. A month later Pharis, fallen into the bottle again, drank herself to death in a binge of epic proportions. Poisoned herself, she had. That was when all these new problems for Cam had started; when the old man had put away the whiskey and moonshine.

No! This wasn't the truth…

"You know it's best if you stay here with me," Mrs. Shimala said, her voice sounding like a snake rustling across dry leaves as she moved to stand directly before him. "You know this. Your mother's abandonment. Your father's drunkenness. Tern's death. It's all because of you."

Cam gaped. She was lying. He hadn't been the cause of all those terrible events.

Mrs. Shimala smiled, vulpine and cruel. "Tern was in that Pathway because of you. He followed where you led. And it was because of your neediness as a child that your mother left your father. Why your father fell into drunkenness. And where he led, your brother and sister followed. You're a curse."

Cam swallowed heavily. Was it true? Was he a curse? He wanted to deny it, but it sounded so reasonable coming from the old woman.

Mrs. Shimala's smile became that of a kind grandmother. "Oh, dear. I've upset you. If you're hungry, I can rustle up some food. Some cookies, maybe. One bite, and you'll never want for anything. I add a special touch to make them lovely." Her smiled transformed from kindly to that of a skull's rictus grin. "But you've already eaten, haven't you? Heart's blood from of one of mine. I know you now." The grin grew wider and wider. Wide enough to engulf Cam's head, his entire body, the world. "I'll be watching."

Cam woke with a shout of terror. His heart pounded. The vivid dream… The events of it faded, but the old woman.
He had never known or met anyone with that name—what was it again?—but she had felt so real. And the terror of her lingered. He swallowed a fresh bolus of fear, remembering the smell from the room.

He knew what it was. It hadn't been pus alone but also the stink of rotting flesh. What had it meant? Who had she been? And why would his mind come up with such a horrifying dream?

Minutes passed, and his panting finally relaxed. The fear no longer gripped him so tight, and he realized that his neck and back were sticky with sweat, but there was also something on his face and chest. Something also sticky, but it wasn't sweat.

Memory returned.

The wolf. It lay pressed against his torso and legs, stiff. Dead for hours then. Its gaze was empty, and its eyes had resumed a normal color.

Cam's next realization was of the others. Scrambling to his feet, he frantically searched about.

His eyes landed on Lilia. She lay unmoving. Her throat and chest had been savaged. Flies buzzed about her. Cam lurched to her, tears tracking over his blood covered face. *Lilia. Why did this have to happen to her? She deserved a good life, a happy life.* With trembling hands, Cam made to lift her up, but he then recalled Master Bennett and Jordil.

He had to find them. *Please Devesh, let them be alive.*

A quick survey showed him three dead wolves… and Jordil. He lay face down in a pool of blood, unmoving. Cam rushed to him, terrified at what he might find. He rolled Jordil over. His face was pale as snow.

"Help me up. He can be saved." *Master Bennett.*

Cam faced about, finding his instructor struggling to rise. Blood coated his face and wounds marred his arms and chest. He looked like breathing wasn't so easy neither.

"Jordil isn't dead," Master Bennett said as Cam helped him to his feet. "Badly injured, but we might be able to save him."

"What do I do?" Cam asked. Master Bennett leaned heavily against him as they went back to Jordil.

"His leg." Master Bennett pointed to a terrible wound on Jordil's calf. Pus-ridden already and swollen, blood seeped from it. "Tie it off with a ligature. I'll heal him as best as I can. After that, it's prayers he'll be needing."

Cam quickly did as ordered, using his belt to bind Jordil's calf. Fear caused him to fumble as he went too fast. Angry at himself, he took a deep breath, forcing out the emotions. Calm settled over him, and he smoothly managed to tie off the belt.

While he worked, a faint yellow glow surrounded Master Bennett. He'd engaged his Ephemera, and his hands hovered over Jordil's head. "He's not too far gone," Master Bennett said, sounding relieved. He grimaced an instant later. "This won't be easy." The yellow glow brightened, pouring from his hands like rain. It fell on Jordil, soaking into him, cleaning the blood off his face, healing wounds Cam hadn't even noticed until now.

The Ephemeral glow cut off, and Master Bennett sagged. "That's all I can do for now," he said. "The rest is up to you. Release the ligature. Find Midwife Spenser." His words spoken, Master Bennett seemed to lose all strength, collapsing into Cam's arms. Only his regular breathing told Cam that he was still alive.

Cam didn't waste another moment. He lifted Master Bennett into the wagon bed, doing the same with Jordil and Lilia. He couldn't have managed this a few days ago, but the Kinesthia Tang was already showing its worth.

But the cost...

"You're a curse," the old woman of the dream had said, and it felt like she had spoken true. Guilt flowed through Cam like a river as he got the wagon rolling. It was all his fault. Lilia would be alive if not for him. She'd only been on this path because of his weakness. And Jordil might end up paying the same grim price. Even Master Bennett.

Maria Benefield's words from months ago echoed in his mind. *"Leave before you hurt anyone else."*

How prescient she'd been. Traverse would have been better off if he'd done as she'd advised. Journeying to the Adept Pathway had been a fool's errand. He was a curse—

With a hard shake, Cam cut off the thoughts. He'd didn't believe that of himself. Not a bit, and that level of self-loathing was unlike him.

There was something else to it.

Again, he shook off the thinking. The sun was lowering, and he didn't aim on lingering in the darkening forest. Those wolves had been rakshasas. Cam hadn't forgotten their red eyes, the color of a Novice. Maybe it meant a boil had formed close by. If so, he needed to reach Traverse as quick as possible.

It was only a few miles back to Traverse, but the ride seemed to stretch for hours. Cam paused now and then to check on Jordil and Master Bennett, and he reached the quiet town in the early evening. Folks were still about, finishing some final few tasks for the day, conversing and appearing content.

But when they caught sight of him—he looked to have bathed in blood—their features transformed to horror. They shouted questions, and he answered as best he could, never slowing. In fact, he got the wagon rolling faster.

But his back itched when he noticed a trail of people following him.

They filled in those who were only now arriving, intent on learning the cause of the ruckus. The story quickly got mangled. People barked speculation, some of them wondering if Cam had been the one to attack the others. In other instances, it had been Master Bennett. Sometimes it had been a quarrel between Jordil and Lilia. Only occasionally were wolves mentioned.

The stories grew wilder, but in all cases, anger was aimed at Cam, surging through the crowd. His eyes flickered over when he caught the harsh glare sent his way by Maria Benefield. She and her sycophants stood by the road, fury on their faces.

"You did this," she shouted, her statement repeated by her friends. "You're a curse!"

Cam shut her out. He had a single task to complete. Reach Midwife Spenser and have her save Jordil and Master Bennett. Nothing would stop him. After that, he had to tell Jordil's and Lilia's families what had happened.

He dreaded doing so. They would hate him, which only made sense. Cam was the bearer of bad news, and who knew what wild, terrible tales they would have heard by the time he had a chance to speak to them.

Minutes later, he reached Midwife Spenser's home. She stood waiting on the porch, likely having been alerted by all the shouting. The midwife had been old for as long as Cam could recall, ancient even in his own father's youth. It was because she was an Adept, a powerful one, too, with yellow eyes that were deeper in color than Master Bennett's. Her gaze passed over Cam.

"What is this?" she asked, her voice firm and carrying rather than quavering like her hunched over frame might have suggested.

Cam dropped from the wagon, quickly explaining. "You have to help them."

"I know my duties, child," she said, gently chiding him. "Bring them inside." She stared at the gathered crowd. "Don't just stand their gawking. Someone help him."

Her words sparked a bevy of hands to suddenly aid Cam in bringing Master Bennett and Jordil inside where they were laid out on a pair of cots.

"What about the wolves?" Cam asked afterward. Midwife Spenser was glowing yellow, her hands hovering over first Jordil—who remained pale as a sheet—and then Master Bennett. "Someone needs to tell the guards. There might be a boil building out there."

"You best see to that," she said, never looking up from her work. "Talk to the mayor. Tell him your story rings true. Tell him I said so."

Cam breathed out in relief. If Midwife Spenser was willing to speak on his behalf, maybe he could nip all these ugly rumors in the bud. Plus, he'd had witnesses, those who had helped carry Master Bennett and Jordil inside.

But upon stepping out on the porch, Cam was unprepared when he discovered a number of people were still gathered. They shouted questions, and he did his best to explain what had happened, trying to keep it simple.

"What were you four doing out there?" someone asked.

The what-for didn't matter, and Cam reminded them about the wolves, the rakshasas on Traverse's borders. That finally got the crowd breaking apart as they fixated on what was important.

Cam was free then to find Lilia's family and tell them what had happened, but first he had to deal with Maria Benefield and her friends.

"I hope you're happy," she snarled. "This is your fault. Master Bennett and the others were helping you dive a Pathway to fix your drunkenness."

Cam's jaw reflexively clenched. "You don't know what you're talking about."

"Then you weren't diving a Pathway?" she scoffed. When he didn't deny her words, a smile of cruel pleasure lit her face. "See what you've done? You're a curse like I said before, and this time everyone will know."

"You say what you want, but I know the truth," Cam replied. And the truth would protect him, especially with Midwife Spenser backing his words. Cam pushed past Maria and her friends.

His next stop, the home of Lilia's parents proved unnecessary. They'd already been informed of her death, and although Cam was able to provide a few more details, including the reason why she'd been out on the road with him, it provided them no solace.

In fact, the reasoning seemed to incense Mrs. Fair. "This is your fault!" she had screamed, throwing off her husband's consoling arms. "You were the reason. She would still be alive if she wasn't your friend!"

In the face of such rage, Cam had no way to defend himself. He left the Fairs and headed home, walking through a town of whispers, finger-pointing, and speculation. Loudest amongst the conversation following him home were the words *"his fault"* and *"curse."*

Cam tried to ignore the accusations, tried to focus on what was important: Master Bennett and Jordil. Midwife Spenser had sounded hopeful when she'd examined them. Their survival was all that mattered. In the face of that, what folks said about his future wasn't significant.

But it sure hurt, and it made him wonder if he really might be a curse.

When he finally arrived home, it was to find Pharis waiting on him. She stood on the front porch, concern clear on her face. Her eyes widened on seeing him, and he understood why. He still hadn't cleaned off the blood.

"Oh, Cam." She drew him into a hug.

The enormity of what had occurred finally caught up to him, and he cried, sobbing into his sister's shoulder. "Lilia's dead," he managed to say.

"I know."

He drew away from her. "I didn't do it. I wasn't the reason for her death." He needed her to hear it from his lips.

"I never figured otherwise."

"Everyone blames me," Cam said. "What do I do?" he asked, desperate. While the lives of Jordil and Master Bennett were more important than his own petty concerns, right then and there, in that moment, they didn't seem so petty.

Pharis shook her head, a hopeless look on her face. "I don't know."

Three weeks later...

"You holding that spot for anyone?"

Cam glanced up. It was Maria Benefield standing in front of him. She wore a dark red skirt with a white shirt under a leather vest, and her wavy, brown hair was set free to frame her pretty face. She smiled his way, her dark eyes sparkling.

Cam did a double-take.

Why was Maria acting like she had anything but hatred for him? He stared at her, trying to reckon what she had planned even as he wished she'd just leave him alone. He had so much on his mind. Lilia's death and Jordil's lingering injuries. At least Master Bennett was back on his feet, although he remained weak and barely able to get out into the community. It seemed healing Jordil immediately after the attack by the wolves had taken a lot out of him.

Cam's worries about Jordil and Master Bennett was why he was here right now, seated on a bench along the border of the town square; from this place where Traverse's finest buildings surrounded a grassy sward that served as the village's heart. He had been watching those taking part in the last spring festival of the season. An elm tree arched over his location, providing welcome shade from the late morning sun, and plenty of people had set up small picnic baskets on plaid blankets, feasting and visiting while their children played. Others worked a spit off to the side, and the smell of roast pig wafted in the air, making Cam's stomach rumble.

But most of his longing was on a small band playing a rollicking set of songs and the young folk who were busy kicking up their heels in dance. It would get more raucous when the sun set, but already there were plenty of people his age out there having a good time.

He'd scowled, though, when he saw Suse Marline, who was engaged to that right prick, Pivot Stump. And Ingold Brest, bouncing around like a fool with Tormick Echo, who rumor said had gotten inside the knickers of plenty of women. They were all children of wealth and privilege, and ever since the attack by the wolves—which thankfully *hadn't* been from a budding boil—they'd made his life difficult.

Still, while Cam might not like most folks in Traverse who were his age, he still wished he could have just once taken part in the celebrations in which they seemed to delight. In the years since that first Pathway, he had been too weak to dance with anyone. Now he could, but there wasn't much dancing to be done for him. Too many folks—not nearly everyone, but enough—blamed him for what had happened to Lilia.

These days, hard stares were the least of the insults sent his way. Loud cursing and spitting was too often aimed at him, and Cam sometimes pondered what he was still doing here. What was there for him in this town? He had Kinesthia, but he couldn't use it like a proper Novice. And in the few conversations he'd managed with Master Bennett since the attack, there seemed little his instructor knew on how to unlock his potential.

All of which had him staring blankly at Maria while she stood there. Cam blinked, suspicion roiling through him. "No." He rose to his feet. "You can sit here if you like."

Maria's smile grew cruel. "I was actually hoping you'd lift off and leave. We don't want you here."

Sliding in to stand next to her was Barth Lord, trailed by Pivot Stump and Tormick Echo along with a whole bunch of others. Half the town it felt like, any family of importance, including Lilia's folks. Cam found them arched around him, faces stern as steel; ready to visit pain on his stupid head.

Cam cursed inwardly. He should have listened to Pharis and never come to this dance. "There ain't no call for this. I'm leaving," he said, holding up his hands, a gesture of placation that galled him. He owed nothing to nobody here.

"You don't get it," Maria said, her tone harsh and full of loathing. "We don't want you *here*. In Traverse. You got Tern killed, and now you've done the same to Lilia. Almost did the same to Jordil and Master Bennett." She tilted her head like a bright notion had come to her. "You really should go. Something bad will happen to you if you don't. I'm just sure of it."

"You're a curse," Mayor Stump shouted. "You bring nothing but trouble. You no-good Folde."

Maria's father shook a fist under Cam's nose. "Worthless, trouble-maker. A curse, just like the mayor said."

Cam stared at the hard gazes all around, memorizing them. Most of the people were quiet, shocked, fearful, and simply watching. It was only a tiny handful who were enraged, but that tiny handful had all the passion, and they cowed the others.

A rotten tomato splattered against his shirt. Several small children shouted at him, calling him names.

"Stop this!" It was Master Bennett.

Cam exhaled heavily, feeling like he'd been granted a reprieve.

Master Bennett was leaning heavily on a cane, and with him was Midwife Spenser. He glared about in outrage. "How dare you! Shouting your blame at a blameless youth. I was there. I saw what happened. We were attacked by rakshasas. They are the ones upon whom you should be venting your anger."

"But none of you would have been there if not for him," Maria said, refusing to back down.

A part of Cam wished someone would punch her in the face and shut her up.

Midwife Spenser looked like she wanted to do exactly that. "Be quiet, girl," she snapped. "Your reach is long, but only because of your voice. Test me, and I'll see that pretty voice snipped."

Her threat only served to stir the angriest part of the crowd. Cam's rising hope crashed when ugly promises were hurled his way. This wasn't going to end well.

"Leave him be," Master Bennett urged.

Cam noted how some of the crowd, the ones not crying for his blood, remained quiet. They still watched, unsure. But the angriest members, like the Benefields and the mayor's family, they weren't having any part of Master Bennett's insistence. Now it was truncheons and stout sticks that appeared. Maria's father was leading their outrage, calling out what needed doing: Cam driven from the village.

Master Bennett faced Cam, grief and regret on his face. "I'm so sorry, my boy. You'll have to go. There's nothing for you here. I can't teach you, and it isn't safe."

Cam had already reckoned the same, and he gave his old instructor a quick hug. "I'll not forget you, Master Bennett."

A sad nod of acknowledgement met his statement, and without another word, Cam darted away from the village square. He ran, hearing the jeering shouts and curse-filled promises as a few people gave chase. The catcalls spurred him to greater speed, running still even when he realized no one was after him. Anger crowded his thinking—fury and humiliation—but beyond it, another clear notion: all the cruel and sadistic bastards who were wanting him gone could go to the unholy hells.

Cam reached the poorer section of Traverse, and there, he finally slowed. He couldn't run anymore anyhow. He panted, his heart racing as fast as a mouse streaking away from a cat. Honor's gift of Kinesthia had solved much of his weakness, but he still had a long way to go before he could run all that far. Soon enough, he reached his father's rundown hovel.

Disregarding the structure's deteriorating conditions, Cam entered through the front door, surprised to discover Pharis inside. She was planning on moving out in a few weeks, but here she was, hands on her hips, standing over their father and Darik, both of whom sat at the kitchen table. An argument appeared to be brewing between the three of them, with the latter two looking like they were just getting started on their drinking since they were still upright and not slurring their words.

Pharis faced him when he entered, noticing his upset. "What happened?" she asked, concern on her face.

Cam's anger still roared in his ears.

"Cam," Pharis said, her tone soft. "What happened?"

He took a shuddering breath and told her. "I have to go. Now." He scowled. "They're likely to burn me out of the house if I'm still around by nightfall."

"Those bastards," his father said, fury in his voice.

Seeing his dad's support had Cam feeling a mite better. Though he was a drunkard, at least the old man loved him. The entire family did. Even Darik seemed outraged on his behalf.

"I've got some money saved," Pharis said. "You can have it. Pay me back by becoming a Crown and rubbing it in their faces."

Cam smirked, some of his anger easing. Wouldn't that be a thing.

Coming home a Crown? No one in Traverse's history had ever managed that. If they had, Traverse wouldn't have been a moderately successful town that wasn't much larger than a village, but a thriving city. Crowns had that kind of influence.

"I'll do my best," he said with a laugh, the last of his anger leaving him. Afterward, it didn't take long for him to pack up whatever belongings he needed. His father made sure to include food, extra coin, and even offered a few bottles of whiskey. Cam was sadly tempted to take the liquor. Clean as he'd been for the past year, he wouldn't mind a drink right about now.

But in the end, he left off the whiskey, not missing Pharis' exhalation of relief when he did so.

Soon enough it was time to go, the middle of the afternoon with the sun beating down. A quick hug with his father and brother led to a longer one with Pharis. A few tears leaked down Cam's face as he turned away from his kin and strode down the rutted lane in front of the only home he'd ever known. He was leaving Traverse, and this might be the last time he ever walked these streets.

And yet, there was also excitement over what was to come, about a future where no one would know him as a drunk, a curse, or a no-good Folde.

He eventually exited the walls of Traverse, thinking and planning. He had a rough idea of where he was going; where to camp for the night; and where he wanted to reach. Charn, the capital of the duchy. He could find work there and learn more about the Way into Divinity. After all, he *was* a Novice Greater. That had to mean something.

However, mostly he prayed for Lilia. For Jordil. No matter if he did attain a vast, bright future, he'd never stop grieving over her death and Jordil's pain.

10

Cam poked at his campfire, watching the stew simmer while re-viewing the day's events. There hadn't been much to it. Just hours of hiking—one foot in front of the other. Mile after mile, just like most every day since he'd been run out of Traverse several weeks ago. The only break in the journey's monotony was whenever he came across a village or town, which were haphazardly dispersed throughout the duchy. They grew up like mushrooms along Brewery Highway, the main road that connected the duchy from south-to-north until the road curled to its end along the southwestern peaks of the Diamond Mountains.

Cam planned on following Brewery until it intersected Coal Pass, which was said to be haunted by many dangerous species of Awakened Beasts. There, he'd best be off joining a caravan, and afterward, he'd come to Vivid Pass, and the large town of Game along the Charn River. A boat ride should then see him to his destination, Charn, the capital city itself.

It was months of travel he faced, but hopefully, it wouldn't be much harder than what he'd already covered. It hadn't been an easy trek so far, but he'd made it, which was something. And he was thankful for the various folk who had helped him on the way. So far, he'd always managed to find work with a local farmer or merchant, doing whatever they needed and receiving payment in food and a night's lodging. Sometimes they even offered liquor, and the temptation for that sweet liquid dragged at Cam like an anchor.

It was because of the lonely march following his banishment from Traverse; where sometimes he was just thirsty and a slug of whiskey would taste fine at the end of a long day's labor or walk.

But he knew better than to give in to those urges.

If nothing else, holding fast to his sobriety also let him hold fast to his meager money and supplies. Best let others pay his way than waste his coin. And if those hiring him might occasionally ask personal questions, like where he was from and such, Cam didn't mind answering. None of those strangers knew him or his reputation, and if they later on learned, so what? Cam would be long gone by then.

That was how his nights in a town went, but the majority of the time, Cam actually spent his evenings parked in the wilds, in between whatever village he'd just passed and whatever village he'd yet to reach. A night like tonight where it was quiet, simple, and serene. Just the way he liked.

He needed that restful peace and solitude after the brutal attack that had taken Lilia's life and nearly stolen Jordil's and Master Bennett's. Add in the way he'd been tossed out of Traverse, and… His jaw clenched. Even now, thinking about it got his dander riled even if his mind was conflicted.

A part of him dreamed about what he'd do to those fine people of Traverse if he ever got a chance. How he'd pay them self-righteous bastards back for how poorly they'd done him.

But another part of him, a kinder, better voice, urged him not to be that kind of person. Dreaming of some vague kind of vengeance was one thing, but really thinking deep and making plans to have it happen was wrong, nor would it make him happy, and really, that's all he wanted out of life: contentment and satisfaction. But that brighter way of living couldn't be found in fantasies of revenge. In fact, as Cam cogitated it would only lead to the opposite.

He'd often ponder those ideas in moments like now and in places like this, a small, empty glade next to Brewery Highway. It was far from anyone or anything, but still regularly used by other travelers given the old firepit centered within the clearing and the small collection of stacked logs close at hand. Thanks to whoever had been kind enough to leave the wood, it hadn't taken Cam long to get a fire started and a beef stew on. Best of all, no one else was about to disturb the peace.

"That smells good," a voice spoke from the treeline. "You wouldn't be interested in sharing some of your food, would you?"

Startled out of his reverie, Cam swung his gaze in the direction of the voice. He peered into the gloom beyond the firelight, eventually making out a figure.

"Sorry for hiding from you," the voice said, a male. "But I've found that in the wild, humans are usually quick on the swinging of swords rather than in the pausing for conversation." The figure stepped out of the darkness, waddling forward before settling himself several yards away, on his rear with legs splayed out.

Cam blinked in surprise. The figure looked like a small bear, except he had an unusual mix of luxuriant white fur over his torso and black colorings over his legs, rounded ears, and around his red eyes. An Awakened Beast, a Novice. Cam might have been alarmed by the bear-creature—he remembered the wolves even as he remembered Honor—but the figure was so... cute.

"What are you?" Cam blurted, reddening the moment the words exited his mouth. "Sorry. I didn't mean to sound so rude."

The figure chuckled, his round belly jiggling. "I'm not offended. There are far too many folk who take offense these days, both humans and Awakened. We'd all be better off if we'd listen with charity. But in answer to your question, I'm a panda bear." He blinked before grinning wide, and if anything, looked even cuter. "And I really am a bear, and I really would love to have some of your delicious stew. I've been subsisting on roots and leaves for so long, I've forgotten what good food tastes like."

Cam couldn't help it. He laughed. The panda bear—he'd never heard of such a creature—had a way about him that made him happy and want to smile. "Of course, you can have some stew."

The bear shifted closer, leaning forward to peer into the bubbling pot. "You wouldn't happen to have bamboo? I love bamboo. Fresh bamboo, stewed bamboo, boiled bamboo, broiled bamboo… it's all so delicious."

Again, Cam laughed. "I'm afraid not, but I got potatoes, carrots, onions, and some dried beef."

The panda settled back on his rear. "My name is Pan Shun."

"Cam Folde."

"I like you, Cam Folde," the panda declared, yawning. "Can you wake me when the stew is ready? The only thing better than eating is sleeping."

Cam smiled at the bear in bemused amusement. "Of course."

Cam sat up with a horrified start, terror seizing his mind. Eyes wide but unseeing, sweat beading on his forehead, heart pounding like a drum ready to burst… *Lilia.* Her death. Throat ripped open. A rakshasa feasting. Darkness descending on Traverse itself.

It was the same nightmare he'd been suffering for weeks now. Every night it happened. Sometimes Tern would be mixed into the dream. Occasionally it was Pharis or his father or Darik. But in all cases, a violet-eyed wolf would tear them apart, laughing at Cam, calling him a curse.

"Are you well?"

Cam didn't respond. He couldn't. He didn't know where he was, much less who had spoken. It didn't matter anyway since his thoughts continued to revolve around the nightmare. He hated remembering those last few minutes of Lilia's life. She hadn't deserved to die like that. And Jordil didn't deserve to lose her. The two of them should have had decades longer of living together ahead of them. He bowed his head, weeping.

"Are you well?" the voice repeated.

Awareness returned to Cam, and he glanced across the campfire to the worried visage of Pan Shun. Cam laughed, a derisive note. "I'm as good as I can get."

"You suffer," Pan said, concern evident in his voice. "If you want, I'd be happy to listen to whatever troubles you."

Cam viewed the Awakened in appreciation, glad for his company.

The panda was a good sort to care so much for him. They'd been on the trail together for a week now, deciding it would be safer to journey together rather than separately since they were both heading to Charn. From there, Pan planned on boating down to the island of Nexus and applying to the Ephemeral Academy. He had his reasons for getting gone from his mountain home, but Cam hadn't bothered pressing him on the why. If the Awakened wanted to tell him, he would.

"It's a kind thing," Cam said in reply to Pan's offer, "but I'm not ready to talk about any of it." Inwardly, he shuddered. Telling Pan about Jordil and Lilia might lead him to talking about his secret fears: that he was a curse to those who knew him. It made no sense for him to believe it, but there were too many tragedies where he'd walked away unscathed, and others had paid a terrible price.

How would the Awakened respond? Right now, Cam had the panda's good opinion, but that could change right quick once Pan found out who he really was.

The Awakened Beast rose to his feet. He didn't look it sitting down, but he was tall, just a few inches shorter than Cam, but dozens of pounds heavier with soft, thick fur. The bear was also young—around seven—which was early into his adulthood for his kind, just like Cam was for his. The Awakened's stubby white tail poked out of his loin-cloth, which had a hole in the back just for it.

Pan went to his packs and withdrew a flute with his human-like hands. He even had four fingers and a thumb opposite, although they all ended in stubby, black claws. "I'm not as good as my master,

Rizfam, but music always makes a heart feel warmer. Would you like me to play?"

Cam smiled. He loved listening to Pan's music, but for whatever reason, the Awakened always asked him first before putting lips to pipes. "I'd love it."

The music came out soft and sweet, a tender melody that reminded Cam of spring sunshine and birds trilling; of hope and an absence of guilt. He relaxed, slouching back into his bedding. A deep breath let him forget about the nightmare. Another deep breath, and he let the music lift him.

The fire had burned to coals, but it still gave off heat, which Cam appreciated. He and Pan needed the warmth. They had pushed into the elevations, the foothills of the Diamond Mountains, camping in a high valley. Moonlight highlighted the heights that sheltered them on all sides, and a lonesome wind blew, rustling some trees, but otherwise the night was quiet.

The song came to an end, and Pan set aside his flute.

Cam clapped, smiling in appreciation. "Thank you for that. The music did help."

Pan might have dipped his head in acknowledgement. "You're welcome." He grinned all of a sudden. "We make a good pair. You, with your ability to cook. And me, with my ability to eat."

Cam laughed. "You bring more than just your mouth. Don't forget your music-making. Without that, I reckon my nights would be a lot more troubled."

Pan chuckled. "Which only proves my point. We make a good pair." His laughter subsided, and seriousness stole across his features. "It is good to have met you. I didn't think I'd ever again have a friend."

It was a glimmer of light illuminating Pan's past, and for just a moment, Cam thought about not nosing into it, but curiosity got the best of him. "You want to tell me what happened?"

Pan flopped to the ground with a huff, his flute still in his hands. "I don't want to talk about it anymore than you want to talk about your nightmare." He stared at the flute, quiet and contemplative. "But

I think I should. I come from the northern reaches of the Diamond Mountains. I told you that, but what I didn't say is that I was abandoned by my family." He glanced up. "That's not true. I wasn't abandoned. I was told to leave."

Cam frowned. "Told to leave?"

"My family… we are all Awakened, guided in how to Heighten our Ephemera as cubs. For my people, it's a ritual and those who can learn what's necessary become Awakened, while those who can't become wild pandas."

Cam leaned forward, listening close to the fascinating explanation. "Is that what happens for all Awakened?"

Pan shook his head. "For other Awakened Beasts, the Heightening can be stimulated by need: love, hate, or most commonly, fear. Or they're lucky enough to find and ingest a plant or even a stone that's rich in Ephemera." He shrugged. "Anyway, many in my family have a Primary Tang of Spirairia. Because of that, we are often seers, and a prophecy about me was spoken from hundreds of years ago."

The panda didn't say anything else, and Cam sat up, hoping to hear more.

"I can't tell you about the prophecy," Pan grumbled. "I'm not allowed to learn it myself. If I ever do, the prophecy itself says it won't come true." A heavy sigh. "My only value is as the panda who enacts the prophecy. That is my sole worth and purpose in life."

A bubble of doubt burbled through Cam. Pan was wrong. He had much more to give than just as an agent of some prophecy. He was kind, generous, smart, and a great musician. So many talents. If anything, Cam wasn't worthy of Pan's friendship.

In that moment, a worm of guilt got Cam to want to talk about his own past. "If we're being honest and all, I guess I should tell you some about myself." It took what felt like hours to tell the Awakened about the events that had brought him here. In reality, it probably only took a few minutes. His life hadn't been that interesting. Enter a Pathway with friends that they had no business diving. Seeing a friend die. Having to choose Plasminia for his Primary Tang. Falling into drunkenness. Life passing in a blur. Honor. Lilia's death. Chased out of Traverse.

When he finished, Cam realized his heart didn't weigh so much. Some of the bitterness that he'd held onto was gone. He inwardly frowned. It couldn't be that easy, could it? Just talking it out with a friend? Be nice if it was true.

Cam found Pan staring at him, empathy on his face. "You have many reasons to resent your lot in life, but it doesn't seem healthy. Would it not ease your heart to let it go?"

Cam smiled. "You may be right, and I'll tell you. Just talking it over might have helped me get it gone."

"I wish it was that easy," Pan said, shutting down some of Cam's hopes. "You can't simply will it away. You also have to replace it with something healthier. You have to refuse to wallow in the mire and want more out of life. To want to do better."

The advice might have annoyed Cam back when he drank, or even a week or so ago when he'd been bitter and angry. A moment later, he realized he was still bitter and angry, but whatever the case, in that moment, he was able to listen and learn.

And what he learned was that Pan was right. While Cam was allowed to be bitter, he shouldn't want to wallow in it. He shouldn't *want* to be unhappy.

"What do you think I should replace my bitterness with?" Cam asked.

Pan grinned. "Food."

Cam laughed. "I should have known."

"And since we're both awake, why don't we have an early breakfast?"

"It's the middle of the night."

"A late supper?"

11

Pan exclaimed with joy when Cam showed him the stand of bamboo he had discovered.

"Bless you, my friend!" the panda exclaimed, jiggling with excitement. Without another word, he plunged into the bamboo trees, which grew along a narrow embankment shouldering Brewery Highway. And soon enough, from within their depths came the sounds of contented munching.

Cam grinned. He'd found the bamboos yesterday when stretching out his legs during his overnight watch. He'd marked the location, which wasn't hard to recall, and this morning, he had led Pan to his discovery. Watching the panda light up with excitement upon seeing the grove had been everything he had hoped for.

While Pan ate, Cam thought about how far they'd come. It had been another week on the road from when they'd talked it out—Pan about why he had left his home and Cam about how he'd ended up a drunk—and the nightmares had ebbed as the journey took them deeper into the Diamond Mountains' daunting foothills. Coal Pass wasn't too far off, and travel wasn't so easy now. Cam struggled getting his breath. There wasn't enough air, and just as bad, his years of weakness hadn't been fixed with just a couple months of roughing it.

Still, it was a sweet time. Peaceful since no one but Pan knew him and his history. No one was around to give him lip for being a "no-good Folde". Or worse, declare him a curse to those around him. He reminisced about Traverse, and the memories led him like a dog running home to recollecting on Jordil's and Lilia's unwavering friendship. And from there, to her mangled corpse.

Cam blinked back tears, pondering again on a mystery he'd yet to solve: why did bad things happen to good people? He knew he wasn't the first person to ask the question, and just like everyone who came before him, he had no answer.

Not wanting to think on it any longer, Cam tried to distract himself by taking in his surroundings. He inhaled a deep breath, absorbing the cool, crisp air of the heights. Placid clouds plodded along a pale, blue sky, and the sun shed warmth, feeling like Ephemera itself after the evening's iciness. He imagined it penetrating into his Source.

The notion had him grinning, imagining it to be true. What if it did penetrate to his Source? What changes might it make? Curiosity got ahold of him. Cam hadn't Delved his Source since he'd left Traverse. There hadn't been any need. It wasn't like he could do anything with his Ephemera. But why not take a look at it now?

His decision made, Cam Delved his Source, noticing right away the pale red, lightning-laced Plasminia. Then below it, there was…

Cam frowned. Below Plasminia, he'd expected to see the small amount of Synapsia he'd gained from Honor's gift, the liquid floating directly atop his ruby Kinesthia, and it was there. But there was something else. Directly under Plasminia and above Synapsia was what seemed like a blood-orange gas. Frowning, Cam studied it.

An instant later, his eyes widened with understanding. Spirairia. He also had Spirairia.

His holler of elation brought Pan running from the grove, eyes wide with alarm and several stalks of bamboo clutched like clubs in his hands.

Cam laughed. "I'm fine. I just discovered something."

Pan lowered his arms, the fear fading from his face. "What is it?"

"I have Spirairia."

Pan tilted his head, looking confused. "I thought you had a Novice Tang of both Plasminia and Kinesthia and a thin sheet of Synapsia."

"I do."

"And now you also have Spirairia? When did this happen?"

Cam shrugged, having no notion. Nor did he figure on knowing what having four Tangs of Ephemera might mean. But it couldn't be common, could it?

"Do you realize how rare it is for someone to develop three Tangs of Ephemera?"

"I've a notion," Cam said, trying not to sound smug.

"I've a notion, he says," Pan mimicked, his arms thrown to the heavens as if in supplication. "It's not so rare that it's impossible, but it's rare enough that most duchies mark all their Novice Primes and provide them greater boons and benefits to see them Advance. It's my goal to get there, too."

Pan's explanation should have made Cam happier, but it didn't. Instead, the joy in his sails stopped blowing. He was a nobody from a small town in the back end of nowhere. He might have it in him to become a Novice Prime, but who would care? In the end, he was still a Plasminian, and his kind didn't get no boons or benefits. Besides, there was also another bigger problem. "I don't have three full Tangs of Ephemera."

Pan waved aside his complaint. "But you could. That's what I'm saying. You might even be the first person to achieve four full Tangs. And if you can Advance them, who knows what you could accomplish? What you could do for all of us? Even if we're safe now, the rakshasas and their boils will always try to claim new territory. And you, with four full Tangs at whatever Awareness, might be able to do more to stop them than an entire squad of warriors."

Cam smiled in wistful delight, his vision going distant as he imagined what Pan was talking about. Imagining himself a hero. Closing deadly boils that entire teams of Ephemeral Masters couldn't manage.

"You see it, don't you?" Pan said, smiling brightly.

Cam wanted to share in his friend's optimism, but optimism was a close companion to hope, and recently for him, hope hadn't been a good thing.

Pan must have guessed the flavor of his thoughts. "Remember who you were several months ago, weak and with every reason to be bitter. Now here you are. Healed of your illness and blessed to travel the world with the handsomest of pandas."

Cam laughed. Pan was right, but even still, he wasn't yet willing to agree. "I might see a bit of what you mean," he allowed. "But in the meantime, light's burning, and we should get going."

Pan agreed without another word, and his willingness to let matters lie was another reason Cam liked him so well.

Soon enough, their packs gathered, they headed off, and while they marched along, Cam reconsidered his discovery. It also didn't take him long to notice the spring in his step, and it was easy to figure out why. Despite his best attempts to crush it down, hope had rekindled in his heart.

"Well, look at that," Pan declared the next day of their travels, offering his happy, tongue-lolling smile. "I had no idea we'd come across something so fortuitous. It's perfect."

Cam looked to where Pan was peering. What was so perfect about this place? They were several miles out from a town called Dander— similar enough to Traverse to be a twin—somewhere well beyond the fields surrounding the place. Currently the cobbled track of Brewery Highway had them in a forest of towering evergreens on all sides, except on the left.

There, a wildflower meadow, acres and acres in dimension, defied the trees, and a small pond glistened. A number of hills huddled around the clearing, but it was the stony rise, black like basalt, split down the middle, and hulking in the center of the glade, which caught

Cam's attention. Craggy and ridged, it rose a dozen times his height and loomed like a small mountain. There was no reason for it to be here. It didn't belong, and from it extended a heavy presence that Cam dimly recognized.

"This area was once a boil," Pan declared, gesturing to the wildflower field and all around.

"How can you tell?"

"The Ephemera is still thick here. You can feel it emanating from the boil's broken core. And from what I can tell, it's only at the Neophyte Stage, which is why whoever lanced it didn't bother taking it. It can only help Novices. No one else, not even actual Neophytes." He pointed to the black rise. "The rakshasas stole Ephemera from whatever beings they could and fed it to the core. Doing so gathers even more Ephemera. While the boil was alive, it likely made this place toxic for all other kinds of life."

It was an interesting explanation, but Cam still wasn't sure why they had stopped here. Plus, he didn't much like being around the dead core of a once-boil. What if there were still rakshasas about? He glanced around in worry.

Pan laughed, his round belly jiggling. "There are no rakshasas," he said, guessing the direction of Cam's concern. "Once a boil is destroyed, the rakshasas linked to it are either killed or they flee and never return."

Cam's fears eased off, but he still didn't know why Pan had them stop here. There were miles more to go before they were supposed to stop for the day, and Coal Pass wasn't going to get any closer just by wishing it.

"Ephemera still emanates off of the core," Pan explained, "and for us as Novices, it's perfect. We can Accrete Ephemera here, and over time, Imbibe it into our Sources."

Cam smiled as his mood brightened. "Gaining more Ephemera means we can become more than we are now."

"We both need to become Novice Primes if we're to attend the Ephemeral Academy."

Cam's smile faded. Pan's plan wasn't necessarily his. Plus, from what he could tell, it sounded like only the rich and powerful attended the Ephemeral Academy. And no matter what Pan thought, even with four Tangs at full Novice, Cam doubted he counted as either. Certainly not the rich part, and doubtful about the powerful as well.

Pan must have caught onto his reluctance. "Even if you don't want to go to the Ephemeral Academy, surely you want to become a Novice Prime."

Cam nodded without hesitation. "I do, but you've got one thing wrong about what might happen to me here. If I Accrete and Imbibe more Ephemera, most likely, it'll turn to Plasminia, which might then Advance me to Acolyte. A Plasminian Tang a full Stage higher than my Kinesthia means I'll be right back where I started from. Weak and worthless."

"No, you won't," Pan said. "To Advance a Stage, you have to answer the deeper questions. For Novice to Acolyte, it's—"

"The difference between selfishness and selflessness." Cam smiled in relief. He'd forgotten about the questions, and without a way to answer them, there was no way for him to Advance. Which was a good thing for now.

"You'll do it then?" Pan asked, catching on to Cam's change in mood. "I have two Tangs beyond my Primary of Kinesthia, but they're only at the beginning. I want to raise them to Novice."

Cam nodded. "Why is it so important for you to be a Novice Prime? Why not add those Tangs later, like as an Acolyte?"

"Because there is no later," Pan explained. "Once your Primary Tang Advances past Novice, whatever Tangs you have is what you'll always have. There is no chance to form any new ones."

Cam had learned the same lesson, but he'd also wanted confirmation. "There is just one other thing," he said. "Can you teach me to Accrete?" Master Bennett had never covered this under his teaching.

"Of course. Accreting is what I'm best at."

"Eating is what you're best at."

Pan grinned. "That, too. Now come. We need to be closer to the core."

They walked through the large, sunny glade, flowers perfuming the air and birds trilling from the surrounding forest. Meanwhile, Cam's heart raced, like he was approaching something terrible and dangerous.

"Accretion is the same for both Awakened and humans," Pan explained as they neared the core. "You close your eyes, Delve your Source, and draw the Ephemera in like a breath. It should settle on your skin and pulling it inward is like drinking through a tube with a stone lodged in it." He hesitated. "Gaining enough Ephemera to Advance a Tang will also expel toxins from your body. The process can be filthy. You might want to take off your clothes."

Cam had learned about this, and he did as Pan advised, disrobing to his knickers. From what he remembered, Advancing Spirairia released a black liquid while from Synapsia came a kind of phlegm, which sounded gross. Kinesthia was associated with a watery serum of some sort, but of Plasminia, no one knew a thing.

They reached the dead core, which was still housed in the towering black rock. Pan plopped on the ground, his belly jiggling like it always did. Cam settled next to him.

"Delve your Source," Pan advised. "Then feel the Ephemera coming off the core. It feels different for everyone, but for most, it's like a light breeze. Then imagine your Source attaching to it, asking the Ephemera to stay on your skin so you can Imbibe it later."

"You act like the Ephemera is alive."

"It is. It comes from the Holy Servants through Devesh and is a part of them and everything else."

Which again raised the question of why bad things happened to good people. But now wasn't the time for weighty discussions. "And this is how most Awakened Accrete Ephemera?"

Pan nodded. "Even humans."

Cam frowned at the panda. "How do you know so much?"

Pan grinned. "I might just be a Novice, but my family is Awakened, and I was taught all the ways to Advance." His smile grew bitter. "I needed to learn if I'm to enact the prophecy."

Cam didn't miss the resentment on his friend's face or his voice, but he let it alone, knowing Pan wouldn't appreciate his prying. Instead, he closed his eyes and Delved his Source. It quickly formed in his mind's eye. Next, he imagined a breeze coming off the core, which was strangely enough, easy to do. It was like the touch of a feather, but there it was. Cam imagined his Source reaching out to the breeze, calling on the Ephemera to collect on his skin, wanting it to remain in place so he could Imbibe it and draw it into his Source.

Hours passed before Cam noticed that nature was calling. He opened his eyes and levered himself upright with a groan. Right away, he felt an oppressive film covering his body. Was it sweat?

"You've done it," Pan said in approval, eyes open as well. "There's a sheen on you."

"It's not sweat?"

"No. It's Ephemera. Can't you tell the difference?"

Cam paused before replying, trying to figure out if Pan was putting him on. Was the sheen he was feeling really Ephemera? It took him a few minutes to answer the question, and when he did, he grinned.

"See," Pan said, sounding smug. "Just listen to me, and you won't go astray."

"Of course, wise master," Cam mocked.

Pan simply shook his head in exasperation.

Cam left him there, and after taking care of his bladder, he resumed his position next to his friend. Pan had his mouth slightly ajar, and a string of drool had collected. Cam smiled. Even then, the panda was cute.

Days after their encounter with the dead boil and its remnant core, Cam found himself still struggling to Imbibe the Ephemera he had collected. Some of it, he'd surely lost since the sheen on his skin wasn't as cloying and heavy as it had been early on. But some, he must have Imbibed since his Synapsia was thicker than before. Just give it a nudge, and he'd Advance and become a Novice Prime. His Spirairia wasn't too far behind, neither.

His success didn't mean any of it was easy, though. The process of Advancing his Ephemera was just as Pan had described—like drinking through a tube with a stone lodged inside. Plus, his Plasminia wanted to transform every bit of entering Ephemera into more of itself, and it was a constant fight to keep that from happening. It was like pulling on the reins of a mule when the stupid animal wanted to go straight but a body needed to go left.

And yet, Cam hadn't given in or given up. Every night, he Imbibed whatever Ephemera he could, bringing it into his Source and fighting his own bloody, fragging Plasminia the entire time.

In addition, his slowly Advancing Tangs brought their own sort of troubles, coming in the form of an increased awareness of the world. There was so much to see, hear, and feel. The slightest breeze brought Cam a flood of information, smells and sounds that he'd never before noticed. Much of it was loud and obnoxious, and the worst stank like an overflowing outhouse.

But it wasn't all doom, gloom, and bad news. There was something good that came from all his hard work. Cam knew himself to be smarter than before. He recollected words and phrases that better expressed how he felt and thought. They were big ones, too; large-coin words, his dad would have said.

Cam didn't much like them. Did he really need to talk like that? He reckoned not. He'd speak like himself, and if big-city folks didn't like it, they could piss off.

"Is this a good place to stop?" Pan asked, interrupting Cam's wonderings.

Cam glanced about. Pan had halted them next to a small clearing amidst a large copse of pine with a fire pit already dug out from where other travelers must have stopped. The setting was a couple miles out from a small village they'd passed a little while ago, and on the other side of Brewery stood fields of barley waving in the wind and golden under the late afternoon sun. Out in the distance, a couple of

Ephemeral Masters with Spirairia walked the crops. Wisps of orange light flicked off their fingers, spreading out onto the plants, and wherever they touched, beetles of the kind that could ruin a field in a day, would lift off with a buzz before falling dead seconds later.

"It's a good place," Cam said to Pan.

After getting their camp set up and their dinner eaten, of silent accord they got to work. Both of them, fighting to Imbibe the Ephemera they had Accreted at the dead core. It wasn't an easy task for either.

An hour later, with twilight upon them and the fields empty, a whistling sound from overhead broke Cam from his meditation. He glanced upward, and his jaw dropped.

Streaking across the sky and descending toward him was a man. A dark cloak fluttered around his form, hugging tight and not rising upward like Cam would have expected. A domineering pressure emanated from the figure, one so heavy that Cam struggled to get to his feet. His legs wanted to give way, but he locked them tight, not wanting to meet this powerful person—whoever it was—on his butt or on his knees. Never again would he be weak in front of anyone.

The man drew closer, and his features came clear. Cam breathed a bit easier. It was Master Winder. A moment later, Cam's easy breathing grew a bit strained. Master Winder seemed angry as a badger.

"What happened to Jordil and Lilia?" the Wilde Sage said as soon as his feet touched dirt.

Cam wanted to answer, but it took all his effort to remain upright. Master Winder's presence was that intense.

"Sir, perhaps you can Cloud your Source," Pan suggested, strain on his face and in his voice.

Master Winder glanced at the panda with a narrow-eyed frown, blinking once. An instant later, the pressure was gone.

Cam sagged in relief. "It was my fault," he said in reply to Master Winder's question. "Lilia died protecting me."

Master Winder's violet eyes flashed like candles. "Tell me everything."

12

It took a bit of time and emotion to explain about the Awakened wolves and Lilia's death, but Cam got through it, pretending he was reciting a story about someone who wasn't him. It was the only way. Otherwise, he knew he'd have broken down and cried.

The death of his friend; Jordil's certain grief... it ached like a blow to the brain, and what he'd said earlier about it being his fault—he knew it wasn't right, but it still felt that way. Sure, it was the Awakened wolves who had killed Lilia, but she had only been on that road because of him. Otherwise, she would have been home, safe and healthy.

"You're a curse." He recollected the words.

"This wasn't your fault," Master Winder said, forgiveness in his voice.

The tone nearly undid Cam, and he fought against a sob. He wanted to be punished, and it was being taken from him.

"It wasn't your fault," Master Winder repeated.

Cam found himself engulfed in Pan's arms, held in a hug. The panda smelled like bamboo, and he was soft and warm. Cam broke down and sobbed. Guilt still ate at him, even though it made no sense. Fury, too. Rage at the world and self-loathing of his role in the death of a close friend. A death he'd never properly grieved. The sobs came harder as he recalled what had happened after his return to Traverse.

Almost as soon as Lilia's funeral pyre had cooled to embers and ashes, he had been cast out from his home. Then had come the simple struggle of staying alive on the road, of walking and working, and constantly making himself fight against the lure of the bottle and a sense of emptiness. There had never been a chance to rest and reflect, and he'd never wanted to, always shying away from his feelings.

No longer, and the sorrow swept over him.

The entire time, Pan held him, saying nothing, but after a few minutes, Cam had himself collected, and he eased away from his Awakened friend. He viewed Master Winder. "What happens now?"

Master Winder pursed his lips. "Why don't you tell me your plans, and then we'll decide."

Cam answered with a question of his own. "Sir, why are you so interested in us? We're just Novices."

"I'm interested because of your potential," Master Winder said. "Now tell what you want to do with yourself."

Further explanations followed. Pan with his dream of attending the Ephemeral Academy, and Cam with his about going to some place where he could start a fresh life.

"I'm still trying to encourage him to come with me to the Academy," Pan added after they both finished explaining their goals.

"What Tangs do you have?" Master Winder asked Pan.

"Kinesthia and Synapsia at Novice," Pan answered, "and after the dead core we visited…"

"What dead core?"

"There was the remnant of a core a few days behind," Cam said. "From where a boil was destroyed."

Master Winder nodded. "I know the one of which you speak. Neophyte only. It was a good idea for you to stop there. The Ephemera still leaking from that broken core can't help anyone but a Novice, and even then, rarely. Did it help the two of you?"

"Yes, sir. It did," Pan said. "I was able to Advance Synapsia, and I Accreted enough that I'm certain that in a few days, I'll be able to Advance Spirairia to Novice as well."

The Sage's eyes glinted with interest now. "Meaning you would be a Novice Prime, and a strong candidate for the Academy." He rubbed his chin. "It seems fortune favors you."

Pan bowed. "My fondest wish is to attend the Academy. I love Ephemera, everything about it. The Way into Divinity. It means everything to me."

Cam snorted. "Don't let him fool you. He doesn't like nothing as much as he does bamboo. He'd drown in it if he could."

"Hilarious, I'm sure," Master Winder said, not sounding the least bit amused. Cam wiped away his smile. "And while your friend was Advancing, what have you accomplished?"

The question was a challenge, the smack of a glove across Cam's face. What had he done with his life? There wasn't much to it other than tragedy and bad luck. But was there really nothing else to him?

While he considered what to say, Pan spoke on his behalf. "He has Plasminia and Kinesthia at Novice."

"This, I already know," Master Winder said, his tone curt.

"He also has Tangs of Synapsia and Spirairia, and he should have one, possibly both, Advanced to Novice in a few days."

Cam found Master Winder's sudden interest in him alarming. He straightened his posture, feeling like it might be right to salute.

"Is this true?" the Wilde Sage demanded.

A precipice over something hungry and ominous seemed to loom, and the danger came from the Wilde Sage. Cam swallowed down a bolus of sudden nerves, speaking in tones of the utmost respect. "Yes, sir. It's true."

"Two Novice Primes," Master Winder mused. "And one of you of even greater rarity. Someone possibly never seen in all history." Again, his interest settled on Cam, who stiffened further to ramrod straight. It might make him look like a broom handle was shoved up his back passage, but better that than have the Wilde Sage mad at him. "You two will come with me. I will sponsor both of you at the Ephemeral Academy."

Master Winder's order made Cam want to protest. He even opened his mouth to do so, but quickly shut it. There was no point. The Wilde Sage had chosen their futures, and Cam figured that no matter his own hopes and dreams, he'd be spitting in the wind if he argued about it.

The morning sun had barely trimmed the horizon when Master Winder woke them. He was soft enough in doing so, just a gentle shake of the shoulder, but this was the Wilde Sage, and his words had Cam scrambling out of his bedroll like rakshasa hounds were on him. For a moment, he was stuck in his blankets and wrenched around to free himself. He likely looked like a clumsy oaf in the process, but all he could think was to get upright and reach his feet. He didn't want to disappoint Master Winder or even *risk* disappointing Master Winder. There were few things in life stupider than that.

Cam finally got himself sorted out, and he faced the Wilde Sage, chest out, shoulders squared. Sidelong, he viewed Pan doing the same. Cam's mouth twitched when the poor panda tried and failed to suck in his prodigious gut. Great word there: prodigious; one he only knew because of his Tang of Synapsia, which nowadays had him feeling bright as a mirror reflecting sunlight.

All the instruction he'd taken from Masters Bennett and Moltin; only now did it seem like he could well enough recall the learning. And a better vocabulary might be a part of it.

Master Winder took the wind out of Cam's self-congratulatory sails when he turned a slight smile his way and asked a simple question. "Now that you're awake, what can you tell me about the Sage-Dukes?"

Other than their names? Not much, although Cam didn't want to admit it. The Wilde Sage likely thought him ignorant enough as it was. Cam looked to Pan, hoping his friend would know the answer. Sure enough, the chubby panda came through.

"I know their names," Pan said, "but that's not what you want to know, is it?"

Master Winder flashed another smile, but not of good cheer, and it was gone before Cam could puzzle out what it might mean. "You're smarter than you look," the Wilde Sage said.

It sounded like a compliment, but Pan stiffened on hearing it. "I try," he said, his voice strained.

"So you do."

It was an enigmatic kind of comment, and Cam glanced at Master Winder, wondering what he meant by it. Next, his gaze went to his friend, whose normally happy demeanor seemed like it was just a few shades from being angry as a sunburn. What had him so upset? Cam didn't know, but his eyes went to Master Winder, outraged on Pan's behalf. He might have glared at the Wilde Sage. In fact, he did so for the briefest moment, before quickly shifting his attention. Best not risk that foolishness.

Instead, he pretended to stare about the small clearing where they had camped, inspecting the fire which was down to ashes and embers; the surrounding forest full of shadows slowly giving way to sunlight; and the sounds of life stirring as birds sang and small critters rustled. All the while Cam waited, exhaling in relief when Master Winder never called him out for his glare.

"What I meant to ask is this," the Wilde Sage said. "What do you know about the history of the Sage-Dukes?"

Again, Pan was the one to answer, but he spoke in a monotone, like he was reciting something memorized. "The nine Sage-Dukes rule the nine great cities on Salvation. It has been thus for as many thousands of years of history as we can recall, although the dukes themselves are not so old. Each new member rules the city of the one he or she replaced, and the one edict all dukes follow is the law of stability. They cherish it above all else and don't allow for any change that might risk their position, privilege, and power."

"Very good," Master Winder said. "You are correct, and it is that stability that dooms us to stagnation. There has been no new Divine in centuries or longer. Meanwhile, the rakshasas seek to grow their numbers every year. If not for the Ephemeral Masters who battle on behalf of the dukes, their boils would fester, threatening many villages and towns."

"All the Sages are limited like this?" Pan asked. "Unable to Advance to Divine? Even you?"

The answer came in a fierce growl. "Even me."

Cam had a question. "Why don't the dukes take the field against the rakshasas and wipe them out once and for all? They're Sages, after all."

"Because just as there are nine dukes, the rakshasas have their own version of Sages, nearly Divines, in fact. Three of them, rulers of powerful boils and their own sort of civilization."

"Shimala, Coruscant, and Simmer," Cam whispered, shivering. He vaguely recalled a terrifying dream in which an old woman named Shimala had trapped him in her house, pretending to offer him a place to stay for the night. Had he really experienced it?

"What do the rakshasas want?" Pan asked.

"Growth and expansion, like all living beings," Master Winder said. "But their perverse view on the Way into Divinity is the reason we can't allow it."

Cam had a notion what Master Winder meant. It was how the rakshasas Advanced; by slaughtering and stealing Ephemera from any they deemed weaker or less worthy. Perverse, just as Master Winder had said.

"Getting back to the Sage-Dukes," the Wilde Sage said. "You should know something more about them. All of them seek to raise Ephemeral Masters, to see them Advance and battle under their banners against the rakshasas. That is the main reason for the Ephemeral Academy. It is a place where their finest young Ephemeral Masters go for training, to rise in Stages from Novice to Glory. Any who attend are Novice Primes, and they can be jealous of their status." Cam swallowed when Master Winder sent a challenging gaze in his direction, exhaling when the Wilde Sage turned away, speaking to Pan. "It can be dangerous for those who attend and don't have the support of a Sage-Duke. You'll have to work hard just to catch up to where they are already starting. Is this what you want?"

Pan never hesitated. "Yes."

Cam found himself once again the focus of the Wilde Sage's attention. "And you?"

Cam answered the question with one of his own. "What kind of dangers?"

Once again, Master Winder gave his cheerless smile. "A good question." He flicked a glance at Pan. "In the future, you would do well to think before answering, my little Awakened panda."

His words must have struck another nerve because Pan stiffened, appearing embarrassed this time.

Cam scowled, not liking how Master Winder insulted his friend.

"You disagree with how I speak to the panda?" Master Winder asked.

Cam realizing he'd been glaring at the Wilde Sage, and rather than shrink in fear, he gazed boldly at Master Winder, letting him see his anger. "Yes, I do. You shouldn't speak to him like that."

For a wonder, the Wilde Sage didn't take insult, instead nodding acceptance. "Hold onto that outrage because your friend will receive far worse insults at the Ephemeral Academy."

Cam frowned in confusion.

Master Winder noticed. "Many Ephemeral Masters don't respect Awakened Beasts the way they deserve. And since too many—not most or even a lot—become rakshasas, that distrust is only amplified. You'll both face that kind of sentiment at the academy."

"What about Avia Koravail?" Pan asked.

"Ah. Her. She's a special case. She is an Awakened orca, who upon reaching Novice, transformed her appearance into one nearly indistinguishable from a born human. It helps that she's beautiful, and it helps even more that when she strode ashore and her potential was recognized, she was adopted by Duke Kelse Vail, the ruler of Saban. As his daughter and likely heir, she is afforded a great deal of respect. She will be in your class, a new student at the academy."

An orca? Cam had seen a pod of them the one time he'd visited the ocean. They'd been massive and majestic. But rather than ask questions about this Awakened orca, there was something else he wanted cleared up first. "And us? You said it would be dangerous for us to go to the academy without a duke sponsoring us. Should we even go?"

"If you have courage, yes," Master Winder said. "And while you won't have a duke to sponsor you, you will have a Sage. My name will grant you admittance and some protection, but I also have certain requirements."

"What kind of requirements?"

"The dukes sponsor Ephemeral Masters to battle the rakshasas. So do I. You will fight in my name. It is a dangerous life." He gazed at them, his visage hard. "Is this still what you want?"

Cam had been thinking on the matter the entire time they'd been talking. The Ephemeral Academy meant a chance to grow and Advance along the Way into Divinity. It was what he had dreamed of achieving since childhood. His answer resounded just a beat after Pan's. "Yes."

After Cam agreed to go to the Ephemeral Academy, the next question was how he and Pan would get there. The academy was on the island of Nexus, a far journey, and while the Wilde Sage could likely fly there and back inside an hour, Cam and Pan most certainly couldn't. They'd have to walk, and at their pace, it would be months before they arrived. Then there was the voyage across the water. Cam had seen the ocean once, and it had stretched endlessly. Lake Nexus might be called a lake, but that was like saying a mountain was a molehill. Both words began with 'm' but that's where the similarity ended. Lake Nexus was as massive as an inland sea, vast beyond measure.

There were other questions, too, like where would he and Pan live on the island? How would they pay for it? What about food? It was probably pricey, and Cam didn't much feel like starving. What kind of work would they have to do? Same with the classes? What would they learn? And how would they afford to pay for their instruction?

He was about to blurt out a river of queries, but Master Winder cut him off with a raised hand. "I will explain more later," the Wilde Sage said, his expression warm. "For now, know that I will pay your fees for attendance, including room and board. Same with a small stipend, so you can enjoy life a bit. It won't be much." His brow furrowed, and his visage grew severe. "I won't have you whiling away your days doing nothing. You will learn and master what is taught, but once you are Glories, I'll complete your education and your training; better than the school ever could."

Cam considered what had been both said and unsaid. Just now, Master Winder had acted like the academy couldn't teach them as well as he could, which made a sort of sense. After all, Master Winder was a Sage, and the likely reason he didn't take on their education himself was because he didn't have the time. They were only Novices and not worth his attention; not like Saira, who was a Crown.

Master Winder clapped his hands, bringing the conversation to an end. "Enough. It's time to leave."

Cam glanced about. He supposed they'd best get to walking then. He was about to say so, but an instant later, his mouth clacked shut when Master Winder waved his hand. The world seemed to shake, although Cam's feet didn't stir any. But something did change. Where the Wilde Sage had waved, a doorway framed into being. It started as a black line right off the ground, before spinning on its axis and exposing a swirling rainbow bridge.

An anchor line.

Cam gasped, unexpectedly thrilled. He had heard of anchor lines—everyone had—but he'd never thought he'd actually see one. It was a miracle only Sages could create.

"Just step through," Master Winder said, "and it'll take you to the academy."

Cam gazed at the doorway, grinning in rising eagerness. It really was an anchor line, and he was about to ride one. One of the most improbable happenings he might have ever hoped to experience in his life.

The excitement had Cam wanting to freeze this moment in his mind, and he stared about the clearing, etching every detail into his memory. The sun stood early in the morning. A breeze, one smelling of rhododendrons and azaleas, flitted like fingers through his long hair and clattered a nearby stand of bamboo. Pan, thinking ahead, had already harvested a number of those shoots, clutching stalks nearly as tall as himself. But for once, Pan's attention wasn't on the bamboo. Instead, he gazed wide-eyed at the anchor line, the same wonder on his features that Cam wore.

"Step through," Master Winder repeated, his patience clearly wearing as thin as a moth-eaten blanket.

Cam quickly made to do as ordered. He ensured his rucksacks were secured to his back, not wanting to risk them flinging about when he traveled the anchor line. Shortly satisfied, he took a fateful step forward...

And his body stretched to the breaking. A harsh noise, like a bird shrieking, echoed in his ears. Lights blurred. The world disappeared, and Cam screamed, his voice torn away, leaving him mute.

Then he was out, stumbling forward, nearly losing his balance. Nausea soured his stomach, and he bent at the knees, gasping, trying to recover. All the while, the bright sunshine in which he found himself had him squinting.

An instant later, Pan came out of the portal, tripping, falling, and sliding on his face, his bamboo scattering. The poor panda groaned, struggling to rise off the ground. His arms shook, and Cam moved to help him, pausing when Master Winder exited the portal. The Wilde Sage moved with the easy grace of old familiarity.

Of course, he did. He probably traveled by anchor line whenever he wanted.

Cam helped Pan rise to his feet. "You alright?"

Pan nodded. "That wasn't fun," he said, looking as miserable as a wet cat.

"No, it wasn't," Cam agreed. His stomach still rumbled now and then, and while waiting for it to settle, he took a gander at his surroundings.

Cam guessed it to be noon, and they stood on a peerlessly white granite shelf that was poised upon a low-lying black cliff above waters—it had to be Lake Nexus—that had an aqua-blue color that Cam had only heard about in stories. There were no boats in view, just the endlessly splashing spray against the shoals and rocks, lofting twinkling rainbows that shined in the sunlight. It was a beautiful sight, but also disappointing in a way.

He had expected more from Nexus and the Ephemeral Academy. Where were all the buildings and such?

Cam turned about, inhaling in sharp wonder. Now *there* was something grand.

Before him rose a nest of hills, spread about the island, every one of them covered by red-tiled, white buildings. The structures were clustered close, stacked atop one another with narrow alleys like charcoal marks highlighting their glimmering brightness. And in the distance, there stood a larger hill with an assortment of buildings, the largest of which appeared to be a massive coliseum. But it was the structure nearest the arena, rising on the flat-topped summit that garnered the majority of his attention. It was a temple, rectangularly shaped and having intricate carvings on its facade and fanciful shapes curling about the innumerable columns marching along its periphery. And surrounding the temple like emerald jewels were green gardens, the color shocking against the stark whiteness of most of the island. All of them hosted statues of heroes.

"Welcome to Nexus," Master Winder said, sounding pleased by Cam's obvious stunned amazement.

13

Cam didn't have a chance to examine the city, which bore the same name as the island. Instead, Master Winder had them striding quickly through various neighborhoods and environs, along streets paved with carefully fitted gray bricks. Cam wanted to stop and stare, and the one place he did was at a view overlooking the harbor. He gaped in wonder at what he saw.

There, on a small set of islands, soared two massive statues, hundreds of feet in height. Cast of alabaster marble, they were of a man and a woman, holding hands across the water, gentle smiles on their faces. The woman wore a sari, the pleats seeming to have movement and the man wore an achkan over a pair of pants.

Cam didn't have to ask to understand who the figures represented. *The Holy Servants, Rukh and Jessira.* They appeared exactly how he would have expected. Both of them beautiful and awe-inspiring.

Master Winder had him hustling along shortly thereafter, and they quickly trekked through the city. Cam still wanting to halt at every new sight, ask a thousand questions about the persons, places, and things they encountered. He'd never before seen so many people in one

138

place, smelled so many foods—where did they get it all?—or heard so many conversations, all piled on top of one another like the buildings themselves. Nexus was a town unlike any other.

No. Not a town. Nexus was a city, and Cam wanted to stop and soak it in.

Unfortunately, there was no halting Master Winder. He had them pressing forward, never slowing, never answering their questions, always urging them on to greater speed. Cam might have asked Master Winder to slow down some, but there was no point. The Wilde Sage had a burr in his britches and they kept on until they reached a large wrought-iron gate with pickets topped by golden finials shaped like leaves. It interrupted a white wall, ten feet tall and marching along the boundaries of what Cam realized was the Ephemeral Academy. A pair of guards warded the way inside, but upon seeing Master Winder, they waved them through.

The world calmed the moment they stepped past the gates. All the clamor seemed to end just a few steps inside. Cam glanced back, wondering if there was some kind of magic to make it happen. But, no. There beyond the gates was the unchanged hustle and bustle of the city. Cam faced inward again, still not sure how it could be so loud in one place and quiet just a few feet away.

He shook his head at the unanswered mystery and took in his new surroundings, able to examine it since Master Winder didn't have them running anymore.

Cam found himself standing in a largely empty plaza with a fountain and a crystal statue of two people in the center. They were smiling, hands clasped and from their off hands came a splashing of water. Again, it was the Holy Servants. A wide swatch of grass circled the fountain, breaking the monotony of the flagstones. But Cam had no focus for the green growth. His eyes were fixed on the figures, warriors in this rendition.

"The Holy Servants," Pan whispered.

"Rukh and Jessira," Cam agreed, staring more closely at the figures. The Holy Servants... weren't they supposed to have eventually settled into lives of peace? Nonjudgmental was what lots of folks said was their greatest quality. Why did they look like fierce warriors then? It was obvious since both had sheathed swords at their waists and a quiver of arrows on their backs.

"Come," Master Winder ordered, guiding them right, circling the fountain and the statues. They ascended a set of stairs that had Cam huffing and puffing and his thighs burning by the time they finally ascended the top.

There, they reached another flattened area of the hill, this one broken into clusters of green gardens with a lot more people. Some were reading books while others played a game with some kind of disc that they flung with a flick of their wrists to one another. The discs floated through the air like they might off and fly like a Sage. Cam itched to learn how it was done. Was it some secret Ephemeral skill? Whatever the case, it looked fun.

His attention shifted again when he found himself in a shadow cast by a long building made of smooth white stones like the other structures on Nexus. The structure extended as long as Traverse's finest inn, and a columned portico lined by rose bushes faced them. More young folk were present on the porch, taking their ease on a plethora of rocking chairs situated at regular intervals. A gentle breeze flitted, cool and carrying the scent of roses in bloom.

A few of the people on their rocking chairs were staring their way, but Cam's attention was on a familiar figure, who stood before the tall, paneled doors leading inside.

Saira.

She wore a welcoming smile, but Cam frowned when he caught sight of her eyes. Instead of the indigo of a Crown, they were the Haunt-blue of a Glory. What had happened to her?

"I give you over to the care of my apprentice," Master Winder said, drawing Cam's attention from Saira. "She will explain more about this school. Do as she tells you. Master your Ephemera and grow." With a final nod, a violet glow surrounded the Wilde Sage as he bent his knees and launched into the sky, swiftly departing.

Cam watched him leave, still amazed at the sight of a person flying.

"Welcome to the Ephemeral Academy," Saira said, moving to stand before him.

He sensed danger. An enemy was close, one he wasn't yet ready to face. Might never be ready to face. Better to hide, grow stronger, and plan.

"What happened to your eyes?" Cam blurted the question, not thinking how it might sound.

Saira's welcoming smile grew strained. "A private situation."

Cam dropped the matter, recognizing she didn't want to talk about it.

She faced Pan. "I'm Saira Maharani," she said, introducing herself. "And you are Pan Shun."

The panda nodded, appearing bemused, which was the same as how Cam felt. How had Saira known the Awakened's name, and why didn't she seem surprised to see them?

She must have caught onto their bewilderment. "Master Winder told me you'd be arriving today. It's a good thing he found you when he did, or you'd have missed the start of the semester."

Cam's frown deepened, and he shared a look of uncertainty with Pan. Had Master Winder anchor lined to Nexus last night? He asked the very question.

Saira chuckled in response. "Master Winder is a Sage. He can communicate across great distances as he wills." Her humor transformed into a more sincere smile. "Let's get you settled. Follow me." She headed into the building before them.

More of the people on the porch were staring in their direction, assessing them like wolves apprising easy meat. Cam could understand why. He was dressed in rough country garb with ratty, old boots that had seen their better days years ago. And Pan only wore a breech-cloth and had a rucksack on his back and a fistful of bamboo in hand. The two of them looked like hayseeds from the back end of nowhere while everyone else was garbed in fine clothing, well made and with no scuffs to muss the sheen of their footwear. A few of the folks on the porch sneered their way, and Cam quickly shuffled out of their sight. They had a right unpleasant way about them.

He caught up with Saira as she was leading them into the building. "This is your dormitory," she said. "You'll be on the first floor."

Cam only had a moment to gawk. They had entered a wide space with floor-to-ceiling windows at the far end. Through them could be seen the bustling city, docks, and the massive statues of Rukh and Jessira in the harbor. And further out, boats looking like toys bobbed on Lake Nexus, which glistened in the sunshine.

Saira led them left, down a wide hallway, paneled in a tan wood and floored in white marble.

"Bamboo," Pan whispered, touching the walls reverently.

Cam chuckled. "I doubt they'd take kindly to you eating the walls."

Pan laughed in reply. "I like all kinds of bamboo, but not any that have been stained and polished."

A couple of students headed their way down the hall and gave them curious gazes. They wore the same finery as those outside, but for whatever reason, they didn't have the same superior smirks on their faces.

Saira was talking, and Cam stopped worrying on anyone else he saw, paying heed to her words. "Those who attend the Ephemeral Academy are the five best Novices from each duchy, occasionally a few more. There is also space for five others who earn a place through the sponsorship of powerful sponsors like Master Winder. Thus, in a matriculating class, there are fifty students, and generally around five hundred in the entire school, spread out over five or so years."

Cam did some quick calculations. "The math doesn't add up."

Saira smiled. "You noticed?" She shrugged. "Every Advancement—from Novice to Acolyte, Acolyte to Adept, and Adept to Glory—is said to take a year, but that's not true. From Novice to Acolyte, it *does* take a year, but Acolyte to Adept is usually completed in anywhere from one-to-two years, while Adept to Glory is anywhere from two-to-four. The average length for full graduation is five years, while geniuses get it done in four. Plus, there are two incoming classes of Novices every year, split six months apart. Thus, the total of five hundred students."

"How long did it take you?" Pan asked. "To reach Glory here?"

"None," Saira said with a smile. "I was trained elsewhere." She continued. "At any rate, beyond the time taken to graduate, you should know that most of the students here also receive special materials from their sponsoring duchies. They are often supplied with tonics and pills to aid their Advancement."

Most students didn't mean all, and Cam doubted he and Pan would be so lucky. "What about us?" he asked, having an idea as to the answer but wanting confirmation.

Saira glanced at him, an enigmatic expression on her face as she paused in front of a dark, paneled door. "There will be opportunities for you to obtain those same materials." She held up a cautioning hand. "But Master Winder won't simply give them to you. They must be earned, based on your performance in the school." Her gaze flicked them up and down. "You will be provided new clothing, however. It should be ready by the time classes start."

"And your role?" It was Pan, and Cam wished he hadn't spoken, especially when Saira's strained expression returned.

"I'll be teaching you how to fight, in both armed and unarmed combat."

Cam hoped the answer would be enough for Pan, but the panda kept talking. "Is it true that at some point, the Ephemeral Master becomes the weapon?"

Saira nodded, the strained look easing off. "Yes, but until that happens, you will mainly be taught the spear and shield along with the staff and short swords."

Cam elbowed Pan, hoping he'd take the hint and shut it.

"This is your room," Saira said, opening the door and gesturing them inside. "I'll see you throughout the week while you get settled in. Then there will be a welcoming ceremony. Classes start right after."

Saira left them then, and Cam watched her depart, wondering again what had happened to her Ephemera. He had heard of Masters who regressed in Advancement but it was supposed to be as rare as hen's teeth.

"Let's go," Pan said, interrupting his thoughts.

Cam grunted, and they entered their quarters, into a room with a dark leather couch centered in the space. It faced a pair of high-backed chairs from across a coffee table. Past the arrangement was a rectangular dining table with seating for six backlit by a broad window that allowed in bright sunshine and a view of the city and lake.

Cam wanted to explore it all, but first he had to catch his breath and regain his bearings. He felt wrung out like a dishrag. Dropping his rucksacks with a thud, he collapsed onto the sofa, thinking on his life.

Yesterday, he and Pan had been wandering Brewery Highway, heading toward Charn, but for Cam, he'd really been heading nowhere fast. Then Master Winder had found them, and with a snap of his fingers, like a mythical asrasin changing reality, they were now students at the Ephemeral Academy.

His altered situation would take getting used to. Ever since the disaster that cost Tern his life, Cam had felt like he'd been running and running and running and getting nothing done. And then out of the clear, blue sky, someone had swooped down, picked him up like a chess piece, and set him down at the famed Ephemeral Academy, giving him an opportunity for which others would have begged and pleaded. He'd never expected in this life or any other to end up here. It was the same as saying he'd like to walk on the moon.

Regardless, Cam's life could now have purpose and clarity, but it was unearned. It wasn't because of anything he'd done, and he wasn't quite sure what to feel about that.

"Why did he choose us?" Pan asked, sounding unusually subdued.

"I don't know," Cam said. He had a vague notion, but that wasn't the same as being sure. He knew Master Winder had been interested in him right after learning he could become a Novice Prime. Beyond that, Cam didn't know much else.

Pan went to sit cross-legged on the ground, meditating, and while he did so, Cam closed his eyes again. He must have dozed because next thing he knew there came a knock on their door.

He scrambled to his feet, about to answer when it swung open. On the other side of the doorway stood a young woman with an appearance unlike any Cam had ever seen. She was tall, powerfully built, and pretty in a dangerous sort of way, but what was most striking was her pale skin and hair that was a mix of white with black spots. She smiled, a flashing of teeth that seemed a bit sharper than normal.

Cam's eyes widened. She was an Awakened Beast.

"Hello," she said. "Professor Maharani asked me to show you the school."

Cam blinked. It took him a short spell to recognize who the girl meant when she said Professor Maharani. *Saira*.

"Thank you," he said, not liking how diffident he sounded. But the truth was, the girl intimidated him. She was nearly his height, and there was something in her Novice-red eyes that said she could bend him like a willow branch if she took the notion. "I'm Cam Folde." He glanced at Pan when his friend didn't offer his own name. The panda appeared mesmerized. He might as well have been drooling, like he was spying a virgin stand of bamboo.

Cam nudged Pan, not wanting his friend standing there like a lump.

Pan shook himself free of his enrapture. "Pan Shun."

"Avia Koravail," the woman said, still grinning.

Cam frowned, trying to recall where he'd heard her name. It came to him a second later. "Wait a second. You're the Awakened orca."

Avia frowned, blinking in surprise. "I don't know if I'm *the* Awakened orca, but I am *an* Awakened orca."

Cam flushed, feeling the fool. "Sorry. I didn't mean to say it like that.

I'd just heard your name before. And of course, you're *an* Awakened orca."

Avia's frown lifted. "In that case, no worries. Just don't call me a fish."

Cam chuckled, taking in her nearly human appearance. "Definitely not a fish."

"Come on," Avia said with a grin. "It's time for lunch."

Cam startled. He'd slept that long?

Avia chuckled. "You looked wrung out when you arrived. It's no wonder you slept away the morning."

She led them out of their quarters, and Cam paid attention this time to where they were going. They traveled a hallway with murals and paintings decorating the walls—scenes of great Ephemeral Masters battling rakshasas, or simple settings of farm life or forests. A few busts stood on plinths, although Cam had no idea who they represented. He knew so little about his world's history.

They exited the dormitory and ran across another young woman—also a Novice—whom Avia seemed to know. She was of medium height and build, intense in appearance and with the typical dark-eyed, dark-haired features of which Cam was familiar.

"This is Jade Mare," Avia said. "She's from Bastion and will also be in our squad."

Cam didn't know what Avia meant by squad, and he asked.

"All Novices are grouped together, five per squad, based on the patron duchy. Those of us who are Awakened Beasts." She gestured to herself and Pan. "Or are sponsored by someone other than the duke of their realm, are placed in their own separate squad, Light Squad" She soured. "Most call us Squad Screwup, though, since we never win at anything."

Cam wanted to smile. Squad Screwup sounded about right for where he belonged. "What don't we ever win?"

"You'll learn more tomorrow," Avia said, "but basically, here at the academy, we are trained and taught how to destroy boils. It's a competition, and to succeed means we get better materials to more easily Advance. That's what Squad Screwup hardly ever wins. Those kind of materials."

What Avia had told them wasn't exactly inspiring, but Cam had faced this same sort of attitude and odds all his life. What was another place and another group of people thinking he wasn't worth the mud on their boots?

"Let's get some food," Jade declared. "I'm hungry enough to eat..." She grinned. "...an orca."

Avia laughed, a trill of joy. "An orca would devour you in one bite, little nugget."

Cam grinned. Avia had a happy way about her, and she made the people around her happy, too. He also found himself admiring her way of speaking. She was an Awakened Beast, but she talked real good, better than him. And in hindsight, he realized Pan did as well. He bet all the folks here did. Maybe he should work on talking better, too?

They set out from their dormitory, crossing the plaza that took up most of what Avia explained was the Secondary Level.

"This is where the dormitories and cafeteria are located," she said. "The level where the entrance and coliseum are located is the Primary Level." She pointed to the temple atop the hill. "That's the Tertiary Level."

Cam only had a chance to glance upward for a moment before Avia had them rushing along.

"Why aren't you in Saban's Squad?" Pan asked Avia as they pressed on.

"First, it's Squad Saban," Avia said. "And second, it's because I'm an Awakened Beast. There's no leeway there, even if I'm an adopted daughter."

There was clear irritation in her voice, and Cam hoped Pan would catch the hint and let the matter drop.

Thankfully, his friend did, but then he stuck his foot in it by asking her a question sure to get her riled. "How did you become so human in appearance?" Pan asked.

Cam sighed to himself. Pan liked Avia. That much was obvious, and because of it, he seemed like he wanted to do nothing but pester her with personal questions.

But Avia surprised Cam by not getting angry. "Lots of people think I achieved it when I became a Novice; that it's a sign of my potential." She grinned. "It's not true. What happened is my mother saved Duke Vail, my human father, when he was only a Crown."

Cam started. How could Avia's mother have saved a duke when he was still a Crown? All the Sage-Dukes were hundreds of years old and had ruled their cities for centuries. "Just how old is your mother?" Cam blurted out, wanting to smack himself as soon as the question left his mouth. Hadn't he just mentally chided Pan for his overly personal questions?

Avia's grin faded, transforming to sorrow. "A couple hundred years old, and she's starting to show her age. And whatever she saved my father from, it still cost him. It's why even as a Sage, he's already failing in his health." She seemed to shake off her grief. "Anyway, the reason I look so human is because my father gifted me with that change. It was a promise he made to my mother. It's easier to Advance as a human than as an Awakened Beast."

Pan grunted. "But Awakened Beasts can Imbibe Ephemera more easily."

Avia nodded. "But Awakened Beasts have more trouble Enhancing their Tangs. For me, it's the best of both worlds." She smiled, shrugging a bit. "And as I am now, I can also help my pod when my mother passes, and later I can help my father by truly becoming his heir. When I'm a Crown, I can be happy."

Cam peered at her, unsure what she meant. Avia already seemed happy, so why would she have to wait and become a Crown to become what? Even happier?

"We're here," Avia said, guiding Cam with a gentle nudge toward a round building with a dome of stained glass. It had to be the cafeteria given the delicious aromas wafting from it. Wide windows circled the structure, no doubt offering an excellent view of the plaza, city, and lake. Entering alongside them were a number of other students, and Cam didn't miss the sneers, smirks, and derision aimed at him and Pan. It wasn't hard to reckon why. Everyone here was dressed so well, while he and Pan wore what amounted to fine rags.

"Sorry," Avia murmured, face red with either anger or embarrassment.

"Sorry for what?" Cam asked.

"You've noticed the looks, haven't you?"

"I've noticed."

"It's humiliating," Pan agreed.

Jade scowled. "It's the way of this place. It's all about lineage and wealth as much as it is about Advancement and Enhancement of your Ephemera."

"And yet, they seem to view you with admiration," Pan said to Avia.

"They admire my father," she replied. "I may be the heir to a duchy—it all depends on if I can reach Sage before my adopted father dies." She flashed them another of her grins. "And if I accomplish that, everyone here will want my goodwill."

It was simple politics then, except at a larger scale.

They passed into the cafeteria, entering a large, open space that was round like the building. A number of rectangular tables were scattered throughout the room, and the din of a hundred conversations filled the air. So did the smells of just as many different types of food, too many for Cam to reckon. A line of students waited at various places where servants piled their plates.

Cam's stomach rumbled. There was so much food, and it all smelled delicious.

Pan twitched. "Do they have bamboo?"

Avia chuckled, pushing them forward. "If they don't, I'm sure they can find you some."

Cam noticed a large Awakened Beast seated alone—a male—but he couldn't figure what kind. His skin was a black-green color, and his features were roughly human, but thick and coarse. He was massive, towering even while seated, although he sat directly on the floor with his legs splayed—similar to Pan—and his red-streaked head bent to whatever he was eating.

"Don't stare," Jade hissed in warning. "That's one of our instructors. Orthosial Shivein, an Awakened turtle. And don't you dare ever call him Orthos. He hates that. He'll go crazy. Call him Professor Shivein."

"Squad Screwup," a proud voice announced over the din.

Cam internally winced. If there was one truth in any school, it was that there was always a bully and his hangers-on. He turned to face the person who had called out to them, unsurprised by what he saw. A young man—tall, well-built, and disgustingly handsome—who grinned in cocky confidence as he sauntered their way. Two others trailed after him.

"Victory Arta," Avia said. "I thought I smelled something rancid."

A fight looked to be in the offing, and Cam fisted his hands, getting ready.

But Victory surprised him. He didn't take offense to Avia. Instead, he threw his head back and laughed. "You better remember me when you become a Sage," he said. "All the kindness I've shown."

Avia grinned, and her reaction had Cam relaxing. "This is Cam Folde and Pan Shun," she said by way of introduction. "And this is Victory Arta, the latest and youngest son of Duke Dorieus Arta of Chalk."

Another noble and possible heir.

Cam noticed Victory sizing him up, and he unconsciously straightened, glad to have a few inches on the noble.

"Rumor says the Wilde Sage is sponsoring the two of you," Victory said.

"Rumor's right," Cam said.

Victory laughed. "Rumor's right," he said in a mocking tone to the others with him. "Don't you just love his country accent?"

"I think it's refreshing," said one of them, a young woman, tall and striking. She held out a hand, which again, caught Cam off-guard. "Charity Kazar. It's good to meet you."

"She's the daughter of Duke Ahktav Kazar of Maviro," Jade said.

Cam, who had been in the process of shaking hands with the young woman, was again caught off-guard.

"I'm Merit Thens," said the third member of their party. He was of medium height and had remarkably unremarkable features. He was currently smiling wryly. "And before Jade can tell you, my mother is Duchess Marsula Thens of Santh."

Cam glanced from one noble to the other. Including Avia, there were four children of Sages attending the Ephemeral Academy in one class? That couldn't be common, could it? He realized no one was including Pan in the conversation. "This is Pan Shun. He's from a tribe of Awakened pandas in the Diamond Mountains."

"Good to meet you," Merit said to Pan, while Victory and Charity ignored him.

"Where are *you all* from," Victory asked, still badly emulating Cam's accent.

"Traverse," Cam replied. "A town in the middle of nowhere in the duchy of Charn. And it's y'all. All y'all if you're looking for the plural."

Victory inclined his head. "Thank you for the lesson in grammar, and it truly was good to meet you. But we have to be going now. Lots of training and all that. You know how it is."

They left with a bevy of breezy smiles and waves, and Cam watched in bemusement as they exited. "They seem nice," he noted, still struggling to reconcile how easy-going the nobles had been.

"They're nice because they don't think we're competition," Jade said in narrow-eyed annoyance. "We're a joke to them."

Cam's own eyes narrowed as he considered the departing nobles in a new light. A flare of competitive fire sparked to life. He'd always hated losing, at least back before he'd become weak. "Then we'll just have to show them how wrong they are."

Avia gave him a companionable slap on the shoulder. "That's the spirit."

14

The next few hours were spent touring the school with Avia and Jade, and Cam tried not to gawk at every fresh discovery. His favorite spot was just outside the library which was bathed in sunshine with birds chirping and a mild breeze blowing. A long view extended out to the gleaming city itself and the aqua-blue waters of Lake Nexus. Gardeners cared for the grass and plants, wisps of red and orange Ephemera curling off their hands as they trimmed and cut.

Cam listened as Avia explained how their classes would be scheduled, and while she spoke, he pondered how long the two women had to have been at the academy to be so familiar with everything about it. He asked the question.

"A couple of weeks," Avia answered. "Most everyone comes early to settle in before classes start."

"You're behind the curve," Jade added, her lips pursed in annoyance for some reason. "I'm guessing you didn't get any extra instruction?"

Cam shook his head. "Truthfully? I never expected to ever end up here. Pan wanted to, but it was more a dream than anything else. We was heading down to Charn when Master Winder found us."

"Why did he choose you?" Jade asked.

Cam hedged, not wanting to talk about Jordil and Lilia. "He knew me from before, and we're both nearly Novice Primes."

"Nearly?" Jade's expression went hard and hostile.

Cam's hackles rose, but he held off from snapping an answer he'd regret. Instead, he raised his hands, wanting to ease her anger, whatever the cause. Jade seemed a mite touchy. "Pan should be there in a couple days, and I'm not far behind."

His answer must have worked because Jade relaxed.

"Is this a problem?" Pan asked, blinking in confusion.

"No," Jade said with a sigh. "It's fine. But we're Squad Screwup, and I was hoping for…"

She didn't finish her thought, but Cam could guess at it. Jade was hoping the newest members of the squad would have more going for them than merely Master Winder's support. Instead, she had gotten herself a hayseed and an Awakened Beast, neither of them skilled in Ephemera and already behind every other student in the academy.

Pan grinned his cute, toothy smile. "Does anyone want a snack?"

Jade chuckled, the last of her irritation fading. "No. But it is time for supper."

After the meal, they returned to Cam's and Pan's quarters where Avia demonstrated something astonishing: indoor plumbing. Cam had only heard stories about such a thing, and he couldn't stop flicking the faucet on and off, watching the water pour forth like a miracle. Same with the toilet, which flushed with a single pull of a slender chain. Then there was the shower with its warm water.

Cam gaped at every new revelation. How was this possible? So many questions burbled from his mouth, and Avia and Jade laughed at his excited queries. It was the way of Ephemeral Masters to have such miracles available to them is all they said before leaving.

The next couple of days passed in a similar vein. Cam and Pan were up early for meditation, each seeking to Advance their final Tangs and achieve the Awareness of a Novice Prime. Afterward was breakfast with Avia and Jade. More meditation followed by time spent wandering the school and better learning the various parts of the campus. Next was lunch. Meditation again. More wandering. Supper, and then a final round of meditation.

On their third day, though, there was a change in their schedule. It was time for the official opening of the school year and a welcoming ceremony for the new students.

Cam was grateful. Boredom had already settled in, like an unreachable itch in his mind. And he was mighty tired of sitting in the same place, meditating or walking around what had become familiar grounds and doing nothing much else.

They would finally start their training, and he was both nervous and excited by what it might mean. While he still didn't see why Master Winder had chosen to sponsor him, he also figured he might as well try and prove the Wilde Sage right in his judgment. He was at the Ephemeral Academy, so why not do the best he could and show up all those who still sneered at him and Pan? And there were plenty of those. Never the higher ranked nobles, like the ones he had met on his first day at the Ephemeral Academy, but instead, it was those who licked their boots.

His thoughts on success, Cam dressed in his best clothes, knowing they were still tattered compared to what everyone else wore. Pan had on his breechcloth, and after a quick breakfast, they were off, heading for the Primary Level where the welcoming ceremony would take place. The sun shone bright, and a lacing of clouds decorated the powder-blue sky. Humidity pressed down, but a mild wind blew now and then, stirring the air.

Cam and Pan descended the stairs to the Primary Level alongside Avia and Jade, arriving early along with a trickling of others. A tall stage had been built near the fountain of the Holy Servants, and a half dozen people were seated there, including Saira. Cam wanted a good view and insisted they get as near to the dais as possible. He led them to the very edge of where they could stand, a roped-off section bordering the grassy sward encompassing the fountain.

Cam was about to wave to Saira, but Jade firmly gripped his arm and shook her head.

"She isn't your friend," Jade had said. "She's a professor. She's above you. Don't forget it."

Cam nodded understanding. "Is that who they are? All the professors?"

"Not even close," Jade answered. "They are the ones who work for the academy itself—our instructors—but the duchies send their own professors, Glories chosen by each duchy for their specific squads. They're essentially private instructors who also spy on the students and make sure they remain loyal."

Cam grimaced. How could anyone learn from someone who might not have their best interests at heart?

He kept his thoughts to himself, and the time near the fountain passed in relative quiet until more people arrived. Soon after, the plaza filled, and a multitude of conversations formed a din.

Pan, who had been munching on a long stalk of bamboo, started when a piercing whistle blasted from the stage. The bamboo comically fell from his mouth, and he glanced around in embarrassment.

Cam grinned at him, but his attention returned to the stage when a middle-aged man with gray-hair and a wrinkled face rose to his feet. He stood tall and strong, and his indigo-Haunted eyes, which edged to violet, proclaimed him a powerful Crown. "Welcome to the Ephemeral Academy," the man stated, his voice booming and fully quieting the gathered students. "For those returning, you know to be silent. For those who are new, now is the time for silence."

Cam was about to ask Avia about the man, but upon hearing the words, he figured it best to keep his mouth shut.

"My name is Lord Font Queriam," the man continued. "I am from Saban, and we are tasked by our great duke, Duke Kelse Vail—long may he prosper—with the management and oversight of the Ephemeral Academy for the next three years. I will be your dean." His eyes might have gone to Avia just then, but Cam wasn't sure. And if it did, he wasn't sure what to make in the Lord's enigmatic gaze. "This school was founded some twenty-five hundred years ago by the first Duke of Bastion as a means to teach and train the next generation in the use of Ephemera. It was when the rakshasas first made their presence on our world known. You will follow in the long history of splendor which attends this academy. Not only will you master your Ephemera and graduate as Glories, but you will also go on to protect our people by destroying boils and killing rakshasas. We will teach you how."

All this time, Cam had tentatively acknowledged his position as a student at the Ephemeral Academy, but until hearing Lord Queriam's declaration, he hadn't truly reckoned what it meant. Now he did, and it stunned him like a blow to the head. He was expected to achieve the Awareness of a Glory? And that was just to graduate? It was beyond his wildest imaginings. And when he became a Glory... just wait until those so-called fine folk of Traverse found out. They'd chew off their lips with jealousy.

His mind occupied by thoughts of a vague sort of vengeance, Cam missed a bit of Lord Queriam's speech.

"...It was around then that the rakshasas first appeared," the dean was saying, "Shimala, Coruscant, and Simmer. The trio of childhood friends who corrupted others into their perverted Way into Divinity. Though they claim to create, their means are repugnant. Murderers all."

Cam recalled the long-ago battle between Master Winder and Borile Defent, the Silver Sage of Weeping, the rakshasa Sage who claimed to create.

"Now, for those who are new here," Lord Queriam continued, "it is time to introduce your professors. First is Glory Orthosial Shivein." The Awakened Beast Cam had seen on his first day at school stood, crossed his massive arms across his broad chest and glowered. "Professor Shivein is an Awakened Beast—a turtle—and he will teach you the use of Kinesthia and fighting, both armed and unarmed."

"Don't ever get on Professor Shivein's bad side," Avia whispered.

"And don't call him Orthos," Cam added with a grin. He remembered the first warning.

Avia offered an answering smile.

"Next is Professor Saira Maharani," Lord Queriam continued. "She will aid Professor Shivein in teaching Kinesthia." Saira also stood, waving briefly to the crowd before reclaiming her seat.

"She's new to the school," Avia said, peering at Saira and sounding curious. "No one knows much about her."

"She was a Crown once," Cam said.

His words earned looks of shock from Avia and Jade.

"She told you that?" Jade asked. "I thought you only met her a few days ago."

Cam shook his head. "I've known her for years, and when we met, even just a few months ago, she was a Crown." He waved his hands, hushing away any more questions. "I'll tell you later." Lord Queriam was talking again, and he didn't want to miss anything.

"Please greet Professor Placido Werm," Lord Queriam said, introducing a paunchy man with shifty eyes, the whites of which glowed the blue of a Glory. "He is in charge of teaching Spirairia."

The professor stepped forward, appearing bored as he waved desultorily to the crowd of students, a possibly contemptuous smirk at the corners of his lips.

Cam didn't like the man's attitude. Professor Werm seemed like someone who was bitter at life and bent on taking it out on others. And given his thick belly and thin arms and legs, he also didn't look like someone who cared to work all too hard.

"He's not much to look at, is he?" Jade asked.

She was talking to Pan, who solemnly nodded his head, appearing sad for some reason. "I don't think he'll go any further on the Way into Divinity than he already has."

Avia scoffed. "That's because he's probably as lazy as a seal in the sun."

Cam wasn't sure about seals—they was some kind of water-dwelling animal—but why would they be lazy in the sun?

He had no time to ponder the matter because Lord Queriam was talking again. "And finally, we have another new instructor, Professor Eveangel Grey. She will teach Synapsia."

A woman with unusual features rose to her feet. She was tall—taller than Saira or even Avia—and had honey-blonde hair. Her skin had a reddish-golden undertone, and while her blue-Haunted Glory eyes beamed with intelligence, her irises were an emerald-green, a color Cam had never seen in a person. She wasn't classically beautiful, but there was an undeniable presence to her, something seemingly more profound than Master Winder's, which made no sense. He was a Sage, while she was a mere Glory.

Cam snorted to himself. A mere Glory. Months ago, he would have bowed and scraped before someone like Professor Grey, and now here he was, scoffing at her Stage of Awareness. Still, even as he examined her, that sense of presence and power faded until she seemed no different than the others on the dais with her.

But that strange presence had been there. Cam was sure of it.

"She's something, isn't she," Avia whispered.

Cam realized she had caught onto whatever was impressive about Professor Grey, same as he.

"No one knows where she came from," Avia continued. "She just showed up a few weeks ago, saying she was from some island chain on the other side of the world or something."

"I bet she's from Sinane," Jade guessed. "They're supposed to be led by a women Sages."

"Saira would know. She's from Sinane," Cam said. Once more, came the looks of interest, this time from others in the audience who had overheard him.

Again, Cam waved aside any questions. "I'll explain later."

Lord Queriam cleared his throat, regathering everyone's wandering attention. "We will now have a demonstration of what is possible with Ephemera. First, Professors Maharani and Shivein will show you what Kinesthian Glories can accomplish." He gestured the two instructors forward.

Pan nudged him, clearly excited and grinning in his happy,

tongue-hanging-out-a-bit way. Cam smiled back before returning his gaze back to the stage. He leaned forward, not wanting to miss what was about to happen.

Saira and Professor Shivein leaped off the narrow dais on which they stood, landing on the grassy sward that had been kept clear of students. The instructors stood a dozen yards apart, bowed to one another, straightened, and faced off. Cam blinked in shock when a blue sheen coated their forms. It was like stained glass.

An instant later, the professors exploded into movement. Heavy punches and kicks were fired, and throws were blocked. They each jumped, soaring dozens of feet above the ground. Spinning about one another, their blows continuing, increasing in speed and ferocity. Shockwaves billowed out. Cam felt it in his gut as his insides shook from the booming sounds.

The dance of violence continued, but no blow actually hit until Saira snapped a sidekick. It landed, echoing with a hollow thud. Professor Shivein slid away from her, his clawed feet digging into the ground until he came to stop twenty feet from where he started.

The kick seemed to signal the end of the demonstration, and the crowd of students applauded. Cam joined in, hooting and hollering, although inside he felt a bit sad. The demonstration had been impressive enough, but he remembered when Saira could fly.

Lord Queriam gestured then for Professor Werm, who dipped his head in acknowledgement. He still held the slightly derisive smile on his face. Was his face set in a permanent sneer because of some injury, or did he really think himself superior to everyone else?

Cam hoped it was the first. If it was the second, he'd likely want to punch the man in the face.

The professor stepped onto the cleared area, head rotating like he was scanning it. Cam shifted on his feet, frowning and uncertain. He only knew bits and pieces about Spirairia.

Cam startled when a voice spoke. *"Watch and learn a different way to fight."*

He glanced around, seeking out who had just talked to him. But no one met his gaze, and his confusion deepened.

Pan pointed toward the professor. "It was him," he said, shock on his face.

"It was who?"

"Him," Pan said, still pointing to Professor Werm.

Cam didn't know what Pan was talking about. "What do you mean?"

"Spirairians can sense our feelings and emotions," Jade explained. "And most Glories with Spirairia can speak mind-to-mind. Telepathy."

Cam had heard stories of telepathy, but he'd always reckoned them fables. He eyed Jade, wondering if she was funning him.

"Observe the proper use of Spirairia."

It was the voice again, and Cam's focus latched to Professor Werm, viewing him in a fresh light. The man might smirk like he was better than everyone else, but if he was a Spirairian and could project his thoughts to everyone watching, then he was a strong Ephemeral Master and deserved respect.

Professor Werm spread his hands. A hazy blue light emanated from his fingers, falling like misty rain to the ground. Where it settled, the ground shivered and shook, turning over, filling in divots and holes where the grassy sward had been ripped apart from Saira and Professor Shivein's demonstration. Fingers of green growth extended, stretched out, filling in the torn and twisted areas.

Cam's eyes bolted wide open, and he rubbed at them, not believing what he was seeing.

But the changes kept on. Fresh shoots of grass, blue-hued, just like the light still dripping from Professor Werm's fingers, exploded in new life. They reached for the sunlight. Another surge poured forth from the professor, and the new grass gained full height, flaring with a final spurt of growth before settling into the same deep green as the rest of the sward. Most everything was fresh and new, with only a few scars still marring the field.

Cam gazed a while longer. He had seen Acolytes and even the rare Adept work the land in Traverse, improving it, protecting crops and such, but they'd never done anything like this. This was simply... He shook his head, unable to come up with the right words to describe what he'd just seen.

But when he stared at the others, expecting to see his own stunned amazement, he was greeted by a surprise. All of them, even Avia, were nodding like what had happened was normal and not anything special. Cam shook his head in disbelief. Just what kind of world had he entered where people viewed a miracle as mundane?

Professor Werm's demonstration must have been done because without another word he rejoined the others. And taking his place directly after was Professor Grey. She smiled at the crowd even as she leaped off the platform. She landed light-footed on the grass surrounding the platform. From her body trailed a wispy blue light, similar to Professor Werm's but denser, like a liquid. She stood stock still for a moment.

Where Saira and Professor Shivein had exploded into movement, Professor Grey simply blurred. Cam blinked, unable to catch hold of her motions. She moved too quick, and he couldn't get his mind to focus on her. She'd stop for a split second, and then she was off. It looked like all she did was swirl around the open expanse of grass.

And then she was done, landing smoothly atop the platform, seating herself with a grace that didn't seem natural. Cam stared at her in jaw-dropped amazement. She had moved faster than an arrow, graceful as a dancer, and—

"She healed the sward," Avia said, sounding every bit as stunned as Cam felt.

"Who is she?" he heard himself ask.

He didn't get an answer, not that he expected one.

Lord Queriam paced to the edge of the dais, interrupting whatever other conversation they might have had about Professor Grey. "And now that you know what is possible," Lord Queriam said, "it is incumbent that you expand your mind and your reach. Seek glory, not what's easy. Begin your Way into Divinity."

After Lord Queriam finished his final exhortation, the students broke apart, and it was time for their first class. While on their way there, Cam had a bit of excitement about him. Mostly he was nervous, worried about how things would go since he was so far behind everyone else. Yesterday, Pan had Advanced his Spirairia and was now a proper Novice Prime, but Cam hadn't yet managed the trick.

He scowled. It was because of Plasminia stalling his progress, and at the rate things were improving, he'd likely need another couple of days to Advance his Synapsia and a week beyond that for Spirairia. Cam continued to fret over his situation, lagging behind the others in his squad, staring sourly at their backs as they chatted amiably while headed to their first class—Kinesthia. It would be taught by Professors Shivein and Saira.

Cam shook his head, feeling low. What was he doing here? Why even bother with Kinesthia or any class? He'd just be wasting his time. All he had coming was humiliation. He had half a mind to head back to the dorm and pack his bags and leave.

That's how it was for him nowadays. Sometimes, like just before the welcoming ceremony, he'd be confident he could make something of himself. Then that confidence would be gone like a blown-out candle, and only anxieties and doubts would remain.

Cam glanced over when he noticed Pan slowing down to pace next to him.

"You can do this," Pan said. "You aren't a Novice Prime, but you will be. Believe it. Believe in yourself."

They were kind words, said by a kind friend, but it wasn't enough. Cam was terrified. "I'm scared, Pan." He wasn't ashamed to admit it. "Ever since I walked that first Pathway, my life has gone sideways. Sometimes good, but too often bad."

"But you're healed of all that," Pan said. "You said so when you gained Kinesthia."

Cam scuffed his boot against the ground. "And it only cost the life of one of my closest friends. I'm scared about…" He couldn't say the rest, his fears about being a curse. Ever since Maria Benefield had first made the claim, the possibility had stayed with him, growing when Lilia died, until it sometimes gained the weight of a surety.

Pan sighed, not speaking for a bit. "Just finish the first day, and see what happens," he said when they reached the stairs leading down to the field.

Cam paused at the top of the flight of steps, staring down at the large rectangular field of grass, several acres in size. It was edged by a tall, ivy-covered wall made of brick and extending several hundred yards on each side. Within the field were rings of dirt marked off by small stones and a track of crushed gravel tracing the very perimeter. This was the place where they would learn to use their Kinesthia.

And Cam could already tell he'd hate it, especially with Professor Shivein and Saira waiting in the center of the field. The instructors wore sleeveless shirts, loose-fitting just like their pants, and ankle-high boots. They had their arms crossed across their chests, and Saira was tapping her foot in impatience. At first, the two instructors had their eyes trained on Avia and Jade, who trotted down the steps without hesitation. Next, Professor Shivein's and Saira's glares flicked to where Cam still stood at the top of the stairs. They looked like they expected him to head down as fast as he could.

Cam didn't want to go. He wanted to be away from here... to run far away. But he couldn't. He'd made promises to so many people in his life; Honor, Jordil, Lilia, his family, Pan, Master Winder, even Saira in a way. To all of them he'd promised to do something worthwhile with his life. With a weary sigh, Cam descended the steps. "Let's go."

Pan let out a relieved huff and followed after him. It didn't take long to reach the field and line up next to Avia and Jade, both of whom Cam was only now realizing were dressed in garb similar to that of their instructors.

"Welcome to your first class," Professor Shivein said, his voice as deep and rumbly as Cam expected for someone his size.

Cam had to crane his head just to meet the professor's gaze, who looked to have about two feet and several hundred pounds on him. He was truly gigantic, with thick, not-quite human features. Next to him,

Saira—a tall woman—seemed puny.

"Let's get started," Professor Shivein continued, his Glory-blue eyes shining in contrast to the dark green color of his pebbled skin. "We don't have to waste time on introductions. You were at the ceremony this morning and know my name, and I was already given yours. The females will work with me this morning; the males with Professor Maharani." He snapped his fingers at Avia and Jade, gesturing for them to follow.

Cam watched them leave, nervous but not fearful—thankfully. This was really happening. He was about to start a class where he had no business being.

He hardly noticed when Saira moved to stand before him. Only when she spoke his name did he snap his head around to face her. "I'm sorry, ma'am. I wasn't listening."

"I could tell," Saira—no Professor Maharani said. "I don't expect to have to repeat myself in the future. Do you understand?" Her lips were thin, angry lines. She wasn't his friend right now. She was his instructor, just like Jade had earlier told him.

"Yes, ma'am," Cam answered. "I'm sorry, ma'am. It won't happen again."

"No, it won't," Professor Maharani said, her tone flat.

Cam swallowed heavily again, struggling with his fears and doubts, wishing he'd never listened to Master Winder or hoping on something good to happen for him.

"We'll begin with getting the two of you in shape," Professor Maharani said. "I saw how much you huffed and puffed on your first day here. Follow."

She set off at a slow jog, and Cam darted after her. Pan moaned, hating running as much as he loved bamboo. But thankfully, they kept a slow pace. Half a lap passed, and Cam started to have hope that he might actually be able to do this. It wasn't a much faster gait than the one he and Pan had kept during their travels. Cam could even breathe easily enough, only sucking wind a bit. Even Pan was able to keep up without too much trouble. He flashed Cam a triumphant grin.

He shouldn't have. They finished that half lap, and Professor Maharani increased the pace. Cam groaned internally. It had been years since he'd really run, and he had yet to find a good reason to break that habit.

An instant later, he recognized that wasn't entirely true. There had been that recent time when Maria and the good folk of Traverse had chased him out of town. That had been a good reason to run. There had been others. Like when he'd teased Farmer Gerald's bull, and the stupid animal had charged through the fence and raced after him. Or when he'd stolen an apple pie cooling on Widow Morton's windowsill. He smiled in memory. The pie had been so delicious.

Pan grunted, sounding pained, his face straining when Cam glanced his way.

"Come on," Cam urged. "You can do this." But privately, he wasn't so sure on his own account. His thighs burned, and his racing heart kept wanting to talk him into slowing down. How much worse must it be for Pan?

"Pandas are built for a sprint," Pan gasped. "Not for long distance running."

Professor Maharani chuckled, looking fresh as if she'd rolled out of bed. "We haven't come close to running a long distance."

It was a promise and a threat all in one, and Cam joined Pan in groaning.

Four laps they ran before Professor Maharani took pity on them and finally stopped. Cam crashed to a halt, bending at the waist, hands on his knees, and panting.

Pan simply collapsed, chest rising and falling, his mouth agape as he gasped. "I'm dying," he proclaimed.

"No, you aren't," Professor Maharani said, an amused smile on her face. "Get some water." She pointed to a couple of large jugs off to the side. "Drink and be back here in two minutes."

Cam helped Pan rise to his feet, and together they stumbled over to the water, drinking their fill. Afterward, Pan fell to the ground again, but that wouldn't do. Cam couldn't let his friend fail, not on Pan's first day at the academy. It was his lifelong dream.

"Come on," Cam said, tugging on Pan's arms, urging him upright. "Professor Maharani is waiting."

"That cursed woman is trying to kill me."

"She'll definitely kill you if you make her wait."

Pan groaned, rising to his feet. "Oh, my life."

Together they stumbled and shuffled back to where Professor Maharani waited. By the time they reached her, some of Cam's breath was back. And while his heart still pounded, at least he wasn't gasping like a dying man.

Professor Maharani still wore an amused smile. "Now that you're warmed up, it's time for your next round of exercises. Do as I do." She dropped to the ground, doing a pushup, her muscled arms flexing. Then in an explosion, she gathered to her feet and launched skyward. "Keep up with me," she ordered. "And next time, wear looser clothing. It should arrive this afternoon. I've seen to it."

It was a kind gesture but doing the exercises she demonstrated wasn't. It was torture.

Still, Cam kept at it, a kernel of his never-give-up attitude flaring enough to temporarily overcome his doubts and fears.

"I know this is hard," Professor Maharani said, finally taking pity on them. "But we need to harden your body. Once you're at your peak, using your Kinesthia will be all the more effective." She smiled wolfishly. "Then you can train properly."

15

An hour of constant movement and constant pain finally ended when Professor Maharani let them go. Cam groaned in relief, lacking the strength to do much more than shuffle away when she told them they were done. His body burned hot enough to start a fire, and sweat poured off him, plastering his hair and coating him like he'd taken a dunk in a lake. He winced when reminded by the professors that they'd see Light Squad again that afternoon.

Cam simply nodded before setting off toward the stairs, grimacing at the climb. How many steps were there? Fifty? A hundred? He slowly ascended with Pan at his side. The poor panda looked done for. His soft fur was matted with sweat, his mouth ajar, eyes glazed, and his waddling gait swaying. In contrast, Avia and Jade, despite also appearing weary, still managed a jaunty jog up the steps, their footfalls light. The two women would likely be off to grab some eats before their next class, which was Spirairia, and Cam considered joining them, but honestly, he really just wanted some sleep… maybe for the next day or three.

However, Avia and Jade surprised him. Rather than head off to the cafeteria, they waited at the top of the flight of stairs.

"How do you know so much about Professor Maharani?" Avia asked.

That's why they had stopped? *Figures.* Everybody, everywhere liked to gossip.

Cam shrugged to himself. There was no reason to keep his past a secret. Still, they didn't need to know everything. He told them an abbreviated version of his life, leaving out Tern's death and other tragedies, but when he finished, he noticed both women staring at him warily. "What?"

"Your primary Tang is Plasminia?" Avia asked.

"Yes," Cam confirmed. He'd been clear about it, so why was she still asking?

"And you're not a Novice Prime?" This time it was Jade.

"Not yet," Cam again confirmed. "But I've Accreted enough Ephemera to get there and then some."

"What does that mean?" Jade asked, narrow-eyed like she had a reason to be suspicious of him. "There's nothing above Novice Prime."

Cam bristled. He didn't know Jade all too well, but he knew she was a noble. She probably had everything in life handed to her. And right now, as tired and worried as he was, the last thing he needed was someone like her judging him. "It means it ain't none of your business," Cam snapped. "Master Winder sponsored me. That should be good enough for you. After all, you've never told us how you became a Novice Prime. Your kin pay your way to your skills?"

Jade stiffened, coming to a stop, glaring. "You don't know anything about me or my family."

"And you don't know nothing about me or mine." Cam shot right back.

Jade's jaw clenched. "Just don't hold the rest of us back." She spun about, her back stiff and angry, leaving him standing there.

Cam watched her go, not caring how she thought of him. Rich girl like that, what did she know about suffering?

"You shouldn't have brought up her family," Avia said, giving him a disappointed look before jogging to catch up with Jade.

Cam blinked in surprise. Why shouldn't he have brought up Jade's family? A moment later, he mentally sighed, realizing he might have just made a big mistake. "I think I just put my foot in it."

"I believe you did," Pan agreed, sounding mournful.

His confirmation wasn't what Cam had wanted to hear, but it did tell him what was needed. "You figure she'll accept my apology?"

"The only way to find out is to offer it."

Cam groaned. He really didn't want to have that conversation.

Cam knew he'd messed up, and it made the walk to their next class uncomfortable. Pan huffed along silently next to him, seemingly unwilling to talk. Or maybe he just didn't have the energy. Cam hoped that was all there was to it. He'd hate to have Pan think poorly of him, too.

"I shouldn't have said that to Jade," Cam said to Pan, wanting to break the quiet.

"You know what to do," Pan grunted. "Just don't take too long in doing it. Do it after the next class."

"Why do I have to apologize?" Cam asked. "Why can't she?"

"She could," Pan said, "but is that what you want for yourself? To wait until the other person does the right thing so you don't have to?"

His words spoken, Pan seemed to run out of breath, and Cam left him alone, lost in his own contemplations. They went to the cafeteria, scarfed down some food and coconut water, which was supposed to be the best thing to drink after exercising, and headed off to Spirairia.

It wasn't a long walk, only a couple of hundred feet to a large building situated next to the canteen. In fact, this was where most of their classes would be held, and Cam had already explored it. Like all the other structures on Nexus, the building was made of white marble and roofed in red tiles. It stood three stories tall and had a floor-to-roof porch that lined the section facing out toward the city. A number of students were about, some mingling and talking, while most were headed toward their next class.

Cam briefly wondered about who these others might be, their stories, hopes, and dreams, but he remained locked on how poorly he had spoken to Jade. She walked with Avia, directly ahead, neither of the women showing any inkling of slowing down or wanting to walk with him and Pan. The cheery conversation from the day's beginning was gone, and Cam grimaced at how he'd splintered their group.

In short order, they reached their classroom, a large, windowed space that held a pair of tables with five chairs angled about them and a lectern and blackboard at front. Otherwise, the room was empty, and it seemed like it was plenty large enough for the practice of Spirairia. The four of them took a seat at the tables, Avia and Jade at one and Cam and Pan at the other.

Cam sighed to himself. The distance between them seemed ever larger, but thankfully, he was able to briefly set aside his concerns when Professor Werm entered.

"You know my name," their instructor began without preamble. He didn't use the lectern, simply facing them. "I'll learn yours as is required. For now, let us start." Just as he had during the ceremony this morning, their instructor had a bored expression, as if what he was doing was beneath him. "What is Spirairia?" Professor Werm asked, rhetorically. "It is the portion of Ephemera that is gaseous and allows an Ephemeral Master to interact with the world without touching it. As such, it is likely the most powerful of the Tangs." He spoke, in the bored cadence of a speech delivered so many times, he'd memorized it.

Cam's dislike for the man increased.

"In this class," Professor Werm continued, "we will learn the mastery of Spirairia, and you will see the truth of my claims." Still the bored cadence. "But first some information." The professor paused. "Do any of you have Spirairia as your Primary Tang?" For the first time, there was a spark of interest in his eyes, doused to disgust a moment later when no one raised their hands. "A pity," the professor said. "Regardless, I will teach you why that was a mistake."

He paced before them, hands behind his back, staring at the ground.

"As I said, Spirairia allows a Master to interact with the world without touching it. How, you might ask." He snapped his fingers. "Because with it, a Master can lift and move objects with his mind. He can understand the feelings or thoughts of others. He can control the elemental forces of the world—fire, earth, water, and air."

All well and good, but how would Cam ever master such miracles when he didn't even have Spirairia at Novice level Awareness?

He broke off his thoughts when Professor Werm started talking again. "And what can you learn through the use of these amazing skills? Create fire and storms, certainly. But also farm, grow, teach, and heal. The things that allow a civilization to prosper. Not everything you learn needs to be about war. But how do we learn these wonderful abilities?" His bored cadence remained. "I will show you. And if you're wise, you'll perhaps even forgo regular Bonds and create a True Bond." He paused again. "Mr. Folde, you don't need to take part in this. I've been made aware that your Spirairia is not yet of Novice Stage." Cam didn't miss the lip curl of contempt.

And while he might have wanted to stop paying attention, there again was that kernel of never-give-up attitude that had been absent most of the morning. He wouldn't back down and quit just because Professor Werm said he could or should. Cam would listen to the day's instruction and one day, he'd master it all.

"Delve your Source and allow Spirairia to enter your mind. It is an acceptance of the world, which means it's an acceptance of yourself. This is the beginning of proficiency. Learn to do this, and all else follows; empathy, telepathy, telekinesis, and the use of elements."

For the first time, the bored tone was gone, and Professor Werm actually spoke with real animation.

"For the elements, it is simple, yet profound. The breath you take is the same as air moving through the world. Blood circulating is the understanding of water's flow. Your feet on the ground tells of earth's permanence. The fire in your heart is the sun's burning heat. But it all begins with acceptance."

In some ways, it was the same advice Cam had received from many,

many people. Accept himself, even his flaws, and he might find an easier way of being. But he also knew that acceptance didn't mean he could think himself good enough as he was. He had flaws, and it was best if he worked on them. Like his drinking. He couldn't get to thinking that accepting he was a drunkard meant it was fine for him to drink to his heart's content. That way led to madness, and he'd lived with enough madness to last a lifetime.

But thinking of drinking, of a shot of whiskey… a swig of the sweet stuff… it was a thought never far from the forefront of Cam's mind, even a year after giving up the bottle, and he wished it wasn't so. He loved liquor too much—he always would—and he hated that craving because if he wasn't careful, that craving would destroy him. *That* was what he had to accept about himself.

Cam glanced at Jade, who sat in her chair, her eyes closed, likely trying to bond with her Tang of Spirairia. He also had to accept that he owed Jade an apology. He only hoped she would listen.

"Jade," Cam called out, wanting to talk to her before she hustled off. Their class on Spirairia had just ended, and he hadn't forgotten their argument or Pan's suggestion. He didn't want to do this, but he had to. "Can we talk?"

"About what?" Jade stood in the doorway, arms crossed and wearing an annoyed expression.

"About this morning."

"What about it?"

Pan and Avia gave the two of them a wide berth, his friend giving him a supportive nod while Avia simply stared hard at him, like she was telling him not to mess up.

After they left, Cam stood fumble-footed in front of Jade, eventually making himself meet her annoyed gaze. "I wanted to apologize. I shouldn't have said what I did. It was wrong of me to judge you like that. I'm sorry."

Some of Jade's anger ebbed, the tightness in her features. "That's kind of you to say now, but it wasn't kind what you said back then."

"I know." Cam wanted to defend himself, explain why he had snapped at her, but it would sound too much like he was making excuses. He'd spoken out of turn, and that was that. "Like I said, I'm sorry. I spoke out of anger and frustration, and you didn't deserve it."

More of Jade's tension drifted off, replaced by curiosity. "Why were you angry?"

Cam smirked. Why wasn't he angry? He had so many reasons. But that wasn't the point of this conversation. "I can tell you if you want, but it's also a longer story than why I have Plasminia." He hesitated. "You might not want me around when you find out. Bad things seem to happen to my friends."

"Now you've got me wondering," Jade said, her arms uncrossing. "It also sounds like I need to know this. Same with Avia." She arched her brow. "I assume Pan already knows?"

"He does."

Jade's face firmed. "Then tell me."

Cam did, explaining what had really happened in that first Pathway, Tern's death, his Plasminia, and resultant weakness. His drunkenness and recovery. The unexpected gift received from Honor. Jordil and Lilia's enduring friendship and her subsequent death.

"I know it's not my fault, but it sure feels that way. Like I'm cursed but those around me pay for it."

Jade nodded. "I can see how you might feel like that," she said, thankfully not trying to soothe his feelings with meaningless words of support. "Your life hasn't been easy, and those around you might have had it even worse. But do you really want to think so hard about the past when you've got this opportunity in front of you? You're a student at the Ephemeral Academy. Isn't that what you should be focused on?"

Cam hadn't considered his situation in quite that light, and he paused before saying anything else.

It only took him a few seconds to realize Jade was correct. He should be fixing his mind on what was in front of him rather than what was behind. And the notion that he was cursed or was a curse, how did that even make any sense? It couldn't be true, and the best way to prove people like Maria Benefield wrong was by living a life worthy of a student at the Ephemeral Academy. "You're right," he said to Jade.

"I know," Jade said with simple confidence. "Just don't go repeating your mistakes. Pray for your friends. Don't act like this life you get to live is a burden. Do that, and you'll be fine."

Again, Cam wanted to say cross words to her; tell her she had no right to judge him. Demand to know what she knew of suffering.

But wasn't that how he'd ended up arguing with her in the first place? Deflecting from uncomfortable questions because ultimately, he wasn't happy with who he was as a person. More importantly, wearing a victim's cloak wasn't who he wanted to be.

Cam managed a halfhearted smile. "I'll do better. I have to. I have to make their lives—"

"I'm not your priest or confessor," Jade said. "Just do better and stop talking about why or how."

He stared after Jade as she marched away, considering her words. Maybe she was right. Those doubts he carried were tearing him down, and he needed to end them. He wasn't weak, and he'd always known he wasn't useless. The ill will of those fine folk from Traverse shouldn't be how he measured his worth. He should do so based on the optimism and hopes of people like Master Bennett and his family.

16

A few more seconds of staring after Jade passed before Cam got himself moving. Their next class was in Synapsia, and it was with Professor Grey, who no one seemed to know much about. The only thing they could tell was that she had arrived a few weeks prior to the term, from parts unknown, and was to be their instructor in Synapsia. Beyond that, nothing.

It was a short walk down the hall to where her class was held, and as Cam encountered other students, not for the first time did he struggle with how he really was a part of this school. It still struck him as passing strange, but there it was.

He entered the classroom and found the rest of his squad already present. They sat around a semi-circular table, and Cam joined them, taking a chair next to Pan, the two of them seated opposite Avia and Jade.

"How did it go?" Pan asked in a stage whisper.

"Fine," Cam replied in the same manner.

Jade snorted, which was better than a smirk, glare, or sneer. *Progress.* "We'll see."

Any further conversation was cut off when Professor Grey arrived. She wore a green sari of all things and a pair of sandals with leather ties looped around her ankles. Her honey-blonde hair was bound in an intricate braid, and Cam was struck again by her appearance. She looked different than anyone he'd ever met, moving with an even greater grace than Master Winder. And most strange of all, her Glory-Haunted blue eyes seemed to glow less brilliantly than the emerald green of her irises. It was always the other way round as far as Cam knew.

Professor Grey stopped within the center of their semi-circular table, gazing at them a moment before grinning, a flashing of her white teeth. "Good morning. I'm Professor Grey," she said, speaking in a confident contralto. "I will be your instructor in Synapsia this year. Why don't you introduce yourselves?"

She gestured, starting with Avia, who stood, speaking her name and which duchy she was from. Next came Jade, then Pan, and finally Cam.

Once they were done, the professor smiled again. "Excellent. And all of you but Mister Folde have your Synapsia at the Awareness of Novice." It was a statement rather than a question. Cam found the professor viewing him with her head tilted like she was wondering about him. "When you Imbibe your Accreted Ephemera, your Plasminia fights you, does it not?"

Cam nodded. "Yes, ma'am."

"And have you learned how to prevent it?"

"No, ma'am." It was his greatest frustration.

"Then why fight it? Allow it to happen."

"If I do that, the Plasminia will keep growing, and I'll be left weak again."

"True, but as a Plasminian, you can Imbibe your Accreted Ephemera and later on transform it into what's needed. The work might then go faster."

"But won't it be impossible to transform? It's my Primary Tang." It's what he'd always been taught. Once Ephemera was added to a person's Primary Tang, it couldn't be changed.

"Again, that's an advantage of Plasminia," the professor said. "It has greater flexibility at changing than the other Tangs. You couldn't have fully transformed your Plasminia to an altogether different Tang, but in this case, it should work." She shrugged. "Try it my way just once and see what happens. What have you got to lose?" Before he could answer, she focused her attention on the other members of his squad. "What can you tell me about Synapsia and its importance?"

Unsurprisingly, it was Pan who answered. "No matter what Primary Tang an Ephemeral Master might possess, Synapsia is the most important Tang."

Professor Grey was nodding. "Yes, but why is that?" She answered her own question. "Because it allows a Master to improve his or her awareness and understanding of the world. It also maximizes a person's self-belief and will, their confidence. And never underestimate the importance of will and self-confidence. My husband is the deadliest warrior any of you is ever likely to meet, and it has nothing to do with his skills in Ephemera. That certainly helps, but what truly sets him apart is his self-belief and his will to overcome, especially his confidence that he *will* overcome."

Cam shared a wondering look with Pan. Just who was Professor Grey's husband?

He didn't have a chance to talk it over, though, since the professor was still speaking. "Synapsia allows a Master to make himself or herself so much greater than whatever Awareness might be in their Primary Tang. Master Synapsia, and you can do greater things than you know."

Avia raised her hand. "Is it true that Synapsia also lets us Advance our other Tangs more easily?"

"In general, yes," Professor Grey replied. "It's because someone utilizing Synapsia is calmer. In some ways, they're smarter; even able to better understand who they are as a person. Synapsia is absolutely critical for your life as Ephemeral Masters. It teaches you to do more with less. And at higher Stages, it even allows for self-deceit, so much so that a person can temporarily raise their other Tangs an entire Stage."

Cam listened, hearing a truth in the professor's teaching. It didn't just sound right in his ears but also in his heart, ringing with the solidity of an iron gong. "When will we be able to use our Synapsia?" he asked. He flushed when the professor stared his way. She wasn't as beautiful as Saira, but there was a light in her eyes, a way of looking at him that both made him uncomfortable and also drew him in. He wanted to stare at her, and at the same time, not have her attention.

"Everyone will start using it today, during this very class," Professor Grey said. "First, I want to review what is possible, even at Novice. With mastery of Synapsia, especially if you're wise enough to Enhance it, your mind will work twice as fast. You should also notice a warning when in danger, a vague tingling that if you're careful to listen, can save your life. You'll also eventually have improved insight into how to use your other Tangs and have greater confidence and even charisma."

"I can already do some of what you're talking about," Jade said, wearing a challenging expression. "Enough of it anyway. So what else can I learn from you?"

Cam expected the professor to get angry about being questioned—Master Moltin back in Traverse sure would have—but Professor Grey didn't seem to show the slightest sign of being flustered. Instead, she answered Jade's question with questions of her own. "But can you use your Synapsia well? Can you use it as automatically as breathing?" She waited on Jade's answer, seemingly curious.

Jade gave a minute shake of her head. "No."

"Then you've not really mastered Synapsia at all," Professor Grey said. "You have much more to learn, and *that* is what I can teach you." She clapped her hands. "Attend if you wish to grow into greatness."

From anyone else, Cam might have smirked at the words and attitude, but they fit Professor Grey, and instead of silently mocking her, he listened closely.

"For this class, I will teach you to properly meditate. I want you calm, confident, and charismatic. Later, you'll learn to improve that sense of danger that I earlier mentioned. There will also be challenges to expand your mind, which will also expand your Synapsia. Puzzles to solve in mathematics, logic, and word association. Bouts of chess and other games of intellect, conflict, and planning." Her attention landed on Jade. "Learning most of what Synapsia can offer but not truly mastering it is a poor foundation. You know this."

Cam had no chance to think about what had been spoken so far since he found himself under Professor Grey's scrutiny. "And while the others are meditating," she told him, "I want you to try what I said. Imbibe your Accreted Ephemera. Let it become Plasminia, and I can show you how to transform it into Synapsia and Spirairia."

Cam leaned away from Professor Grey. Why was she staring at him like that? So intense? It was oddly frightening.

Maybe she noticed his fear because she chuckled, the intensity smoothing away. "I'm sorry if I scared you just then. It wasn't my intent. My husband tells me I can be frightening to those who don't know me."

Cam didn't know what to say, but he sure hoped he'd get to know the professor well enough that she wouldn't frighten him with just a look. Then again, the professor could likely frighten him no matter how well he knew her. She just had that way about her, of coiled danger and power.

After Synapsia was lunch, which passed in a blur, but Cam was heartened when Jade and Avia chose to sit with him and Pan. While he'd apologized, and Jade had accepted, some people just pretended to forgive while holding onto the grudge. Thankfully, Jade seemed like the better type, letting bygones be bygones.

After shoveling down their food, it was then time for their afternoon class on Kinesthia. As before, Professors Shivein and Maharani—Cam still wanted to just call her Saira—waited for them in the same grassy field as in the morning. The sun stood a little past its zenith and shined a bit too much warmth. Cam took his time getting down the steps to the field, wishing for a breeze to kick in and cool things down.

It didn't, of course. Wishing for weather was a surefire way of getting the opposite.

The heat continued to steam the air, and Cam just knew his brain would likely broil in the afternoon Kinesthia class. It would be even worse than in the morning, but at least he was unlikely to get bent out of shape and tell off one of his classmates.

His thoughts distracted; Cam almost didn't hear it when Professor Maharani—she should still be Saira—started talking. When he did start paying attention, he nearly cursed out loud.

"We won't be running, lifting, or anything like that," Saira— Professor Maharani! —said. "That's for the morning. In the afternoon, we'll work on your coordination and balance. Eventually, we'll include gymnastics and certain types of martial training, such as wrestling, boxing and other forms. But for now, we'll dance. Choose a partner."

Cam looked to Avia and Jade, surprised when they paired up. When Professor Maharani said to find a partner, he figured it would be a man and a woman dancing together; not a woman and a woman and a man and a man.

He mentally shrugged. Oh, well. It didn't really matter.

Cam faced Pan, chuckling a bit at the detritus of bamboo shavings littering his friend's fur. They were everywhere; small pieces, big pieces, medium sized pieces.

"What did you do?" Cam asked, gesturing to the bamboo shavings. At lunch, he'd been so engrossed with his own food, he'd paid no mind to what anyone else had been eating.

"I was hungry," Pan said, sounding defensive.

"Well, maybe so, but I reckon you got the best of them bamboos. You look like you sent them through a woodchipper." He pretended to peer into Pan's mouth. "You don't have any saws hidden in there, do you?"

Pan chuckled. "No, but wouldn't that be wonderful? I could likely eat thrice the amount of bamboo I can now."

Cam nodded in sage agreement. "Maybe even five times."

Professor Shivein walked up on them, looking as grumpy as a turtle with no shell, which was exactly right for the Awakened Beast. "I'll be working with the two of you this afternoon," he said, his deep voice shaking Cam's innards. "You will follow my movements as best you're able. Pay heed."

Cam held out his hands for Pan to take, figuring they'd be doing couples dancing. He grinned, thinking on who would lead and who would follow. Pan was about to take his hands in his own, but Professor Shivein surprised him.

"That kind of dancing will come later," their instructor said. "For now, you need to master these movements. Attend."

Professor Shivein began to dance. His hands were held slightly away from his torso, and he took lilting steps, a leap and a twirl ending in a scissors kick. Professor Shivein landed lightly on bent knees, barely stirring the grass. Another twirl and other movements followed, all of them graceful and controlled.

Cam's eyes bulged. How did someone so big move with such dexterity, such delicate precision? It was uncanny.

"This is only a part of what you will be expected to do in the coming weeks," Professor Shivein said, having come to a halt and striding back to them. This time, his footfalls were heavy and ponderous like his frame.

"Can we use our Kinesthia?" Pan asked.

Cam had interest in the answer. He'd never been taught to actually utilize any of his Tangs. He had some ideas on how to make it happen, but a notion wasn't the same as actually knowing for true. Plus, all he had was Plasminia and Kinesthia, and until Professor Grey's class, he thought he couldn't actually use his Tangs.

"Today is a day to understand your strengths and your weaknesses," Professor Shivein intoned, crossing his tree-trunk sized arms across his equally massive chest. "Do your best with your natural abilities. Eventually, you will get to use Kinesthia. Go."

Now that the professor had finished answering Pan's question, he apparently expected them to get moving. Cam prepared to do so, glancing over at Avia and Jade, who had already started their motions. They moved nearly as gracefully as Professor Shivein.

He grumbled to himself. In comparison, he and Pan would likely look like a pair of lumbering bears.

The thought had him chuckling even as he got going. Pan *was* a bear, a panda bear, but still a bear.

"What's so funny?" Professor Shivein barked.

Cam stiffened in alarm. "Nothing, sir," he quickly answered.

"Then wipe that stupid smile off your face and start dancing."

Cam nodded, red-faced since everyone had glanced over at him after catching Professor Shivein chewing into him. It wasn't just that it was humiliating, but also because Cam didn't like folks yelling at him. He'd never handled it well back in Traverse, and he didn't like it any better when it came from Professor Shivein, who acted every bit as no-nonsense as his appearance implied. For a moment, Cam cast a longing look at Professor Maharani. She wasn't nearly as brusque or rough.

Even as Cam finally began emulating Professor Shivein's steps, he realized his earlier assessment had been wrong. He was the only one looking like a lumbering bear, stumbling and bumbling like a fool.

Pan moved with an uncanny grace. Chubby as he was, he grinned in pleasure as he spun and sprang about in a way Cam couldn't.

"You are weak now, but you aren't hopeless," Professor Shivein said softly, sneaking up on Cam. "Don't give in to your doubts. You can do this."

His words of encouragement offered, the professor moved on, but Cam stared after him, touched by his kindness.

The rest of the day passed smoothly enough, and the rest of Cam's squad even got a chance to practice at Bonding their Spirairia and Synapsia Tangs during the other classes. Avia and Jade could already do the latter, and Pan could do the former. But Cam couldn't do either.

He had hopes, though.

During Professor Grey's class, he had done as she'd suggested. He'd Imbibed the remaining Ephemera he had Accreted from the core of the dead boil. It hadn't taken that long either, and right now his Plasminia felt full to overflowing. But just as Professor Grey had said, there wasn't any sense it would transform his life to ruin. In fact, it felt like his Plasminia was just waiting for him, like it wanted him to do some bit of work with it.

And Cam planned on doing just that, soon as supper was over.

He tore off a chunk of chapati and used it to spoon some chole and a bit of spiced potatoes. The food was hotter than what he was used to, but it was also delicious. Fact was, his poor tongue was scolding him for what it had been missing out on all his life.

Distracted by supper and classes, Cam paid scant attention to Pan, Avia, and Jade, who were going over what they'd managed to figure out by Bonding to Synapsia and Spirairia. He might have offered some input of his own, but he had other issues on his mind, like what else Professor Grey had told them this afternoon.

She had spoken to them about Enhancement; what it meant and how to do it. For Spirairia, it involved condensing while still leaving it gaseous. Professor Grey claimed there were even some gases that had the density of metals, and if an Ephemeral Master managed that, they'd be mighty tough for anyone to handle. Cam had trouble believing that—the part about gases being dense as metals—but Professor Grey had said it with such conviction, that he felt like it had to be true. Synapsia was also condensed—it being a liquid and such—and according to Professor Grey, the most potent form it could manifest was when it was as dense as quicksilver. Kinesthia, a solid, required the opposite of Spirairia and Synapsia, which meant it actually needed to be made *less* dense, enough so it would actually float on some gases.

As for Plasminia, strangely enough Professor Grey knew how to enhance that Tang, too. It wasn't because she knew more than everyone, but because she simply knew how to find the information a person might need. It was a gift she had, and Cam had heard that instructors from other squads were already seeking her out, wanting her help in finding whatever missing piece of knowledge they or their students required.

In Cam's case, the information came from a chunky book she had lent to him. It had been written centuries ago by an anonymous author, who claimed that throughout history several Sages had experimented in the creation of Plasminians. Unfortunately, all of them had failed in whatever they sought, and their experiments—reading between the lines, it sounded like torture—merely confirmed what was already widely known: Plasminia was worthless.

However, for Cam there was useful information, specifically on how to Enhance Plasminia. According to the book, it was straightforward and simple; an Ephemeral Master just had to slow down the lightning, which was otherwise bouncing around chaotically. Cam didn't know how it was done, and the book hadn't offered any further insight, but it sounded right.

Other instruction that Professor Grey gave was a rough estimate of how Enhancing their Tangs could improve the ease with which they could use them. She said there were three States a Tang could hold within each Stage of Awareness: Silver, Gold, and Crystal. She also said—and Pan confirmed it—that for a Novice of the Silver State, they could Bond their Ephemera about four times with sixty seconds of cooldown between uses before it slipped away from them. It was the same as useless as far as Cam was concerned. But for Gold, it was half a minute between uses and at Crystal, the time was fifteen seconds or thereabouts.

Of course, after those four uses a Novice couldn't Bond the Tang they'd been using at all for thirty or more minutes. It was a longer cooldown, and there was no getting around that, no matter how Enhanced a person's Tangs.

Professor Grey had also said that the cooldowns shortened with every Advancement and so did the number of usages. A Silver Acolyte, for instance, had eight uses with ten seconds between each one before the Bond broke and a longer cooldown of a quarter-hour started. For Gold Acolytes, it was five seconds, and Crystal was half of that.

It was something worth aiming for, and Professor Grey—Cam really liked her—wanted all of them to reach Crystal in all their Tangs while Novices.

"That is what will be done in my class: learn to Accrete, learn to Enhance, and master your mind with exercises," she had told them that afternoon, right before class dismissal.

"I'm ready for a nap," Pan announced, patting his stomach and smoothing his white fur as they were finishing supper.

Cam was drawn out of his thoughts. "Meaning you ate too much."

Pan chuckled. "You know me too well. And it wasn't even too much bamboo this time. It was the noodles."

"You just love food," Cam replied, stifling a yawn and recognizing he was also tired.

A hiss from Jade woke him some. A trio of girls was headed their way.

"Not them," Avia groaned.

The girl in the lead was short, curvy, and pretty enough, except for her nose-in-the-air attitude of arrogance. Meanwhile, the other two were tall, lean, and had the brainless scowls of idiots. Cam didn't have to be told that the three of them were bullies and that they were trouble.

"Well, look who it is," the short girl in the front and apparently the one in charge said to Jade. "The leader of Squad Screwup."

Jade stood, towering over the shorter girl, a smart decision. A bully should never be faced while seated.

"You have something to say to me?" Jade challenged.

The short girl snorted. "Like I'd waste my time talking to someone like you."

Cam frowned in bewilderment. Wasn't that what she was doing? He looked to Pan for guidance, but his friend just shrugged.

"I don't know why your family bothered sponsoring you," the short girl continued. "They were probably stupid enough to think they could get their money back if you failed. Fools."

The two tall girls behind her chuckled, a mean sound to their laughter. "Yes, you should just quit and save them from wasting their money when you fail," the girl on the left said.

"Why would I do that?" Jade asked, feigning confusion. "Didn't you just say we can't get our money back if I fail?"

Cam laughed, while all three girls reddened, facing him with identical scowls.

"And who are you?" the short girl demanded. "Someone who fell off a turnip truck."

Cam grinned. "Nope. We"—He indicated Pan— "fell out of a portal. Master Winder sponsored us. And don't go recommending we drop out on him. He don't seem like the kind who accepts quitting from his Novices."

The short girl didn't seem to know what to say and settled for a glare and huff. It was sad, really. The short girl, whoever she was, wanted to bully Jade and by extension the rest of them, but she just wasn't any good at it. Maria Benefield would have chewed her up and spit her out like a piece of gristle.

"Just stay out of our way," the short girl finally retorted.

"We're in different squads, remember?" Jade said, talking like she was speaking to a simpleton. "We will always be out of your way."

Her comment earned another scowl and huff before the three girls finally let them be.

"Who was that?" Cam asked, once he figured the retreating girls were out of earshot.

"Kahreen Sala," Jade nearly spat. "Her family is one of the wealthiest in our duchy, and mine is indebted to hers."

"She doesn't seem very nice," Pan observed.

"That's because she isn't," Jade replied. "We'd do best by staying away from her and her pets."

"Unless they test us," Avia declared, speaking for the first time since Kahreen had made her presence known. "I'm not the kind to back down." She smiled, a deadly flashing of teeth, some of which still looked orca-sharp.

Cam gulped, making a note to never get on Avia's bad side.

17

Cam yawned mightily. "I'm sleepy," he declared to Pan.

The two of them stood outside the doors to their quarters, alone and with the hallway darkened for the evening. Everyone looked to have retired for the night, although a few conversations could still be heard drifting along the corridors.

"The day isn't done yet," Pan said. "We still have lots of studying to do."

Cam's mouth automatically curled into an expression of disgust. Studying was about as bad as cleaning an outhouse—it had to be done, but no right-thinking person looked forward to it. And Cam was right-thinking. He liked reading adventure stories and such, but having to go through a textbook... he'd rather stick his arm in a bear trap.

The notion had him glancing at his friend, a panda bear. He hoped no one had ever tried to lay out a trap for Pan and his people.

"I took copious notes," Pan continued, "but in the days to come we should also go to the library." He marched into their quarters, turning on some wall-mounted lanterns by twisting a small handle on their front surfaces. They didn't use oil lamps at the academy, but some kind

187

of Ephemeral lights.

Cam followed him inside, slump shouldered. *Studying.* He didn't want to do it, but if he wanted to reach a higher place in life, he'd have to. And it started with figuring out what everyone else at the school seemed to already know: the theory and practice of Ephemera.

"I've got a lot to learn," Cam said. "Can you help me?" He'd already asked a lot of Pan during their time together, and a large part of him wondered what Pan got out of their friendship. Not much by his reckoning.

But unsurprisingly, Pan just grinned at the question. "You're my friend. Of course, I'll help." He plopped on the floor, short, chunky legs splayed as he pulled out a stalk of bamboo he must have had hidden somewhere. Soon enough, he was munching away.

Cam peered at Pan in bemusement. "How are you still hungry?"

Pan shrugged. "I'm not, but eating bamboo calms me. And I want to be calm when we review the notes I took. It's the best way to learn."

While Pan ate, Cam decided to get cleaned. They didn't only use buckets and baths to wash up here. They had showers, which was a luxury only the wealthiest in Traverse could afford. But Cam's clothing was soiled, and he didn't much like the notion of washing away his grime and donning dirty garments.

It was then that he noticed the packages on the table, which turned out to be the clothes that Saira—Professor Maharani! —had promised would be delivered today. Cam perused the items, grateful for Master Winder's generosity. There were several sets of clothing for their Kinesthia classes; some comfortable clothes for regular use, and a sturdy pair that almost felt armored.

There was a similar set for Pan, although Cam wasn't sure he'd ever wear any of them. He seemed to like his breechcloths just fine.

"What's this?" Pan asked, coming alongside Cam. "New clothes."

He sounded a sad note, and Cam glanced at him, wondering why. "What's wrong?"

"I'll only need the clothes if I reach Glory Awareness. That's when Awakened Beasts take on a human form if we so choose… except for the rare cases like Avia."

"But everyone who goes to the academy gets to Glory, don't they?"

Pan shook his head. "Not everyone. A large proportion do not. About four out of ten, in fact."

Sixty percent succeeded? That was it? It sounded so low. The entire time, Cam had just assumed everyone who attended the Ephemeral Academy got to the high ranks of Advancement. His jaw firmed. Well the odds could be better, but they weren't nothing. Cam would just have to make them work for him.

"I'm going for a shower," Cam said. "You want to study afterward?"

Pan nodded, still staring at the clothes like they might jump up and bite him. Whatever had him bothered, Cam hated seeing his friend so forlorn. He clapped Pan on the shoulder. "When we reach Glory, it'll make the struggle all the more worthwhile. We'll get it done."

Pan straightened some. "Hurry up and shower. I want to study."

"Won't take but a few shakes of a cat's tail." Cam grabbed his clothes, entered his darkened room, which held a bed, dresser, and a desk and had a window overlooking the city. He twisted the knob on the wall-mounted lamp, figuring it would turn on the light. Sure enough, it did, and able to see now, he sorted the clothes in the dresser before heading off to the bathroom. A quick shower later, he re-entered the main room, where Pan was sitting on the ground, going through his notes.

"You want to take a quick bath?" Cam asked.

"Later," Pan said. His earlier sense of being disheartened was gone, and an intense focus seemed to have taken hold. He patted the ground next to him. "Sit. We should start with what Professor Grey said about your Plasminia."

That's right. The first thing Cam needed was figuring on how to transform his Imbibed Ephemera and become a proper Novice Prime. He was just getting himself settled when someone knocked on the door. Cam frowned, sharing an uncertain glance with Pan. Who would be stopping by this late? Avia and Jade? Shrugging to himself, he went to the door and opened it.

Outside stood Jade, and with her was a man about Cam's age. Dark-haired and dark-eyed like most everyone, he was lean, goateed, and had an air of mischief about him. A number of rucksacks were at his feet.

"This is Weld Plain. He just arrived," Jade said. "He'll be staying with you."

Cam tried to make sense of what was being said. "With us? Why?"

"Because I'm the fifth member of your squad," the man said, stepping forward, thrusting out his hand, and grinning. "And like the pretty woman said, I'm Weld Plain, but I'm far from plain. Master Winder says hello, by the way."

Cam shook the man's hand without thinking, flabbergasted. He hadn't expected a fifth. His eyes went to Jade, who was staring at Weld, an indecipherable expression on her face. Her eyes flicked the man up and down, pausing on his buttocks. A flush crept across her face. "Well, good night then," she said, quickly departing.

"Come on in," Cam said to Weld, introducing himself and Pan. "I guess you get the third bedroom."

He indicated the doorway, but the man made no move toward it. Instead, he paused in front of Pan. "What are you studying there, panda?"

Cam stiffened. Pan had a name.

"I'm studying my notes from today's classes."

Weld nodded understanding. "Good thing to do. You Awakened Beasts need to get in all the work you can."

Cam's irritation transitioned to a flare of anger. So far, he didn't much like Weld Plain, who was far from plain.

"But none of y'all need to worry about anything now that I'm here," Weld proclaimed. "They're training us to destroy boils, and I aim to be the best there ever was. I'll carry y'all across the finish line whether you need me to or not."

"Destroying boils requires a team," Cam said, trying to tamp down his anger.

Weld laughed like he'd just heard the silliest thing. "I don't need no team. When it comes to Ephemera, I'm the best you'll ever meet."

Pan snorted. "Better than Master Winder?"

"I will be one day, little panda," Weld answered.

Cam's dislike solidified.

Cam settled himself next to Pan, ready to resume his studies, but he noticed Weld eyeing them in confusion.

"You two really going to sit on the ground like slugs?" Weld asked. "Let's go drinking. The night's young. There might be some fine fillies needing a ride." He thrust his hips, leaving no confusion as to what he meant.

"You buying?" Cam asked. On the tip of his tongue was the desire to head out with Weld. No matter how little he liked the man, a drink would be finer than any fillies right around now.

Weld's easy grin was Cam's answer. "I got the coin. Master Winder talked my dad into letting me come here." He brayed laughter. "I've got plenty of money coming in from both the Sage *and* my old man."

Cam stared at Weld, tempted even if he knew it was wrong.

Just a pint in a pub, maybe a shot or two. How much could that hurt? And after that, he'd head right on back and get his studying in.

"I can tell you want to come," Weld said, wearing a confident smirk. "Let's go."

"We need to study," Pan interjected. Cam caught his head shake out of the corner of his eyes.

"Wasn't talking to you, panda," Weld said, eyes locked on Cam. There was a silent urging in his stare.

With a forceful-feeling lurch, Cam managed to thrust away his imaginings of those alluring drinks he so badly wanted. "Pan's right. We have to study."

Weld threw his hands in the air, wearing an air of disgust. "Fine. Stay here you boring bookworms." He gathered his packs and headed for a bedroom, luckily the empty one. He dropped off his rucksacks and immediately headed out again. "Last chance," he said, standing by the front door.

Cam shook his head. "No, thanks."

"Looks like I joined the wrong squad," Weld muttered over his shoulder as he departed.

"I don't think I like him," Pan said.

Cam didn't either, and he said so. He also didn't want to think about Weld. Instead, he struggled on overcoming the temptation raised by the newest member of their unit—a tumbler full of amber loveliness.

He closed his eyes, thinking of himself healthy and hale, standing in a sunny meadow. And with every second of his imagined vision, the allure of alcohol faded and was finally gone.

"What do I need to know?" Cam asked, pointing to the papers spread out before Pan. "And what did Professor Werm mean about True Bonds?"

Pan pursed his mouth. "One, I don't know what Professor Werm meant by True Bonds. I'll find out. And two, you need to learn everything since right now you know so little." Pan grinned, taking the sting out of his all-too accurate comment. "Let's review what Professor Grey said about Plasminia."

He passed over several sheets of paper, which Cam perused. He wanted to get the reading done as quick as he could. However, while giving the pages a gander, Cam found himself getting interested in spite of himself. He was also happy to see he remembered what the professor had taught. Or at least Pan's writing said he had.

An interesting note captured his attention. "Did she really say a Plasminian can sense Ephemera more easily than other Masters?" He pointed out the lines Pan had written.

Pan peered at them a moment, his lips pursed as he seemed to shape the words while reading them. It was a habit Cam had noticed before, and for a moment, he wanted to pinch Pan's mouth shut. Maybe bop him on the nose. Just because it would be funny and cute. He controlled himself, though, keeping his hands in his lap, although he couldn't keep the smile off his face.

"She did say that," Pan eventually said, thankfully overlooking Cam's humor. "She also said that it would mean you could find the cores of a boil easier than other Masters except Spirairians, who have a similar ability. If nothing else, it would make you useful to any unit out hunting rakshasas."

Cam grunted acknowledgement, considering what it might be like to actually be useful for once. It was a sight better than being a no-good Folde like how the fine folk in Traverse referred to him. He'd be worthy of respect, which was the only thing he'd ever really wanted in life. "Good to know," he eventually allowed, going back to reading the notes.

There next came some information that had him uneasy the first time he'd heard it. "Professor Grey says she wants us to solve puzzles and play games to improve our minds?"

"She did," Pan said, not looking up from the notes he was reading. "Chess and other games like that."

Cam closed his eyes, already loathing what was to come. His father had tried to teach him to play chess once, but between the old man's drunken explanation and Cam's own lack of enthusiasm, the rules hadn't stuck. Nor had he wanted them to. Those few times playing had been enough to tell him how little talent he had for the game.

Pan glanced his way. "You don't know how to play chess, do you?"

"I know some of the rules."

Pan rose to his feet. "There's a set in our quarters. I'll teach you." He waddled over to a hutch pressed against a nearby wall and withdrew a rectangular box. "Come on," Pan said, going to the dining table.

Cam followed, feeling like he was heading to his funeral. He didn't want to play chess. It was as boring as watching a pot boil.

An hour later, Cam had the rules down and three losses under his belt. He also had a newfound appreciation of the game. Chess had an elegance that touched him in some indescribable fashion. It was planning mixed with the recognition of patterns, and his younger self simply hadn't seen it. He did now, and if he wanted to succeed at the academy, he'd have to learn to plan and recognize patterns.

By then, it was late, and Cam wanted some sleep. He stifled a yawn, saying goodnight to Pan. Before hitting the sack, though, Cam also wanted to try to shift some of his Plasminia to Synapsia like Professor Grey's book said he could.

He sat cross-legged on his bedroom floor, settling his mind. *All is Ephemera and Ephemera is All.* Unbidden came the thought, and Cam closed his eyes, focused on Delving his Source and Bonding his Tang of Plasminia—another lesson from Professor Grey.

It took no effort for him to slip into his meditation and let his Plasminia slip into him. When he opened his eyes, he knew lightning coursed a circuit around his irises. Now to transform it into Synapsia, which Professor Grey's book said could be done through will, understanding, and acceptance that All is Ephemera and Ephemera is All.

Cam closed his eyes again, maintaining the Bond with Plasminia. The Tang flowed through his Source, lightning circling and darting, never resting long. Capturing a portion of it was a challenge, and it took Cam many fruitless minutes before he managed it. And as soon as he did, it slipped through his fingers like a wriggling fish.

He scowled. It wasn't going to be easy, but he had no sense of giving up. Tonight, his resolve was strong, and he spent more time reeling in his Plasminia, trying to hold it in place. A number of missed chances had him glowering, but still he refused to quit. He'd get something out of this work, even if he had to stay up all night.

Finally, likely an hour into his efforts, he was successful. His will overcame his Plasminia's efforts to get free. Cam held a portion of his Primary Tang in his mind's eye, staring at it, studying the way it flitted about like a lightning-wreathed bee. He imagined it buzzing, seeking a way out.

He frowned. But was that truly what it wanted? While he gazed on the Plasminia, it trailed what might have been a gas. *Spirairia.* Sometimes Cam could see a liquid or even a solid within its heart. *Synapsia* and *Kinesthia.*

All is Ephemera and Ephemera is All.

The phrase was true, and like the twisting of one of those knobs that activated the wall-mounted lamps, a light went off in Cam's mind. He felt a shifting in how he viewed reality. At the same time, a pressure extended into his mind, and he grimaced, clutching his head. It felt like it was about to split open. Only an instant it lasted, and when it was done, the flickering mote of Plasminia had transformed, becoming liquid while the lightning faded and fell away.

Cam stared at the wall, seeing nothing, focusing on what he'd accomplished. Had he really done it? Rising awareness of his success brought a smile to his face and a sense of victory and joy to his heart. He *had* done it. He had gained the tiniest drop of Synapsia from his Plasminia, and although it was only the first step in a thousand-mile journey, Cam was happy.

The work would be its own reward—so Cam told himself—and he got back to laboring, his resolve like steel. Several hours later, he was surprised and elated when he achieved the success for which he had been hoping. His Synapsia flared to a carnation-red. He'd Advanced it to Novice.

Cam pumped his fist, wanting to shout with joy, but he held his voice down. Pan was asleep, and he could always share his good news in the morning. Nevertheless, a single thought circled endlessly through his mind. He was a Novice Prime.

And he wasn't done yet. He focused on his Spirairia. Before the night was done, he'd Advance it to Novice, too.

18

Cam stifled a yawn, blinking bleary eyes. He'd been up late, but in the end, it had been worth it. The work was done. *At last.* Three weeks ago, he'd Advanced Synapsia to Novice, and that same evening, he figured he could do the same for Spirairia.

But it hadn't happened. Hours he'd spent at it before finally giving up, and the night following had also been a failure. Three weeks of failures he'd endured before last night, he finally got the last of his Tangs—Spirairia—to Novice. It had flared to a blood-orange color, flowing like a fog, and his relief knew no bounds.

Thank Devesh! Cam's lack of success for those three weeks had started to eat at him, the disappointment leading to an erosion of confidence, which was the last thing he needed since thinking the worst about himself was something with which he already struggled.

But maybe last night's achievement might help him firm his self-confidence. Pan figured it should, but the panda always thought the best about folks.

Cam glanced askance at his friend, grateful to have him in his life.

Along with the rest of Light Squad, they stood at attention for their first class of the day, Kinesthia. Today, it seemed they would practice archery since they all held bows in hand and had a quiver of a dozen arrows on their hips. Meanwhile, planted in the grass at a distance of twenty yards were a line of round targets with a red circle at dead-center and circles of different colors surrounding it. There were five targets in total—one for each of them—with bales of hay positioned to catch any stray arrows.

The morning sun beamed down from a cloudless sky, warming the world and glistening on the dewy wet grass. A kind breeze kept down the humidity, but sweat still beaded on Cam's brow.

It didn't bother him much, and he was able to keep his attention focused on Professor Shivein and Saira—Professor Maharani! —who were going over the basics of archery.

Cam knew most of what the instructors had to say. He'd been using a bow since he was a boy, hunting food for the family as far back as he could remember. His dad had taught him, and some weeks, what Cam had hunted had been their only food. Of course, his skill at using the bow had dropped like a rock when he'd lost his strength to Plasminia and alcohol, but it would likely come back quick.

He hoped so anyhow. There had to be something where he was as good, or better than everyone else.

"You have your targets," Professor Shivein said. "Get to it."

"Will we be allowed to use our Kinesthia?" Avia asked.

Of all of them, she was the only one willing to question their Awakened instructor. The rest of Light Squad found Professor Shivein to be intimidating.

"If you can maintain the Bond, then yes," Professor Shivein said to Avia. "Use whatever Tang you wish."

Cam sighed. He could Bond Kinesthia. It wasn't hard, but holding it was something else. He just wasn't good enough, only able to maintain the lightest of Bonds to any Tang for half as long as everyone else. He also had to wait twice as long to reforge the Bond, but at least his final cooldown was the same length of time.

"I'm not looking forward to this," Pan said, staring at his bow like it was rotten food.

"You got nothing to worry about, panda," Weld said, grinning cocky as a rooster. "As long as I'm around, I'll see you safe. You just keep that pretty fur clean and eat your bamboo. It's what you're best at, right?" He brayed like a jackass.

Cam wanted to punch Weld. "Tell you what," he said, anger getting the best of his mouth. "You think you're that good, then let's put a little bet on it."

"What kind of bet?" Weld asked.

"Archery," Cam said. "Whoever does the best wins and whoever loses has to clean the bathroom tonight."

Weld grinned. "You got yourself a deal, son."

Cam hid his glee. Weld came from money, which raised an obvious question. Why would a rich boy like him ever bother learning how to use a bow? He wouldn't, which meant Cam was fixing to feed Weld a whole mess of humble pie. "The rules are simple," Cam added. "The most arrows on the target wins."

"What if we have the same number?"

"Then it's whoever has the most arrows close to center."

"Is this a wager?" Saira asked, approaching them with eyebrows arched. She had apparently overheard their conversation. "If so, then I'll be your judge."

Cam was privately relieved. He couldn't ask for a better judge, although it probably wouldn't matter. Weld wasn't an archer. He had no reason to be, which meant his best way to win would be by chirping in Cam's ear and distracting him. But he wouldn't be able to do that with Saira around. Cam nodded to himself. He had this wager won.

The rest of the squad must have also heard what was happening, and curiosity had them pausing their practice and gathering close to watch the wager, even Professor Shivein. Cam glanced at them. Avia appeared excited; Pan apprehensive; while Jade flicked an admiring glance at Weld's backside. She did that a lot, and she flushed when she caught Cam noticing. He inwardly shook his head. What did Jade see in Weld? The man was handsome enough, but he was also a braggart and a jackhole.

"You can take the first shot," Weld said, looking like he didn't have a care in the world.

Cam grinned to himself. Weld's cocky attitude was about to look mighty stupid. It was what Cam told himself, trying to build up his confidence as he Delved his Source, reaching deep to his ruby-red Kinesthia. His co-ordination and balance immediately improved. So did his strength. It seemed like he could jump high enough to launch himself over the wall surrounding the field, and his movements felt smoother and easier than they ever had in life.

He nocked an arrow, sighting along its length. An exhalation to breathe out his worries. He could do this. *Focus.* The target was everything. A final exhalation, and Cam let loose.

The arrow whistled, landing with a thud. It quivered just off the center of the target. A smattering of applause met the result.

"Nice shot," Weld allowed, stepping forward. He faced his own target, nocked an arrow and lifted his bow. His movements were assured and practiced.

A pit yawned in Cam's stomach. Weld knew what he was doing. The other man exhaled; the bow steady. A release, and his arrow landed near dead-center, closer than Cam's first try.

More applause clapped out from the other members of Light Squad while the pit in Cam's stomach yawned wider. He was in trouble.

Weld grinned his way. "Your turn, son."

Cam tried not to let the words touch him. He had to stay calm and focused. But it was hard to do with his nerves jangling.

"You can do this," Pan whispered.

His friend's belief helped Cam regain some of his lost composure. He nocked an arrow, sighted along it. *Exhale.* Release. The arrow hammered home, a bit wider than the first shot, but at least it was on the target.

Nevertheless, the claps were fainter this time.

"Not bad," Weld allowed. "But not good enough." He nocked, sighted, and released in one smooth move. The arrow landed directly above his first.

Cam still had Kinesthia, but it wasn't enough. He needed more. He Delved his Source, Bonding Synapsia this time. He struggled to hold it when a headache bloomed like a thorny rose. His vision blurred in and out, finally lurching back into focus. And once Cam could see properly again, the world seemed brighter. Serenity settled his nervousness, and confidence seeped into his being.

He nocked an arrow, aimed, and released it in the blink of an eye. His mind worked fast enough for him to track the bolt's flight, and he knew where it would impact without having to wait and see. It smacked with a dull echo, dead center. This time the cheers were louder, Avia shouting encouragement.

Cam grinned her way, glad for her support.

Weld whistled in mock appreciation, stepping to the line. But he should have kept quiet since his next shot went well wide of his first two or any of Cam's

Cam didn't waste any time. At any moment, his Bonds would break. He had to get this done as quick as possible. He stepped forward, aiming and releasing as soon as the arrow was lined up. It carved into the target, dead-center again, right next to the last one.

Weld scowled, but he, too, somehow regained his composure. His next shot was close on to his first two.

Cam stepped up to the line. His focus was the best it had ever been. His mind worked faster than it ever had. A bird lifted off a branch in the corner of his vision. He could count the number of wing beats needed to get it aloft. The experience was better than any drink, and he sighted another arrow.

It landed just off center this time.

Weld's arrogance was gone. He got to the line, and this time his arrow hit close to the first two. He had four arrows close to center compared to Cam's three. Weld was winning.

Cam's confidence wasn't shaken. Not in the slightest. He was going to win this bet. No chance he was cleaning the bathroom tonight. He let loose his arrow, smirking at Weld after it hit dead center, landing so close it caused his other three to quiver.

They traded shots, and on his final arrow, the twelfth, what Cam feared to happen finally occurred. The last of his four Bonds with Synapsia and Kinesthia broke. He was on cooldown for the next half hour. He had nothing but his talent to lean on. But some of the confidence given to him by Synapsia stayed with him. He didn't let himself think about losing. He lifted the bow, exhaling, breathing out tension. The center of the target firmed in his sight. *Release.*

The arrow landed just inside the target's center. Cam sighed in relief, smiling even as the rest of Light Squad cheered his success, even Jade.

"We're down to the final arrow," Professor Maharani said. "Cam has the lead, but Weld can still tie."

Cam stepped directly behind Weld when the other man got to his line. "You best get ready to clean the bathroom tonight, son," he whispered.

Weld turned around with a grin, shoulder-checking Cam, moving him back. "Don't get to counting your chickens. It ain't over." He lifted his bow, sighted along the arrow, holding the pose, exhaled, and released. His last bolt landed just outside of the target's center.

Cam whooped, screaming his triumph. Pan was hollering while Avia tried to congratulate him. But Cam hardly heard her or Saira's confirmation of his win. Joy filled his mind, hardly letting up even when he saw Weld's crestfallen expression.

Victory came so rare to him, and he couldn't get enough of it.

Cam's good feelings lasted the rest of the class, but some of the shine rubbed off when he realized he hadn't won the archery contest with a whole lot of grace. He shrugged it off. If Weld wanted an apology, he'd be waiting a mighty long time.

Their next class was Spirairia, and Professor Werm arrived shortly thereafter, which was a minor miracle. Usually, he was late by a couple minutes, but not today, and he got to lecturing as soon as everyone got settled. "Mr. Folde, I am told you have Spirairia Advanced to Novice. Is this correct?"

"Yes, sir," Cam said, glad to be able to say so.

"In that case, you can actually join in the instruction today," Professor Werm said. Like was his norm, his tone was mocking, but Cam caught an underlying respect in there as well. The professor stared at him a bit longer, his Glory-blue, Ephemeral eyes unblinking. "As I've told you throughout the term, Spirairia requires acceptance. Meditation is the best means, but you also need to find your own, best path forward. I've taught you what I and many other Spirairians have learned, but ultimately, your means of using the Tang, of accepting yourself, is an individual requirement. I will help as I can, but this first, most important lesson is one you must master on your own. Begin."

Professor Werm was talking about how he meditated by breathing in through his left nostril and out through his mouth. Somehow that centered his mind, allowing a better Bond with Spirairia. There would come a time when such breathing exercises weren't needed, but for now, Cam had no other choice but to do as Professor Werm suggested.

But before he could start, Weld got his attention. "Celebrate your win today," he said, "but you better believe I'll get you back." He grinned, but it wasn't a pleasant smile. Cam made to reply, but Weld waved him quiet. "We don't need to talk. I just wanted to let you know. Now shush. This work isn't easy."

Cam leaned away from Weld, surprised and annoyed. The mild threat didn't bother him, but the final words did; Weld's claim that the work wouldn't be easy. This from the man who learned and mastered teachings on his first attempt. Then what did that mean for Cam?

He mentally shook his head. Best find out now instead of later. He closed his eyes, Delving his Source. Spirairia flowed like a blood-orange fog just under his Plasminia. And while Cam could Bond it, using it was another matter. It was like Professor Werm said: first he had to gain acceptance in some way.

Which wasn't going to be easy. Cam didn't like himself, didn't like his past and how he'd responded to his disappointments.

Not having any other notion on what to do, Cam kept his eyes closed and Bonded Spirairia. At the same time, he Bonded Synapsia. The Tang had helped focus his mind during the archery contest. Maybe it would help him now.

As before, a headache pressed his scalp with long fingers of pain, but Cam persisted, waiting it out. Soon enough, the pain subsided enough for him to think again, and with Synapsia his thoughts came sharper, clearer, faster.

He knew on a rational level that he wasn't at fault for the deaths of Tern and Lilia, but how to translate that into his emotions? He studied on it, wondering how to go about changing his feelings. Or maybe he shouldn't change them? Maybe that was the point of using Spirairia. He had to accept those feelings and accept those personal failings.

But how?

Not really having a proper notion and figuring he had nothing to lose, Cam started the breathing exercises Professor Werm had taught them. In through his left nostril, out through his mouth. It was harder to do than it sounded, impossible in a lot of ways, at least to do it correctly.

But Cam kept at it, helped by Synapsia's focus.

A minute later, his Bonds to both Tangs broke, and he had to wait out the short cooldown before he could go again. While paused, Cam continued practicing his breathing, although he continued to come nowhere close to getting it right. The cooldown ended, and Cam fixed to work again.

Another minute slipped by. Another failure and another cooldown. Cam grimaced. It was impossible to breathe like Professor Werm said, and he wondered if he was actually accomplishing anything. Worse, he only had two more uses of his Tangs before he hit the longer half-hour cooldown, so he figured he best make them count.

"I like to imagine what I wish my world was like," Pan said.

He'd explained this before, about how he'd learned to properly Bond Spirairia, but until now, Cam hadn't listened much. It seemed pointless since it didn't do him any good. Until today, he'd been utterly unable to Bond Spirairia whatsoever. But now, with Spirairia at Novice, Cam listened closer.

"After that," Pan continued, "I think about the life I have and how I can render the mistakes of the past useful to make that better reality come true."

Cam thanked his friend for his advice and set to using it as soon as his cooldown ended. Bonding both Spirairia and Synapsia, ignoring his pounding headache, he imagined a world in which Lilia and Tern had never died.

But that wasn't a world he could have. The past was written, and it couldn't be changed.

He set off then to a different dream. In this one, he was a Glory, helping folks in need, ridding the world of boils, and settling disputes by making a good peace among those who disagreed. That was what he wanted to do, and in order to do it, he had to Enhance his Tangs, Advance his Awareness, and learn from those who could teach him.

Those teachers weren't just his instructors at the academy neither. They included Pan, Avia, and Jade. His family, too, especially Pharis. Honor and Jordil. Even Lilia, despite her death. Her spirit and good cheer lingered in his memories. Cam could learn from all of them.

It was a kind of acceptance, and for the first time in a long time, the faintest flicker of peace flashed across his mind.

In that instant, his Bonds broke, but Cam didn't let a little thing like that hold him back. He continued to dream like Pan had advised, wanting so much to make this world of his imagination come true.

That evening, Cam was up late, studying with Pan. There was a notion he wanted to discuss. "Professor Werm seems certain that Spirairia is the most important of Tangs," he noted. "But I think he's wrong."

"It's Synapsia," Pan said without a moment of hesitation. "If I could have chosen it when I had a choice, that's the one I would have wanted."

Cam wouldn't argue. He felt the same way. But Professor Werm's declaration continued to ring in his mind. He frowned, trying to figure on why their instructor might feel the way he did. "Do you think it has to do with what he was talking about with farming and healing and such?"

Pan shrugged. "Maybe. But even then, Synapsia guides Spirairia."

"No, it don't," Cam said. "Synapsia makes a mind work faster and better. A person might even be said to be smarter. But the guiding for doing what's right. Of caring for the land and people…" Cam pointed to his heart. "That comes from here. And it's Spirairia that can do more than any other Tang at seeing it through."

Pan looked like he was fixing to reply, but just then the door opened and in stumbled Weld, drunk as a skunk.

"Fellas," he said, slurring his words, lofting a bottle of whiskey. "Who wants a shot? He wandered toward Cam, who sat at the dining table. "What about you? You didn't want to drink with me when I first came here. What about now?"

Cam's mouth went dry. His eyes locked on the bottle, and his hand twitched. He wanted that drink—hated the want for that drink—and he didn't care that Weld was leering at him like he'd solved some puzzle.

"Maybe you should sleep it off," Pan suggested to Weld.

"I wasn't talking to you, panda," Weld said, his gaze meeting Cam's. "I was talking to my friend."

With an effort, Cam shoved aside his need. "I think I'll pass," he said, his voice hoarse.

"You sure?"

Weld passed the bottle under Cam's nose, and he automatically took a whiff. The desire rose again, but this time, he was ready for it. Cam suppressed the want. "I'm sure."

Weld scowled. "You two are as fun as watching an old woman bathe in a sauna." He swallowed a slug straight from the bottle. "I'm going to bed." He stumbled off, tripping over his feet. A cracking sounded out, and Weld collapsed, clutching his ankle, screaming in pain. "Fragging hells! I think I broke my ankle."

Cam viewed his intoxicated and injured flatmate, momentarily wondering if this was how he had appeared when he'd been stumbling around drunk. It was likely the case, and he had no idea how Pharis had put up with him. He sighed at Weld's shrieking. "We best take him to the infirmary."

Several days later, Weld was off his crutches, healed right quick by the doctors in the infirmary and able to rejoin Light Squad.

On his flatmate's first day back, Cam was scribbling notes as fast as he could, writing in the leather-bound folio Professor Maharani had purchased for him. He had asked for it on his second day at the academy, and already, a little over three weeks into his schooling, he was making a large dent in filling out its pages; so much so that he'd likely need a new folio in another month.

"Lancing is what this entire institute is dedicated toward accomplishing," Professor Grey was saying. It was their second class of the day in Synapsia, and in the afternoon, she often included lectures on history, naturalism, and theories on the use of Ephemera. She also touched on other topics, such as philosophy, which for her seemed to focus on the universal notions of fraternity and forgiveness.

Cam didn't know if he could manage either—fraternity or forgiveness. He sure didn't consider the fine folk back in Traverse to be part of his fraternity, and he sure wouldn't be forgiving them for what they'd done. Only for his family could he see himself offering those vague but powerful notions. And as he calculated matters—beyond his true family, such as Pharis, Darik, and his father—those he considered close enough to be his brothers or sisters were either those in this room or people like Master Bennett. His gaze caught on Weld. Well, most everyone in this room. Weld could take a leap off a bridge, and Cam wouldn't much mind.

"I'm still unclear on one matter," Pan said.

"What a surprise," Weld muttered in a stage whisper.

Cam glared at the man. Weld did that a lot—made others look bad on purpose, and Cam figured it had to do with how gifted he was. Weld was better than any of them at using his Tangs. Stronger, faster, and deadlier with Kinesthia. His mind worked quicker with Synapsia. And he already had some ability with telekinesis and empathy with Spirairia. But his gifts only made him arrogant, and they sure didn't make him the leader he seemed to think he was.

There were also times when Weld was asked by a fellow student for the answer to a question. Sometimes the man might tell them what sounded like the right reply, and usually, it was close. But later on, Cam or Pan or whoever would discover the answer wasn't quite right. It was always a subtle difference, nothing enough to prove any wrongdoing on Weld's part, but it did make a body suspicious.

Plus, Cam couldn't figure that Weld was a good person. Not after he'd taken an immediate loathing toward Pan, poking fun and mocking him at every turn. One of the gentlest, most generous, and most caring people Cam had ever met. There was no call for that. None at all.

As a result, Weld's behavior sparked a burning dislike in Cam, and it was a dislike that went both ways. Cam knew that he and Weld might be heading toward a busting of fists, and he welcomed it.

In his weeks of schooling, he'd walked a spell on the Way into Divinity, raising all his Tangs to Novice and learning to Bond them, too. And although he probably didn't stand much of a chance against Weld, so what? Bullies only needed challenging since most were braggarts with a lot of bark but not much bite.

And speaking of braggarts, it was time Weld got a taste of his own way of talking. "Be quiet," Cam whispered to Weld in the same stage whisper the jackhole had used on Pan. "The rest of us want to learn how to do more than pick our noses."

His comment earned a snigger from Avia and Jade while Weld reddened in anger or embarrassment. Cam didn't care which.

Professor Grey ignored their interplay and spoke to Pan. "What are you uncertain about?"

"How do boils form?"

Professor Grey wore a sad smile. "Ah. That. Some say it was a mistake made by the Holy Servants; that in their zeal to allow all beings to have a chance to Advance, they didn't think about how the Ephemera they birthed—"

"I thought Ephemera came from Devesh?" Cam interrupted.

"Ultimately, it does," the Professor said, "but for this answer, we will pretend that the Servants, seeking to be like our Holy Creator, birthed Ephemera. And in so doing, in trying to inspire their creations into a state of Creation, they didn't see how their Ephemera could find a way to strive for that same sense of Creation."

Cam had never heard of such a thing, and based on everyone's confused expressions, no one else seemed to either. Professor Grey spoke like Ephemera had a mind of its own, like it had a purpose outside of Devesh and His Servants.

"Ephemera seeks itself," Professor Grey continued, "and unfortunately, in some of those areas where it thickens like a stew, rakshasas have learned to thrive. And in those places, they warp the natural world, creating a boil. In some cases, the boil is of such potency that most normal humans can't survive in those regions. Ultimately, it is all part of a natural process in which creation through destruction is occasionally necessary to restore health to the world."

Some of what she said Cam had already heard; that sometimes in order to change for the better, a person, village, city, and even a duchy needed to undergo creative destruction. It was a phrase that sounded good and rational, but it left out the emotion. It couldn't be simple and fair for those involved, especially those who got more of the destruction end of the stick and less the creation part.

"Is that why Divines sometimes allow themselves to die?" Pan asked.

"No Divine ever died," Weld scoffed, taking the opposition to Pan's belief like he always did.

"Actually, they have," Avia said. "There's plenty of documentation."

Weld shrugged, looking contemptuous. "Agree to disagree."

"She's right," Jade said. "There's been plenty of reports about it throughout history."

Weld's reply was to fold his arms and smirk like everyone else was stupid and he was so very smart.

"Good answer," Cam said to Weld. "You definitely proved your point that time." He made sure that the mockery was bright and clear.

"You're one to talk, gimp," Weld said with a sneer.

Cam tried not to let the insult rile him. Gimp was what Weld sometimes called him on account of how much weaker he was than everyone else. Of course, Professor Grey implied that he wouldn't have that same handicap at the higher Stages of Awareness, but until then, he'd be disadvantaged.

"We're moving afield," Professor Grey said. "Getting back to Pan's question, what I said is only one possible explanation of why boils exist. Others have their own opinions, but in the end, it doesn't matter. Boils exist, and it is your job to destroy them. It is the reason for your training here at the Third... I mean the Ephemeral Academy." She paced in front of them. "If a boil isn't destroyed, it will be grown by the rakshasas that feed on them. Anyone know how?"

"Their cores," Cam said, having had direct interaction with one.

Professor Grey smiled. "Exactly. A core draws in and transforms Ephemera, which feeds the rakshasas, who in turn, feed the cores. A core will then expand a boil's area of influence, but if you destroy it, the boil and the rakshasas subsisting on it will usually die. In addition, an Ephemeral Master of a higher Awareness than the core can purify it. We can then use the core to Advance both humans and Awakened Beasts. The core becomes a force for creative change, but in a kinder and gentler way."

"Is it true that Coruscant, Simmer, and Shimala exist in a boil outside of Salvation?" Pan asked.

"You're talking about Hell," Weld said, for once not sounding so cocksure.

"It is the greatest boil," Professor Grey replied. "And no one from Salvation knows how to reach it or where it is."

Weld leaned back in his chair, extravagantly stretching and clasping his hands behind neck. "Well, if we ever do, once I reach Sage, I'll be the one to destroy it."

Cam rolled his eyes.

19

The semester raced by with the first six weeks gone as swiftly as the beating of a hummingbird's wings. In that time, Cam made sure to write home to his family and friends, letting them know how he was doing and what he was learning. That included the very first instances in the use of weapons, including staffs. He figured Master Bennett might be proud of the latter. There were also spears and shields, and Light Squad had begun training with all of them early on in the semester. The staff was a weapon Cam enjoyed. It felt easier than a sword, more natural to him. Other than Jade, the rest of Light Squad felt the same way. She, of course, had been raised to fight and knew something on how to use every weapon.

But Cam also recalled how at the Awareness of a Glory, the person became the weapon. What they were learning now wasn't always going to be what they needed later.

That was a concern for years from now, and until that time, while Jade trained off to the side with Pan—the two of them taking on Professor Shivein—Cam, Weld, and Avia were to spar against Saira.

He made a note to himself. He'd call Saira "Professor Maharani" in public, but in the privacy of his mind, he couldn't help but refer to her by the name from when they first met.

His decision made; he glanced around. It was a lovely morning for a brawl. The weather was cool and dry. A gusting wind blew, and puffy clouds drifted. It would be getting on to autumn soon, and Cam looked forward to when winter's proper cold would bite down. And in the distance, Nexus' white buildings gleamed and the aqua-blue waters of the lake scintillated in the warm sunshine. The massive statues of the Holy Servants loomed over the harbor and the city like titans promising protection.

Saira faced them from a distance of twenty feet, staff in hand, wearing a sleeveless tunic and waiting on them. Even in repose, her muscles rippled, but that was the least of her strength. She'd once been a Crown, and she still had the body of one, refined, stronger, and more durable than any Glory.

"Whenever you're ready," Saira said, staff twirling in her hands.

"We should charge her as a group," Weld suggested. "It's only to first touch. One of us is bound to get in a lucky blow."

"We'll get in each other's way," Avia disagreed. "We should spread out and attack from all angles."

They set to arguing, which Cam ended by speaking over the other two. "We wait too long, she'll attack us first. We'd be better off going at her from different angles; far enough apart so we don't tangle our staffs, but close enough that we can support each other."

Weld looked ready to argue the point, which was normal for him. Truth was it was normal for everyone in Light Squad but Pan to dismiss Cam's suggestions out of hand. He was the weakest of their group, and an adage old as time said the strong should lead the weak.

Cam didn't reckon it was as smart as it sounded. He had useful advice to give, and he was tired of the rest of them—Pan excluded—not listening when he had words to say. "You know I'm right," he told Avia, hoping to appeal to her better side. "Isn't that how a pod would attack? Hit and run. Not in a cluster, but also not all spread out."

"But she's a Glory," Weld said, "and you said she used to be a Crown. If we attack separately, she'll still be plenty fast enough to crush us."

"No, she won't," Cam countered. "She said she'd only fight using Novice-level abilities."

"I agree with Cam," Avia said, bringing the argument to an end. "We do it like he said."

"Then Weld should take the center," Cam said. "He's our strongest. He can support the two of us if we get in trouble. Avia, you'll be to his right, and since Saira is right-handed, you might have a chance to land a hit on her weaker side."

"You'll take her strong side?" Avia asked, sounding doubtful.

"I'll do my best," Cam said with a shrug. "Let's get it done. And Bond Synapsia, not just Kinesthia."

"Yes, mother," Weld said, sarcasm leaking out of his voice.

Cam disregarded it. He Bonded Synapsia and Kinesthia—thin as his links to them were—knowing and accepting the headache that always happened whenever he linked to two Tangs. His vision blurred—again, typical—but once it cleared, he spread away from Weld and Avia, trusting them to do the same.

He studied Saira, who still waited patiently, knees bent, but her staff was no longer twirling. Instead, it was held diagonally across her body at the ready position. Bonded to Synapsia, Cam's mind worked quick enough to count the few loose strands of her ponytailed hair as they flitted in the breeze.

With a frown, his examination focused on Saira's hair. The tie holding it together was loose. If he got close enough, could he somehow remove it? Or better yet, maybe Avia could while Cam and Weld held Saira's attention. If they could, it might be all the distraction they needed in order to win.

He called the others over before they could attack, explaining his change of plans.

"How's she supposed to get that hair-tie off?" Weld asked.

"She gets close enough to use Spirairia." Cam peered at Avia. "Can you do it?"

Avia gave a firm nod.

Then this is what we'll do." Cam explained.

They spread out again, same formation. At ten feet, Weld screamed inarticulately, rushing forward. Cam darted after him. Weld swung wildly at Saira, who blocked smoothly. Cam flicked a stab at her gut. She batted his staff aside. Avia joined the fray, sending out a testing slap. Weld swung hard once again.

His recklessness cost him. Saira defended, rode her staff down Weld's, bruising his knuckles. A quick thrust got him in the gut. He grunted, folding over. A first hit on him. Weld was out.

Cam aimed a thrust at Saira's elbow, but she easily blocked. Her counter threw him off balance. But it got her out of position, enough for Avia to close. She swung a vertical chop. Saira braced and blocked.

Suddenly her ponytail came loose. Her long hair wreathed her face. It was the distraction Cam needed. His horizontal slash took Saira at the hip. She grunted, not going down but waving off the rest of the match. She'd taken a hit. It was over.

Cam whooped, sharing a look of exultation with Avia. He hadn't expected their plan to actually work.

"Reset. We go again," Saira said, looking peeved as she tied off her hair, this time more securely.

"Maybe we should listen to you more often," Avia said to Cam, approval on her face.

The next class of the day was a surprise. Rather than meet in their normal room, Professor Werm led them out into the fields surrounding the academy.

"Let us discuss farming," he said, pacing like he always did, hands clasped behind his back. His head was bent like he was lost in thought, but there it was still, the sneer of contempt always on his face.

Cam didn't know why Professor Werm felt the way he did; nor did he care. During his time at the academy, he had begun to recognize what was and wasn't important. And liking Professor Werm wasn't important. As their instructor, he did a good enough job teaching

Spirairia, which meant Cam didn't care two hoots of an owl if the man smirked, sneered, jeered, laughed or anything else. He could get his point across and show them what they needed to learn.

Today's topic, though, was unusual. Unexpected, actually. What good was farming when it came to lancing boils? Professor Werm didn't look ready to answer just yet, and Cam glanced about. He and the other members of Light Squad stood outside a greenhouse that reflected the rays of the mid-morning sun. Around them were small fields of corn, wheat, beans, and a few other crops; all of them segmented into nice square plots. A few Masters were out amongst the growing greens, checking them for mites, bugs, diseases, and whatnot.

Cam had never much paid attention to a farmer's life, but he knew it could be uncomfortable, especially on a hot day like this where the weather had him wishing for a shower. After Kinesthia, it was always the case that he'd be soaked in sweat and grime. And while Cam was fitter and faster than he'd ever been, he was still weaker than he wanted to be. His one consolation was that at least he finally had the strength of his build. It brought him some comfort, especially since everyone else was coated in a layer of sweat just as he was. Everyone but poor Pan, whose fur was soaked and matted. Maybe he ought to consider shaving.

Cam snickered to himself. Pan naked of his fur would be hilarious.

"You are wondering why we are discussing farming," Professor Werm said. "We do so because without farmers, there is no food. And without food, we die." He flashed a smile that looked like a grimace of pain rather than anything pleasurable. "There are other reasons, and you'll learn them today. Bond to your Spirairia and observe."

Cam did as instructed, Delving his Source and Bonding Spirairia.

As soon as he did, any lingering stress seemed to breathe out of him. He smiled at the loss of tension he hadn't even known he was carrying. The world itself felt more alive when Bonded with Spirairia. The fields glowed brighter, and Cam could sense the life flowing through them. His awareness of those around him also increased—Pan's gentle curiosity and Avia's intense desire to succeed, so similar to Jade's. Maybe that was why they were such good friends? There was also Weld's full-bore confidence but it overlay his unmistakable uncertainty.

But Cam couldn't remain in this blessed state for long. Only a few minutes to hold the Bond, unlike Plasminia, which he could maintain for as long as he wanted.

He set aside his concerns about his limitations when Professor Werm led them to a fallow portion of the field of crops. From a pocket in his jacket, he withdrew a withered acorn, cupping it in both his hands. "This came from an area contaminated by a boil. In most ways it is ruined with no possibility of sprouting. Watch."

Cam peered closer. From Professor Werm's hands wisped a stream of blue light, his Ephemeral Spirairia. It held a purity of life Cam had not yet seen from anyone else; so bright when viewed while Bonded to Spirairia it might as well have been liquid sunlight. The Ephemera poured into the acorn, and the nut seemed to suck it up, expanding, filling out until it shone healthy, no longer withered.

Professor Werm dug a small hole in the loose soil, planting the acorn. More light poured from his hands, drifting off his fingers. He looked to be playing a melody on a musical instrument only he could see.

Seconds later, a sprout pushed out of the ground. The shoot of an oak. It trembled, rising higher, thickening, glowing the same color as Professor Werm's Spirairia. Finally, the blue light flickered out from their instructor's hands. The last drip landed on the oak, and it might have flashed brighter one last time before it settled into the normal pale green shade of a new shoot.

"What lesson did I teach you?" Professor Werm asked, and for once his face didn't contain its usual mocking sneer. Instead, he wore an unexpected expression of profound weariness and humility.

The shape of his features took Cam aback. He'd never figured to see such meekness on the professor's face. Cam got so caught up in thinking on what it might mean that he didn't have time to think on the question asked.

But as usual, Pan and Jade *had* thought about it.

"The lesson I learned is that even what we consider useless can be redeemed," Pan said.

Jade built off Pan's response. "And healing can be more important than simply slaying."

Professor Werm smiled at their answers. "You are correct. When you destroy a boil, you will help many people. Certainly any villagers or townsfolk who live close by. But what about the land itself, the area the boil contaminated? You owe it no obligation. You can just walk away with no heaviness on your conscience." He paused. "But this is our world. Why not help and heal when you can? It costs little and serves the highest goals of Ephemera. Heal the land, and you'll serve, which is what the Holy Servants ultimately taught was *our* purpose. Life and creation. That is the duty of a farmer, and an Ephemeral Master who so chooses can keep farmlands healthy, bring dead fields to life. Even Acolytes can help small villages thrive. Your lives don't have to be about dealing out nothing but death. You can create as well. Isn't that a higher ideal?"

It was the onion-peeled exposure of a profound, warm layer under the professor's constant smirk of superiority. It was the same as when Cam had found out the man's private passion was growing tiny trees planted in small pots. They had been no more than several feet in height and their trunks only inches in width, but they still had the shape of their towering cousins in the wild. It had been a revelation to know such a thing was even possible, and just like then, Cam viewed Professor Werm in a fresh light. Who was he underneath his rough exterior?

Who were any of them?

The question had Cam reflecting on Weld. His overflowing confidence hid a deep-seated anxiety, and Cam wondered if that meant anything. Could he and Weld find a better way to be? They hadn't yet brawled, but they also didn't much mask their dislike, and in Cam's case, contempt.

Professor Werm withdrew five more shriveled acorns from his pockets, passing them out to the students. "By the end of the semester,

I want to see you improve these nuts. And by the end of the year, I want to see them sprout."

Cam's heart fell. This wasn't going to be easy.

"Think on what I said," Professor Werm said. "You are dismissed."

Professor Werm's demonstration had Cam lost in wondering for the rest of the morning. He barely listened to what was said in Synapsia, losing a few games of chess to Pan, and was last to solve a numbers-related puzzle.

The last stung, but it also failed to snap him out of his funk. Until this morning, he hadn't ever given much consideration to the other ways of Ephemera, how it created life, supported it, and made things better for everyone. It had taken Professor Werm's demonstration to show him how restricted he'd been in thinking of his future. He could do so much more with his gifts.

In such a light, creative destruction also had a better meaning. So did what he'd taken as his private mantra: *All is Ephemera and Ephemera is All.*

It took his second class in Kinesthia to knock him out of his meanderings. Professor Shivein and Saira waited at their normal field, and she flashed a welcoming smile as Cam and the others descended the steps.

Weld nudged Cam. "She's smiling my way. If she wasn't one of our instructors, I'm sure there's a lot of fun things we could do together." His leer explained exactly what kind of fun things he had in mind.

Cam made sure Weld saw his eye-roll. A woman like Saira wouldn't have anything to do with a braggart like Weld.

Avia must have felt the same way. "Didn't you say something like that about Professor Grey? What did she do again?" She tapped her lips, pretending to muse out the memory.

Weld stammered. "Professor Grey took it the wrong way is all."

"What? Took it wrong that you said *'Eveangel, honey'* to her?" Avia chuckled, cold and cruel. "You're lucky she only reprimanded you. If it had been me, I'd have ripped your head off."

There was a savagery to Avia's words, and Cam figured she was telling the truth. She had been an orca, a predator, and she would have visited carnage on anyone stupid enough to speak to her so disrespectfully.

Weld's unease became an oily smile. "Then it's a good thing I'll never talk to you like that or call you 'honey' because you're anything but sweet."

Avia didn't reply, although the slight flush on her face gave away her irritation.

Cam might have said something to Weld, but Jade was shaking her head his way, warning him to stay out of it. He sighed and did so, although he wouldn't mind putting a boot up Weld's ass.

It was a pleasant image that lasted until they reached their instructors.

"Hurry up and get in line," Professor Shivein chided. It was the first thing he always said, morning or afternoon. "We'll be practicing couples dancing. Avia with Pan. Weld and Jade. And Cam with Professor Maharani."

"What are *you* going to do?" Avia asked. "Practice flying?" She grinned at Professor Shivein, the only one brave enough to joke with him.

Professor Shivein snorted at Avia. "A turtle doesn't need to be a bird. Now off with you." He left them then, heading toward the stairs leading away from the field.

As soon as he left, Cam headed to where Saira waited for him. "Guess you're stuck with me," he said with a smile.

"How will I get over my disappointment?" she replied in a dry tone.

Cam chuckled. He might have to call her Professor Maharani, but they still had their relationship from before the academy. He wasn't sure what it had been, but it was the same now as then; close enough to friendship that he could relax around her.

And seeing Weld scowl his way only made him feel better about it.

"Are you ready?" Saira asked.

"What style of dancing are we going to practice?"

"Bhangra."

Cam grinned. It was his favorite kind of dance, although he liked all the others, too—the formal waltz, the simple twist, and even the romantic ballroom. Truth be told; however, he'd only practiced the latter with Pan, not having the gumption to carry on like that with Avia or Jade, and definitely not with Saira. Holding any of them so close for so long would probably cause him to faint.

"I figured you'd like that," Saira said. "Now stop smiling like an idiot. Let's get to work."

"I'm ready whenever you are."

Saira's skin glowed with the deep blue sheen of her Kinesthia, and she replied by naming the steps they would practice.

Cam nodded once he had the steps memorized, waited a moment longer to Bond to his Kinesthia, taking a few seconds to get used to his improved balance, speed, and power. He Bonded Synapsia, too, accepted the eye-burning ache of holding two Tangs. No one else felt that pain like he did. For them, holding two Tangs was nothing, but for Cam it hurt like needles stabbing his eyes.

But in the end, the pain also wasn't important. He needed Synapsia if he wanted to keep up with Saira.

She gave him a crooked smile of approval. "Bonding two Tangs… daring. And you'll need it."

Her words spoken, they were off. Saira set a swift tempo, and Cam worked hard to maintain her pace and rhythm. Her arms rose and fell in a complex but smooth motion, and she swayed about gracefully. Cam knew his own movements were rough and ready in comparison. A leap was coming, and Cam bent his knees, launching himself as powerfully as he could. Four feet he rose, and he might have patted himself on the back, but Saira was several feet higher than him. She could have kicked him in the face if she wanted.

Cam shrugged it off, refusing to falter. He knew these steps, had drilled them into his muscle memory. Another leap, and this time Saira didn't jump so high, and they looked like actual partners.

On they went, Cam losing himself in the dance, riding the flow. He moved in perfect synchronization with Saira, having no difficulty when they came together and he had to put hands on her waist and lift her. He supported her when she twirled around his hips. Just another part of the dance, but so far, everything still came smooth and easy. It was like he was relaxed from a few fingers of whiskey.

The thought of drinking nearly tripped him, and he reddened with embarrassment, thrown out of the flow; having to focus in order to stay in time with Saira. It wasn't so easy now, and for the rest of the dance, he struggled like he was laboring under a log. He imagined he looked that way, too.

They finished, Saira facing him in the pose in which she'd started. She let her hands drop. "What happened?"

Cam didn't want to admit his weakness, but Saira already knew about it. "I was just thinking how easy it was to dance with you," he answered. "It was like I was free and easy from having a couple of fingers of whiskey."

She nodded, lips tightening with understanding and empathy.

Which only made the situation worse. Cam didn't want Saira's—or anyone's—pity.

Somehow, Saira must have realized it. The empathy fell off her face. "For someone who never danced and had no training in using your body, you've come a long way," she said. "At this rate, you should be ready for the demonstration at your mid-term testing."

She was talking about the middle of the year examinations, which were supposed to assess a Novice's mastery of body control and power. Other squads were planning on some kind of martial display, while Light Squad—apparently at Master Winder's insistence—were going to dance. Cam wasn't ready for it, but he'd hopefully get there.

"We're going again," Saira said, face hardening. "Get in position."

Cam gladly did so. He'd much rather experience Saira's bark than have her pity.

20

Cam stared at the withered acorn he'd received from Professor Werm earlier in the day, pondering it before setting it aside. He closed his eyes then, recalling the instructions from the anonymously written book on Plasminia that Professor Grey had loaned to him. The advice was on how to Enhance Plasminia, centering on slowing it down and cooling it off.

But what would happen to all that heat when he did? Would it blow off of him like he was some kind of fire?

Professor Grey hadn't known the answer. She had simply smiled. "Try it tomorrow and find out," she had said. "You might be surprised."

But Cam didn't want to wait that long. He'd read the book, and he wanted to know. Now. As a result, here he was, alone in his own room, late at night after studying at the library. He had caught up with the rest of Light Squad in most scholarly pursuits, including basic knowledge about Ephemera.

But in practical usage, he was lacking.

There was only three and a half months to go until their mid-year tests, and he needed to get better. He needed to Enhance his Ephemera.

The others were figuring out how, and while none of them had climbed past Silver, it was only a matter of time. Jade thought she might break through to Gold in another couple of months. Avia and Pan were a few strides behind their most intense member, and who knew where Weld was. He refused to say, only smiling a smug grin whenever anyone asked.

Although hadn't Professor Grey frowned at Weld the other day when he had made some joke about how well he was doing? Maybe Weld wasn't as far along as he wanted everyone to think.

Cam shook off thoughts about his flatmate. Weld didn't matter. He was nothing but a malcontent and a braggart. Instead, he kept his eyes closed and Delved his Source, especially his Plasminia. There it was, flickering with lightning. It formed a circuit around the entirety of his Source, too fast to be anything but a blur.

He had to slow that down, and also fix his attention on his Source itself. It was still lumpy in shape; not the smooth globe said to power Sages. Cam wanted that, too. He wanted it all, and Professor Grey said every Enhancement to his Plasminia at every Stage would make that dream closer to reality.

But first he had to practice how. The book had provided some guidance, but Professor Grey didn't want him doing anything on his own. She wanted to be there when he made the attempt.

But Cam was impatient. He wanted to try this tonight. So, he studied his Plasminia, wondering about it. The book suggested several options on how to slow the Tang, each one vague and each one mentioning that it all started with *imagining* Plasminia forced to slow down.

Maybe if he pretended to dam up the Tang? Wouldn't that slow it some?

Having nothing else to lose, Cam imagined his hand dipping into his Source, blocking the Plasminia.

It must have done something because the lightning-flowing Tang bent around an invisible object, going up, down, and around it. Excited, Cam widened the imaginary block.

Immediately, his skull ached, like someone was beating on it from the inside out. He clutched his head, jaw tightening from the pain, letting go of the imaginary block. The pain receded in slow stages until all that was left was a dull throb. Minutes passed before even that was mostly gone, although a lingering echo of it remained.

When his head no longer ached, Cam reassessed what must have happened. The block had been too much. Plasminia couldn't come to a full stop. Doing so would cause the pain he'd just felt. A wetness formed on his upper lip, and a swipe revealed a yellow-tinged bloody fluid. It reeked like nothing Cam had ever smelled. More of it leaked out of his nostrils.

Seeing all that redness... Cam swayed from where he sat cross-legged on the ground. It had him light-headed. Moments passed before he felt steady enough to rise to his feet, all the while trying to hold the liquid back. It dripped through his fingers, threatening to get on his clothes. Frag! A quick rush to the bathroom, and just in time, he managed to lean over the sink, letting the liquid pour out.

He gagged on the rotten egg stench, running water over his face and cursing himself out. He had to be more careful. He might have done some serious hurt to himself like that. He really should have waited until the morning like Professor Grey had said. The leaking fluid—whatever it was—eventually slowed to a drip, and Cam pressed a washcloth to his nose. Again he gagged. The stink was so bad, but hopefully pressure would get it to stop.

He glanced at himself in the mirror, shocked at the splotchiness on his face. A bunch of small blood vessels had burst, and if he looked closely enough, the same held true for his sclera. Although, there it was harder to notice given their Novice-red color. Fresh cursing followed, and he hoped Pan didn't hear. Pan didn't like when he cursed.

With the washcloth still held to his nose, Cam shuffled through the common area of the quarters, headed back to his room. Figuring that was enough experimenting, he checked his Source, wanting to make sure he'd done nothing else to himself.

What he saw caused him to pull up short. His Plasminia had slowed, not markedly but enough for Cam to know it wasn't his wishings. Had his mad workings actually done some good?

Like a flicked on Ephemeral light, Cam realized then what the fluid from his nose meant. It was yellow bile, the excrement and foulness as his body was purified and better able to house Enhanced Plasminia. It was supposed to stink like a skunk marinated in rotten fish. And by Devesh, it sure had.

For a moment, Cam wondered if he should try again at blocking his Plasminia. Not entirely this time but just a bit, maybe leave a sieve for it to go through. The patient part of his mind warned against it, but the part that was wanting to get things done faster—the part that always believed that if a person wasn't first, they were last—urged him to take a chance.

In the end, he couldn't say no to progress. Plus, wasn't experimenting supposed to be some kind of important part of studying the world?

Whatever the case, Cam figured he'd best be off experimenting over a sink. If there was more of that yellow bile, he didn't want it fouling his bedroom. He returned to the bathroom, mouth curling in disgust at the lingering odor of the yellow bile. He wisely decided to disrobe. No reason to let that stink get on his clothes.

Once ready, he Delved his Source. There it was, and there was his Plasminia, still rotating like a top on fire, but definitely slowed some.

Should I really be doing this? It was a final cautioning note, but Cam answered by imagining his hands—no, a net with fine strands and openings settling in front of the Plasminia.

Again, his head swelled with pain, but not like before. This time, it was endurable, so Cam stuck with it, leaving the net in place. The pain built, but it wasn't nothing he couldn't handle.

Abruptly, Cam vomited. It was yellow-tinged blood, and the taste of it was worse than the smell. He gagged even while hurling up whatever he'd eaten that night. More vomiting followed, thankfully landing in the sink. There was more of the yellow bile leaking from his eyes, ears, and nose.

A reflexive feeling in his back passage had Cam snap his head up in alarm. *Oh, no!*

He raced to the toilet, dropping his drawers and landing on the seat just in time. A gross volcano exploded out of his back passage. His belly cramped. He sensed the yellow bile flowing even through his urine. His bladder emptied, but the yellow bile still poured from his nose, his mouth, his very pores.

Cam sat on the toilet, head hunched and miserable, promising to never again do what he'd just done. His head throbbed, and his entire body ached like someone had taken a shine to beating him with a stout stick. And then there was the stench… it was awful, lingering in his nose, his mouth. The yellow bile crusted his hair and skin in a foul layer.

"What is that disgusting smell?" Pan asked, standing at the doorway. He had his nose firmly pinched.

Weld leaned around the corner, peering over Pan's shoulder. "What the fragging hell did you do?"

"Yellow bile," Cam said, too tired to keep his head up.

"Just how much came out?" Pan asked.

"All of it." A beat later. "I think."

"Oof! What is that smell?" Jade asked, waving her hands in front of her face and wearing a look of absolute disgust.

Cam winced. The sun was shining. A puffy array of clouds filled the sky, and a gentle wind blew in from Nexus Lake. But all the breeze did was swirl the stink that had remained clinging to his skin like a smelly cloak. He had showered and showered and showered again last night, but it hadn't done enough. The stench of the yellow bile remained, and all night while sleeping on the floor—there was no chance he'd sleep on his bed with this kind of stink on him—he'd dreaded the morning to come.

Well, that morning was now, and as lovely as the day had dawned, as normal as the walk to his squad's first class of the morning should be—Kinesthia—everything was different. His eyes hurt from the sun's brightness, and his skin stung from the clothes he wore. Even the wind hurt. Same with his hearing, which ached whenever someone spoke. And Devesh, why did his sense of smell have to be as potent as a bloodhound's just now?

As a result of how he was feeling and smelling, Cam had skipped breakfast, joining the others when they were about to descend the stairs leading to the field where Kinesthia was held. He'd known the reaction his smell would cause, but that didn't make it any less embarrassing.

Avia pointed at him, her nostrils pinched shut, eyes slitted in a pained expression. "It's him. He smells like a dead sea lion rotting on a rock with decaying garbage dripping out of every orifice."

Cam did a double-take. That was quite the vivid picture.

Weld grinned like he had a secret to spill. He even seemed like he was going to throw an arm over Cam's shoulder but thought better of it at the last instant. "Our boy..." he pointed to Cam, "...decided to Enhance his Plasminia last night." He laughed. "He had yellow bile streaming off him like rivers of pus."

Another vivid picture.

"You didn't!" Avia said, sounding horrified. "What if you'd hurt yourself?"

Cam reddened, hoping no one would ask if he *had* hurt himself because the answer would have been yes. Right now, his head felt as stuffed as an overly-filled down pillow, and his balance was off. He could barely walk a straight line. Worse, while he'd managed to wash off the disgusting yellow bile, a lot of it must have remained on his skin, invisible but clearly present. He could certainly still smell it in his nostrils and on his breath. It was there with every whiff he took. Even his urine this morning had still carried yellow bile's stink.

"It isn't that bad," Pan said, trying to put on a good face. "At least he did Enhance his Plasminia."

Cam gave him a grateful smile. While Pan hadn't helped him clean up—he pitied his flatmates over the lingering stench in their bathroom—he had fetched him fresh clothing. As for Cam's small clothes from last night—he'd burned them. Just a quick Bonding to Spirairia, which had occurred more easily than ever before, and it was done. His first true use of that Tang.

"You did hurt yourself, though, didn't you," Jade accused. "You just wait until Professor Grey finds out, buddy boy."

Cam sighed. How did she know he'd hurt himself?

"Finds out what?" Saira asked when they arrived before her and Professor Shivein. She gagged an instant later, and Cam's sigh became a pained exhalation.

"Good Lord above," Professor Shivein declared. "Which one of you died?" He glared at the five members of Light Squad.

Cam raised his hand. "It was me, sir," he said. "I mean, I didn't die, but I'm the reason for the stink. I Enhanced my Plasminia. It's the yellow bile."

"And you didn't think to take a shower?" Professor Shivein asked.

"I took five of them, sir. But the smell won't go away."

"Well, stand downwind of us," Professor Shivein said, pointing vaguely at a direction and distance far away from the rest of the class. "And go take another shower as soon as we're done."

"Yes, sir," Cam said, drifting downwind of the others at a distance of twenty or so feet."

"Thank Devesh," Weld said with feeling. "I think my nose wanted to kick my ass."

Pan viewed him in confusion. "How would that even be possible?"

"It's a figure of speech," Weld explained.

"A dumb one," Jade replied.

"Enough chatter," Professor Shivein said. "I want to get through what we'll be doing over the next few months." His glare fell on Cam. "And as soon as we're done, I want you off to see Professor Grey. She might have a notion on how to rid you of your stench."

Cam wilted. It wasn't his fault he stank so much. Well, it was, but that didn't mean everyone had to give him such a hard time about it.

"It's time to start training for the mid-year testing," Saira said, speaking loudly enough for Cam to hear from where he stood. "All of you have come far enough that we can do so. There will be a martial exhibition, and you'll also be expected to lance a boil created by Lord Queriam. But even before all that, if you do well enough in your classes, there's a chance to receive a tonic created by your sponsors. It should lift you from Silver to Gold Enhancement in your Primary Tang. Earning the tonic, winning the martial exhibition, and lancing the boil should be your only focus from this point on."

Cam listened with half an ear. All of this he already knew. Instead, most of his attention was given over to Spirairia. He could Bond to it, but the flash of fire last night had been the first time he'd been able to truly use it. And it had happened without thought, coming instinctually. What about now? Why not test to see what he could do with it?

There was a small pebble by his foot. Could he move it? Professor Werm had them practicing doing something similar, over and over again. The others could already manage the trick, but not Cam. What about now, though?

He Bonded Spirairia, felt motions in the world, potentials for power, a line linking him to the pebble. A simple thought caused the small stone to tremble. A second later, it ceased moving, falling still. Cam frowned. It was close to what he wanted but not quite there. He refocused, and this time, when the pebble shook, it also rose off the ground, only a few inches before his concentration shattered.

"Cam Folde! Are you paying attention?" Professor Shivein roared.

Cam nearly jumped out of his skin, hastily firming his posture, chest out, shoulders square, arms locked to his sides. "Yes, sir," he hollered. He replayed what had most recently been spoken, grateful that he could recall it. "You were talking about the demonstration we'll be doing at mid-year. The dancing we'll do for our martial exhibition. You also said that the exhibition can include our instructors, and that Sai—I mean Professor Maharani will take part."

Professor Shivein grunted, a low-toned intonation that shook Cam's insides even from where he stood. "Well, I'm glad to hear the yellow bile didn't poison your hearing," Professor Shivein said. "Now, if you don't mind, get yourself gone to Professor Grey. Your reek is making my nose want to jump off my face and hide."

"Yes, sir." Cam hustled away from the field, praying that Professor Grey would have a way for him to get rid of the stink of yellow bile. Or at least mask it somehow.

"Oh, goodness," Professor Grey lurched away from Cam the moment he entered her classroom. "You Enhanced your Plasminia, didn't you?"

It was a statement rather than a question, but Cam nodded anyway. He couldn't make himself meet her gaze. How much he stank was mortifying. Everything about it. The walk here had felt like a slow-motion trudge of one foot after the other, each step an exercise in humiliation as everyone—and it really had been everyone—had pitched away from him the moment he got within sniffing range.

A flick of Professor Grey's eyes, and the door into her classroom shut. She must have done something else because a slight breeze started up. It cleared the air, removing the stench of Plasminia. Cam straightened from the hunched over pose he hadn't realized he'd been holding.

"How did you get rid of the stink?" he asked.

"I didn't," she replied. "It's still there, but the breeze is carrying it away. The only way to get it gone is to Enhance your Plasminia to Gold along with the Spirairia. Bonding to it and Kinesthia should let you cleanse your skin. I'll tell you how."

Cam didn't think to question her or ask her how she knew so much about his Primary Tang. So far, everything Professor Grey had told him had been the absolute truth. He reckoned this would also be the case. Which left him in a bit of a quandary. Enhancing Plasminia he could do—although he shuddered over the pain he'd have to carry and even more about the yellow bile he'd lose from all orifices—but Enhancing Spirairia was a different kettle of fish. He knew how it was done, but so far, he'd never had call to actually do it. All he knew was that Enhancing the Tang resulted in black bile. And given the stink of yellow bile, he had no want for another flavor to contaminate his body.

Professor Grey must have sensed his dislike for what she proposed.

"I'll teach you what you need to know in order to help with the biles."

"Will it stink as bad?"

"The black bile? No. It smells like mud."

"Mud? That's it?" That didn't sound so bad, and it also sounded monumentally unfair. "What about Synapsia and Kinesthia?"

"A swamp and iron."

Cam glowered. "So no one else is ever going to stink like me? Why does it have to be Plasminia that reeks so bad?"

Professor Grey's eyes went cold and distant. "Some decisions, I'm sure, weren't made without proper forethought." She shook off whatever weirdness she was pondering on. "Regardless, that's what you have to do. And you'll do it here. Start with Plasminia. Slow it to Gold, and then we'll work on condensing Spirairia."

Cam startled. "You expect me to raise both Plasminia and Spirairia to Gold before the rest of the class gets here?"

"All is Ephemera and Ephemera is All," Professor Grey replied. "The Tangs are just your mind's way of making sense of reality. It doesn't have to be the only means. Remember when you Imbibed your Accreted Ephemera? You let it transform into Plasminia and made it into what you needed?"

Cam nodded.

"Then think on that lesson while you work."

"Now?" Cam knew his voice had a whiny tone, but he couldn't help it. Doing this would be disgusting. Plus, for whatever reason, as beautiful and forceful as Professor Grey might be, she always seemed more like a motherly figure than anything else. And if anyone could listen to a grown man whine, it had to be a mother.

"Yes, now," Professor Grey said with a chuckle. "I'll watch and make sure you don't hurt yourself."

Cam sighed, seating himself on the ground, closing his eyes. He Delved his Source, seeing again how Plasminia was slower than before. It still raced, but more like a bunny's legs blurring rather than those of a centipede where one movement bled impossibly fast into another. Again, he imagined the fine net, placing it into the rotating flow of his Plasminia. He noticed something else then as well. His Source didn't have as much of a distorted appearance. It was rounder with a few bulges here and there, but smoother overall. He found himself grinning.

"Your Source is more like a proper globe, isn't it?" Professor Grey said.

Cam's concentration shattered, and with it his net dissolved. How did Professor Grey always know what he was thinking? He mentally shook his head. It was probably just another one of her bizarre quirks. He focused again on his Plasminia, on getting his net in place.

The lightning-laced Tang slowed the moment it hit the net, and a headache sprung up.

"Bond Kinesthia," Professor Grey said. "Strengthen your body. And relax the image slowing your Plasminia. Let the Tang flow through more easily."

Cam did as she instructed, and the pain lessened.

But he had no time to celebrate his accomplishment. Despite doing like the professor said, here came the stink of the yellow bile, pouring out of him, his eyes, ears, nose, and… His eyes flared open in panic. He hadn't thought this through. Just like last night, he had the sudden urge to go to the bathroom, ejecting the yellow bile from both directions. Same with his mouth. And the sensation showed no sign of letting up. He was about to make a huge and humiliating mistake.

"All is Ephemera and Ephemera is All." The professor's voice soothed him. "Use the yellow bile. Return it to your Source. Use it as fuel to condense your Spirairia. Pull on it. It will come back to you. Start with your tears. Imagine them rolling into the orbits of your eyes, re-entering your body, deep into your Source."

Cam kept his eyes shut and didn't bother talking. Talking meant he'd have to open his mouth, and if he did that, he'd vomit. Instead, he did as Professor Grey instructed. The imagination of what she described wasn't easy. The visions kept wanting to slip away, like greasy eels escaping his grasp. But Cam held fast, not letting them go. He had to do this, inspired to succeed by the pressure on his bladder and his back passage.

Pain built again, but this time it was in his muscles, deep in his bones, and still Cam persisted. Time passed—he didn't know how much—but in the end, he managed what Professor Grey wanted. His tears of yellow bile dried, re-entering his Source where Plasminia wanted to take it back. He relaxed then, feeling like he'd run up a mountain and rolled down the other side. Fatigue weighed him down, and his body was sore like a rotten tooth.

"Don't let that selfish Tang reincorporate the yellow bile," Professor Grey said. "Push it down into your Spirairia."

Cam gritted his teeth, letting go of his net. This time, he imagined gripping his Source tightly and pushing the yellow bile down lower. His mind held the imagining, and it seemed to work. Spirairia flared, the Tang a mite less gaseous.

Seconds later, he got another encouraging bit of news.

"Keep going," Professor Grey urged. "You're doing well. A few more hours, and you'll have finished with whatever yellow bile you've extruded. After that, I want you back at your flat. You'll need rest. Sleep the rest of the day, and then start it up again tomorrow morning. And this time, do it outside." Cam imagined the professor's lips twitching and her emerald eyes flashing with humor. "I'm sure your flatmates will appreciate that."

Cam still didn't dare reply. Instead, he kept at his task, which was as hard as a billet of steel and hurt like that same billet dropped on his fool head. More time passed, an hour at least. Longer actually since he finally had to stop when the other members of his squad knocked on the door and entered.

"He still stinks like roadkill," Weld observed.

"Worse than roadkill," Jade agreed. "Roadkill dead for a week."

That was Cam's signal to leave. He'd gotten most of the yellow bile used up. There was no more pressure anywhere, and best of all, not only was his Plasminia slower, his Spirairia was clearly denser, which explained the slick layer of black bile covering his skin. It meant he'd done it. And although he still stank—he knew he did—his accomplishment might mean great things for him in the future.

After Synapsia, when everyone else left for lunch, Pan stayed behind. He had questions.

"Did you need anything?" Professor Grey asked, noticing him still waiting in the classroom.

Pan cleared his throat. Professor Grey didn't scare him like she did Weld. Nor was he in awe of her like Avia. He appreciated the professor; her knowledge and clear kindness toward the Novices under her care, but he wasn't intimidated by her.

Well, maybe she intimidated him some… Or maybe even a lot.

Pan cleared his throat again. "I wanted to ask you about the book you gave Cam. The one on Plasminia. I had a chance to read it, and I have concerns."

Professor Grey lifted a single brow. "Oh?"

Pan cleared his throat a third time. "Yes, it's about the other Plasminians in history. It has me worried for Cam. It doesn't seem like the odds are in his favor."

Professor Grey blew out a breath. "I see. What exactly are you concerned about?"

Her voice was soothing, and so was her demeanor, but there was something to Professor Grey that had Pan nervous. "It's about those who used Plasminia as their Primary Tang. According to the book, they were all weak, just like everyone says. The book also says none of them Advanced to Acolyte. Does this mean there is a hard cap in how far Plasminians can Advance?"

"The short answer is no. There are no hard caps," Professor Grey said. "The likely reason for the lack of Advancement is because they didn't receive the proper teaching after forming their Plasminia Tangs. At least, that's the lesson I take from the text, especially since a few did manage to add Kinesthia Tangs and lived out normal lives. They were like Cam; lucky enough to receive the care and attention from someone who could properly help them."

"Why didn't those Sages who did those experiments know this?" It was something Pan had never understood.

"Because they weren't exactly kind and caring. They were torturers. They forced the creation of Plasminians simply out of curiosity and did grotesque experiments on them." The professor's Glory-hued eyes flashed. "Those Sages were rakshasas in everything but name."

Pan made a snarl of disgust. He hadn't known, and while he knew some so-called good people could act in ways to make even a rakshasa blush, it still shocked and horrified him.

"But even today, did you know that every few decades, there is some poor unfortunate who chooses Plasminia as their Primary Tang?" Professor Grey asked. "They die shortly thereafter, usually after only a few years. Cam was lucky in that regard."

She was speaking about Cam's diving of an Adept Stage Pathway and the gift given to him by Honor, the Awakened squirrel. Cam truly had been fortunate in coming across her, but until he'd read the book and speaking to Professor Grey just now, Pan hadn't realized just how fortunate.

"It's a shame, really," Professor Grey continued. "The only reason no one helps those other Plasminians is because they lack the resources and the knowledge." She cocked her head. "Was there anything else?"

There was. It was something Pan had often wondered about, and an entire chapter had even been devoted to it in the book. "What about those who formed Plasminia as a Secondary Tang?"

Only then, after he asked the question, did Pan realize how the information must have been obtained: the torture of more innocents. Generally, Pan was mild-mannered, but what those Sages had done made him see red. They deserved to burn.

An instant later, Pan came to himself, discovering Professor Grey holding his hand, staring at him in sympathy. "I know. I feel the same way. And I also know the deeper question you're meaning to ask. What is the purpose of Plasminia?"

She gave his hand a final squeeze, and it was as though she pushed the anger and anguish from him, leaving him calm.

"If nothing else," Professor Grey continued, "Plasminia allows a person to sense Ephemera even more acutely than a Spirairian. It's a powerful skill. And the reason that so few managed the trick in forming a Secondary Plasminia Tang—less than two in ten—is likely the same reason as I mentioned before: lack of knowledge, kindness, and knowledge."

Pan relaxed further on hearing her explanation. It meant that Cam was in good hands because if there was one thing Pan felt sure about Professor Grey, it's that she was knowledgeable, kind, and caring.

21

It took Cam a full week to finish Enhancing his Plasminia and Spirairia to Gold. It was a week where he wasn't allowed to attend any of his classes because none of his instructors and classmates could put up with his smell. No matter how well he managed to slow Plasminia and use the yellow bile to compress Spirairia, there was always a residual amount left on his skin. And he couldn't risk washing it off; not when he still needed it to finish his Enhancement. Even the smallest portion could be important.

What it meant was that Cam spent the week walking about with a nearly visible miasma floating around him, a stench that contaminated everything, including his flat. Nothing could cover it up. And even though Cam Enhanced outside, he still had to come inside to sleep. Then the reek would seep everywhere. Incense burned by the logs, fresh flowers on every table, and windows thrown open… none of it was enough. At some point, the stench seemed like to have penetrated the very walls.

It got so bad that Weld ended up moving out, which Cam took as a good thing. Pan, however, being a good friend, stayed. But how he managed to put up with the stink was a mystery.

Thankfully, there came a day when Cam's Plasminia and Spirairia reached Gold. It was a morning like any other, but in a flash, his Tangs changed. Both of them remained red, but now they each had a distinct golden undertone. On seeing the change, Cam had shouted in relieved joy.

Not only had he Enhanced two of his Tangs, but he could also finally get himself cleaned, just like how Professor Grey had told him. He Bonded Kinesthia to harden his skin. Next, he Bonded Spirairia, using it to scrape himself clean, collecting the last of his yellow bile at his feet and burning it. Five times he did it before even Pan couldn't smell the stink anymore. Cam went a sixth and seventh time just to be sure.

And when it was over, Cam's gratitude knew no bounds. He finally didn't stink any more. He could finally resume his classes, and the one he looked forward to the most was Synapsia with Professor Grey. He wanted to show her what he'd done.

She glanced at him when he walked in, lifted her nose like she was testing his smell, and smiled. "What took you so long?"

"I had a lot of Plasminia to Enhance," Cam answered.

"I see. When you Enhance it to Crystal, consider using the yellow bile to condense Synapsia and loosen Kinesthia."

Cam brightened. He'd have a Crystal Primary Tang and three Golds.

The same calculation seemed to have occurred to Jade. "Just what will he be able to do with three Gold Tangs and a Crystal one?" she asked.

"It's never been done, so your guess might be as good as mine," Professor Grey said.

"Well, he better be able to do something," Weld said. "As many classes as he's missed and as weak as he is all around, he needs every break he can get." He grinned. "We can't carry you forever."

Cam flashed the other man a look of irritation. "No one's ever carried me. I get by on my own work." He glanced at Pan, Avia, and Jade. "With some help from my friends."

"I'm not your friend then?" Weld asked, scowling.

"I didn't say that," Cam replied, although it was true. "But you haven't exactly tried to make yourself liked."

"What—"

"Argue about it on your own time," Professor Grey cut in. "Get to your tables. Today you'll play chess using timers. Set them at ten minutes. Avia will play against me. Go."

Cam and Pan shared a table and a chess set while Jade and Weld did the same.

"I think I've got you today," Cam said, grinning at Pan, who grinned back in his infectious way, eyes crinkled and mouth agape with pointy teeth showing.

"You'll never get me," Pan said. "I'm too fast. Like lightning."

Cam barked laughter. "We'll see about that."

They fell into the routine of the game, each one making moves after only a moment of thought and slapping the timer to close the hourglass marking their ten minutes. Back and forth it went, and Cam could see he was losing, down a pawn and having a weaker position for his master pieces.

But he hadn't yet lost. There was a way. There had to be.

He Bonded Synapsia, just like he knew Pan had likely been doing. And while he couldn't use the Tang as well as his friend could—Cam was still limited by his Plasminia—maybe today it would be enough. It seemed like it might. His awareness of the world had never been so great, and movements that should be a blur—the fluttering of the wings of a fly—slowed enough to be seen. Best of all, his thoughts came clearer and so did his ability to plan.

"You've lost," Jade said from a little distance away.

"Not yet, I haven't," Weld replied, peering intently at the board.

Cam glanced at the other two. Weld was only down a single pawn, but he was also three moves from checkmate. It was inevitable. He just didn't see it.

And until this morning, Cam wouldn't have either. He was better than Weld at most games of intellect, but he had nothing for Jade or Pan. Only against Avia could he come close to holding his own, and even then usually not. But the patterning of Jade and Weld's chessboard made sense today in a way he'd never before seen.

Cam returned his attention to his own game. There wasn't much time left on his Bond, and he needed to focus. A short while later, he saw a possible exit from the traps Pan had laid. He advanced a rook four spaces, supporting two pawns now.

Pan made no comment, simply stared at the board, frowning. It was only during these sorts of games that Pan's desire to win fully showed. Just as much as the rest of them, he hated to lose. He simply hid it better. Pan made his move, still frowning.

Cam still had his Synapsia Bonded. Seconds ticked by as he studied the board. The exit was still available. He moved, immediately slapping the timer. He had a little over four minutes left in the game, while Pan had a bit less. By then he also had to let go of Synapsia, but as soon as his two-minute cooldown ended, he engaged it again.

Five moves more they each made. Cam was on cooldown again from his Synapsia, but hopefully Pan would take most of the remaining time on his next move, and—

Pan's move came within seconds.

Cam cursed. He didn't know what to do. With his Synapsia locked away still, his mind moved like molasses. Pan's advance of a bishop disrupted Cam's plan, and he couldn't see what to do next. There was only a bit over a minute left on his timer, but Cam didn't panic. He could do this. His heart beat slow and steady with no sense of nerves, and he stared at the board, trying to unlock the pattern, to see if a way to victory still existed. He peered more closely. It looked like advancing his knight would get him a few moves closer. He did so.

Pan smiled at him. "You should have moved your bishop to where you moved your knight."

Cam Bonded Synapsia and immediately saw what Pan meant. Two moves and he would have had checkmate. As it was, in one move Pan would have the game. Cam tipped over his king, glowering over his mistake.

"You shouldn't feel bad," Pan said. "You did well."

Cam shrugged, not wanting his friend's attempt at making him feel better. What he wanted was to win. "Let's play again."

"So then Tern was running fast as a streak of grease," Cam said, wanting to make sure he got the timing of the story down. It wouldn't be as funny otherwise. "He was way ahead of us, completely winning the race." Now came the heart of the story, and he grinned, slowing the pace.

Light Squad was having supper after finishing off their classes. Cam had played Pan a couple more times in chess, and the next time he got a draw. The time after, with no more Bonds to Synapsia available to him, he got trounced as hard as a little brother mouthing off to his older siblings. Cam didn't mind. He'd held off Pan in one game and come close in another. It was progress by his way of measuring.

Afterward, the squad had headed down to the cafeteria for supper. The place was packed with all manner of folk, mostly students, but also a few more Advanced Masters; including a few Crowns, who usually had a retinue of hangers-on. Those last were easy to pick out. They stared awestruck at the Crowns, like they had hung the sun, the moon, and the stars. Stupid fools. Rukh and Jessira had done the hanging of the firmament.

Cam picked up the story again, figuring he'd paused long enough. "But then like an idiot, Tern looked back."

"Why did he look back?" Pan asked.

It was the perfect question, and Cam could have kissed the panda for asking it. "Because the jackhole wanted to make fun of us. And when he looked back, he never saw the pond he was running toward. It was covered with a layer of scum. You know what I mean?" Everyone at the table nodded. "Tern only had time to get off one squawk before he went down, like a bag of rocks." He laughed in remembrance.

"Why is that so funny?" Avia asked. "He fell into water. Isn't that a good thing?"

Cam leaned back in his chair, hands behind his head. "For a fish, sure."

"Not a fish," Avia said.

Cam ignored her comment. "And not if the water contains leeches, and not if one of them got a hankering for Tern's privates. Which one of them did. And once Tern realized what had happened, he screamed so loud, a flock of pigeons took flight, a hound dog bayed, and I bet folks could hear his shrieking from a mile away." He laughed hard, remembering the events like they were yesterday instead of ten years ago. It had been a fine day, the first day of their first year of schooling.

His humor dried into disappointment when he caught Avia and Jade staring at him in perplexion. Same with Pan. Only Weld laughed, which was worse than no one laughing. Cam didn't care if Weld thought the story funny. He'd wanted his friends to. "Guess you had to be there," he eventually allowed

"I had a friend do something like that once," Weld said, grinning and leaning forward like he had a big secret to tell.

Cam tried to hide his eyeroll. Of course Weld had a story just like his. He always did, and in his stories, the events were always twice as big, twice as bold, and twice as dangerous. Always wanting to show another person up was the kind of fellow Weld was.

But Cam held his tongue. He didn't want to start an argument at the end of such a good day. So he listened, nodding along, smiling, and waiting for Weld to get to the point when his friend or whoever it was did something grander than Tern. He even made a game of it, trying to figure on what would happen. Maybe Weld's friend—wait. No. It was Weld being chased, and Cam guessed it would be by a rakshasa or a pack of wolves.

He grinned to himself when Weld said it was a rakshasa. Now would come the fall or whatever, and Cam made a bet it would be some forgotten pit lined with spears and a nest of snakes at the bottom.

Nope. Just scorpions. No spears. But Weld's scream scared off all the critters, including the rakshasa and also caused an earthquake, which luckily smoothed out one wall of the pit. Amazing thing that.

Weld was able then to stroll on out of the pit.

Cam privately scoffed. What a load of bull. And based on their expression and silence, everyone else seemed to be thinking the same. Weld didn't see it. He never did. He just grinned proudly, looking like he'd claimed first place in some contest. Cam might have said something then, but he wanted their supper to stay civil, so he kept quiet even while inwardly mocking Weld's stupid story. Cam's at least had been true—other than the scream scaring off a flock of birds. Still and all, the shriek had been mighty loud and impressive, and he smiled inwardly at the memory.

His humor ended when he noticed Pan of all people glaring a hole at Weld. Cam viewed his friend in worried surprise. What was Pan fixing to do? Cause a fuss? He had plenty of reason to do so. Weld had done nothing but tease and mock Pan ever since coming into his life.

"You're lying," Pan declared at last. "None of that happened."

Weld's smug humor fled. "What did you say?" His voice came out low and harsh.

Cam tensed, ready to defend Pan if it was needed.

"I said, you're lying," Pan repeated. "You always tell these stories, right after someone else's, but yours are always an exaggerated version. I think you make them up."

Weld seemed to relax. "I don't know about that. Maybe you're just jealous because I'm living such an exciting life, while you… What's the most exciting thing you've done, panda? Hunt some bamboo?" He brayed like the jackass he was.

"I impressed the Wilde Sage," Pan answered quietly.

"So did I."

"And I earned my Novice Prime on my own. No one paid for tonics or put me in a place for it to happen."

Weld's face got ugly again. "And what have you done with all that you've impressed and earned? Landed in Squad Screwup?"

"So have you," Cam said, not wanting Weld's anger landing solely on Pan.

"Oh, ho. The Sage of Plasminia speaks," Weld mocked. "I lapped you in Kinesthia today, weakling. I dance better than you. I'm better with Spirairia."

"You're not smarter than me," Cam said. "And whatever advantage you have in Kinesthia and Spirairia, you're losing it. I'm gaining on you, and soon I'll be the one lapping you." He had no idea if that was true, but in the moment it sounded right.

Weld scoffed, leaning forward. "The day you lap me is the day I lick your yellow bile straight from the tap, doesn't matter from where."

Cam leaned just as far forward, refusing to back down. He stared Weld from inches away. "Then you best get to practice licking."

"Are you threatening me?"

"No need," Cam said, gaze still locked on Weld. "You're not as far ahead of me as you were, and we all know it. I might still be the least member of our squad, but Jade has passed you by in everything. So has Avia, and Pan's not far behind. You've gone slack in your studies, and if you don't get your head on straight, you'll be lucky to still be in Squad Screwup after the mid-year testing."

The statements came out harsh and guttural, but every word felt right, like they'd been building over all these months and just needed to come out. Cam watched as Weld fumed but said nothing. The other man glared, his jaw clenching.

"I don't need to listen to your bullshit." Weld dipped his head to the women. "Ladies."

With that, he stomped off.

"You think that was wise?" Avia asked, speaking into the worried silence left by Weld's departure. "Antagonizing him like that?"

Cam had no doubts that what he'd done was right. "It might not help Weld none—what I said—but he needed to hear it."

After the dust-up with Weld, the dinner conversation wound down pretty quick. Avia and Jade headed to their quarters a few minutes afterward, and so did Cam and Pan... following a few helpings more of the fixings, of course. They returned to the dormitory, which was relatively quiet. A few students were coming in while several others were going out, all of them conversing quietly. Softly lit Ephemeral lights illuminated the corridors.

Cam wondered where Weld was staying these days. He'd never bothered to learn.

"The flat doesn't smell any longer," Pan said in surprise, sniffing the air when they opened the door to their quarters.

"I left all the windows open," Cam said. "Nothing clears out a space like nature's goodness."

"Wise," Pan grunted. He waddled into the room, plopped to the ground, and started gnawing on a chunk of bamboo he had brought home from the dining hall.

Cam shook his head. Pan and his bamboo. It didn't seem like he could go ten minutes without chowing down on his favorite food.

While Pan crunched away, Cam went to the windows on the far end of the room and closed them before settling on the floor.

"I'm worried about Weld," Pan said around a mouthful of bamboo.

It was a feeling Cam shared. "He had to hear what we told him. I don't like his bragging, but he used to be able to back it up. He can't now, and it's going to lead to trouble for us."

"Us?"

Cam nodded. "We're a squad. Meaning we have to work together if we want to succeed, especially with our first test from Lord Queriam coming up next month. We're supposed to lance a make-believe boil and learn where we need to improve. But if Weld isn't up to snuff, we'll be so busy helping him out that we might not be able to see to our own weaknesses." He wasn't sure if what he was saying made sense, but Pan managed to figure it out.

"You're right," Pan said, shoulders slumping and looking disheartened. "We'll fail the test and not even know why. All because of Weld."

Cam pursed his lips. It wasn't entirely fair to blame everything on Weld. Easier, sure, but not fair. After all, what about Cam? Was he really good enough to stand with Pan, Avia, and Jade? Weld might be a weak link, but it didn't mean Cam wasn't one, too. He could break just as easily as any of them. In fact, more likely since he'd already broken once in his life. Given himself over to drinking, and that lingering desire had never really left him and likely, it never would.

"When it comes down to it, any of us can fail," Pan said, surprising Cam out of his morose thoughts. "I was sent from my home because of a prophecy written generations before I was born. It makes me feel like my only role in life is to enact that foretelling and not live for myself."

"That's not true," Cam immediately disagreed. He'd heard similar statements from Pan, but until tonight, he'd never said nothing about it. "You've got worth, and if you don't believe it yourself, then believe me. You're a good person—"

"Panda."

"Shut up. You're a good panda-person, you deserve happiness on your own terms."

Pan shrugged. "Maybe."

"Ain't no maybe about it. You're a good panda-person," Cam insisted. "But what's this got to do with you failing?"

"Nothing probably, but knowing you were sent out into the world like I was…"

"It makes a body doubt their worth, don't it?"

Pan nodded, looking solemn and sad. He had his flute in hand, fingering a mournful tune. It had been a while since Cam had heard Pan's playing, and it saddened him to hear his friend sounding out such a lonesome song.

"Well, I'll tell you now and I'll tell you again. You're worth a thousand of me," Cam proclaimed.

"And now you undervalue your worth," Pan said, using his flute to wag at Cam. "I've listened to you speak of yourself like you don't deserve anything but a bad fate. You think you're cursed. You say it like a joke, but inside, you're worried it's true." A wag of the flute. "It's not. You aren't a curse. What happened wasn't your fault, and you didn't cause it." Another wag. "Lay the blame for what happened to your friends at the feet of those who deserve the blame."

"Tern's momma blamed me," Cam said. "And I sometimes wonder if my own didn't leave on account of me. Did I need too much? Was that why she left?"

"She left because she wasn't fit to raise you. She abandoned you. She wasn't a good mother."

Everything Pan said was right, and Cam knew it. He just wished he could rid himself of that last niggle of uncertainty.

Pan sighed. "I wish you could see yourself as I see you. I wish you could see yourself as Avia and Jade do."

In the midst of his doubt, Cam's interest perked. He had some notion that Avia and Jade liked him well enough, but what did they actually feel about him? "What have they said?"

"They think what you've accomplished is amazing."

"Really?"

"Yes," Pan said with a nod. "We all think so, even Weld. You are a Plasminian, the first of your kind to reach the heights that you have."

"Some heights," Cam scoffed. "I'm a Novice. That's the lowest Stage of Awareness for anyone on the Way into Divinity."

"You're a Novice Prime," Pan corrected. "And be honest. What do you think your chances are of reaching Acolyte? Or Adept?"

Cam didn't want to say. Speaking his expectations felt like a surefire way to invoke karma. Then all his good fortune would be stolen in the flicker of a cat's tail.

"Cam?" Pan persisted.

"Pretty good," Cam growled, having to force the words out.

"Pretty good at which," Pan said, not letting the matter go.

Cam exhaled heavily, still nervous about saying the secret hope he had in his heart. "Pretty good at reaching Adept." He had a feeling he'd be able to make a pretty good stab at answering the questions that led to the bottlenecks in Advancement.

"Then believe you can. And when you do, remember this conversation as you rise to Glory. It can be done. You can do it, and when you do, you'll be the first Plasminian in history to have done so. The rest of us are Synapsians and Kinesthians. We're common, but you. You're unique. And I can't wait to see what you can manage, especially since Professor Grey says your true power will come when you Advance to the higher Stages of Awareness."

Cam heard the words, wanted to believe them, but it wasn't in him to think of himself as anything unique, interesting, and important.

But hadn't he already done all three?

With a lurching of his thoughts, Cam reconsidered Pan's words, recognized that his situation *was* unique, and that what he could achieve might also prove to be both interesting and important. And… He cut off that line of thinking. Karma lay in that direction.

"How about this?" Cam suggested. "I'll stop believing I might be a curse if you start believing that you deserve happiness and a chance to live for yourself."

Pan grinned his toothily infectious grin, his pointy canines visible. "You promise?"

"Promise."

"Then I will do so." He held out a hand, and Cam shook with him. "In this, we will be brothers."

A wave of emotion caught Cam off-guard, and he had to blink back watering eyes. "We already are brothers."

Pan pressed his forehead against Cam's, nodding solemnly. "Yes. We are."

22

Force of habit had Cam sniffing himself. It had been three weeks since he'd Enhanced his Plasminia, and he'd yet to stop checking on his odor. Better safe than sorry as he figured things. He also checked his pockets again, making sure he had his money bag on his person. It was the twelfth time he'd confirmed it, but he had to make sure. He wasn't used to having much coin, but by managing to last in the academy for as long as he had—half a semester; two and a half months—he'd also earned an extra stipend from Master Winder.

Saira had been the one to let him know, passing the money to him this afternoon, right after the two of them had practiced couples dancing. Over time, Cam had learned to overcome his nervousness about holding her, Jade, and Avia so close. He'd actually done pretty well this afternoon with nary a single fumble-footed misstep. The improvement in his co-ordination only went to prove that dancing helped train a person, teaching balance and form in a way different but necessary from martial exercises.

He couldn't wait to write home and tell everyone about it. Him. Cam Folde. Dancing with nobles. They'd be proud.

"Are you ready?" Pan asked, wearing his best breechcloth and harness.

Before answering, Cam gave himself a final look-see. He'd trimmed his shaggy beard to an even length and cut his mess of hair to nearly scalp short. Add in his white shirt, tan pants, and dark boots, all of which were his finest items, and he looked fairly presentable. A last look, and Cam nodded to Pan. "Ready."

They left their quarters, moving through a crowd of people in the building's hallways and foyer. Tomorrow was their first day off since the beginning of the school term, and everyone had the same goal in mind: a night out on the town. Weld was already gone—making himself scarce as soon as classes ended—but since Cam and Pan had each earned an extra stipend, they had decided to join Avia and Jade for dinner.

The other members of their squad were waiting for them out front.

"You look nice," Avia said to Cam, flicking her gaze up and down.

"Much better than usual," Jade agreed. "Handsome under that rat's nest."

Cam grinned. "Careful there. I might get to thinking you're flirting with me."

Avia chuckled. "There's no thinking about it. Jade's definitely flirting with you."

Jade laughed. "Only if flirting means teasing a friend."

Cam smiled in response. "Well then, one good turn deserves another. I think you both look lovely." It was true. Avia, with her pale coloring, was striking in her dark blue pants and shirt while Jade wore a blouse and skirt that fit her right fine.

"What about me?" Pan said in a whining tone.

Cam laughed, pulling his friend into a hug and kissing his forehead. "You're the loveliest, most handsome of all of us, young panda-person."

His comment earned him one of Pan's infectious grins, an expression that never failed to make Cam feel better about the world.

They headed out, exiting the academy, which Cam was shocked to realize he'd never done until just now. The bustling streets of Nexus were filled with folks going about; some simply heading home while others were probably traveling on important business. A late day sun cast angled light on the white buildings, leaving them glowing, and a breeze blew off Lake Nexus, bringing a heady mix of briny water, floral aromas, and the mouth-watering smells of seared meat.

Cam's stomach growled in agreement with his mouth. He was hungry. Then again, he was always hungry. All the exercise he endured had his appetite raging. He only hoped it wouldn't take all his money to feed his belly.

"Where's Weld?" Jade asked, peering about like she might see him hiding somewhere.

"He wasn't able to come with us tonight," Pan said, diplomatic as usual, although Weld didn't deserve it.

Cam couldn't help snort derision. "He's off drinking with his friends is what he said he was going to do." He knew his words made Weld look bad, but he couldn't find it in himself to care.

"Meaning we *aren't* his friends," Jade said, her features becoming intense.

Cam shifted, uncomfortable now with how he'd phrased things. He should have thought it through a bit better.

"With his drinking friends," Pan added, still the diplomat.

"I see," Jade said, although by the set of her features, she was likely still annoyed by Weld's absence.

"How did your dancing go with Professor Maharani?" Avia asked, thankfully changing the subject.

"You mean how'd it go on account of how I'm slower and less skilled at using my Tangs than all y'all?" Cam asked.

Avia blushed but nodded minutely.

"You don't have to worry about hurting my feelings," Cam said with a laugh. "I know my limitations better than most anyone. But in answer to your question, the dancing went fine. I doubt I'll ever have her grace, but you never know. At least I can keep up with her nowadays."

"Weld didn't seem very happy to see you two dancing together," Pan said, laughing with an evil chuckle—at least for him, even though he still came off as cute.

Cam smiled, recalling Weld's expression. "He never likes seeing Sai—I mean, Professor Maharani dancing with anyone else." Cam sent a grin toward Avia. "I noticed a certain Awakened was staring at us, too."

"Avia? Who was she staring at?" Pan asked, sounding honestly confused.

"Both of us," Cam said. "I think Avia appreciates beauty in whatever form."

"A few compliments and you think yourself beautiful?" Avia teased.

Cam shrugged. "I'm only repeating what people have told me."

"That you're beautiful?" Jade asked with an arch of her brow. "You wish you were, but at best you're handsome in an intimidating way."

Cam was about to disagree when Avia raised a hand, calling for silence. "Beauty and power are not bad things. As an orca, I like people who are intimidating."

"Is that why you like Professor Grey?" Jade asked.

Avia grinned, shivering in excitement. "She's the most intimidating person—human or otherwise—I've ever met."

"More intimidating than your father, the Sage-Duke of Saban?"

Avia seemed to reconsider. "Well, maybe not him."

It made sense. No Glory, no matter how interesting, was the equal of a Sage.

Cam's ponderings ended when they reached their destination, the Blind Pig, an inn and restaurant that Jade had chosen. While the eatings was supposed to be excellent and the prices reasonable, on first examination it didn't look like much. The restaurant portion looked to be a hole-in-the wall space, leaning on the downhill slope of a busy, cobblestone street and taking up the bottom floor of a narrow building. There was a small seating area inside and more tables and chairs outside with a couple of servers hustling about, carrying drink and food orders.

Again, Cam's mouth watered, this time for the alcohol he could smell. He desperately wanted a sip. But a sip would turn into a swig.

Then would come a number of shots, and he'd be lost.

Avia and Jade made to get a table, but Cam held them back. "I know it's a lot to ask, but do you mind not ordering anything stronger than water?"

They knew about the shame he carried and hadn't shown much judgment about it. He held his breath, hoping they still felt the same way.

They impressed him by simply nodding like it was of no account.

"Water it is," Jade promised.

It didn't take long for the waiter to get them seated outside, which was their preference. The night was warm but dry with the sun getting ready to set and a nice breeze swirling the air.

Cam shifted in his chair, nervous. The hole-in-the-wall exterior didn't do the Blind Pig justice. It was a fine restaurant, and Cam had never eaten in one before. He wasn't sure what to do. Fact was, he'd never eaten anywhere but at home, in the kitchen of some slop house where he'd picked up work during his long walk along Brewery Highway, or in the academy's cafeteria. What did folks do when they actually sat down at a place like this?

His answer came soon enough when a different waiter came by, asking what everyone wanted to drink. They all chose water, but what Cam appreciated was the fact that the man didn't bat an eye at Pan's presence, even though there weren't no other Awakened on staff or eating at the restaurant. It also turned out the first fellow who had seated them was actually someone called the host. It was strange, having one person fetch patrons to their table and another fetch the food.

Cam cast aside the oddities of rich folk when Avia wanted to hear more about how his dancing with Saira had gone.

"You really do call her Saira, don't you?" Avia asked.

Cam shrugged. It was how he thought of her, and he doubted that would ever change. "It's what she told us to call her in the Pathway."

"You're lucky she was there," Jade said. "What were you thinking? Entering a new Pathway without any training or equipment."

Cam shifted in his chair, not wanting to talk about it. From what he'd learned since, especially at the academy, he had a much better idea of just how stupid he and his friends had been. They were lucky all of them hadn't died. "We weren't thinking," he allowed. "We all wanted a different life, and we thought the Pathway would get us there."

"We've all got our private wants and haunts," Avia said.

"I know I do," Pan agreed. For once, his infectious smile was nowhere in evidence. "My purpose in life is to fulfill a prophecy that I'm not even allowed to know."

Irritation poured through Pan's voice, and Cam could empathize. The prophecy and what it meant had to burn like a wound. Add in the abandonment by his family, and the whole thing had to feel like a dagger to the gut. Even worse, from what Cam could suss out, Pan loved his family and seemed to think that only by enacting his prophecy would he earn back their love.

It wasn't true. Pan was worthy of love no matter what any prophecy said, and if his family couldn't see that, then they were the ones who weren't worthy.

Avia, curious about everyone and everything—mostly because she was a terrible gossip—had a few more questions for Pan, and afterward, it was Jade who told about her past. It was a strange kind of dinner to have; to go over their history in ways none of them had ever done in their near three months together.

It was fascinating, too, and sometime during their talking their meals arrived. Cam listened close to the others even as he stuffed his mouth, only vaguely noting how delicious was the fare. Any other time, and he'd have savored it and made embarrassing sounds of pleasure. But his mind was occupied by the stories being told as the members of his squad spoke about their lives before the academy.

"Your father *was* a Crown?" Pan asked Jade, who merely nodded.

A bitter scowl twisted her lips. "Was a Crown and now he's a Glory. After my mother and sisters died, he lost his understanding about what it means to be a Crown; his certainty about his purpose in life. He regressed from a Crown Prime to a mere Glory Greater. The family lost a lot of prestige when that happened."

"Is that why you work so hard?" Cam asked. He'd noticed it from the first day. Jade took notes, studied without quit, and worked relentlessly at mastering everything their instructors taught. They all did, but none of them had Jade's intensity. Cam hoped she didn't break under her self-imposed pressure.

Jade nodded in answer to his question. "I'm like Avia. We both need to succeed if we ever want to be happy. Me to restore my family's name and fortune, and her... for her own reasons."

It was a signal for Avia to share, and she seemed to acknowledge their silent urging. A sip of water first, though, and she spoke of her life in the ocean as an orca. It sounded happy, although Cam pulled away from her when Avia spoke of her joy in the hunt. Her eyes seemed to widen, grow darker with a predator's pleasure, as she described how she'd ambush a seal, the blood in the water... A moment later, she reddened in embarrassment. "Anyway, I Advanced to Novice right around then—my mother found me a bed of plankton steeped in Ephemera. It tasted awful, but at least it triggered the change. You know the rest afterward. I was sent away to live with Lord Vail, who adopted me and gifted me with this human form." She gestured to herself, her features flat, holding off repressed grief. "And Jade is right. I work as hard as I do because it's the only way to make the loss of my family and the ocean a worthwhile sacrifice. I'll never be a member of the pod again, but I can protect them as a Crown and even more as a Sage."

Cam mentally shook his head at the ambition of those in his squad. Pan to fulfill an ancient prophecy, and Jade and Avia who sought at a minimum to become Crowns. And what about him? What did he want?

The conversation died down, as each of the others seemed to withdraw into private places of sorrow and regret. But from a nearby restaurant on the other side of the street, Cam heard a familiar voice full of conceit.

It was Weld. He was seated with several young men and women, all of them hanging on his every word. "Everyone was watching, all the squads because I was holding my own against the Glory teaching our unit. But when I went to do a hip-toss, my ankle went out. I tried to hold on, but then it snapped. You saw me limping around a few months ago, right?" Nods met his question. "Well, that's why. And when my ankle broke, it sounded like a tree cracking." He shook his head as if trying to rid himself of a bad memory. "Everyone just stopped. They knew the injury was bad. But you know what I said to them?" His audience leaned in. "Get me some whiskey because if my ankle needs to be set, I'd rather be drunk." Roars of approval met his response.

Cam stared at Weld in astonishment. The bald-faced liar. That wasn't what had happened. Weld had been drunk and tripped over his own feet.

Just then Weld glanced over, catching sight of Cam listening in and rather than show the slightest remorse, he lifted a glass in a toast.

Cam bobbed his head in brief acknowledgement, doing his best to hide his contempt. He knew Weld wasn't someone trustworthy, but this… this was pathetic. The others in Light Squad hadn't noticed Weld, and Cam didn't want them to. He didn't want their happy night of sharing to turn into one where they talked about Weld. Thankfully, the other man and his crew left just then, heading off somewhere down an alley.

After Weld departed, Cam raised his glass of water in a toast to the rest of Light Squad. "I want to say some words. No matter how we ended up here, I'm glad it's the three of you who're in my squad. I don't think I could have come this far without you. To all of us and Light Squad!"

Jade grinned, raising her glass. Same with Avia and Pan, all of them smiling through their private pain. "To Light Squad!"

23

Cam stared at Pan in consternation when they got home that night. "You really want to study now? This late? When we have all day tomorrow to do it? Why not wait until then?"

He and Pan had just returned to their quarters after the evening out with Avia and Jade, and Cam was ready to call it a day. He'd plodded back to the dorm, weary from a long day and content with an evening spent with friends out dining. Even running across Weld again, this time on their way in, hadn't ruined his mood. Not much anyway. Not until Weld gave them his typical leer, proudly displaying a bottle of whiskey to Cam like it was a prize, and saying he was heading out once more and no one should expect to see him until tomorrow morning at the earliest. That's if Cam believed Weld's claims about his success with women, which he didn't.

"You don't think Avia and Jade will be studying?" Pan asked. "When we have only a month to go before Lord Queriam's test?"

Cam sighed. "They will." Which meant he and Pan should, too. It was the only way they could keep up with Avia and Jade. "Let's go do it then."

They gathered their belongings and hiked to the library, along a brick pathway lit by Ephemeral lights that shone down from tall, black posts. The academy was quiet for once with only a few others out and about. Trotting down to the Primary Level, they circled past the fountain of the Holy Servants and quickly approached their destination, the library.

It was a massive structure, square, blocky, and ivy-covered. Rising four stories, this late with the sun long since set, it was clothed in shadow, except for some lights shining out of various windows on each floor.

Cam and Pan reached a pair of doors made of glass and entered a simple foyer leading to an expansive room with a ceiling soaring to the second floor. Bright lights illuminated the space, which contained a number of tables and chairs, and beyond them were rows of shelves holding innumerable books and volumes categorized in a way Cam was only now starting to reckon. A dozen students were scattered around the room, some looking up when he and Pan entered.

Among their number, just like Pan had figured, were Avia and Jade, sharing a table and already studying. Cam feigned to not notice Pan's smug smile.

Pan nudged him. "Just admit I'm right, and I won't bring it up again."

"You're right," Cam said with a chuckle, not able to rouse any bit of annoyance toward Pan's I-told-you-so attitude.

They joined Avia and Jade, who glanced their way.

"Glad to see you studying," Jade said. "We all need to be cracking the books if we want to succeed at Lord Queriam's challenge. It's only a month away."

Cam scowled on thinking about her words. "We'd have a better chance at winning if Weld spent more time studying than he did carousing. He said he was heading out when we was heading in."

"I think he does study," Pan said. "There's no other way to explain how he can still do so well. For a while, I was catching up to him, but not anymore."

Cam paused in the midst of responding, considering Pan's

statements. What he said made sense. Weld was fitter and faster than anyone but Avia and the most effective member of Light Squad in his use of Spirairia. It was only with Synapsia that he trailed them, but he should be trailing them in all ways given how much time he declared that he spent as a lech.

Cam's anger stoked as he realized Weld had been playing him for a fool. All along, the snake had been working as hard as any of them, hiding it, though, pretending to have some amazing ability to learn and master his use of Ephemera based on a single instruction. And Cam had believed him, thinking Weld was some kind of genius, better than him and making him feel smaller because of it.

"Weld is the kind who feels best by making others think they're less than him," Avia said, agreeing with Pan.

Cam let the anger build, allowed it to crest for a few seconds before exhaling it out. He didn't need it. It wouldn't help him in his Way into Divinity. Weld could keep his petty lies. They didn't matter. Cam had his own work to do, and he best get to it.

He cracked open his folio, Weld already forgotten as he set to review the day's material. Before starting, though, his eyes misted as he thought of how proud his family must be to know where he was. Masters Bennett and Moltin, too. And as for those arrogant bastards who'd forced him from Traverse, they wouldn't know what to say. They'd have nothing *to* say.

But Cam would. He'd tell them to go bugger themselves. It wouldn't matter if a boil was about to burn their fragging homes.

His mind dancing on dreams of retribution against those who had done him wrong, Cam had trouble focusing. Minutes were wasted until he realized what the problem was. Revenge was a dish best served cold, but for Cam, it wasn't a dish he ever wanted to serve. In fact, he felt dirty just thinking on it, like it made him unworthy of his calling.

With a mental nod of agreement, Cam put aside his ugly fantasies. The studying came a whole lot easier then, and he was able to make some headway.

In the midst of it, he realized that Saira was seated a few tables over.

He'd never learned why she'd regressed in her Advancement, and he'd never figured out how to ask the question. It was likely deeply personal, but the curiosity burned inside him. But just as he considered going over and talking to her, a quartet of wealthy students whom he recognized ambled toward their table. Cam grimaced on seeing them.

At their head was Victory Arta, the young, disgustingly handsome son of Duke Dorieus Arta of Chalk, and striding next to him was Merit Thens, the blandly forgettable child of Sage-Duchess Marsula Thens of Santh. On Victory's other side was Charity Kazar, tall, prone to smiling, and about as beautiful and striking as Saira. She was also of noble lineage, and in her case as the daughter of Duke Ahktav Kazar of Maviro.

Cam didn't mind none of those three.

Instead, it was the final member who earned his grimace. Kahreen Sala, a short, pretty, and petty woman from a wealthy family in Bastion—the same duchy as Jade. Cam didn't like her any more than he would a flea-bitten dog sleeping in his bed. He'd never had a pleasant interaction with Kahreen Sala, and he likely never would.

Victory grinned at them. "How are y'all doing?" he asked, in a passable country accent. He must have been working on it.

Cam found his lips curling up. It was hard to dislike Victory. "I'm finer than a frog's hair. You?"

Victory guffawed, earning him a scolding look from one of the librarians. "Finer than a frog's hair? Tell me you just made that up."

"Love to, but from where I come, that's just the right thing to say to a question like that."

"It's the perfect thing," Merit added with a teasing smile.

"Country bumpkin is what you mean," Kahreen said, chuckling like she'd just said something clever. "Can someone tell me, why we are talking to Squad Screwup? We all know they aren't going to last the year."

"Because they're hoping to dump you off on us," Jade said, smiling sweetly at Kahreen and rising to her feet. "As poorly as you've done this semester, they don't want your stink getting on them."

Kahreen's face went hard. "What did you say, peasant?" she demanded, a red-shine gloss coating her body.

Cam gaped in shock, struggling to decipher what was happening. Kahreen had Bonded Kinesthia. If she used it against Jade, she could be expelled. He rose to his feet. "I'm sure it was all just a misunderstanding," he said to Kahreen, wanting her attention on him. "There's no reason to get expelled over this."

"I'm not afraid of losing my place here," Kahreen snapped.

"You should be," Cam said, lowering his voice. He reached for the only argument he figured might get inside Kahreen's way of thinking. "What do you think your chances are of marrying into high nobility wearing that kind of stain?"

His question must have broken through Kahreen's outrage because she deflated some, gazing at Victory, Merit, and Charity in hope and uncertainty.

"He's right," Charity said. "Let it go."

Kahreen's jaw clenched, worrying Cam that she'd do nothing of the kind. "I'll let it go, but I won't forget it."

Jade smirked, arms folded across her chest. "Any time you need a reminder—"

"Be quiet!" Cam snapped at her. He'd almost calmed the pot from a boil, and Jade was trying to simmer it up again.

"You watch yourself, peasant," Kahreen said, clearly wanting to get in the last word.

Before Jade could say anything, Charity took Kahreen by the arm and basically hauled her away, Merit following.

"I'm surprised you got her to back down," Victory said, staring at Cam in surprise. "Kahreen's temper usually gets the better of her."

Cam scowled at Jade. "So does Jade's."

"Only when it comes to people like Kahreen," Jade said.

Victory nodded his goodbye and headed after the others.

Cam exhaled in relief. "That could have gone a lot worse."

"You really need to learn to shut it around her," Avia said to Jade once Victory was gone.

Jade slumped in her seat. "I know, but something about that girl makes me want to punch her."

Cam knew what she was talking about. There were plenty of people back in Traverse he wouldn't mind punching.

"You did well," Saira said, coming to stand by their table and likely having overheard the entire conversation. "Keeping the peace is an important part of what Ephemeral Masters are meant to do."

Cam smiled, glad for her encouragement even as his curiosity from before got the best of him. "I was meaning to ask you something," he said. "It's about when we first met." The moment the words were out, he wanted to call them back. Now wasn't the time to go poking and prodding into Saira's private affairs.

But she didn't do anything but stare at him for a few seconds, her blue eyes, which had once been indigo-Haunted, seemingly peering into his heart. Cam forced his feet still, not wanting to shift under her scrutiny. "Walk with me," she said at last.

Cam cursed himself and his curiosity even as he followed Saira. He really shouldn't be doing this. It was none of his business why she had gone backwards in her Awareness. If she had wanted to tell him the reason, she would have done so.

"What did you want to talk about?" Saira asked when they reached a small alcove.

It was private enough, distant so no one could overhear their conversation, but plenty close for Cam to sight his friends. They watched him, uncertainty on their faces. He shared that uncertainty, and while a part of him considered asking some made-up question, he couldn't do it.

He wanted to know the truth about Saira because whatever had happened to her felt like it had something to do with him, like he'd somehow been responsible. The possibility ate at him, and he couldn't leave the situation be.

Before his courage failed, Cam spoke what was on his mind, the questions pouring out. "When we met, you were a Crown, and now you're a Glory. Was your regression because of me? Did something happen to you in that Pathway? Was I the reason?"

Saira didn't answer at once. "This is what you wanted to know?" she said after a moment, her eyes flashing, possibly in anger, the expression at odds with the placid expression on her face.

Cam wanted to apologize and slink away, but his courage held him upright and in place. "I've always felt like I might be the cause of your loss, so I figured maybe I could also help you Advance again."

Saira's eyes widened into a look of surprise. An instant later, she broke out in laughter, the humor fading only when she realized Cam didn't find the situation quite so funny. "You don't think it's somewhat silly or even arrogant for a Novice only three months or so into his training to think he can help someone Advance in Awareness from Glory to Crown?"

Silly was being kind, and Cam tucked his head in embarrassment even while a nugget of nerve kept him from turning tail. "It's silly, but that's also not a no. Can I help?"

"No. The Way into Divinity is a private road that we all must travel in order to find the deeper truths underneath this material we call reality." She plucked at her sleeve as if in demonstration. "It is a lesson my mother taught me when I won the victory that let me leave Sinane and in order to fight the rakshasas in the rest of Salvation."

This was new, and Cam made a note to ask Pan if he knew what kind of victory Saira might have won.

"She also told me that by leaving Sinane, I would always be unhappy with how limited my understanding would become. She said that in the rest of the world, people desire the fruits of their labor too devoutly to let go of the unreality of existence."

It was a heavier answer than Cam had expected, and he had no idea what any of it meant. He also didn't have a chance to think on it since Saira was still talking.

"My departure from Sinane was a disappointment for my mother, and I imagine I'm still a disappointment. I'll return when I'm a Sage, but she fears it will never happen. So do I. Those are my limitations, and if you can help me overcome what I know I've lost by leaving Sinane, and the loss of the unwavering certainty I once had in Rainen." She shrugged. "I'd welcome the assistance."

Cam blinked, overwhelmed by the information, especially Saira's loss of faith in Master Winder. It was the only statement that made sense in her flood of words. "What happened to Master Winder?"

He didn't think she'd answer at first since she glanced aside, staring at a window that reflected their images. Turning back to him, she spoke. "Master Winder is my master just as much as he is yours, and where he leads, I follow. So when we pulled you out of the Pathway five years ago and he said the only means for your survival was with Plasminia, I believed him. I helped him. I helped you. But I've come to wonder if we might have been wrong. If there might have been another way for you to live. Which would mean that the years you spent weak and eventually infected by your addiction to drink could have been avoided."

Cam heard what she was saying, and a part of him might have been angry at Master Winder, but what was done was done. More importantly, there was no way to know if the Wilde Sage might have been wrong. Cam was alive, and he had a chance at a life he could never have dreamed of having. It was enough. "Why are you telling me this?"

Saira smiled wanly. "Do you know how an Ephemeral Master Advances from Glory to Crown? They must understand when to hold fast to certainty and when to doubt. It isn't an easy Awareness to achieve, one of the two blockages that prevents the rise to Sage. I had it, but when we encountered you again, and I truly considered your situation. I lost it. I lost it because I lost certainty about what I thought I knew."

Cam stared at Saira, sifting her words, most of which he couldn't fathom, but there was one kernel he knew for truth. He *had* been the cause of Saira's regression. At least, his situation had been.

She must have seen the guilt on his face. "It wasn't your fault. It was no one's. I will regain my Awareness of certainty and doubt." Her lips quirked. "Of that, I have no doubt. Neither does Master Winder. He believes that by teaching at the academy it will soon be restored."

Cam hoped she was right. The fact was, he was a simple man, and he had no advice to give or even assurances to offer about such deep questions like certainty and doubt. It was beyond him. "I'm sorry," he said, not sure why he was apologizing.

"You don't have to be. Now go get some work done. Lord Queriam's test is in a month. I expect you to succeed. Good night." Saira paused just as she turned to leave. "I would prefer if you didn't speak on these matters to anyone. I'm a private person, but some of this touched on your life. It's the only reason I told you anything."

"My lips are sealed tighter than a bullock's buttocks during fly season."

Saira's tight-lipped expression transformed into one of amusement. "That sounds vaguely foul," she said with a soft chuckle.

She left him then, and Cam returned to where the others waited.

"What was that about?" Jade asked.

"I promised not to talk about it." He held up a hand to stop the deluge of protests ready to shoot his way. "Don't bother. I don't break my promises."

Over the next day, Cam couldn't get Saira's explanation of what happened to her out of his mind. She didn't blame him, and he didn't blame himself either, but he still felt guilty. It was strange, having emotions that made no sense. Or maybe it wasn't guilt he felt, but regret?

Cam couldn't rightly tell, but it wasn't until the afternoon class on Synapsia, that he was able to really focus on anything else. The weather was cool but sunny outside, and the windows closed up tight against a rattling wind. An autumn squall looked to be building on the horizon, but Cam's attention was on Professor Grey.

She had a new challenge for them this afternoon. Instead of playing games of intellect or solving math or linguistic problems, she had challenged them with a different sort of puzzle.

"You have ten Ephemeral Masters in your unit," Professor Grey said, "and you're facing fifteen rakshasas. How do you defeat them?"

"What rank are the rakshasas?" Jade asked.

"Novices. Both the rakshasas and your forces," Professor Grey answered, her green irises glowing brighter than the blue of her Glory's Haunt.

Avia had a hand raised like she always did, although Professor Grey never seemed to care if any of them did or not. "Where is the core located?"

"Unknown, but somewhere close," Professor Grey answered. "The rakshasas are defending it."

"What about the terrain?" Pan asked, sounding diffident like he usually did whenever he spoke to Professor Grey.

"A temperate forest full of hardwoods and dense brush."

Weld leaned back in his chair. "So, to sum it all up. We're outnumbered. We don't know where the core is, and there isn't any visibility." He sighed dramatically. "If we don't approach things right, we'll be buggered. Doubly so if we go into that forest. We have to draw the rakshasas out."

Jade and Avia were nodding in agreement, while Pan stared at his desk like he didn't want to venture an opinion.

Well, Cam did. Weld's summation wasn't complete, nor was his solution the only one available, especially since they hadn't yet learned all they needed to know.

Before he could say anything, though, Jade was talking. "Weld is right," she said. "If we enter the forest, the rakshasas will pick us off."

"What about if we sent scouts first?" Pan offered.

"That's actually a good idea, panda," Weld said, sounding condescending.

"Before we send scouts, what's our position in relation to the rakshasas?" Cam interjected.

"What do you mean?" Professor Grey asked.

"We can see the rakshasas since we know there are fifteen of them, but what kind of rakshasas are they? Do we have the high ground? Do we have clear line of sight to the rakshasas? How far away are they? Are we on foot or do we have horses? What kind of weapons do we possess? What weapons do the rakshasas have?"

Professor Grey offered a crooked grin. "Is that all you wish to know? How about asking how to defeat the rakshasas?"

Cam thrust his jaw out obstinately. "I'm not asking anything like that. Just some basic pieces of information. But I might have more I want to know afterward."

Professor Grey nodded. "You mistake my humor for mockery. It wasn't the case. I was happy to hear your questions. And in answer to them. The rakshasas are chimpanzees. Your forces are crouched on a rocky hill from a hundred yards away. You don't have horses or a clear line of sight. The rakshasas have bows, arrows, and spears. You have the same weapons along with swords. Is that enough information?"

Weld looked ready to say it was, but it wasn't.

"Not nearly," Cam said. "Can we guess the location of the core?"

"She said we didn't know," Weld said, sounding exasperated.

"I'm not asking for a location," Cam snapped back. "I'm asking if we can *guess* a location."

"You think it's in a clearing a couple hundred yards behind the chimpanzees," Professor Grey replied.

"Can we see it from our position?"

The professor hesitated. "We'll say you can."

"Well, if it's just a bunch of monkeys, we can charge them," Weld said. "Run right through them. Take them head on and get to the core and lance it."

"It might work," Avia mused with Jade nodding in agreement.

"I don't think it will," Pan said, speaking soft like he didn't want to call no attention to himself.

"Why wouldn't it, panda?" Weld challenged.

"He has a name," Cam said, irritated on Pan's behalf. "Maybe learn it. And he's also right. It won't work. Or at least, it might not. We need more information."

"What else do we need to know?" Weld asked, a frustrated whine to his voice.

"Are we fresh for the fight? Are we armored? Are the chimpanzees armored? Is there a heavy wind, or can we use our bows? What kind of lighting is there? Is it daytime or getting toward night?"

"You're fresh," Professor Grey answered. "It's morning. You're armored in leather. Same as your enemy. The wind isn't an issue."

"If it's bright, then we definitely don't charge," Cam said. "Chimpanzees are stronger than us, and we're only armored in leather. Their nails might get through. There's no reason to fight them on their terms, especially if they'll just scatter into the trees when we approach."

"Then what do you suggest?" Jade asked.

Before answering, Cam had a final question. "How good are we with our weapons? And do we all have Synapsia?"

Professor Grey's eyes seemed to flash in approval. "Proficient, and yes."

The answers Cam had hoped to hear. "Then we pepper them with arrows."

"From a hundred yards out," Avia said, sounding doubtful.

"Bows are only good to fifty yards or less," Weld added.

"For Neophytes," Cam said, irritated some that he was having to explain all this. It was so basic. "We're Novices. If we Bond Synapsia and Kinesthia, our accurate range is two hundred yards."

Weld looked like he wanted to argue, but then his thinking must have at last caught up with his mouth, and he clicked it shut. Cam's answer also seemed to flummox the others. Jade and Avia wore pensive expressions.

Same with Pan. "I would have never thought of that," he said to Cam, sounding impressed.

Avia grinned. "You're sneaky good at this; planning attacks, I mean. Well done."

Cam did his best not to preen under their approval. He only knew the questions to ask because of all the readings he'd done with Master

Moltin about military-type stories.

"Agreed. It is well done," Professor Grey said. "But the battle isn't over. While your plan would have substantially thinned the enemy numbers, what happens next?"

"Charge?" Weld said, his tone hesitant and weak.

Cam didn't answer at once, slowly piecing together what he would want to do afterward. "Instead of charging, we could send in half of our warriors while the other half remain outside the treeline. The ones rushing in could draw out the chimpanzees where the archers could cut them down."

"Excellent," Professor Grey said, and there was no mistaking her approval this time. "Everyone take note. Charging straight ahead is usually the choice of last resort. Better to plan a way to victory that minimizes your own losses and maximizes those of the enemy."

24

The next month passed by as swift as a dog chasing a rabbit, and here it was now, Lord Queriam's assessment. Cam stood with the rest of Light Squad. They had descended a long staircase that took them dozens of feet below the lowest-tiered seating in the arena, reaching the floor of the coliseum. Cam stared about like a country boy who'd never before seen a girl.

This was his first time at the massive arena, and he gazed about in wonder. The coliseum's seating rose in tiers of staggered benches—empty now but sure to be full during the actual mid-year testing. An ivy-covered wall, massive in height, marked off the acres-large pitch with tall grass swaying under a billowing wind that signaled a coming cold snap and winter's eventual coolness. Above it all loomed a gray, gloomy sky.

Cam hoped the dismal weather wasn't some kind of prognostication about Light Squad's chances today. He wanted to win this challenge. He wanted Light Squad to win.

His gaze went back to the pitch, figuring on how the assessment would happen. It was only then that he finally figured on why the arena was structured the way it was. By having the pitch well below the seating, everyone in attendance could easily view what has happening atop even the tallest hills.

Regardless, on the far side of the gigantic field lay a set of low-lying hills, grass covered and steeply sided with narrow ravines separating them and moss-covered boulders protruding from their shoulders. On quick scan, it looked there was only one passable way through to whatever was on the other side. Cam guessed it would be the boil's core, and Light Squad would have to find a way to climb those hills and lance it.

It wouldn't be an easy trek, fighting up that single ravine. The defenders would have all the advantages. They wouldn't have to lug Light Squad's shields, short swords, and spears up a hard incline. They could just sit there, comfortable and in control of the heights, firing off arrows at any attacking force. It would be a massacre to take that route.

But what other option was there? Cam tried to see a way forward, but none came to him. He wracked his mind, imagining one plan after another, disregarding them as soon as they appeared. None of them would work, and eventually, he exhaled in frustration. There had to be a way through. He just wasn't seeing it.

Cam Bonded Synapsia, got his thoughts running quicker, and stared with fresh eyes at the hills, hoping for the insight that had previously eluded him. Again, he examined the terrain, explored possibilities, kept at it until he lost the Bond. Again, he sighed.

At least no one else was about. The other squads would have to handle this challenge in their own time. None of them would be allowed to take notes or see how anyone else fared first. It was supposed to be a blind test. But those other squads were sponsored by their duchies, the children of wealth and privilege, and the information they needed would almost certainly be passed on to them by their private instructors.

No matter. Light Squad would overcome this test. Someone in his unit would solve the puzzle of those hills. They had to.

That's what Cam tried telling himself even as butterflies fluttered in his stomach. He shivered, nervous as a long-tailed cat in a roomful of rocking chairs because what had him especially anxious was that Light

Squad didn't have a true leader.

Avia, Jade, and Weld still fought over that title, and Cam could understand why. They were the most skilled and powerful members of the unit, but in the end, their squabbling worked against their team. Light Squad lacked direction and focus, and it was largely because Avia, Jade, and Weld weren't the leaders they needed.

Cam figured he might be able to take on that role. He could often see what needed doing. There were plenty of times during their practices when he figured out what the others had missed, but it took a fair bit of wrangling to get them to follow his lead. Over the past few weeks, they'd finally started listening, and Cam hoped it would be the same today.

He turned his attention to the other members of Light Squad. Pan and Avia stared about wide-eyed while Jade seemed curious and eager. Weld, on the other hand, pretended to be bored. But based on how his eyes kept flicking about, he was just as excited as everyone else about being here.

Cam snorted in annoyance. *Poseur.*

Ever since finding out Weld worked nearly as hard as any of them—even if he pretended he didn't—it was still depressing how easily skills came to him. For Weld, it was basically hear it once, practice it twice, and then there was mastery...

Perhaps it wasn't quite so simple, but it sure felt that way to Cam who had to struggle for every scrap of ability.

Fragging Plasminia. Why couldn't he have been a Synapsian? Or even a Kinesthian?

Cam shook off his irritation and wants. It was pointless to wish for them. Like his daddy used to tell him, if wishes were leaves, he'd be under a bare-naked tree, drunk out of his mind.

Instead, he focused on his breathing, setting aside all burdens. The assessment would soon start, and he aimed to be fit and ready.

Minutes later, their professors and Lord Queriam arrived. At a gesture from the Crown, Light Squad approached. Cam noticed the instructors wore placid expressions, but Professor Shivein and Saira seemed to have some nerves going on. Same with Professor Werm. The only one who seemed as calm as a winter lake was Professor Grey. She could have been strolling through a garden for how even-keeled she appeared.

As for Lord Queriam, he had his hands clasped behind his back and seemed bored. What was going on in that mind of his? What did he have planned for this test? Lord Queriam was the one in charge of creating the false boil. As a Crown, only he had the necessary Awareness to make it so.

For a moment, Cam wondered what it must be like to wield so much power. Flight, telepathy, telekinesis, a nearly indestructible body… Could a person like that even relate to a nobody like him?

Cam's eyes drifted to Saira. She had been a Crown once, and because of his presence in her life, she had lost that Advancement, and while she didn't blame him, Cam felt like she should. She'd gone from having Lord Queriam's Grace to teaching Novices.

Lord Queriam cleared his throat, roping in their attention. "The boil I shall simulate will be on the far side of these hills." Cam smiled to himself, glad to have guessed correctly. "The defenders will be lower-level rakshasas, a mix of humans and Awakened Beasts of Novice Stage like yourselves. You have your weapons and your shields, and so will your opponents. Be quick about the task for you have thirty minutes to succeed or fail. Are there any questions?"

Headshakes from the others, but Cam had some. "How many defenders are there?"

Lord Queriam answered. "Ten."

"Do we know their spacing? Are they all hiding along that one path into their hills?"

"That's an issue you'll have to learn on your own." The lord's answer was curt, and his patience appeared thin.

Still, Cam had more questions. "Is the entire coliseum in play?"

Lord Queriam exhaled as if in frustration. "No. You can't climb into the seating and come in from behind the hills."

"But can we climb the seating at all?"

Lord Queriam stared at him, hard-like, and Cam tried not to fidget. "I don't know why you would bother, but fine. You can climb the seating, but your approach *must* be from directly in front of the hills."

It was the answer Cam had expected to hear, but there was a possibility in there, too. "Yes, sir," Cam replied.

"If there are no more questions…" Cam kept silent, not missing Lord Queriam viewing him with a clear expression of *shut up*. "Then your assessment begins… Now."

"There's only one path forward," Avia said as soon as the instructors left the pitch.

Weld was nodding. "If we go with shields up, we can defend from arrows."

"And that's probably the worst they'll have," Jade agreed. "They're Novices. They can't touch us with Spirairia from any kind of distance."

Cam had stepped back while the others argued, still gazing at the hills, pondering a notion.

Pan moved to stand next to him. "What are you thinking?"

"A way to win." And that couldn't be a straight ahead charge uphill with no idea of where the enemy was or what they could do. There had to be a better way. Cam stepped into the argument between Avia, Jade, and Weld. "We need to know how the rakshasas are deployed."

Weld scoffed. "How are we supposed to figure that? They're on the heights, hidden behind rocks."

Cam smiled at him. "We get to a higher height." He called out orders. "Pan. Avia. Climb back up. Get to the seating. To a place higher than the hills. Locate the rakshasas."

"That's… actually a good idea," Avia said, seeming impressed.

Cam caught Jade viewing him the same way, but other issues occupied his mind. He continued to stare at the hills, frowning, judging. Once Pan and Avia could tell them how the rakshasas were spread, only then could they plan their attack.

"It won't matter," Weld said after Pan and Avia left. "Knowing how the rakshasas are fielded. We still have to fight them while they've got the high ground."

Weld was right, but it didn't mean they shouldn't suss out some other line of attack. Cam continued to study the terrain. All the hills were steep except for that one path, but a person with enough strength could... Excitement built. Yes. That might work, but it would depend on how the rakshasas were positioned.

Moments later, Avia and Pan returned.

"Four rakshasas on each side of the path," Pan said. "All of them with arrows and spears."

"The final two are back with the core," Avia added. "None of them have shields. They're all lightly armored."

It was better news than Cam had expected, but only if Light Squad could exploit it. "They're all facing downhill, toward where we are now?" he asked. "They ain't looking in any other direction?"

"I don't think so," Pan said.

Jade scowled. "Why are you so interested in where the rakshasas are looking? We already know where they are, and we still have to charge their location."

Cam didn't bother answering her. Instead, he pointed out what he'd seen. "See that shelf branching off the main path? It's thin, but it goes all the way over to that ridge. If some of us get over and up there, they'll have clear line of sight at the rakshasas, and this time, we'll have the high ground."

"It won't work," Weld said, his tone doubtful, but at least for once he didn't sound like he already had all the answers. "The rakshasas will see what we're doing."

Cam shook his head in disagreement. "Not if they're focused on the ones attacking." He pointed again. "Plus, there's an overhang above the shelf most of the way. It should keep whoever is going hidden."

Weld grunted, staring at the area in question. "You might be right."

"Yes, but it still leaves a question," Jade said, looking like she'd bit into a lemon. Cam guessed she just didn't like that it was his plan they seemed about to follow instead of hers. Well, too bad for her. She needed to think better from now on. "Who is actually going to use that ledge."

"Our best climbers," Cam answered. "You and Weld. The rest of us will keep the rakshasas focused on us. Once you get to the top of the ridge, if it ain't a far shot to the core and them last two rakshasas, kill them and then kill the core. Otherwise, pepper the ones pinning us down."

Weld flashed Cam an unexpected grin. "Well look at you, taking charge." He snorted, laughing a little. "Only makes sense I suppose, you being the runt of the litter and all. Who else would be in charge of leading Squad Screwup."

"Light Squad," Pan corrected. "Squad Screwup may be what others call us, but we shouldn't do the same. We should name ourselves after what we want to believe is best. And I say our best is Light Squad. We'll bring light to the darkness and destroy boils that threaten our people."

Weld rolled his eyes, but in the end, he didn't deny Pan's sentiment.

"Just don't take too long," Avia said to Jade and Weld. "It's a good plan, but we don't have hours to see it done."

"We'll kill them all," Weld said, all confidence again. "Fact, we might even have a nice picnic laid out for you by the time you reach the top."

"It's bad karma; talking like we've already won," Jade warned, an opinion Cam shared.

For once, Weld took her chiding in stride, not snapping at her or making a cocky comment.

Cam had a few final orders. "We'll circle in from opposite sides toward that path," he said. "Split their attention. Rush in hard, shields up. We don't want to lose anyone to a stray arrow before we reach the hills."

This time, no one questioned him. They all just nodded like what he'd said was right and sensible, which it was.

Still, it was odd having the strongest members of the unit listening to his call. Cam liked it. He liked being of use. Now it was time to show Light Squad why they should keep on listening. "Move out. Jade and Weld to the left. The rest of us to the right. Go!"

Light Squad rushed toward the path, wooden shields above their heads. It made for an awkward run, but Cam was glad they did so. Arrows fell around them, poorly aimed, but a couple thunked into their shields.

Soon, they reached the base of the hill. Weld was about to ascend, but Cam held him back. "Wait." He stared upward, tracing a path. There was protection from the rock faces that jutted out. It would guard against arrows, but only if they moved swiftly and in proper pairs.

He quickly explained what he wanted, receiving nods.

"You have twenty minutes left," Lord Queriam shouted.

Plenty of time. "Weld and Jade," Cam barked. "You're up. Then Pan and Avia. I'll bring up the rear."

Weld grinned. "That's about where runts belong; behind their betters."

Cam scowled. Even if there wasn't anything mean in Weld's tone or features, he wasn't in the mood to listen to the man's jibes. "Shut up and move out."

No one argued. Everyone simply launched themselves up the trail like they were supposed to. Cam shook his head in wonder. Was this what it was like to be a Sage? To have everyone do as a person said without any back talk? He could get used to that.

Cam rested under an overhang, panting like a dog in heat. His pulse pounded in his ears, but a minute of rest, and he'd be good to go. All those months training under Professor Shivein and Saira had paid off. He had ascended the hill, keeping up with the others, dodging, holding a heavy shield over his head, and staying turtled as he crab walked upwards.

In fact, they'd all made it. None of them even taking a nick. The next part of their plan was already underway, too. Jade and Weld were racing toward the ridge overlooking the enemy forces, and as he waited on them, Cam crouched low and glanced down the trail.

He could see the length of the pitch, to a shaded box where the instructors watched. Meanwhile, uphill of Light Squad were the rakshasas, a mix of humans and Awakened foxes. They had arrows at the ready, but were thankfully terrible shots, usually missing by yards.

Better yet, since the rakshasas had their attention stuck on him, Avia, and Pan, Cam reckoned a shift in tactics worth the risk. He gestured Avia over. "The rakshasas ain't looked once at Jade and Weld," he told her. "Follow them. Pan and I will keep their attention."

She gave him a doubtful look. "You sure?"

"Sure enough. Go. Catch up to Jade and Weld. Kill any rakshasas you see." He offered a grin. "Unless you feel like saving some for me and Pan."

Avia ventured a quick smile before timing the arrows and moving to the shelf. Cam watched her inch along the lip of stone, chest and legs pressed against the stony hill as she shuffled sideways. A bend in the rise, and she was lost to his vision. In the meantime, Pan had continued to hold the rakshasas' focus, darting his head out from behind where he hid, firing arrows in return.

Cam got back into the flow of events as well, doing the same as Pan. They kept their little game of peekaboo going.

But shortly, a vague tingling broke into his satisfaction. Something was off. But what? Cam frowned. He needed to think better. He Bonded Synapsia, and the increased clarity of thought cleared his mind. He recognized what was missing.

The rakshasas weren't shooting enough arrows.

Cam peeked around the overhang, knowing he'd draw fire. He just had to hope the rakshasas wouldn't get lucky. They didn't, and staring upward, Cam realized what had him troubled. There were only four rakshasas shooting at him and Pan. Only the Awakened foxes. None of the humans were visible.

Cam's eyes widened in alarm as realization swept over him. The humans must have sighted Jade and Weld, possibly Avia, and were off ambushing them. The others would be mowed down unless he and Pan defeated the Awakened foxes.

A particularly close arrow had him ducking behind the overhang even as he evaluated a new plan. He signaled to Pan, telling him of the change. "Switch positions with me. I need you to draw their fire. Just keep your head out where they can see it. When they look to shoot at you, I'll take them down."

"You can do that?"

"I can," Cam said. He was the best archer in their squad. "But I don't know how long my Synapsia will last, so we best be quick." Cam peered out, drawing a couple of bolts. "Go!"

He and Pan switched places on the trail. Cam now hunched behind a low-lying boulder that gave some protection against the rakshasas. But a lucky shot could still take him out since he wouldn't be able to use a shield. *Please don't let the rakshasas improve their aim.*

Pan ducked out from behind the overhang and the rakshasas sighted on him. Cam marked two of their numbers. He had a clear line on them.

A deeper Bond to Synapsia than usual allowed him to focus like never before. A foxlike rakshasa, upright and small with a red tail, swelled in his vision. It was almost like he could reach out and touch the creature. Cam added a Bond to Kinesthia, straining under the twin uses of Ephemera. A headache was building, but there wasn't no time to worry on it. His better balance let him nock an arrow, draw it full, and release.

The rakshasa cried out, vanishing in a scintillation of light and ringing chimes.

Cam was already moving to the next Awakened fox who'd stuck his nose out a mite too far. An instant later, this one also went up in an explosion of light and tinkling sound. Cam drew attention from the two remaining rakshasas. A few arrows clattered against his boulder. Close, but it also left the rakshasas vulnerable. Cam had an arrow at the ready. Release. A shout and ringing of chimes. Best he'd ever done with a bow. Nock, aim, and release. A cry of pain from the final rakshasa, but nothing else. No chimes.

Good enough.

Cam had taken the rakshasa in the right shoulder. The creature wouldn't be firing arrows at them. "Come on," he urged Pan.

Pan lumbered out from behind the overhang, and together, they sprinted up the hill. Cam kept his Bonds, tracing the quickest path, knew exactly where to place his feet. He rushed the slope, quicker than Pan. A split second to kill the rakshasa he'd earlier injured.

"You have five minutes left!" Lord Queriam shouted.

Cam disregarded the warning. He had to crest the hill. Jade, Weld, and Avia could already be dead. It might only be him and Pan. *Fifteen feet to the peak.* Synapsia brought it into tight focus. Cam's mind worked swiftly, half again as fast as normal, planning. Ten feet. Heart crescendoing. Breathing heavy. Fatigue wanting to weigh him down, but he didn't let it. Couldn't let it. Only winning counted. *Five feet.*

Cam summited the hill, and his gaze immediately went to where he expected to see Jade and Weld. Just as he feared, they were pinned down by the four human rakshasas and a pair of Awakened foxes. The last two must have been the ones next to the core.

Pan reached his side, mouth open and heaving hard.

"Take out the rakshasas to the left," Cam told him, the plan having formed during their ascent. "I'll take the ones to the right."

Pan sketched a hasty nod.

Cam already had his bow ready. Synapsia was still with him, but it couldn't be for much longer. Nock, aim, release. A rakshasa died. Another one was spinning around.

He might as well have been moving in mud. Nock, aim, release. The rakshasa was down. One more to go.

Pan, on the other hand, struggled with the rakshasas to the left, all three of whom were still in the fight.

Cam prepared to help him. With an abruptness that felt like his head had rammed into a wall, the clarity and quickness of his thinking was gone. His Synapsia was gone. A headache vise-gripped his skull, graying his vision. Cam fell to a knee, nauseated. Distantly, he noted Pan holler in triumph. The ringing of chimes told the story of his friend's success.

A moment later, a leaden weight pressed on Cam as he lost Kinesthia. A wet blanket might have been draped over his body. He couldn't move. Breathing was a challenge. And he gazed in incomprehension at his shoulder. An arrow bloomed there. Blood leaked in a river down his torso. *His shoulder!* The pain of it. Cam went to clasp the arrow, yank it free.

His strength left him, and he fell over on his side. He saw nothing but the stony ground. Dirt and pebbles pressed against his cheek. Somewhere Pan was shouting. None of it mattered. Cam wanted to sleep a bit. He closed his eyes.

Cam awoke with a start, sitting up, shocked and fearful. Where? A hand went to his shoulder. The test. Getting shot. It wasn't real, but it had hurt bad enough to feel like it was. And the shadow of it remained, slowly fading. Strength returned, and Cam rose to his feet.

He glanced around. He was on the pitch again, but this time there were no hills, and the coliseum floor was nearly level with the lowest-tier seating. Jade, Weld, and Avia celebrated in jubilation while Pan peered at him, concern on his face.

"What happened?" Cam asked.

Pan's relief was like the dawn. "You took an arrow to the shoulder," he said, "but your distraction gave Avia, Weld, and Jade the time to take out the final three rakshasas." He grinned. "Then it was just a stroll to lance the core."

"We won?" Cam asked in disbelief.

His attention went to Lord Queriam, who wore his usual impassive expression while the professors appeared relieved.

"Congratulations on your victory," Lord Queriam said. "A close-fought win. I expect your instructors will want after action reports from each of you. Learn from this. The challenge wasn't meant to be so difficult."

Cam couldn't seem to get his mind to work, but that last statement roused his attention. He shared a wondering look with Pan. The assessment wasn't supposed to be hard?

25

Cam shifted in his chair, nervous and uncomfortable. He and the rest of Light Squad were gathered in their classroom for Synapsia, and they all looked like he felt. It was in contradiction to the happy, warm sunshine pouring down since the brightness didn't touch Cam's heart. He was worried.

Hours ago, Light Squad had completed their first assessment, lancing a boil created by Lord Queriam, and right after, they'd composed their after-action reports. Professor Grey currently sat at her desk and was reading what they'd written. Cam wondered how she'd react. The plan had been of his devising, so whatever mistakes they had made were because of his lack of foresight.

One that immediately jumped to mind was sending Avia, Jade, and Weld along that shelf of rock. Instead, if they'd held their position near the overhang, the five of them could have picked off their enemies given how the rakshasas couldn't hit the side of a barn from five feet away. If nothing else, it would have been a safer plan.

Professor Grey set aside the last of the reports, arranging them neatly before addressing them. "First, let me congratulate you. Your victory wasn't as simple as Lord Queriam would have you believe. In addition, his decision to make the rakshasas barely functional when it comes to archery isn't a situation you're ever likely to face. And finally, while there was no risk of death to you, there was danger."

Cam grimaced. He still remembered the pain of being shot.

"So, the decision to skirt that lip of stone and gain the high ground was a smart one. It was safer than simply charging uphill. Even with suppression fire from your allies, those exposed could have taken heavy casualties. Indeed, the other path was safer, and yet, it somehow failed. Why is that?" She tapped the papers in front of her. "None of you make mention of it in your after-action reports."

Cam didn't know what she was talking about, and he looked to Weld and Jade, who wouldn't meet his gaze. He frowned upon seeing their reaction. What had happened when they reached the top of the ridge?

Jade finally spoke. "We attacked the rakshasas defending the core instead of taking out the ones shooting at Cam and Pan."

"Why was that a mistake?"

Weld slinked deeper into his seat, fascinated by something on the ground.

"Because we didn't account for the wind around the core," Jade said.

"That was only the beginning of your errors."

"Our misses got the attention of the human rakshasas holding the pass," Jade said. "We should have shifted our aim, but we continued to go after the Awakened foxes next to the core."

"And then you were pinned down by two foes."

Cam scowled, annoyed at Jade's and Weld's stupidity. Rather than following the plan and killing the rakshasas closer at hand, they'd gone for glory.

Avia also wore a glower of irritation aimed at Jade and Weld. "They stayed too long in one place, did too little, and got pinned down."

Cam continued to scowl, angry at what Jade and Weld had done. But he couldn't let the guilt fall entirely on them. It didn't sit right, and it also wouldn't do their unit any good. Light Squad had to fight as one, and any blame needed to be shared. "The plan was mine," he said.

"So, if anyone's at fault, it's me for not being clearer on what needed to happen."

"The hallmark of a good leader," Professor Grey said, dipping her head in approval.

Cam appreciated her statement, but any goodwill he felt was ruined when Weld snorted in derision.

It earned the other man a flinty glare from Professor Grey. "You have a different opinion of what it means to be a leader?" she asked, staring Weld down. "Your incompetence nearly cost you, and yet, Cam won't let you take the entire blame. He shields you until you can learn from your mistakes." Her narrow-eyed gaze remained lit on Weld, who seemed to wither. "So, tell me Mr. Plain, in what way did I err in saying Cam has the hallmarks of a good leader?"

Cam stared at the professor in surprise. He'd never seen her get so angry before.

Weld mumbled something, but Cam couldn't make it out.

"What was that?" Professor Grey snapped.

"You didn't err," Weld replied, speaking a bit louder.

"I didn't err in what?" Her tone remained sharp and acidic.

"You didn't err in saying Cam has the hallmarks of a good leader."

"Well, thank you for that," Professor Grey replied, the acid in her voice no less potent.

She shifted her attention from Weld, and he seemed to exhale in relief. It was a sentiment Cam appreciated. He hoped to never get on Professor Grey's bad side. Just this small view of her annoyance was frightening.

"I don't like when she's angry," Pan whispered as an aside. "It's scary."

Cam nodded agreement.

"There were other mistakes," Professor Grey said. "Not enough of you Bonded your Ephemeral Tangs. Spirairia isn't of use yet, but Synapsia and Kinesthia—all of you should have Bonded with them during as much of the battle as possible. So, why didn't you?"

Cam wanted none of the professor's basilisk-like attention, but he couldn't stay quiet and let someone else get barked at. "I didn't think to co-ordinate the usage of our Tangs. It was my oversight."

"Yes, it was, Mr. Folde," Professor Grey said, her tone stern. "But why didn't anyone else think of it?"

"Because we weren't thinking," Jade said. "Not in the way we have to."

"Then what *was* on your mind?"

Jade dropped her gaze. "Glory," she muttered.

Finally, Professor Grey's anger cracked. "Glory is the worst reason to enter a battle. The accomplishment of your goal and survival should be your only focus. Do them both, and the glory follows. Not the other way around. Am I clear?"

A chorus of "yes, Professor," met her query.

"There are other aspects of your battle that could have gone better," Professor Grey said. "We will review them here, and in your other classes."

"Should we have held our position?" Avia asked. "At that overhang where we split the squad. Should we have held there? The rakshasas had terrible marksmanship. We could have drawn them out. Let them miss and kill them in response."

"That is what Lord Queriam intended," Professor Grey said. "He wanted you to charge the rakshasas and kill them just the way you described. It would have been a swifter, surer win, but it would have also taught you bad habits."

"Like charging a fortified position?" Cam asked.

"Yes," the professor said. "And in the real world, you're unlikely to run into enemies incompetent enough to allow you to overrun their position when they have the high ground *and* the numerical advantage. It's best to never get into the sloppy habit of disrespecting your enemy. That way lies tragedy."

The rest of the day passed pretty much like the class with Professor Grey, and upon looking over the other members of Light Squad, Cam realized they were still feeling down about it. Repeatedly reviewing their mistakes and having the blame laid on Jade and Weld didn't make anyone feel good. It had been a team effort, and as a team, Light Squad had made errors. Cam sure had—the co-ordination of their Ephemera being the most obvious—and he'd tried to accept the fault.

But it didn't seem to do much good. Pan stayed quiet the rest of the day, Weld remained unusually reserved, and Jade and Avia spoke in hushed tones instead of bright and sparkling like they usually did.

At breakfast the next morning, Cam noted a lot of the other Novices wearing that same hang-dog expression. From what he'd overheard, it sounded like many of the other units had ended up struggling to complete their tests, same as Light Squad.

The dirge-like atmosphere made a mockery of the sunny day, although with the cold wind blowing, maybe it was a proper attitude for everyone to have. Success at the cost of quite a bit of failure.

But that attitude wouldn't be any good for Light Squad. They shouldn't feel so wretched about what was ultimately a win.

Cam still remembered how he used to encourage Jordil, Lilia, and Tern back before Plasminia and drink had stolen his self-confidence. He'd gained much of it back, but was it enough to inspire Light Squad? To light a fire in the hearts of his unit given their sorry-sack expressions.

No way to know but to find out.

"Listen up," Cam said, encouraged when everyone glanced his way. "We accomplished our mission yesterday, and we lost no one. I call that a win. That's the only after-action report that counts."

"You took an arrow to the shoulder," Jade said, sounding a bit skeptical.

"I'd have lived, though, right?" Cam argued back. "And that's what matters most. That's all that matters. It's what Professor Grey said: get the job done and live. Well, we did that." He made himself meet everyone's gaze, forcing confidence into his features. Devesh, this was harder than it used to be. It used to come as natural as breathing. Still, it seemed to be working since everyone's broken-hearted expressions lifted a mite, even Weld's.

"We made a lot of mistakes," Pan volunteered, sounding diffident.

"Sure we did," Cam agreed. "But ain't that what these tests are for? To learn so we don't screw things over when it's really important."

"You really think we did well?" Avia asked.

Cam chuckled, as if he thought her question was ridiculous. "Let me ask you something. In all the after-action reports, did we once get asked why we didn't win? Or why one of us died?" He answered himself. "No. And that's my point."

"I heard a couple of the squads actually failed," Weld said. "And at least one lost most of their members before the survivors lanced the core."

"Then just imagine how bad *their* after-action reports must have gone," Cam said.

The mood lifted, and smiles replaced the dour frowns from before.

"So, hear me out," Cam continued, feeling his way toward what needed saying. The attempt reminded him of tired, old muscles he'd not used in a while stretching and contracting, coming back to sore life, exposing him to awareness. And in the moment, that awareness was speaking on how his squad needed vinegar to go with the sweetness. "We succeeded in what we wanted done yesterday, but there were mistakes, and those mistakes, we'll work on. Next time we run one of those tests, our after-action reports won't only be about blame or mistakes, but about successes, too." He hoped that would be the case, but he honestly had no idea how these things worked.

"You better be right," Weld said with a shudder. "Last thing I want is for Professor Grey to light into me again."

On that, Cam whole-heartedly agreed. While he hadn't been the focus of Professor Grey's ire, the backlash had been bad enough.

But back to the sweet. "Come on then," Cam said. "Professor Shivein is likely getting impatient with us. We don't want to make him wait."

Jade chuckled. "That would be a disaster." She inclined her head his way. "Lead us to class then, oh great leader."

Everyone laughed, and they exited the cafeteria, shortly reaching the stairs descending to the Kinesthia field. Cam trailed after them, feeling better about himself and his squad. Maybe the person he'd once been—the person he had actually liked—was still hidden away somewhere under all the drinking and disappointments he'd experienced since that terrible Pathway.

Pan smiled, holding up for him. "You did well," he said, throwing an arm around Cam's shoulders and briefly hugging him while bumping foreheads. "I keep telling you to believe in yourself, and after what you just did, you have to see how everyone else believes in you, too."

Cam hugged Pan back, wiping at eyes grown misty. "I couldn't have done any of this without you. Thanks, Pan."

"Of course. That's what friends are for."

Later that night, Cam lowered himself to the dewy-wet grass next to Pan, the two of them the only ones present at the field where they held the class on Kinesthia. The sun was fixing to set, and a soft wind blew. In addition, there was an early winter chill in the air, causing Cam to shiver. He should have brought heavier clothing. Then again, clothing would be a problem for what he had in mind.

Pan didn't have any of that trouble. He had his soft, white-and-black fur to keep him warm and seemed utterly content, munching on a stick of bamboo. He smiled toothily when he caught Cam's attention.

Cam couldn't help but smile back. "You don't have to be here, you know?"

"And let our leader challenge himself with no one to support him? Never." Again came the infectious smile.

Cam chuckled, but his humor cut off when he noticed two figures approaching. *Jade and Avia*. What were they doing here?

"I told them about what you had planned," Pan explained, still chomping away on his bamboo.

"He said you were going to Enhance your Primary Tang, and we figured we should do the same," Jade said when she and Avia arrived. "You being our leader and all." She offered the same teasing comment she'd taken to using ever since Lord Queriam's first challenge.

"You're never going to let that go, are you?" Cam muttered, but there was no heat in his voice. He didn't mind their teasing since the day had gone well. A lot of it had to do with him, which brought a warmth to Cam's heart.

"Not now. Maybe not ever," Avia replied, settling herself on the ground next to Cam.

Cam chuckled at her comment. "You might want to get upwind of me," he suggested. "At least twenty feet away."

Avia quirked her head.

Pan scrambled to his feet. "He's right. When he Enhances Plasminia, he'll smell like he did before."

"Devesh, no," Jade said, sounding horrified. "Should we even be here?"

Probably not, although Cam wished otherwise. However, he knew how bad Enhancing Plasminia made him smell. "You don't have to stay here, but if you really want to grow as Ephemeral Masters, you should Enhance your own Primary Tangs. It doesn't matter where you do it."

Jade sighed. "Here is fine." Nevertheless, she moved a long distance away.

So did Pan and Avia. They all murmured something to one another, but Cam stopped paying them any mind. He disrobed, seated in his drawers, and with his eyes closed... although he wanted to peek to see what Avia and Jade were wearing. Were they in their small clothes, too?

He chided himself for thinking on what he shouldn't be thinking. But Avia and Jade sure were easy on the eyes.

Focus. It was a little over a month before the martial exhibition, and a few days prior to that would come some kind of final conference to test out how all the Novices were doing. Cam wanted to show well, which meant Enhancing his Tangs. Be better than anyone else.

And there was a way to make his dreams a reality. Ever since he'd first Enhanced Spirairia to Gold, he'd been doing the same for Synapsia and Kinesthia. They weren't too far off either. A push harder, and he might get them to Gold and Plasminia to Crystal.

He'd just have to accept the stench.

Cam left off his ruminations and Delved his Source. There it floated, still a lumpy potato but getting closer to a globe than it used to be. And on the surface was his Plasminia, golden-tinged and glowing red, rotating swiftly and surely, but slower than before.

But Cam needed it even slower.

Using his metaphorical net, which had grown familiar with use, Cam dipped into his Primary Tang, imagining it slowing. It was harder than it had been at first, and he had to hold his concentration longer. An itch on his face nearly tossed him out of his focus, but Cam kept at it.

Minutes passed, and since his Plasminia showed no sign of slowing, Cam imagined the net getting tighter.

A vise crushed his head. Blood tinged with yellow bile flowed from his nose. His eyes threatened to bulge out of his head, and Cam's skull felt like it was about to crack open.

The net was too tight. Cam relaxed it a smidge, and after a while, he saw what he was wanting. Plasminia slowed. The same headache as before gripped him, but this time, it wasn't nearly so throbbing; clamping tight to his temples, forehead, and neck, but tolerable.

Cam prepared himself, and soon enough, here came the yellow bile, stinking like nothing living ever should. It leaked out of him, from every orifice, and he had to control the need to vomit. It was the smell… Cam nearly gagged on that alone, but he held in his gorge.

All is Ephemera and Ephemera is All.

He chanted the truth he didn't fully understand, and at the same time, he inhaled deep, seeking to wrench the yellow bile back into his Source. While this part had become easier with practice, it still remained as hard as grasping a slippery eel. Nevertheless, Cam persisted, and inch by inch, he returned what had leaked from his nose, from his eyes, and his ears back into his body. Another inhalation, and even deeper it went, all the way back to his Source.

The momentum built, and the pressure on his bladder eased.

Nausea faded. The yellow bile on his face dried, and once it re-entered his Source, like it always did, Plasminia tried to take it in and speed up. Cam wouldn't let it. Through sheer concentration and will, he kept to what he needed, pushing the yellow bile past his Spirairia.

Synapsia was flowing languid, but when the yellow bile touched it, the liquid Tang flared, growing thicker. It condensed just like Spirairia had. Cam pushed on. He wasn't done yet. He kept on condensing Synapsia. It glowed brighter and brighter, eventually flashing golden.

Cam smiled to himself, distantly noting a mucus-like liquid coat his skin—the phlegm produced when Synapsia Enhanced. It had a swamp-like smell, which mixed unpleasantly with the ongoing stench of the yellow bile.

But he set aside his regard for the reek. Even when his Synapsia lit up golden, Cam wanted it condensed even more, wanted it as Enhanced as much possible. However, there came a time when the Tang resisted his further attempts at increasing its density, and he had to let off.

His work, though, wasn't yet complete. Next would come Kinesthia, and this part would be the most difficult yet. Instead of condensing Kinesthia, he had to loosen it. Doing so would maintain the Tang's strength but also give it greater flexibility.

Before starting, though, Cam reassessed himself. He had been Enhancing for hours now; was certainly tired enough for it to be so. And only when convinced he had the energy to persist in his effort did Cam resume the work. He inhaled heavily, settling himself as he briefly reviewed the instructions from the anonymously written book that Professor Grey had found for him.

It was time.

Cam slowed Plasminia once again, swiftly injecting the extruded yellow bile down into Kinesthia, heating it and causing it to vibrate. From his skin came the purging of serum, a clear, thin liquid having the iron-sharp smell of blood.

It was the first step to Enhancing Kinesthia.

But it wasn't the final step. Cam continued to work until the solid Tang at the core of his Source transformed. While it stayed ruby red, it now had the additional hint of a golden color, ripening, growing lustrous until there was no more serum to remove.

Cam was about done then, but before opening his eyes, he examined his Source. There were protrusions aplenty still, but the globe-shape had become clearer. The only disappointment, which really wasn't much of one, was that his Plasminia hadn't Enhanced to Crystal. It would have to be a job for another night.

Satisfied and happy, Cam finally opened his eyes. Right away, he noticed Pan still seated where he'd been before, softly playing a light melody on his flute. Meanwhile, sometime during the night, Avia and Jade had left.

Cam groaned, rising to his feet. His body was stiff as a board, and he stretched, arching his back. Once he could move without moaning, he headed toward his friend.

"Stop right there," Pan said, opening his eyes. "Get rid of that smell first."

Cam sighed. "That bad?"

"Even worse since you've got the stink of two other Enhanced Tangs on you now."

Cam took a whiff of himself. Ugh. Apparently, his wretched reek was the sweet smell of success.

26

"When did you get so good at this?" Weld asked with a scowl.

Cam hid a proud grin. Following last night's Enhancement of Synapsia and Kinesthia to Gold, he'd immediately noticed an improvement to himself. Even without any Bonds, his mind and body worked better. He had increased recall, his muscle memory was sharper, and his ability to ferret out solutions was increased. As for the Bonds themselves, they were stronger, too.

Everything about him was better, and the improvement currently had Weld on his back foot and any of his usual boasting was long since silenced. Cam had pasted him three straight times in a timed competition of figuring out how to separate a trio of bent nails wrapped around each other.

Bonded or unBonded, Cam felt like the answer was obvious. It was simplicity itself to solve the puzzle, and the quickness by which he did it had Weld annoyed.

"That's enough," Professor Grey said. "Shift opponents. Get your romano sets."

"I'll see you later," Weld promised.

"And you'll lose later," Cam said, his confidence bolstered by today's performance. Weld grumbled and scowled, but so what? He'd lost. Cam waved him off like he was a fly, earning a final glower before the other man departed to take on Pan while Jade slipped into his vacated seat.

"I hope you're not trying to pick a fight with Weld," she said.

"Nope. Just giving him a taste of his own medicine."

"It's a fifteen-minute game," Professor Grey said. "Set your timers. Avia, you'll play me."

Cam silently wished Avia the best of luck. Winning against Professor Grey in romano was impossible.

The game centered around twenty different types of soldiers battling across a landscape, seeking to destroy the enemy. It featured two, or sometimes three opponents, with the roll of dice and assorted calculations meant to determine the victor. Cam enjoyed the game, the tactics and strategy involved. It had taught him much about small unit combat; had taught all of them, although the others continued to lag in truly understanding the fundamentals of combat, at least compared to how he saw it.

He turned around and found Jade already getting her side of the board ready. She had chosen black, which wasn't typical for her. Jade usually wanted white, which—just like in chess—got to roll first. It probably had to do with her aggressive nature.

Jade arched her brow when she caught him staring. "What? You earned white by becoming our leader. You've done well." She gripped his hand, squeezing it briefly. "Thank you."

Cam flushed, flustered by her approval. Jade had always been kind enough to him, but she'd never gone out of her way to be especially friendly. He peered at her, noticing she had her hair unbound. It framed and softened her already pretty features.

"It's your move," Jade said, drawing his attention away from her face.

Cam blinked. Oh, right. The game. He hit his timer, getting it running as he set his attention to the board. He shifted a pair of scouts, and then it was Jade's turn.

They played quickly, and while Cam tried to keep his mind on the game, his thoughts flittered to another topic. No woman had liked him much growing up, and there was no reason any of them should. He was from a poor family, drunk more times than not for a few years, and physically weak, which most young women likely didn't find attractive. As a man, there hadn't been a lot to recommend about him.

But how much of that was still the case? He was still from a poor family, but a person couldn't choose their parents. He had his sobriety, and nearly as important, he was a student at the finest Ephemeral school in the world. The last was a miracle, but it was a miracle Cam had made himself worthy of receiving. So maybe he was also worthy of attention?

His thoughts spiraled to a conclusion just as Jade pressed her timer. It was Cam's turn, and he studied the board with fresh eyes. A Bond to Synapsia slowed the world. Jade's shifting aside a lock of hair was as languid as a woman fanning herself in the heat. Pan and Weld appeared still as stones. And there was Avia, concentrating on her board, a fierce look of determination on her face.

Professor Grey glanced his way, moving like she normally did. Even a quick turning of her head was graceful. She dipped her head his way, apparently recognizing that he had Synapsia Bonded.

Cam looked back to his board. He had a game to win. Jade had advanced three of her archers. They would soon threaten his knights, who would likely win, braced as they were behind a large rock. Still, it would be a terrible exchange for him. He studied the board, figuring on his next set of steps. Once a strategy was in place, Cam made his move, slapping the timer.

Jade frowned, slow like the motioning of her hand a little while ago.

Minutes felt like they had passed, but when he glanced at his timer, it had only been seconds. With Synapsia at Gold, time moved like molasses. Cam wondered. *Is this how everyone else sees the world with Synapsia?* If so, it was as intoxicating as a healthy swig of whiskey.

Jade made her move, retreating a quintet of archers, blocking a planned advance of knights. It also put his cavalry in danger. A few quick moves between them, and each time, Cam shifted to add support to his knights, making it harder for her to accept the exchange. But he still couldn't get her archers out of the way.

It was fine. Cam had his pieces ready. He could accept the loss of his knights now if she took it with her archers because it would leave her general exposed to his scouts. A quick peek at Jade, but she didn't look like she'd seen it. Her eyes were focused on the wrong side of the board, likely planning to advance her own cavalry. She'd overwhelm him then.

But first, he silently urged her to take his exposed knights. And do it fast. His Bond to Synapsia was running out. He could still perceive Jade's movements as being slower, but not as much as before.

Cam's next move blocked Jade's archers. He hid a relieved exhalation when she finally rolled her dice in order to attack his knights. Not surprisingly, he lost. But then they were rolling for him to kill her archers. He took them. She killed a couple of his scouts. But the move opened a path for three of his horse. Her general was threatened.

Jade's eyes shot open. "How did you…"

Cam tried not to grin, although his mouth did twitch a bit. "It's your move."

He had her in a precarious position, and she knew it. Jade took longer on her next move, and by the time she finished, Cam's Bond to Synapsia was gone. He was on cooldown.

It didn't matter. He knew what he had to do, having played out a number of steps in his mind. Two scouts cut off her archers. Jade ignored the offering, moving her cavalry at a straight-ahead charge.

Cam took the paladin defending the general. "Check."

Jade studied the board, quickly seeing what he had planned. There was no way for her to protect the general, and she turned the piece over, smiling at him. "When did you get so good?"

Cam laughed. "You know, that's exactly what Weld asked me just before you sat down."

"And?"

"Last night. When I Enhanced Synapsia and Kinesthia to Gold."

Jade boggled. "You Enhanced both of them in a single evening? Impressive. It's hard enough to Enhance a single Tang at a time, and here you are doing all four."

It was true. Cam's way was harder. But his success from last night had him grinning. "And if I'm lucky, I might-should get Plasminia to Crystal."

"Might-should?" Jade chuckled. "You and your country dialect."

"It's charming, ain't it?" Cam made his drawl even thicker.

"Not like that, it *ain't*. But honestly, four Tangs at Gold is… What can you do now that you couldn't before?"

"I think I can actually use my Tangs the same as everyone else. When I had them at Silver, they barely helped with anything, but now that they're Gold, it's like they're…" He couldn't come up with the right word.

Jade's lips twitched into a smile. "Enhanced."

Cam laughed. "Exactly."

"I wonder what you'll be able to do when you Enhance Plasminia to Crystal."

Cam shook his head. "No idea," he replied, but he certainly had his wishes for what it might mean.

"Let's see what you can do," Saira said, gesturing Cam forward.

She had agreed to meet him after supper, at the field where the class on Kinesthia was held. A stiff wind, cold and ill, whipped about. A bit of daylight remained as the sun lingered high enough to shed some illumination. There should be plenty of light to spar against Saira.

In the weeks after Cam had Enhanced Kinesthia and Synapsia, he had undergone a slow, steady increase to his abilities. And now he wanted to know just what he could do now with all those improvements. For one, he could more easily Bond any of his Tangs, but what about two of them at the same time? In the middle of a fight, especially? That had never been easy for him, an anvil to the head really, which was irritating since for everyone else it was hardly even a nuisance.

But he figured he might have a way forward now. It was advice from that book Professor Grey had found, and Saira had agreed to help him test it out. He could have waited until tomorrow, but he didn't have the patience to hold off.

"You're leaving this late, aren't you?" Saira asked.

"You mean since the conference is tomorrow and the martial exhibition is the day after?"

She nodded.

"As it is, I think I can hold my own," Cam said. "But I want to do better than just 'hold my own.' I want to excel."

"And you want to see how much you can excel?"

"I think I have a way forward."

"Show me."

Cam responded by Delving his Source and tried something he'd never before attempted. First, he Bonded to Plasminia, and the moment he did, weakness caused him to nearly collapse. His muscles wanted to sag like bags of jelly. Cam nearly fell to his knees, but before he dropped, he Bonded Kinesthia. Fresh strength rapidly replaced the weakness, and Cam grinned.

Two Tangs Bonded, and it was no challenge. But what about three? He needed Synapsia for the sparring to mean anything. Going against Saira or any opponent with just Kinesthia would do him no good. His mind had to be as swift as his body.

Cam attempted the third Bond, wincing in anticipation of the eye-burning pain…

But it never happened. There was nothing but the silence of his mind. Cam opened his eyes, not even realizing he had them closed until he met Saira's gaze. She had her head tilted, a posture of consideration and challenge.

Cam's body burned with fire. A shroud of red light covered his body, indicating his use of Ephemera. But best of all, it was like Kinesthia and Synapsia were finally working together the way they were always supposed to as his mind sped like a racehorse given its head. So many possibilities, more than ever before.

Saira didn't bother with any Bonds. She didn't need to. Not as a Glory. "Be ready," she said, stepping forward since Cam hadn't. She threw a measuring left-hand jab.

Cam slapped it away. Another jab. This one harder and faster, closer to landing. Cam shifted to his right, away from her power. He'd felt it enough times to be wary. Saira angled, cutting him off. He checked a testing kick. Lifted an arm, accepting a straight right on the shoulder. No pain.

Confidence built. Saira's punches weren't coming slow. She was throwing with ill intentions. Not as hard as she was capable. Saira was a Glory, after all, but she was definitely aiming to hurt more than before.

And Cam was keeping up. He circled, defending a takedown, stuffing it. He tried for a plum, but she slipped out like a fish. A push off from a follow-on knee nearly set him on his butt. Saira was strong, and Cam's lack of balance cost him. She rattled him with a left cross. He twisted from the rest of the combination—a straight right and left hook.

"You're doing better," Saira said, "but you can't always give ground. Sometimes you have to stand and trade."

Cam took her advice to heart. He planted his feet, and when she came in range, he let loose with a savage left uppercut. Had it landed, it would have gotten Saira's attention but not much else. A Novice hitting a Glory, even full force, would be like a grasshopper running into a horse.

But the left didn't land. Neither did the follow-up straight right.

Stars bloomed in Cam's vision. He'd taken a shot to the head. His mind blanked. His thoughts fractured. He knew enough to retreat, automatically moving to his right. Distance and time. He needed both, achieved both.

His mind clicked back on. Saira waited on him, not pursuing, hands at her side, peering at him in concern. She had given him the time to recover.

"What happened?" he asked, he felt dull, like he'd dipped his mind in a barrel full of tar.

"I got you with a left hook. It came over your right."

Cam scowled. "I need to be faster."

As far as he knew, it was true, but Saira's next words told him he was wrong. "Timing beats speed," she said. "That's why my punch landed, and yours missed. That, and I have a lot more experience at this than you do." She lifted an eyebrow in challenge. "Go again."

Cam shook his head, wincing at the motion. He reached for his cheek which ached. His whole head hurt, and his mind still didn't feel like it was likely to work right anytime soon. "Better not," he answered.

Plus, even if he wanted to go again, his Bond to Synapsia and Kinesthia was already fraying, shorter than the normal time when he held them. Which made sense. His Plasminia allowed him to more easily Bond one Tang at a time, but there was a price. He burned through the Bonds faster than he otherwise would.

Saira approached, offering him a smile. "You actually did well for a few seconds."

Cam blinked at her, feeling stupid like she'd hit him again. Her smile lit her face, making her even prettier than normal. No. Not pretty. Saira had always been beautiful, and a smile on her was like blessed sunshine on a cloudy day.

Something of his thinking must have leaked onto his face because Saira's smile became a frown. "What's wrong?"

Cam breathed out in relief. Saira hadn't realized he was thinking of how beautiful she was. Right then, he wanted to shake himself. What kind of idiot was he? Just a few weeks ago, he had been admiring Jade, and now here he was having similar views about Saira. Best knock those moon-brained considerings out of his head.

"Nothing's wrong," Cam said. "I was thinking on what would happen if I got Plasminia to Crystal. I've been working toward it."

Saira stared at him a bit longer, frowning like she wasn't sure whether to believe him or not. She eventually shrugged. "Will that make you weaker again?"

Cam didn't think so, and even if it did, he no longer feared the outcome. The weakness hadn't happened when he got Plasminia to Gold and Kinesthia was still Silver. He mentioned it.

"That's good," Saira said with a nod. "Just stay with your plan then, but please don't take any risks."

Cam frowned in confusion. "What kind of risks?"

"The kind where you end up hurting yourself. You're a Plasminian. Other than that book Professor Grey found for you, there isn't much we know about what you should and shouldn't be doing."

"I'll be careful," Cam promised.

"I know you will," Saira replied. "What do you have going on the rest of the night?"

"Enhancement."

"You think you can get Plasminia to Crystal? Before the conference tomorrow?"

Saira was talking about the upcoming gathering of all the squads, the assessment to see which Novices had progressed the furthest prior to the mid-year testing in two weeks.

Cam nodded. He actually thought he could do even more than Enhance just one Tang, but it was best not to speak too proudly. Karma was sure to hammer him low if he did.

"Get some rest," Saira advised. "And make sure you clean yourself before tomorrow morning. That yellow bile is absolutely foul."

"Yes, ma'am," Cam replied. The yellow bile and its stink. Yes, it helped him, but not for the first time did he wonder why it had to smell so bad. Couldn't the Servants have chosen some less disgusting method to Enhance Plasminia?

"I'll see you tomorrow then," Saira added, striding off.

Cam waited for her to get gone before he took off his shirt and pants. No chance he'd want Saira to see him in his drawers. He sat cross-legged on the ground, the already present dew quickly soaking his small-clothes. He shrugged off the mild discomfort, closing his eyes, and Delving his Source.

First, he created the figurative net for Plasminia, making it finer than ever since slowing his Primary Tang took ever more effort. He kept at it and Plasminia eventually slowed enough to create a headache and the yellow bile.

Cam was ready for them both. By now, he was used to the pain as well as the nauseating stench and other sensations caused by the bile. He didn't let any of it distract him, though. Instead, he worked steadily, recovering the yellow bile, his force of will hauling it home to his Source where he sent it lower. Down to his Synapsia and Kinesthia where he let the yellow bile sit inert, doing not much of anything.

In the meantime, Plasminia had lost some of its red-gold luster, taking on a glassy sheen. A shiver of excitement coursed through Cam. It was happening. Plasminia was Enhancing to Crystal.

Quickly getting back to work, Cam extruded more yellow bile, and Plasminia continued to slow further. The glassy sheen took on a greater clarity. More bile, and a ringing in his head signaled the change this time. It sounded like glass tinkling. His Plasminia still glowed red, but rather than a golden undertone, it now held a glassy quality.

A moment only did Cam allow himself to bask in his accomplishment. The first member of Light Squad to Enhance a Tang to Crystal.

And he wasn't done yet.

Cam continued to Enhance Plasminia, getting it to a mirrored sheen, working until it was as bright as he could manage. By then, there was plenty of yellow bile coating his face, wanting to exit through his bowel and bladder. Cam focused, drawing it back into his Source. He packed as much as he could into Kinesthia, joining it with whatever other bile he'd already collected.

More hard work awaited, but before he began, Cam took a deep breath. *All is Ephemera and Ephemera is All.*

The phrase helped him focus, and once he felt prepared, Cam Enhanced Kinesthia. The yellow bile heated the Tang, causing it to vibrate until serum poured from the pores of his skin. The iron-hard scent of blood wafted into his nose.

On Cam worked, falling into the labor, losing track of the hours, and not halting even after a glassy finish replaced Kinesthia's golden underglow. More heating of the Tang, loosening the bonds holding it solid. A cycle of heating and vibration, purging as much serum as he knew how. He labored long, but there came a point when Kinesthia finally transformed, ringing like a bell and gaining the same mirror-shine as Plasminia. A bit longer until no more serum extruded from the Tang.

Cam yawned, wanting to call it a day, but when would he ever get another chance like this? He poured the remaining yellow bile into Synapsia as well, enough to Enhance it to Crystal, unwilling to stop until it was done.

More hours passed, but all Cam knew was the desire to condense Synapsia. He fell into the rhythm of his work. The yellow bile collapsed Synapsia in on itself, causing it to lose its gold luster and lighten in color. On his skin, phlegm mixed with serum, a disgusting combination, but a shower would get rid of it.

Finally, the ringing sound Cam had been hoping to hear sounded, and Synapsia had the glassy sheen of Crystal.

Cam wanted to rest then, but he had a final push to make. He best do it now or it might never happen. He continued to condense Synapsia until it approached the density of Kinesthia. The last of his yellow bile was used, and finally the Tang had the brightness he wanted.

Three Crystal Tangs. It had to be a rare achievement. And even if it wasn't, Cam couldn't have done any better. He was proud of himself. Only Spirairia needed further Enhancement, and Cam had an idea on how to make that happen.

As he levered himself to his feet, stiff as a brittle branch, he realized it was deep into the night. No one else was about, and the world was as quiet as a cavern. Cam closed his eyes, enjoying the privacy and stillness, looking forward to explaining what he'd done to Pan.

He smiled then. Earlier in the evening he'd been in a hurry to test himself against Saira, but now, a pool of patience seemed to extend from his Source. It calmed his mind, letting him know the truth: he'd done something momentous.

27

The next morning dawned gray and dismal with heavy clouds scudding across the sky. The day looked to be cold and dreary, and through the window in his quarters looking out on the city, Cam spied folks hustling about, wearing cloaks and coats. Some even had mittens, gloves, and scarves, which meant it was chilly out, and winter might have finally settled on Nexus.

Winter, he thought with a wistful longing. Cam loved the cold, the frosty weather, his breath pluming in the frigid temperatures, and warm drinks to chase away the chill. He frowned on thinking of the last, knowing what kind of drink best drove away the cold. It wasn't one he could have.

Regardless, even if he couldn't drink fine wine, winter's cold would be welcome.

"Are you ready for today?" Pan asked.

Cam broke off his ponderings on the weather. Last night, he'd finished what would have seemed impossible before coming to the Ephemeral Academy. He'd Enhanced three Tangs to Crystal, and to-day, he'd have to demonstrate his success for all the other Novices and their instructors to see. Yes, he was still a Plasminian, but given his Enhancements, he didn't reckon on embarrassing himself any longer. Fact was, he'd likely shine.

"You'll do well," Pan said, grinning his cute grin, his pink tongue and canines visible.

Cam smiled back, unable to help himself and not really wanting to.

Pan's grin widened, his eyes crinkling in pleasure.

Cam's smile became a frown as a question occurred to him. *Does Pan grin like that on purpose?* To get people to smile back at him? Cam's eyes widened. *He does.* "You little trickster. You do that on purpose."

Pan wore a look of innocence. "Do what?"

But Cam could see the abashed acknowledgement lurking on Pan's face. "You know what I mean. Smiling like you do. All cute and adorable. You do that on purpose to make people smile back."

"Why is it wrong if I do?"

"So you admit it?"

"Only if you can tell me why it's wrong."

"It's wrong because…" Cam didn't rightly know why it was wrong, and in fact, he kind of thought it was right. Sure, some might say it was being manipulative, but he didn't think that's what Pan was aiming for. Pan just wanted to bring joy into the other people's lives. What was wrong with that?

Pan waited, looking a bit worried, which got Cam to feeling bad. He didn't want his friend feeling fearful on his account. "There's nothing wrong with it," Cam said.

Pan grinned again, just like he always did, cute and infectious, and Cam responded just like he always did, with a happy smile of his own.

"Have you figured anything new you can do with three Crystal Tangs?" Pan asked, plopping on the ground, a green stick of celery in hand.

"You might not want to eat that," Cam said. Celery tasted like the wall of an outhouse—only if someone was stupid enough to lick one. The celery or the outhouse; made no difference which one.

"Why not?" Pan asked, munching mightily. "Mmm. Tastes almost as good as bamboo."

Cam shook his head in pity. Anyone who liked the flavor of celery had to have a sense of taste that worked worse than a millhouse over a dry creek. Then again, Pan did love bamboo, and the one small bite Cam had taken of that woody grass had left an impression. He had instantly sworn off ever trying it again.

"You didn't answer my question," Pan said. "Is there anything new you can do with your Tangs?"

Cam shook his head. "Haven't tested it yet, but I figure I'll be able to do what you and the others can do at Gold, which is a far sight better than where I started. I ain't going to complain."

"It is better, and you have come far," Pan said. "I'm glad you're finally allowing yourself to recognize it."

Cam smirked. "You're one to talk."

Pan tilted his head in confusion.

Cam explained. "How many times have I heard you talk about how your only worth is in fulfilling your kinfolk's stupid prophecy?"

"It's not stupid," Pan protested.

Cam wasn't willing to concede the point. As far as he was concerned, that prophecy was an anchor tied around Pan's neck, and his fragging family had tossed him out into the waters and let him drown. He couldn't forgive them for what they'd done. What kind of people shoved their child into the wilderness because of words spoken hundreds of years ago or longer? Words that Pan wasn't even allowed to know?

Utterly bollocks as far as Cam was concerned, and he said so to Pan. It didn't matter how upset it might make his friend. Pan needed to hear what Cam had to say. "You're always going on about how your best worth is to fulfill this prophecy, but you're wrong. You deserve happiness on your own terms."

Pan drooped. "It's how I was raised," he said, his voice a pained whisper.

Cam might have wanted to say a further piece, but the hurt in Pan's voice hauled him up short as guilt replaced righteous anger. Cam sat next to Pan, threw an arm around his friend's wide shoulders. "I'm sorry if I spoke out of turn."

Pan stared at the nubbin of a celery stalk left in his hand. "If I think about myself any other way, I'm afraid I won't fulfill the prophecy, and worse, my life will have no meaning." He lifted his gaze. "I don't want to think about myself like that."

"Then you won't," Cam said, trying to muster certainty into his voice. At the same time, he silently swore obscenities at Pan's family. They had him so messed up inside. He actually thought what they had done was the best thing for him.

A short time later, he and Pan gathered their belongings and headed off to the cafeteria, joining a line of other students.

"Maybe you can tell me again what it's like to Enhance three Tangs to Crystal," Pan said. "That way, I might learn something for myself."

Cam laughed. "Enhancing them to Crystal wasn't fragrant. I can tell you that much."

"I know," Pan said. "I could smell it when you came home."

"I took three showers," Cam said, knowing he sounded defensive. "I even burned it off my skin before I came home."

"But you didn't burn your small clothes," Pan said. "They stank."

"That bad?"

"That bad," Pan confirmed. "But you don't stink this morning."

Cam smiled. "You're a good person—"

"Panda-person."

"Right. A good panda-person. Don't let anyone else tell you different."

The gray gloom persisted throughout the morning, and a blustery wind kicked in, carrying the briny smell of the cold sea, salt, and fish from the distant harbor. Cam and Pan had joined the rest of Light Squad, and they stood alongside one another in a corner of the Kinesthian field. All the Novice squads had come together here, a crowd of a hundred or more, all of them murmuring and muttering, appearing as unsure of what was happening as the members of Light Squad. All of the instructors were present as well: Professors Grey, Shivein, Werm, and of course, Saira. There were a bunch of other Glories, too; folk Cam didn't recognize, but he figured they were probably the private instructors from the other squads. They stood in huddled groups, close to the units they taught and trained.

And over it all was a buzz of excitement; not heard but sensed. After last night, Cam had increased his empathic ability, and even without Bonding to Spirairia, he had a notion what others were feeling. Avia had a predator's anticipation, which made sense. She was an orca and a hunter. Pan was steady as always, but uncertain. Weld was edgy and nervous, and Jade... Well, she had the strangest emotion. Anticipation and concern.

"What do you think this will be about?" Weld asked, appearing worried and sounding unusually humble.

Cam shrugged, having no answer to the question and not much wanting to talk. Whatever happened would happen. They'd have to accept it and deal with it as best they could. The rest of Light Squad seemed to share Weld's concern, though, including Pan, who chewed his lower lip in worry.

Cam gently rubbed the center of Pan's forehead, between his eyes, knowing how much his friend liked it. It was soothing, and soon enough, Pan's eyes slitted. Seconds later, there it was. Pan grinned, like a rainbow after a storm.

Cam let off rubbing Pan's forehead, distracted by Jade's sense of anticipation and concern. "What do you know about what's going to happen?" he asked her.

Jade started. "How did you...?" She waved off the explanation he was about to offer. "Nevermind. We're supposed to show what we can do with our Tangs," she said. "It's an assessment for the other instructors to offer guidance to those who aren't directly under their tutelage."

"That's all?" Light Squad's instructors had already told them the same thing. "What's the point of that?"

Weld was the one who answered. "The point is supposedly so the instructors can guide students who aren't their own, teach them how to improve their Enhancements before the mid-year testing. But that isn't it, though. It's really for the richer squads to show off how far they've come. Politics by other means. But what they don't know is that Squad Screwup has come just as far. We've all got our Primary Tangs to Gold. Not every squad can say that."

"I heard Victory has his Primary *and* a secondary at Crystal," Jade said.

"So do Merit, Charity, and Kahreen," Avia said.

"Kahreen!" Jade said, sounding outraged. "How? She's lazier than a snake in the sun."

"But she's wealthy," Avia said. "Money can buy Enhancement for even the laziest of snakes."

"Speaking of snakes," Weld whispered, gesturing with his chin.

As if speaking about them brought about their appearance, here came Victory, Charity, Merit, and Kahreen.

Victory looked every ounce the perfect scion of a Sage-Duke. He walked with a swagger, and people moved aside at his approach. For reasons he couldn't explain, Cam was glad that he stood taller than the other man. Broader, too.

Next to Victory was Charity Kazar, tall and graceful. She moved with an assured serenity, her footsteps light and clipped without a single wasted motion, smiling, seemingly pleased and proud of herself. Then again, she was the beautiful, talented, child of a Sage-Duke. She had reason to be smug.

Walking alongside them was Kahreen Sala; short, curvy, and also the child of privilege and wealth. Even if her parents were only Glories, they had money enough to allow Kahreen to achieve whatever Enhancement she needed.

And like he often did, trailing after was Merit Thens. He remained unremarkable in appearance but was every bit as talented as Charity and Victory. And he, too, was the child of a Sage-Duke. He skulked like a shadow after the others, though, glancing about, his expression unreadable.

"Are you ready for the assessment?" Victory asked on reaching Light Squad. The noble beamed a confident smile.

"We're as ready as a steak over a fire," Weld said, smiling right back. "What about you? I hear you've got yourself to Crystal on your Primary Tang."

Victory's smile didn't wax or wane. It stayed steady, like Weld's acknowledgement didn't mean nothing to him. "It's true, although Charity, Merit, and Kahreen managed the same."

"What about the rest of your squads?" Jade asked, seemingly bored, but through his empathy, Cam could sense her agitation.

"Everyone is at least Gold," Charity said. "What about yours?"

"We're all Gold," Weld said.

"But no Crystal?" Kahreen said with a vindictive smile.

"We're Enhanced enough to have won our first challenge," Weld said, which didn't really answer the question. "We lanced the boil Lord Queriam tested us against with no deaths. What about your squad? How did y'all fare in that test?" He tilted his head as if he didn't already know the answer.

On hearing his question, Charity's smile went brittle. So did Kahreen's.

"We'll lance the boil that matters," Charity said, granting them a graceful incline of her head. "Good luck. Our professors might be able to help you improve your Enhancement. You should listen to them." She departed then, looking as fine when leaving as she did when approaching. Cam watched in admiration until Pan nudged him.

"Close your mouth," Pan said.

Cam clapped shut his jaw.

Kahreen wore a plainly false expression of support. "But what *our* instructors teach usually costs a lot of coin. Tonics and such. I'm so sorry you won't be able to afford them." She waved at them, smirking broadly as she sashayed away.

Victory might have grimaced at Kahreen's parting comment. Cam couldn't tell before the noble addressed Light Squad. "Just remember,

while no one expects much from Light Squad, I'm sure you'll do fine."
He tugged Merit after him, and they departed.

At least Victory and the others hadn't called them Squad Screwup.

"Three squads with Crystals," Jade spat. "We'll be so far behind in
the rankings." Tension and unhappiness sprayed from her like waves
off a rock, and Cam now understood why. If there was someone who
hated losing, it was Jade. It didn't matter what the game or reason; she
wanted to win at all costs, or at least see the other fellow lose.

Her upset had Cam grinning. He had a secret that would make her
happy.

Jade noticed his humor and scowled at him. "What's so funny?"

"I have three Tangs at Crystal," he answered.

"Bullshit," Weld stated.

"Bulltrue," Cam replied. "I raised them last night. Plasminia,
Kinesthia, and Synapsia."

"You really have three?" Jade asked, hopeful longing filling her
features.

Cam nodded.

A slow smile of delight spread across Jade's face. "They'll be so
angry."

Cam chuckled, glad to have brought her some joy.

Minutes later, orders were shouted, and each squad was sent to a
different set of instructors. For Light Squad, it was the professors from
Victory's unit. All of them were men, and all of them were tall and
powerfully built, just like Victory. They wore impassive expressions,
their arms crossed over their chests, and their Glory-blue eyes were
flat and disinterested. All in all, they didn't look too friendly.

One stood in front of the others. "We will test you," he said, his
voice as gravelly deep as his build suggested it would be. "Who is your
strongest?"

Avia, Jade, and Weld glanced at one another, likely thinking on who
should answer.

Their hesitancy earned the ire of the professor. "Step forward," he
ordered, pointing to Jade. "After you, the other girl. Then you." He

pointed to Weld. "Next, the panda." He smiled mirthlessly at Cam. "And you're the Plasminian. You'll go last. We know your capabilities."

Cam didn't let the jibe get to him. By now, he'd heard it all. It just meant a whole lot of folks would soon be eating an entire murder of crow.

Jade stepped forward, and Cam sensed the professor engage his Spirairia, using it in a way they hadn't been taught. "Bond your Tangs." A few seconds later, the professor—who still hadn't introduced himself—grunted. "Gold in two Tangs. Well done." He gestured for Weld, testing him straightaway. "Gold in your Primary. Silver in the others. Passable. We will have some advice for you on your Enhancement." Avia also had two Golds and a Silver. Same with Pan.

Cam watched the scenario play out, waiting until he was gestured forward.

"Bond your Tangs," the professor ordered.

Cam did so, Bonding Plasminia first and then Synapsia to calm him enough to Bond Kinesthia and then Spirairia. It was a strain, but he gritted his teeth, clasping tight to his Tangs. A wash of someone's touch, like a feather playing on the surface of his mind, flicked across his Source.

The professor's eyes widened, and he glared at Cam. "Impossible. How are you doing this, boy?"

The other professors locked their attention on Cam, and his legs trembled under the weight of their Glory-Advanced Awareness. Weren't they supposed to Cloud their Sources?

"What is impossible?" one of the other professors asked.

"He has three Crystal Tangs and one at Gold," the first one declared in his gravelly voice.

The other professors meant to assess Light Squad began murmuring, all of them abruptly interested in Cam. Same with a mess of other squads and professors who must have overheard.

Cam glanced at the rest of his unit. They all gazed at him with a mix of triumph and pride—even Weld—while Pan smiled like he'd seen the best stand of bamboo in existence.

"Is this true?" one of the professors from another group asked, drifting over along with a number of other students and instructors.

"It's true," the lead professor said. His eyes snapped to Cam. "Unless it's a trick. Keep the Bonds. Let's make sure."

Cam's brow broke out in a sweat. A dull headache started, and while he very much wanted to let the Bonds go, he couldn't. Not yet. He managed to hold them, just long enough for another feathery touch, but right afterward, the Bonds fell apart, and Cam exhaled explosively. He hunched over, gripping his knees, panting, his head throbbing fierce. Exhausted, gasping like he'd broken the surface of a lake just before running out of air.

"Well?" he heard someone ask.

"Three Crystals and one Gold."

Cacophony ensued.

Whatever joy Cam might have had in surprising the Glories quickly died. He flared his nostrils, annoyed at how many people he didn't know suddenly wanted to talk to him, mostly to learn his secrets. They yelled, demanding he explain what learning he'd stolen; what herbs, tonics, or drinks he'd used.

Now the right—or rather *wrong* kind of drink would have actually done him harm, but even the kind the other students were hollering about wasn't anything he could have ever afforded. Not unless he sold off a body part.

It took a while to get all the hooting and hollering sorted out, and it didn't surprise Cam that it was Professor Grey who made it happen. She had that kind of presence; one that caused even the powerful instructors of Victory's squad to stand down when she called for silence.

"I know you all wish to know the secrets of how a Novice managed to achieve three Crystal Tangs, but there isn't any," she said. "It was hard work and the advantages of being a Plasminian."

"What advantage?" Kahreen asked. "Plasminians are weak.

Everyone knows this."

Cam rolled his eyes, especially when she brayed like a jackass after finishing her little speech, looking around for support. But there was none to be found. Professor Grey only had to turn her gaze on the girl, and Kahreen drooped like a leaf of lettuce left out in the sun.

"Plasminians have disadvantages aplenty," Professor Grey said. "But when it comes to Enhancing their Tangs, in this one area they have a benefit unknown to other Ephemeral Masters."

"You know this how?" the lead instructor in Victory's squad asked.

"By close reading of history and a book I discovered in the library," Professor Grey said. "I've used its teachings to guide Cam, and the practical application of its instruction indicate that the information it contains is correct. Witness Cam Folde. He proved the book's veracity. Now, it's time to finish this evaluation. Disperse and return to your squads and instructors." She clapped her hands as if the conversation was at an end, and shockingly, the other students and professors drifted away.

Cam glanced at Victory's instructors, all of whom frowned his way. He straightened, refusing to be intimidated.

His posture earned him a grunt of approval from the lead professor. "You have nothing to learn from us," he said. "And given how well the rest of you are progressing, especially without any supplements, I doubt we have anything to teach you either."

"There is one thing," another instructor said. "If your Sage benefactor offers you a tonic meant to Enhance a Tang, use it on your Primary—everyone but the Plasminian. It will make Enhancing all the others easier."

The head instructor nodded in agreement before gesturing them off.

As one, Light Squad bowed to the instructors before leaving the field. Other groups were headed out as well, and there was a bottleneck at the stairs leading away. The students chattered in excitement, most of them buzzing about the mid-year testing only a couple of days off. Everyone was expected to maximize their Enhancements prior to the examinations, and Light Squad was no different. And if they all received the promised tonic, Cam figured most all of them should have at least one Crystal Tang.

"Are your Tangs really Enhanced to Crystal because of the yellow bile?" Weld asked. "Professor Grey didn't give you some extra supplements or pills?"

"The yellow bile is my only advantage."

"What do you mean?" Jade asked, looking honestly curious, although Cam had explained this to her before. Then again, Jade didn't listen much if it didn't have anything directly to do with her.

"Meaning that I can use yellow bile to Enhance my other Tangs," Cam said.

"And let me tell you," Pan said with feeling, "sharing quarters with him, especially with my sensitive nose, is no easy task when he's in the midst of meditating and Enhancing."

"It's why I moved out," Weld confirmed.

"Maybe you shouldn't have," Avia noted. "Of all of us, you're the furthest behind. One Gold and two Silver Tangs. If you'd stayed, maybe you would have pushed harder at Enhancement."

Her comment earned her a scowl from Weld.

Cam cut in before the man could say anything annoying. "Did you see Kahreen's expression when she found out about my three Tangs?"

Jade laughed in delight. "She looked like she swallowed a lemon. And even better, we're now ahead of all the other squads. We actually have a chance to win some acclaim and maybe even some prizes."

"And we need them since not all of us are rich," Avia agreed.

"Wait," Pan said, feigning being confused. "You mean swallowing a lemon *isn't* Kahreen's normal expression?"

Cam broke out in laughter. "Never change," he said, throwing a companionable arm over Pan's shoulders.

28

"What happens now?" Cam asked.

Light Squad had been given the rest of the day off, but a message had been passed for them to meet back at the Kinesthia field after lunch. They stood there now with everyone else gone. The only ones still present were Light Squad's instructors, who quietly conversed in a small island of their own while Cam and the rest of the unit waited off to the side.

The cloudy day had persisted in its gloom, and a chill wind whipped about, tugging at his clothing. It was the kind of weather Cam loved. The only thing better was if snow was in the offing. Then, when the world shined with sunlight reflecting off the powdery white, and the brilliant air was hard and clean… it was magical.

"I think our sponsors are coming," Pan said, guessing at the answer to Cam's question and seeming nervous over the possibility.

Then again, his guesses were usually right, and as if Pan's spoken words called him into being, a whistling sound from high in the grayness overhead became the figure of a man in flight. Seconds later, it was clear who was descending.

Master Winder. The Wilde Sage. Cam hadn't seen him in months; not since he'd been dropped off at the academy.

"He brings a tonic for all of you," Professor Grey said, having strode to their side. "Including for Avia and Jade. He's taken on the role of their sponsors in this regard."

"Why?" Avia asked, and based on Jade's expression, she was wanting to know the answer, too.

"Because you've all done well, and you're all worthy," Professor Grey explained. "Any other reasons he might have will be for him to discuss but know that both your families approve."

She stepped away just as Master Winder touched down, and Cam relaxed at seeing the Wilde Sage's proud smile.

"You've done well," Master Winder said. "Most of you." His eyes rested on Weld, the lowest ranked of them, who faltered upon meeting the Sage's gaze. "For this work, I bear gifts." From a pocket, he withdrew five small, sealed bottles, willowy and hour-glassed, tinted green. "One for each of you. We will discuss what should be done with them."

He gestured, and as one, every member of Light Squad accepted a bottle. Cam held his up to the sunshine, trying to peer inside. It was a liquid that had the consistency of dark wine.

An abrupt surge of yearning for the taste of alcohol—

No. He shoved away the desire even while acknowledging it would always be with him, hanging over his head like a curse.

"We'll start with Jade," Master Winder said. "She has achieved the greatest level of Enhancements along with Avia and Pan."

Professor Grey cleared her throat. "You are incorrect. The one with the greatest Enhancements is Cam. He has three Tangs at Crystal: Plasminia, Kinesthia, and Synapsia."

Master Winder's shock on hearing Professor Grey's statement was as bright as sunshine on a snowy field. His mouth didn't drop, but his eyes did widen and a hint of disbelief filled his bearded face. His reaction was surprising. Until now, Cam always figured the Wilde Sage knew everything there was to know about everyone. But it was clear he didn't. He could be confused by the unexpected just like anyone else.

"This is true?" Master Winder asked.

Cam nodded, drawing himself proud. "Yes, sir. Last night. Only one that's missing is Spirairia."

"And it is at Gold?"

Again, Cam nodded, a grin flickering across his face. He wasn't as strong as the rest of his squad, but that would change. Over time and with hard work.

Master Winder's smile filled out, becoming kinder. "You are a surprise, Mr. Folde. The tonic you hold… drink it on a full stomach." He raised his voice, talking to them all. "It's best to wait until the evening. Darkness and quiet are your allies. You don't want any distractions. The process of force raising a Tang isn't easy. There will be lethargy and fatigue like you've never felt. You'll want to give in to sleep. Fight it. The tiredness is in your mind. Don't let it limit you. Have a friend on hand for encouragement. The process will consume several hours."

"Yes, sir," Cam said, although Master Winder's advice had been aimed at their entire group.

"Well done," Master Winder said, speaking his final words to Cam before gesturing for Jade. "Let us speak. Your Primary Tang is Synapsia. You have it and Kinesthia at Gold. Raise Synapsia to Crystal, and you should have an easier go of raising Spirairia to Gold as well. After that, work on Kinesthia. Two Crystals and Spirairia at Gold is a strong start, and if you're lucky, you might have a chance to raise the last to Crystal, too, before you Advance to Acolyte."

"Yes, Master Winder," Jade said, bowing her head more humbly than Cam would have ever expected her to do.

Master Winder next spoke to Avia. "Your Primary Tang, Kinesthia, is at Gold. Same with Synapsia. This is where things grow tricky. Normally, you must Enhance your Primary Tang above the others, but doing so isn't what you need. Raise Synapsia first. Hold it there. Fight however you must to make it happen. It will be confusing, like walking through a darkened cabin, trying to avoid the nails at your feet. Get to the end of the hallway, and at that point, you should be able to Enhance Kinesthia. You'll then have two Crystal Tangs and can even work on Spirairia."

Avia paled. It wouldn't be easy doing what Master Winder suggested.

"Pan," Master Winder said, drawing Cam's friend forward. "You will do the same as Avia. The two of you should work together."

"Yes, sir."

Master Winder might have sighed when he faced Weld, who had his shoulders thrust back like he was standing at attention. But there was no hiding the green around his gills. "Mr. Plain," the Wilde Sage began. "Your Primary Tang is Kinesthia, and it's at Gold. The rest are Silver." The disappointment in his voice was obvious. "Your task is the hardest since you've travelled the shortest distance. For this reason, on this one occasion, I will gift you another tonic." From his pocket, he withdrew another bottle. "You will do as Avia and Pan. Raise your Synapsia to Gold with the first tonic. Then raise it to Crystal with the second. The tonics won't last long, but if you push past the pain, you can use your improved thinking to Enhance Kinesthia to Crystal. Your path will be more difficult, agonizing in many ways, but it will serve you right for slacking. Work harder from here on out. These tonics aren't meant for the lazy or the witless."

Weld ducked his head, red-faced and embarrassed, which he should be feeling. He'd started the term as their strongest member, and if he didn't change his ways, he'd soon be the weakest. And Light Squad had no room for someone who couldn't pull their own weight.

Master Winder raised his hands, calling their attention. "There are other matters to discuss as well. Please stay. I want you to more fully understand your purpose at this school."

The field grew silent as Master Winder prepared to address their unit, and Cam straightened, glancing at Pan. They shared a look of expectation, neither of them able to hide their curiosity and neither of them bothering. What was the true purpose of Light Squad? Cam had cogitated on it; talked it out with Pan, but they'd been unable to come up with any good answers. The solutions were there—Cam and Pan could feel them—but they were as invisible as no-see-'ems—the tiny swamp-living insects that bit hard as a mosquito.

Cam wondered if Master Winder's answers might bite just as hard.

They'd even considered asking Saira about it. She would be the one to know, but asking her didn't sit right. It would be similar to having her betray whatever she knew of Master Winder's plans. And Saira was too loyal to do the Wilde Sage shady like that.

Master Winder's eyes rested on Avia and Jade. "I've chosen every one of you for Light Squad this year; even those who aren't in my direct sponsorship. I spoke to your families about it, ensuring that you would be enrolled in this particular semester."

Cam frowned inwardly. That didn't make any sense. Master Winder had only lucked into him and Pan a week before the academy year started.

"Some of you were a lucky find," Master Winder said, seemingly talking directly to Cam's thoughts, his eyes drifting from him to Pan. "And if I hadn't found you, I might have shelved my plans for a time. But I took a gamble, and my gamble paid off." He stood silent a moment, like he was thinking on deep matters. "This world is in danger. You know of the boils. What you don't know is there are more of them every decade, every year. More rakshasas than there are of us, Ephemeral Masters. It grows ever harder to keep them in check. And the Great Rakshasas—Simmer, Shimala, and Coruscant..." He spat the names like a curse, "...grant their lessers aid and comfort, while our own Divines are nowhere to be seen."

Master Winder paced, head down, intensity written into his face and carriage. "So it falls on us, the Sages of Salvation, to save the world, and so we shall." He glanced at them. "I have taken a lead in this role. I field teams to lance boils, and they perform Devesh's work. We've attacked over a dozen boils in the past few years, lanced all of them. Far greater success than the units fielded by the other Sage-Dukes with only half their morbidity and mortality."

Cam viewed Pan, mouthing, *"morbidity and mortality?"*

"The number of injured and killed," Pan whispered as an aside.

Master Winder's hearing clearly picked up the explanation. "Exactly so, Mr. Shun. We are better trained because I demand the training. I don't demand perfection, but I don't accept anything less than the best from the men and women under my protection." His gaze landed hard on Weld, who shrank like a beaten dog. "They get the same from me."

Cam lifted his chin, proud to be a part of whatever plan Master Winder was telling them. All his life, he'd wanted a chance to be more than his disrespected surname, more than his prior drunkenness and weakness.

He had that now. Here at the Ephemeral Academy. A chance to make the world a better place.

Master Winder wasn't done talking. "This will be done by getting the best out of you. Listen to your professors. They will teach you, as well or better than the instructors placed by the Sage-Dukes. Your strengths will be strengthened. Your weaknesses tempered. Your flaws folded and removed. You will become warriors worthy of the name."

Professor Grey stirred, looking uncomfortable on hearing the last, and on the verge of speaking.

The Wilde Sage continued uninterrupted, though, his voice growing in power. "Do as I say, and you'll have a chance to achieve glory and greatness. More, you'll have a chance to fight for what is right and protect those who need it."

Cam was nearly vibrating in excitement. It was everything he'd ever wanted out of life. To make a difference and be someone of note. He clapped vigorously, leading the rest of Light Squad in a cheer.

Master Winder lifted his hands, calling for silence. "But like a newly forged sword, you need a proper test. Something more than martial exhibitions and challenges. To learn how far you've truly come. In this case, it's a newly discovered boil, but one you should be able to easily handle. It should prove to be an excellent training exercise. There are some dangers involved, but overall, the boil is something Light Squad can handle. I've discussed the matter with Professor Maharani. She will give you greater details."

"Where is the boil?" Jade asked. "And how long will we be gone from the school?"

"As I said, Professor Maharani has the details," Master Winder said.

"Suffice it to say, that you won't be leaving on this mission until after the mid-year testing. Afterward, lance the boil, and you'll prove worthy of my ongoing sponsorship."

"The students are worthy already," Professor Grey said. "They shouldn't have to face this kind of danger."

"I appreciate the advice, Professor Grey," Master Winder said, "but the danger is slight. The boil is lightly defended, and the students will be under my direct supervision and care. Just as importantly, Light Squad needs the practical experience."

"And who will command?" Professor Grey asked.

"Cam will command," the Wilde Sage answered. "I've heard the reports. He has good instincts for tactics."

On a day where he kept wanting to stand ever taller and prouder, the last comment had Cam craning his neck and shoulders, stiffening like never before.

"Professors Maharani and Shivein will support them," Master Winder said to Professor Grey. "You and Professor Werm aren't trained for combat. You would only get in the way."

"I do have experience," Professor Grey said, the first lines of anger hardening her features.

All this time, Master Winder hadn't bothered facing her. He finally did. "Not enough for what I require. You will stay here. Is that understood?"

"Yes, sir," Professor Grey said, the anger gone from her face and her features smooth as a winter's lake.

"Can you do this?" Master Winder asked.

Cam realized the Sage was talking to him. "I can."

"And your drunkenness? Is it under control? I won't have a commander, or anyone under my sponsorship with such a glaring weakness."

"I have it under control," Cam said, hiding his humiliation as best he could. He pretended he was a cool, winter lake, just like Professor Grey. "I haven't had any alcohol in over a year and a half."

"Good," Master Winder said. "Then you won't fail yourself, or me."

This time, Cam didn't want to straighten in pride. The words sounded too much like throwing bones to a loyal dog. Well, Cam was many things, but he was no one's dog. Anger and embarrassment coursed through his veins, but so did the competitive streak that rose up at times, such as now. He wouldn't fail himself, Master Winder, or anyone else ever again.

"I must go," Master Winder said, addressing Light Squad as a whole. "Your testing begins in a few days, the martial exhibition, and I expect victory. And recall again which Tangs I want you to Enhance. I expect to see you all with at least two Crystals the next time we meet." He rose into the air, elevating before exploding upward in a rush of speed and a booming of air.

Cam watched him leave, and a part of him was disappointed that the Sage couldn't stay for the mid-year tests. Despite Master Winder's harsh statements toward him at the end of the visit, Cam had a deep desire to impress the man.

His disappointment must have shown. "He is busy," Saira said, coming to stand alongside him. "There are places that require his help. Boils that threaten small towns that the dukes can't defend."

Cam set aside his petty concerns. "Why not?"

"Because the dukes don't always have enough Glories and Crowns to defend the smaller cities and towns."

Cam's confusion must have shown.

"You heard Rainen. It's about numbers. It's easier to walk the path of a rakshasa; to murder and steal than do as we do." Saira hesitated a moment. "And I know what he said at the end, bringing up your drinking wasn't something you enjoyed hearing, but it's his way. He doesn't want us getting too proud. And if the others see how he's willing to give you grief—the one who has come the furthest and has a chance to be the strongest—they'll think long and hard about what he'll do to them if they dare be lazy." Her gaze settled on Weld. "They need you as an inspiration."

"How are you feeling?" Cam asked Pan.

"Nervous but willing."

"Same here," Cam said with a bark of laughter.

The two of them sat on the floor, next to the dining table in their quarters. The clouds from earlier in the day had broken apart, and the evening sun poured through the windows. It was shortly after supper, and the rest of Light Squad was present, too.

Even Weld, which was a minor miracle. Cam reckoned for sure their cockiest member would be off drinking and womanizing. He snorted to himself. Weld likely wanted to do just that, but after being told off by Master Winder, some wisdom must have penetrated the fool's thick skull.

In fact, Weld was strangely quiet tonight, staring at the two tonics the Wilde Sage had given him. He swirled one of them about, glowering at it, lost in brooding thoughts. It sounded complicated what Weld would have to do; Enhance Synapsia to Gold and then Crystal before working on his Primary Tang of Kinesthia.

Then again, if Weld had worked harder throughout the term, he wouldn't be so far behind. A man could have all the talent, but if he worked lazy, then he had no one to blame for his hardships but his own self. It didn't mean Cam didn't empathize—he did—but that empathy only stretched so far. Weld had to find his own way forward.

Besides, Cam had other matters on his mind. He glanced at his slim hourglass bottle; the tonic that had the thickness of wine. Cam's mouth watered on thinking of the heavenly drink, but he automatically shoved down the need. Work needed attending, and he wouldn't sit around staring at a bottle like a mooncalf idiot.

Cam rose to his feet, drawing closed the blinds. Master Winder had advised darkness when imbibing the tonic. "I'm fixing to take my tonic," he said. "Soon as I do, I don't want no one bothering me or talking in my ear."

"We won't," Jade replied. She peered about, fierce as a falcon. "The same holds true for me. When I upend the tonic, don't talk."

Pan shifted on the floor, munching on a bamboo shoot. "Maybe we should take the tonics at the same time?"

Cam shook his head in disagreement. "Master Winder said we should have friends on hand to encourage us when we're weak."

"I don't need any encouragement," Jade declared.

Cam stared at her, surprised by her cocky attitude. It wasn't usually like her.

"Mind if I go first?" Weld asked. His voice had come out hoarse as a rasp across wood. "I've got two tonics to take, and I doubt either will be easy." He glanced around the others. "Do you think you can watch out for me? I'll take one, and try to—"

"Do more than try," Cam growled, angry for reasons he couldn't explain. "Get your Synapsia to Crystal. Fight like you've never had to. You do that much, and I'm sure you'll make it. But use any of this *try* nonsense, and you'll faceplant. You understand?"

Weld viewed him askance before eventually offering a shallow nod.

"As for going first, no," Cam said. "Those of us who have the least work will take our tonics, and once we've seen to what's needed, we can help you."

"Are you sure about this?" Pan asked as an aside.

"I'm sure," Cam answered. "Focus on yourself. Be ready." He held up his tonic, readying to unstopper the wax seal.

Jade had her own bottle in hand as well.

Cam grinned to the room at large. "See y'all on the other side of Crystal." A quick pull, and the wax seal came away with a hiss. A pungent smell filled the air, harsh with the smell of brine but softened by the perfume of flowers. It wasn't the most appetizing of aromas. Staring down at the liquid, through the remnant of the broken seal, Cam still couldn't tell just what color the tonic might be. It moved heavy, though, like it had a greater weight than what he expected.

Shrugging casually, he upended the bottle, draining it in one go. Immediately, his stomach clenched around a taste that was worse than the smell, reminding him of yellow bile. His vision grayed, went white, brightened again. Shimmers filled his sight while a fire poured outward from his center. It spread in a flash to his toes. Contracted back to his center, rose through his throat, into his heart. Spread again, condensing. Again, his gaze grayed, went white. The sensations stretched like fingers, toward his Source. Reaching into it, providing a possibility.

The curdling in Cam's stomach settled while at the same time, a need for sleep soothed away his worries. But Cam recalled what Master Winder had warned. The tiredness wasn't real. It was a limit, and he wouldn't let it define his heavens.

Cam Delved his Source, watching with eyes closed as it brightened under the influence of the tonic. The ongoing siren-song lullaby was refused. He would sleep after the work was finished. Spirairia required condensing, and Cam got down to the business of doing it.

The tonic continued to flare, a locus of energy, and Cam gathered it fully into his Source. He used it to condense Spirairia, stoking it, working it like dough. Never stopping.

Time lost meaning, and all Cam knew was the labor at hand. He kept at it. Compressing Spirairia, stiffening it. On and on he went, until finally, Spirairia flared to a silvery, reflective brightness, tinkling like a tiny bell. He'd Enhanced the Tang to Crystal, and he smiled to himself in satisfaction.

Cam opened his eyes to a room draped in silence. Avia and Weld were alert, nodding his way when he awoke. Otherwise, they had then attention on Pan and Jade, who were also still working.

Thinking on everyone's needs, Cam fetched a number of tall glasses of water. They'd likely have some thirst. Afterward, he settled in to wait.

29

Cam tugged at his clothes. Loose fitting as they were, the bright saffron color of his pants and vest along with the carnation red shirt and silver buttons were a mite louder than he was comfortable wearing. His normal garb was usually bland and boring, not this peacock array of clothes, which he didn't like. There was also an ornate, bronze sword on his hip, a dull prop, but it, too, had too much shine.

Fact was, if Cam's kinfolk ever saw him dressed like this, they'd pull a muscle laughing.

Grimacing over the situation, he glanced about where he stood with Light Squad, all of them waiting just outside a stage where the martial exhibition was taking place. Back here, the lights were turned down and dimness held sway, but a hustling of people broke the monotony. Other units had already gone onstage and demonstrated their skills, and in a few minutes it would be Light Squad's turn. A musty smell had Cam rubbing his nose, and he hoped not to have to sneeze. The last thing he needed tonight was a distraction. Or maybe that's exactly what he needed.

Once again, Cam ineffectually tugged at his clothing. Why couldn't his garb have been bland, like Cam himself? He wasn't exciting enough, nor did he have the confidence to carry off these clothes.

But Weld did. His clothes fit him like a glove, which made sense given the man's cockiness. Of course, the sickly expression on his face told the truth about his state of nerves. Weld wanted to get this over with just as bad as Cam.

Pan, who also wore the same clothing, seemed the most rested and relaxed, which was unnatural. Usually, Pan was full of anxieties.

"You feeling good?" Cam asked, checking in on his friend.

"Better than ever," Pan replied with his typically toothy grin. "After the other night, enhancing Synapsia to Crystal, everything seems right as rain."

Cam grinned at his friend who had used one of *his* favorite phrases. "Everything might be right as rain, but these clothes ain't what I'd call subtle." Another tug. "Or comfortable."

"You look fine," Saira said, moving to stand next to him. She wore a silk sari, pleated and folded close around her ankles. It was a deep purple color with a gold blouse that left most of her abdomen exposed. Metal bangles of various colors graced her wrists and around her ankles were slender, silver chains. They tinkled with every step she took. Her dark hair was gathered in a braid piled atop her head, and she had a sheathed sword at her waist as well.

Avia and Jade were similarly attired, and all three women looked beautiful tonight. Of course, they were beautiful on any night.

Cam cut off his thoughts. He didn't need to be admiring the women in his life like that. "I don't know about me looking fine," Cam said in reply to Saira's comment, "but I'll be happy when I can change out of this finery."

Saira's lips twitched into a smile. "Looking fine. Finery. Did you mean to say that?"

Cam cocked his head like he was pondering the matter. "You know. I think I did."

Saira chuckled, patting his upper arm and giving it a light squeeze. "As long as you can take humor in a situation, you'll do well."

Cam didn't think so. Some situations just weren't funny. "Do you have many dances back where you came from?"

"In Sinane? We have them all the time. Every month there's a different reason to have a celebration." Her smile became broader. "My favorite is the Festival of Spring. Some call it the Festival of Love. It's where we're supposed to let go of any mistakes and regrets made in the past year; to end any conflicts we might have with others; and forgive and forget. People celebrate by dancing through the day. Lovers throw colored powders on one another. It's so beautiful."

It sounded like something out of a dream, but Cam could never imagine taking part in it. It was too much for a country boy like him. "I'm sure you'll get to celebrate it again." He mentally winced the instant his condescending words left his mouth. Saira missed her home, and it often sounded like she thought she'd never get to go back.

Sure enough, just as he feared, Saira took his words badly. Her smile became wistful and brittle. "I'm not so certain about that," she said. "In order to go home, I have to become a Sage, and since I regressed, that's going to take a lot longer than my mother would have ever expected of me. If I'd never left Sinane, I might have already managed it."

Her explanation had Cam curious. "Then why'd you leave?"

Saira appeared to shake off her rough memories. "Because the world required a daughter of Sinane to help protect it against the rising dangers. And while I could have become a Sage had I stayed home, it would have been as a weaker version of what I wanted. My mother is a Sage Greater—she has her Primary Tang at Sage and another Tang at Glory, but I want to become a Sage Prime: my Primary at Sage and another at Crown. There hasn't been one in Sinane in generations."

"Why is that so important?"

Saira's distant expression focused on him, and Cam had to force himself not to step back under the intensity of her blue-eyed regard. "I had a dream once. It woke me in the middle of the night. I only wanted to go back to sleep, but it wouldn't leave me in peace. I tossed and turned, and the whole time, the dream kept unspooling. There were visions, words, songs, and all of them had the same meanings."

She didn't say right away what that was, and Cam waited for her to explain herself.

"They boiled down to several simple truths," Saira continued. "The first one, I'm sure you know: *All is Ephemera and Ephemera is All.* The second was this: doubting one's certainty can be the highest form of growth."

Cam wasn't sure what to make of Saira's admission. The first part sounded correct, but the second… wasn't that why she'd lost her Awareness as a Crown? Doubting Master Winder and herself?

His disbelief must have shown because Saira's expression became a knowing smirk. "You can say what's on your mind."

Cam explained what he'd been thinking. "Why would you want to be doubting anything else when you already gave up so much by doing it once already?"

"An excellent question," Saira admitted. "And my mother would agree with you. It's a large reason for her disappointment in the choices I've made. She wanted me to follow in her footsteps; not this journey I've undertaken. Her disappointment is a large reason I can't go home until I become a Sage Prime and show her why my decision was the right one."

It wasn't the first time Saira had said she was a disappointment, and just like it had in times past, it sounded wrong. Saira was an amazing person. She was kind, compassionate, generous, and on top of that, despite being intelligent as a whip and beautiful as a new day dawning, she was humble and good.

"Well, if your mother is ever disappointed in you, then she's wrong," Cam said. "You're wonderful."

"Well, thank you," Saira said with a soft smile. "And by the way, did it work?"

"Did what work?"

"Did I distract you?"

Cam realized the conversation *had* distracted him, and he chuckled at what she'd managed. "That was sneaky."

"But it worked?"

Cam chuckled ruefully. "It worked."

"There are only two more squads before us," Saira said. "Let's watch them together?"

"Yes, ma'am."

"And Cam?"

"Yes, ma'am?"

"Relax."

Talking it out with Saira helped soothe Cam's nerves, and he gazed onstage, watching Victory's squad. After them would come Charity's group and then Merit's unit.

And finally would come Light Squad. Usually, they would have been the first group out there since the lowest ranked unit always went first. But this year, with Cam's position as the Novice with the most Tangs at Crystal, Light Squad would be the one to go last.

Cam watched the proceedings alongside Saira, and he glanced back when the others joined them. Weld hung back, still looking green around the gills. His normal cockiness was as absent as leaves on a winter-bare tree, and Cam eased back to talk to him. He didn't want Weld vomiting all over himself, which the other man looked like he might be fixing to do. Cam also needed Weld's best. The only way they could win the exhibition was if each of them was on point and giving their all. Worrying about not vomiting was no way to do the latter.

"You're looking a bit rough," Cam noted to Weld. "Anything I can do to help?"

Weld grimaced. "I'm not nervous," he said. "Not much. It's just those tonics from the other day. Fixing what was wrong with me hurt pretty bad." He winced as if in demonstration of his pain. "I haven't been sleeping much."

Cam frowned, not liking what he was hearing. "You still hurting?"

"No. I'm fine, but getting my Synapsia to Crystal, holding it there and getting Kinesthia to the same..." He shuddered. "I never want to go through that again."

"I know what you mean. Growing can be painful. But so far, the journey has been worth it, even with all the heartaches I've experienced."

"Really?" Weld asked, sounding doubtful.

Cam shrugged. "A lot of folks wouldn't think so, but I can't say that I'm unhappy with the person I've become. If I hadn't suffered, then I wouldn't be me."

"And your friends would still be alive. I heard what happened to them."

Cam's gaze sharpened. "I said if *I* hadn't suffered. I didn't say I wanted my friends dead. If I could become as I am right now—even with my addiction to drinking—and have my friends alive… I'd take that in a heartbeat."

From within the folds of his clothes, Weld pulled a small, silver flask. It was hourglass-shaped, just like the bottles that had contained the tonics, and on unstoppering it, the aroma of alcohol filled the air. "Don't mind me."

Cam's mouth watered. His eyes glazed. That drink. How badly he wanted some. With a forceful, and by now, automatic repression, he pushed off the desire, taking a careful step away from the other man.

Weld took a long pull. "Want some?" he asked, innocence on his face as he held out the flask.

Cam's jaw clenched. He didn't know why Weld would make such an offer. He clearly knew about Cam's weakness. The answer came with the spread of a sneer across Weld's face. It was an intentional bit of cruelty on the other man's part. "Go frag yourself, you jackhole," Cam said.

"Takes one to know one."

"What's that supposed to mean?" Cam demanded, seeing red. He got close to Weld, right in his grill.

"You think I didn't see how you looked at me the other night. Sure, you got yourself to Crystal on your own, and Master Winder might have been disappointed with me, but you didn't have to treat me like you did."

This was why Weld was acting like this? For getting called out the other evening? It was pathetic. The red in Cam's vision deepened. His eyes narrowed, and he wanted to do nothing but punch the smirk off of Weld's face. With a controlled exhalation, he breathed out his anger. Now wasn't the time.

"You're right about one thing," Cam said. "Master Winder *was* disappointed with you, and if you're the reason we don't win tonight, what do you think he'll do next?" He snorted. "Enjoy your drink."

Weld continued to sneer. "I know what I have to do, and I'll do it. You go on and romance Professor Maharani. Or should I call her Saira, like you do?"

Cam closed his eyes, praying for patience. He knew what Weld was about now; anything to get under Cam's skin. It wouldn't work. Drama was the last thing Cam wanted, especially with the martial exhibition coming up.

"You best know your role," Cam advised. "If you don't, or if you try and sabotage us, I'll make sure you're off Light Squad."

"You don't have that kind of pull," Weld scoffed.

"I don't, but Saira does. And seeing as how I'm *romancing* her, I'm sure she'd listen to what I have to say. After all, I'm the highest ranked member of Light Squad, and until the other night, you were the lowest."

"Without me, there's no way you'll lance that boil."

"You think we can't recruit someone to take your place? Everyone in Light Squad has at least two Crystal Tangs. Other folks are noticing. Wondering what it's like to hitch their wagon to ours. So, yes, we can replace you. It won't even be hard. We'll probably have people beating down the doors." And truthfully, it might even be a good idea given Weld's attitude. He'd always been too proud of himself and difficult to deal with. But this? Cruel behavior over a barely-there slight? He wasn't the kind of person Cam wanted in his life.

His words must have finally penetrated Weld's thick arrogance because the other man's face went pale. "You wouldn't kick me off the squad; not right before the martial contest."

"Maybe so. But it would still be a better problem than dealing with you," Cam said, staring Weld in the eyes, wanting the other man to see how serious he was. "Are we having an understanding?"

Weld dropped his eyes. "We are."

It wasn't good enough. Cam needed Weld to say it. "And what understanding is that?"

"I'll work hard, and I won't give you any more trouble."

"No, you won't," Cam agreed. He left Weld stewing there, returning to the rest of Light Squad, who eyed him askance, concern on their faces. They must have picked out the tension between him and Weld, especially since Cam's face always gave away his emotions.

"Is there a problem?" Pan asked, viewing him in worry.

"Not anymore," Cam replied.

Saira stared his way, flicking her gaze at Weld. "Will he be alright for the dance?"

Cam eyed Weld, who was staring at the floor. His expression of unhappiness was as obvious as the bright colors of his clothes. "We'll see." If Weld failed them, then he'd find out that Cam hadn't been lying about having him removed. "If he's the reason we falter, we'll have to replace him."

"I hope it doesn't come to that," Saira replied.

Cam wanted to agree with her, but if it turned out to be necessary, he also wouldn't hesitate in getting on with it. The only one who might not agree was Jade. She liked Weld—for reasons Cam couldn't decipher—and of all of them, she'd be the one who would be most upset.

He shrugged to himself. It was a bridge he'd cross if and when he needed to. For now, there was the martial exhibition coming up. He'd best concentrate on that.

It was time. Cam breathed out any last lingering nerves, imagining there was no room in his heart for it. He and Light Squad would complete this exhibition and win because they'd worked too hard. No chance they'd lose. A quick glance around the small theater in which the exhibition was to take place showed him it was a full house. The room was packed, and Cam could make out a few of his instructors seated in the middle rows, while up front was Lord Queriam and some other rich folks based on the quality of their garb.

Another last examination, this time to the back, showed Weld no longer seeming so nervous. Instead, a fearsome concentration held sway over the man's features.

Cam scowled. Weld had best not mess up. The more Cam thought about finding someone to replace him, the more it made sense. Why deal with someone who gave him lip for no cause, picked on Pan for no reason, and was cruel enough to offer a recovering drunk a sip of whiskey?

No reason at all. But it was something he'd have to account for later. Right now, there was the dance.

Light Squad entered the stage, lined up in two rows, each man opposite a woman. In Cam's case, he faced Saira, waiting on the music to start. She had her knees bent, arms overhead, and hands in a pose. He matched her positioning, concentrating on the first movements. He didn't want to get this part wrong. For whatever reason, the opening steps weren't hard, but if he was to make a mistake, that's when it would happen.

A quick grin on Saira's part broke through Cam's concentration, and he realized he'd tensed up, shoulders locked with nerves. He smiled back, shaking out arms and legs before getting back into the proper position. Once ready, he Delved his Source, Bonding Synapsia and Kinesthia.

Time elongated. The world slowed. He could count the dust motes floating in the air. The murmur of the audience became intelligible as he pieced together individual conversations. Folks were wondering why Light Squad had the honor of performing last in the martial exhibition.

Well, they'd learn soon enough that Light Squad was the best damn unit they'd see this evening.

A second later, the music looked near to starting. It was played by a small band of musicians that the academy had hired for today's exhibition. Until now, the musicians had been sawing away on their instruments, keeping their fingers loose. But now they'd gone quiet.

Cam viewed them briefly. There was a fellow playing the tabla, another behind a set of drums, a fiddler, and a pair on guitars—a standard and a four-string. There was also a mandolin player, but he didn't strike Cam as a musician only. The man had skin the color of tea touched with milk and moved with an undefinable grace.

The music burst forth, and on the opening notes, Saira and Cam leaped upward in unison. He kept pace with her, in both height and speed, matching her movements, which hadn't been the case a month ago. They swirled around each other, arms and legs twirling.

Cam relaxed into the motions once the first few steps were out of the way, falling into the rhythm. He let it flow through him. The tabla and drums framed a heavy beat. A deep bass set out from the four-string guitar, and the fiddle wailed while the mandolin notes circled above. The music carried Cam, driving him forward and onward.

Then there came a part that required exquisite timing. Cam focused anew, not wanting to mess this part up. Thus far, Light Squad was demonstrating explosive movements, but it would grow ever greater in just a few seconds.

"Sai!" Saira shouted. It was a signal, and with a smooth motion, she drew her sword.

Cam did so as well. They rang their blades against each other's, still dancing. Still swirling, but every fourth beat, they clashed again. Saira swept her blade low. Cam leapt it, went into a front roll, and she leaned away from a thrust. He pulled away from her riposte. They reset before going at it again.

Their movements shifted Light Squad's line, and for a few beats, Cam faced off against Jade.

Another shift, and once again, he faced Saira. *Shift*. And he faced Avia. *Shift*. Back to center and dancing with Saira, who shouted again.

With a slamming of swords into scabbards, their blades were sheathed. The music slowed, and Light Squad slammed to a halt. But only an instant. They moved next into a measured pace, matching the sedate tempo. Now was the demonstration of control.

Cam's hands went around Saira's waist. He lifted her overhead, and she arched into a layout. A spin, and he set her down. Her hands went around his waist, and without any effort, she lifted him while he mimicked her posture from seconds earlier.

They flowed into the waltz; formal, dignified, and restrained. Half a minute later, the tempo rumbled, becoming staccato. The dance's pace increased until with a burst, Light Squad was swirling about as swiftly as they ever had. They ended in a single line this time, dancing in rhythm, facing the crowd. Cam distantly noted the audience was grinning in clear delight.

The music became a thundering, repeating chorus, and Light Squad kept up. The final few seconds. Cam held hands with Saira on one side and Pan on the other. And on the last note, everyone leaped and landed as one.

The demonstration was over, but Cam continued to hold hands with Saira and Pan as the crowd cheered riotously. The audience appeared overwhelmed with joy, many of them, including Lord Queriam, wiping away tears. Cam didn't know what was going on. His heart pounded. He grinned wildly, and his breathing wanted to come in heavy pants, but he refused it. He kept his attention outward, staring shiny-eyed.

Had Light Squad really impressed the crowd so much?

Saira briefly squeezed his hand, and Cam finally broke from staring outward, looking her way.

It was the most natural thing to draw every member of Light Squad, including Saira and Weld, into an embrace. They'd given their best. Cam knew it, and he also knew even if they didn't win the demonstration, they'd made a lasting impression.

A year ago, he'd have never imagined himself in a grand city, impressing Ephemeral Masters and rich folk. It told him a truth that he struggled to reconcile, and maybe he never would. But in that moment, he reveled in how far he'd traveled and how much further he might yet go.

All is Ephemera and Ephemera is All.

30

"To Light Squad and to kicking ass!" Cam saluted the members of his unit, all of whom had come together at the Blind Pig, the inn they'd taken to going whenever a gathering was in the offing.

Even Saira was present. Same with Professors Shivein, Grey, and Werm. They'd all come to celebrate the victory earned during the recently finished martial exhibition. It was late, but the streets of Nexus remained packed with folks out and about, going to see friends and loved ones, or just out to enjoy the city. The smells of a hundred different foods, and the raucous cries of people having a good time filled the air.

The only person not having a good time seemed to be Professor Werm who sat in a corner, nursing a beer, and viewing the world in his strangely calm, detached manner. He still wore a slight sneer, but by now Cam reckoned it wasn't a sneer so much as just the way the man's mouth was shaped. Meanwhile, Pan, Avia, and Shivein were off in a corner laughing over something, while Weld and Jade were having what looked to be a fierce discussion. Cam had a notion what it might be about. *Weld's behavior before the exhibition.*

He dismissed them from his thoughts, especially Weld. Right now, he didn't have much use for the man. Instead, Cam kept his attention on Saira, who was talking to him about the exhibition.

"I didn't think you were so heavy," she said with a chuckle as her cerulean eyes sparkled amidst the blue that demonstrated her Awareness as a Glory. "I barely got you lifted over my head."

"Am I really that heavy?" Cam asked, genuinely confused.

Saira's eyes boggled. "Have you seen yourself? You're taller than nearly every other Novice and built like you've been carrying logs your entire life."

Cam rubbed the back of his neck. "I don't know about logs, but there have been some heavy weights in my life."

Saira's humor transitioned to a tight-lipped expression of empathy. "I know."

Cam silently cursed himself. He shouldn't have said that. He preferred seeing Saira happy than having her feel sorry for him. He forced a quick grin. "It's not a problem. I'm a student at the finest Ephemeral school in the world. I've got good friends. And I've got wise teachers. Those weights aren't so heavy anymore."

"Wise teachers?" Saira chuckled. "Devesh, you make me sound so old."

During all the time he'd known Saira, Cam had never bothered learning how old she was… or dared ask her really.

She must have guessed the question on his mind. "I'm thirty-two."

"Only twelve years older than me?" The difference wasn't that much, and maybe when he closed the gap in Advancement, he could—

"Twelve years older but a hundred in worth and experience," Professor Shivein said, intruding on their conversation and slipping in between them like he belonged.

Cam wanted to shoot Professor Shivein a glare of irritation, but he knew better. The turtle likely wouldn't take it too well.

"Professor Maharani is worth every one of you Novices," Professor Shivein said. His words were slurred, and the alcohol on his breath explained that the professor was either drunk or well on his way to it.

Cam's nostrils flared on smelling the alcohol.

Before Cam could respond to Professor Shivein, Weld sidled up to his side. "Can I talk to you?" he asked.

Cam had a guess as to what it might be, but he didn't plan on making it easy. "About what?"

"Something private. I think you know."

"Sure," Cam said, seeing now how his guess was right. "There's an alley nearby."

They left the party, weaving between traffic until they reached the darkened alley, which reeked of urine and refuse. No one was about, though.

"What did you want to talk about?" Cam asked, leaning nonchalantly against the alley wall.

Weld didn't look like he could hold still. He twitched, arms moving, hands restless. He finally settled on folding them behind his back. "About what I did and what you said. I told Jade. She said I'm lucky you're nicer than she is. She said she would have ripped my head off for doing something like that." He scuffed a boot against the ground. "I don't think she respects me much right now."

Cam stared at Weld in disbelief. "And it took talking to Jade to tell you what you did was wrong?" He snorted in derision. "So, what did you want to tell me? And make it something that I don't already know. Because from where I'm standing, you're scum. You're full of yourself. You're lazy. You speak poorly to Pan. And you're thin-skinned and cruel enough to entice a drunk to drink. So where does that leave us?"

Weld's jaw clenched, like he was the one who'd been wronged. But he surprised Cam when he exhaled and his anger seemed to flee, replaced by regret. "You're right. I am all those things. And I can't say I'll change, but I'll try. I'll work hard. I'll stop speaking poorly to Pan, and I'll never again do what I did to you."

"And what's that?" Cam pressed, arms folded. "What did you do?"

"I tried to hurt you in the worst way possible," Weld said, not dropping his eyes.

Cam had to give the man credit. At least Weld could hold the gaze of the person calling out his wrongs. "Yes, you did," Cam agreed. "And from where I come from, we don't forgive or forget; not for something like that."

"I'm not asking for forgiveness or forgetting. I'm asking for a second chance. Please."

Cam would have liked nothing better than to tell the man to stick his *please* where the sun didn't shine. But how could he? Hadn't Cam received exactly that kind of grace by all the people who loved him? They hadn't abandoned him when he'd slipped into alcoholism. Then there was Honor's gift? She'd given him his life back.

How then could he not offer the same to Weld?

He couldn't, but it didn't mean his patience needed to be endless. "Second chance is your last chance," Cam said. "You mess with me again. You mess up again, and you're done with Light Squad. Am I clear?"

"Crystal." Weld's lips quirked into a smile. "See what I did there? Crystal because of your Tangs."

Cam gazed at him, flinty and without a hint of a smile. "It's too soon to be trying to joke around with me," he replied. "Let's head back to the party before folks start wondering if we're murdering each other."

The next morning dawned cloudy but unseasonably warm. It was still winter, but it felt like spring with humidity in the air, and the promise of green things growing. Cam had spent the early hours writing home, telling his family and friends about the martial exhibition Light Squad had won.

Afterward, it was time to head to the coliseum. Cam walked behind the rest of Light Squad, rubbing the top of his head and wishing he'd taken the time to get his hair trimmed. He didn't like it any longer than long stubble, and right now, it lifted as high as his knuckles.

Thinking on his hair gave way to thinking on the day to come. Although, Light Squad was ranked ahead of everyone else, for some reason, they were also the ones scheduled to go first in the martial competition. It made no sense, stinking of unfair politics, which, come to think of it, was about how the world worked.

At least they had better armor. Master Winder had seen to it. It was red in color, just like their Awareness, lighter and more flexible than that with which they had been practicing. Cam hoped it would make a difference; anything to help.

Pan drifted back to join him. "Are you feeling as nervous as I am?"

"Why are you nervous?"

Pan's ears drooped, and his usual good cheer was nowhere to be found. "Because I don't pull my weight."

Cam's eyes shot in the direction of his friend, outraged on his behalf. "Any of the others feel that way about you?"

Pan shook his head. "Only me." He hesitated. "And maybe Weld. He's not been acting right ever since the exhibition last night."

"Weld." Cam tried not to sound like he was cursing when he said the name. They'd kept clear of one another after last night's conversation, including at breakfast this morning when Cam hadn't bothered engaging Weld in any kind of talk. He was willing to give the man a chance, but that didn't mean he had to be friendly with him. Weld had a long ways to go before Cam saw him in a different light.

"What happened between the two of you?" Pan asked.

Cam vacillated in how to answer. There was one thing about knowing what Weld had done, and another in spreading gossip about him. Speaking those kind of words could ruin Weld's reputation, and there likely wouldn't be any coming back from that. Cam didn't think that was in Light Squad's best interest. "We had a disagreement is all," he answered. "You know how Weld can get. I set him straight."

"A good thing then," Pan said, still seeming down in the mouth.

They fell silent as they continued onward, coming across other students headed to the coliseum. Cam called greetings to them. He briefly wondered how many folks would be out watching them this morning. He doubted it would be a whole lot. In times past, the arena would be packed for the later tests, but the first ones were for unskilled teams, and most people wouldn't bother waking so early.

"You think we'll win?" Pan asked, his anxiety drifting off him like smoke.

Cam draped an arm across Pan's shoulders, having seen enough of his friend's sad-faced expression. "Let me ask you something," he said, speaking loud enough so his voice carried. "What's the worst that can happen today?"

"We fail," Pan replied.

"But we aren't going to fail," Cam said. "Ain't no way Devesh will let us fail, not after all we've been through. We're too good." The others had slowed down, glancing back to listen to him. "You hear me," he said to the rest of Light Squad. "We're too damn good. This boil ain't no more of a challenge than any we've already overcome. Think about it. Pan's a panda-person from some backwater in the Diamond Mountains, where folks have him believing his life ain't worth nothing unless he fulfills some fool prophecy. Avia used to be a fish."

"Not a fish."

"Whatever," Cam said, ignoring Avia's feigned outrage. "Then there's Jade, who's from a once-prosperous family, but now all their eggs is in one basket. Worst of all, they're counting on a girl to get them back their wealth."

"What's wrong with a being a girl?"

"Nothing," Cam said. "But we know girls ain't as tough as boys."

Jade slowed and landed a bruising punch against his shoulder. "You sure about that?"

Cam tried not to wince after the punch landed. It had really hurt. "No. Not anymore," he said, pretending to peer at Jade, like he was studying her. "You sure you ain't a boy in disguise?"

"I'm sure. What about you?"

Her reply earned Cam jeers, even from Weld, and he took in the mockery in good nature, happy to see Light Squad showing some signs of life. Cam raised his hands, calling for quiet. "And we can't forget Weld." He had to be careful here. Weld wasn't a friend and roasting him might not go over like Cam wanted. "He was once the best of us, then he became the least. But we all saw him dancing fine last night. He kept up, and that's something." Cam stared Weld in the eyes. "You won't let us down, will you?"

"No, sir," Weld said without the slightest hesitation or mockery in his voice. "I won't let anyone down."

"Keep your word, and you won't have no trouble," Cam said, still maintaining eye contact.

"What about you?" Pan asked.

"What about me?" Cam replied.

"Exactly," Jade said with a teasing grin. "What about you? You're too big and tall to move with anything but the grace of a drunk buffalo."

Cam pretended to scowl. "Does the buffalo have to be drunk?"

"You know he does," Jade said, looping an arm through Cam's as she viewed the rest of the squad. "We have an Awakened panda who thinks his only worth is to fulfill a prophecy. A fish—"

"I'm not a fish!"

"—walking on dry land," Jade continued. "A man too cocksure for his own good. Me, someone with the weight of a family's expectations. And then we have our leader. Someone we can best compare to a drunken buffalo."

"Why's the buffalo got to be drunk?" Cam complained once again.

"You know why," Jade said. She still had her arm looped in his.

"There you have it then," Cam said. "We've gone through more hard knocks than any other unit, which means winning the boil ain't going to be a problem. We'll get it done and celebrate again." He stared at the others, making sure to meet their gazes. "I had a mighty good time last night, and I aim to do it again. Y'all with me?"

Light Squad shouted their approval, earning strange looks from those close at hand. To hell with what those other folks thought.

"To Light Squad," Cam shouted.

"To Light Squad!"

Light Squad exited a small holding room and entered the coliseum, descending to the pitch like they had on their initial test. It was still early in the morning, and only a few people were around. They offered scattered cheers at Light Squad's arrival. Cam stared about at those in attendance, figuring the early-risers must think they were either getting the worm or they had some other reason to be here. Whatever that was, he had no notion. Nor did he care. He was just glad for their presence. At least someone would be around to watch Light Squad conquer and achieve.

Just then, his eyes caught a glad sight. A huge leaderboard was framed to the retaining wall surrounding the coliseum grounds. It took up a large section and listed the various Novice units and their rankings. Light Squad's name sat squarely at the top.

An instant later, another sight had him less happy. It was the weather. In the short time since breakfast, heavy clouds had rolled in, and a soaking might be in the offing. If so, Cam wanted to get started before the weather took a rainy turn.

"Not a lot of people around," Pan said. "Which is sad for them. There won't be a lot of people around who can brag that they saw the legend of Light Squad unfurl." He offered his happy smile.

"Their loss," Cam agreed as he led Light Squad onto the coliseum grounds. A heavy fog clung to the floor, unnatural and making it impossible to see what they would have to fight against.

Cam turned to face Lord Queriam, who stood in a covered booth. With him were Light Squad's professors, all of them standing and smiling, applauding enthusiastically. It brought a lump to Cam's throat to have their support.

Lord Queriam raised his hands, calling for quiet, which didn't take much given the sparse crowd who appeared half-asleep or hungover. Cam knew the latter feeling all-too well. He also knew the best way to get past a hangover was to get rip-roaring drunk.

Not now, he thought, automatically shoving away the desire.

Lord Queriam began speaking. "To those in attendance, the first unit we have facing the mid-year challenge is Light Squad. They have done remarkably well, winning the martial exhibition. In addition, one of their members, Cam Folde, is the highest ranked Novice in memory, having all three of his Tangs—" He paused when Professor Grey said something to him, leaning toward her. "Of course. My apologies. Novice Folde has all *four* of this Tangs at Crystal, including Plasminia. That is correct. He is a Plasminian."

At this, the small audience murmured. Cam caught a number of them shooting him surprised and wondering glances.

He rolled his eyes. Yes, he was a Plasminian, but it didn't call for people to act like he was bizarre because of it.

Lord Queriam spoke again. "The other members of Light Squad have achieved similar qualities of greatness with all of them possessing two Crystal Tangs. Most impressive, would you not say?"

Polite applause followed his question.

Lord Queriam stared about, seemingly offended at the lack of a more enthusiastic response. With a gathering of his dignity, he continued. "They will be the first unit to address the boil. The first to make the attempt at conquering rakshasas. Their only information is this: of the enemy, there are fifteen."

"Fifteen?" Weld cursed under his breath. "We're outnumbered three-to-one."

"Which is no different than the odds we'll face in the wild," Cam reminded him. "If Lord Queriam was feeling properly peckish, we could have been on the wrong side of twenty rakshasas."

"It's still worse than the two-to-one odds we had last time we were here," Weld reminded them all.

Cam shrugged. "The odds are the odds. Whining about them won't do us no good. We got fifteen rakshasas to kill, and by Devesh, we'll kill them all." He faced Light Squad, his expression fierce. "Am I clear on this? We'll kill them all. No excuses."

Pan gave a firm nod. Same with the others. "No excuses," they replied.

"Let us see if they succeed," Lord Queriam said, winding down his speech. With a gesture, the fog shrouding the coliseum floor swirled as if caught in an eddy. It quickly tore apart, and a setting similar to the last time Light Squad had attempted to lance a boil faced them.

A single hill, towering with a near vertical cliff, loomed directly ahead, and a solitary trail snaked upward. It looked to be a hard climb.

"Take a count," Cam ordered. He had a spyglass in hand, using it in place of Kinesthia, which could have brought every aspect of the cliff into sharp relief. But it was also better to save the Tangs for when the battle was begun.

The rest of Light Squad stood close at hand, all of them using spyglasses as well, questing their gazes along the ascent, searching for the rakshasas.

"I see five coyotes," Avia said.

"Mark them," Cam ordered.

"All five are halfway up the trail," she replied. "Three on the left and two on the right."

"Weapons?"

"Bows."

Cam nodded. It made sense. The coyotes would try to pin them down with their arrows. He also reckoned they'd be a mite better with their aim than the rakshasas that Light Squad had faced when last they had lanced one of Lord Queriam's boils.

"Four elk," Weld said. "Further upslope. Can't tell what kind of weapons."

As big as elks were, they likely weren't handling bows. They'd be the ones wearing heavy armor and fighting with war axes, hammers, and antlers.

"Three bears," Avia pronounced. "Right next to the elks."

Cam cursed. Just how many powerful rakshasas was Lord Queriam throwing their way?

"Two bulls," Weld added. "Downslope of the other heavy rakshasas."

Cam's cursing became florid. This test had gone from difficult to nearly impossible. Worse, there was a final rakshasa for which they had not yet accounted.

Pan was the one to pick it out. "A tigress, toward the rear. She must be the one closest to the core."

Cam frowned, thinking on how to attack the rakshasas. They could charge uphill, but the coyotes would pick them off given that nearly vertical ascent they'd have to take. But what about those boulders a dozen yards upslope? If they could get there, they'd have some protection. He measured the distance to the rocks, gauging how far they were to the coyotes.

Suppressing fire from a pair of archers at the base behind those outcroppings, and…

A plan came together, and Cam explained what he had in mind. "Once we kill the coyotes, we close so we can pepper the bears with arrows. They'll want a piece of us. Get them angry enough, and they'll charge straight down. The bulls might even follow. The elks won't. They're too sensible."

"What about the tigress?" Weld asked.

Cam pondered, rubbing his chin. "Tigers get riled pretty easy, but they're also cunning. She'll hold back, try and ambush us."

Quiet settled on Light Squad as they considered the slope ahead of them and the plan to conquer the boil.

"Well, at least it's a plan," Jade said at the end.

"It'll work," Cam said, a surge of energy rippling through him, leaving him excited and without any doubts. He wanted the others to feel the same way. "We got this," he said, punching Pan in the shoulder. "We're going to burn them." He leaned his forehead against Avia, wanting her to feel what he was feeling. "You hear me? Come on!" He slapped her shoulders. "No chance we'll lose!"

She must have caught onto his energy because she snarled back at him, full of intensity. "No chance we'll lose!"

Cam moved off. "No chance," he replied, fist-bumping Jade's shoulders. "No chance! Say it."

"No chance!" Jade growled, fist-bumping his shoulders in turn.

"No chance," Cam said, addressing Weld.

"No chance!"

"No chance we're going to lose!" Cam shouted.

"No chance!" Light Squad roared back.

31

Cam slammed against a large boulder, huddling low. He wanted to ascend higher up the hill, but the fragging coyotes were on them like green on grass. And like he reckoned would be the case, the aim from the Awakened Beasts was much better this time. Cam's shield was already pincushioned with a half a dozen arrows. Same with everyone else's, and right now they were trapped—*fragging coyotes*—stuck at the base of the hill.

Light Squad's initial plan of having three of their members ascend while a pair of archers countered the coyotes had quickly fallen by the wayside. Any time any of them stepped clear of the boulders, the coyotes targeted them. It was an impossible situation, and the only obvious option seemed to be a straight-ahead charge.

Cam couldn't allow that. Light Squad would be ruined if they did something so stupid. There had to be another way forward. Maybe if—

"What do we do?" Weld shouted, crouched behind the same boulder as Cam. "They're all over us." The first hints of panic warped his voice.

Fragging Weld. Most times he was cocky as a rooster, but put him in a little danger, and he melted like ice on a hot griddle.

Cam gestured to Avia, who crouched close at hand. A couple feet away, on the other side of the trail, was Pan and Jade. "Can you punch arrows out of the air?" he asked her.

She cocked her head in question.

"I'm fixing to poke my head beyond the boulder. Soon as the coyotes start firing my way, can you push their arrows aside, so they don't murder me?"

Avia gave a firm nod. "I can do it." She jabbed Weld with an elbow. "We both can."

Weld grimaced, rubbing his gut where Avia had elbowed him, but he also nodded agreement.

Cam took a settling breath. *Here goes.* He leaned past the boulder. No arrows came at him, and he edged a bit further out. Still no arrows. A quick peek showed him the coyotes had their attention elsewhere, on Pan and Jade who were peeping above their boulder, keeping the rakshasas' focus.

Perfect.

Cam was ready; already Bonded to every one of his Tangs; bow in hand and an arrow on the rest. His eyes intent, a coyote's chest seemed to swell in his vision—a kill shot. A smooth pull brought the bow to full draw. A split-second to adjust his aim and release.

The arrow was still in flight, but Cam already had another arrow at the draw. The coyote he'd been targeting went down. The other rakshasas yipped in anger, shifting their attack on him.

Arrows whistled his way. Cam forced himself to remain still. Trusting Avia and Weld, he sighted his next target, a burly coyote, out in the open. Arrows fell around Cam, their paths twisting, missing him by inches. He released, ducking behind the boulder when an enemy arrow thudded right next to his foot.

He peeked out again. The burly coyote was down, and the remaining rakshasas launched fire at him. An arrow nearly took out his nose. Cam pressed back to the boulder.

"Two of them are out from cover," Avia noted, peering over the top of their boulder.

Cam hoped Pan and Jade could take advantage.

They did, not needing him to tell them what to do.

"They got one," Avia said. "The other one is trying to get back behind cover. He's—"

Cam didn't bother waiting on what she had to say. He rolled out from behind the boulder, rose to his feet, aimed, and released.

The arrow took a retreating coyote in the back.

Another roll brought Cam bumping against Pan. "Fancy meeting you here," Cam said with a grin. "I hear these parts are some kind of dangerous."

"What makes you say that?" Pan asked. "Just because some lunatic is shooting arrows at anything that moves?"

"I wouldn't compare those rakshasas to lunatics. Seems a mighty unfair thing to say about lunatics."

"I wasn't comparing the rakshasas to lunatics. I was comparing you to a lunatic."

Jade snorted, chuckling. "He's right. And if you're feeling any crazier than normal, you want to take down that last coyote?"

Cam levered himself upright. "I got a better idea. I'll be bait for the coyote. Soon as he steps clear of wherever he's hiding, put him down."

"Yes, sir," Jade replied, sounding serious.

"And none of this 'yes, sir' garbage," Cam said with a scowl.

"Yes, sir," Jade replied, lips twitching into a smile.

Cam sighed. "Just kill the coyote."

"Yes, sir."

Cam huffed. A moment later, he darted out into the open, waving his hands like a fool.

Frag! The coyote came out from behind an overhang far overhead. But worse, the bears were heading downhill. As fast as they were moving, they weren't but seconds away from making contact.

"Fire at will!" Cam shouted. "Kill those bears!"

He unlimbered his bow, distantly noting when Weld put down the last coyote. The bears, black-furred and massive brutes, rumbled downslope, not more than a dozen yards away. Cam aimed and fired as fast as possible. Two arrows, and there was no more time. Two bears were down, arrows peppering their hides. The last one also had a couple arrows protruding, but not enough to threaten the Awakened Beast.

Short swords then. Cam focused on Synapsia and Kinesthia, wanting as much speed as he could manage. Time stretched, dilated. Dust clouds hung in the air. The bear slowly grew in his sight, the red eyes prominent. He controlled his breathing. His heartbeat remained slow and steady. Just like always when it came to battle.

"Brace for impact!" Cam shouted. The bear sighted on him. Cam hunkered low. Right before the bear got in range, he darted forward. A duck under a swiping paw, and he was there. A straight thrust, directly into the bear's chest.

But not a kill shot. Cam lifted his shield against the counter—

—and was blasted off the ground, airborne. The world twisted. He tried to right himself, but still landed with a jolt. His helmeted head smacked the ground. For a moment, his vision blanked, came back into focus.

Cam blinked, first seeing stars and then Pan's concerned visage. "Are you alright?"

Cam tried to answer, managing only a mumble. His head wouldn't work correctly, hurt something fierce. Nausea gripped him, and Cam rolled over, vomiting. Afterward, he felt a smidge better. "Help me up." He groaned when Pan got him upright, closing his eyes when the world swayed and twisted. Seconds later, while the nausea still messed with his sight, Cam felt stable enough to take stock of the situation. "What happened?"

"You killed the last bear," Weld said, looking steadier, the panic gone from his voice. "The bear just didn't know it before he nearly knocked your head off."

"What about the rest of the rakshasas?" Cam asked.

"Holding position," Weld replied.

"Not quite," Avia clarified. "The bulls pulled back. They're standing next to the elk."

"Then we've still got four bulls, three elk, and the tigress," Cam mused. "Do they have bows?"

"If they do, they haven't used them yet," Pan said.

Cam nodded, studying the fifty-yard ascent. "They'll roll rocks on us." He pointed out a likely spot for the ambush. "Right when we reach that chokepoint. We'll be single file going through there."

"What if we give them a different target?" Jade suggested.

"I'm listening."

"A pair of us fire arrows. We arc our shots since we can't see them, but we still keep them pinned down."

"The others get in close and finish them while the rakshasas are distracted," Cam mused, rubbing his chin."

"Seems too easy," Weld noted.

"Tell my head it's too easy," Cam replied. "Jade and I will lay down the suppressive fire. The rest of you hustle uphill. I want them seeing Weld and Pan. Avia, stay hidden behind them. Cut them down when they ain't looking."

"And if the tigress attacks?" Weld asked.

"Then you'll have to hold until Jade and I get to you," Cam answered.

A few final instructions, and Weld, Avia, and Pan surged upslope. Cam immediately began launching arrows. It was a hard shot, but he didn't need accuracy. He only needed the rakshasas not looking down while the others got through the chokepoint. Even still, a couple of pained grunts from atop the hill told him he might have gotten lucky.

Even as he fired, Cam kept an eye peeled on his people hustling through the chokepoint. They were almost there. Just then, rocks the sizes of cantaloupes ripped down the hill, moving like they'd been fired from a ballista. Right at the chokepoint, they went, a barrage.

A roar of pain told him Pan had been struck. Cam hoped he wasn't too badly injured to fight.

Jade aimed and fired, steady and without letting up. "They're through."

"Go!" Cam barked. "I'll cover you."

Jade launched herself up the hill. Cam kept on firing arrows, and once she was through the chokepoint, she darted to safety.

Cam held onto his bow and sprinted. Bonds to Kinesthia and Synapsia helped him rush upward. But it was Plasminia, coursing like a fire through him, that had him going even faster. He'd done this before, but not to this extent, and doing so meant he'd burn through his Bonds in less than a minute.

Which was fine since at his pace, he moved in a blur. The world should have been a smear given his swiftness, but he could see everything. Every clod of dirt flung upward. Every flicker of light reflecting off dull stones thrown at him. Nothing escaped his attention, and every placement of his foot was sure. He leaped, from one boulder to the next, several yards with each stride.

Four vaulting steps, and he was through the chokepoint. The sounds of battle atop the hill carried to him. Ever swifter he rushed. A final jump, and he landed on the crest of the peak. The bulls fought Avia and Pan, the latter looked to have had his shoulder broken. Meanwhile, it was Weld and Jade against the elk. The tigress prowled forward. Cam didn't hesitate. He rushed the feline. Plasminia burned in his veins. Same with Synapsia and Kinesthia. And as fast as his mind was working, it was easy to see what the cat intended.

He rolled under a disemboweling swipe, unsheathing his sword in the same motion. A horizontal cut opened a deep wound across the tigress' chest. She growled, launching forward, swiping and swinging unfurled claws.

Cam blocked with his shield, throwing her last blow off the center line. A thrust took the cat in the throat. She gurgled, falling backwards. Cam put her out of his mind. Jade was down, blood soaking her chest. Weld was hobbling, looking like he could barely stand as he retreated from a single elk, who also wasn't moving too good.

Avia and Pan were also down, a bull standing over them. The rakshasa had a rivulet of blood leaking from a deep wound to its hip.

A decision was needed, and Cam made it. He bashed the elk threatening Weld off balance. "Get to the core. Lance it," he ordered.

"But—"

"Do it!" Cam shouted, facing off against the elk and the remaining bull. They stood between him and the core—but not Weld.

Weld finally got his ass in gear and disengaged. Cam prevented the rakshasas from going after him. The bull snarled, swinging his war-hammer in a vicious arc. Cam easily dodged. His Bonds weren't going to last much longer, but he only needed them to last long enough. If Weld lanced the core, everything would be over.

Cam threatened the bull with a sword. The rakshasa bit on the feint, lifting his warhammer to block. Cam spun on his heel, the sword sweeping in a horizontal slash. The injured elk tried to shift, but its leg gave way. Cam disemboweled the creature.

He sensed what was coming from the bull and fell over on his back. Rolled to evade pounding blows. Got to a knee. His Bonds frayed and came apart. He caught a punishing blow on his shield. It barely slowed the warhammer, shattering apart into splinters and pounding into Cam's chest. He was hurled onto his back, at least four ribs broken, struggling to breathe.

The bull loomed overhead, readying the killing blow.

What in the hells was taking Weld so long?

Even as the question passed across Cam's mind, the bull took a stumbling step away from him, appearing confused. Moving slowly. It was the opening Cam needed. He surged to his feet. A single thrust to the chest ended the rakshasa.

And as soon as the blow landed, Cam collapsed. The pain in his chest. His breathing grew shallow; his mind faint. Although they had taken three casualties, Light Squad had won.

The world faded to black.

Or maybe it was four casualties.

The world returned in fits and starts. Memory returned first. Cam clutched his chest, expecting pain, but… there was nothing. He took a testing breath, still anticipating injury. Again, nothing. Not a hint of his broken ribs. At that point, he levered himself up onto his elbows, eyes immediately going to his team. Pan and Avia were already up, while Jade was only now groaning to wakefulness. Weld stood near her, hand out to help her rise.

Cam got to his feet. "How you doing Jade?" he asked.

Before she could answer, the world shifted as the hill on which Light Squad stood smoothed, receded like it was melting. The rest of the pitch rose, swiftly forming an unbroken grass flooring. Only now did Cam hear the thunderous applause and the whistling cheers. Light Squad had won, but it hadn't been a cheap or easy victory.

Only Weld had managed to live through long enough for them to claim the win. The rest of them had died. It was a terrible math, the deaths of so many in order to claim what was barely a victory. And yet, the folks who had watched acted like they'd done something grand and glorious.

Cam's attention went to Lord Queriam's box. Their instructors were cheering just as wildly as anyone, including Professor Werm. It might have been one of the few times Cam had seen the man unabashedly happy. And more surprising, even Lord Queriam was smiling, clapping politely but clearly pleased.

What was going on? Cam looked to rest of his squad, hoping one of them had an explanation. Shrugs met his questioning gaze.

The last of the hill dissolved, and Light Squad now stood upon the coliseum floor, staring at Lord Queriam, who was calling for quiet. "We have just witnessed one of the finest exhibitions of courage and stamina in the history of this illustrious academy. You all know why. This particular challenge is one that no one in the past several hundreds of years has conquered. In fact, the last victory was won by a squad led by Rainen Winder, the Wilde Sage himself. Thus, for good reason, is this challenge called the Unwinnable."

Cam shared wondering gazes with the others. The Unwinnable? He'd heard of it. It was legendary in its difficulty. Had Light Squad really faced it? And more importantly, won? It seemed impossible—Cam's mouth quirked—or rather, unwinnable.

Lord Queriam was still talking. "For succeeding where no one has in centuries, Light Squad will earn thrice the normal acclaim for their success. Congratulations and well done!"

The doors leading out of the coliseum grounds opened then, a clear signal for Light Squad to depart. Before they exited, though, Cam viewed his instructors one last time. Professor Grey caught his gaze, and inclined her head in respect, while Professor Shivein gave a fist pump, and Saira and Professor Werm both simply smiled before bowing slightly.

Light Squad departed the coliseum, and as soon as they entered a small holding room, Jade shrieked, an unusual sound coming from her. "We won! Fragging yes! We won it all! Both challenges!"

Cam grinned at Jade, having briefly forgotten her competitive nature. Then again, he had that same burning desire, the way he used to feel when younger. Victory's sweet sensation swept over him, and he roared triumph. "I told you!" he shouted to the rest of Light Squad. "No chance we were failing!"

"No chance!" they shouted as one, all of them lost in jubilation.

"We should celebrate," Pan said. "Another night at the Blind Pig!"

"Unholy hells but it'll be fun," Weld declared.

"Let's see the rest of the tournament first," Cam suggested. "See who's coming in second place."

Jade grinned. "Now that's a plan."

The squad made to exit the holding room, but before Weld left, Cam held him back. "You did good."

Weld shrugged, looking like he was aiming to appear humble. "All I did was walk to the core and lance it. The rest of you did the hard work."

"We all did hard work," Cam corrected. "And without you, we wouldn't have made it out with the victory. Accept the praise."

Weld seemed like he had something else to say, but he swallowed down whatever it might have been. "Thank you." He hesitated. "Are we square?"

"Not even close, but one day, we might get there."

"I guess that's the best I can expect."

Weld left him then, catching up with Avia and Jade, throwing his arms across both their shoulders, and having them promptly shrug him off. Cam chuckled. Weld would never change, not the heart of him, but if he could do better, it might be enough for Cam to give the man some trust. Either that, or he'd give him enough rope to hang himself.

Pan was waiting for him outside the room. "Your plan worked."

Cam laughed. "My plan? It was our plan. Everyone contributed. Everything we did was a full effort from the squad."

"Without your leadership—"

"Stop," Cam ordered, not wanting all the acclaim to go his way. The rest of the squad had to know and feel that they'd earned this win; not just him. "I came up with the bare bones of a plan, but it was Light Squad as a whole that improved on it and executed it. We wouldn't have won if any of us hadn't given our best."

"So you say," Pan said, grinning in the toothy, mouth-agape way that made him look so cute. "I'm just glad you're our leader."

Cam laughed, throwing an arm over Pan's shoulder, drawing him close and kissing his forehead. "Come on. Let's go see how the other teams do."

"Yes, sir."

Cam groaned. "Not you, too."

The rest of the day passed swiftly with roughly half of the other Novice units succeeding in their test. The best showing came from Victory's squad, who managed a win with three surviving members. It was enough to earn them second place.

Afterward, Victory, Charity, and Merit approached Light Squad just as they were heading out to the Blind Pig. The day was done, and the clouds from the morning had long since broken apart. Twilight had settled on the land, and the last light of the sun streaked the sky in purples and blues. A crisp wind blew, smelling and feeling of spring, which was still months away. Thick clothing was all that was needed to keep warm, although Jade was tucked into a heavy coat. She felt the cold worse than anyone Cam had ever met.

"Just how in the fragging hells did you end up ahead of us?" Victory demanded, appearing upset for the first time since Cam had known him. Always before, he was relaxed and certain, like he was secretly amused that Light Squad was even fixing to compete against him and the other nobles. Well, it was about time he reckoned matters correctly for once.

"We heard you only had one survivor in your test," Charity said, looking as irritated as Victory.

None of them had been around to witness Light Squad's win or its importance, and just as Cam was about to explain it to them, Weld spoke first.

"We did only have one survivor," Weld said. "Me. And the reason I survived to lance the boil was because Cam came through with a great plan."

"That still doesn't explain why you're still ahead of us," Victory said.

"It's because of the test we faced," Cam said. "The Unwinnable."

"The Unwinnable?" Merit repeated, sounding shocked. "Meaning *you* beat the Unwinnable?"

"We sure did," Cam replied with an easy-going grin. But his easy-going feeling shivered when he caught Charity eyeing him like he was a piece of meat and she was a hungry lioness. Cam shifted away from her, uncomfortable with her regard, placing Jade in between the two of them.

"You lot are full of surprises," Victory said, some of his good cheer returning.

"Where are you going now?" Charity asked, her focus still stuck on Cam.

"The Blind Pig," Avia said. "It's become our unofficial place to celebrate. There's supposed to be music and dancing tonight."

"Really?" Charity smiled at Cam, toothy and frankly frightening. "Maybe I'll stop by. Save me a dance?"

Cam managed a smile, although he knew it was sickly. "Of course."

With that Victory, Charity, and Merit departed.

"I think that young woman has an unhealthy interest in you," Pan noted.

Cam had to agree, and he honestly had no idea why it was so.

"You better be careful around her," Jade advised with a chuckle. "Next thing you know, you'll be waking up in her bed, signing away your life to serve her father."

The waking up in Charity's bed part didn't sound so bad. It actually sounded enticing, but the rest was terrifying. "Let's go," Cam said, not wanting to talk about it any longer.

Shortly after, they left the campus and entered Nexus' busy streets. Folks hustled along, chased by a brisk breeze that threatened rain. The wind swirled the noisome stink of refuse from darkened alleys, mixing it with the more appealing scents of spices and seared meats that drifted out of the various restaurants and food stalls set along the street corners and intersections.

It didn't take them long to reach the Blind Pig, and when they arrived, Cam was surprised to see their instructors present as well, just like last night.

Professor Grey greeted them all with a warm embrace, her green eyes twinkling. "I wanted to congratulate every one of you. You've done well."

Professors Werm and Shivein offered their own congratulations.

Then it was Saira's turn. "When we learned the test you were to face, none of us held much hope for your success."

Professor Grey cleared her throat.

Saira grinned. "Well, one of us did, but she always sees the best in people."

"Only the ones who are the best," Professor Grey said. "And we also don't want to keep you. Get something to eat. The music is about to start, and I plan on dancing."

Cam blinked. He couldn't imagine Professor Grey dancing with anyone. Who would be worthy of dancing with her? Although... Cam eyed a man standing close at hand. He moved with a predator's grace, like a stalking leopard. Hadn't he been playing a mandolin at last night's martial exhibition? Cam wasn't sure, but the man and Professor Grey moved off.

"The music is about to start," Saira said, breaking into his thoughts. "I heard it's a group of singers. Young men. Prettier than most women." She quirked another smile. "The girls go insane over their aggressively suggestive dancing."

Cam tried to decipher what that might mean.

Saira laughed at the confusion likely evident on his face. "You'll see what I'm talking about. Go on. Get something to eat."

Just before leaving her, words spilled from Cam's mouth. "Save me a dance?" He had no idea where the question came from. It just seemed to blurt its way out before he could think them over.

"It wouldn't be appropriate," Saira said. "Besides, we've already danced together. The martial exhibition."

Cam knew enough not to say anything more on the matter. Instead, he shifted the conversation. "You know, when I first came here, I thought I deserved every bad thing that happened to me."

"And now?"

"And now, I think I'm doing better. I'll always be a no-good Folde, and I'll always have some weaknesses, but I also have my strengths." He looked to Pan, Avia, and Jade. "And I have my friends. That makes all the difference."

"Friendship, fellowship, and faith do make all the difference," Saira agreed in a solemn tone.

She was right, and for the first time in all the years Cam could recall, he was content.

32

It had been a week since the mid-year competitions, and Cam didn't like the attention it had generated. Lots of folks had their eyes on him now, well-meaning nobles and such, who seemed fascinated by his four Crystal Tangs and how he'd done in the martial exhibition and tournament. They stopped by his table in the cafeteria when he was trying to eat or asked him questions when he was heading for class.

Charity was part of both groups, and while she wasn't the worst of the lot, she scared him the most. Or maybe intimidated him was a better way of putting it.

Right now, she was sitting close, wedged in between him and Pan at their second class on Synapsia for the day. Any closer and her leg would be pressed against his. He noticed her viewing him askance, like she was trying to figure out if he was a tasty critter. The late afternoon sunlight beaming through the classroom windows highlighted her pretty features, but the hungry expression on her face struck him as disturbing. Jade was also flicking a stare at him every now and then, and Cam couldn't figure what was on her mind. Whatever it was, she didn't seem happy. He'd have to ask her about it later.

"What do you think this means?" Professor Grey asked, pointing to the blackboard where she'd written a phrase: *creation occasionally requires destruction*. It was something she had told them a time or two, but with this, a combined class that included Victory's and Charity's squads, she apparently wanted to go over it again.

Silence met her question, until Pan slowly raised his hand, licking his lips, nervous like. Cam understood the reason for his anxiety. Ever since the combined classes had started, the Novices from the other squads kept on about how Pan was a know-it-all, which might even be true. But so what if it was? Pan studied hard. It wasn't his fault he knew better than most.

"Yes, Mr. Shun," Professor Grey said.

"It means that destruction doesn't always have to result in loss," Pan said. "Sometimes it removes what's unnecessary so better, healthier growth can occur."

Someone from Victory's team muttered about all-knowing pandas, which caused Pan's ears to sag.

Cam was about to respond in defense of his friend, but of all people, it was Weld who spoke first. "If you don't like it that Pan knows so much, then maybe you ought to consider cracking a book every once in a while."

"I read plenty for what I need," replied Gorn, the member of Victory's team who had muttered about Pan. He was a short, stocky man, fiery, and easily angered. A noble, of course, and with the dark hair and dark irises of most every person Cam had ever met. In fact, the only one without those features was Professor Grey.

"Doesn't seem like you read plenty," Weld replied. He was seated next to Jade, smirking at Gorn. "If you did, you wouldn't have so much trouble parsing out such an easy phrase."

"Moving on," Professor Grey said, sounding like she was trying to rein in the brewing argument.

"Maybe I'm not as smart as you fine fellows, especially your pet Beast," Gorn said. "But any time you want to have a go at me, I'm right here."

Cam stiffened. There was no call for speaking about Pan like that.

"I'm no one's pet," Pan growled, sounding as furious as Cam had ever heard him. "You want to start trouble with me? Fine. You start it. And I'll finish it."

"I said we're moving on," Professor Grey said, a burr to her voice.

"Any time, jackhole," Gorn said, ignoring Professor Grey. "I'll take those bamboos and shove them so far up your back passage, you'll be tasting them til summer."

Cam shook his head at Gorn's stupidity. The man was a fool. When Professor Grey said, "moving on," a person best move on. Otherwise, they'd get the rough side of her tongue. It might not sound like much, but it was plenty bad.

Professor Grey moved, not so much in a blur, but all at once. One instant, she was on one side of the room. The next, she was looming over Gorn. Her eyes fairly crackled. "You will keep a civil tongue in your mouth, or you will leave this class right now."

"What's the problem, honey?" Gorn said with a smirk. "You got it hot for the panda or something?"

Cam's jaw dropped. Gorn hadn't really said that, had he? And to Professor Grey of all people. Her posture had gone stiff and fury filled her eyes. Cam couldn't help but anticipate Gorn's coming misfortune. He deserved it.

"Leave this class right now," Professor Grey said, "and never come back."

Gorn leaned back in his chair, hands behind his head, the appearance of smug nonchalance. "I don't think you know who my daddy is," he said, sneering now. "I'll stay in your class because my teachers—my real ones—want me to. You kick me out, and they'll be mad. Then my daddy will hear about it, and then *he'll* be mad. At you. You won't want that."

Professor Grey's posture relaxed. "Last chance. Leave on your own two feet."

Gorn chuckled. "See. What we're having is a failure to communicate. What you need is—"

His voice cut off as he disappeared. So did Professor Grey. Cam blinked, trying to figure out what had happened. His questioning gaze went to Pan, who shrugged, seeming just as confused as Cam.

Professor Grey reappeared, standing at the head of the class.

Victory was red-faced and looking upset. He probably liked Gorn just as little as everyone else, but as the leader of his squad, he had to stand up for his people. "What did you do to Gorn?"

Professor Grey turned a raptor's gaze upon Victory, who blanched, sinking into his chair. "What happened is that I just provided an excellent example of what this phrase means." She gestured to the blackboard. *Creation occasionally requires destruction.* "You see, I've just partially destroyed your squad by removing a member. And in doing so, I've also given your unit a chance for creation and greater growth."

"You can't do that," Victory said, gathering more courage than Cam expected him to have. Had the situations been reversed, he would have never had the gumption to talk back to Professor Grey.

Cam shivered when Professor Grey smiled, showing her teeth. "I can and I did, and as to what I did... well, your friend wanted to inform his father about my behavior. Now, he has a chance to do so."

"Gorn is from Valkin," Charity said, frowning with the same confusion Cam was feeling. Surely Professor Grey wasn't saying she'd returned Gorn to his home. That would have required an anchor line, a power only possessed by Sages and the most powerful Crowns.

"Sometimes it isn't what you can do, but what your friends can," Professor Grey said.

Her enigmatic reply did nothing to solve the riddle of what had just occurred, but one thing Cam was sure about—if he didn't already know—was this: never rile Professor Grey.

After the class on Synapsia, which thankfully finished without any more drama, Cam shot out of the room. Getting away from Charity was foremost on his mind, and bless Pan for holding the noble back, asking something inane about the city of her birth. Cam used the distraction to race straightaway to the cafeteria where he inhaled supper before lighting home to his quarters. He didn't want to talk to anyone since these days those kind of conversations always dragged around to his future plans.

He was a Novice. That was it. He didn't have time for future plans or prospects. All he wanted was to Advance to Acolyte and work on his weaknesses. Right now, that meant reading on what he didn't know, and every day that pile of ignorance grew larger. Fact was, the more Cam learned, the more he realized how little he really knew. There was a mountain of information to master, and the only way to get himself atop that peak was working harder than anyone else.

An hour later, Pan showed up at their quarters, the rest of the squad trailing after him.

"We're going to the library," Pan announced. "Do you want to join us?"

Cam glanced up from the book he'd been reading. "Can one of you run interference in case Charity shows up?"

Weld smirked. "She sure is mighty interested in you these days. Don't she know you only have eyes for Professor Maharani?"

Cam grimaced. Ever since the dancing exhibition, it had become a joke among the others, to tease him that he had the likes for Saira. The worst part was much of it—probably most of it—was true. He did like Saira. It was hard not to. But he felt some of the same for Jade and Avia. All three women were smart, caring, and attractive. He'd be blind and stupid not to wonder about them now and again.

But as for Weld's comment about Saira… Cam had a ready reply. "Only problem I see with that is Professor Maharani don't have the likes for me."

The room fell silent, everyone's eyes bulging in disbelief. Cam grinned at their responses.

"So you admit it?" Pan said. "You do like Professor Maharani."

Cam didn't see the harm in acknowledging the truth. "Of course, I do. But she's our instructor. She don't see me that way, and she never will."

"But if she wasn't our instructor?" Jade asked.

"Then we might be having a different conversation."

Weld barked laughter. "I have to tell you, I'm actually relieved. I was starting to wonder about you. Whether you were even human. There are so many beautiful women in your life, but all you see are books and Ephemera."

"I see women," Cam said. "But there's other things I got to finish off first. First thing is I've got to become worthy of them. Which is why I'm fixing to wander over to the library right now. Who's with me?"

"I'll walk with you," Jade said.

The others had to go and collect their books, but all of them agreed to head over as soon as they could.

Cam and Jade left then, encountering a number of people in the hallways or just loitering around the building. The campus was similarly busy with students moseying about or hanging out in the green areas. In spite of the darkness settling across the island, many folks were out playing games or socializing. Maybe it was because it might be their last time to do so before winter's cold finally arrived. Right now, the weather was temperate and mild, which Cam didn't like. Winter should be bitter cold and snowy, not this disgusting pleasantness. Even the evening breeze blowing off the lake—humid and pregnant with a sense of growth—conspired against him, reminding him of late spring.

"I love this weather," Jade said with an appreciative grin.

Of course, she would. Jade hated the cold. Eyeing her, Cam was reminded of something he wanted to ask. "You seemed upset with me earlier. Did I do something?"

"When was this?"

"In Synapsia, you kept giving me the stink eye."

"I wasn't giving you the stink eye," Jade corrected. "I was giving it to Charity. I know you're not comfortable around her. Especially with her almost sitting in your lap."

Cam chuckled in relief. "That would have been something, wouldn't it?"

"You would have liked that?" Jade asked, viewing him in seeming disappointment.

Cam shrugged. "Like Weld said, there are a lot of beautiful women in my life, and I'm a man. I notice them." He smiled, noticing Jade's rising annoyance. "But I ain't dumb enough to involve myself with a woman like Charity Kazar. She'd chew me up and spit me out if I was rooster-stupid to get tangled with her."

Jade laughed. "Rooster-stupid. You made that up."

Cam waggled his eyebrows. "It's charming, ain't it?"

"I'm sure it is," Jade said with a warm chuckle. "Anyway, at least you're smart enough to not to get involved with Charity, even if you're stupid enough to have become infatuated with Professor Maharani."

"She's someone worth getting infatuated with," Cam said.

"Idiot," Jade muttered, although the smile on her face told Cam she wasn't being serious.

"What about you?" Cam asked. "You got any special man in your life? Back home or here? I notice Weld always makes sure to sit next to you these days."

"That's because Weld wants what he can't have."

"Really?" Her response surprised him. "Because early on when he first joined Light Squad, I thought you had eyes for Weld. I never could figure what you saw in him."

"His backside," Jade promptly announced. "His is especially fine." Cam stared in astonishment. Did women really look at men like that? And all this time, he thought only men saw women that way.

Jade laughed when she caught sight of his surprise. "You're not the only one who notices beauty."

"You also never answered my question," Cam said.

"Do I have a special man in my life? No." Her expression became strained. "There was a time when I would have had a number of suitors, and I still could have them, but..." she shrugged, falling silent, like she didn't need to tell him any further what she meant.

"But what?" Cam asked, not knowing what she was trying to say.

"It would have always been a political marriage. And since I'm from a fallen house, those interested would have been vultures wanting to pick my family's carcass clean. I want more out of life and a future husband than that."

It was more information than Cam had expected to hear. "I wasn't asking if you had a husband picked out. I was just wondering if you had a man in mind who you wouldn't mind spending time with."

"Are you asking to spend time with me?"

Cam swallowed heavily, hoping it was too dark for anyone to make out his abrupt pallor. He liked Jade, but the two of them having that kind of relationship would be a bad idea. It would do neither of them a bit of good. They didn't need the distractions that a relationship might cause. "Not that I wouldn't be honored—"

Jade burst into laughter. "You should see your face. You looked like Shimala had crawled into your dreams." She continued to wheeze with amusement, breaking into fresh laughter whenever she looked his way.

Cam watched her hilarity in annoyed silence. Was the idea of the two of them having a relationship really that funny to her?

Jade finally got her guffawing under control, and she sobered when she realized he wasn't laughing. "You're a wonderful person, Cam, but you know my truth. I have to become a Glory at the least, but a Crown would be even better. It's the only way to save and restore my family honor. Nothing else matters until then." She smiled. "Even a relationship with a charming hick."

Cam viewed her, trying to hide the sorrow he felt on her behalf. What she had just said was a sadly familiar refrain, one echoed by Pan and Avia. They all seemed to share a common notion that their happiness would only be accomplished once they achieved something of importance. Cam didn't think it was true, but how to get them to see it?

Later that night, after finishing their studies in the library, Cam and Pan returned to their quarters. It had been a long day, but there was time enough to get a bit more work done.

For instance, there was still the acorn Professor Werm wanted them to revive, and in this task, Cam had hardly managed any progress. Pan was further along. So were Avia, Jade, and Weld, but none of them looked likely to succeed if they didn't make a concerted effort to see the work completed.

And for Cam, he knew he suffered a much heavier burden. During the martial competition, he had burned hard with Plasminia, making his Synapsia and Kinesthia work that much better—nearly like everyone else's—even if for a far shorter amount of time. But he'd yet to figure on how to do the same with Spirairia.

He glanced at Pan, who made it look so easy. He wasn't reviving the acorn, but just doing the regular exercises Professor Werm wanted them to practice. Pan was using Spirairia to float a round rock in the air, up and down, up and down, over and over again, getting himself used to the work. Then he was sliding it across the floor, back and forth, back and forth. Finally came loops.

There was a practical use to the exercise—more than just shifting arrows out of flight—such as tripping opponents or pinning their feet to the ground. Professor Werm also promised to eventually teach them how to grow, heal, and nurture the land. Cam looked forward to that. After all, what was the point of living if the natural world was left unprotected?

"I'm off to bed," Pan said.

Cam wished him a good night but remained awake. He couldn't yet do nearly as much as Professor Werm wanted from Light Squad, but he was bound and determined to get there. It was why he continued to labor away after Pan had called it a night. Cam didn't have the ready skills of the others, so the only way to stay with them was to outwork them.

But, Lord Devesh, he wished he could catch some sleep.

Cam sighed. He recalled then what his daddy used to say about wishes, but he didn't bother on finishing the quote. Instead, he focused on the acorn. His cooldown had just ended, and he Bonded Plasminia and Spirairia, seeking how to use the former to intensify the latter. A fruitless few minutes passed until the Bonds disintegrated. Cam grimaced. He wasn't getting anything done, and the frustration had him wondering what he was doing wrong.

His annoyance built, but with a forceful shove, Cam pushed aside his irritation. It wouldn't do him any good to approach his problem with anger. Instead, he focused on his Source, knowing that in order for him to become the equal of the rest of Light Squad, he needed Plasminia to increase the usefulness of his other Tangs. He'd figured the trick with Synapsia and Kinesthia, but what was holding him back with Spirairia?

As he pondered the matter, a realization struck him. He'd used Kinesthia more effectively only when he'd also been Bonded to Synapsia. What if that was the key? It was the first bit of optimism he'd felt in a while, and he tried to contain himself. He shouldn't let his hopes rise for no reason.

But as soon as his cooldown ended, he couldn't help but grin in anticipation when he Bonded to Plasminia, Synapsia, and Spirairia. As soon as he did, his mind sped and the world stretched. Everything sounded slower. Moved like it was in molasses even as he felt like his thoughts were swift enough to grasp any and all things. Nothing was hidden from his reckoning.

And the initial notion that had him Bonding three Tangs was right. He could sense its correctness, even as he engaged Plasminia, Bonding more firmly, cascading its energy deeper into his Source and having it touch both Spirairia and Synapsia.

His mind instantly raced faster. Spirairia brightened, and a different kind of world became apparent. A tangled web of light and possibilities. Touch one thread, and touch a life on the other side of creation. The woven world was what Professor Werm called it, a world Cam had never before seen. And while he'd never be a master of this Tang, it also didn't matter.

He had a simple task in mind.

Cam focused on the acorn in his palm, lifeless to his eyes, but not to his Spirairia enhanced senses. A wispy, white light, stretched like frayed cotton, flowed into and out of the acorn, which wasn't actually dead; not entirely. Nothing was entirely dead. There was always some possibility of life.

He frowned then, wondering on the strange idea. Everything was possibly alive? Even a stone, a cup of water? Surely not. He wasn't thinking things true. Or maybe the truth was that everything was possibly dead?

No. That wasn't right either. Cam shook his head. And it, too, didn't matter. The acorn was all that concerned him, and he focused on it, intent on driving what needed to happen. The wispy light, whatever it was—possibly Ephemera?—it was the key. It swirled into the acorn but didn't seem to remain long, flowing out as soon as it entered, like water chasing through a wide-open channel.

Cam needed to change that, and he reached out with Spirairia, touching the acorn and the wispy light. He needed it to remain inside the acorn, to collect within it.

And like it wanted to do nothing else, the wispy light sank into the acorn. Some of it still leaked out, but not as much as before. The acorn brightened like when Professor Werm had first shown Light Squad what was possible with Spirairia. Not to the same extent, but similar in a general way.

All too soon, Cam's Bonds broke apart, leaving him feeling like he'd run a dozen miles uphill. But he smiled anyway. He'd managed what he'd wanted. The acorn had filled out the tiniest fraction, no longer appearing quite as withered. And while it also wasn't as healthy appearing as Pan's acorn, that was fine. For Cam, this was still a huge step forward, and working at it every night, he could actually see himself succeeding at Professor Werm's task.

33

Over the next few days, while Cam had thought he'd reasoned out the secret on how best to harness his Tangs, he learned it wasn't exactly the case. Plasminia still burned through his Bonds too quickly, and he wasn't sure what to do about his old curse.

Looking for any kind of help, Cam had decided to talk it over with Professor Grey since she seemed to know everything about anything. She'd heard him out, nodding understanding at his explanations and worries before searching through her bookshelf. An "aha" moment later, and she had a slim volume in hand, thumbing through it.

"It's the first of a three-part autobiography from Goranth Vinger, the Wilde Sage three generations prior to Rainen," she had explained when Cam asked about the book. "As an Acolyte, he had three Tangs at Crystal, and he struggled with maintaining his Bonds." She pointed to a passage. "What he did was utterly boring. He practiced Bonding his Tangs over and over again. In any spare moment, even when eating, he would Bond and fight to maintain their integrity. Over time, it worked. His Bonds strengthened. They were never weak again."

"Will it work for me?" Cam had asked. "The book you found on

Plasminians said I won't be the equal of everyone else until I'm a Glory."

Professor Grey had shrugged. "Who can say. That book you're referencing is a mix of grotesque experiments, theory, and guesswork. So far, it's been accurate, and nothing in it says that Goranth's teachings won't work for you."

Put like that, it hadn't been much of a decision. Cam wanted to be the equal of everyone else, whatever it took. Especially because what if he never got to Glory? It happened. Lots of Masters peaked at the lower Stages of Advancement, and Cam reckoned he shouldn't trust that he'd be one of those destined to achieve greatness.

Instead, he'd be better off doing as Professor Grey had told him. In addition to studying and learning all that he'd never been taught, mastering the use of his Tangs, and bringing the dead acorn to life, he also had to harden his Bonds so they didn't come apart so easily.

But doing all of that… where was the time?

It was why Cam was up so early. In the hours before dawn, Cam figured he could get some of that new and extra work done before breakfast. The world outside was quiet and dark with nothing stirring the silence. It was a perfect time to meditate and focus on his Bonds. He could also use the time to work on the acorn.

Unfortunately, something in his labor must have woken Pan.

"What are you doing?" Pan asked, coming out of his bedroom.

"Sorry if I was making too much noise," Cam said. "I didn't mean to disturb you."

"It's alright," Pan said, flopping down next to where Cam sat cross-legged on the floor. "But you didn't answer my question. What are you doing?"

Cam explained the problems with his Bonds and how to fix them. "So, on top of everything else, I've got this other work to do."

Pan gently bumped his forehead against Cam's, resting it there a moment, his soft fur, smelling clean and woodsy, soothing rather than tickling. The gesture was one that carried over from early on when they'd first met, and for whatever reason, it always brought Cam a measure of peace.

He breathed out then, releasing tension he'd not known he'd been experiencing. "Thank you," Cam said. "But I don't know if you can help me with this. I have to do it on my own."

"I can be there to support you," Pan offered, an unexpectedly serious expression on his face.

Cam smiled. "I appreciate it, but I don't want you interrupting your rest on my account. Go back to sleep."

Pan whuffled. "You carry all these burdens, but they won't feel as heavy if you have someone sharing the pain with you."

"How can you share my pain?" Cam asked.

Pan grinned. "By just being here. Letting you know you're not alone. Don't discount the power of friendship." He reached to the table where he had his flute. "Plus, music can tame even the most savage of humans."

Cam laughed. "I think your phrasing there needs fixing."

"I said it correctly."

"I still don't want you worrying about me. It'll only make me feel guilty," Cam said.

"Is that really the reason? Guilt?"

"What other reason is there?"

Pan didn't answer in the way Cam expected. "All of us in Light Squad share certain traits. Many of us believe our best road to contentment lies in doing what our family needs. For me, it's fulfilling a prophecy. For Avia, it's becoming the true heir to her human father and saving her pod."

"Of fish." Cam grinned.

"She's not a fish," Pan replied with an answering smile. "And Jade needs to become a Crown to restore her family's honor. As for you… you fear you're cursed. Have you never wondered if we're all of us wrong?"

Cam had wondered. He'd often thought the same as Pan, but the trouble was that knowing of a problem wasn't the same as solving it. Cam had come far, but he hadn't come far enough. His wounds still troubled his mind, and so did his craving for alcohol.

But Light of Devesh, he sure hoped that one day, he'd find some measure of healing and just be happy with his life.

Cam sighed. "You're right. I still get stuck on thinking of myself like that. Some days, I don't, but other times, I…" He shook his head, unable to formulate the right words.

"Other times you're afraid?"

Cam nodded, morose because Pan was correct. He tapped the side of his head. "I know up here that I don't deserve a bad fate. That I'm not cursed." He pointed to his heart. "But right here, I'm yet to be convinced. Same as you and your prophecy."

"It seems like we're both broken," Pan agreed. "But getting back to this new task you need to take on, I can still help. I can share the time with you, even if it's only music you need. Friends help each other."

Cam stared at Pan, touched. What had he done to deserve a friend like him? "You saw the best in me when I figured few others did. I wish there was something I could do to pay you back for all you've done for me."

Pan smiled. "Friendship isn't a business transaction. You don't owe me anything."

"Maybe so, but if there's anything you need, I hope you aren't ever too proud to accept whatever help I can give."

"I'm nothing if not humble."

The final class of the day—Synapsia—was over at last, and Cam slouched his way out of his seat. His eyes wanted to shut, weighed down by fatigue and lack of sleep. He was tired, worn out from running on three or four hours of sleep a night for the past three weeks. Cam had taken Professor Grey's advice to heart about how best to strengthen his Bonds, doing as she'd told him, working and working and working until there was no time left to work. Every waking hour given over to what was needed. Study, train, grow, strengthen his Bonds. On and on, a never-ending cycle of labor that left Cam struggling just to keep his eyes open.

His tiredness was showing in his classes, too. He wasn't strong enough for Kinesthia, aware enough for Spirairia, and alert enough for Synapsia.

"Cam, a moment of your time," Professor Grey called out as he was about to follow the rest of Light Squad out of the classroom.

The others shot him querying looks, but Cam didn't know what to tell them. And even if he did, as dull as his mind was working, he wasn't sure he'd be able to properly explain it anyway.

After everyone else was gone, Professor Grey addressed him. "How have you been doing? I know you aren't getting enough rest."

Cam smirked. Of course, he hadn't been getting enough rest. With all he had to do, where was the time to sleep?

"You misunderstand my comment," Professor Grey said, taking in his smirk. "I know you haven't been getting enough rest, but sometimes that's not to your benefit. The question I ask is has it been worth it? Are you making progress?"

Cam *had* been making progress. Not a lot at first, barely any, but over the past week, he'd started to notice that his Bonds were lasting longer, the use of his Tangs smoother. But was the gap between him and Light Squad any less? That he couldn't tell.

And Cam wanted that gap closed as quick as possible. Word had come from Master Winder. He wanted Light Squad out in the field soon; to lance the boil he figured they could handle. Saira knew everything about it, and she'd be accompanying them when they headed out in the next few days.

But was it a good idea? Although he'd been filled with excitement when he'd first heard of it back before the mid-year examinations, Cam wasn't as certain. Light Squad was a Novice unit. Were they really ready to take on any sort of rakshasas? Cam wasn't sure, but no one else seemed worried, not even Pan.

"Cam," Professor Grey prodded.

He realized he hadn't yet answered her question. "It's been worth it."

"And yet?" Professor Grey asked, her eyes piercing and wise.

"I'm afraid," Cam admitted. "Master Winder wants us in the field. There's a boil he wants us to destroy. He says it's a simple training exercise, and…" Cam licked suddenly dry lips.

"And what will you do about it?" Professor Grey asked, her voice soft.

"Do as I'm told, I guess."

"You have the right to labor, but you shouldn't worry so much about the fruit of it."

Cam frowned, not sure what her comment meant.

"There are great truths that can lead to service," Professor Grey said, still speaking in riddles. "Among them is the idea of detachment, and by this, I don't mean disinterest, but acceptance of what will be. I've mentioned this before. Those are among the challenges every Ephemeral Master faces as they Advance in Awareness, but the underlying answer behind all these questions—be it the passage from Novice to Acolyte or Sage to Divine—is the truth that impels us. You need to find that truth."

Cam still frowned, unclear as to what the professor was talking about and how it would help with his dilemma.

Professor Grey chuckled ruefully. "I'm not making sense, am I? There is so much for you to learn, and I recognize your fear. It exists in everyone, but it need not. Remember All is Ephemera and Ephemera is All. Do you know what this means?"

"It means that everything contains Ephemera?"

"No. It means everything *is* Ephemera, and everything is ephemeral. Nothing lasts. No one. You are born, you will die, and that which you are will return to Devesh. But you will endure in the Most High."

Cam understood this on an intellectual level, but he still wasn't sure how this was supposed to help him with his upcoming journey. "I don't want to die," he said at the end. "Not now. Not ever."

"And you won't. You never will since you are also Ephemera."

"But I'll just be a part of Devesh when I die. I want to be me."

"That's because you fear dissolution. But such a fear is meaningless. You have never been only you. You have always been Devesh through the Atman graced within you—your soul inside—your true self. And that will live on." She touched his shoulder, poking it. "This isn't you. It never was. And the key to your journey in the Way into Divinity is to find out how to shed it and retain your ability to serve."

Cam found himself growing interested in spite of his worries about the upcoming travels. "How do you know this is true?"

Professor Grey offered an embarrassed grin. "How do you think? By reading, especially the teachings from the Servants. Those are meaningful, especially the treatises that speak of the three *Gunas*, the three aspects of reality. The first is *Sattva*, which represents goodness and purification. The next is *Rajas*, that which is passion and activity. The final is *Tamas*. Darkness and ignorance; the inertia that inhibits our growth."

"And let me guess. *Tamas* is the worst aspect of reality."

Professor Grey gave an enigmatic smile. "Perhaps, but that is for you to learn on your own."

Interesting but not nearly useful for what Cam was facing. "Anything else in those teachings?"

"The only other one to give you hope is that in one treatise, simply titled *Avatara*—Descent—there is a promise that during a time of turmoil and tribulation, the Servants will descend and re-establish divine law."

Cam sighed inwardly, disappointed. He wished he had Professor Grey's faith. But he'd learned his own hard lessons and waiting for magical beings was a fool's gamble. Better to rely on his own wit and will. He said as much.

"So be it," Professor Grey said. "But if you take any lesson from our discussion, recall that the key to selflessness versus selfishness— the means by which a Master Advances in Awareness from Novice to Acolyte—isn't so difficult to comprehend. It begins and ends with this notion: all actions should be done without selfish attachment to their outcomes."

That sounded… impossible and frankly, somewhat ridiculous. In fact, Cam doubted if any Ephemeral Masters took that answer as a means to Advance from Novice to Acolyte. "Ephemeral Masters are pragmatic; not ascetic," he said. It was the gentlest way he could think to disagree with Professor Grey and not sound like he was dismissing what she had to tell him.

"True," Professor Grey replied. "And how many Divines have been birthed in the past thousand years? How many Sages in the past several centuries?"

"That's because of politics. The Duke-Sages don't want any competition. They kill anyone who rises to Sage."

"So some claim, but what about the rest of the world? On other continents, there are still Crowns who Advance to Sage, but even then, it is infrequent. Perhaps once a century or less. There might be a reason for that. And certainly there has to be a reason for the dearth of Divines."

"And you think it's because the Ephemeral Masters aren't taking the right lessons in how to Advance."

"I am not alone believing this. It is written in the treatises I earlier mentioned. When you return from lancing this boil, you might want to read them. They aren't long, but they contain wisdom."

Cam didn't respond at once. Instead, he recollected everything Professor Grey had told him, picking at it. She'd never led him wrong before, and there had to be a reason for what she was saying now; this fundamentally philosophical discussion that seemed to have no bearing on his struggles with Plasminia and the journey he would soon have to make.

The next morning dawned sunny and bright, but the seeming warmth was a lie as a biting breeze gusted. It swept across the campus, rattling bushes and trees and heaved winter's dry, bitter scents and a welcome return of the cold. Cam loved it, so happy with the chill weather that he didn't even remember he was supposed to be tired from staying up late and getting up early.

He strode next to Avia—the two of them side-by-side—while Jade,

Weld, and Pan walked on ahead, the five of them headed to Kinesthia.

"This boil we're supposed to lance," Avia began, sounding annoyingly chipper. "Master Winder mentioned it weeks ago, but by now, I thought he must have forgotten about it, you know?"

Cam grunted, not wanting to answer; not wanting to think about it. To him, lancing a boil as Novices continued to concern him and talking to Professor Grey yesterday hadn't really settled his mind any.

What had she been going on about anyway? All that talk about detachment and selflessness. Cam had pondered on it last night, even discussed it with Pan, and what he'd come to conclude was that it made no sense. Either that or he and Pan weren't wise enough to figure whatever lesson Professor Grey had been trying to impart.

"You're awfully quiet," Avia said.

Cam viewed her askance. Did she really not fear what they would have to face? "And you seem very cheerful," he replied. "Don't you know what's waiting for us at the end of that road we're taking?"

"You mean the boil," Avia said, shrugging with admirable nonchalance. Cam wished he could be that carefree. "If Master Winder says we can lance it, then we can lance it."

Cam wasn't so certain, but he also didn't want to spoon-feed his own unsurities to Avia. "I know it's supposed to be a simple training exercise with plenty of support, but I'm still nervous."

"About what?"

"About us being tossed from the nest when we ain't ready."

"Ain't ready," Avia teased with a grin, her eyes twinkling. "You know, when I walked ashore, if I could have chosen a country accent, I'd have done it in a heartbeat. It's so evocative." She sighed melodramatically. "Instead, I got stuck with the same boring accent that everyone has."

"Not the nobles," Cam replied. "They have their own way of talking."

"Yes. It's like this," Avia said. She hooded her eyes, drooped her lips, and wore an arrogant, self-impressed expression. "Stiff upper lip and all that, my boy. Why don't you come around the castle some time? We'll have tea or some such."

Cam broke out in laughter. "How do you do that?"

Avia grinned. "Lots and lots of practice. Plus, I'm a noble myself."

"Yes, the daughter of Duke of Saban, but somehow you got stuck in Squad Screwup."

"I'm glad for where I ended up," Avia said.

"Me, too."

They paced along in silence then, marching through the campus, among other students who were headed for their own classes. Their conversations drifted to Cam every now and then, but it was of mundane matters: the food served at breakfast, the cold weather, who was dating who, how to Advance.

On hearing the last, Cam recalled again Professor Grey's talk from yesterday. About how a person shouldn't worry so much about the actual outcome of their work. That they should try to succeed at it, but not worry if they didn't. Or was that what the professor had actually been saying? If true, it sounded so dry and pointless, and if there was one thing Cam didn't think about Professor Grey, it was that she was dry and pointless.

"You're doing it again," Avia said, interrupting his thoughts.

"What's that?" Cam asked, still distracted.

"You're off in your own world. We're talking, and the next thing I know, you've got this far-away expression on your face." Avia pouted. "If I didn't know better, I'd think you thought I was boring."

Cam blinked, his mind returning to the here and now. Did she really think he thought she was boring? If so, she was wrong. Cam liked Avia. She was smart and charming and—although she hid it sometimes behind her cheery demeanor—she was a deep thinker.

Avia grinned. "You really thought I was being serious?" Her smile gave way to a gently chiding, mocking expression. "Oh, Cam. Don't ever change, my silly, innocent hick."

Cam couldn't figure if Avia was teasing him now or giving him a compliment. Maybe a bit of both?

"I know you like to think things through," Avia continued. "It isn't because you're bored with me or Pan or anyone. It's just the way you are."

So, it was a little bit of teasing and a little bit of a compliment. "What about you?" Cam asked. "You like to hide it, but you do the same."

Avia's smile faded. "I suppose so, but humans don't like Awakened Beasts who are smarter than them."

Cam considered her words, which rang true. Pan was given a hard time by other Novices because of how bright and curious he was. The same likely held true for Avia. While she looked very human, there were clues that she wasn't, and that difference would always be held against her. And there was also jealousy to consider. Avia was the adopted daughter of the Sage-Duke of Saban, and that adoption would have spurred mountains of envy from most anyone in her father's duchy. And for an Awakened Beast it must have been a nightmare.

Isolating as well. It made Cam wonder. Was Avia really so happy? Or was it a facade to protect herself?

"You're doing it again," Avia noted.

"I'm sorry," Cam said, meaning it in many different ways.

Avia cocked her head. "I know you want to be supportive, but do you really think I want your sympathy? Would you want mine for the ills you fight?"

His alcoholism. His worry that he was a curse. No. He didn't want anyone's sympathy for that, and Avia would feel the same about her troubles. "I wasn't offering you sympathy," he told her. "I was offering empathy. I feel for you because I can imagine what you've experienced. That's all."

"Acceptable," she allowed after a moment.

"Have you ever not been isolated because of your status?" Cam asked.

"Ah, a personal question. And in answer to it, yes, I've always been and always will be isolated because of who I am. I'm an Awakened Beast who happens to be the adopted daughter of Duke Vail, but with Light Squad, I don't feel it so much. Light Squad is my pod."

Cam smiled, glad for her response and drawing her into a hug. "Just don't make those clicking noises like orcas are supposed to do."

"That's called talking," Avia said in an exaggerated tone, like she thought Cam was an idiot.

He smiled, cheered out of his worries for a moment. "I didn't think fish could talk."

"Not a fish," Avia corrected.

34

Cam sat at the dinner table in his quarters, staring out the window but unable to see much else beyond the twinkling lights from the harbor. It was dark out; quiet, too, except for the chirping of crickets and a soft wind sighing through the boughs. From the hallway came a brief spurt of laughter; a pair of students, their conversation carrying but cut off when they either wandered away or entered their rooms.

"So, let me make sure I understand," Weld said, interrupting his thoughts. "You really want my help with this? With Spirairia?"

Cam sighed to himself. Yes, he needed Weld's help, and he didn't appreciate how happy the other man seemed at the prospect. "It ain't only like that. I can figure it out on my own, but it might take me too long."

Pan, seated on the floor, munching on a stalk of bamboo like he always did, nodded in agreement.

Weld smirked. "I'm sure you're right, but it's also not every day that I actually have one up on you. Let me take the win."

Cam grimaced in annoyance, making sure Weld saw it. It was late. Cam was tired and his patience short. Worse, his day wasn't done; not by a long spell. He still had his Bonds to improve, but it was also time to get back to working on the acorn.

That was the help he needed from Weld. Somehow the other man seemed to have an insight into how it was done.

Professor Werm had guided them as best he could, but there was something Cam just wasn't understanding. A book in the library supposedly could help, but it was missing and the librarians figured it likely lost.

Which meant Weld might be Cam's only hope. He needed whatever Weld knew, anything to shorten the labor. Because weeks ago, while Cam had thought he'd figured out the secret to healing and growing his acorn, his way was proving too hard. It left him worn out like a farmer hitched to his own plow.

It couldn't go on, and in the end, Cam had to swallow his pride and ask help from someone he didn't fully respect. He'd made the request at supper tonight, the evening before their departure from the academy. Tomorrow, they would set sail to lance a boil, but before they left, Cam wanted to know how better to grow his acorn. He didn't want to wait until they returned. It might even be something he could largely get done during Light Squad's travel.

So with his figurative hat in hand and no other option available, he had asked for Weld's help, surprised when the other man had readily and happily agreed.

Cam should have known it wouldn't be so simple. Weld wouldn't have said yes if he hadn't seen some kind of benefit to be gained. And here it was. Weld finding amusement in the situation and likely to use it as a wedge for however long he felt like.

Well, if it got Cam the knowledge to fix his acorn, then so be it.

Pan had glanced up at Weld's words, taking a definitive crunch of his bamboo. "Is it really that important for you to feel like you've won something against Cam?" he asked after swallowing down his food.

Weld's grin grew wider. "You know it is. I've been the slow man in our squad the whole time I've known you. And our boy here has been the golden child. So, yes, I'm wanting to feel like I've won something."

Golden child? The unholy hells was he talking about? Cam was a golden nobody. He inwardly shook his head at the notion; not that it mattered none anyhow. "Fine. Then you've won something. Now, can you teach me how to do what you're doing?"

"Why now?" Weld asked. "Shouldn't you be focused on the boil we have to lance?"

"Because I want to know before we leave," Cam said. "Are you going to help me?"

"Hold that thought." Weld closed his eyes, holding a meditative pose while also pretending like he was basking in some unseen glory. "I'm ready," he said, opening his eyes. "Now. In order to grow your acorn, you need to Bond to Spirairia and Kinesthia—"

"You think I don't know that?" Cam said with a frustrated growl.

"Have you tried it while also holding Synapsia?" Weld asked.

"Of course." It had been advice from Professor Werm.

"How much of a Bond have you been forming?" Weld asked. "You don't need a whole one. Just a portion of Synapsia; only enough for the clarity of thought needed to fully Bond to Kinesthia. That way, you'll have the stamina to maintain the Bond to Spirairia."

Cam blinked. A limited Bond? He'd never tried anything like that before.

"How did you figure on using Synapsia in such a limited fashion?" Pan asked.

"Trial and error," Weld answered. "It wasn't easy, but once I realized the secret, growing the acorn became an order of magnitude more effective."

Cam tilted his head, frowning. "When did you figure this out?"

"A couple months ago."

"Then why haven't you progressed farther with the acorn? It sounds like you could be nearly done with it if what you say really is orders of magnitude more effective."

Weld scowled. "Let's just say I fell into some bad habits. You know what I mean?"

Cam did know, and he'd already said his piece about Weld's laziness.

There was no call on repeating it. Weld had listened, and he'd made changes. He was working hard, growing stronger every day.

Pan stood. "Do you mind if I join you?" He didn't bother waiting on them to respond, rushing to his room and returning with his acorn in hand.

"If we're ready, then I want both of you to start by Delving your Sources," Weld instructed. "Don't form any Bonds, though. I'll tell you which ones to create and when to create them."

Cam Delved his Source, visualizing it in his mind's eye.

"Now," Weld said. "Create a Bond with Synapsia—the lightest you can manage—and only after that, create one with Kinesthia. *Then* comes Spirairia. The Bonds build off each other. One makes the next easier."

Cam formed Plasminia first—he was a Plasminian, after all—and then the Bonds like Weld said. He immediately noticed the difference. Holding Spirairia was far less difficult, not needing every ounce of concentration. And the Tang itself felt more solid, more usable.

There was a brief odor as well, a flash of a rotten something that came and went so fast that Cam wasn't even sure it was real. When it didn't recur, he mentally shrugged. It was likely his imagination.

"Reach for the acorn," Weld ordered. "Can you see the glow that flows through it? It's Ephemera. Or at least that's what Professor Werm says. You have to convince it to stay inside the acorn. That's what will bring it back to life."

The last part Cam already knew. But his way had been so difficult and halting in speed. This time, it happened much more rapidly. He might even get this done by the end of the year like Professor Werm wanted.

"You're doing well," Weld said, laughing when he noticed Cam's surprised expression. "Listen. You're a Plasminian, and I doubt anyone like you has come as far as you have. That's worth something."

"That's what I keep saying," Pan said, nodding vigorously.

"Well, panda, maybe he'll actually listen to one of us this time," Weld said.

"I don't like it when you call me 'panda,'" Pan said, a burr in his voice.

"Well you are a panda," Weld said. "Just like I'm the one who brings prettiness to Light Squad."

Cam wanted to sigh in disgust. Just when he was thinking Weld might be turning over a new leaf, there was the arrogant jackhole he'd gotten to know so well. At least he was calling them Light Squad instead of Squad Screwup.

"Avia and Jade are prettier than you," Pan replied.

"You won't get no disagreement from me," Weld replied. "But I still bring prettiness to Light Squad."

This time Cam rolled his eyes and shook his head in mock sorrow, again making sure Weld saw it.

Weld left his old quarters feeling pleased. Cam and Pan had been forced to ask him for help. And best of all, they'd admitted he knew more than they did, at least on this one matter, which had him whistling a bawdy tune.

Sure, they might think they surpassed him in other ways, but not tonight. Tonight, was Weld's, and he loved the sense of victory coursing through him. Cam and Pan thought they were better than him, but they weren't. He'd just proved it, and he couldn't wait to tell Jade what he'd done.

Weld knew she liked him—he'd caught her staring—and maybe this would impress her enough to let him kiss her. And if he impressed her even more, maybe she'd let him have more than just a kiss.

He gave himself a mental nod. *Yes.* That's exactly what he'd do. And all it would take would be to study that book Professor Werm had wanted them all to read, the one about Spirairia. Weld smirked. The others in Light Squad had gone to the library looking for it, not realizing Weld had already found and stolen it away to his quarters.

Served them right for looking down on him.

Cam awoke with a start. By the barest of margins, he kept from gasping and drowning. Icy water and darkness enclosed him like a prison. His eyes widened in terror. Where was he? He spun in a circle, desperate to figure out which way was up.

A pinpoint of light flickered into being. He swam for it, pulling hard, praying it would lead him to air. His lungs burned. His vision grayed. The need to breathe became overwhelming.

He surfaced with a gasp, gulping down sweet air while floating on his back, unable to do much else. He was just relieved to be alive. A few moments later, finally over the shock of his confusion and near-drowning, he took in his surroundings.

A dark cavern filled his vision, the ceiling rising overhead, glowing with some kind of moss. The light he'd seen. He twisted about. There was no easy exit to the cave. Hard walls, sheer and rising straight from the water, met his searching gaze, but at the far end, there appeared to be a shore of some kind.

Seeing no other option, Cam swam toward it. It was a long ways there, and he had to stop and tread water a few times to recover his stamina. Not being used to swimming so far, it was hard exertion, and by the time he reached the shore, his heart was pounding and his lungs were expanding and contracting faster than a blacksmith's bellows.

Cam emerged from the water, collapsing on wet sand, unable to do anything but lie there.

He shivered while he waited on his breathing to settle and his heart to slow. The water had been as cold as a winter lake, and the air wasn't much warmer. He needed a fire, anything to raise his temperature.

But the sand was so comfortable. Why not just rest here a mite longer; maybe take a short nap.

No. *That way led to death. He had to get up and get moving. With a groan, Cam stumbled to his feet, dizzy for a spell. It passed soon enough, and he was able to take stock of his situation.*

The shore on which he found himself was only twenty yards in length and a quarter that deep. Water lapped at his feet, and he couldn't tell if there was an exit to be found. The glowing moss did little to dispel the darkness; instead, casting brooding shadows that covered the walls along the shoreline like lacunae of darkness. There was an oppressive nature to them, making him imagine the menacing eyes of a giant spider.

But the shadows were likely the only way out of the cavern, and Cam needed that exit. He was freezing and he hoped even just getting his body moving might help warm him. Resolved to free himself of this place, Cam searched along the shoreline for a way out, peering about, feeling with outstretched hands and fingers. Anything to get gone from this cavern where a silent, malignant regard seemed to spear him. It wanted his blood.

No. It wants my Ephemera. To make a husk of me.

Cam shivered at the imagined thoughts and fears, but somehow sensing they were right. He glanced down to where the water lapped at his feet, a malicious animal toying with its prey. Cam frowned. Wait. He was on the edge of the shoreline, and only minutes before the water hadn't reached so far.

Cam's eyes widened in horror. The water was rising to fill the cavern. He increased the pace of his search.

There! He sighted a tunnel, just large enough for him to fit through. Cam squeezed into the passageway, ignoring the rotten smell of something dead emanating from within. The alternative, after all, was drowning.

Nevertheless, his gorge rose as the stench inside grew progressively worse. The reek was enough to make his eyes water, a near visible miasma. And yet there was nothing to see. The darkness within the tunnel was as depthless as any Cam had ever encountered, so black that light and color seemed an illusion, something he might have conjured once in a dream but not in truth.

But his lack of sight didn't matter. The water had reached him even in the tunnel's throat, tugging at his feet, kissing his ankles.

Cam pressed on, feeling his way forward. Seconds later, his questing hands abruptly ran into the tunnel's end. Panic began to rise. He felt about him. The walls pressed close, only a few feet apart. He pushed out in all directions. There was nothing but jagged stone. No way out. Only hard, enclosing walls, darkness, and icy water where he would drown.

A weight pressed on his heart, telling him this was the end. That there was no hope. Cam sagged, a sob in his throat. How had he ended up here? He should be at the Ephemeral Academy, among friends and a chosen family. Confused and lost, he prayed for salvation, closing his eyes and lifting his head to where he knew the sky must be. Somewhere far above him.

He did so even while knowing there was none to be found. Not for him, a no-good Folde, a curse to others. A soft exhalation, an acceptance of life's passing, and Cam opened his eyes.

A light glimmered high above, a dim white circle. Cam's heart lifted with hope. The sun. It was a way out, and he had to climb if he wanted to live. Sparing an instant to Delve his Source, Cam Bonded Kinesthia. A surge of energy raced through him as fresh strength infused his muscles.

Without a moment to lose, Cam braced his arms against the dark walls surrounding him, raising his legs—calf deep now—out of the water. He pressed them against the walls, and by slow increments, forced himself upward, climbing to the light.

Rise and brace. Rise and brace. *That was the entirety of his existence. And as he rose, the dank stench of rot and death waned. The silence within the cavern and tunnel was replaced by Cam's harsh breathing as he fought to escape. To live.*

Rise and brace. Rise and brace. *His legs burned. His shoulders felt afire, but Cam knew that to give in to weakness now would mean his death. He had to keep on.*

And slowly the light grew stronger, the hole through which it beamed, wider. Cam paused then, only a moment to shake out his arms even as the ache in his legs increased. Then he was off again.

Rise and brace. Rise and brace.

Only a few feet further.

Cam exited the darkness and emerged into the light, pitching forward; out of the hole, eyes shut, unable to handle the glorious brightness.

A snarl of dissatisfaction might have echoed out of the passage from which he'd just climbed, but following it was the mocking laughter of a wicked crone. That and a whisper. "I know you, boy."

Cam shivered, this time in terror. He'd heard that voice once before, but when it was, he couldn't recall. He rose to his feet, staring down into the hole, wondering at how he had come to be in this place. And how to get home.

His attention next went to the world at large. Cam stood on a plinth that rose like a ragged nail from the very edge of a tree-covered island where snakes hung upon every branch and rustled through every shrub. Cam's mouth curled in disgust. Anything that could walk without legs had to be a rakshasa.

He didn't want to look at the snakes any longer, so he turned his gaze to the ocean. It was an odd color, a dark red with areas where it seemed to have clotted and the water moved in thick clumps. An iron-tang stench suffused the air, and realization swept through Cam. The ocean was made of blood.

A hard wind whipped, and Cam stumbled. Arms windmilling, he plummeted, screaming.

Cam awoke with a start, sitting up in bed, finding himself in his quarters, back at the Ephemeral Academy. The dream. It faded even as he tried to recall it, emptying from his awareness until all that was left was a vague sense of disquiet.

He settled back in his bed, his heart pounding, trying to find peace and rest. *What had just happened?*

The next morning, Cam awoke, sore and tired like he'd run five miles uphill with a sack of rocks bouncing on his back. There was a lingering sense of disquiet, but he couldn't figure out why. Whatever the reason, he couldn't lay in bed doing nothing. Today was the day they would be journeying off to go lance a boil.

Joy.

With a tired sigh, Cam rolled out from under his sheets and got himself ready. Pan was up by then as well, and after grabbing a quick breakfast in the cafeteria, the two of them met up with the rest of the squad near the front gates where Saira and Professor Shivein waited.

Also present, which was somewhat a surprise, were Professors Grey and Werm. But they were there to merely wish Light Squad safe travels, briefly hugging each of them before it was time to get rolling.

"We've secured accommodation on a ship," Professor Shivein said. "It should take us three days on the lake to reach our port. Following that, we'll have another two weeks to reach the boil. Any questions?"

Weld raised his hand. "Where exactly is the boil?" he asked in a calm, collected voice. While he was still cocksure as a rooster, at least he leavened it nowadays with a bit of pretend humility.

"Why do you ask?" Saira asked with a teasing smile. "Are you afraid we'll get you lost?"

Weld shook his head. "Nope. Just like to know where I'm going is all."

"It's a village called Surelend," Professor Shivein replied. "Several weeks southeast of Corona. Any other questions?" He didn't wait but an instant before cutting off all conversation. "Good. Let's go." He hiked his packs over his broad shoulders, and they set out.

Cam kept quiet during the short trip down to the docks, sullen and stuck on wondering why they were doing this. Meanwhile, the others chattered away like magpies.

"Are you still bothered by what's to come?" Saira asked. She'd slowed down to walk next to him.

Cam shrugged, not wanting to admit his fears, worried it might make him sound like a coward to her. "Some of that, but I also didn't sleep well last night. Not sure why. There's other things."

"Like your Bonds not being strong enough and how you're worried you're falling behind the rest of the squad?"

Cam stared at her. He'd never mentioned any of that to her.

"I was a Crown," Saira said gently. "That means something, and one thing it means is that I understand the nature of Advancement, Enhancement, and Ephemera. I know what you're going through."

Cam grimaced. He hadn't wanted Saira to know about his troubles because in all the years since they'd first met that's all he'd ever been to her: trouble. At some point, he wanted her good opinion.

"I also spoke to Professor Grey. She told me the advice she gave you, on strengthening your Tangs." Saira peered at him, hard and intense. "Is it working?"

Cam vacillated. Did he want to admit the truth? Or would doing so cause karma to kick him in the teeth. "It's coming along," he admitted in the end. "I can't say for sure when I'll catch up with everyone else, but I'm a sight better now than I was before."

Saira nodded. "Maybe we can shorten that time. You have two weeks with no classes and no library studies. Work on your Bonds as much as you can. But don't shirk Spirairia. I'm not as skilled in the use of it as Professor Werm, but I know enough to help you if you need. Do all this all day, every day. While we're traveling, I want you doing nothing but Bonding and practicing."

"Yes, ma'am," Cam said. "I will."

They walked in silence then, and shortly after, reached the busy docks. Cam halted. It was a scene of chaos with a cacophony of curses and shouts as sailors loaded and unloaded an armada of merchant vessels. No one seemed to want to listen to anyone else, everyone yelling at once. It was a wonder anything got done. Then there was the pungent stench of brine and fish. Cam's nose wrinkled. He'd never liked that smell, although he'd been told that a person eventually got used to it.

Moments later, they boarded a single-masted schooner, wide all the way down to the waterline. Cam viewed it in amusement. If a ship could be said to appear pregnant, it was this one.

The captain, a beefy fellow with a handlebar mustache, got their cabins sorted. Cam, Pan, and Weld would be in one, while Saira, Avia, and Jade were in another. Professor Shivein, being as big as three of them on his own, got his own space.

Cam glanced at the small room he would be sharing with Pan and

Weld. It was filled out with four bunks—two-atop-two—and each one with a footlocker. All the furniture appeared to be nailed to the floor to keep them from moving during a storm. Best of all, the din from the docks was down to a muted roar here.

"I want to go see the rest of the ship," Pan said. "Want to come?"

Cam was tempted, but there were other things that needed doing first. "You go on. I'll catch up in a bit." Pan cocked his head in question, but Cam didn't answer straightaway, not wanting Weld to know of his problems. "I'll be meditating," he added, hoping the vague response would be answer enough.

Pan nodded understanding, while Weld barked in disbelief. "What for? You can take a day off, you know?"

"I know," Cam said, "but I need to get this done. Plasminians have to work twice as hard as the rest of you." He shooed them off. "Now, get gone. Explore the ship. I'll be out soon."

Pan dragged Weld after him before the other man could say anything else, and with a grateful sigh, Cam seated himself on the floor. He closed his eyes, Delved his Source, and Bonded all his Tangs.

It was another opportunity to grow. That's what he told himself even as the pain built while he held onto all four Bonds. He made the connections as deep as possible and did his best to prevent them from fracturing. Pressure built in his head, labored his breathing and his heart, but he ignored the pain, stretching his limits.

35

Following the three-day journey by a boat that brought them across Lake Nexus' blue waters, Light Squad disembarked in Warren. It was a small town hugging the lake's southern coast and situated somewhere between Santh and Corona. From there, they traveled by foot, each of them with a mule to haul their supplies and Saira and Professor Shivein leading them.

It would have been a whole lot faster and easier if Master Winder could have transported them by anchor line, but this was a training exercise. According to Saira and Professor Shivein, the Wilde Sage wanted them trekking the whole way to Surelend so they'd gain a proper reckoning for what it meant to be out in the field. Besides that, there was also a limit on how often even a Sage could form an anchor line.

Cam wondered if maybe that was why Master Winder flew so often.

Nevertheless, Cam wanted to get the journey done with as quick as possible. Walking wasn't such a bad thing, but it gave a body too much time to think. And Cam had much to think about, including his unsettled sleep from several nights before—it still gave him the daytime shivers, and he had no idea why. Not to mention the battle at the boil.

Worry for Light Squad. How to keep everyone alive.

It was too many bad thoughts, and already Cam just wanted the battle over with. He'd do his best and that would have to be enough. Do his best and he'd have to believe the rest would fall into place.

His view on the matter—his unconcern about victory or defeat and focusing instead on simply doing his best—reminded him of what Professor Grey had advised before they'd set out. And while Cam had yet to reconcile what she'd taught as being anything like what he really wanted, maybe there was some kernel of truth in there for him to learn.

He brooded on the topic, wondering about his future as he stood with his back to the campfire. It was their first night on the mainland, and a soft breeze sighed through the limbs and leaves of the trees surrounding the small clearing in which they'd stopped for the evening. It stirred the campfire, causing embers to glow, sparks to flare, and lofted the earthy aroma of turned dirt and manure from the farmlands close at hand.

The fields belonged to the folks from the small village they'd encountered a little ways back, and with early spring already here in this part of the world, the farmers were getting ready to plant. It was warm as well, and Cam had long since shed his thick layers of clothing, exchanging them for a simple shirt and rugged pants.

He sweated a bit despite the lighter clothing, wishing for winter as he and Professor Shivein shared the first watch. While the rest of the squad slept, Cam traced his instructor's movements. Professor Shivein paced out past the firelight, but as big as he was, he was hard to miss, even in the deep darkness holding sway in this isolated part of the world.

Finishing with his circuit around the camp, Professor Shivein ambled back to the fire. Cam viewed him with a question on his face. In the weeks of journeying after he'd been chased out of Traverse, he'd never encountered anything dangerous out in the wilds. Even predators such as wolves and bears hadn't proven to be much of a problem. So why had the professor spent so much time making sure it was safe?

Especially since Cam doubted there was anything deadlier than a fox out there.

"Nothing to worry about," Professor Shivein said, his voice a husky whisper. "And I can see by the expression on your face that you're wondering why I wasted so much time making sure about that."

Cam furrowed his brow, wondering how the professor had known.

"It was written all over your face," Professor Shivein explained with a grin that softened his heavy features.

He gestured for Cam to follow him away from the fire, and they strode past the light, entering the darkness beyond until they were well away from the others. Cam gazed heavenward, to vivid stars appearing like a beautiful smear of light against the darkness. It was something he'd not seen in his months at the academy since the city's own illumination tended to drown the starlight.

"Do you know much about turtles?" Professor Shivein asked, speaking now in his normal rumble.

Cam didn't. He'd hunted turtles when there was no meat on the table, but he figured that wouldn't be an item he'd be smart about admitting to Professor Shivein. "Other than they're born from eggs..." He shrugged.

"Well, let me tell you. I'm what you call a leatherback," Professor Shivein said, drawing himself up proudly. "We're the biggest turtles in the world. The longest lived and the wisest. But hardly any of us survive to reach adulthood. One out of a thousand. I was one of the lucky ones."

Cam had never considered how challenging life might be for a turtle. In truth, he'd never pondered the situation; never saw a need to. He did now. "Why is it so hard?"

"Because from the moment we're born, we're threatened. Crabs, raccoons, birds, even driftwood—and those are just the dangers we face as hatchlings. When we enter the ocean... that's where we encounter the true terrors. Nearly every fish that swims and many other types of creatures see us as a tasty snack. That's why so few of us reach maturity." His eyes went soft and sad. "I saw nearly all of my brothers and sisters dead before we even hit the water, and the dying didn't stop there. In my entire clutch, I was the only one to reach a year in age." His focus settled back on Cam. "That's why I was so careful about the safety of the campsite. It's bred into me."

Cam appreciated the insight, but why was Shivein telling him this? Other than Avia, none of them knew him well, which made him opening up to Cam all the stranger.

Professor Shivein grinned again, his large blunt, white teeth flashing. "We'll likely share many watches before we reach the boil. Better you know the reasoning for why I'm so cautious now than always wonder and think me a fool."

Cam protested. "I'd never think you a fool." Professor Shivein was a Glory, and that alone accorded him respect in Cam's eyes. Plus, the professor was plain intimidating, and there was no chance Cam would ever mock the man, not to his face or even behind his back.

"No. I suppose not, but you'd think it, and you'd be right to do so. Which is why I told you what I did just now. The only reason I survived during that first year was because I managed to Heighten my Ephemera. I Awoke. It was when a barracuda chased me. Fear was in my heart, and I wanted to survive, but I knew it was hopeless." Once more, his gaze went to the past. "That's when I saw the truth. My life will never end. I will always be. Some part of me. All is Ephemera and Ephemera is All. I didn't have the ability to think the phrase, but I felt it, and in that moment, my Ephemera Heightened, and I was changed. I became a Novice and doing so allowed me to out-swim the barracuda."

"How long ago was that?" Cam asked. He'd always wanted to know and since the professor was being talkative…

"One hundred and fifty years." Shivein's attention focused once more on Cam. "Ephemera is a powerful ally. Honor who you are and what you have, and you have a chance to go far."

Two weeks later, on a morning that began with rain and a stiff wind, Light Squad finally reached their destination—the village of Surelend, except it wasn't really a village. It was more akin to a small town, similar in a lot of ways to Traverse.

During Light Squad's travel here, Cam had read whatever information Saira and Professor Shivein had about Surelend, and as they approached, he studied the place, comparing it to what he'd learned. As he expected, encircling the town was a ten-foot stone wall with an iron-banded, wooden gate gaping inward. And waiting to greet them there were several figures, including a tall, handsome woman—the mayor based on the descriptions Cam had read—along with a prettier, younger version of herself. Likely her daughter.

"Light Squad, I presume," the handsome woman said. "Welcome to Surelend. I am Mayor Lightwell." She gestured to the young woman with her. "This is my daughter, Marta. She will serve as your guide. We've secured accommodations for you in our finest inn. I imagine you'll want to rest first before scouting the boil."

"The travel here has been difficult," Saira agreed. "And a few hours of rest would do us good."

"I'm sure it would," the mayor agreed. "And after your rest, we would all be grateful if you destroyed the boil as swiftly as possible. The rakshasas grow bolder by the day. They've already destroyed several nearby farms."

"We'll get them gone," Weld said, bold as always and flashing a confident grin at the mayor's daughter, who quirked a winsome smile back.

Cam frowned to himself. He didn't like Weld much, but the man sure knew how to talk up and charm a girl. It was a skill he wished he had.

"How did you know when we would be arriving or who we are?" Pan asked, speaking the question that was also on Cam's mind.

"The Wilde Sage informed us," the mayor replied.

Cam furrowed his brow. He had figured Master Winder wouldn't be on hand for this lancing. Had something changed?

He made a mental note to ask Saira about it later, but for now, he followed as Marta led them to a prosperous looking inn. It was a mix of bricks and stone on the first floor and framed in timber on the upper. The entrance opened into a large pub smelling of freshly fried bacon and woodsmoke from the large fireplace where a fire merrily crackled. There was also the salivating smell of beer and alcohol.

Cam nearly wandered to the bar to order a pint, but with a by-now instinctive shove, he pushed away the longing.

A portly man, the owner, got their rooms organized—all of the men in one and the women in another with Professor Shivein having his own.

"Will you be alright staying here?" Pan asked, somehow recognizing Cam's battle with his addiction.

"I'll be fine." Cam said. "Let's grab some grub. I don't know about you, but I'm tired of hardtack and dried meat. I want some real food."

Pan chuckled. "No disagreements from me."

They rejoined the others in the pub, and when they arrived, Cam was surprised to see Marta still with them. He would have figured she'd have other work to do. His gaze fell on Weld, who sat next to her. Or maybe she just wanted to chat up the handsome Novice from the Ephemeral Academy.

Cam shrugged to himself. It wasn't his business.

An unclaimed chair waited between Marta and Saira, and Cam seated himself there, catching the attention of a waitress and ordering breakfast. He was about to talk to Saira, but before he could, Marta faced him.

"I don't think we've been introduced," she said with a smile.

"I'm Cam Folde," he said in a polite tone, ignoring Weld's flush of annoyance, likely at Marta paying attention to some other man. "I caught your name when we entered your fine town. It's a pleasure meeting you."

"Fine town?" Marta's smile remained, and she twirled a lock of hair around a finger. "I don't know about that, but I'll admit it's finer now that you and your squad are here to save us."

"We'll do our best, ma'am," Cam said, leaning on his best manners.

Marta chuckled warmly. "Ma'am? That makes me sound so old." She faced Weld again. "Your friend was just telling me about Light Squad. From what he says, you've got a few years on me. Maybe I should call you, 'sir.'"

"Absolutely not," Weld said, inserting himself into the conversation, his grin looking a bit desperate. "Cam doesn't hold to such formality. Isn't that right, brother? We're all equal here."

From the other side of the table, Cam caught Jade rolling her eyes, and Saira coughing lightly into her hand, suppressing a laugh.

"Even though you're the leader?" Marta asked Cam with a lift of her eyebrows. "The one who makes sure your squad always wins?"

They'd been talking about him? What for? Cam looked to Jade, wanting some guidance and only received a leering grin.

"Indeed, Cam is the leader of Light Squad," Saira said, saving him from having to reply. "As such, he and I have some private matters to discuss."

She rose to her feet, clearly expecting Cam to follow her. He did so, not missing the disappointed expression Marta sent his way. Shrugging, he followed Saira to a corner table, a good distance away from anyone else.

"You're welcome," she said, taking a chair.

"What am I thanking you for?" Cam asked, seating himself as well.

Saira smirked. "That young woman is on the prowl for a husband. Do yourself a favor and don't *ever* find yourself alone with her. She'll have you crowned with a wreath of flowers and wed faster than you can say saffron."

None of that made any sense, and Cam shrugged minutely, in neither agreement nor disagreement. "Was there really something you wanted to talk to me about?"

"Actually, yes. It's regarding a decision I've made. I've been speaking to Professor Grey, and from what I've learned, Plasminia is far more powerful than I realized."

Cam frowned, not sure where this was headed.

"It's a Tang all true Ephemeral Masters would be wise to seek, but for myself, I can only gain it as an Adept or lower," she added. "Apparently, it's the only Tang one can add beyond Novice."

Cam's jaw nearly dropped. "You plan on regressing again? Because of what Professor Grey said?"

Saira inclined her head.

"And you believe in her?"

"I believe in her knowledge, that book on Plasminia theory she shared with you." Saira cocked her head. "I actually read it once. A long time ago, but it seemed so fanciful, flying in the face of everything we know about Ephemera."

Cam frowned in surprise. "My first experiences with Plasminia weren't so good, but I've always wondered about the nobles. Why didn't any of them choose Plasminia? They have access to tonics, cores, and maybe even Pathways, so there's no reason they couldn't have added Kinesthia later on like I did."

Saira nodded her head. "There have been nobles with that kind of access who made that choice, and every one of them were either unable to form that Tang of Kinesthia or they died in the process. It's an old story, which is why no one ever chooses Plasminia as their Primary Tang. Everyone fails at it." She peered at him, serious. "You were lucky in what you accomplished. You and that other man, Fetch Deville."

Cam hadn't known, and he offered a private prayer to Devesh for seeing him succeed where others had apparently failed. A worrisome notion occurred to him. "Will you also need luck?" he asked. 'Forming a Plasminia Tang?"

She smiled. "It's not my Primary Tang, so I should be fine." She hesitated then. "There's something else I want to talk to you about. You've been unsettled ever since learning about this boil, and I think I know why. It's because you worry you're a curse." She shook her head. "You're not."

Her words unexpectedly touched Cam, gave voice to his private fears while also providing him solace. He wished he knew what to say in response. Right now, the only things coming to mind sounded utterly sappy.

"You're not being overly sentimental if you say, 'thank you,'" Saira said, still smiling.

Cam chuckled ruefully. "Is it really so simple for you to figure what I'm about to say?"

"Only because you're a friend."

Cam mentally grimaced. *Friend.* One of the worst words a young woman could use to describe a young man. "Then getting back to your regression," he said, wanting to shift the conversation. "How does it happen?"

"It's nothing more than a conscious choice. Anyone can do it."

"And if you want to Advance?"

"I'll be a different person. I'll also have to discover new truths."

"The questions we have to answer to Advance in Awareness?"

"Correct." Saira ticked off the questions. "To Advance to Acolyte is to understand the difference between selfishness and selflessness. For Adept, it is to balance passion and rationality. Glory requires the knowledge of giving versus receiving. Crown, as you know, is certainty and doubt. Sage is having the awareness of reality compared to falsehood."

"And Divine is knowing the difference between permission versus acceptance."

"A question no one has successfully answered in many, many centuries."

Cam nodded, pondering still what would happen to Saira when she regressed. Worried for her, if truth be told.

"And the important part for you is this," Saira said. "When I regress, I can gift my Ephemera, and it's best if I gift it to a worthy person or persons."

Cam frowned. "Who would you give it to? Professor Shivein?"

She smiled, bright and beautiful. "No. I would give it to you. You and the rest of Light Squad. I'm a Glory. I have enough Ephemera to raise all of you to Acolyte. That's assuming you discover your personal answer about the difference between selfishness and selflessness."

"You would do that for us?" Cam asked, his eyes widening in

astonishment.

"As I just said. You're a friend. Of course, I would."

"And there's no risk? Why don't older, dying Masters do that for their children?"

"It's not so simple," Saira said. "To begin with, it takes a great deal of skill. At least the skill of a Crown, in their youth and at the peak of their power. I can't imagine a Crown in such a situation giving away their Ephemera. Second, the recipient still has to know themselves well enough to Advance. Otherwise, it does them no good."

Several hours later and roughly five miles from Surelend, Light Squad lay on their bellies, atop a low hill overlooking a river gorge. Behind them extended rolling farmlands of spring wheat and the first plantings of corn. Some of them—too many, including the farmhouses—had been burned to blackened husks. The work of the rakshasas.

Cam vowed to see the farmers avenged even as he scooted forward on elbows and knees, studying the river gorge ahead of him, seeking to gain the enemy's measure. The rest of Light Squad did the same, all of them gazing downward into the ravine, which was lined with broken boulders and scattered clumps of evergreen trees. And along its base flowed a narrow river, trickling and gurgling. A wind wafted, tugging on Cam's clothing and carrying a mineral scent.

This was where the boil was located, in a cave on the far side of the gorge, only a few feet off the ravine floor with a wide trail leading to it. The rakshasas hadn't bothered clearing the copse of scrub pine forty yards out front. A bad decision. The trees would provide cover, but would it be enough?

Cam continued studying the layout of the land, tracing a path to get Light Squad to the copse of pine trees. That's where matters became difficult. There was no further cover, and Cam didn't and never would like the notion of a straight-ahead charge along an open path.

A screaming sound from high above had Cam darting his eyes

toward the sky. There was a man up there, rapidly descending.

"It's Rainen," Saira said before Cam could order Light Squad to prepare themselves.

Cam bit back a scowl as Master Winder alighted. The Wilde Sage showed no care that he'd given away their position and presence to the rakshasas.

"You face twenty-eight rakshasas," Master Winder said without preamble. "Fifteen are Novices, comprised of ten humans, two elk and three coyotes. Another five are Acolytes; four humans and a vulture. There are also five Adepts—two humans, two deer, and a snake—and three Glories; all of them mountain lions." His mouth pursed. "It's a lot worse than I expected."

Cam didn't like those odds. "We're outnumbered over five-to-one. Is that why you're here? To kill the rakshasas so we don't have to risk ourselves?"

"Life is a risk," Master Winder said. "And you're right, the odds aren't as favorable as I had hoped, but I still think the experience might do you good, having Light Squad try to lance the boil. And while there will be injuries, know that I'll protect you if things get too dangerous. I'll leave the decision to you."

"In that case," Weld began. "We'll—"

Cam cut him off, not ready to answer Master Winder's unspoken question. "How will you protect us?"

"I'll provide overflight control," Master Winder said, "I'll be watching everything. However, there is a risk. Nailing, the Sage of Warring Thunder, the rakshasa who rules this area, might monitor the situation as well. And Nailing is served by two other Sages."

"Then you would also be outnumbered," Pan noted.

"Correct, but remember your lessons. The rakshasas are more numerous than Ephemeral Masters, but they aren't nearly as skilled."

It brought Cam some hope that they could actually defeat the rakshasas and lance the boil. But there remained a lingering doubt. "You really think this is important?"

Master Winder nodded. "You can't learn to truly fight until you're in a real fight. But you want those first engagements to be as controlled as possible. This boil is stronger than I originally intended, but it's one I still think you can handle. And I can still control the situation so it remains as close to non-fatal as possible."

Cam viewed Light Squad, all of whom nodded his way, even Weld. He faced Master Winder. "What do you advise?"

Master Winder smiled. "Why don't you tell me your plans, and I'll tell you my advice?"

"We were going to surprise them," Weld muttered, sounding bitter. "Kill them when they weren't looking." He scuffed a boot against the ground. "Looks like there's no chance of that happening now."

Master Winder flushed. "Yes. Sorry about that. You'll have to work around that limitation." His gaze settled on Cam. "What do you intend to do about it?"

Cam shared Weld's irritation, and largely for the same reason.

Regardless, what was done was done, and he'd just have to accept it and move on. He Bonded Synapsia, sending his vision questing to the other side of the ravine where the rakshasas had clearly noticed Master Winder's arrival. A number of them stared toward the hill on which Light Squad stood, pointing and gesturing. Plans flittered through his mind, added and discarded in mere moments. His eyes flicked about, and he considered options…

Seconds later, he had the beginnings of an idea. It would focus on misdirection. His eyes went to Master Winder. "You're not going to kill them for us, but you'll be there overhead, right?"

Master Winder nodded.

"Then how about in the middle of the battle, you let them see you leave."

Master Winder's eyes narrowed. "Tell me what you have in mind."

36

It didn't take long for Light Squad to have a plan in place, and it was like Cam had originally intended; it was all about misdirection and deception. Partway into the battle, Master Winder would depart the field, seemingly abandoning Light Squad. And when the rakshasas saw this, hopefully they would grow bold enough to leave the safety of their cavern in order to destroy their enemy. But it would be a mistake because out in the open, Light Squad had the advantage, and would, in turn, crush the rakshasas.

There were a few final details to iron out, and Cam met with his professors and Master Winder to discuss them.

"Are we sure Nailing won't show up when you leave?" Cam asked Master Winder.

"I'm not, but it also doesn't matter. I won't actually be gone. I'll be close enough to sense whatever is happening here, including if Nailing—the Sage of Warring Thunder began life as a buffalo, by the way—enters the battle. He'll come by anchor line, and I can sense the formation of one of those from a hundred miles away. If he comes, I'll be here to protect you."

It was exactly what Cam had wanted to hear. Satisfied, he was about to order Light Squad into position, but a strange curiosity flickered through his mind. Something about which he'd long been curious. "Why are you called the *Wilde* Sage? Why not the *Wild* Sage." He spelled out the different spellings.

Master Winder's eyes widened. "That's what you want to know?" Upon seeing Cam wasn't joking, the Wilde Sage threw his head back and laughed. "You are an interesting fellow." His eyes shined with humor and a smile remained on his face. "It's because of the founders of my line, William and Serena Wilde. Salvation's first Divines. They might have Advanced beyond even that Stage by now since they don't live among the current Divines."

"I didn't think there was anything beyond Divine."

"You mean like Servants?" Master Winder asked with a quirk of his brow.

"Well, sure," Cam allowed. "But that's Rukh and Jessira. They're unique. There ain't any others like them."

"And yet, it's said that they don't want to be unique. That they want others to Advance and be as they are. Servants who can then become proper Creators."

It was odd, having a theological discussion with Master Winder on the eve of battle, but Cam's natural nosiness egged him onward. "And you think William and Serena, the founders of the Wilde line—"

"It was their surname," Master Winder corrected. "It's why I and those Sages in my lineage that came before me name ourselves the Wilde Sages. It is to honor them."

Cam accepted the correction with a quick dip of his head. "And you think they became Servants?"

Master Winder shrugged. "Maybe. Those in my lineage believe that they helped Rukh and Jessira create Salvation but afterward, no one knows what happened to them. The Holy Servants gave us their philosophical views through *A Warrior's Sorrows* and a bit of their biography in *The Song of Devesh*. And it's in the latter that we have confirmation of William and Serena. They're mentioned. Apparently, they were students of Rukh and Jessira, eventually became their friends, but what happened to them afterward, we don't know."

"What do *you* think happened?"

"I think we should stop conversating so much about William and Serena and get your squad ready for battle."

Cam smiled at Master Winder's attempt at wittiness. "Conversating? I didn't think you had it in you to talk country. And you almost even got the accent right."

"Consider it the next skill I wish to learn," Master Winder said. With that, he ascended into the air with a whoosh.

Cam was rocked backward by the billowing air of the Sage's departure. He continued to stare upward until Master Winder was merely a blob floating in the sky. Only then did he face his squad, who stood arrayed about him, close at hand. He eyed them and the world all around, freezing the moment in his memory.

It was early afternoon, and the rain from earlier in the day had drifted south. Clouds still covered the sky, but in the distance, it seemed like they'd broken apart and ragged sunshine beamed down. A good omen. A worse one, though, were the pair of vultures circling the river gorge.

Cam did his best to shake away his morbid thinking. He didn't have time for it anyhow. "Anyone have any questions?"

"I think we've gone over it enough times," Weld said.

"Yes, and because of that, everyone should know how this is going down," Cam replied. "There won't be any mistakes on our side; not because someone didn't know where they were supposed to be. Everyone clear?"

"Crystal," Pan said.

"Shivein and I are heading out now," Saira said. "Give us about five minutes to get in position. Good hunting."

"Good hunting to you, too," Cam replied.

Saira and Professor Shivein Blended—a talent of the Glories—becoming nearly invisible against their surroundings as they set off.

"We'll follow in a few," Cam said to Light Squad. He frowned then, noticing for the first time their nervousness. Strange. All this time, they had been the ones who hadn't seemed to have a lick of fear about coming out here to destroy the boil, while Cam had been filled with nothing but a stomach full of worries. But now, on the eve of battle, he was calm and content as a cat with a belly full of milk. No anxieties roiled his middle.

He wanted the squad to share in his lack of anxiety. "Listen. You heard Master Winder. The rakshasas outnumber us, but they don't have our skills. Their numbers won't do them any good. We'll take them because we've out-trained and outworked them. They'll fall, and we'll stroll on out of here. You hear me?"

A halfhearted set of assents met his words.

The response wasn't good enough.

Cam stared each member of Light Squad in the eye, forcing them to meet his gaze. "Believe me when I say this. You're the finest students at the Ephemeral Academy. All of you have at least two Crystal Tangs. No other squad can say the same, and I guarantee you, those damn rakshasas can't say that neither. You hear me?"

He shouted the last, and this time a stronger cheer came in response to his question.

Better, but still not quite there.

"We're the best squad there ever was. We've fought like no one else. We won everything set before us. The martial exhibition. The Unwinnable. And these rakshasas sure ain't un*killable*. We're going to end them. Believe me and believe in yourself. Ain't no chance we're going to lose!"

This time, Light Squad answered with a resounding roar. "No chance!"

They were ready.

Cam cursed when he loosed a tumble of stones while belly-crawling down the slope. The rakshasas better not have heard him. So far that seemed to be the case since the enemy remained huddled inside their cavern. Their caution likely had to do with Master Winder still in the skies above the boil. They probably feared what he might do if they exited their cave.

However, whether they were hiding deep inside their cavern or closer to the entrance was an answer Cam didn't know. He had no idea as to their deployment. Light Squad had tried to find out when Saira had closed in on the cave, but she'd been driven off. Blended or not, the enemy Glories must have sussed out her presence, sending a storm of elemental fury her way. In the next few minutes, though, when Master Winder exited the scene, they should have that information.

Cam glanced ahead, making sure everyone was in position. Jade and Avia, their most powerful close-in fighters, crouched behind a pair of boulders. In the meantime, Cam, Weld, and Pan huddled behind boulders of their own, bows in hand. It would be up to them to pepper the rakshasas who emerged from the cave. And when they gave chase, Jade and Avia would cut the creatures down from behind. During it all, Saira and Professor Shivein would do their best to keep the enemy Glories, Adepts, and Acolytes out of the fray.

That was the bare bones of their plan, but it all depended on the rakshasas coming out. Cam didn't like any notion where Light Squad had to blindly enter the cave. Nothing good would come from such a decision.

Cam continued to study the cavern's entrance, looking for anything else that might give his unit an advantage. An instant later, he wanted to smack himself in the forehead. An overhang extended over the opening. Light Squad could collapse it. Doing so might not kill any of the rakshasas, but it could split their forces and keep any reserves out of the battle.

He glanced to where he knew Saira was supposed to be, waving in her direction. He hoped she'd look his way.

Seconds later, she materialized next to him. "What is it?"

Cam pointed to the overhang, quickly reviewing what he had in mind.

Saira nodded. "I'll pass the word on to Shivein. One of us will see it done." She raced off, disappearing as she Blended again.

Shortly thereafter, the screaming sound of Master Winder exiting the battlefield echoed across the ravine. Cam glanced to the skies, witnessing the Wilde Sage rapidly departing, heading south, climbing at a steep angle. He would reposition miles away from the sensory range of the Glories, but close enough to engage if Nailing and his Sages entered the fray.

Cam's attention resumed on the cave, hoping the rakshasas would take the bait. He nocked an arrow, laying it on the rest, waiting.

His wait wasn't long. A stirring from the cave's entrance revealed a number of rakshasas edging out, shields at the ready. Cam Bonded Kinesthia, and his vision heightened, bringing the rakshasas into sharp relief. He could see their eyes.

The ones who had exited the cave were a mixed bunch. Five Novices—three humans and two coyotes—along with an Acolyte—another human—and an Adept, this one a deer. There was also a mountain lion Glory stalking behind them.

Saira and Professor Shivein attacked, fireballs howled and splinters of ice screamed, hammering at the rakshasas.

The Glory gestured, and a shield of glowing, green webbing flared to life. The elemental attack smashed into the protective barrier with an echoing boom. Cam felt it reverberate in his gut, but against the rakshasas, the barrage did no damage. The enemy Glory unsheathed a sword, roaring orders. Another Glory exited the cave along with two more human Novices and Acolytes each along with a snake Adept.

Cam held off from attacking, gesturing for Pan and Weld to do the same. With that green webbing, it would have been a waste.

Saira and Professor Shivein were on the move. Steel slugs boomed off their hands, tracing a ripping line across the ravine, exploding around the rakshasas. The shield rocked with a concussive roar, flared, but still didn't take any damage.

Or had it? It seemed to be lighter in color.

Another Glory, the final one, exited the cavern. All three were in the open, and an elk and coyote Novice followed out, too. The first Glory gestured with his sword just as another wave of attacks pounded into the shield. Rumbling echoes filled the ravine like thunder.

Saira and Professor Shivein moved erratically, attacking from different angles.

The rakshasas split, one group moving toward Saira. The other going after Professor Shivein. It wasn't exactly what Cam had wanted, but it would do. Pan seemed to have figured it out, too. Same with Jade and Avia. As one, they lifted their bows. The webbing only protected the rakshasas as they advanced. It was weaker on the flanks and absent from behind. Weld didn't seem to realize, and Cam had to gesture to him, miming what he wanted.

Weld, once again a bit wild-eyed at the battle's beginning, thankfully figured it out pretty quick.

A hollow boom, different than before, rocked the ravine. Cam's vision went back to the cave. The overhang slowly slumped down with a grinding crack, slamming into the ravine's floor. The ground shook, and dust billowed in a plume, obscuring the cave's entrance. Cam reckoned it would be pretty much obstructed now.

Too bad none of the rakshasas seemed to have been caught up in the overhang's fall. But it got the attention of one of the enemy Glories. The mountain lion glared in the direction of where the attack had come from. He gestured, sending black lightning crackling toward Professor Shivein. Their instructor grunted in exertion; hands extended as his own glowing web—also green—came to life. It protected him, the lightning splashing across the shield in a shower of sparks.

Two of the enemy Glories targeted Saira, seeking to cut her down. As they pressed forward, the lower-Staged rakshasas were exposed. The glowing webbing didn't currently extend to them. Cam rose, aimed, and released. So did the rest of Light Squad. Two of the human rakshasas—Novices both—went down, crying in pain.

The rest of them sighted in the direction from which the arrows had come. The Adepts hung back, supporting the Glory, but the rest charged.

"Fire at will!" Cam shouted. He managed to launch two more arrows before the rakshasas were too close.

None of the arrows got through, caught on raised shields.

Cam dropped his bow, grabbed his spear and shield, and dropped into a skirmish line with the rest of Light Squad. Together, they prepared to receive the surging rakshasas, a mix of Novices and Acolytes.

Cam offered a final prayer for Light Squad's survival before Bonding fully to all his Tangs.

The world slowed as Synapsia engaged. The rakshasas seemed to run as if in mud. Cam could make out every droplet of saliva spitting. Spirairia took hold, and he saw the woven world. So many options to change reality with a flex of his will. Kinesthia connected, and Cam's muscles thrummed with strength and power, a false sense of indestructibility as he faced the onrushing rakshasas.

"Spears forward!" Cam ordered.

Moving in unison, Light Squad readied themselves, shields braced and short spears set. Cam had a wish that the stupid rakshasas would just impale themselves. After all, they were foolish enough to charge spears with only swords. In addition, their armor was a mishmash of leather with some metal in their most vulnerable places. Light Squad, on the other hand, was fully kitted with chest plates, pauldrons, vambraces, and greaves.

The rakshasas shouted like lunatics, and at an order from one of the Acolytes, they split their formation. Some of them looped wide.

"Bend!" Cam shouted.

Light Squad shifted with Weld and Jade, who held the ends of their line twisting to face the rakshasas who sought to encircle them. They continued shifting until they formed a rough circle, keeping the enemy from attacking their backs.

The rakshasas closed and mayhem ensued.

Cam focused on what was before him. He stabbed at a human

Novice. The blow didn't land but sent the rakshasa stumbling away with a cry. An Acolyte moved swiftly into the breach. She aimed a strike with her sword. Cam caught the attack, flung backwards by the powerful blow. He lost his balance, briefly falling to a knee. Bracing himself on the ground, Cam shoved himself upward, grabbing a handful of dirt in his shield hand.

The Acolyte was on him, while the Novice circled to attack Weld's blind side.

Cam shouted warning. Weld heard, and he retreated, gaining distance. The enemy Novice pulled away, glaring at Cam. The Acolyte was back. Cam flung the dirt he still held in the rakshasa's eyes.

The Acolyte snapped her shield around, preventing the crude attack from blinding her.

It was distraction enough, though, and Cam closed the distance. His shield slammed into the rakshasa's. They circled, fighting for position. Cam thrust with his spear. The Acolyte twisted out of the way. She aimed her own thrust, her short sword giving her better leverage close in. Cam had to retreat. The Acolyte rushed him from the right just as the Novice re-entered the fray, charging hard from the left.

Using Spirairia, Cam lifted one of the Acolyte's feet. He barely got it off the ground. At the same time, he stepped forward. His shield cracked into the rakshasa's. A well-placed foot was set behind the rakshasa's lifted one. A hard shove, and the Acolyte was on her back, shouting in desperate fury.

The enemy Novice was there. Cam slapped aside a looping swing. The uncontrolled blow had the rakshasa off balance and unprotected. Cam hammered a front kick into the Novice's gut. The air exploded from the rakshasa's lungs, and he folded over himself, struggling to breathe.

Again, Cam couldn't take advantage of his enemy's momentary weakness. The Acolyte was on him again. Swinging and thrusting, rage on her face. Cam gave way, looking for a way to win. His mind raced. Right now, all he was doing was holding off the enemy. He needed to end them, especially since his Bonds would likely fail quicker than theirs.

A distant shout took the decision out of his hand. One of the Glories was calling on the lower-Staged rakshasas to retreat. At a barked command from the Acolyte Cam had been battling, the enemy disengaged from Light Squad. They retreated in good order.

Cam scowled. They'd done no damage to the creatures. Other than the few rakshasas they'd arrowed early on, the enemy had only taken a few nicks and cuts. He was about to order a charge at the rakshasas, but he saw a better opportunity.

"Cover me," he shouted, rushing to where he'd dropped his bow and quiver of arrows.

Pan followed, also with a bow in hand.

"The Adept." Cam pointed out the deer rakshasa. The creature had drifted away from the Glory's side, no longer within the bubble of green webbing and without a visible shield. "Target it. Maybe we can distract it enough that Shivein can take it down."

Setting an arrow on the rest, Cam focused on the deer. His sight tightened on his target, the creature's chest. His vision narrowed, to where the beating heart would be, protected as it was by leather armor; imagining the bolt penetrating deep. With an exhalation, he released.

The rakshasa must have sensed the attack. It crossed its arms, and the arrow slammed into a glowing, green webbing. It wasn't as bright as the one produced by the Glory, but it was strong enough. Pan's arrow was also halted, breaking apart into splinters.

But their attack did its job. The Adept was facing them. The weakness to the side of its shield was in Shivein's direction, and their instructor took full use of his chance. A jolting line of jagged icy spears roared from his hands.

The deer tried to spin around, but it was too slow. The spears of ice caught the creature in the flank, ripping it apart. The enemy Glory closest at hand snarled in anger, pointing at Cam and Pan.

Cam's stomach hollowed. He knew what was coming. "Run!" He raced behind a nearby stout boulder, falling flat to the ground and covering his head, fingers laced. Hopefully the others would be smart enough to do the same.

A fusillade of metallic bolts screamed, pounding into the boulder, carving it up, sounding like non-stop peals of thunder. Chips of stone along with larger lumps slammed into Cam. Even with his armor, he'd be bruised good.

After seconds that felt far longer, the attack ended. Shivein must have taken off the pressure. Cam peeked up from where he lay. His boulder had been blown apart. Hardly any of it remained. And if Cam had only hid behind it instead of lying low, he'd have been blasted apart, too.

Devesh, that had been too close.

Before getting to his feet, Cam surveyed the battlefield, taking stock. His ears rang, and he smacked the side of his head, wanting his hearing normal. At least the rest of the squad had come through with only scrapes and heavy bruising. They were still in the fight.

Meantime, Saira and Professor Shivein exchanged fire with the Glories, their attacks sounding like a rumbling rockslide; dull, though, since Cam's hearing wasn't yet right. Lightning crackled and the assaults from Light Squad's Glories pounded out a staccato rhythm. Boulders, heavy stones, and dirt were flung into the sky in a never-ending series of explosions.

As for the enemy, the lower-level rakshasas hadn't halted their retreat. They stood next to the snake Adept, awaiting orders maybe. Frantic movement from within the blocked cave indicated that their reserve was still trying to get out.

Well, that just wouldn't do.

37

Before taking the attack to the enemy, Cam first dashed away to safety. Once he was behind a new boulder, he called out orders. "Get those Novices! Pin them down!"

Hopefully, the Acolytes would have to extend their protection to their weaker members, and maybe it would give Saira and Professor Shivein the opening they needed to kill the more powerful rakshasas.

Cam rose to his feet and took careful aim. His Bonds still held. Through Synapsia, he was able to maintain a locked-in focus. And with Kinesthia, his aim was steady and unmoving. Not even the slightest tremor. He released an arrow, setting another on the rest before the first shattered against a hastily raised, green shield.

From the cavern, the crumbled remnants of the overhang moved. Cam shifted aim. A human Adept pushed his way out of the cave. Covered in dust and dirt, he was busy scowling. Cam launched an arrow. It whistled toward his target.

The Adept gestured frantically. A shield flared to life, catching and severing the arrow. But the arrowhead itself continued to tumble in flight, punching into the rakshasa's shoulder. He clutched his wound, falling back into the cave, shouting in pain and anger.

Fresh arrows were incoming. Cam ducked behind his boulder. Most of the Novice rakshasas were firing at him. A quick peek showed him the enemy had pressed out from the cave, leapfrogging forward. The Glories continued their own assault against Saira and Professor Shivein. None of them were able to spare the attention to do anything other than defend and attack one another.

The battle was changing to one of attrition. Following that first engagement, Cam liked Light Squad's chances. He recognized that the Ephemeral Masters *were* far stronger than any single rakshasa at the same level of Advancement. But he also didn't figure on simply gambling the battle on something that still felt like a wish and a prayer. The tide needed turning.

But how?

Cam examined the situation while the rest of his unit took potshots at the rakshasas, devising and discarding multiple possibilities in the span of seconds. Where were the rakshasas weakest? Their initial plan to draw them out had worked, but they needed something else. Something more.

Just then, Cam's Bonds frayed and snapped. The world lurched, moving too quickly for him to take in all the details of the wildly shifting battle. Fragging hells! It was madness, and he couldn't make any sense of it. His cooldown was two minutes.

Panic threatened, and Cam's heart raced. Fear he wasn't used to feeling spiked in his heart. It made no sense. Every other battle or fight, he had remained unflustered. Nothing had bothered him.

But this was a different kind of battle. This was real, and there were real consequences of life and death. His life and possibly his death, and that of his unit. It clarified the stakes like nothing else ever had.

Cam breathed deep, eyes closed, struggling to control his fear. Another deep breath, and the panic receded. A final breath, and it was gone. Cam's heart beat steady and slow as an old man's walking pace. He opened his eyes.

"They're advancing!" Weld shouted. He was pressed against a

boulder, close at hand and sounding on the edge of panic.

"Hold your position," Cam sounded out, voice calm. An idea formed, and there was nothing to it but to get it done. He searched about, locating the rest of his team. "Jade. Pan. Advance to the right. Get within fifty feet of them. Aim at the Acolytes. Ignore the Novices for now. Get them following you." He turned to the other members of his squad. "Avia. Weld. Shadow Jade and Pan. Come in from their left. But hang back. When the Acolytes give chase, cut down their Novices."

"We could use your help," Jade said, scowling at him.

He figured on the reason for her glare. She must think he was going to hide while the rest of them risked their lives. Outrage surged at her lack of faith, but Cam reined it in. Light Squad needed him steady and sharp, not furious and out of control. "And you'll have it," he said to Jade in a cool but sharp tone. "Now, get into position."

Jade scowled a final time before giving a sharp nod of assent and running off in the direction Cam had ordered.

Seconds later, Saira raced across the ground toward him, apparently having a lull in her battle against two of the enemy Glories. She looked to nearly be flying, although she'd lost that ability when she'd regressed. "We're holding," she said, halting briefly next to him. "But you and Light Squad need to shift the odds, or we're going to have to call on Rainen."

Worry rose. It wasn't what Cam had expected to hear from her. He had thought she and Shivein could overcome the enemy Glories. "How long can you hold out?"

"Ten, fifteen minutes. Not much longer than that."

His cooldown would be over well before then. "We'll change the odds."

"I'm counting on it," Saira said before rushing off.

Cam returned his attention to the battle unfolding before him. Pan and Jade were in position, but they hadn't gone unnoticed. Rakshasas fired arrows in their direction. None hit as Pan and Jade hunkered down behind boulders. They waited, and as soon as there was an opening, they straightened, launching their own attacks at a pair of

Acolytes. Shouts and orders echoed across the ravine as the enemies took shelter.

Soon enough, the rakshasas prepared their counterattack. They raced from boulder to boulder, advancing. Pan and Jade feigned panic and fell back in what appeared to be an uncontrolled retreat. The Acolytes and a handful of Novices whooped in excitement and gave chase. Cam silently urged them on. *Keep coming.*

Weld and Avia, unseen and forgotten, rose from their hidden position just as the rakshasas raced by. A pair of Novices went down, arrows in their backs. The rest of the rakshasas halted their charge, crying out warning. They swung their shields about, shifting to defend against Weld and Avia.

Pan and Jade took the opportunity to halt their retreat and reset themselves. They managed to kill an Acolyte and a Novice.

Cam's Bonds were off cooldown, and he hastily reformed them. He breathed relief as the battle's chaos slowed to a crawl. He had all the time in the world to figure what was happening.

And what was happening had him scowling in concern and self-recrimination. Every member of Light Squad had just lost their Bonds at the same time. He should have realized. His oversight... They could all be killed because of his stupidity.

A quick examination calmed him some. It looked like many of the rakshasas had also lost their Bonds. But not all of them. A couple of them—a Novice and an Acolyte—still lurched in the eye-blurring motion of those using Kinesthia.

Light Squad would be easy meat if those rakshasas managed to close with them. Which they wouldn't. Cam would make sure of it.

"Fall back!" Cam ordered his squad. "Back to the treeline." He broke from cover, moving slower, pretending he didn't have his Bonds. He raced toward the remaining rakshasas, hoping to get them focused on him.

The elk Novice and the initial Acolyte who Cam had fought took the bait. They angled toward him. Cam timed their slow movements, keeping an eye on his squad and the enemy. The two rakshasas who still had their Bonds had retreated back to the Adept for some reason. But more of their kind were spilling out of the cavern.

Saira and Professor Shivein sent a volley of fire as the rakshasas exited, but the enemy Glories protected them. Their shields flared, dimming some as thunder cracked from the impacts. Dirt plumed upward, obscuring the sky. But Cam didn't need to see it clear to know that the shield held. Worse, with the arrival of the fresh rakshasas, Saira and Professor Shivein would be hard-pressed. Their attacks hadn't yet waned, but they couldn't last too much longer.

Light Squad had to even the odds.

Which they could once they were off cooldown. But Cam could also get those odds closer to even on his own. He just had to convince the rakshasas to keep on coming on.

The Acolyte and Novice would soon be in reach. Cam deepened his Bonds, and fresh strength and speed enhanced his muscles and mind. He spun about, shooting toward the unprepared rakshasas. Shock and fear appeared on their faces, a slow-motion dropping of their jaws. Cam felt like he had all the time in the world to stab forward with his spear.

The leaf-shaped blade took the Acolyte in the throat. Cam spun about, braced himself. He blocked an overhand swing from the gigantic elk. The creature leaned into the attack, grunting in effort. Cam pushed the rakshasa off balance. Before the elk could recover, he bashed the creature in the face, blinding him. The rakshasa never saw the gut-thrust coming. Cam angled his attack upward, punching the spear into the elk's chest. He ripped his weapon free, leaving the rakshasa to fall, facedown with blood pooling.

A second Acolyte approached, the coyote Novice with him. They moved just as slowly as the other two rakshasas, but Cam wasn't fooled. The woven world showed him the truth. Though they didn't have the tinge of color around them that indicated someone using Ephemera, nevertheless, Cam could tell they held Bonds.

He gave way, edging so the Novice would reach him first. The coyote rakshasa accelerated, closing well in advance of the human Acolyte.

Cam sent a lazy, horizontal swing with his spear, angling his shield outward and out of position. He all-but begged the coyote to kill him. The rakshasa fixed on doing just that. The coyote darted at him, shield in position to block Cam's lazy swing and aiming a gut-thrust.

Cam snap corrected. He brought the spear low, aimed at the coyote's unprotected legs. At the same time, his shield bashed out to counter the rakshasa's thrust. The rakshasa's sword banged with a dull thud into Cam's shield; hard, chipping off chunks. Meanwhile, his spear cut deep into the enemy's thigh, slicing to the bone. The coyote screamed, collapsing, blood pumping from a deep wound. He might bleed out if he wasn't healed.

The Acolyte arrived. But he didn't attack at once; nervous, licking his lips.

For the first time, Cam had a chance to more closely examine one of the enemy. The rakshasa was a man in his middle years, gray haired and features unremarkable. There was nothing evil seeming about them. He could have been someone's father or grandfather. A simple farmer or tradesman. So, why had he chosen the rakshasa's version of the Way into Divinity?

A question for another time.

The coyote wasn't dead, and Cam aimed to change that. He moved to the side, hoping to shift the enemy Acolyte the way he wanted. Cam looked to his right, away from the coyote. He telegraphed his attack, even feigning movement in that direction. The rakshasa shifted, nearly out of position.

Another glance to the right, and the Acolyte moved even further, his hips pointed away from the coyote. Cam rushed at the wounded rakshasa, too fast for the Acolyte to get turned around. The coyote was rapidly weakening, but dead was even better. A quick plunge of Cam's shield crushed the coyote's throat.

The Acolyte roared in outrage, and Cam fled him, giving ground.

Other rakshasas were heading his way, and he couldn't afford to get tangled with this one. He darted away from the pursuing Acolyte, gaze flicking to the treeline. Weren't the others off cooldown yet? He could use their help.

As in answer to his question and need, arrows whistled past Cam, coming from the pine trees. The Acolyte halted his chase, hastily raising his shield. He was blind to what was in front of him. Cam rushed back at the distracted rakshasa. He didn't need to kill the Acolyte but incapacitate would work. He stabbed the rakshasa in the ankle and immediately shot off to the side.

The Acolyte howled, hopping about like an injured bunny. His shield lowered as he bent over, clutching his damaged ankle. A pair of arrows dropped him dead. At the same time, a brief, brutal scream from further away showed that one of the charging Novices—another non-descript human—had taken an arrow in the chest. The rest of the rakshasas retreated like their britches were on fire.

The short lull allowed Cam to survey the scene. Light Squad erupted out of the treeline, finally off of cooldown. Cam saw where they could be of best use. Professor Shivein looked ragged, battling against a Glory, a pair of Adepts, and four Novices. Saira—fighting two Glories, the final Adept, and three Novices—was in even worse shape. Her hair was scorched, her armor battered and burned, and blood caked her face and dripped from a wound on her right shoulder.

There were also two Acolytes, a human and a vulture, who didn't appear able to fly. They had no one protecting them. And Cam could tell they were on cooldown. They were only fifty yards away.

Light Squad could kill them and then support Shivein and Saira.

Cam faced Light Squad, snapping instructions. "Avia. Pan. Get to Saira. Take the pressure off her. Weld. You're with me. We'll do the same for Professor Shivein."

"What about me?" Jade asked.

"You'll be with me and Weld. But halfway to Professor Shivein, you and I will break off and kill those Acolytes. They're on cooldown."

Jade made to look at the Acolytes. "Don't look," Cam barked, not wanting her to give away the game.

"How can you tell they're on cooldown?" Weld asked.

"I just can," Cam said. "Now move out. Hustle. Our Glories are taking damage."

"Be careful," Pan said to Cam before he and Avia dashed off to bring relief to Saira. If nothing else, they could pin the Novices attacking her. Maybe even the Adepts.

"Come on," Cam urged, leading Jade and Weld at a sprint toward Professor Shivein.

The enemy saw their approach, shifting about. Seconds later, the Novices were firing on them.

"Shields," Cam called out, although it proved unnecessary since Jade and Weld already had theirs raised.

The bolts thunked into their shields. Another volley was similarly blocked.

"Hold position," Cam ordered. He had a new idea, and he got the three of them behind a single, massive boulder.

The Acolytes had gone to help their brethren who were attacking Saira. They must have seen Avia and Pan since both rakshasas were pointing at them. But what Cam had noticed is that the Acolytes had their backs turned on him.

"I see it," Jade said, an arrow aimed.

Cam got his own on a rest, sighting down the bolt. As he concentrated on the shot he wanted to make, the world seemed to stretch. The feathers of the arrow tickled his cheek. The air held still. The sun broke from a scattering of clouds, and a sunbeam seemed to freeze as it extended to touch him. The day was peaceful, except for the explosions and cascading dirt.

Cam released his arrow at the same instant as Jade and Weld. The bolts were still in flight when the three of them launched a second sequence. All six arrows punched into the backs of the unsuspecting

Acolytes. They screamed in pain, stiffening, stumbling, and slumping over dead.

"That'll do," Jade said, sounding pleased.

Cam nodded. "Let's go help Professor Shivein."

The three of them sprinted to where they saw their instructor battling hard odds.

A warning flared in Cam's mind. "Down!" A concussive hail of stones ripped a line over where Cam and the others had been only an instant before. "Move!" Cam guided the others to a boulder. Just in time as the stones slammed into where they'd been lying. The attack continued, pounding at them.

Seconds later, it relented. Cam ducked his head out, quickly pulling back when an arrow nearly took him in the eye.

The single look told him enough, though. The Glory and his Adepts were still engaged with Professor Shivein, while the Novices had been moved to defend against Cam, Jade, and Weld.

"Drop the Bonds," Cam said.

"What!" Weld protested. "We'll be in cooldown."

"No, we won't," Cam said. "We'll be able to re-Bond immediately. Just when the rakshasas enter cooldown."

"We can't kill them if they're still protected by the Glory," Jade argued.

"Yes, but the Glory will have to extend his shield over them," Cam explained. "It'll make it weaker for when he faces Master Shivein. The Novices will come at us then, figuring us easy picking without our Bonds. Now do what I said."

There was no argument this time. Cam let go of his Bond as well, hating how the world seemed to crash into his head. So much sound and shaking. In that instant, a line of explosions rocked the ravine. A quick peek showed him one of the human Adepts had been singed bad but was already healing himself.

"We need to keep the attention of those Novices," Cam said. "Fire at them."

Weld and Jade did so, but without Kinesthia, their attacks lacked their prior fine focus. Many of their shots went wide or were smoothly deflected or evaded. The rakshasas countered, and when they did, Cam and the rest of the squad barely got out of the way. It was mostly a matter of sheltering behind the boulder.

While he hunkered behind the stone, Cam did some rough calculation. He'd Bonded thrice with all his Tangs, which meant he had one more time to go before he hit the much longer cooldown of over a half hour. The rest of Light Squad were on the same schedule. As for the rakshasas, he had to believe they were on their next to last Bonds, too.

Arrows clattered against the boulder.

Come on. Send them after us.

Cam took another look. The Novices didn't look to be moving anywhere. But the Adepts… Light Squad had a better angle on them.

"Go after the Adepts," Cam said. "Get their attention. We need those Novices after us."

It was strange, wanting to be attacked, but it was also their best chance of ending the rakshasas. Plus, there was Nailing to consider. If he ever showed, who knew what reinforcements he might bring?

Cam adjusted his aim. He knew his arrows wouldn't do much, but a distraction might still help Professor Shivein. Weld and Jade followed his lead. Three arrows rattled against the shield, which didn't even flare in response, so weak had been their attack.

But they got the attention of both Adepts. One of them—the one who'd gotten singed—pointed them out. Cam didn't need to warn anyone to run. The three of them bolted, diving behind a more distant boulder.

Just in time as a wall of flames washed against the stone they'd previously been hiding behind. The Adept turned his fire on their new boulder, and Cam had to belly crawl backward as the rock heated, turning red in seconds. A bore burned through, and a pencil-thin line of fire lanced over his head. Jade screamed. The fire had sliced along her back.

Cam grabbed her, dragging her with him as he backed away. Weld was with him. They found another boulder, thicker and taller than the last one, and waited out the flames. Jade looked in bad shape. She groaned, barely able to move. *Please be fine.* They couldn't do anything for her now, though. First, win this battle, and then see to healing her.

The fire ended within seconds that felt like hours, and Cam took a quick glance. At last, the Novices were charging in their direction. And the fragging Adept who'd burned Jade was dead.

38

Cam's attention snapped to Jade when she moaned. Burned as badly as she'd been, she needed help.

"I can heal her. She'll be fine." Master Winder said, speaking into his mind like Professor Werm once had. *"Finish this battle. Win."*

Cam nodded, relieved that Jade would be seen to. And Light Squad *could* win this battle. They just had to do it quick. Cam studied the remaining rakshasas, calculating what was needed to finish them off. Seven Novices, no Acolytes, a pair of Adepts, and the three Glories.

Light Squad couldn't do much about the more powerful rakshasas, except distract them, but that might be all Saira and Shivein needed to finish the battle. So how to end those Novices? That was the key that Cam had to solve. They had to be at the end of their Bonds, but so long as they remained protected by the Adepts and Glories, there was no way to kill them.

Cam frowned, trying to figure on what might work.

"Jade is hurting," Pan said, interrupting his assessment. He and Avia had broken off trying to reach Saira, reconnoitering with the rest of the squad. "Is there anything we can do for her?"

"Win," Cam said. "Master Winder let me know. He'll protect and heal her. We just have to finish this." Even Saira could likely heal Jade since it was an Adept-Stage skill.

"What do we do?" Weld said, his earlier fear having subsided.

Cam didn't know at first. He observed the Novices staying well back of the Adepts and Glories, who were darting about, evading and attacking Professor Shivein. A notion came to him. The Novices were undefended. "Pan, you and Weld get behind the Novices. Soon as you see them slowing, you'll know they've lost their Bonds. Close with them then, so the Adepts and Glory can't so easily kill you without killing their own. There's a pile of rocks you can hide behind, too." He pointed them out. "If the Adepts or Glory attack you, I'm sure Professor Shivein can put them down."

"What about the two of us?" Avia asked.

"We're doing the same, except on Saira's side."

"The Novices are fighting right next to the Glories over there. We won't be able to get close."

"Which is why we'll be right on Saira's hip. We'll do the same as those enemy Novices. Pester the Glories, and if Saira can get them to chase her, we can kill the Novices while she kills the Glories."

Avia grinned. "You sure you just don't want to be on Saira's hip?"

"Now's not the time," Cam chided.

"What about Jade?"

"We have to leave her," Cam said. He carried her off a short distance, to a half-moon ring of tall boulders, setting her down carefully. Cam hated having to abandon Jade like this, but what other choice was there? He checked in all directions, grunting in satisfaction when he figured no one could easily get to her here. "She'll be safe. Master Winder will watch out for her," he said when he rejoined the others. "Move out."

He and Avia sprinted, both of them hunched over, making a smaller target. Cam hoped the Glories didn't notice them. If they did, from this distance, there wasn't much he and Avia could do to defend themselves. His heart pounded out his worry, both for himself and Avia and also for Pan and Weld. He shot a brief glance to where the other two should be advancing, catching a quick sight of them. Then they were gone, hidden by a mound.

He sent a quick prayer their way even while resuming his attention on the direction he and Avia were headed. An instant later, they reached Saira's side, rolling in from behind.

"Good to see you," Saira said when they arrived. The area around her was nothing but rubble and ruin. Long scorch marks and jagged craters. Saira stood amidst it like a queen of battle, out in the open, daring the Glories to attack. "You have your Bonds."

"The last of them," Cam said. "What do you want us to do?"

"Find me a way to end this," Saira said, cool and calm. But Cam could tell the effort she was expending. Saira might look like a queen of battle, but she'd taken damage aplenty. Burns, wounds—and by the way she was limping and holding a hand close to her body—maybe some broken ribs.

"We can do it," Cam said. He'd already seen the opening. There were no rakshasas defending the cave. The way inside was clear, which meant the way into the core was as well. And the rakshasas were out of reserves. At a flat out run, he and Avia should be able to make it in there. The enemy Novices might even follow, but Cam wasn't worried about them. If they pursued, he and Avia would kill them.

What was more important was lancing the core. Doing so would greatly weaken the rakshasas. He flashed another glance at the cave, distracted by white lines moving in eddies, in paired spirals, drifting out from somewhere inside. The vision left him, and he shook off wondering about the brief image.

"Can you keep their attention?" he asked Saira.

"I've already got their attention. Whatever you're going to do, do it fast."

"Yes, ma'am." Cam turned to Avia, telling her what he had in mind. "We circle wide so they can't tell what we're about. Soon as we reach that ring of stones, we run flat out. You see where I mean?"

Avia gazed along the length of his arm, nodding. "I see it."

Just as Cam was about to set out, a warning flared in Cam's mind. "Wait," he said, holding Avia back.

The enemy Glories attacked. They hurled arrows of ice, rent the earth, and set the air afire. The world became a howling storm, but none of it did any harm. As long as they stayed still, Saira's shield protected them.

The assault ended.

"Now," Cam ordered, leading Avia in a stop-start fashion. They darted from one boulder to the next, crouched low and hopefully hidden from the rakshasas. Raced across open ground, toward the ring of stones, which grew larger painfully slowly. Cam counted the seconds, which ticked by like minutes.

Saira's counterattacks rang out like some titanic smith at her anvil, ferocious and echoing. Cam caught a glimpse of what she was doing. From her hands exploded fiery bolts that impacted like an avalanche. A metal spear extruded from the ground, dirt falling off like a waterfall. It accelerated, wailing like a banshee, blasting into the rakshasas' shields, which flared brightly and dimmed afterward.

The Glories gave way to Saira, spacing themselves apart.

Cam reached the ring of stones immediately behind Avia. They paused an instant. "Now we run for it," he said.

Avia grinned. "We got this."

Cam wished Avia had kept her mouth shut. Bragging on a matter was a surefire way to take one on the chin. It was like asking karma to come and kick them in the face, which was foolish since karma was happy enough to do that on her own.

Sure enough, just as he and Avia approached the cave, enemy Novices peeled off in their direction, four of them, three humans and an elk. All of them angry as a raccoon with a sore tooth. They'd get to the cave nearly at the same time that he and Avia did.

But maybe there was a way to slow them.

"Arrows," Cam ordered.

He and Avia continued to sprint, nocking arrows, aiming, and loosing. It should have been impossible having any kind of accuracy or even finding the coordination to do something like that. But with Kinesthia and Synapsia, what should have been impossible wasn't.

The enemy Novices had to raise their shields, and it slowed them some. *But not enough.* Cam and Avia fired again, and as before, the rakshasas defended, running even slower now. They also weren't firing back, which told Cam something. Although the red haze around their forms indicated they were using Ephemera, the rakshasas were also about to lose their Bonds. They'd be on cooldown soon.

Time to kill them then.

Cam dropped his bow and drew his short sword, wishing for his lost spear. No help for it now. An adjustment to his run had him aimed at two of the human rakshasas. Avia could handle the other two, including the elk since she'd been smart enough to keep her spear. He rolled beneath a diagonal slash; rose to block a thrust from the other rakshasa. A parry and Cam had to step back, mentally cursing. When would the rakshasas lose their Bonds?

He hammered aside a lazy chop. The rakshasa overextended and paid for it by losing several fingers, screaming. Cam kicked him in the gut, shutting off his caterwauling. But before he could finish the rakshasa, the other one was there.

This one had more skill, and Cam found himself on the back foot. He blocked most swings with his shield, which was being whittled down to little more than chips of wood. The other rakshasa was back in the fight.

Perfect.

The injured rakshasa ran at Cam. The fool had his sword aimed like a lance. Cam batted it away and shoved the Novice into the other rakshasa. Both went down in a tangle. Excitement got the best of Cam. He wound up and swung hard, like he was fixing to use a club. He missed both rakshasas, who got themselves sorted out, reset and ready, even the injured one, who moved to flank.

Cam feinted at one, then the other. The injured rakshasa went to raise his shield, but he was a split-second too slow. A thrust took him in the throat. Cam sensed danger at his back. He spun away from a furious swing that would have decapitated him. Cam faced off against the final rakshasa, the more skilled one. He gave ground, blocked a thrust, a chop, and another thrust.

The rakshasa's sword bent on his shield, and the tip got stuck. Only for a bit, but as the Novice tugged on his weapon. Cam let go of the shield. The lack of resistance had the rakshasa falling away from him. The enemy Novice landed on his backside.

This time Cam didn't swing like he was fixing to knock the rakshasa's head off. He thrust, fast, straight, and true; no motion wasted, puncturing the rakshasa's armor. His sword slid home into the enemy's chest. The rakshasa cried out. Another thrust silenced him.

"Nailing is coming. I'm blocking his anchor line for now, but you need to finish this!" Master Winder again.

Cam shuddered. An enemy Sage was a disaster.

Immediately, he looked to Avia. One of the rakshasas was dead, and she faced off against the elk. Blood dripped from a heavy wound she'd taken to the forehead, and she swayed. The elk kicked. Avia barely blocked with her shield, but it still fractured, breaking apart into splinters, rocking her off her feet.

Cam ran at the elk, slowing to grab the shield from one of the fallen rakshasas. The elk saw him coming, licking his lips and looking uncertain. He stepped back. Cam went straight at him. He dove beneath an overhead slash; landed right next to one of the rakshasa's hooved feet.

Just where he wanted to be. The woven world flared in his sight. With Spirairia, he pinned the Novice's foot to the ground. It was the farthest he could reach with the Tang. Far enough, though, and when the elk tried to kick him, his foot barely budged.

Cam slashed out. His blow sheared the rakshasa's tendon at the ankle, and the elk collapsed. Avia was back in the fight, approaching from behind. A thrust through the elk's chest, and the fight was over.

Avia sagged, and Cam noticed her looking upset with him. "I

thought you said their Bonds were going to break," she said.

"I thought they would," Cam said with a shrug. "When we lance the core, maybe it'll happen then."

Avia nodded. "Let's get this done. I'm so tired."

Cam led the way to the still partially obstructed cavern, quickly making his way inside.

There, he discovered a roughly carved tunnel, one lit by widely spaced Ephemeral lanterns. Shadows pooled in the passage's sharp edges, and everything was covered in dust from when Saira had brought down the overhang. There was a long table in what appeared to be a cooking area and a painting of a buffalo, an Awakened Beast, above a place where the tunnel narrowed. Wasn't Nailing a buffalo? And was the painting of him?

Cam dismissed the stray observation.

A number of rooms with cots and foot lockers split off from the main corridor, but Cam disregarded them, too. He and Avia hustled deeper inside, to where a tingling told him he'd find what they were looking for. Soon enough, they reached the end of the tunnel and discovered a blue globe resting on a white pedestal. The boil's core.

Again, Cam noted white lines—Ephemera perhaps—drifting outward from the core in paired, helical spirals. The image flashed apart when he blinked, leaving him confused. What was that about?

An instant later, when the vision didn't reappear, Cam decided it wasn't important. He'd think on it later. For now, lancing the core was all that mattered, and it shouldn't even be that difficult. It was a simple application of Kinesthia and Spirairia. Except Cam had never done this, and he honestly didn't know if he had enough control of either Tang to see it finished.

Luckily, he had Avia with him, who must have seen through his hesitation. "I'll do it," she said.

Cam stepped back, watching as she placed both hands on the core. Her brow furrowed in concentration, and she seemed to apply pressure on the core, more and more of it. Her hands shook, her Novice red eyes glowing brighter. The core vibrated, trembling in a way that was different than the motion of Avia's hands. A single pinging sound indicated the formation of a crack.

Avia had created a single point of weakness, and her will seemed to redouble. Another ping echoed in the hallway. Avia stabbed in with Spirairia, enhancing the cracks. Seconds later, with a hissing scream, the core was lanced. The blue glow emptied, dispersing into the air, and when it was finished, Avia held a dull, white stone.

"Let's see the rakshasas fight now," she said, smiling with satisfaction.

"Come on," Cam said. "Light Squad still needs us."

Avia held onto the core as they raced back to the cavern's entrance.

When Cam exited the cavern, it was to a very different battle. Saira was finishing off the last of the Glories, and Professor Shivein was doing the same on his side. Pan and Weld—the latter hunched over and clutching his chest—had gotten the better the Novices with whom they'd been tangling.

Everything looked to be fine for Light Squad, except for a rip in the sky. It was a hundred feet out from the cavern entrance and twenty feet above the ravine's floor. An anchor line. And through it emerged a man hairy as a bear and wearing nothing but a pair of pants. His muscles bulged, and he was massive enough to make Professor Shivein seem small. A braided beard hung down to his chest, and thick brows shadowed his violet eyes—eyes which told who and what he was. Nailing, the Sage of Warring Thunder.

And following on his heels were two more Sages, a man who might have started as a mountain lion like the recently killed Glories, and a woman, who flicked her tongue like a snake. They stood to either side of Nailing.

Master Winder shot down out of the clear sky, stopping with a crack of thunder between Cam and Avia and the enemy Sages. He appeared small in the face of their size and might, but Cam knew Master Winder was stronger on an individual basis than any of the rakshasa Sages. He had to be. Otherwise, this was fixing to be a mighty short fight.

Cam felt it just as much as saw it when Nailing turned his violet eyes on him and Avia. There was a pressure to the rakshasa's gaze. It was a weight similar to what Cam had once felt from Master Winder, but this one held a restrained malice. It growled at Cam, ordering him to bend the knee and give way to the Sage's will.

No. It was a single word that Cam repeated over and over. He'd give way to no one, and he'd never bend the knee. Maybe it was being too proud, but Cam would take on that sin and live with it. What he couldn't live with was ever being weak-willed enough to buckle under the pressure of someone else's expectations.

Staring defiance in the face of the Sage's promised destruction, Cam refused to bow. And Avia appeared to take courage from his unwillingness because she stood upright as well.

The Sage blew out an exhalation, seemingly amused. But when his gaze moved to the core Avia held, his humor faded, replaced by a flash of anger in his violet eyes.

"You'll want to direct your attention to me," Master Winder said.

Nailing's eyes moved off of Cam and Avia, and he shuddered when the Sage did so, muscles noodle-weak from what had felt like a fight for his life.

"And you should have never directed your attention to me," Nailing said, his voice as deep and rumbly as his build suggested it would be. Cam felt the tones rattle his innards like an avalanche rumbling from a distance. "You mess with the bull, and you'll get the horns."

Master Winder folded his arms, clearly unimpressed. "You're still using that trite phrase? This many years later? Don't you find it silly?"

Nailing smiled, cheerlessly. "Many have said so. It was among the last words they spoke in this world."

"Meaning you killed them," Master Winder said.

"Of course."

The female Sage with Nailing slithered forward. She definitely must have started off as a reptile of some kind. "And now that you've said your piece, it is time to tear you into pieces."

Master Winder boggled at her a moment before throwing his head back in derisive laughter. "Tell me she didn't just say that," he exclaimed once he got his humor under control.

"I most certainly did," the female Sage hissed. "What of it?"

"It's silly. That's what," Master Winder said.

Cam frowned. If he didn't know better, he'd have sworn Master Winder was delaying the Sages.

Master Winder continued speaking to the snake-like Sage. "You really need to—"

"Are you going to talk us to death then?" Nailing interrupted. "Is that it? So we won't kill you right now?" He snorted in disgust. "You, Rainen Winder. The unkillable killer of rakshasas. The terrifying Wilde Sage. The man whose name is a curse among my kind. And yet, here you are, finally on the wrong end of a predicament, and what do you do? You talk because you don't want to die. You make jokes hoping we'll take pity on you. It's disgusting. I expected more from you, Rainen Winder."

"I know you won't appreciate my humor," Master Winder said. "And I'm not trying to talk you to death." A black line split the sky, twenty feet from where Master Winder floated. "I was waiting for him."

The anchor line rotated, exposing a rainbow-filled doorway into infinity. And through it stepped a slim, elegant man, white haired but smooth featured. His eyes glowed violet, and he exuded power no less than that wafting from the other four Sages. Avia's gasp told Cam who it was.

Her father, Kelse Vail, the Sage-Duke of Saban. His presence changed the dynamics of the situation, and Nailing knew it based on his furious glower.

"An interesting soiree you're holding," Duke Vail said, speaking to Nailing. "I know I wasn't invited, but I felt sure you simply forgot to send me an invitation."

"You think this old weakling is enough to save you?" Nailing asked, gesturing rudely at Duke Vail.

"Try me and find out just how weak I am," the Duke replied.

Cam truly hoped Nailing wouldn't. He remembered the battle between the Wilde Sage and Borile Defent, the Silver Sage of Weeping. The destruction they'd visited on the forests north of Traverse. Cam had been lucky to survive their war, and he doubted he'd be so lucky a second time.

Nailing didn't reply at first, his eyes resting on Duke Vail, flitting back to Master Winder. "You might win, but it will cost you."

"And you'd still be dead," Master Winder said. "Your boil here is destroyed. Fight us now, and your greater one will be as well. You lost. Accept it or you'll lose even more."

The female Sage glowered. "You think yourself so smart, don't you?" she hissed in fury. "There will come a time, *Wilde Sage*, when your wisdom fails you. And when that happens, we will be there to carve out your heart."

Please, let her shut up, Cam thought.

Duke Vail lifted his brows in mock horror. "That's quite the vivid portrait you just painted, my dear. But until then, I insist you depart. We wouldn't want this situation to become any messier than it already is." His visage hardened, and in that instant, he transformed into the powerful Sage-Duke the world knew and respected, rather than the light-hearted fellow he had been pretending to be.

The female Sage stiffened. She might have stormed past Nailing, but the Sage of Warring Thunder extended an outstretched arm, blocking her.

"You've won this round," Nailing agreed, "but there will always be another." He gestured, and an anchor line split the sky.

Cam urged them to depart before they could change their minds. *Come on. Leave.*

The female Sage was the first to exit, followed by the mountain-lion who hadn't bothered talking. Before he left, though, he seemed to stare at Cam and Avia for a moment. A smile might have wisped across his face, too fast for Cam to be sure before the Sage was gone.

Nailing was the last to leave, and before he exited, he offered a hard stare at Master Winder. "The world never stops turning. Our day will come."

Master Winder and Avia's father didn't bother responding. They simply stood on the air, observing until Nailing's anchor line closed. Cam watched as well and had the odd feeling that this wouldn't be the last he'd see of those Sages.

The anchor line collapsed, and silence reigned within the ravine.

Cam abruptly bent over at the waist, gripping his knees as a relieved laugh burbled through him. They'd survived. They'd won. It was all that mattered. That and seeing to the healing of Light Squad.

Avia, though, shivered. "Did you see their eyes? I never thought a Sage's eyes could be so violet. They seemed sharp enough to cut diamonds."

Cam straightened with a grin. "That's because they weren't violet. They were violent. Get it?"

Avia punched him in the shoulder, chuckling softly. "Idiot."

39

After Cam and Avia's brief conversation, silence descended over the ravine. Nothing but a lonesome wind and the sound of dirt trickling to the ground like rain from where it had been tossed about by the Glories during their battle.

And though the battle hadn't taken much time—only about fifteen minutes—it felt a lot longer. Cam wanted to lie down and take a nap—not a dirt one, but any other would do—but there was work to be done first. After sending Avia, Weld, and Pan off to where the Duke was healing Saira, he hustled over to Jade.

Fear knotted his throat when he saw her. She wasn't moving; still as a corpse and pale as one, too. The fear crested until Cam noticed Jade still breathing. She was only unconscious then. Maybe she had taken a blow to the head along with the burns she'd received, and if so, hopefully Master Winder could heal both injuries.

The Wilde Sage arrived just then. "Go to Duke Vail. I'll see to Jade."

Cam exhaled in relief, nodding acknowledgment to Master Winder. "Thank you, sir." He shuffled to where the Sage-Duke was healing the other Novices.

Professor Shivein had also arrived by then. "A hard battle," he said. His face was slicked with blood, and bruises were already darkening his skin, including an eye, which was swollen shut. He didn't seem able to walk too good either, and one of his wrists was clearly broken.

"Are you going to be alright?" Cam asked.

"I'll be fine."

"You sure?"

Professor Shivein quirked a crooked grin, ghastly given his swollen cheeks and lips. "I'm sure. Go see how your friends are doing."

"Yes, sir." Cam went to Sage-Duke Vail, who had just finished healing Avia. She still didn't look fully right, but at least she looked a mile righter than she had a few minutes ago.

"How's Jade?" Avia asked when her father was finished with her.

"Unconscious," Cam responded. "Master Winder is healing her." He turned to the Sage-Duke, intending on asking what was to happen now.

He waited, though. Duke Vail was tending to Pan, who was covered in dirt and had a crusting of blood along a hip. One of his hands seemed broken as well. At least, Cam guessed it must be given how swollen it was. Thankfully, it didn't take the duke long to see to Pan, and by then Master Winder joined them, setting Jade down.

"It was a harder battle than I expected," the Wilde Sage said, addressing Light Squad. "The Glories who Nailing sent weren't the newly Ascended that reports indicated. They must have been further along in their Way into Divinity."

Saira grimaced. "All of the rakshasas were stronger than we thought to find."

"And we almost died, sir," Cam added.

"I would have protected you," Master Winder said. "And Duke Vail was close at hand. The risk was far less than you think."

"We could have still been killed," Cam replied, disliking the explanation. "Nailing had two other Sages with him."

"And the moment they attacked, I would have defended," Master Winder said. "I won't allow harm to come to my charges. I would have kept you safe. And know this, if Nailing had attacked me, the block on Vail would have immediately ended. The Sage of Warring Thunder wouldn't have been able to maintain it. He would have been in trouble, and he knew it."

"Then all that talk from him about fighting you and father?" Avia asked.

"Mere posturing," Duke Vail replied.

"And after this battle, Nailing needed to posture," Master Winder said. "He lost some of his most promising rakshasas. He won't be able to so easily replace those he lost."

"Neither would we," Saira said. "We wouldn't be able to replace Light Squad if they'd been killed. We should have brought another unit to support them."

"If I'd known how dangerous this boil was," Master Winder said, "I'd have destroyed it on my own. I wouldn't have even bothered with another unit."

"And we did win," Cam reminded Saira, forced to contradict her because he wanted Light Squad to understand what they'd accomplished. It had been their hard work, determination, and bravery that had seen the boil lanced.

"And now that we know how difficult it is to battle the rakshasas, we'll train even harder," Pan added.

"That's the spirit," Professor Shivein said. "You won, and your tactics were excellent and decisive. You should celebrate."

Cam didn't know about any celebrating. It had been a close-fought victory that could have ended in tragedy. But nevertheless, maybe Light Squad should think on enjoying their triumph. They should appreciate it. "You're right," he said to Professor Shivein. "We won as a unit, and we should celebrate that fact."

Even as he spoke, he tried not to look at Jade's bloodless face; tried not to recall the injuries so many of them had endured. Or the killing. He had killed both humans and Awakened Beasts, and even though they were rakshasas, actions had consequences. Currently, Cam wasn't completely at peace with himself over what he'd done—killing humans and Awakened Beasts—even if he rationally knew there hadn't been an alternative. Back at the academy, maybe he'd have time to think about what he might be feeling or should feel. Or at least write an after-action report so he could express those thoughts and do better next time.

But that was a private mess. For now, he wanted Light Squad to know their worth.

"Indeed," Master Winder said. "This was a victory, and Light Squad should take heart in their accomplishment." He addressed them, beaming. "Shivein is right. You were brilliant, and I applaud what you did here."

"Perhaps so," Duke Vail said. "But remember, there have been no rakshasas who've Advanced past Crown since you killed the Silver Sage of Weeping. It was a terrible blow to their power and prestige."

Master Winder cocked his head in confusion. "Your point?"

"My point is that we shouldn't take these kinds of risks if it puts our future best and brightest at risk. You know what Avia can become. Same with Saira, once she reclaims her certainty. Jade also has it in her to become a Crown. So does Pan. And that says nothing of your Plasminian. We have no idea what he might manage."

Cam held himself unmoving, shocked by what Avia's father had just said. The Sage-Duke knew of him. Did others, too? And if so, why? He was just a Novice from the back end of nowhere.

Master Winder didn't respond at first to the Sage-Duke. "You know I don't risk my people unnecessarily," he said at last. "As I said before, I would have never allowed them to come to harm."

Duke Vail might have responded, but Saira interrupted their conversation. "While you think about what next to do, I'm returning to Surelend with the Novices. They need rest."

Both Sages hastily straightened, their features contrite like they'd been scolded.

"Of course," the Sage-Duke said. "Give me a moment with my daughter before you leave."

"I have words for you as well," Master Winder said to Saira, drawing her off.

Cam watched them a moment, shaking his head. What was this about going to Surelend? There were two Sages standing right there. Couldn't one of them anchor line Light Squad back to the academy?

Pan wandered over to his side, catching hint of his upset. "What's wrong?"

Cam explained.

"I'm sure they have their reasons."

Cam shrugged. "Maybe." There was something else he wanted to share with Pan, something Cam had thought hard on since he'd learned of it. "Saira is going to regress further. She wants to create a Tang of Plasminia, and the only way is if she is an Adept. Professor Grey's advice."

Pan's eyes boggled.

"I'm thinking maybe the rest of y'all should also form a Plasminia Tang. If Saira thinks it's that important…"

"Then we should think it equally so," Pan finished. "But how would we do it?"

Cam smiled. "All is Ephemera and Ephemera is All. We'll figure it out."

Cresting a final rise, Cam sighted Surelend in the distance. Over the past several hours, Light Squad had trudged the miles long hike back to the village, and by now, the sun was fixing to set. Cam wanted to do the same, just collapse in whatever bed or floor he could find and call it a day.

But first, he had to see to Jade, get her washed up and settled. Then he had to take care of Weld, who had a couple of broken ribs. His breathing was labored, but he was fighting through the pain, never complaining, which was impressive.

Cam had never figured Weld would have that kind of grit. Pan was helping him, and the two hobbled along like an old couple. Avia's injuries hadn't been so bad, and Duke Vail said she'd be fine after a night of rest. Same with Saira and Professor Shivein, even though their injuries had been a sight more severe. Then again, they were Glories, and Glories healed faster than Novices.

Jade groaned just then, and Professor Shivein pressed a finger to her forehead, a surprisingly gentle touch, until she fell back asleep. It was for the best. Jade had only awoken briefly, and her burns, which Master Winder insisted would heal without a scar, were still red and inflamed. It was best if she slept through the pain.

Minutes later, a dip in the road led to a rise, and there were the gates of Surelend. They were closed, but Cam caught sight of a pair of guards peeking through a narrow slit. They whispered excitedly, and seconds later, hauled open the gates, shouting questions.

"The boil is lanced," Cam said. "We'll explain it to your mayor. She can tell everyone else. For now, know that you're safe."

His words resulted in shouts of joy and excitement. The guards made to shake the hands of every member of Light Squad, although they didn't go near Professor Shivein when he growled at them. Folks from houses close at hand poked heads out of windows, asking about the commotion. From there, it didn't take long for word to get passed. Then it was a mess of people pouring out of their homes, praising Devesh, the Holy Servants, and Light Squad—in that order.

Cam didn't mind sharing the credit with those that were divine. Fact was, he'd have done the same. Still, what had him annoyed was when the good people of Surelend got in his way. He just wanted to get to the inn and see his unit abed and resting.

Thankfully, Mayor Lightwell came along and quickly gained control of the situation. Her daughter, Marta, was with her. "I hear congratulations are in order," the mayor said, smiling brightly and with tears in her eyes.

Cam looked to Saira, thinking she'd want to be the one to talk to the mayor. She must not have since she had her attention on Jade. Cam shrugged inwardly. "It was a close-run battle," he told the mayor. "But in the end, the rakshasas were vanquished, their boil lanced, and even their Sages were sent running with tails between their legs."

Weld mustered enough courage to grin at Marta. "And when he says tails between their legs, he's not lying. The Sages who showed after Cam and Avia lanced the boil were all Awakened Beasts."

Marta smiled brilliantly at Cam. "You lanced the boil? I should have known it would be you."

"It was actually Avia," Cam said.

"But you played a hero's role," Marta insisted.

"We were all heroes," Cam replied. While he appreciated Marta's obvious interest, he didn't know how to respond. Girls back home didn't like him, and it left him uncertain around them—unlike how he felt around Jade, Avia, and Saira, but they were different. "And I don't mean to be rude, but we've got injured. Master Winder has healed them, but they need rest."

"Of course," the mayor said, clearing the area around them with a single shout. "Follow me."

Cam trailed after the mayor, leading Light Squad through a throng of folks who continued to shout their praise. He ducked his head, embarrassed by all the fuss.

"Handsome, brave, *and* humble," Marta said, smiling at him through hooded lids. She'd slowed, pacing alongside him. "What other secrets do you have?"

Cam truly wouldn't have minded getting to know Marta, but her forward behavior was too off-putting. He also feared Saira's advice from earlier in the day—had it really only been just this morning?—about Marta marrying him before he knew what was happening.

Avia slid up on Cam's other side. "Can I talk to you for a minute?" she asked, before addressing Marta. "It's regarding Light Squad. You understand."

Marta inclined her head. "Of course." But a flashing of her eyes displayed her irritation even as she stepped aside.

"What did you need to talk to me about?" Cam asked.

"Nothing," Avia said with a smile, clutching his arm possessively. "But you looked like you could use a rescue."

Cam laughed. "You ain't lying about that." He told her what Saira believed was Marta's motivation.

Avia listened with a serious expression. "I wouldn't know about human mating customs," she said, "but from what I do know and what I could tell, that's about right."

"Is that why you're holding my arm like you own it?"

Avia flicked a glance at Marta, who'd briefly looked their way. "It gets the message across."

Cam exhaled heavily. Here was Avia, only a few years removed from swimming the seas as an orca, and already she knew more about the dance between men and women then he did. Or at least she knew how to swim those treacherous waters.

The notion struck him as odd, thinking on talking to women like it was swimming in treacherous waters. What did that say about him? He mentioned it to Avia.

She gave him a sympathetic smile. "You'll figure it out."

"Maybe so," Cam allowed, "but that's not the only thing that's got me bothered."

"What are you talking about?" Pan asked, coming up on his other side.

"My trouble with women," Cam said.

"What trouble," Weld scoffed. "Avia and Jade like you well enough. Maybe even Charity. And then there's the mayor's daughter panting after you, too."

Cam gave Weld a hard stare. "Just to be clear. Avia and Jade aren't panting after me."

"No, we aren't," Avia said, although she hadn't relaxed her grip on his arm. "And also to be clear, I'm holding your arm like this so Marta thinks you're mine and will leave you alone."

"What about me?" Weld complained.

"I can hold your arm," Pan offered to Weld with a toothy grin, reaching out.

Weld waved Pan's grasping hands away. "Stop that," he said before addressing Cam. "I just mean that you've got plenty of women interested in you. So, what's this trouble you're talking about?"

"Back home, no girl ever gave me the time of day."

"They would now," Weld said. "You're a Novice Prime. You're the leader of Light Squad. We're ranked ahead of any other squad in our class, and we just lanced a boil. Lots of women are going to find you plenty attractive."

Cam grunted. While he reckoned Weld was right, it was still strange. Even stranger was having this conversation in the first place. He had more important matters he should be handling. He told the others so, and they drifted away, everyone but Pan.

"You're about to deflect," Pan said, speaking first. "You don't like praise because you don't think you deserve it. It's the same reason a woman's attention makes you uncomfortable. But I think you do deserve it. Without you, I think we would have been slaughtered today. We're only alive because of your leadership."

"He's right," Saira said, striding up to them. "If not for your planning, none of us would have walked away from that boil. The fact that we all did is amazing. And that we'll all recover from our injuries is nearly miraculous."

Cam ducked his head, eyeing her askance. He'd reasoned out the same as what she'd just declared, but to have her actually say so… Perhaps it *was* time for him to have more belief in his worth.

The next morning, Cam made sure to take a bath. The night before, he'd been up late, ensuring everyone else was seen to. After that, he'd collapsed in his bed and fallen fast asleep, not waking until well past dawn. And when he did, only then did realize how dirty he was; covered in sweat, dirt, and blood from scrapes and cuts to which he'd not paid any mind. Plus, he stank, and sniffing himself convinced him to get out of bed and make straight for the inn's bathhouse.

Even though his stomach rumbled rather fierce, he couldn't imagine eating while covered in filth. The attendant at the bathhouse was an elderly Novice, and she quickly filled a tub and had it steaming in no time. Cam discarded his clothing, easing into the bath with a sigh of relief.

But his relief was short-lived when the water quickly turned to the color of mud. Nevertheless, he scrubbed and scraped at himself until there was no more dirt to be found. A fresh tub of water to make sure the last of the filth was washed away, and he was clean.

Afterward, Cam headed downstairs to the common room. The windows were thrown wide, letting in the bright sunshine and the sparkle of an early spring morning. The perfumed scent of flowers planted in wooden boxes under the windows drifted inward, mingling with the smell of crisping bacon. There were a couple merchants finishing their breakfast, and Saira was also downstairs, seated alone in a corner, looking like she was just getting started on her meal. The rest of Light Squad was probably still asleep. Yesterday had been a rough one for all of them.

Cam sat next to Saira, ordering breakfast when a waiter came around.

She peered at him in curiosity. "How are you feeling?"

"Likely better than you," Cam said, indicating the bruising still marring her face and the way she held an arm stiff by her side.

"You've got your own wounds," Saira said, sounding like she was talking about a matter other than any injuries Cam might have suffered during the battle.

He chose to look past whatever she might have implied. "Can I ask you about Master Winder?" He wanted to talk about what had been bothering him since yesterday.

"You can ask, but I can't promise I'll answer."

Cam held back a grimace. He should have figured she'd say something like that. Master Winder had been the one to train her and show her the world. Of course, she'd be loyal. Still, maybe she would be willing to tell him a bit of what he wanted to learn. "Would he have really defended us like he said?"

"He would have," Saira interrupted. "Don't ever doubt it. He would have saved us if we showed signs of losing."

"But we were in real danger."

"Every one of us is in danger," Saira countered. "That's what it means to battle rakshasas. At least in this time and age. We fight so that those who come after might not have to fight so hard. So that everyone can live free and pursue their own happiness."

Rather than inspiring Cam, Saira statements disquieted him. Was the endless war against the rakshasas going badly? Or at least worse than he'd assumed. He asked.

Saira's mood lightened into a smile. "Of course not. We're winning. Or at least we're not losing. And hopefully together, we can end this destructive conflict."

Cam felt a weight lifted. "Then there is hope."

Saira laughed. "Of course we have hope. There is always hope. Hope is the greatest of gifts." She reached into a pocket, withdrawing the cracked core Avia had brought out of the cavern. "We also have this."

Cam frowned, recalling the white wisps wafting off the core that he'd seen in the rakshasa's cave. "I might have seen something before Avia lanced it," he said, going on to explain about the wispy, white paired helical spirals.

Saira frowned. "I've not heard of anything like that. I can ask Professor Grey. She might know."

"If anyone would, it's her." He gestured to the core. "What good is that anyway? You never explained."

Saira handed him the core. "It has enough Ephemera to let you and most of Light Squad maximize your Ephemera while you're still at Novice."

Cam frowned, confused by what she was saying. "I thought we already were maximized."

Saira chuckled. "Oh, Cam. You have so much more potential for growth. This core is a large part of why Master Winder wanted you and Light Squad to destroy that boil. With it, you can reach your absolute peak by Imbibing more Ephemera. You aren't yet at your peak capacity. That way, when you do Advance to Acolyte, your ongoing room for growth will continue to be so much greater. It's a mighty opportunity you've been given."

Cam hungered for what she was offering, but caution held him back. "You don't think it's too mighty?"

This time it was Saira's turn to frown in confusion. "What do you mean?"

"Just that. Is it too powerful? This is a core that was used by Glories and Adepts. Can we even use it?"

"You can," Saira said with confidence. "With my help, it shouldn't be an issue. I told you I wanted to regress to Adept. In doing so, I'll give you and the others my Ephemera. Before that happens, though, I'll teach you how to *accept* Ephemera."

Cam's memories went to Honor, the Awakened squirrel who had gifted him with the Ephemera he needed to heal. He hoped wherever her memories had taken her, she felt the way Cam was living his life was worthy of her offering. "Accepting Ephemera is painful."

"It can be," Saira said. "It was for you, but I also suspect some of that had to do with the nature of your problem."

"My Plasminia."

"Yes. Your Plasminia has been the great obstacle that has trapped you all this time, but I also think—and Professor Grey concurs—that it can be of great benefit to you as you Enhance and maybe even Advance."

She was right about the former, but Cam wasn't sure how Plasminia would help him Advance. Increasing Awareness required answers to deep philosophical questions. A problem for the future, however. "Can we get Plasminia Tangs for all the others?"

Saira smiled, holding up the core. "With this? Absolutely. I intended for Light Squad to do so anyway. We'll discuss it further once we return to the academy later today."

"How are we getting home so soon?" Cam asked. "Does Master Winder plan on anchor lining us?"

Saira nodded. "He couldn't do so yesterday. Traveling by anchor line when severely injured can be dangerous. We should be fine now, though, including Jade."

Cam tried not to stiffen when he noticed Marta enter the inn. "Just how soon can he get us home?" he asked, recognizing he sounded desperate.

Saira glanced to where he was looking before turning back to face him. She smiled knowingly. "How about I stay here with you? I'll protect you from the scary, pretty girl."

"Very funny," Cam muttered.

Saira's response was a knowing chuckle.

40

It turned out that Master Winder wasn't the one to return Light Squad home to the Ephemeral Academy. Instead, it was Sage-Duke Vail. Cam heard some talk between Saira and Professor Shivein about how the Wilde Sage had to put down another boil somewhere east of Maviro. If true, Cam worried for his mentor. Did the man ever get a chance to rest? Or was all his time taken up with fighting rakshasas?

The truth seemed to likely lean toward the latter, and it gave Cam an even greater appreciation for Master Winder than he already had.

"That's a lovely sight," Pan said, interrupting his thoughts as he exited the anchor line and moved to stand alongside him.

They stood in the same location as when they had first arrived in Nexus, and Cam turned his attention to the city, which rose in the distance, a beautiful view of white buildings roofed in red tiles, reflecting the sunshine bathing the island and the towering statues of Rukh and Jessira in the harbor. But in spite of the cloudless, sunny sky, there was a nip to the air, which brought a smile to Cam's face. A calm wind fingered his clothes and his close-cropped hair, conveying a bevy of scents, including the tang of brine. His nose twitched, and the glad smile wiped clear from his face. There was also the reek of offal and waste, which seemed to cloud the air, even at a distance. He'd forgotten how bad a city could sometimes stink.

The rest of Light Squad arrived, and they set off for campus, walking the streets of Nexus. Things didn't feel right for Cam as they traveled. The folks here seemed so happy and unaware of the dangers lurking out in the world. It was so normal and innocent, and for a time, he wished he could say the same for himself.

But hiding away from trouble didn't make it vanish. He'd best remember that, especially since he'd spent years hiding from his troubles at the bottom of a bottle.

They pressed on and eventually reached the academy.

"I'll take Jade to the infirmary," Professor Shivein said when they reached the Secondary Level. He held her in his arms where she remained unconscious. Her burns weren't nearly as red and awful, but they'd still hurt something fierce if she woke up just then. "The rest of you have today and the next few days off. Get some rest. Heal."

Weld groaned. "I don't think I'll be ready for classes that soon."

Cam empathized. Weld looked nowhere close to being healed. Every few breaths he flinched, like the slightest movement triggered fresh pain.

"How are you feeling compared to yesterday?" Saira asked him.

Weld took an experimental breath. "Better," he said, "but it doesn't mean I'm feeling good."

"I wouldn't expect you to," Saira replied. "But every hour, the healing Master Winder laid upon you will work faster and more thoroughly. You'll see what I mean."

"Will Jade be healed just as fast?" Cam asked.

"No," Professor Shivein answered. "Given the severity of her burns, it might take her a week to fully recover." With that, he left them, carrying Jade to the infirmary.

"Go rest," Saira told the rest of Light Squad. "And remember to drink plenty of water and get enough food. Your bodies need both."

A chorus of muttered "Yes, ma'am," met her words, and she left them, heading down to her quarters. A bunch of students gave them curious gazes, but Cam ignored them. He didn't feel like talking about what Light Squad had just gone through. None of them did, not even the usually boastful Weld. They simply walked in silence to their dorm.

"I'll see you at lunch?" Avia asked once they arrived at the dormitory.

"We'll be there," Cam answered. "Weld?" For some reason, he felt a need to draw the other man into their unit.

"I'll be there."

They separated then, and Cam and Pan shortly reached their quarters.

"Thank, Devesh, we're home" Pan said, collapsing to the floor. Somehow, somewhere, he found a stalk of bamboo, and he began munching contentedly. "I missed this."

"Missed what? The bamboo?"

"Yes, the bamboo. But also just being here. I wasn't sure we'd ever see it again."

"None of y'all seemed too worried when we found out about the boil," Cam reminded him, sitting down next to his friend.

Pan wore a solemn expression, speaking slow like he was talking to a dull child. "That's because we were stupid."

Cam laughed. "Then next time someone tells you to do something dangerous, remember this lesson."

Pan sobered. "I hope there isn't a next time. At least not this year."

Cam was praying in the same vein, but his mind was also on other problems. He'd gained far greater confidence in his skills and his ability to lead Light Squad, but what about for who he was as a person? Did he still worry he might be a curse? Cam wasn't sure, which was sad in its own way.

"What's going on?" Pan asked. "You seem to have a heavy burden weighing you down."

Cam smirked, derision directed inward. "Since you've known me, when *haven't* I seemed like I have a heavy burden weighing me down?" It was another sad truth. Cam had found happiness and purpose at the Ephemeral Academy, but always lingering in the back of his mind was the worry that his joy would be ripped away from him.

"We've both felt that way, don't you think?" Pan asked, still munching on his bamboo. "Carrying heavy burdens. They're like a haunting. A spirit that whispers lies. And we believe them. It ends up a wound that we use to define ourselves."

"And it ain't true," Cam said. "None of it is. I'm not a curse, and I don't deserve a miserable life." And since he was recognizing that truth, he might want to forgive himself for his weakness, have faith he deserved happiness, and that it would be his if he wanted. Not everyone got a chance at making that choice, and he should be grateful that he was one of the lucky few who did.

"No, you don't," Pan said by way of agreement. "And my life shouldn't be dictated by a prophecy made long before I was born. I should be allowed to find joy in whatever I do, whether it has anything to do with Ephemera or the prophecy or not."

Cam fixed Pan with a stern gaze. "So, what's stopping you?"

Pan smiled. "Nothing. What about you?"

Cam considered the question and realized an answer he'd long been lacking. "Nothing. I want to be happy, and I deserve to be happy."

Pan nodded. "We both do. And we'll make it so."

Having a day off was bizarre. Until now, the days at the Ephemeral Academy had melted together, one after the other with no variance between them. The work had kept Cam too busy to worry about having nothing to do, but the next morning, he lacked that structure and found himself feeling lost. Pan was off at the library, and Cam might have joined him, but he just didn't want to.

He felt empty inside, the events from Surelend continuing to prey on his mind. He'd been the least injured of Light Squad, but the terrors of what might have been, of what he'd done—the killing—lurked like its own kind of rakshasa in his thoughts. Imaginings of all those bad things weren't simple to resolve, and he couldn't shake them off.

He sat there awhile, re-reading the letters from home that had arrived while Light Squad had been in the field. It was his first set, and he cherished them. Everyone seemed to be doing well, although Jordil's missive had been brief.

Cam understood. There wasn't much in Jordil's life to see him happy right now, and he prayed it wouldn't always be the case.

But after reading the letters over and over again, basically memorizing them, there wasn't much else to do in the quarters. Cam sat alone, brooding while the morning sunshine streamed in. He recollected how back in Traverse, at a time like this, whenever he had too much time on his hands and too many worries on his mind, the solution had been a pull of whiskey or moonshine to wash them away. And right now, a drink sounded mighty fine.

With a grimace, Cam pushed the siren song away. He needed to find something to occupy his time and his mind. Maybe he should go visit Jade. It was better than pining alone here in his quarters.

His decision made, Cam set off, leaving his dormitory and entering the campus. It was quiet out since most of the students were in class, and a short trek later, he reached the infirmary, which was housed close to the cafeteria.

The hospice center was an easily overlooked ivy-covered building, small and tucked away in a corner of the campus with a surrounding of flower gardens. Upon entering, Cam was greeted by a wide, well-lit hall. A woman in a gray smock over a black robe sat behind a desk. Using a set of scales, she was carefully measuring a powder, weighing it into a glass container.

"What can I do for you?" she asked, not looking away from her work.

Her brusque tone had Cam feeling nervous, like he'd been caught by Master Moltin doing something wrong. "I'm here to see my friend. Jade Mare."

"Third room on the left," the woman said. "She already has a visitor."

"Who is it?"

The woman sighed, sounding put upon. "I don't know. Why don't you run along and find out?" It was a question posed as a firm suggestion.

"Yes, ma'am." Cam ducked his head and hustled along.

Three doors later, he entered a room with sunlight brightening the space. There was room for a single cot and a chair. The first was occupied by Jade who looked heaps better than yesterday. She'd been burned bad, even on her chest, but through the thin gown that hung on her like a cloak, Cam could see the injuries were well on their way to healing.

Avia sat in the chair. "Hello, Cam."

Cam smiled at seeing them. "Well look at that. It's my two favorite girls."

Jade and Avia stared at him for a second, each other for a moment, and promptly broke out in laughter.

Cam reddened, knowing he'd stepped in it, but not knowing how. The laughter kept on, and eventually it got him feeling peevish. "What's so funny?" he demanded.

"You," Jade said. "Calling us your favorite girls. We all know that's not true."

What was Jade going on about? Sure, the phrasing was clumsy, but why wouldn't Avia and Jade be his favorite girls? "Well then who else could be my favorite girls?"

Jade stared at him like he was an idiot. Even Avia, who was usually kinder to him, was viewing him like he was exceptionally stupid.

"Who?" Cam demanded.

"Professor Maharani."

Cam cut her off. "Now, just hold on. There ain't nothing between me and Saira."

"Nothing on her end," Avia said, "but you can't say there's nothing on yours."

Cam stared at Avia in betrayal. How could she? Sure, he'd admitted his feelings about Saira to Light Squad. And sure, Saira was beautiful. And sure he'd dreamed about her and him a time or two or ten, but that's all there was to it. Dreams. There was no way to make them real, and he knew it. Even if Saira really did regress to Adept—and he had thought hard about how he might catch up with her level of Awareness—he'd never be worthy of her.

"You have been thinking about it, haven't you?" Jade said, grinning wickedly at him like she'd just been gifted a new toy.

Cam wasn't about to grace her gossiping with an answer. Plus, the best way to stop a gossip was to not gossip. "I came to check on you, but it looks like you're fine." He made to leave.

"Please don't go," Jade said, pretending to be panicked. "We won't bring up your feelings about Professor Maharani again." She grinned wickedly at him, though. "Or should I call her Saira?"

"That would be inappropriate," Saira said, sweeping into the room.

Cam stifled a mortified groan. How much had she heard? With her Glory ears, it might have been everything. He glared at Jade. What a disaster. There was no other way to put it. And it didn't make Cam feel any better to see Jade and Avia go white like they'd lost every drop of blood. After their needling, they deserved to have some terror.

"We were just joking about calling you Saira," Jade said. "We wouldn't actually do it."

"I'm sure," Saira said, her voice flat. But a twinkle in her eyes told Cam what he'd been fearing. She had heard, and she found it amusing. "And I'm also sure you weren't gossiping about me."

Hearing her question had Cam wanting to find a hole, crawl into it, and never come out. Meanwhile, Jade and Avia went pale again.

"No, ma'am. We weren't gossiping about you," Avia said.

"Excellent. Now that we've settled that you weren't gossiping about me, tell me how you're doing?" Saira said to Jade.

"Much better," Jade answered. "The burns healed through the night. They're mostly a bad itch now."

"Good. Let me see." Saira leaned in closer.

Jade looked like she was about to slip the thin gown off her shoulders, which was Cam's signal to get gone. "I'll be stepping over to the library," he said, nearly tripping on his own feet to leave the room as quick as possible.

After leaving the infirmary, instead of going to the library, Cam decided on a detour and went to see Professor Shivein. He had a question he wanted answered, and he reckoned now was as good a time as any to ask it.

Professor Shivein had offices in the building where they had Synapsia. It was a cramped space, rich with the smell of moldy paper and old person. A large desk hunkered in the center of the room, bracketed by bookshelves full of neatly organized trinkets: a few odd items and two score or so of books with heavily creased spines. There was also a painting of an ocean scene next to a curtained window with the drapes closed.

As a result, the room felt gloomy, and the only illumination came from a single Ephemeral lamp on the corner of the large desk. It stood like an island, amidst some carefully stacked papers.

"What can I do for you?" Professor Shivein said, fully healed and not bothering to look up from the book he was reading. He was at his desk, and although it was big, it looked small with him seated behind it.

"I wanted to ask a question?"

Professor Shivein didn't answer at first. Instead, he used a strip of leather to carefully mark his place in the book. Only then did he look up. "What is it?"

There was a burr to his tone, and Cam shifted, uneasy all of a sudden. "Do you know of anyone who created a Plasminia Tang later in their Advancement?"

Professor Shivein stared at him without answering. "You're thinking of finding a way for Light Squad to gain a Plasminian Tang."

Cam wasn't surprised by his instructor's guess. Professor Shivein was smarter than he let on. "When I use Plasminia, it lets me accelerate the use of my other Tangs. They all work better."

"But the price to pay is that your Bonds don't last as long."

"Yes, but I'm hoping that won't be the case for the others. Their Primary Tangs aren't Plasminia."

Professor Shivein steepled his long, thick fingers. "It's an idea worth exploring," he said. "But why bring this question to me? Why not ask Professor Grey? She is likely better able to answer this kind of question than I."

"I was going to ask her," Cam answered. "But I also thought I'd get as many different opinions as possible."

"That's usually a good idea, but in this case, her opinion is the one that matters most." Professor Shivein shrugged. "But, no, I haven't heard of anyone gaining a Plasminia Tang later on in their Advancement. I also think you will soon find an answer to your real question."

"What real question?"

"Whether gaining a Plasminia Tang will weaken a person who already has Kinesthia. Professor Maharani has spoken to you about her plans to regress?"

Cam nodded. "She's mentioned it." He still couldn't figure whether it was a wise decision but coming from someone who had once been a Crown, he'd have to trust she knew what she was doing.

"Then you know the reason why she wishes to regress. She wants a Plasminia Tang. When she succeeds, you'll have your answer as to whether it will weaken an Ephemeral Master who already has other Tangs. Unless the other members of Light Squad gain a Plasminia Tang before she does." He shrugged. "Regardless, you'll have an answer." Professor Shivein had been leaning back in his chair, but now he sat forward. "Now. I have a question for you."

"What is it?" Cam asked, struggling to keep the nervous quaver out of his voice. There was just something so-very intimidating about Professor Shivein.

"When you gained Kinesthia, what happened?"

Cam's eyebrows lifted in surprise. That was what Professor Shivein wanted to know? "It was painful. The Ephemera that Honor—she was the Awakened squirrel who—"

"I know who she was."

"Well, the Ephemera kept wanting to become more Plasminia, and my Source warped holding so much. Keeping it all together was the hardest thing I've ever done." Cam chanced a joke, hoping the professor would find it funny. "Other than giving up my drinking."

The professor didn't crack a smile. "I imagine so."

Cam mentally sighed. He doubted he'd ever get the professor to like him much. "Anyway, it was hard to concentrate on what needed to happen with all that pain. I sure wouldn't want to have to do it a second time."

"You might have to," Professor Shivein said. "When you Advance, it will be your Plasminia that does so first. The other Tangs will have to be Advanced later. You might find yourself struggling with your earlier weakness. Which leads me to ask a final question. What would you say if I were to offer you *my* Ephemera?"

Cam blinked, stunned and unable to respond at first. "Why would you do that, sir?" he was able to say at last.

"Because I think Professor Maharani has the right of it. If I want to Advance, first I may need to regress. I need Plasminia. For people like Werm, being a Glory is all they hoped to accomplish. For me, I have always wanted to become at least a Crown Lesser, an Ephemeral Master with a Tang at Crown and another at Acolyte. A Crown Greater would be even better—a Crown Tang and one at Adept—but beggars can't be choosers. But to regress…." The professor shrugged. "There is no certainty that I can gain what I hope, and so the risk may not be worth it."

Cam nodded, although he wasn't sure what any of this had to do with him.

As if sensing Cam's confusion, Professor Shivein continued. "Did you know that there are thousands of Awakened Beasts in the ocean?"

"There are?" Cam hadn't known.

"The ocean teems with life, especially along the coral reefs of the Suspific Ocean near the city of Maviro. It's beautiful there. One of my favorite places. So much life and so many things to see."

Cam couldn't imagine, having no frame of reference. "It sounds challenging," he ventured to say.

"Oh, it is. Completely and utterly. But it's also why I Advanced. I learned much in those deadly places, faced death regularly… it teaches you something."

"What's that?"

"Mortality." Professor Shivein barked laughter. "And that it's also a stupid way to train. There's too much luck in risking death to Advance and not enough merited gain. It's a stupid flip of a stupid coin." He shook his head in disgust. "So once I reached Acolyte, I searched for a different way.

Cam kept silent, wanting to learn more about Professor's Shivein's past.

"That's when I met Corona, the Sage of the Fiery Sun.

Cam frowned, recalling all the current and past Sage-Dukes he'd read about. "I don't know him or her."

"Her. And you wouldn't. She was a rakshasa."

Cam's eyes widened. "*You* were a rakshasa?"

Professor Shivein nodded. "I was still an Acolyte when Avia's father found me. He had a soft spot for ocean-dwelling Beasts." He smiled in apparent remembrance. "He let me live, and he also taught me a lesson. The lesson gave me the answer I needed to understand the difference between passion as opposed to rationality. It's the reason I left Corona and joined Sage-Duke Vail. He and his Crowns trained me until I gained my Adept Stage Tang and also one at Acolyte. I was an Adept Prime. From there, I reached Glory, and at Glory, I have been stuck for decades."

"And by regressing, you think you can break through whatever is holding you back?"

"Exactly."

It made sense to Cam now. When Professor Shivein regressed, he could gift the Ephemera he could no longer house in his Source to someone else. But why would he choose Light Squad? Cam asked the question on his mind. "And how can you? You aren't a Crown, and I thought you needed a Crown's knowledge to make a gift like that."

"We'll cross that stretch of water when it's time," Professor Shivein said. "And as for why I would choose Light Squad... it's because there is no one worthier."

41

After a week in the infirmary, Jade was finally released and allowed to resume her classes. She moved without any gingerness or stiffness, and if she had any lingering pain, Cam couldn't tell. He was just glad she was fully healed and back with the rest of the squad. He'd missed her—they all had—and he even forgave how her loose lips had made him uncomfortable around Saira. The fact was, Jade was a gossip, but she didn't mean any harm.

Right now she was laughing at something Pan had said, sitting with Light Squad at their usual table in the cafeteria for supper. The din of the many students conversing, shouting, and laughing declared it a happy time, but Cam felt removed from it.

His mind was on Light Squad, focused on how to improve himself and the unit. He never wanted to see any one of them come so close to dying like they had at Surelend.

As he measured situations, the only good things to come from that boil were gaining the core and having Weld finally work on becoming a proper part of their group. He was spending more time with them, even sharing study sessions after classes, something he'd never before done.

Cam glanced around the cafeteria, noticing some folks staring their way. There were a lot of unfamiliar faces, which made sense since a good number of them were newly arrived a few weeks ago as part of the mid-term class. So far, Cam hadn't talked with them much, being too busy with his own work and getting his mind used to the repetition of classes and learning. Not that the new students likely cared about talking to him. They were all nobles since the mid-termers didn't have an equivalent to Light Squad—Dark Squad in their case.

Nevertheless, some of the newer students were viewing Cam and the others in curiosity, while others were giving them the stink eye. There was one brute in particular, nearly Cam's height and even thicker if that was possible. He glowered at them like someone on Light Squad had stolen his money.

"Who's that?" Cam asked Avia, gesturing with his chin at the glowerer.

She took a look over, a sour expression taking hold. "Card Wolver. He was at the school last year but was injured halfway through and had to withdraw."

"Why's he staring so angry at us?"

"Because he was injured in an intra-squad test against last year's Light Squad."

An immediate question formed in Cam's mind, and he couldn't believe he'd never thought about it before. "What happened to them? Last year's Light Squad."

"They graduated."

"Graduated? After only one year?"

Avia shrugged. "They became Acolytes, and Master Winder—he sponsored them—must have thought they were ready for the field. From what my father tells me, they're part of a larger unit with Adepts, Glories, and even Crowns. They sometimes even get the core when they lance a boil, which helps them gain Ephemera."

Was that what Master Winder intended for this year's Light Squad as well? Cam glanced around the table. Of them, he, Pan, and Weld would have to leave if Master Winder refused to sponsor them next year. Avia and Jade, having their own means, would be allowed to stay. But what squad would the two of them join? The ones from their home duchies? He supposed so, but what bothered him the most was the notion of their separation. They'd come too far as a unit for him to want them separated just yet.

"I've heard that most of last year's crew are already edging toward reaching Adept," Jade added, speaking into their conversation.

"Any of them die?"

"Not so far," she said.

"Well, that's a relief," Cam said, glancing again at Card Wolver.

Card must have taken offense, though, because he stiffened, looking like he was wanting to confront Cam.

Well, come on then, Cam silently urged, not breaking gaze with Card. It wasn't his way to pick a fight. He was usually one to avoid them and keep the peace. But he also wasn't in the mood to put up with some new student's arrogance.

Card strode over to Light Squad's table, Victory hastily following after him. Cam frowned, his eyes narrowing. Was Card with Victory's squad then?

"You got a problem with me, boy?" Card said, arms braced on Light Squad's table and leaning in on Cam. "Because if you do, I'll be happy to fix it."

Cam stood, not liking having someone looming over him. He faced off with Card, glad for his extra inches even while trying not to pay attention to how thickly built the other man was.

Weld glanced up from whatever he was laughing about with Pan, his expression abruptly serious. Everyone at the table reacted the same way. They stared at Card, silent but steady.

"There ain't no call for a fight," Weld said. He stood, moving up on Cam's left even as Victory waited at Card's side. "We were just celebrating a friend's recovery."

Cam appreciated Weld's stepping in. It showed he truly thought of himself as a member of Light Squad.

Card sneered "Maybe you think there *ain't* no cause for fighting, but your boy staring me down says otherwise."

Cam bristled. Card had a noble's way of talking, but just then, he'd made sure to sound like he was country. It was an insult, and Cam didn't like it. He didn't like this man, and he might have said something he would have regretted, but from the corner of his eye, he caught sight of Pan minutely shaking his head. That small gesture soothed him, allowing Cam to breathe deep and regain a measure of calm. "Listen, I'm sorry I was staring too hard at you," Cam said. "I was thinking about something—"

"Shut the frag up!" Card snarled, stepping closer. "You eye me again, and I'll break you. Believe me, boy." He shoved past Cam, making sure to knock him hard in the shoulder.

Cam barely felt it, wise enough to Bond Kinesthia right before the impact. He stared after Card, simultaneously amused and irritated by the man's antics. Did he really think his mean-mugging and bullying attitude was frightening?

Victory had yet to leave. "Sorry about that," he muttered. "Card comes from an old line of powerful Ephemeral Masters. They don't care much for anyone who doesn't have a lineage just as old."

"Is that why he's such a jackhole?" Cam asked.

Victory sighed. "You don't know the half of it. Imagine having him on your squad. Arrogant, prickly, and absolutely sure of himself."

"Is he as good as he thinks he is?" Jade asked.

"Maybe better," Victory answered. He stared off in the direction Card had left. "I have to go. Make sure the git doesn't go and punch a wall for not moving out of his way." He swiftly departed, leaving the table silent.

"Well, I'm not hungry anymore," Pan announced into the silence left after Card's and Victory's leave-taking.

"Me neither," Cam agreed. "I'm heading home."

"What are you going to do?" Jade asked.

"Grow my acorn. It's hard."

"That's an interesting way of putting things," Avia said, doing little to stifle a grin.

Cam feigned a scowl. "You know what I mean. I was talking about Professor Werm's—"

"I know."

"What about you two?" Weld asked Avia and Jade. "Want some company?"

"We're studying in the library," Jade answered. "We want to learn some techniques. Shore up some weaknesses."

"Techniques on what?" Pan asked.

"Spirairia," Jade answered. "It's our weakest subject."

"That's because Werm is our weakest instructor," Weld said, which was the truth, although Cam didn't like saying so. "If we had a set of instructors like the nobles can afford, we might not have had so much trouble with the boil at Surelend."

"Our professors are good," Cam defended.

Weld disagreed. "If they were that good, they would have been scooped up by one of the Sage-Dukes."

"There was a time not too long ago when the nobles didn't have their own instructors," Jade said. "Everyone received the same teaching."

"What changed?" Cam asked, curious.

"The rise in the number of rakshasas," Jade answered. "A couple of centuries ago, there were more boils than there are now, and the poaching of talented Ephemeral Masters became a problem. The private instructors were meant to prevent that."

Cam had already heard some of this, but after experiencing Surelend, he reviewed the information with fresh insight. "It still seems short sighted."

"The duchies have great instructors," Weld said, apparently stuck on disagreement. "You met them. Victory's teachers are amazing."

"What about Professor Grey?" Avia asked, the same question on Cam's mind. "She knows more about Ephemera than anyone, maybe even some Sages."

"She doesn't know more," Cam corrected. "She just knows where the best information is."

"Same difference," Avia countered.

"I don't want to talk about Professor Grey," Weld said with a shudder. "She knows a lot, but—"

"But nothing," Cam cut in. "You're not thinking it through. We're Light Squad, the ones everyone used to call Squad Screwup. Yet, we're the ones ranked first among all Novice units. We're the ones who've won every competition the school has thrown at us. We're the ones who won the Unwinnable. We're the ones who lanced a true boil even though we were outnumbered four-to-one. And we're the ones who have at least two Crystal Tangs for each member. No other squad is even close to us." He shook his head. "And you think they have better teachers. No chance." It was what had become Light Squad's private chant, and Cam saw them remembering. Weld, too. They all straightened, eyes bright. "And I have an idea for how to make us even better," Cam continued. "I've talked it over with our instructors, the ones who guided us this far." He made sure to hold Weld's gaze. "What do y'all think of forming Plasminia Tangs?"

Perplexed expressions met his question.

"How would it help us?" Pan asked.

"When I Bond all my Tangs and also use Plasminia, it makes the others work better," Cam explained. "My Bonds also don't last as long but ending a fight quick-like seems worth it."

"Who did you talk about this with?" Jade asked, appearing curious instead of dismissive.

"Everyone," Cam said. "All the professors, and they all think it's a good idea. Saira and Professor Shivein are even planning on regressing so they can gain a Plasminia Tang as Adepts. They think it can help them Enhance their other Tangs and make them more powerful when they Advance back to Glory. Possibly even help them reach Crown."

"Really?" Avia said, sounding skeptical. "How? They would have to answer the deeper questions again in order to Advance."

Cam shrugged. "It's what Professor Shivein said. He might be wrong. But for you lot, what's more important is that I don't think you'll suffer the weakness that I'm stuck with since all y'all have different Primary Tangs and your Kinesthias are already at Crystal. It should protect you." Cam stared at the rest of Light Squad, gauging their responses. Everyone but Avia appeared curious and open to the possibility.

"How is this possible?" Pan asked.

"The core we lanced at Surelend," Cam answered. "It has enough Ephemera for you to create a Tang of Plasminia."

"And you?" Jade asked. "What do you get out of all this?"

"After you're done with the core," Cam began, "I'll Imbibe what I can to maximize how much Ephemera I hold before Advancing. We can discuss it further in my quarters. I can answer whatever questions you have then. Figuring I know them, of course."

"Why don't we ever meet in their quarters?" Pan asked, pointing to Avia and Jade.

"Our quarters are a mess," Avia quickly said.

Jade arched a brow. "And whose fault is that?"

"Moving on," Avia said, flashing a smile even as she flushed. "Talking it out in your quarters sounds like a great idea."

"I'm not sure I'm available for that tonight," Weld said with a smirk. "I promised to tell some young ladies stories of my derring-do. You know how it is."

"Yes, we do." Cam stared at Weld in disappointment. Just as much, he was disappointed in himself for believing the man could change.

"Wish me luck," Weld said, doffing an imaginary hat.

"Luck in what?" Avia asked, but Weld was already gone.

"Luck in drinking and fornicating," Pan said, answering for the swiftly departing Weld.

Cam snorted in amusement. "The drinking part I don't doubt. But I'm not convinced he's doing much fornicating. He's more talk than walk."

Jade laughed. "It would be a neat trick if you can walk while you're doing it." She grinned Cam's way, which she often did whenever Weld disappointed her.

"I wish he stayed and trained with us," Avia said, frowning and obviously unhappy. "Leaving like he just did… it's such a jackhole thing to do."

"That's because Weld is a jackhole," Cam said. "And you haven't said what you think about my idea."

"Weren't we going to talk about it in your quarters?" Jade asked.

"We could, but you and Avia also want to go to the library," Cam replied. "We can talk here. The cafeteria is nearly empty anyway." He gestured about, to where only a few other tables held patrons.

Jade shrugged. "I've already thought about it," she said. "I actually started thinking about it when you Enhanced your other Tangs so easily."

"So did I," Pan said. "I had even planned on asking Professor Grey for her guidance in how it might be done."

Cam exhaled, relieved the others were seeing things his way. Well, everyone but Avia. He turned to her.

She viewed him, still uncertain. "You're sure that Plasminia will help us Advance?"

"I'm not, and it's for the exact same reason you're worried about it," Cam admitted. "But having Plasminia should still help you Enhance your Tangs no matter your Awareness." He grinned, wanting to lift her tense mood. "The only downside I could cogitate—"

"Wait. Did you say cogitate?" Pan appeared scandalized.

Cam frowned, unsure about Pan's reaction. "Yes. Cogitate. Like reckon, think, or imagine."

Pan shook his head in sorrow, muttering about misused words.

Cam shrugged, addressing Avia once again. "Anyway, the only downside I could *figure*…" he held Pan's gaze before turning back to Avia "…is you'll stink. The yellow bile doesn't wash off."

Pan groaned. "It'll get all over my fur."

Jade didn't seem to have any such reservations. "How do we do it? Won't we need more Ephemera?"

Cam slowly smiled. "You mean like the Ephemera remaining in the core we earned by lancing that boil?"

"It's still not that easy," Pan said. "If we aren't careful, we can take in too much and rupture our Sources."

"Which is why Saira is going to guide us," Cam replied.

"That's something only Crowns know how to do," Pan countered.

"You mean someone like Saira? Who was once a Crown?"

Pan's face lit with his infectious grin. "I see someone's been thinking things through."

Cam chuckled. "I promise not to do it again."

Several nights later, Light Squad was ready to gain everyone a Plasminia Tang, even Weld, which Cam counted as a minor miracle.

They met in Saira's quarters, which was on the Primary Level. Upon entering, they found themselves in a large room with a kitchen near the front, but deeper into the space was an area for dining with a high-gloss table and matching seating. Next to it, a leather sofa and several high-backed upholstered chairs clustered around a low-lying table. Warm Ephemeral lamps provided cozy lighting, and the smell of orchids perfumed the air, wafting from the various flowers potted in tall vases in several corners. A pair of doors led off to a bedroom and the bathroom.

Saira was dressed casually, seated on the couch and talking to Professor Grey. Her hair, usually braided and pulled back, hung loose about her lovely face, and she wore a pale, yellow lengha that trailed to her ankles, a matching choli, and a sheer red scarf. She was as beautiful as Cam had ever seen her, and he forced himself not to look her way. Mostly because he knew he'd stare. He also remembered Jade teasing him about Saira, and how she'd overheard. The last thing he needed was for an unfortunate miscommunication to be proven true.

Professor Grey said a final few words to Saira before rising to her feet. It seemed to be a signal because Saira stood as well. So did Avia and Jade, who had been seated in the high-backed chairs. "I hear congratulations are in order," Professor Grey said.

Cam didn't know what she was talking about, and he shared a look of confusion with Pan, who stood alongside him.

Professor Grey laughed warmly. "I'm talking about the reason why you're all here. Incorporating a Plasminia Tang into your Source is a wise decision."

Her gaze lingered on Weld, and he straightened from where he'd been leaning on the dining table. "Thank you, ma'am," he said.

Professor Grey tsked. "So formal, Mr. Plain."

Weld grinned. "I figured it might get me on your good side."

"We'll see," Professor Grey replied. "There is literature on forming new Tangs. It's easiest as a Novice and nearly impossible at any other time. For Plasminia, in some ways, it can be even harder. You risk much, but it is a manageable risk, especially since Professor Maharani and I have separately reviewed how this will occur. With courage and will, I think all of you have an excellent chance for success. But before we begin, are there any questions?"

"Are you the one that's going to guide us?" Cam asked.

"Actually, that will be both of us." It was Saira who answered, and her tone had a bit of a bite. "I was a Crown, and I still have my old dexterity in using Ephemera. Professor Grey has similar skill."

Cam reddened. He hadn't meant to make it seem like he doubted Saira.

"Take a look at the core," Saira said, turning away from Cam and seemingly dismissing his inadvertent slight. She placed it on the dining table, giving them a chance to inspect it.

They gathered around, each one moving in close, and when it was Cam's turn, he scrutinized the core, noticing some differences from what he had expected to see. When Avia had lanced it, Cam had thought it was a dull white color, but looking at it now, he realized it held an iridescent sheen, shimmering under the light of the Ephemeral chandelier directly above and giving it a sense of movement.

"We'll start with Pan, and then Avia," Saira said. "As Awakened, the two of them should be the most adept at pulling Ephemera into their

Sources."

Pan took up the core, staring at it like it contained all the secrets of Ephemera... which Cam supposed, it might.

"Delve your Source and Bond Spirairia," Saira said. She took the core from Pan, cupping it in both hands. "When you have the Bond, place one hand on mine and give the other to Professor Grey." The professor moved to stand alongside Pan. "I will act as your guide and filter the core's Ephemera, while Professor Grey will help keep your Source intact so you don't harm yourself."

Pan licked his lips, clearly nervous, but he did as Saira told him.

"Do you feel the Ephemera? It's right beneath the core's skin, underneath the glowing aspect."

Cam reckoned she meant the iridescent part of the core.

"I do," Pan said in response to her question.

"Then touch it with your will and Spirairia. The Tang will want to connect with the Ephemera in the core. Let it."

"I can see it," Pan breathed, licking his lips again.

"Concentrate now. Pull your Spirairia back into you. It should draw some Ephemera with it."

Pan frowned hard, concentrating like Cam had never seen him.

"Don't strain so much," Professor Grey advised. "Relax. The Ephemera will come to you at its own pace."

Working off an idea, Cam forged a Bond with Spirairia, letting it fill his vision. The room brightened in a white sheen that drowned all shadows. Some of it came from the Ephemeral lamps, which shined like suns with light streaming in and out in a never-ending river. But most of it came from the core, which glowed so gloriously that it almost had a sound like it was singing.

In addition, thick trails of wispy light flowed sedately into Pan, much of it blocked by Saira's hands before it resettled in the core.

"Don't let it become Kinesthia," Saira cautioned at one point. "It will want to, your Primary Tang. This is another use of your desire and dedication. You have to imagine the Ephemera entering you gaining energy, gaining speed and becoming Plasminia."

"How?" Pan asked, although Saira and Professor Grey had both covered this during the week when they'd discussed what was going to happen tonight.

"Heat it," Professor Grey answered. "Use Spirairia."

Pan frowned even more fiercely than before.

"Careful," Professor Grey cautioned. "Not so hot."

Pan's jaw clenched like it did when he was trying his level best. He didn't want to fail, and Cam silently urged him on to success. Minutes later, Pan gasped. "I have it. A Plasminia Tang."

Cam started. That quick? When he'd taken hours to do the same when forging a Kinesthia Tang? He exhaled in irritation. It seemed his Plasminia caused more issues than he realized.

He set aside his annoyance when he noticed Pan's exhaustion. Sweat matted his friend's fur, and he looked ready to collapse. Cam darted forward, prepared to support Pan, guiding him to the couch where he dropped with a groan.

"My head hurts," Pan said, clutching a hand to his forehead. "And it feels like I ran a mile uphill with a sack of rocks on my back. Is this from the Plasminia?"

"I don't know," Cam said. "Maybe it's just from you frowning so hard."

Pan smiled. "I should practice meditation next time we try something like this."

"Next time?" Cam shook his head. "You got yourself a Plasminia Tang. There won't be a next time. You've already succeeded at what you needed doing."

Pan's smile widened. "I did, didn't I." He sobered a second later. "I hope the others are just as successful."

Cam did, too, and he left Pan then, wanting to watch and support the rest of the squad. Avia was the next to touch the core, and Ephemera breathed into her, filtered by Saira. A half hour later, Avia gasped just like Pan had. She, too, had a Plasminia Tang at Silver, and she, too, was left drained and depleted by the endeavor.

"How are you feeling?" Cam asked, knowing the question was

stupid as he guided Avia to the sofa.

"About as well as I probably look," Avia grumbled.

"That bad?"

"That bad."

Cam left her there, next to a sleeping Pan. Next it was Jade's turn and then Weld. Both of them struggled far harder to gain their Plasminia Tang, taking a few hours each. But in the end, they, too, were successful.

Cam viewed Light Squad, envying how relatively painlessly and quick they'd created their Plasminia Tangs.

Although…

From the way the others were laid out, Cam reckoned they weren't feeling like they'd gotten off all that easy. Nor did they likely yet appreciate what they'd managed tonight.

But they would. He just had to teach them.

"They'll need to rest for a bit," Saira said, moving to stand next to him. "Are you ready to Imbibe?"

Cam shot her a startled gaze. "Now?"

She quirked a smile. "What better time is there?"

42

The next morning at breakfast, Cam frowned in concern when he caught Pan staring at his bamboo in distaste. He'd never seen Pan stare at food like that, especially bamboo, which he had always previously viewed with nothing but contentment.

"What's wrong?" Cam asked.

"I don't feel so good," Pan said, sounding miserable. "Ever since last night, my stomach is all rumbly and bumbly." He held his belly, like he was fixing to be sick.

Avia nodded, looking just as miserable. "I was sick all night. I couldn't even hold down water."

"Same," Weld said, pale and sickly appearing. "I swear my guts tried to crawl out my mouth."

A disgusting image.

Jade didn't seem to be any better, and she stared disconsolately at a glass of orange juice. It was the only thing she had on her plate, which was saying something. Jade liked to eat nearly as much as Pan.

Cam eyed them in worry. What if they ended up weak like him? Or if their poor sense of well-being only got worse? "Is the nausea any

480

better than it was last night?"

Pan shrugged minutely. "If it is, it's not by much. I think I'll skip class today." He groaned, rising to his feet. "Can you tell the professors what's happened?" Without waiting for anyone to respond, he shuffled off, likely heading back to their quarters.

Cam watched him depart, his worry becoming fear.

"Is this what you felt like when you had Plasminia?" Jade asked him.

"Some, but I wasn't sick like what you're saying," Cam replied, still staring after Pan. "I was mostly weak and couldn't do anything. Walking too far was a chore."

Jade clutched her gut. "Well, if you were sick like me, I can see why you went to drinking so much. This feels awful."

"Do we have to take on any more Plasminia?" Weld asked, his tone morose.

"Didn't you get your Tang to Silver last night?"

Weld nodded.

"Then you're fine," Cam said. "You'll have to Enhance your Plasminia, but the good news is that you can use the yellow bile you'll extrude to Enhance your other Tangs, too." He quirked a smile. "Of course, you'll have to get used to stinking like a dead skunk."

His teasing didn't quite go over the way he hoped since no one smiled, but at least it had Weld groaning theatrically. "The ladies will just love that."

"It'll get better," Cam said, hoping he was right. "Maybe you should take the day off. I'll come by and check on you. Bring some food. Yogurt and bread, maybe."

Mumbled affirmations met his suggestion before Light Squad stumbled to their feet and plodded out of the cafeteria. Cam watched them, chewing his lower lip with worry, figuring on what he had to do. First, he'd want to cancel Kinesthia and then ask Professor Grey—if anyone was likely to know any solutions, it would be her—for some advice. Saira, too. Maybe even Professors Werm and Shivein.

Victory was just entering the cafeteria when Light Squad was exiting, and he drew away from them in comical shock. An instant later, he hustled over to where Cam was finishing his breakfast.

"What happened to them?"

Cam, still sick about the entire situation, didn't want to talk about it to Victory. "They listened to my advice," he said, self-directed sourness in his voice. At Victory's expectant expression, he sighed. "I'll tell you about it later."

He left the cafeteria, breakfast uneaten as he hustled to the Kinesthia field where he explained the situation to Saira and Professor Shivein. It didn't take much convincing before they agreed to cancel the morning class.

"But you'll be here in the afternoon," Saira told him. "The others can't train, and I know you want to help them, which is fine. But you also don't need to spend the whole day sitting around doing nothing. Be back here after lunch."

Cam quickly agreed with her before rushing off to find Professor Grey. She had quarters in the same building as Saira, but Cam had never been there. Instead, he'd always been able to find her in their classroom. Which was where she was this time, too.

Her face brightened when he entered, but her welcoming smile quickly faded. "What's going on?"

Cam explained.

"Is that all?" Professor Grey said with a warm laugh. Her humor immediately set his mind to ease. "It's to be expected when forming a new Tang. It wouldn't have mattered if it had been Synapsia, Kinesthia, or Spirairia. They would have felt sick as…" Her lips twitched. "A Kesarin kitten who ate too much chocolate."

Having no notion as to what she was referring, Cam mentally discarded it as part of Professor Grey's strangeness.

She waved aside his confusion. "Never mind. Just know that what they're experiencing is normal. Make sure they get plenty to drink, and they'll be fine soon enough. Soup would be good, too."

Cam breathed out in relief. It was exactly what he had been hoping to hear. "So nothing they did is going to hurt them permanently?"

"Of course not. Was there anything else?"

Actually, there was. Cam had planned on asking her during Synapsia, but now was as good a time as any. "I'm adding more Ephemera to my Tangs before I Advance—assuming I can Advance."

"You can, and you certainly will. Both add more Ephemera and Advance."

Cam knocked on Professor Grey's wooden desk for luck. "Maybe so, but I won't be counting on certainty in nothing."

"You should count on it. You're better off approaching the idea of Advancement with confidence and surety; not doubt and skepticism just so you don't have to face disappointment. That way doesn't lead to greater happiness or satisfaction, Cam. And knocking on wood doesn't ward off karma's touch." She tilted her head. "Do you understand what I'm saying?"

"I think so," Cam said, hesitant to say he actually didn't. All his life, he'd thought of karma as the bad things that happened to a person who got too proud. It sounded like Professor Grey was saying elsewise.

"Some people think karma is the union of cause and effect," Professor Grey said. "The resultant consequence of thoughts, words, and deeds. Even attitudes. But it isn't fate. It doesn't change by knocking on wood and pretending you aren't hoping to achieve something of merit."

Cam wore a faint grin. "I understand that, but I also don't want to call down bad luck."

"And you won't, but rather than hope for or against an outcome, you're better off expecting one. In some ways, it frees you from the concerns about your actions. By living in such a fashion, it becomes one of the means by which a person can achieve *moksha*, spiritual freedom. Action without concern for an outcome since you already have an awareness or belief in what will be. It is only when we fear the results that karma catches hold of us."

Cam carefully considered her words, eventually shaking his head in disagreement. "That's not something I think I can do."

Professor Grey smiled. "It's not something many can. I can't. Not always, but it is what we should strive to accomplish. To find a balance where you can live without fear of failure. Live with selfless devotion to a righteous cause, and you will have a chance to achieve something remarkable." She shooed him away then. "Now off you go. Check on your friends, and I'll see you in a few hours. My class isn't cancelled for you."

"How are y'all feeling this morning?" Cam asked.

It was a week since everyone in Light Squad had gained a Plasminia Tang, and while their recovery had been as quick as Professor Grey had said would be the case, they'd been off their best game during that time. Their speed, balance, endurance, even control of Spirairia and sharpness of their minds. None of it was as good as before.

This morning, though, Cam sensed a spring in everyone's step, all of them looking fit as a fiddle.

And if they were to have chosen a day to get right with the world, this was it. It was a beautiful morning with the sun shining like a beautiful woman's smile, beaming through the sky's blue field and puffy clouds stretched out like cotton balls. A pleasant breeze seemed to whisper to Cam to go play like when he'd been a child, and the warmth felt like a blessing on his skin. And while Cam loved the winter, there was an undeniable magic in the air when spring finally came around. He felt grand enough to want to dance and sing.

"I'm feeling great," Pan said in answer to Cam's question.

Jade agreed. "I haven't felt this good in a long time."

"Same," Avia added with Weld agreeing a beat later.

Cam grinned, happy to hear it. He led Light Squad at a trot down the steps toward the Kinesthia field. His mood soured, though, on seeing who was waiting for them down there. It was Victory's squad, including Card Wolver. Arrogant, gruff, prickly, and thin-skinned. Card Wolver was a jackhole of the highest Advancement.

"I'm guessing we're going to have a combined class with them," Cam said, not bothering to hide his unhappiness.

"The professors never mentioned it," Pan said.

"They probably didn't know," Cam said. "This is Victory we're talking about. The son of the Sage-Duke of Chalk. He could have wrangled this together last night or even this morning, and the professors would have had to go along with it."

"Or it's because of Card," Avia said. "With his family and their pull, you never know."

"It's to be a combined class today," Saira said without preamble when they arrived. "Light Squad against Squad Chalk."

"You'll be dueling as a unit," Professor Shivein said. "It won't be in any place other than this field, so planning shouldn't be an issue."

"They outnumber us," Cam pointed out. Even after Professor Grey had removed Gorn, with Card's addition, Squad Chalk had six members.

"You shouldn't have any trouble with that," Victory said. "You lot won the Unwinnable, and from what I hear, you lanced a boil housing nearly thirty rakshasas."

"Must have all been Neophyte rakshasas," one of his crew muttered.

Cam didn't let the teasing get under his skin. "Believe what you want. But we're not going against you when you have numbers on us."

"But you will," Saira said, striding forward. "This is per the request of Duke Arta himself. He wants to know how well his son and his Novices from this year can do against the famous Light Squad." Cam shot her a look, and she quirked a crooked smile. "Your reputation is growing."

What reputation? Cam glanced to Avia and Jade. Did they know what Saira was talking about? The other two merely shrugged, which was a less than helpful reply.

"Your goal is to defeat the other squad," Professor Shivein said. "You'll use padded staffs." He handed them out from a small collection that he must have brought to the field and dumped in a barrel. "Professor Maharani and I will name those who are out of the fight. When you hear your name called, drop to the ground, and do no more."

"What about armor?" Cam asked.

"We've provided that as well," Saira said, pointing to a collection of gear next to her, all of it leather. There were helmets, chest plates, and greaves. "Squad Chalk. You'll start at the north end of the field. Light Squad, to the south. Separate and on my mark, we'll begin."

"Good luck," Card smirked, after the Chalks got geared. "Not that it'll do you any good." He stretched extravagantly, displaying his muscles.

Cam snorted in contempt. Muscles didn't count for much when dealing with Ephemeral Masters. Cam had come across plenty of skinny folk—Adepts and higher—who looked like a stiff wind would blow them over. And those same folk could bend steel with their bare hands.

Let Squad Chalk be confident then. It would only make them easier to defeat. As Squad Chalk got geared, Cam studied them; three men and three women. He didn't know them well, but he'd taken their measure. They were skilled but fought as individuals. Most had at least one Tang at Crystal.

But so did Light Squad—all of them—and everyone in Cam's unit also had Plasminia. It was time to make it work for them.

He stared at the Chalks a bit longer, seeking out their weakest members. They would be the first to fall. His eyes shifted to Victory. And take him down and there went their leader. Finally, there was Card Wolver, the wild card. He might have a scary sounding name, but in the end, it would be Light Squad who would attack like a pack of wolves. Once the others were out of the way, they'd take him down and kill him.

His plan settled, Cam faced Light Squad. "Bunch close. Protect each other's flanks. Target their weakest members." He indicated them by name. "Get them out of the way first. Then Victory. Avoid Card as much as possible. We don't know how good he is. Save him for last."

Everyone nodded understanding, and they Bonded their Tangs. Time dilated, creeping by in a crawl. Cam's thoughts raced but remained in control. He felt powerful enough to snap his staff in half, and the wispy lights he'd grown accustomed to seeing filled his visions. The world was full of Ephemera. Or maybe better to say the world *was* Ephemera.

"Fight!" Saira shouted.

Light Squad ran in a clustered formation, Cam at the head, and the others winging off on either side. The Chalks raced forward in a ragged grouping. It would make Cam's plan even easier to execute. He shifted the direction of his run. Light Squad smoothly bent, aimed like an arrow at the pair of Chalks to their right. The shift in direction twisted them away from Card and Victory.

The two units came in a clash of hoarse shouts and wood cracking. Weld and Jade, paired up to the left of Cam, took on one of Light Squad's targets, a woman. Jade pressed her, a set of horizontal swings ending on a push. When the woman tried to retreat, Weld slapped her feet out from under her. A thrust of the staff, and she was done.

To Cam's right, Avia and Pan forced a Chalk straight back. The two of them gave him no room. It was a short series of swings, coming from both sides. The man tried to run, but he only made it two steps. Avia tripped him, slammed her staff against his back, and it was over.

Only seconds had passed, but the rest of the Chalks were on them, looking angry as a nest of hornets. It didn't seem to matter that *they* were the ones outnumbered now.

"Fall back!" Cam shouted. Light Squad retreated, refusing to engage the Chalks. They gained distance. Cam flicked a quick peek at Victory's squad, waiting until their line was ragged again. "Hard left!"

Light Squad sprinted at the one Chalk who had surged ahead of the others. It was a woman, a powerful fighter. Avia and Jade engaged, pincering her. Each sent a quick feint and a slash. The Chalk had no notion of what to do. She reacted to both sides and had a split second to retreat. Pan didn't give it to her. A wide swing brought her down.

At that point, the remaining Chalks ground to a halt. Everyone but Card, who stood centered in his unit.

"Wait!" Victory shouted at him.

Card didn't listen. He charged straight on.

Cam smiled to himself, adjusting his plan. "Fall back!"

Light Squad did so, giving ground.

Card sprinted harder, separating himself from the rest of his unit.

"Soft right!"

Light Squad knew the maneuver. It brought Jade and Weld at Card, and they attacked him in unison. First, Jade with a slash. Weld with another. A feint from Jade pulled Card off-balance. He got back in position, defending against a thrust aimed at his chest. Card was doing well, but he never accounted for Pan. When he did, he finally recognized his danger. He spun to the side, seeking room.

Cam and Avia were there to cut him off. Card pretty much ran himself onto Cam's staff, falling over in a heap. He was "killed," declared so by Saira.

Card didn't take it well, though, wanting to rise and re-engage.

But Saira was on him, a foot pinning him down, glaring. "I said you are out."

The remaining two Chalks hadn't come any closer, and Light Squad faced them.

"Give up now," Cam said with a cheerless smile. "Or do you really want the bruising that comes with losing?"

Victory's answer was a scowl followed by his staff flung to the ground. "You won this round, but we're going again."

"Fine by me," Cam said. He already saw ways that Light Squad could outmaneuver the Chalks.

The two units reset, both of them—including the Chalks this time—taking a few minutes to figure on a plan.

The planning didn't do Victory's unit any good. Light Squad defeated them and did so a third and fourth time, winning every encounter without taking any losses. Two more times after, they went at it, and the Chalks lost on each occasion. At least on the last one, they finally took down a member of Light Squad.

Jade fell to Victory, while Cam took a punishing thrust to the chest from Card. His ribs felt bruised, making breathing a chore, but what hurt worse was Card sneering down at him. His sneer lasted just until Pan swung a staff into his stomach, launching the jackhole onto his backside.

Cam was glad to see the other man humbled and hunched over in pain; not reckoning there would ever be any kind of world where he'd have warm feelings for someone like Card Wolver.

Later that afternoon, Victory approached Light Squad while they were having lunch. With him were Charity, Card, Merit, and Kahreen. None of them wore the friendliest of expressions. In fact, they looked right peeved. The rest of Light Squad noticed, and they tensed, their conversating drifting off as everyone went quiet.

Cam could reckon why Victory and Card seemed upset, but what about the others? What had their fur so ruffled?

He made to rise, but Victory bade him remain seated. "I wanted to congratulate you on your win this morning," the nobleman began.

Cam noted how the others in Victory's group had fanned out behind him. This wasn't just a congratulations then. This was a confrontation.

"But I also wanted to let you know that it will never happen again."

"I guess we'll see when we see," Cam replied.

"We want another chance at you," Card said, shoving forward. "A formal contest. Us against Light Squad." He sneered the name. "We'll prove you're not as good as you think you are."

"We don't think we're that good," Jade said. "We know we are. Or did you forget about this morning when we dusted you."

Her statements earned her a scowl from Kahreen and Card.

What a surprise?

"Then you're willing?" Card asked, still frowning.

Cam pondered the offer. A formal challenge? He'd read about them, but he'd never thought Light Squad would ever take part in something like that. "What do we get out of it?"

"You'll get teachings to increase your abilities," Victory said.

"We have good teachers," Cam replied.

"In everything but Spirairia. Werm is good, but he's no warrior."

"Professor Werm's teachings are good enough," Pan said. "We've all used them to excellent effect."

Kahreen sneered. "What teachings? The one where you move rocks around? Or learn to grow a tree?"

"Moving rocks saved our lives," Pan said. "I held a rakshasa's arm to his side. Just long enough for Weld to kill him. And the growing of trees helps us become good stewards of the land. That's worthy knowledge."

"What would you know?" Kahreen said, arms folded.

"More than you," Cam replied, dismissing her and her stupidity. "It doesn't matter what Spirairian teachings you have since we're limited in what we can do with that Tang. We're only Novices."

"But building out those talents now helps later," Victory countered. "We can see it happen. We'll even toss in twice your usual month's stipend."

Cam glanced at the rest of his team, wanting to know what they thought about all this. Nods of approval met his gaze. Exactly what he was hoping to see. Still, Cam wasn't yet ready to give a full answer. "We'll think about it."

"Think quick," Victory said.

"And while you're thinking," Kahreen said, scowling, "what do we get out of it if we win?"

"First of all, I never agreed to anything," Cam said. He grinned at her annoyance, stretching out his legs because he knew his lackadaisical posture would irritate her even more. "As to what you get, well, you nobles finally get a win over us. That should be enough for y'all, right?"

"Fair enough," Victory replied.

"What's the challenge?" Weld asked.

"Your unit against our best," Card said with a predatory smile.

Cam now understood the presence of Charity and Merit. "Meaning the best of all your units."

"Unless you don't think you can take us," Charity said, speaking for the first time as she feigned to buff her fingernails.

Cam had grown up poor, and what it taught him was never to take the first offer. That instinct served him then. "If we're going that hard, then we want more than just teaching. We want your manuals, the ones that teach those techniques even more quickly."

"That's a lot to ask," Card growled.

"It's a lot you're asking from us," Cam replied.

"Deal," Victory vowed, interrupting Card. "And the challenge is defeating the other in a classic lancing competition."

"Who defends?" Cam asked, controlling his glee. The challenge offered so much to Light Squad. Even if they lost, it didn't matter. It wouldn't cost them hardly any face. But if they won... Only a fool would turn down a match like this.

"We both defend," Victory answered. "Whoever lances the other team's core first wins."

Pan spoke, wanting a clarification. "What if we lance your core, but all five of you are alive and only one of us is? Who wins then?"

A few minutes of debate followed Pan's question, but in the end they had a set of rules in place. Lancing the core would count for twelve points, and the number of players alive at the end would count for four points each. The math worked out so if a draw happened, victory would go to the lancing team.

"Whenever you want, we're up for it," Cam said.

"I heard about your challenge," Professor Werm said, standing in front of the academy's farms for that afternoon's class in Spirairia.

Cam raised his brows and shared a look of surprise with Pan. Word traveled fast.

"You'll be facing the very best noble Novices," Professor Werm continued. "They'll have received tonics and training none of you can afford. I can help with that. I'm not a warrior, but I know a way for you to win."

"Then why didn't you teach us this before?" Weld complained.

"Because what you are expected to learn at the academy is meant to provide an immediate use of Spirairia, but only as a warrior. However, what you *should* learn is something otherwise. It's a longer path, but one that will gain you maximum mastery of Spirairia in all areas, be they war, growth, or healing. It's called a True Bond, something most people don't bother learning these days."

"Why not?" Pan asked. Based on the way his head was pitched to the side, he already knew a bit about this True Bond.

"Because it's hard to learn," Professor Werm said. "It's even harder to master, and at first, it isn't any quicker to use than the Bonds you already have. It's also like rolling a rock to the crest of a peak, watching it roll down the other side, and never getting frustrated that you can't balance it. Eventually you will, so long as you don't pound the crest to a flattened shape."

So far, what Professor Werm was telling them was underwhelming at best. "Then what's the point?" Cam asked.

"Because a True Bond is more focused, more efficient, more utilitarian, and once you have it mastered, it'll last far longer than your current Bonds. It also allows for a slightly greater use of your weakest Tang. At the highest Stages, such as at Crown, this can be important."

Cam's ears perked, his mind fixed on something Professor Werm had just said. One of his greatest weaknesses was how short his Bonds lasted in comparison to those of others. "Then let's get to work."

Professor Werm glanced around. "Is this what everyone wants?"

The members of Light Squad sought each other's gazes, questioning. But for Cam the answer was evident. He wanted to learn this True Bond. It overcame one of his greatest deficits. And in the end, the rest of Light Squad felt the same way.

Professor Werm began his instruction as soon as the decision was made. "Delve your Source, and imagine your breath unifying Spirairia, Synapsia, and Kinesthia into a single Bond. And then draw that Bond into your body."

This wasn't like anything Cam had ever done. The instruction flew in the face of all their prior teachings. And it only made sense that during that hour of class, none of Light Squad managed what Professor Werm was saying because it was impossible.

But Professor Werm didn't seem upset by their failure. "We'll work on it twice a day and by month's end, you'll have it," he promised.

Cam didn't think so. Not based on what they'd just done. Or rather, *not* done. But just as his doubts threatened to spiral into certainty, he recalled Professor Grey's teachings regarding how he should expect success rather than wish against failure.

The instruction settled his nerves, and he closed his eyes, seeking a semblance of confidence, praying for it, too.

43

"**W**e've got so much to learn," Cam groaned after he and Pan returned to their quarters. It had been an eventful day, what with the combined class in Kinesthia, accepting a challenge at lunch, and learning an entirely new way of forming a Bond in the afternoon.

"At least you don't have to Enhance any of your Tangs," Pan said, plopped as usual on the floor and crunching on bamboo.

"About that. I can give you guidance, but we'll want to be outside."

"I know," Pan said, his ears drooping. "That smell is going to ruin my fur."

A knock on their door produced the rest of Light Squad, all of them here to learn on how to Enhance Plasminia.

"Y'all ready to work?" Cam asked, forcing a chipper tone.

Weld sighed. "You don't have to sound so happy that we're going to smell like you used to."

Cam laughed. "I'm not happy, but there has to be a word about taking pleasure in the misery of others."

"Which is the same as being happy," Jade said in a tart tone.

She might be right, but the others had sure given him the business back when he and yellow bile were making such a stink of things. He didn't see a problem with him chuckling a bit over them having to endure the same as he had.

"We'll be outside," Jade added, taking Weld's hand and tugging him to follow.

Cam viewed them through narrowed eyes. Jade had said she wasn't interested in Weld before—just his backside—but now she was? It seemed so anyway. Ever since Surelend. But why? What did she see in the man? He had started off lazy, never hiding how much he liked to chase skirts and drink too much. He was a liar, too—Cam hadn't forgotten how Weld had explained to his drinking friends on how he'd hurt his ankle in a sparring match when the truth was he'd stumbled over his own feet when intoxicated.

So what was the appeal?

He shook his head. It also wasn't none of his business, but the truth was he was envious of Weld. He sure wouldn't mind it if a woman just once stared after him like Jade did Weld. And Marta and Charity didn't count since their interest in Cam was purely mercantile.

Avia moved to stand next to him, also watching Jade and Weld as they stood on the balcony. "Sometimes I think Jade wouldn't mind having a relationship with Weld, but then he says or does something that only he could say or do, and the spell is broken."

Cam smiled faintly. "Then he's an idiot."

"That he is."

Cam glanced askance at Avia. He'd gotten to know her pretty good in the months since they'd joined the academy, and as far as he knew, she wasn't romantically interested in anyone. Did she know how much Pan pined after her, even if these days he hid it better?

"I'll be outside," Avia said, moving on to join Jade and Weld.

"I've noticed something," Cam said to Pan, who had remained behind. "You know how I Imbibed more Ephemera from the core? When I did so, I realized that I don't have to fight it when Ephemera wants in. I can just let it happen."

"Why is this a surprise?" Pan asked.

"Because it's like Ephemera is alive. Like it knows what it should be, and it gets done."

Pan smiled. "What if it is alive? Wouldn't that make a lovely explanation for your favorite phrase? All is Ephemera and Ephemera is All."

Cam chuckled. "Yes, it would."

They rose to their feet and stepped out onto the back balcony where the others waited.

"If you don't want your clothes to get fouled," Cam began, "you'll have to disrobe to your undergarments. And sit down. It's best to Enhance when seated."

Jade stripped without hesitation, and Cam tried not to stare at her curves, her rippling muscles, and her taut abdomen. He barely succeeded, even while telling himself that he was a young man and young men were supposed to look. They just needed to be discreet about it. Although, even then, women probably didn't like it much.

He scowled inwardly when he noticed Weld giving Jade and Avia boldly admiring glances, which wasn't the slightest bit discreet. "Everyone turn around so you're not facing each other. I don't want any peeking at privates going on."

"I don't mind anyone peeking at my privates," Weld said with a leer.

"Even me?" Cam asked, brow raised.

With a sour complaint, Weld turned around, facing outward.

"Now to business," Cam said. "Delve your Sources. First thing is slowing Plasminia. See how it's spinning? I imagine putting a net to slow it down. Try that."

"A net?" Jade asked. "Why not a windmill or a waterwheel? That way the Plasminia slows down when pushing against the object, and you can imagine the yellow bile leaching out?"

Cam stared at her a moment, shocked and wanting to hit himself. Why hadn't the book ever mentioned that? Or even better, why hadn't *he* ever thought of that? "That's a good idea," he said, infusing a hearty note to his voice.

Everyone got to work, and minutes later, Cam could tell when they succeeded. The stench of yellow bile filled the air.

"My head feels like someone's hitting it with a hammer," Jade complained.

"It only gets worse when the blood starts to leak," Cam advised. "So, don't go too hard. What you're doing for now is enough."

Cam's nose wrinkled as the reek grew riper. Gah! Did his own yellow bile stink this bad? It was a wonder folks hadn't passed out whenever he'd walked by. He stepped away from the others, breathing through his mouth, struggling to hold down his gorge.

Only when he was sure he wasn't going to be losing his supper did he speak again. "Next, imagine inhaling the yellow bile back inside. Imbibe it, but whatever you do, don't let it become Plasminia. Take it to whichever Tang you have at Gold and Enhance it."

"This is impossible," Weld complained. "How in the unholiness did you do this?"

"He did it because he had no choice," Pan said. "It's also why he's our leader."

The words of support had Cam straightening, smiling, and unthinkingly inhaling deep.

He nearly vomited as he took in a deep whiff of the yellow bile.

Several nights later, a knock on the door distracted Cam. He'd been seated on the floor, feet atop his knees, struggling to create a True Bond. No one else was about, and he had the quarters to himself.

The knocking repeated, and Cam rose with a sigh, answering the door. Outside stood Saira and Professor Grey. Cam blinked, staring at them, wondering why they were here. A moment later, his mind got going. "Sorry about that," he said with a shake of his head. "I wasn't expecting to see you is all."

"No worries," Professor Grey said, sliding past him in her graceful manner. "We wish to help you with your challenge."

"It's why we're here," Saira added, stepping inside as well. "We were speaking," Saira said. "And Professor Grey has an idea that I think you should try."

"In this, I will act as your guru," Professor Grey said with a smile.

Cam frowned. "My what?"

"Your teacher." Professor Grey clapped her hands, wanting quiet. "Have a seat."

Cam resumed his position on the ground with Saira and Professor Grey following suit.

"Now that you've increased your overall Ephemera, I want you to try something different," Professor Grey said. "It should work. Delve your Source, but don't form any Bonds. Focus on Plasminia and slow it down again."

This was something Cam had already done. He said so.

"Correct, but that doesn't mean you can't improve it. I'm not speaking only of Plasminia in this regard. For example, a diamond is a precious gem, but not all diamonds are as precious as the next. Some are of higher quality and contain fewer flaws. That should be your goal here: to make your Crystal Tangs of higher quality. Doing so will make them all more answerable to your needs."

Cam didn't think to question whether Professor Grey was right or not. But he did have a question. "How do you know so much?"

"Because I'm old, and I've read a lot," Professor Grey replied. "Now try what I said."

Professor Grey didn't look old. She appeared Saira's age. He stared from one woman to the other, comparing them.

"You're delaying," Saira admonished.

Cam recognized she was right. He was delaying. Probably because this was another new concept, and he already had so many to learn. It had him feeling a mite fidgety over the matter.

Still, if anyone knew what was best for him, it was Professor Grey. With an exhalation and a firming of his resolve, Cam set aside his questions, ignored his concerns, and closed his eyes. Another breath, and he Delved his Source, visualizing it in his mind's eye. Plasminia spun in a wild dash, lightning flickering.

From there, rather than a net to slow his Plasminia, Cam did what Jade had suggested. He formed the image of a water wheel. The Plasminia slowed, the lightning continuing to chase itself in a mad sprint, but definitely slower.

"You're doing well," Professor Grey said. "You won't have much yellow bile, but whatever is formed, don't waste any on your skin. You should have the control needed to hold it inside."

"We'd both appreciate it if you held it inside," Saira said, and Cam could hear the smile in her voice.

As Plasminia slowed, the yellow bile filmed on the surface of his Source—only a bare amount compared to what he'd originally had earlier in the school year—and unsurprisingly, just like Professor Grey had said would happen, it wasn't difficult for Cam to hold it in place. He willed it, and it occurred.

"Guide the bile inward," Professor Grey instructed. "Send it to Kinesthia. Make the Tang lighter."

Again, Cam did as instructed, immediately feeling better. Stronger and more aware of his body, and when he opened his eyes, the world had greater clarity even without Bonding to Kinesthia. His lungs filled with less effort, and his heart didn't beat as hard or as fast. He took a deep breath, appreciating how fully he could inhale.

Until now, he'd never known what he was missing. And here he'd thought that he'd already been healed of Plasminia's weakening effects. "Is this how everyone feels?"

"Not quite," Professor Grey said. "You still have improvements to make, but it can only happen if you continue what you started tonight. You can do this to your other Tangs as well. You'll then narrow the gap between your abilities and those of everyone else."

"Thank you," Cam said, humbled that she'd taken the time to help him.

"No worries," Professor Grey said, repeating her words from earlier. She rose to her feet. "And now that you understand the process, I trust you can manage it on your own?"

"Of course," Cam said, rising to his feet and seeing her out the door.

Saira didn't appear ready to leave yet, remaining by the dining room table. "The advice I have is of a different nature," she said. From within the folds of her lehenga, she withdrew the core they had lanced near Surelend. "There is still some Ephemera within it," she said. "You've Imbibed most of it, and I want you to Imbibe the rest. But this time, don't let it transform into Plasminia. Force it into Kinesthia. Saira raised a hand, forestalling any questions Cam might have, and he had a lot. "Your body struggles with your vast quantity of Plasminia, and your mind spends an enormous effort compensating. But if you increase Kinesthia, your body will be healthier. Your mind could then focus more readily. Everything will work with greater rhythm. Afterward, you'll find it simple to pour more Ephemera into Synapsia and Spirairia."

Cam took the core. "What about the others?" Cam asked. "Can't they benefit from more Ephemera?" He didn't want to selfishly use up the core for only his own benefit.

"For now, the others are balanced, but they'll receive more Ephemera when I regress and pass what I have on to them. This is only for you. Put your hands on mine."

Cam wiped his suddenly damp palms on his pants. He'd held Saira by the waist when they'd danced but putting his hands on hers always seemed more intimate for some reason.

She held the core, waiting on him. "Is something wrong?"

"No," Cam said, firming his voice. He placed his hands atop Saira's. "I reach with Spirairia?"

"Just like always," she said with a soft smile.

The smile nearly undid Cam, making him want to stare into her blue eyes. With a forceful rejection, he got back to work. Seconds later, he was reaching into the burning bright core with Spirairia. He imagined himself touching that glimmering brilliance, drawing it forth.

And there was no pain or difficulty in doing so. The Ephemera within the core leached out, entering Cam's Source as simply as if he was drinking hot soup. He only had to make sure to sip carefully so as not to burn himself.

Cam was about to remark on the simplicity, but he'd forgotten

Saira's advice. Just then the Ephemera he'd Imbibed transformed into Plasminia, leaving him weaker than only moments before.

Saira noticed, frowning. "You forgot, didn't you?"

Cam nodded.

She sighed. "Which is pretty much the opposite of balancing." Without waiting on his reply, she held out the core. "Let's try it again."

"Yes, ma'am," Cam replied, reaching for the core.

A few days later saw Cam frowning, puzzling out a passage from the book he'd borrowed from the library—Professor Werm's suggestion. It was a theory on Ephemera and Tangs. For the most part it didn't contain anything beyond what Light Squad had already been taught, but there were some elements he hadn't quite grasped. For instance, the section about True Bonds, their flexibility and eventual ease of use had him particularly excited. As a Glory, he'd simply have to *want* to utilize a skill, and it would happen, instinctually like moving his arm. There wouldn't be the focused effort that he had to nowadays put forth.

He glanced away from the book, imagining what it would be like. When he did so, his gaze fell on Light Squad, who sat outside on the balcony, still striving to Enhance their Plasminia to Gold. So far, none of them had succeeded, but they'd only been at it a week. Surely one of them would succeed fairly soon.

In the meantime, since they didn't need his advice any longer, Cam had remained inside to study.

Nevertheless, he would have enjoyed being out there. It was a lovely night, a beautiful spring evening with the academy quiet, and a whispering wind soughing through the boughs. The lights of Nexus twinkled in the distance like stars. And it likely also reeked outside given the fact that Light Squad was Enhancing Plasminia. *The yellow bile.*

Cam had wisely kept the windows closed to save his nose from torment. He had also kept the lights turned down, too, wanting as few distractions as possible when practicing on making a True Bond. He was nowhere close to succeeding, but the last time had been his best attempt yet.

An hour later, the others in Light Squad re-entered the quarters, clothed and not stinking too much. Cam had already shown them how to burn off whatever yellow bile lingered on their skin, or in Pan's case, his fur. The others left right away.

"You're not going to bed?" Pan asked once everyone was gone.

"I can't," Cam said. "Forming a True Bond isn't going to be simple. And with me and Plasminia, it'll be doubly so."

"Not when you Imbibe Ephemera," Pan countered. "Didn't you tell me that comes pretty easy for you?"

"It does, but it always wants to become Plasminia, which isn't helping with keeping me balanced."

"All of us might have that trouble," Pan said.

Cam wanted to smack his forehead. Pan was right. All of Light Squad had Plasminia Tangs, and if theirs were like his, it might be greedy when it came to adding Ephemera.

"You forgot, didn't you?" Pan said, smiling, a pair of sharp little teeth peeking out of the corners of his mouth. Pan always was so cute when he smiled like that, and it never failed to make Cam happy.

It didn't this time either, and he laughed. "I did forget."

"And you're still going to stay up late?"

Cam nodded. "You heard what Professor Werm said. The True Bond isn't faster or quicker, but it can last longer. And you know what my biggest problem with Ephemera has always been."

"How long your Bonds last compared to everyone else's."

Cam nodded. "With a True Bond, maybe I can close that gap."

He caught Pan viewing him in consternation. "Even now, you still feel like you're behind?"

Cam hesitated in answering. Ever since the expedition to Surelend, his confidence had grown. He'd killed his fair share of rakshasas, and it had him figuring that while he might seem soft during practice, when lives were on the line, he showed hard. It brought him self-assurance, but he was afraid to express it, still thinking karma would find out and humble him.

He smiled. Wasn't that what Professor Grey had told him *wasn't* a proper way of viewing karma?

"What's so funny?" Pan asked.

Cam explained. "And, no, I'm not believing myself falling behind the rest of y'all."

"Good. Because you aren't failing yourself."

"I said falling. Not failing."

"I heard," Pan replied. "But for you, it's the same thing. You know I'm right. Part of your underlying fear, your haunting and your lie."

Another topic that Cam had thought on quite a bit. And what he'd reckoned was that his friend was wise and correct. He said so.

Pan smiled. "You should listen to me more often then. I'm very smart."

Cam chuckled. "Sure you are. Humble, too. But like all of us, you need to take your own advice. You know what I mean?"

Pan's smile gave way to a brittle despondence. "I know, but it's difficult. Contemplating the world in a way that's different from how you've always known."

"But we aren't talking about the world. We're talking about your inner self. How you think about yourself as a person."

"It's the same thing. How I consider myself becomes how I consider the world."

"Which doesn't change what I'm saying. You've got to sip your own medicine."

"I have, and I will," Pan said, staring at the ground a moment. His eyes flicked back to Cam. "This wasn't the conversation I wanted to have tonight."

Cam chuckled. "It isn't what I wanted either. We're treading deep waters. I doubt any of my kin other than Pharis ever bothered cogitating on such matters."

Pan's mouth twitched into a smile. "There you go again with your country way of speaking."

"What? Cogitated or kin?"

"Both," Pan said.

Cam shrugged, offering a crooked grin. "Consider it part of my charm."

"You have a lot of charms," Pan said. "Your hard work is one of them."

"It's the only way I can see to getting to where I need to be."

"Which is?"

Cam froze. Where did he want to go with all this work? What did it mean? What did he want to achieve? He'd only ever considered surviving the academy and gaining strength. But what was the purpose?

As he pondered the matter, he came to a surprising conclusion.

Surprising because his greatest goal was a selfish one. He wanted to master Ephemera; to become the best Novice in the academy. To outshine everyone since he'd never outshined anyone. Not back in Traverse and not here. He'd always been behind, and he wanted to do more than just catch up. He wanted to race past everyone and become the best. It didn't matter how small-minded it might seem. It's what he wanted right now.

"What is it?" Pan asked, apparently sensing the realization.

Cam told him. "All along, my goal was to not be weak anymore. Or that I wanted to get out in the world and help folks. Those aren't lies. I do want the last, but for the first, I'm not afraid of being weak anymore. I'm not weak. I'm strong, and now I want to be the best."

Pan chuckled. "It's not as surprising as you might think. It might even be a natural transition. Going from being weak to feeling normal about yourself to wanting more."

"The funny thing is I think I can actually make it happen."

"I don't doubt it," Pan said. "And you shouldn't either. Underneath all your uncertainties and fears, I've always figured there was a kernel of self-confidence. And when you fully embrace it, you'll achieve something great."

It was comforting, hearing Pan speak his support, and Cam didn't reply at first. Instead, his memories—like they often did—went to his family, Master Bennett, and Jordil... all the people who loved him.

What would they think of his ambitions if they knew?

"One thing you should understand," Pan continued. "While you want to become the best of us, in some ways, you already are. You lead Light Squad. You are the only one who could have found us a path to victory in the mid-year testing. We would have failed the Unwinnable without your planning. And we would have died in Surelend without your leadership. Believe it."

"I do," Cam said, and for the first time, he recognized that the words were true. His doubts might still bubble to the surface now and then, but confidence in himself and his future was slowly replacing most of them.

It was a far distance he'd already traveled, but peering ahead, there was even more ground he wanted to cover. And by Devesh, he'd cover those miles no matter how rugged or difficult.

44

More weeks passed, during which Cam continued to Enhance his Tangs. He Imbibed the last bit of Ephemera from the core, too, and the work left him feeling strangely satisfied, like all his life, he'd been wobbling and unsteady, and now his body moved in sync to his wants and needs.

The rest of Light Squad also worked at Enhancing their final Tangs to Crystal, and in the midst of their effort, they all managed to form a True Bond as well. It happened a month before the challenge, and the first to accomplish the feat was Weld—the man had talent when he applied himself—and the last, surprisingly, was Pan.

But what it meant was they'd now finally have a chance to learn how to make use of the True Bonds. All of their instructors would teach them, but it was Professor Werm who would go first.

He stood before them, the class taking place outside the greenhouse like he preferred. "Form a True Bond," he ordered.

Cam Delved his Source, seeing it in his mind's eye. There was lightning-laced Plasminia. Gaseous Spirairia, having an oppressive weight as it drifted. Then was Synapsia, liquid, turgid, and dense as quicksilver.

And finally, Kinesthia, solid but having a sense that it could float on air.

Once Cam had the vision fixed in his sight, he pulled on the Tangs. That was the key. Rather than push down and forge a Bond, which is what was typically done, he had to pull one forth. And rather than seek one Tang at a time, a True Bond required him to latch onto all of them at once.

It was a balancing act, delicate and difficult, but now that Cam knew the trick, it came quickly, no slower than the separate Bonds he used to forge. New strength poured into his muscles. His reflexes twitched, ready to have him explode in any kind of movement. Insight filled his racing mind, and the world expanded while also drifting to a crawl. He had time enough to ponder the meaning of life if he wanted. At least it felt that way. And then there was the woven world, the Ephemera crowding his vision, ready for him to seek out and touch creation, but only from a short distance.

Professor Werm nodded, clearly pleased. "Until now, when it came to Spirairia, you have been limited. Your grasp was limited to the rule of five. You could affect the world at a distance of five feet; be it the creation of elemental forces—fire, earth, water, or air—or telekinesis. There, your limit in force was also five pounds. How much you could lift and how far you could move it. The same held true in terms of empathy. Five feet." He paced before them. "With a True Bond, your limits are the same but the length of time you can maintain your use is twice as long. Your use of Synapsia and Kinesthia is also enhanced."

Weld raised a hand, polite for once. "Why doesn't everyone learn to do this?"

Professor Werm answered with a question of his own. "In the month you've spent mastering it, have you learned anything else?"

Weld glanced about like he needed confirmation for what was obvious. "No," he eventually allowed.

"That's why," Professor Werm replied. "You're only at the beginning of your education in the use of True Bonds, and already you're losing time to others. And that loss doesn't end any time soon. It'll take you a year or longer to master what others will accomplish by the end of this term."

Cam had already suspected as much, but it hadn't changed his opinion on what was best for him. For all of them. Holding a Bond longer could be the difference between life and death out in the real world. However, on hearing Professor Werm's explanation, a new concern cropped up. "Meaning the teachings and manuals we receive…"

"Will do you no good until next year," Professor Werm said, confirming Cam's fear. "You'll be as unskilled as Novices even as Acolytes."

"How long will we be behind?" Jade asked, a thrust of her jaw indicating her upset.

Cam sympathized. Of all of them, Jade wanted to Advance as soon as possible. For her, it was necessary. Advancement meant gaining power, fortune, and reclaiming her family's prestige. And while Advancing could still happen as quick as she might want, gaining power wouldn't. Nobles respected power more than they did the mere rank of an Ephemeral Master; meaning an Acolyte who was as unskilled as a Novice would still be a Novice in their eyes.

Professor Werm answered Jade's question. "Your growth will pick up once you attain an Acolyte's Awareness, but it will remain slower than that of other Ephemeral Masters. In fact, you won't truly close the gap until you at least become a Glory. Assuming you reach that level of Advancement."

Jade scowled.

Professor Werm tried to placate her. "I know True Bonds are frustrating. Worse, there will even come a time where you won't be able to go back forming a Bond to each individual Tang like you used to."

Jade's scowl deepened. She folded her arms over her chest, peeved. "Then what's the point? You made it seem like True Bonds were some amazing skill that would tip the balance in our favor. All the instructors did."

"And we aren't wrong," Professor Werm said. "But proper mastery of a True Bond requires time and patience. You won't have the abilities of other Ephemeral Masters at first, but at the Awareness of a Glory, you'll start to exceed everyone else. You'll know your mind, body, and the world in ways they can't. Your weakest Tang will be stronger than it should be since your Bond will be a unified whole. Theirs will be separate. At that point, it will be you who has the advantage."

Cam felt the need to speak since Jade still appeared plenty upset. "Using True Bonds as Novices has no disadvantages. We're still just as good as everyone else, including Victory's group. The only difference is we can last longer. Remember, this isn't a challenge among Acolytes. We'd have made a different choice if it was."

"We're still not going to learn as fast," Jade countered.

"But we won't need to. Not for the challenge," Cam said. "We're fighting the best Novices in our entire class. For that, we need every advantage, and there's nothing much more advantageous than going full out while the other fellow has to bend over at the knees to catch his breath."

"Or her breath," Avia corrected.

"Or her breath," Cam conceded. "And think about this," he added to Jade. "When we win, we'll receive some expensive manuals and techniques that none of us, except Avia, could have ever afforded. But that's only if we win, which wouldn't have been the case given who we'll be facing."

"But we have you to lead us," Pan said to Cam, sounding as doubtful as Jade. "The other squad won't. It could have been enough to achieve victory even without a True Bond."

"I don't think so," Cam replied. "I know my worth, and I'm not worth that much." Small chuckles met his comment. "Trust me on this. You trusted me this far. You all have Plasminia Tangs. You took them on even though they might have weakened you at first. Now, they're barely a hindrance."

"Speak for yourself," Weld said. "Mine still gives me fits and takes away my coordination."

"You never had coordination," Avia countered.

"The ladies say otherwise," Weld replied with a waggle of his brows.

Groans broke out, relieving some of Cam's concern. But he wasn't thinking on letting the matter drop just yet. "We need the True Bonds.

Give them time. We're playing the long game. And True Bonds and the prizes Victory's squad will hand over will make us mightier than anyone. Y'all with me?" Muttered assents met his question, so he repeated it in a shout. "Y'all with me!"

This time, the affirmation came loud and clear, including from Jade and Pan.

"Look lively," Professor Shivein shouted.

It was the afternoon class in Kinesthia, and Cam wiped the sweat off his brow even as it poured down his face, chest, and neck like a bucket had been upended over his head. He'd always sweated like a pig, ever since he was little. It was a big part of why he liked winter so well. Less chance of sweating through his clothes.

And he surely wouldn't mind some winter cool right about now. While an intermittent breeze kept the weather reasonable, it did nothing for the spring sun—so hot in Nexus—which blazed down through an empty blue sky.

Cam chugged water from a canteen. They'd completed most every afternoon exercise, but if he wanted to finish strong, he needed to first quench his thirst. He drained most of the canteen just as Saira called out to get their attention.

"Wind sprints!" she shouted. "Full length of the field. Five sets of four. Get to your marks."

Imagining himself going flat out for a quarter-mile would have sounded insane to Cam when he first arrived. Having to do it four times in a row with only twenty-second breaks in between and repeating it a minute later would have signaled his death knell.

But nowadays, while he'd still be winded from the exercise, he wouldn't be dead or even mostly dead. None of them would, not even Pan. Light Squad had progressed a great deal since that first day at the academy.

And of them all, there was no doubt that it was Cam who had gained the most during his time at the school, nowhere near the peak condition in which he now found himself. He had stamina and strength to burn, but it never hurt to keep adding on to what he already possessed.

Nevertheless, for today's wind sprints, he'd be lucky if he finished within five seconds of the others. His big body just wasn't built for running, neither sprints or long distance. His poor form didn't help him any either. He had long legs, and that was it. He couldn't move them in the coordinated way he wanted.

"Go!" Saira shouted.

Cam took off, next to last, only ahead of Pan and Weld, who were both somehow always slow out of the block. Avia, like always, had the lead with Jade right behind. Then Weld would come on like a house on fire. But it was Pan who would eventually catch them all. With every yard, his short legs would dig in, moving in a blur, getting him rumbling along faster and faster.

And just as Cam predicted, even as Avia and Jade steadily pulled away, Weld passed Cam by, grinning at him and flashing a peace sign. He always did that. *Jackhole.* And here was Pan, focused and determined, blowing past Cam, making him feel like he was moving through mud.

He screamed inside, frustrated. He wasn't supposed to, but he formed a True Bond, tired of the losing. A fresh burst of power and energy filled his legs. His mind sharpened, focused and remembering. There was a way to run, a form to take, and while Cam had listened, he'd never learned. He did so now. Using his better recollection, he forged memory into his muscles.

Cam ran more fleetly than ever before, powered by the True Bond, but this time his form was actually closer to correct. His arms pumped, hands slicing the air. Knees lifted, coming down, propelling him forward. He caught Jade. Surged past Avia. They shot him outraged stares, forming True Bonds as well. Cam grinned when he caught Weld, flashing him a peace sign. *Fair's fair.* Only Pan was ahead.

They hit the end of the field, touched the chalk line, and were off, back to the other side.

Pan lost the lead. Slowing and reaccelerating wasn't so simple for him. Cam kept pumping his arms, arrowing his hands. Lifted his knees. Remembered to hold still his neck. He didn't need his head wobbling around like one of those funny looking dolls.

His form improved with every stride, and while the others also had True Bonds now, they struggled catching Cam, only recovering a few yards on him. The finish line was but thirty yards away. Twenty.

Exultation filled Cam. He was going to win! A broad grin spread across his face.

From his right pounded the drumming of feet. They struck the ground in a blistering rhythm. Ten yards from the finish, Pan roared by, grinning cheekily at him. Cam's jaw dropped, his concentration broke, and he tripped, plowing into the grass. His head hadn't yet cleared the finish line when everyone passed him.

Cam pounded the ground, cursing loudly. He'd been so close.

"Twenty seconds to rest," Professor Shivein shouted, laughing at Cam. "And next time, no one Bonds or I'll have you running until we've gassed you good."

"Come on," Pan said, offering a hand up. "You were close to catching me that time."

Cam took Pan's hand, rising to his feet. "Close only counts in games where it matters," he muttered, still angry with himself.

"Get your breathing under control," Pan said. "We have a lot more running to do."

He was right. Cam didn't need to be acting like a baby about not winning. There was always another chance, and this time, with or without a True Bond, he wouldn't come in last. He focused on his breathing. *Deep breaths, in and out.* Seconds passed, and his bellowing lungs no longer filled and emptied so fast. His pounding heart slowed. He had his breath back.

Just in time.

"On your marks," Saira shouted. A pregnant pause. "Go!"

Cam shot off. No True Bond this time, but he was determined not to need one. He kept his focus on his form. Arms, hands, knees, placement of his feet. Head on straight. Nothing else mattered. The world shrank to himself—his body—and no one else.

Here was the chalk line. Cam slowed, bent to touch it, and raced off to where the instructors waited. Arms pumped. Knees lifted high. He landed on the balls of his feet. Pushed off his toes. The end of the race centered in his vision, coming closer.

A final surge saw Cam cross it, and he coasted to a stop. Arms behind his neck, panting again.

Only then did the world outside return to him. Shouts of encouragement and groans of disappointment. Cam had no idea how he did, but from Pan's excitement for him, he must have done alright.

"What happened?" Cam asked, still breathing heavy. "Who won?"

"I did," Pan said, breathing just as hard. "Then Jade. But you beat Weld and Avia."

Cam grinned, elated.

"Twenty seconds," Professor Shivein said.

Cam's elation fell away. Not coming in last only once wasn't good enough. This had to be the new standard. He never wanted to come in last in anything.

Twenty seconds later. "Get to your marks!" Saira shouted.

Cam paced to the starting line, reaching it alongside the others, getting poised to sprint.

"Go!"

He was off again, focused. Nothing existed beyond his form, beyond the need to win.

"What's this meeting about?" Weld asked, flopping into a chair set out on the balcony.

Light Squad had finished their classes for the day, but before heading to supper, Cam had asked them to come by his and Pan's quarters. It was a week before the challenge, and he wanted to discuss their approach to the confrontation. Light Squad sat in a circle, on the chairs usually surrounding the dining room table. Everyone except for Pan, who munched some celery while seated on the ground.

Before answering Weld, Cam's gaze went to the gleaming city of Nexus in the near distance, and beyond it, to the statues of the Holy Servants. To the bold, blue lake and the sunlight glistening on the waters. It was so beautiful here, even with the thick clouds and a wind pregnant with moisture and telling a tale of a storm to come. From what Cam heard, spring squalls came fast to the island and blew hard. And as if they sensed the pending storm, birds soared across the sky, all of them winging south. Light Squad wouldn't be able to get much extra training in at the Kinesthia field if the rain fixed to fall like a lot of folks predicted.

But neither would Victory's team, Squad Nobility—a stupid name; too on the nose as far as Cam was concerned.

"We're meeting to go over the other team," Cam said at last, answering Weld's question. His eyes flicked to a couple of nearby balconies that were occupied. *Good.* Cam wanted them that way. "We need to think on their strengths and their weaknesses."

Jade exhaled in derision. "If it's weaknesses, then the obvious one is Kahreen. I don't know why or how she's on their team."

Cam had done some investigating, and it seemed his initial impression of Kahreen—based mostly on Jade's dislike and contempt—had been wrong. "She isn't who you think she is," he told Jade. "She has two Tangs at Crystal and the other at Gold. And it ain't all because of her rich kin. From what I hear, she works hard."

"He's right," Avia said. "There are some people who pretend they never do any work or study. But then, when it's time to demonstrate their skill, they do very well. And it's because all along, they actually *were* trying hard; they *were* studying diligently. They just don't want anyone to know it. Kahreen is like that."

Cam's eyes flicked to Weld, who was nodding along to Avia's explanation. There was no flush of guilt on his face, even though he used to do the same thing.

Jade scowled. "That's not the Kahreen I know. She's lazy, selfish, self-centered—"

"And none of that matters," Cam said, cutting her off. Jade hated Kahreen, and once she got to talking on the topic, she could rant for hours. "Kahreen is skilled, and we have to respect her. Her Crystals are in Spirairia and Kinesthia, which means she's slippery and strong. I expect the Nobles will use her as a scout."

"Merit will also be a scout," Weld said. "He's a noble, and he's always around Victory, but you ever notice how you hardly notice him?"

Pan nodded his head. "He watches from the back."

"Which means he likely *won't* be a scout," Cam said. "Scouts observe and report, but Merit just observes. Whatever he sees, he seems the kind to keep it to himself."

"You mean like a leader?" Avia asked with a frown. "I don't see it that way. Not with Victory on the team."

"Don't forget Charity," Jade said. "She's just as strong-willed and charismatic as Victory."

Weld grinned at Jade. "Is charismatic your way of saying you think she's beautiful? You aren't wrong. She's as easy on the eyes as Saira." He turned his attention to Cam. "What do you think? You've seen more of Charity than the rest of us. Or I should say, *felt* more of her. Wasn't she nearly sitting in your lap a few months back?"

Cam flushed. After the mid-year tests and Surelend, Charity had made clear her interest in him, but it was the curiosity of a cat looking to play with a mouse. There was nothing romantic about it. Charity probably just wanted him to join her father's duchy upon graduation, and it seemed like she might be willing to use every one of her womanly wiles to see it happen.

Thankfully, most of that interest had subsided once the challenge had been made.

"Charity is likely the other scout," Avia said, saving Cam from having to reply. "She's fast and cunning, but I've noticed she tends to defer to Victory."

"I've always wondered about that," Jade said.

Cam had a notion on the topic. "It's probably because she's observing like Merit. But in her own way," he said.

"Rumor also says that Duke Kazar, Charity's father, is interested in Victory as a husband for her."

There went Cam's notions about Charity using her womanly wiles on him. No chance of that if she was possibly pledged to Victory. It would be too risky.

Cam tossed aside his considerations about Charity and Victory. "The only one whose role I can't figure is Card. Will he follow Victory's commands?"

"He will," Avia said, sounding certain. "His family is sworn to Victory's. Have been for centuries. He'll do what he's told."

"He's also a lot smarter than he lets on," Pan said. "A few times in the library, I've walked past his table and looked at what he was reading. It was high-level concepts. From what I could tell, he isn't interested in just learning techniques through manuals. He wants to understand first principles."

Cam wouldn't have minded studying first principles himself, but where was the time? He had so many other things to learn first.

"And I wouldn't be so sure that Card does what Victory tells him," Weld said. "Remember the Kinesthia class that started all this? When we took down the Chalks? He didn't listen then."

"I think he will this time," Cam said. "The stakes are too high."

"How should we handle them?" Jade asked.

Cam flicked his eyes to a nearby balcony and noticed some folks had grown quiet. They were listening in. *Perfect.*

He leaned forward toward the rest of his team. "We got some folks peeping down on us," he whispered. "Don't look! They'll likely tell everything they hear to Victory, which is fine since I'm fixing to lie just now. Y'all just go on like you agree with me." He received nods, some hesitant, others firm. Cam leaned away from Light Squad. "So, this is how I'm thinking Squad Nobility will be deployed. Victory will lead, but he'll lead from the front. He and Kahreen will scout with Charity hanging in the back with Merit. And holding the line, defending their core will be Card. He's powerful enough to be trusted with something like that." He spoke some more, pretending to go over how he wanted Light Squad to engage the nobles. He clapped his hands, calling an end to the meeting. "Now that we've got that done, let's get some eats," Cam said.

He hoped his deceptive information, which would almost surely be given to Victory, would help Light Squad in some way. But even if it didn't, it was fun thinking about Squad Nobility chasing their tails, trying to reckon Light Squad's true plans.

45

On the morning of the challenge against Victory's unit, Light Squad entered the cafeteria to a chorus of jeers. It didn't surprise Cam. Everyone else at the academy were nobles, so of course they'd be cheering for their own kind, Squad Nobility.

"Don't let them upset you," Cam said to his unit. "Just get some eats. Nothing heavy. Then we're off to the arena."

The jeers continued as Light Squad ate while listening to promises of how Squad Nobility was going to take them apart. Cam tuned out the crowd, fixing his attention on his food and powering through his meal. Even Jade, who sometimes seemed to eat slow enough for the sun to rise and set before she chewed a bite, finished her breakfast just as fast as the rest of them. They put their trays away then and exited the cafeteria.

The sun shone down amidst a sky full of a scattering of clouds. So far, other than a squall last week, it had been days of wonderful weather, and Cam's eyes went as they usually did to Lake Nexus' glorious blue waters, scintillating in the sunshine. The white stones of the city itself reflected the light like a soul reflecting Devesh, shiny-bright and ethereal. Or maybe he should think it Ephemeral.

Cam grinned to himself at the notion.

"Campus is quiet," Weld noted, indicating the nearly empty area through which they walked.

There had been those jeering folks in the cafeteria, but out here among the buildings, other than flowers blooming, bees buzzing, and birds trilling, there was hardly any movement to be seen, much less any souls wandering about.

"That's because everyone is probably down at the arena," Pan said.

Weld grunted, shrugging. "Figured as much."

That was it from Weld. No crabby comeback. Just a simple, honest-to-goodness response. It was a change in the other man, and Cam was glad for it, glad that Weld had finally let go of his antipathy toward Pan. It must have happened sometime around the mid-year testing, but Cam hadn't noticed it much until fairly recently. It made him happy.

What had him less pleased was the nervousness wafting off Light Squad like fog lifting from a cold lake. That same anxiety didn't touch Cam. He was calm as a cow in a green, grassy field. "Let's take a walk. Burn off some energy."

Cam led them off campus, and they exited the main gates, where the streets close at hand seemed duller than usual. Emptier in some way. It didn't matter that the city was bustling like always, filled with vendors, merchants, and all sorts of people shouting and carrying on. There was an absence of energy this morning.

Or perhaps it was the silence that fell wherever Light Squad passed. They'd been identified.

How or why, Cam didn't know since they weren't kitted out in their armor and bore no banners stating their names. Instead, all they wore was nondescript clothing.

But nevertheless, there was a judging Cam sensed, of people assessing Light Squad and their chances. Why they cared, he had no notion, but he reckoned it probably had something to do with the thrill of witnessing competition. But then why weren't these people at the arena?

Cam shrugged off his concerns. It didn't matter. He took to pointing out places in the city, pretty sights, and interesting-looking people they encountered. Anything to lift Light Squad's minds off the
challenge.

It seemed to work. The nervousness ebbed, and Cam brought Light
Squad back to the campus where they soon reached the arena. There,
the stillness in the streets close to the school gave way to a festive atmosphere. Streamers of smoke wafted from open-bedded wagons
where meat was being seared and vendors shouted about the quality of their food. Illusionists—masters of sleight-of-hand—performed
their trickery, competing for attention with musicians and minstrels.
A quartet of young folk, features similar enough to name them siblings, demonstrated astonishing acrobatics.

But as Light Squad neared the arena, the performers fell away, and
there were only the crowds, who were lined up in preparation to enter
the coliseum through black, marble gates with entablatures filigreed
with carvings of vines. Many even had statues out front of Ephemeral
Masters caught in heroic poses. The people heading inside cared for
none of the fine stonework. Instead, they chatted in a happy drone,
all of them thrilled for the unexpected holiday. They also didn't give
Light Squad a second glance, so caught up were they in their own
excitement.

Cam glanced at the arena. He'd been here plenty, but the view of
the structure still struck him with awe. Formed of white marble like
the rest of Nexus and shaped like an oval bowl, it towered overhead,
soaring to touch the sky. Open arcades, their columns decorated and
fanciful, circled the structure at every level, and through them Cam
glimpsed the audience already in attendance. Light Squad's challenge
wasn't the only event happening today. There were other exhibitions
that would occur first—other squads demonstrating their skill in archery competitions, feats of strength, one-on-one combats, and racing
events.

Cam circled the arena until he reached a narrow gate, cast in
wrought-iron and warded by five guards. This was Light Squad's

point of passage, and they entered a tunnel walled in white marble and brightly lit by closely spaced Ephemeral lanterns. The corridor led them deeper into the coliseum with doors branching off on either side. But there was one farther along that was their destination.

It opened onto a room set aside for Light Squad. A number of plush chairs were scattered around the space along with a few tables holding water and some fruit. However, it was the armor and weapons that held Cam's attention.

"Get kitted," Cam ordered.

Minutes later, with only a murmuring of conversation, everyone was ready, and Cam led them through a door on the room's far end. It opened onto a small, private viewing area from which Light Squad could watch the other exhibitions. Their entrance didn't go unnoticed as a buzzing of expectant conversation and excitement rose from the audience.

Cam distantly noted the crowd's response, disregarding it. Instead, he fixed his mind on the challenge to come, the plans needed to win. Was there anything he'd overlooked? A different way of attacking? Of defending?

The questions chased through his mind until he noted Squad Nobility's arrival. They had a private viewing area as well, located in the most distant part of the coliseum from where Light Squad stood. Cam stared at Victory, holding the other man's gaze, refusing to give way first.

Their battle of stares ended when Charity tugged on Victory's sleeve, drawing his attention away even while she flicked a glance at Cam.

Cam shrugged at her, raising a questioning brow. Right now, he had none of his usual nervousness regarding Charity Kazar because right now Charity Kazar was merely an enemy to be defeated. And he would defeat her.

Several hours later, with the sun at noon, the other exhibitions wound down, and Lord Queriam rose to his feet, gesturing for quiet. He stood a quarter way around the arena from Light Squad, upon a private balcony, which he shared with all of Light Squad's professors and those of Squad Nobility. Using some Crown skill, his voice echoed to every corner of the arena, a conversational tone rather than a booming shout.

A brief review of the rules followed, and upon finishing, Lord Queriam waved a hand and the arena's floor transformed. The pitch descended, and where there had been dirt and grass, there now stood a winter forest with snow on the shrubs but relatively clear ground. A narrow valley, ridged and rocky, drooped down from a pair of treed hills; each topped by a tall flag—blue for Squad Nobility and red for Light Squad. The peaks rose on opposite sides of the valley, their summits wreathed in fog.

"The cores will be found atop each hill," Lord Queriam said. "That is where each team will start, and the challenge will begin. Good luck."

Minutes later, Light Squad exited their viewing area, descending down a long set of stairs to the arena floor before clambering to the heights of their peak. They clustered around the red flag, at the base of which was a similarly hued stone the size of a pomegranate. It gave off a sensation, a vibration that Cam could feel if he concentrated. In the near distance, atop their own fog-covered hill was Squad Nobility, but of them, only vague outlines could be seen. But he noted a similar vibration from their direction as well. Was it their core, too?

Cam didn't have time to ponder the matter, because even as he made to study the layout before him, he realized there were no rules against moving the core. It changed everything.

He gathered Light Squad. "We're going to take the core and hide it. There's nothing that says we can't."

Smiles and smirks met his remark.

Cam addressed Pan. "Take the core. Keep it on yourself. You're the best at hiding, so hide yourself somewhere they won't look."

Pan didn't look too pleased about that. "But I want to fight. I want to contribute."

Cam empathized with what Pan was saying. "I know, and you'll be doing both. Believe me. This isn't about one of us against any of them. This is all of us against all of them. And when we win, we win as one. We all do our part." He addressed the others after Pan perked up some. "I know you think those nobles have techniques and mastery on us, but they don't. And they sure don't have our heart. All along, we've out-worked them. We've out-trained them. We're wolves. They're rabbits. Ain't no chance a bunny is going to beat a wolf. You feel me? No chance!"

"No chance!" Light Squad shouted back, getting fired up. Weld shared fist-bumps with everyone while Jade smacked her forehead against Avia's, both of them growling out their readiness.

"Listen!" Cam shouted to regain their attention. "Here's what's going to happen. Weld and Jade. See those two rises right across from each other." He pointed to a pair of low tors, waiting on them to nod acknowledgement. "Split there. You can still cover one another, but I want early contact with Charity and Kahreen. They'll almost surely head along their own ridge. Let them see you and bring them back to that ravine there." He pointed again. "That's the goal. Hustle through. Avia will be on the heights. She'll arrow them. And when they retreat, they'll run straight into either Weld or Jade. I'll be trailing farther back as the reserve."

"Card will likely also be trailing," Jade reminded him.

Cam nodded. "Probably so. Either him or Victory. But I'm guessing one of them and Merit will be coming on toward our hill from over there." He indicated a smooth path. It descended from the peak of Squad Nobility's slope, disappeared in the valley, and ascended again until it ended where Light Squad stood. "The nobles might have learned to fight as a unit, but they still want glory. They'll battle that way. Separate. I'll ambush whoever they send." No one disagreed, which was a good thing. Cam needed Light Squad to have confidence in his plan. "Let's go over it one more time."

"We got it," Weld said, though sounding a note of complaint.

"Which is why we're going over it again," Cam snapped at him. "I want us all on the same page. None of us forgetting what we're supposed to do." He reviewed the plan once more. "And remember, we can hold our True Bond from the beginning to the end. They can't. They likely won't Bond at all until they see us. We'll get to our positions first and whoop them!"

Lord Queriam's voice carried across the coliseum. "The challenge begins... Now!"

The fog lifted, and Weld and Jade descended the hill while Pan grabbed the core and hustled away toward a ridge. He looked to be making his way toward a cave. Avia stayed by Cam's side, and he watched the other summit.

After a minute. "Go," he said to Avia. She raced after Weld and Jade, bow on her back along with her shield, a closed quiver on her hip, and a short spear in her hand.

Cam continued to observe the opposite slope. He frowned when he saw Merit running down the smooth path, heading straight for him. As for the other four, Victory was with Card and Charity with Kahreen. The two pairs ran, one behind the other, heading toward the ridge Cam had pointed out. Victory and Card shot left where they'd encounter Weld, while Charity and Kahreen went right, straight at Jade.

In either case, both of Light Squad's scouts would be outnumbered. It wasn't what Cam had expected, and he cursed. Weld and Jade had to make it back to Avia or everything was ruined.

Cam slipped his spear into a holster on his back and unslung his bow. Only then did he form a True Bond. Time stretched. The world came into focus, and his mind sped. His balance felt as perfect as he could have ever hoped, and he hustled downslope like a mountain goat. Straight to where he figured Weld, who tended to panic at the beginning of most conflicts, would encounter Victory and Card. If he did so again, there was no way Card wouldn't go straight after him, looking for the kill with no thinking about anyone else.

He just had that way about him.

It wasn't easy going, covering the rough terrain, but minutes later, Cam jerked to a stop. A shout had come from up ahead, to his left. *Weld*. Cam adjusted course, going faster, viewing exactly what he'd expected to see. Weld ran, fear on his face with Victory and Card right on his tail.

Cam dropped to a knee, sighted along the length of an arrow. With a whistle, it was on its way. The sound alerted Card, who got a shield in place. The arrow thunked into it. Card's gaze went to Cam, and he smiled as wolfishly as his last name.

Weld sprinted past Cam's position, and together, they raced off. They had to get to the ravine. Same with Jade. Only then would the odds be even.

Card and Victory pounded after them, their breaths steady but loud. Cam ran harder, lifting his legs like he'd learned. The gap opened. He caught Weld.

Jade sprinted into view. A couple arrows stood out from her shield. Charity and Kahreen must have taken a few potshots. They hadn't yet arrived. It gave Cam an idea.

"Jade!" he shouted, gesturing. She saw and joined them, and together all three raced into the ravine.

"Attack!" Cam shouted. He, Weld, and Jade skidded to a stop, getting behind boulders before facing the onrushing Victory and Card. Avia leaped down and joined them.

Cam ordered Jade and Weld after Victory and Card, spears and shields in place. Here came Charity and Kahreen, the latter looking angry enough to bite off someone's face. With no hesitation, Avia went after Squad Nobility's women.

"She's mine," Kahreen shouted, moving to engage.

Charity paused a moment, scowling at Kahreen before joining Victory and Card, who were holding their own against Weld and Jade.

Cam hunkered behind a boulder. He'd been forgotten. "Retreat!" he shouted to Weld and Jade.

They fell back smoothly, likely recognizing what he had in mind, sprinting through the ravine, around the corner, and past his position.

Cam rose and stepped into the breach. He loosed an arrow. It would have taken Charity in the chest, but directly before impact, the air shimmered, and the arrow dissolved.

The work of Lord Queriam, a prevention of actual killings. Still, Charity cried out once before collapsing to the ground, "dead."

Victory and Card momentarily halted. Before they could get their bearings, Cam ran away from them. Jade and Weld stepped out from where they'd been hiding behind some boulders, blocking Victory and Card.

Cam didn't stop running. Avia was fighting Kahreen, and he aimed to improve those odds. Exiting the shadowed ravine, he entered sunlight and snow.

Just in time to see Avia take a kick to the knee. She limped, moving badly. Things didn't look so good for her. Kahreen preened, her back to him, as she darted in and out at Avia.

Avia defended but was only seconds from going down. From twenty feet away, Cam fired another arrow. Kahreen heard it, tried to get around and block. But the arrow hit with a meaty thunk into her thigh. Kahreen screamed, silenced when a shimmer caught Avia's spear thrust to her throat.

A pained cry from behind. *Jade.*

"Get yourself ready!" Cam shouted to Avia, not waiting for acknowledgment as he raced back to where he'd left Jade and Weld. The former was down and dead, while the latter was trapped between Card and Victory.

"Fire!" Cam shouted.

Both nobles spun about, shields at the ready. Avia launched a pair of arrows, one on top of the other. It was the momentary distraction Weld needed. Rather than run, he attacked Victory, backstabbing him. Card roared in rage, but on seeing Cam coming after him, he finally decided to retreat, darting away, toward the ridge where Cam could sense the vibration from Light Squad's core. Could Card feel it, too?

And Merit was nearly upon them as well. It had to be him given the vibration rushing in their direction. It seemed the nobles had also decided to move their core.

"Merit's coming," Cam shouted to Weld. "Get downhill, right side of our tor. Stop him there. Avia, go with him. His orders given, Cam shot after Card, hoping to catch him before he reached the ridge where Pan had gone. He ran along the shadowed ravine before exploding back into sunshine. A rubbled slope had him leaping over boulders, rolling under a natural stone bridge.

Card was ahead. He could hear the other man's pounding footsteps. Where was he going? His path was circling left, heading downslope, drawing him toward the tor. The same place Cam had sent Weld and Avia to stop Merit. Except Card would come on them from upslope.

No. Cam clenched his jaw in frustration. He'd have to catch Card before then. And he could. Card's Bonds had to be coming apart by now while Cam could tell his wasn't anywhere close to fraying.

He dug deeper, searching for another burst of energy. Knees lifted. Balance corrected as his feet slipped on shale. A hand went down to push himself upright. On he went, running on the edge of disaster. Seconds later, Card came into view.

He was sprinting hard, but Cam was closing the gap, inch by inch, second by second. An instant later, Card's speed slowed dramatically. His Bond was broken. Cam smiled to himself. It would be all-too easy to end him now. As he darted forward, Card spun about to face him, desperation on his face.

Cam frowned inwardly. Something was wrong. Card looked like he had no hope, but his spin. It had been too quick. Too controlled. He was feigning he'd lost his Bond. *Fair enough.*

Cam unlimbered his spear, entered range, and aimed a lazy sweep. Card easily avoided it, and his counter came as a hard thrust. If Cam hadn't been expecting it, it would have taken him in the chest. As it was, he got his shield around, throwing the thrust off-target. Cam circled, looking for an opening.

Card didn't give him one. His form shimmering Novice red, he sent forth a rapid-fire series of slashes and thrusts that had Cam retreating. The blows came fast. Even with Synapsia, Cam could barely keep track of them.

"What's wrong?" Card asked. "No more tricks to save you?"

Cam didn't bother replying. *Focus.* Here came another series of attacks. Cam defended, turning aside the blows, more readily this time. A third wave, even easier to defend. They battled on, and Card started to slow.

Seconds later, an arrow bloomed from the other man's shoulder. He cried out, and his shield dropped. Cam aimed a thrust. It would have taken Card in the chest. As before, however, the air shimmered, and the spear never made contact. Nevertheless, Card "died."

Cam glanced back, seeing Avia standing upslope. She'd been the one to launch the arrow. "I thought I told you to help Weld."

She breathed heavily, heavily favoring her injured leg. "Figured you could use it more."

Cam shrugged. "Come on then. We need to save Weld before he gets himself killed." He could sense Merit, or who he figured must be Merit. The vibration wasn't moving much, which meant Weld had him deadlocked. He made to sprint again, but his speed wasn't there. The True Bond was fraying, and Cam let it go. A short cooldown now was better than one in the middle of battle.

As a result of his slower pace, Avia was able to keep up with him.

"How do you know where to go?" She asked.

"I can sense their core. Ours, too." He counted down the seconds of the cooldown, keeping his attention on the vibration he took to be Merit. The cooldown ended. Merit was on the move again, racing upslope toward the ridge.

Cam's cooldown ended, and he moved to cut off the noble. Ahead was a dry stream bed, and from what he remembered from studying its path, if he followed it, he should find himself ahead of Merit, directly placed in between Pan and the noble. Together, he and Avia could take him down.

Moments later, Cam exited the bed, leaping onto a rugged trail. Just in time.

Down the steep slope, Merit turned a corner. He grunted on seeing Cam. "Should have known you'd be here."

"Where you headed?" Cam asked, getting an arrow on the rest of his bow. Shooting downhill, he'd have a better chance at Merit than the other way around. He launched the arrow. Merit blocked with his shield. That was fine. Here came another one. Merit blocked that one, too.

"I can do this all day," the noble declared.

"No, you can't," Cam said. "Your Bond is going to break. Card's did."

Merit laughed. "You're smart. Your plan might even work if I hadn't just formed a new Bond. I can fight long enough to kill you and anyone else still living on your team."

Cam sent another arrow whistling downslope. "You never said where you were headed."

"Same place you're trying to protect," Merit said. "That panda of yours has your core."

"He's a panda-person," Cam said, knowing Merit wouldn't get the joke.

Sure enough. Merit shrugged. "Whatever. I'll kill him and get the draw."

"Or I'll kill you, and we'll take the win," Pan said, stepping out from further upslope of both men.

Cam had sensed his approach, and he nodded appreciation to his friend.

"Well then," Merit said. "You finally decided to stop hiding."

Pan shrugged. "Hiding while your team was dying. It seemed like a good tradeoff."

"I don't suppose you'd be willing to surrender, would you?" Cam asked.

Merit scoffed. "I can take the two of you."

"What about the three of us?" Avia asked, joining Cam and Pan.

Merit scowled. "I killed Weld, and the rest of my team only managed to kill Jade?"

"You might want to rethink the surrender part?" Cam said, signaling Pan and Avia. "Or we'll just kill you." Three arrows blistered in a staggered approach toward Merit. He blocked the first two. The third punctured an ankle.

The noble grimaced but didn't go down. But another three arrows were already on their way. Merit's concentration failed, and he was only able to block one bolt. His other ankle sprouted an arrow, and so did one of his arms. He toppled just as a third volley reached him, "killing" him.

46

After Merit was put down, Cam became aware of the roar of thunderous applause sweeping across the arena. He gazed about in shock and wonder, having forgotten about the crowd, but they'd been there the entire time, witnessing the challenge. And their exuberant reaction pulled him out of the mindset of the conflict. He continued to stare at the crowd, slowly regaining his bearings, fixing his thinking on what had just happened.

Light Squad had won.

The notion repeated in Cam's mind, a couple more times before fully taking hold. A bolt of energy surged through him, and he whooped, drawing Pan and Avia into an embrace. It didn't matter that he'd had no doubts beforehand as to the outcome. He *knew* Light Squad would win. But thinking so and actually doing so weren't the same thing.

"We won!" he shouted, joy coursing through him, reflected in Pan's and Avia's reactions.

The hills, valleys, crags, and hollows flattened as Lord Queriam returned the arena grounds to their normal state. Jade and Weld could soon be seen, standing not too far off, looking pleased as a peach in summer. Squad Nobility, on the other hand, looked as unhappy as a quintet of cats dunked in water.

Cam called over the other members of his team.

"We did it!" Jade shouted, elation in her voice. She jumped into Cam's arms, and he swung her around. She followed by embracing everyone else. Weld didn't seem to know what to say or do. He was both happy and unhappy, which was strange.

Cam couldn't reckon what was going on with him, so he figured on just telling him the truth as he saw it. "You did good," Cam said.

"I didn't have anything for Merit," Weld replied, explaining the source of his unhappiness

"You had enough," Pan said. "He may not seem it, but Merit is likely every bit as strong as Card. Better than Victory, for sure."

"What about me?" Victory asked, striding over to them. He must have heard the last part of Pan's statement.

Hopefully, the crowd's continuing roar of approval hadn't let Victory hear the entirety, though. Cam didn't want to have to explain anything that the noble might take to be an insult. "We were saying you're not going to like having to give us those techniques and manuals," Cam answered.

Whatever else Victory might have said was cut off when Lord Queriam spoke in a shout. "People of Nexus, you have borne witness to a spectacular exhibition of skill, talent, and cunning. Light Squad. The first unit in hundreds of years to conquer the Unwinnable. Light Squad. The first Novice squad in decades to solo kill a boil. Light Squad. Here they stand, proving they are the pre-eminent unit in this year's class. Show them your appreciation!"

The crowd roared again, hollering and cheering.

Cam's eyes watered as he gazed upon the sea of people, all of them shouting enthusiastically for him and his unit. It was like nothing he'd ever expected or experienced. A chant was soon taken up. "Light Squad! Light Squad! Light Squad!"

For once, Cam was the one who was grinning wide, infectious, and happy when he spoke to Pan. "Can you believe this?"

Pan answered with a laugh and a hug. "You deserve it. You worked harder than any of us. Without you—"

"We both deserve it," Cam said. "All of us." He gestured, telling Light Squad what he wanted.

They formed a line, him in the middle, facing Lord Queriam. Their instructors were there, too, applauding joyously, even Shivein and Werm. Professor Grey smiled wider and clapped harder than anyone else. Saira might have been somewhat more reserved, but only by a little, especially since her cheeks were wet with tears.

Cam had Light Squad bow as one to their professors, low to the ground. He wanted the instructors to know how much their time and teaching was appreciated. Without them, they couldn't have done this. Without them, Cam wouldn't have been worthy of any kind of applause.

Professor Queriam had some more speeches to make, but Cam wasn't listening. His father hadn't won many things in life, but one lesson he'd always wanted Cam to recognize was the importance of treating those who'd lost with dignity and kindness. He had Light Squad face Squad Nobility and shake hands with every member and offer them words of respect.

Cam didn't think Kahreen would accept his regard, but she surprised him by shaking his hand in a firm grip, meeting his gaze. There was none of the egotism or arrogance he'd grown used to seeing. Instead, there was appreciation. "You keep working like you have been, and I'll find a place for you in our house. We'll treat you better than Master Winder. Better than any duke even."

"Not better than my father," Charity said. Once more Cam found her staring at him like a vixen might an unguarded henhouse.

Cam didn't respond to either woman, not knowing what to say. Instead, he moved on to the next member of Squad Nobility.

"You showed better than I thought you would," Card said, after they shook hands. "I can take you one-on-one. Don't ever doubt it, but that isn't your strength, is it?"

It might have been best to simply accept Card's semi-compliment with some mumbled agreements, but Cam was feeling too fine and full of himself to let a remark like that go uncontested. "My strength ain't in one-on-one combat," he said to Card. "But test me when we're Adepts."

"Why wait?" Card said, a challenging glint in his eye.

"We still need your manuals and techniques. But once we have them…" Cam offered a slow, hungry grin. "Then you're mine."

Card opened his mouth to respond, but Victory talked over him. "Now, that's the spirit my father would want," he said. "Come see me sometime. We should talk about your future."

"I think we should talk about Light Squad's future," Merit said. "Your success isn't because of one person. It's because of who you are as a unit."

"I'd be happy to talk, but what about the manuals?" Cam asked, wanting confirmation on why Light Squad had agreed to the challenge in the first place.

"You'll have them," Victory agreed.

"And the coin you promised?"

"That, too," Victory said with a feigned scowl of annoyance.

Cam smiled. "In that case, how about we celebrate tonight? Dinner. All of us."

Merit chuckled. "Our squad doesn't have much to celebrate, but I'm happy to join you for a free meal."

"Meaning Victory is buying?" Weld said in a cheeky tone.

"No. That would be Kahreen," Victory said.

They all laughed—except for Kahreen, of course. By then Lord Queriam had finished talking, and the crowd began to break apart, chunks here and chunks there, drifting toward the exits. The two teams filed out of the coliseum as well, each unit headed to their private rooms.

"How did you know where the core was?" Jade asked as they were exiting the arena floor.

Cam explained. "The book Professor Grey lent to me on Plasminians. You know the one. It told me once that Plasminians and Spirairians have a talent for sensing Ephemera. Cores are condensed areas of Ephemera. I had to trust my instincts. I think Merit has that skill, too. He's a Spirairian, after all."

"A good skill to have," Weld said, sounding approval.

"A good skill for a good leader," Jade said.

"She's not wrong," Avia agreed, laying an arm over Cam's shoulders, hugging him briefly. It reminded him of when Pharis did the same. "You did well."

"I'm only as good as the people with me."

Pan nudged him in the stomach. "I think Avia is trying to give you a compliment. Just be quiet and accept it."

Cam laughed. "I can do that."

Boisterous laughter filled the Blind Pig. Other Novices had found out the squads from the challenge would be celebrating that night, and a whole bunch of them decided to show as well. Most every one of them was currently well past the point of getting liquored up and full-on drunk, slurring their words, laughing at stupid jokes, and stumbling about.

Even Light Squad wasn't immune. To make Cam's life easier, they had originally meant to only drink water, but with everyone else having a grand time, the liquor was soon flowing down their throats, too. Pan and Avia were talking animatedly, their eyes shiny, movements exaggerated, and their voices loud. With them was Merit, smiling faintly while he sipped whiskey, listening like he usually did rather than speaking. Jade and Weld were laughing, his arm around her waist, the two of them flushed and excited as they leaned in close to Charity and some of her friends, talking over the challenge.

Feeling like a visitor to the celebration of someone he didn't know, Cam sat in a shadowed corner where no one paid him any mind. He observed the crowd, their happiness, watching in a mixture of emotions. Who would he have been if not for Honor and that Pathway?

Lilia would still be alive, but what about him? Would he still be in Traverse, having eventually gained the community's respect?

It was certainly possible, if not probable.

He sighed. The past was written and there was no way to change it. Better to simply accept what was and not dwell on what might have been. Beside, shouldn't he be thinking about the present? Light Squad's triumph and the reason for tonight's party? Lilia wouldn't want him brooding on the person he'd once been. She would want him focused on the person he was and could yet be.

"You're not drinking?" Victory said, holding two mugs of ale, offering one.

Cam didn't reach for it. Instead, he nudged out a stool for Victory. "I don't drink."

"Why not? Some kind of moral issue?"

"No," Cam said. He intended on leaving it there, something vague, but the melancholy of the moment had him unburdening himself. "There was a time when I thought myself worthless. I made myself into what I believed."

"What are you saying," Victory said, and his sharp gaze told Cam that he hadn't drank more than he could handle.

"It's means I can't drink anymore. Ever."

Victory didn't respond at once, taking a large swig of his ale. "Pity. I wouldn't mind sharing a drink with you. You're alright for a peasant." He grinned to take the sting out of his words.

Cam snorted. "And you're getting to be a decent sort for a stuffy noble." He gestured with his chin, to where Card stood with folded arms, glowering at the world. "At least you are compared to that git. Does he ever smile?"

Victory briefly glanced to where Cam had indicated. "I think he forgot how. Probably when that broomstick got shoved up his back passage."

Cam laughed, his humor ceasing an instant later when Charity stumbled in their direction.

"There you are." Her words were slurred and her face flushed. "What are you doing hiding in a corner?" She flopped into a chair.

Cam stood, afraid she'd try to sit in his lap. The last time she had, only Pan "accidentally" spilling water on his britches had gotten her off of him. "Victory and I were just figuring on whether your boy, Card, knows how to smile."

Charity made a moue. "He's not 'my boy,'" she replied. "And I couldn't care less if he knows how to smile, laugh, or suck his own—"

"Charity!" Victory cut in.

Like he'd known they'd been talking about him, Card came over. "Am I hearing right that Light Squad used True Bonds during the challenge?" he asked without preamble, addressing Cam.

"You heard correct," Cam answered, unsurprised that Card knew about True Bonds. It had been an unknown topic to him, but nobles like Card probably had all sorts of learning to which none of them was yet privy.

Card shook his head, looking disgusted. "Meaning we lost to people that were fighting with a handicap."

"No, you didn't," Cam said. "If anything, the True Bonds gave us an advantage."

"Card's right," Victory disagreed. "The reason no one uses True Bonds is because it makes you weaker."

"Yes, and no," Cam said, glad to have something to talk about. Anything to take his mind off the drinking going on all around him. "At Novice, we aren't weaker. We're just as strong, and the Bond lasts twice as long. But as we Advance, mastering our abilities will be harder. At Acolyte, we'll still only have the skills of a Novice. We won't close the gap until we're at least Glories."

"Then why do it?" Card asked, seeming genuinely curious.

"Because the Bond lasts twice as long," Cam repeated, like it was obvious. "Being able to fight harder and longer might be the difference between life and death."

"So could having better skills and abilities," Victory countered to Cam's earlier point.

"You're right," Cam said, "but it's a risk I'm willing to take. The entire team did."

"This is so *boring*," Charity said with a huff, wandering off to where Jade and Weld now seemed to be having an argument.

Cam watched them as they talked animatedly at one another. Whatever was going on between those two, it didn't seem healthy, at least not for Jade. He just didn't know what to do about it. Worse, there might not be anything he *could* do about it. Whatever had Jade glitched over Weld seemed like something she had to recognize and solve on her own.

"It still doesn't make sense," Card said to Cam, clearly confused.

"Well, if that doesn't make sense, wait until you find out that the rest of Light Squad has Crystal Tangs of Plasminia."

"No!" Victory said.

"Yes," Cam said, smiling. "Our professors advised and approved of the decision." He hedged. "It was mostly Professor Grey."

"Professor Grey," Card said, his voice full of unexpected admiration. "I spoke to her once. She's someone worth listening to."

"Besides, Plasminia doesn't make us weaker," Pan said, arriving with Avia and intervening in their conversation. He spoke louder than normal, his eyes bright from the liquor he'd consumed. "Well, it makes Cam weaker, but he's our strategist, not our fighter. He gets us where we need to be if we want to win."

"And we want to win," Avia added.

"And you really think this is the best approach?" Card asked.

"It's worked so far," Avia replied.

"My head feels like someone bounced rocks off of it yesterday and picked up again this morning," Pan said, looking pathetically cute as he slouched along next to Cam.

It was the day after the challenge, and Light Squad was making their way to the morning's final class. Other than Weld, who was whistling away at some tune, and Cam, who hadn't been drinking, the other three members of their group looked like something a cat might have dragged in. Classes so far—Kinesthia and Spirairia—had been painful as a burr in the backside for them.

It was all because of drinking too much, especially when they weren't used to it. Cam briefly wondered if he might suffer the same problem. After all, he hadn't touched alcohol in many months now.

"Did you drink extra water like I said?" Cam asked Pan.

"I couldn't," Pan said, despondent. "I wanted to, but even the thought of drinking makes me sick."

"Did you at least sip some?"

Pan nodded.

"Then keep doing that. You'll feel better soon."

"Is that the wisdom of experience?" Jade asked, her tone cross.

Cam shrugged. "It worked for me, but you don't have to listen if you don't want to." He tried to keep his tone level, but it was hard. Jade had been waspish toward him all morning. Well, not just him. Everyone, really. Especially Weld.

Speaking of Weld… he seemed happier than usual. Chipper as he whistled away. Smug even. Cam's eyes narrowed as his gaze went back and forth between Weld and Jade, wondering…

Jade caught him staring, and she wandered over to walk next to him. "Nothing happened that I didn't want to happen," she said to Cam, speaking in a hush and somehow guessing his suspicions. "We kissed. I wanted to. I might have wanted to do more, but…" She shrugged. "Maybe next time I will."

"Meaning you're planning a next time?" Cam hoped not. Weld didn't deserve a woman like Jade.

"Devesh, help me. I don't know." She rubbed her face. "He's wrong for me in so many ways. I know it, but I also can't seem to fix my feelings."

Cam gazed at her, not having a clue on what to say. "You like him that much?"

Jade chuckled darkly. "I can't stand him, but that doesn't mean I don't also want him." She shook her head. "It makes no sense. It's stupid. But thinking and feeling aren't always the same things."

Cam considered his years of drunkenness, of knowing how wrong it was and not being able to do a thing about it. Not wanting to either. He reckoned whatever mixed-up emotions Jade had toward Weld had to be something like that. He only hoped it didn't lead to self-destructive behavior, like his drinking had done for him.

He continued to worry about Jade as Light Squad entered the classroom for Synapsia. The cheery sunshine—bright enough to blind Cam for a moment—caused Pan, Avia, and Jade to groan. They covered their heads, eyes barely open as they slumped into their chairs. The whole time, Weld whistled his jaunty tune.

Professor Grey was waiting on them, empathetic humor on her face. "It looks like some of you had too much fun last night. Which means you'll be no good for anything this morning. So, why don't we have a discussion." She went to the windows, adjusting the blinds so they fell, shrouding the room in dimness.

Pan made a note of relief. "Thank you, professor."

"Of course." She strode back to the front of the class in that effortlessly graceful way of hers. "You can thank me properly by paying attention. Now. Who can tell me how a Novice becomes an Acolyte?"

Cam knew the answer. Everyone did. They'd covered it plenty of times by now. "A Novice becomes an Acolyte when they understand the difference between selfishness and selflessness."

"Those are merely words, Mr. Folde," Professor Grey said. "What do they actually mean?"

It sounded self-explanatory to Cam, and he frowned, not knowing how else to answer.

"Think of it this way," Professor Grey said, taking in his confusion. "What does it mean to be selfless versus selfish? Or better yet, is selflessness in all things your best and truest state?"

Usually about this time, Pan, the smartest of them, would chime in and answer the question, but right now, Cam wasn't sure his friend could even state his name if asked. Meanwhile, Jade and Avia stared straight ahead, appearing to be in private worlds of hurt. And Weld was no use. He never knew any—

"Selflessness is living for others," Weld said. "While selfishness is living for yourself." Cam stared at him in shock, and Weld caught him looking. He shrugged minutely. "I'm smarter than you think."

"Since when?" Cam asked.

Professor Grey cut off whatever Weld might have said in response. "You are correct, Mr. Plain. Those are the basic differences between the two. What about my second question? Is selflessness in all matters your best and truest state?"

Cam didn't think so. Very few things were correct in their most absolute sense. Devesh being the Most Holy was one, but there wasn't much else. Not even the truism of the sun rising in the east and setting in the west since there were stories of a time in Salvation's mythic past when the sun never rose nor set. Instead, it just hung in the sky, unmoving and blazing like the unholy hells until an unknown boy and his dragon had set it into motion. Then had come Rukh and Jessira to bring the world to life.

The same had to hold true for selflessness. It couldn't be for the best in all circumstances, although the world would be finer if it was. "Maybe it isn't true all the time," Cam said to Professor Grey. "But it should be."

"Really? Even if you sacrifice everything you have for others and live to regret your life after?"

Cam could tell she was referencing Tern. Early on in the academic year, he'd told everyone in Light Squad and their instructors what had happened to make him a Plasminia. "I would have regretted not trying to save Tern."

"And well you should. You were right to try and save him. Your mistake was not recognizing your danger, and that ignorance was what led you to a situation where there is no good answer. You couldn't be selfish and live with yourself. But what if you *had* been selfish, and Saira had saved Tern? What then?"

"She couldn't have saved him," Cam said, "but let's pretend she did. I wouldn't have felt as bad, but I'd know I was a coward whose friends couldn't count on him."

She nodded, accepting his answer.

"I wouldn't have felt like I was a coward," Pan said, speaking without looking up. "If I couldn't save my friend, and I knew I couldn't save him, then why would I want to risk death? We'd both die, and no one would live to regret anything."

"But I didn't know I couldn't save Tern," Cam said.

"Then Professor Grey is right," Avia said. It might have been the first time she'd spoken all morning. "You were ignorant, and it led you to a situation without any good answers."

"And that is what you must strive to avoid," Professor Grey said. "Learn. Gain wisdom. Gain knowledge. Grow so you're never without options. And consider this. Selfishness need not be evil. For example, if you had the means to feed a hungry man, would that not be good?"

Cam sensed a trap, but he couldn't see it. "Yes."

"What about teaching him to grow his own food but offering little of your own?" Professor Grey asked. "Which is kinder? Giving him what you have so you're both hungry? Or finding him a means to feed himself? Both can be simultaneously selfless and selfish. It depends on your notion of charity, yes?"

"It's a balance then," Pan said.

Professor Grey's smile was like a sunrise. "Correct, and finding that balance is the answer you need. It is how you Advance from Novice to Acolyte. And the answer isn't unchanging. It moves and shifts with your years and wisdom; in time with who you are and want to be. Accept these truths—that your answers to life's questions may not always be right; that doubt, which isn't always a sin, can be a blessing—and you'll have no trouble finding your own way to satisfying that first question."

47

For some reason Professor Werm was present for their first class of the day in Kinesthia. He'd never been there before, and Cam wondered at his presence now. He stood slightly before Saira and Professor Shivein, wearing his permanent smirk and appearing like he was the one who was going to lead their class this morning.

It was a week since the challenge, and spring was completely present, warming away any final chilly weather until winter felt like a distant, pleasant memory. The sun blazed down, not quite with summer's heat, but near enough to make Cam unhappy. Worse, no wind stirred the air, leaving the campus muggy from the flash thunderstorm earlier in the morning. The trees with their full foliage, the green grass, tall and thick, and the beautiful flowers in bloom made the uncomfortable weather a bit more bearable, but Cam wouldn't have minded a cool wind to lift the heat and humidity.

"Please, have a seat," Professor Werm said.

Cam shared an uncertain shrug with Pan. It wasn't what they normally did in Kinesthia. In fact, it was the opposite since it seemed like they were about to receive a lecture instead of working their bodies.

543

He mentally shrugged. They'd find out what was going on soon enough.

Cam seated himself, Pan and Jade to his right and Avia and Weld to his left.

Professor Werm spoke then. "I gave each of you an acorn at the beginning of the year," he said, displaying a wilted nut in his hand. "Your goal was to heal and grow the acorn into an oak. I'm sorry to say that won't be possible. Not this year." His lips tightened. "You've mastered forming True Bonds or come close enough. And at this point, you likely can no longer even cast the simpler Bond to just Spirairia. Meaning your progress will slow dramatically compared to other Novices. You won't be able to master your abilities well enough to heal the acorn like I challenged."

Light Squad had already figured on this, talking about it once or twice.

Cam raised his hand, gaining Professor Werm's attention. "Does this mean we won't graduate from our first year even if we Advance to Acolytes?" That was one thing none of them had reckoned might happen.

Professor Shivein was the one who answered. "In the opinion of the academy, if you Advance to Acolyte, then that's what you are: an Acolyte. But you'll be learning and mastering lessons others will call remedial for a long time after your Advancement."

The statement settled some of Cam's concerns.

"Does Master Winder approve of what we're doing?" Pan asked.

"Master Winder will have words to say, I'm sure," Saira said, dodging the question rather than answering it. "Your task is to concentrate on your work because there is a lot more to do. We're going to focus on fine muscle control this morning. Professor Werm will help."

"This is a kind of art in which all movements are slow and controlled," Professor Werm said, going on to demonstrate motions that didn't seem too hard. It was some swirling of his arms and legs. Nothing spectacular. "The goal isn't just to use your body, but also your Spirairia and Synapsia. You'll want to use the wild Ephemera that's all around.

Draw it inside, and although you can't capture it into your Source—not easily—allow it to blend with your True Bond. Then move as I do." He continued demonstrating.

Cam wanted to smirk, but he knew it best not to. The professor made it look simple, but it was probably anything but. In fact, Cam figured that when he tried to do as the professor was doing, he'd look like a bear trying to dance on ice.

"Gather," Professor Shivein said, a solid clap of his hands. To his side, he drew Cam, Weld, and Pan while Saira saw to Avia and Jade.

"The first movement," Professor Shivein said. "It may not seem like much but pay attention. Right hand ready to block. Left up high for a knife hand. Do you see?" He moved slowly, controlling his breathing. "Form your True Bond so you can properly utilize what we're teaching you."

"And what is that?" Weld asked.

"Control," Professor Werm answered. He'd started out with Avia and Jade and was now seeing to their group. "If you can learn it, it can make mastery of any aspect of Ephemera quicker. Even with a True Bond."

"Especially with a True Bond," Professor Shivein added. "You know these punches and throws already, and we'll eventually have you spar, but for now relearn them in this slow, measured way. Do it until your form is perfect. Then we'll go faster."

Cam formed a True Bond. He waited a beat, getting familiar with time's dilation, his strengthened muscles, and Ephemera's vast tapestry. It seemed like every week, he saw more and more of the woven world. Rather than catching mere wisps here and there, now it was as if everything glowed with Ephemera. It moved and bound creation, and since his journey was still young, there would be a time when what he currently saw would no doubt seem as dull and lifeless as a world without color.

A consideration for another time. Cam pushed away thoughts of the future and began mimicking Professor Shivein's motions.

But it was every bit as hard as he'd figured it would be.

He knew where his arms and legs were supposed to be, the balance needed, but going slow like this was difficult. Every instinct urged him to go faster. His mind and body wanted him to as well, but he kept his pace deliberate, recognizing how his earlier skepticism or even contempt for what Professor Werm had demonstrated was his arrogance talking.

"I can't do it," Weld complained.

"You can," Pan said. Of the three of them, he seemed to have the most grace with this kind of motion. Which made no sense since Pan wasn't exactly graceful.

"Remember to draw in the Ephemera touching you," Professor Werm told them.

Cam had forgotten and swiftly corrected his mistake. He inhaled deeply, allowing the wild Ephemera to penetrate his skin, enter his muscles, and grant him the control he lacked.

It worked because while his mind continued to race and his body still wanted to explode into movement, a pressure kept him feeling heavy, slowing him enough to move like he wanted. Cam grinned in delight, continuing on. Over time, he began to feel a burn in his legs, stomach, and shoulders. Holding the poses was harder in its own way than explosive movements.

"Good," Professor Shivein encouraged. "Master this art, and it will take you far in your Way into Divinity."

"How long will that be?" Cam asked.

Professor Shivein smiled. "Rukh Shektan was once asked that question by a friend who wanted to know how long it would take to become a master of a warrior's craft. Do you know Rukh's answer?"

"A lifetime," Cam said with a smile, having read the passage during a study session in the library.

Professor Shivein nodded. "And so it was. Just as mastery of Ephemera will take a lifetime. All art is mastered over a lifetime, but never perfected. Even living well takes a lifetime."

Later that same day, after a more standard class on Spirairia with Professor Werm, it was time for Synapsia. This, too, appeared to be typical since when Light Squad filed into their usual classroom, Professor Grey was already waiting for them. It was a truth that no matter how early Light Squad arrived, she was already there.

Professor Grey shut the door, muffling the conversations of all the other students trampling along and heading to their classes. She also drew the blinds, closing them for the most part and blocking the warm sunlight. Immediately, the room was cast in shadows, dulling the heat pouring in from outside and leaving the space more comfortable. Dust motes floated on stray sunbeams, shifting endlessly.

"Take your seats," Professor Grey said. "We will do something different today. I want everyone to form a True Bond."

Cam, seated between Pan and Avia, did as he was bid without hesitation. If Professor Grey said to do something, he did it. There was never a thought of questioning her.

Professor Grey paced before them, hands clasped behind her back, the dust motes moving aside for her. "You were wise to forge True Bonds. Same with your decision to add a Plasminia Tang. The reason centers around a truth you should all know. Do you know what it is?"

She gazed at them, her eyes intense, and Cam tried not to slink into his seat. When Professor Grey stared at them like this, her attention could be hard to handle.

Nobody seemed to know the answer, but Cam thought he might. He forced his posture upright and answered. "All is Ephemera and Ephemera is All."

Professor Grey nodded. "Very good, Mr. Folde. But what does it mean?"

"That everything is of Ephemera, which is why the word 'All' is capitalized."

"Is All a reference to Devesh?" Pan asked with a tilt of his head.

Professor Grey smiled, warm and open. "It is, and All is Him."

"Even the rakshasas?" Jade challenged.

"*All* is Him," Professor Grey repeated. "They are of Ephemera as much as you and I. It is their use of Devesh's Holy gift of Himself, the immortality of All things, that is the difference between you and them. A rakshasa's Way into Divinity utilizes a Tang titled Klevonia. Why can't you use it?"

The answer came in stages to Cam. "We can, but…"

"But what, Mr. Folde?"

He frowned, trying to parse his thoughts together. "But we'd have to practice the Way into Divinity that the rakshasas use, and isn't it antithetical to our own?"

"Antithetical?" Pan said, smiling in his direction. "Look at you, using big words."

"You think the rakshasas Way into Divinity is antithetical to your own?" Professor Grey asked. "And that's why you can't use their Tang?"

Her response couched as a question told him that he wasn't on the correct path.

"Or maybe we can use their Tang, but…" Cam's inspiration fluttered to a stop, and he slumped in his seat. "I don't know."

"But you were so close," Professor Grey murmured. "The reason you can't use Klevonia has nothing to do with separate Paths into Divinity. It has to do with choice. We choose the Tangs we use, but what if there were no need for things such as Tangs?"

The question earned a snort from Weld—of course. He was seated next to Jade, had tried to throw his arm over the back of her chair, but she'd flung it off. Beyond that, he should know better by now than to dismiss any of Professor Grey's questions or pronouncements.

"Divines don't use Tangs," Cam said, chasing after his earlier thinking once again.

"Correct," Professor Grey said, leaning forward like she was silently urging him to find the rest of the answer.

"We aren't Divines," Weld said.

"No, but they weren't always Divines either," Cam said, wanting the other man to shut up so he could think. "They were like us once. Novices, but when they Advanced to Divines, they no longer needed Tangs because All is Ephemera and Ephemera is All." He continued to pick away at the answer until… He broke into a grin. "Meaning there's no need for any kind of Tangs. We *can* use Klevonia if we wanted because in the end, it is still of Ephemera."

"Exactly," Professor Grey, smiling his way, which had Cam wanting to cheer for himself. "And the earlier you recognize this truth, the greater your chances of surpassing the Awareness of a Divine."

"What Stage is greater than Divine?" Jade asked.

"Holy Servant, for one, but prior to that, there is another, written about but with no true confirmation. It is called Heavenly Heathen, and history writes that there have only been two of them."

"Heavenly Heathen?" Cam blurted. "That's a terrible name."

"I didn't choose it," Professor Grey said, appearing cross for some reason. "The two who first achieved that Stage decided upon the name."

"Who were they?" Avia asked.

"We've spoken about them a few times," Professor Grey answered. "The founders of Winder Rainen's lineage. William and Serena Wilde. Myths say that they were the first and only Divines to Advance beyond that Awareness. Myths also say that later on, they followed in the footsteps of their gurus, Rukh and Jessira, and became Holy Servants in their own right."

Professor Grey spoke on, regarding a few more topics, and after the class ended, Light Squad exited the classroom and building.

They made their way toward the cafeteria, joining a campus full of strolling students. Most of them were dressed in light clothing, and they laughed easily. The morning's mugginess had been driven away by a gentle breeze blowing off Lake Nexus, and the day had transformed into one that was beautiful. Puffy clouds wandered the rich, deep blue sky, which was almost indigo, and flowers bloomed, waving their petals under the influence of the wind, their lovely fragrance filling the air.

"How does Professor Grey know so much?" Pan asked.

"It's strange," Jade said, sounding agreement. "How can one person have read so much? Or maybe she's the world's finest librarian." She chuckled.

"Sometimes, I wonder if she's more powerful than my father," Avia said, her voice quiet.

Weld scoffed. "She's just a Glory."

"Does she strike you as just a Glory?" Cam asked.

"Then what is she?"

Cam shrugged. "Maybe she's a Divine in hiding? I don't know."

"We could use a few new Divines on our side," Weld muttered. "Make it a whole lot simpler to deal with the rakshasas."

On this, he and Cam were in perfect agreement.

Three weeks after the challenge, Light Squad chatted and joked among themselves as they headed for their first class of the morning. Clouds had rolled in overnight, and a gusting wind blew, smelling of moisture as it swirled the Kinesthia field's tall grass, rustled the trees, and whipped about in occasional heavier gusts.

Cam figured a storm might be brewing. Another spring squall perhaps since in the distance, heavy waves crashed higher than normal against the piers of the city docks. But if so, the storm didn't look to be making landfall until somewhat later in the day. Plenty of time to finish the class on Kinesthia, but Spirairia would have to be held indoors instead of by the greenhouse like Professor Werm often preferred. And then—

"What's he doing here?" Weld growled, interrupting his thoughts. It was easy to see who he was scowling about.

Card Wolver was standing in front of Saira and Professor Shivein, arms folded, watching Light Squad enter the Kinesthia field. His features were blunt and hard to read, but he seemed annoyed.

Then again, being annoyed seemed to be Card's normal mood, so who knew if this was any different?

"I'll be joining Light Squad," Card declared when they reached him.

"You're joining what?" Cam asked, sure he'd heard that wrong.

"And who invited you?" Weld said, glowering like Card had stolen his drinking money.

"He asked to join," Saira said, "and I granted permission. You now have six members. It makes sparring and other training simpler."

"You'll finally have someone to dance with," Avia said to Weld with a snicker.

"Listen, pretty lady," Weld said. "I dance plenty at night. I've never had any complaints."

"Enough," Card snapped. "I didn't join Light Squad to listen to a fool's obvious failings. I came to learn how you five have continued to defeat your betters."

Weld squawked, preparing to reply, but Cam elbowed him in the gut. "Let it go," he said before addressing Card. "If you want to join Light Squad and learn our ways, you might want to stop thinking of yourself and others like you as our betters. Jade and Avia are every bit as noble as you, and even if they weren't, even if they were peasants like me and Weld, it wouldn't make you better than us." He kept his eyes locked on Card's, not retreating an inch.

Card stared right back. The tableau held for a few seconds longer. No one spoke. But in the end, it was Card who looked away first. "As you say, peasant. I am here to learn from you. You and Light Squad handily defeated the best of the noble class. I will accept that I am not your better. For now."

"Well, that's mighty kind of you," Weld said with a scornful snort.

"I'm sure you boys wish to mark your territories," Saira said, "but we have work. Jade. You and Pan will spar. Weld goes against Avia. Card against Cam. No weapons. Get your gear on." She pointed to shin guards, helmets, and leather chest pieces.

Cam wasn't the best at unarmed combat, but even just a few weeks of learning Professor Werm's slow, controlled movement-based art had done him a world of wonders. He wasn't yet able to hold his own against Jade or Avia, but he could manage against Pan and Weld. Let's see what Card could bring. He had his reputation, but Cam had fought him during the challenge. The man was impressive, but he wasn't an Adept in hiding.

"Are we allowed to Bond our Tangs?" Cam asked before they got started.

"Do as you will," Professor Shivein said. "Just don't hurt one another too badly."

Card smiled, the grin of a predator. "I promise not to hurt the runt too badly."

"Who you calling runt?" Cam demanded. He stared down his nose at Card, who was a few inches shorter.

Card didn't reply, merely cracking his knuckles.

Cam rolled his eyes at the display even while creating a True Bond. He retreated until his mind and body were one, falling into the rhythms of what Professor Werm had taught. *Control. Detachment.*

Card came forward, flicking a lefthand jab. Another. A testing kick.

Cam didn't bite. He figured the other man was trying to gauge his distance and gain a sense of his timing. Another lefthand jab, and Cam circled to his right, away from the power loaded up in Card's dominant hand.

He sent a questing kick to the other man's calf. It was checked. Card had his Bonds going as well, but it wouldn't do him any good.

"You know your Bonds won't last as long as mine," Cam told him.

"Is that how you'll win? Through a coward's ploy?" Card asked.

Cam smirked at the obvious attempt to get a rise out of him. But in truth, he didn't intend on outwaiting Card. He intended on beating him. A jab had Cam leaning back. Card shot behind it, trying to snag a single leg. He latched on. Cam hopped up, leaning on Card's shoulders. Made the other man carry his entire weight. It was mostly to avoid the coming sweep.

As soon as the attempted sweep was done and gone, Cam braced off his leg, twisting, getting chest-to-chest with Card. He shifted. Card followed, but...

There. His grip slipped, and Cam got his leg free. Just in time to eat a hard right. His vision blurred, but he followed his training and his instincts. He gave ground, circling right. A left hook nearly took off his head, but Cam shifted minutely and avoided the blow.

His vision cleared. He snapped off a jab of his own, catching Card but doing no damage. The man ate the punch and kept on coming. *Fine*. If Card's head was a rock, what about his body?

Cam ripped a hook to the stomach—Card didn't even grunt—followed with an uppercut that missed. Card tried a step-in elbow. Cam leaned away, taking a softer blow on the very end. Again came the attempt for a single leg. Cam defended better this time.

He briefly held a plum clinch, but Card shrugged out of it, firing another jab followed by a left kick to the body. The last blow landed. Cam grunted, trying not to show his pain.

But Card moved like the wolf in his last name. He knew when his foe was injured. He pressed forward, getting in close. Cam grabbed wrists, checked a rising knee. Chest-to-chest again. Cam slammed a shoulder into the shorter man's face. Again. A third time.

Card broke away, not liking that position. Cam was the one to press forward this time. He feinted a shot at Card's legs followed by a slow jab. The whole time he kept his eyes on the other man's legs. It got Card moving, thinking. Another feint for a shoot. Card's arms dropped. Cam slammed a kick into Card's head, stunning him.

"Time!" Saira said. "Switch partners. You have fifteen seconds to rest."

"You got me good at the end," Card said, sounding both admiring and surprised. "I thought you were just the strategist for Light Squad."

"He is," Pan said, joining their conversation, "but that doesn't mean he can't fight."

"I lose more than I win," Cam said with a shrug. "Which is fine for now."

Card barked laughter. "You show me someone happy with losing, and I'll show you a loser."

"Rukh said that," Cam replied. "But who said I was happy with losing? You sometimes learn more from losing than winning."

"He's right," Saira said, overhearing their conversation. "Success without losses can make a person complacent."

Card scoffed. "So what should I have learned today?"

"Don't ever take your opponent lightly," Cam said.

48

Another month at the academy passed in a blur. It was a month of making the best of having a new member of Light Squad, one who wasn't easy to get along with. Card Wolver was either the youngest codger Cam had encountered, or he was just an absolute grump. The other option—that he might maybe, somehow, possibly be a decent sort underneath his gruffness—was too stupid to allow. The only good part about it all was how much Weld disliked Card. He cared for him less than anyone else in Light Squad, but Cam didn't care to learn why.

The month with Card also saw Light Squad continue to figure on how to use their True Bonds better. It wasn't so much learning new skills as it was on quickening their old ones. They also had to catch Card up on how to make the Bond. Once he was told by Professor Grey what the reasoning was, he quickly changed his grumpy tune about what he thought was right and wrong when it came to the topic.

It was clear as day that Card respected anything Professor Grey had to say about Ephemera, or most anything, really. She might have even been the reason he'd ditched Victory's unit to join Light Squad.

Cam didn't know, and he didn't care. He had worries of his own. And he was thinking on them on a morning like any other. Light Squad was practicing at the Kinesthia field. It was sprints, lifting, and other exercises meant to increase stamina and strength. Beyond the hard training, a pleasant chill filled the air, but Cam wasn't feeling pleasant. Nor did he care for the deepening spring or the early fog lifting from the overnight rain.

His mind was focused on how to reach Acolyte, and so far, he had no notion. It didn't make him feel any better that no other Novice had Advanced either because it was only a matter of time. Those who were likely to reach Acolyte would do so soon, and he wanted to be in that category.

"We only have three more months to Advance," Pan said during a break in the exercises, speaking like he could read Cam's mind.

"I know," Cam replied after chugging water. "It's all I can think about."

"You're right to be worried," Card said, not looking as wrung out as Cam felt. "You are a Plasminian, and there has never been one who Advanced in Awareness to Acolyte."

"Which means I'll be the first," Cam vowed.

"I'm sure you will," Pan said, offering his encouragement like he usually did.

"I sure hope so," Cam replied with feeling. "I hope we all do. Professor Grey says we can, so I have to believe it's true."

Card nodded. "If Professor Grey says you can, then you will."

"What does Professor Grey say?" Jade asked.

Weld trailed her like a lost puppy. During the past month, their relationship—whatever weirdness they had going on—had taken another turn. This time it was Weld who stared after Jade instead of the other way around. It gave Cam hope that maybe—finally—Jade wasn't so fixated on her feelings for Weld. But he also figured it wasn't so likely as that. Those two had a bizarreness between them that defied normal reckoning.

"If Advancing to Acolyte was just a matter of will and

decision-making," Pan explained in reply to Jade's question between munches off a stick of celery.

Cam didn't want to know where he might have been hiding the food since Pan didn't wear much in the way of clothing.

Any comment was disrupted by a high-pitched scream from over-head. The noise had everyone sighting the sky, although Cam already knew what the roar meant. Master Winder was stopping by to visit.

Cam straightened, not wanting to be hunched over any when his sponsor visited.

Master Winder landed, appearing no different than before: hand-some, hair trimmed short, fit, and of medium build. But there was a worry lurking on his face, a deep concern that had Cam fearful. Anything that could cause the Wilde Sage to be worried couldn't be good news.

Master Winder marched over to Saira and Professor Shivein, bark-ing at them right when he got there. "Rumor says you've taught the Novices the True Bond? Is this true?"

"It is," Saira said calmly, not backing down or appearing the least bit intimidated. Meanwhile, Professor Shivein looked like he wanted his shell back so he could hide inside it.

Master Winder blew out a frustrated breath. "Why?"

Cam eased off a few paces away from Master Winder and Saira. So did everyone else. All of them shared expressions of mingled worry and even fear.

"Because it's what's best for them," Saira replied. "All of their pro-fessors agreed to this, even Werm, and you know how conservative he can be. This is how they can become their best selves."

"But only if they survive," Master Winder said, his voice now as even-keeled as hers. "You know how dangerous their lives will be. They need every advantage we can give them."

"And I'm giving them that advantage," Saira said, growing a mite hot. "Their lives are not yours to spend as you see fit. They have dreams and aspirations—"

"I spend no one's lives," Master Winder snapped. "You of all people should know better. And True Bonds would be perfect for them if they had the time to grow to Glories with no danger. But even then, they still need to train in live situations. And those exercises can be dangerous. So again, I ask why?"

"Because Golden, this continent, is not overrun by boils and rakshasas," Saira said. "Not like Sinane nearly was. You and the Sage-Dukes have done well to keep the situation under control. So why not allow the younger generation to learn in a slower, better fashion? We have the time, do we not? Besides, you yourself use True Bonds."

"I started when I was an Adept," Master Winder said, rubbing his chin. "And had to relearn all I'd learned prior to that."

"And yet, the True Bonds made you a more powerful Sage."

Master Winder's eyes seemed to go distant. "Yes, they did. They most certainly did." His attention seemed to snap back to the here and now. "How well have they learned?"

"The True Bonds?" Saira asked. "Well enough. They're nearly as fast at forming them as they once were a regular Bond. Only the newest member of Light Squad, Card Wolver, is still learning. He's smart, though. He'll catch on."

Master Winder nodded. "Excellent. Then they can help with another training exercise. This one will be dangerous, not just for Light Squad but also for you and Shivein. I need the two of you."

"What's going on?" Shivein asked.

Master Winder glowered at nothing for a moment before pinching the bridge of his nose, seemingly collecting himself. "A challenge unlike any other. One not seen in many decades."

"What kind of challenge?" Cam asked. He didn't want to speak out of turn, but he led Light Squad. It was only right for him to ask the questions that needed answering.

"The dead core that you and Pan came across is alive again," Master Winder said, shaking his head in self-directed disgust. "We should have destroyed it completely, not just lanced it. There are now three rakshasa Sages defending it, including Nailing. And as close as it is to Coal Pass, they can bisect the duchy of Charn if we don't stop them.

There are other rakshasa Sages building their own power within the duchy as well, which means Sage-Duke Shun won't be able to help us. We'll have to deal with Nailing on our own."

"Light Squad has to deal with a Sage?" Weld asked, providing the stupid question of the day.

Master Winder scowled. "Of course not. That task falls to me. I'll give you more details as I learn them, but Light Squad won't be expected to take part in any battles. Nevertheless, I need your help. Gather whatever supplies you feel necessary. I'll anchor line you to where you should be. We leave in two days."

An instant later, he soared into the sky, lost to sight within seconds.

"Well," Card said. "Maybe I should have stayed in Victory's squad."

Later that day, after supper and with darkness having fallen, Cam called a meeting of Light Squad. They gathered in his quarters. In addition, their professors were also present; all of them meeting in order to discuss what to do about Master Winder's proclamation from earlier in the day. Cam wanted to review what they'd need in order to survive the coming battle. He sure hoped someone had some good answers.

"Thank you for coming," he said, settling next to Saira on the room's leather couch.

"Of course," Professor Grey said, seated on the other side of the coffee table in one of the high-backed chairs with Professor Shivein in the other one.

"I'm not certain what I can do to aid you," Professor Werm said. He shared the dining room table with Card, Weld, and Jade. "I am no warrior, and I don't have the education of one, either."

"You can still give us advice," Cam said. "You know more than most about True Bonds. What limits we might have because of them."

"Before any of that, the question we must answer is what will Avia and Jade do?" Saira asked.

"What do you mean?" Avia asked, seated on the floor alongside Pan. For once, he wasn't munching on anything.

"I mean, Master Winder isn't your sponsor," Saira replied. "He isn't in charge of your status. You don't need to do whatever it is he wants of Light Squad." She turned her gaze to Card. "The same goes for you, Mr. Wolver."

"I'm going," Card said. "The Wilde Sage might simply want us in reserve for mop up duty, but it's still an opportunity. I just never expected to have one come my way until I was at least an Adept. I won't run from this."

"Do the other noble Novices feel this way?" Cam asked him.

"The ones who want to Advance into greatness do. Victory, Charity, and Merit, for sure. A lot of them actually."

Cam had never known. "So when we lanced a boil…"

"They were jealous and impressed."

"Why is it so important to them?" Weld asked.

"Because of the core," Card answered. "Even after it's lanced, it still contains enough Ephemera for a Master to Imbibe and possibly reach their maximum potential."

"Which we did," Pan said.

"And that's why I'm coming," Card replied.

"There's no guarantee we're receiving another core," Cam reminded him. "Chances are we won't."

"What about the two of you?" Saira asked Avia and Jade.

"I'm going," Avia answered, like the question shouldn't have required asking.

"Same," Jade added.

"And you know we're going," Saira said, indicating herself and Professor Shivein. "Rainen sent some further information."

"Master Winder needs us," Professor Shivein added. "This boil is far more dangerous than the one at Surelend. As you heard, it is defended by Sages, not Glories. There will be Crowns there, too. More rakshasas than we've ever fought in a single battle before. Master Winder will have to wage an all-out assault."

"I wish I could come," Professor Grey said, sounding upset.

"Why can't you?" Weld asked in a tone just short of a demand.

"I made a promise long ago to not raise my hand against another," Professor Grey said. "To abstain for a time from violence. It is my dharma."

She was holding to her principles, and Cam could respect that. But still, he knew how powerful Professor Grey likely was, and having her fight alongside Saira and Professor Shivein would have eased his mind.

"Regardless," Professor Shivein said. "Master Winder wants Light Squad to help in other ways. To help with evacuation of a nearby town, care for the wounded, and fight only as a last resort. As much as possible, he wants you out of danger, but danger might still find you. Be cautious when we arrive."

It was the most Cam had ever heard Professor Shivein say in one go, and the unexpected compassion and warmth had him blinking, teary-eyed.

"So, we're all going then?" Cam said, repeating the question for the sake of repeating it rather than actually needing the confirmation.

"One thing you should understand," Saira began. "I don't know how the battle will proceed, but even if we're victorious, if you—particularly Master Winder's charges—are injured too badly to Advance to Acolyte, you may not have a place here next term."

Cam shared a startled look with Pan before blurting out a single word. "Why?"

"Will Master Winder really do something like that?" Avia asked, speaking on the heels of his words.

"Rainen has commitments and decisions that have led him to behave in ways that he once didn't," Saira answered.

Cam wasn't sure what that meant, but it didn't sound good for him and Pan. "Behave in ways that he once didn't? That doesn't inspire a lot of confidence," he told Saira. "And you regressed from Crown to Glory because of doubts about what he told me to do."

"You can trust him," Professor Shivein declared, his voice firm and certain. "While closing boils and killing rakshasas is his main focus, he'll still do his best to see you safe."

Cam wasn't so sure about that.

Saira must have caught on to his skepticism. "You are right to have doubts, but in this Shivein is right. If Rainen says he will keep you safe, then he will keep you safe."

"But it also means we have to succeed on both fronts," Pan said. "We have to help with this boil, no matter how small the danger to ourselves, and we have to Advance."

"And you can do both," Professor Grey said. "You have it in you. Trust yourselves." She stared about the room, her gaze resting on each member of Light Squad. "You have accomplished mighty deeds. I don't need to list them."

"We don't mind if you do list them," Pan said with a cheeky grin.

Cam chuckled. He would have expected Weld to say something like that, not Pan.

"I don't think that's necessary," Professor Grey said with an answering smile. "But you have a leader who can keep you safe. Your own abilities are without equal at your Stage. You are strong and courageous. Those are the qualities that saw you win all these other times. And those same qualities will see you through this Trial as well. Have faith in one another."

Cam's glance fell on Weld. He had faith in every other member of Light Squad—even Card. But Weld? He wasn't so sure he felt that way about him. But he also wasn't fool enough to let any part of his thinking show on his face.

"Professor Grey is right," Cam said, meeting the eyes of each member of Light Squad. "We've accomplished mighty deeds, which means *we* are mighty. And whatever boil Master Winder wants us to help lance, we're going to lance it! Ain't no chance we're going down! You hear me!"

"No chance!" Light Squad roared in answer.

"No chance!" Cam repeated.

"No chance!"

The meeting in Cam and Pan's quarters ended once Light Squad had a list of materials they'd need to take with them on the expedition. Since traveling would be via anchor line, they could pack light. They'd want all their weapons, though. A handful of short spears for everyone—wouldn't hurt to have a spare or three—swords and shields and bows with at least a few quivers full of arrows.

"I'll see you in a little while," Professor Shivein said to Cam.

"Yes, sir."

"Mr. Folde. A word," Professor Grey said after Professor Shivein exited.

By now the living room had emptied, including Pan, who was in his room.

"Yes, ma'am," Cam said, wanting to stand at attention for some reason.

"You did well," Professor Grey said. "You gave your squad purpose, certainty, and hope. Not all commanders can manage such a trick."

"Thank you, ma'am." Cam said, unsure of the conversation's direction. Not that he minded Professor Grey's praise. He loved it actually. It reminded him of a momma's kind words. Of course, to really know if that was true, his own momma would need to have stayed a part of his life instead of walking out like she'd done. Not that he ever thought of her much. He hadn't thought of her in years, in fact. But who would he be if she had remained home to raise him?

He shook off musings on his momma when Professor Grey gave him an assessing gaze. "I wasn't simply speaking to hear my voice when I said you're a good leader. I hope you realize that."

"I think so," Cam replied, immediately noticing the hesitancy in his voice. He firmed his tone. "I know so." He wasn't the person he'd been when he'd arrived at the academy, uncertain, frightened of failure, and nearly convinced he was a curse to those around him. Some small part of him still might feel that way—probably always would—but in terms of confidence when it came to battles… in that, he was solid.

Professor Grey cocked her head, like she could peer into his mind. "I think you do. And I'm pleased to hear it. But recall what I said about the fruits of your labor."

"To think on them without concern?" It still struck Cam as an impossibility.

"Yes," Professor Grey replied. "It's easier said than done, but it helps when you're sure that success will occur. When your mind is unoccupied about fears about the future because there is only room for the expectation of success."

Her words confirmed some of what Cam had come to believe as well.

"There can be weakness in such a way of thinking, though," Professor Grey continued. "What happens if you do fail, and inevitably, you will? In such a circumstance, you may break."

This, too, Cam had considered. "I won't."

"You won't fail? Or you won't break?"

"Both."

"Ah, yes. The ignorance and optimism of youth," she said in a teasing tone, sobering a moment later. "We will talk more when you return. About the next step on your Way into Divinity. Learning your truest self."

"My truest self?" Cam didn't know what she meant by that.

"Meditate upon it. Trust what you see within your heart. Then you will know."

After Professor Grey left, Cam hustled to the cafeteria where Professor Shivein wanted to meet with him. The campus was quiet and dark, except for the lighted pathways. The moon shone amongst a nest of stars, like a diadem in a crown. Cam paused a moment to stare upward. Funny. Until now, he'd never considered the moon in that way, probably because he'd seen it all his life. But it was lovely. The entire heavenly sky was, with the lustrous stars shimmering like a curtain of light.

Cam continued to stare a moment longer, enjoying the nightscape. The gauzy clouds highlighting the moon's iridescent sheen. The wind, cool but not cold, pulling at his clothes. The small gatherings of students, murmuring and laughing. And the stillness and peace of being alone but not lonely.

He pushed off his appreciation, recalling the need for haste. Moments later, he approached the cafeteria, which was open at all hours, even in the middle of the night. The lights inside were turned down, though, and the area around it was empty of anyone but a few crickets chirping. Inside, Cam discovered a handful of workers cleaning, sweeping, and prepping, but all told there were less than a quarter of the number of employees who usually filled out the cafeteria during its busy hours.

And other than Professor Shivein, there were no patrons within. A chair was pushed out for Cam, and he seated himself.

"We've spoken some about my past and my future," Professor Shivein began. "And I've spoken to Saira and Professor Grey, too. And what I've come to accept is that if I wish to Advance, then first I must regress. I must become an Adept and form a Plasminia Tang."

It wasn't the conversation Cam had expected them to have. He had come here, thinking they'd talk about the battle they'd soon have to face. So, what came out in response to Professor Shivein's announcement wasn't Cam at his brightest. "I thought you'd already decided that."

Professor Shivein quirked a grin. "I was still wavering on the matter. Like I told you once. I wasn't sure the risk would be worth it. But, you see, the thing is, once I was freed from my life as a rakshasa, I've always wanted to help destroy boils."

"Why didn't you?" Cam asked. Professor Shivein was a Glory, after all.

"Because while I'm a Glory, I'm merely a Glory Greater. Only my Kinesthia is at Glory Stage. My others are at Acolyte. I'm weak."

"But I've seen you use Spirairia at much greater potency," Cam protested.

"When you're an Adept, you can 'borrow' Ephemera from one Tang to strengthen another. For a short time, I can utilize Spirairia as if it was Advanced to Glory. Certainly not to the potency and expertise of a true Spirairian, but enough to defend myself. And with Kinesthia at Glory, I can impress my mandate and enforce my will on my immediate surroundings." He waved aside Cam's raft of questions. "I'll explain some other time."

Cam closed his mouth with a click. He itched with curiosity. They'd never discussed any of this in any of their classes. In addition, while Cam could believe many things about Professor Shivein, weak wasn't one of them. But still, if he really was just a Glory Greater, then how he reckoned himself was in some ways true. For a Glory, he was weak. It also explained why he was willing to regress and claim a Plasminia Tang.

But it would also cost him. Pain and loss of power were the least of what he would have to pay. The worst would be the possibility that he couldn't Advance again later on. It could easily happen. It all depended on if Professor Shivein could find an answer to the question separating Adepts from Glories. To understand the proper difference between giving and receiving, which was also the first block in eventually becoming a Sage.

"Why do you want to destroy boils so bad?" Cam asked.

Professor Shivein stared at him like he'd offered a question only Weld could be stupid enough to ask. "Because they're evil. Rakshasas are evil. I know this better than most."

"What is evil?" Cam asked. He had a pretty good notion, but it was always good to ask someone who'd lived more.

"That's a deep question," Professor Shivein said. "One I don't know how to properly define with words, but I can answer it based on actions. And the actions of a rakshasa are evil. We must oppose them. They steal the very essence that makes us divine. How is that not evil?"

"It's not right," Cam said, thinking on Lilia's death. The rakshasa wolves who had murdered her had been evil, and they had to be opposed, just like Professor Shivein was saying.

"What do you want to do?" Cam said. "Not about opposing evil. We've planned out what we can about the boil we're about to face. I mean, what do you want to do? About regressing. If I can help, I will."

Professor Shivein gave a grave inclination of his head. "I told you that I would grant Light Squad my Ephemera. I'm going to have to go back on my promise. Saira will need it more than you."

"For when she tries to Advance back to Glory."

"Exactly. No offense intended, but she is a special person. Worthier than the rest of you."

"No offense taken." Especially since Cam agreed with Professor Shivein.

49

"**Y**ou have everything?" Cam asked Pan, who was seated on the floor like always.

"I think so." Even as he said the words, Pan rifled through his packs, checking one last time. A moment later, he nodded. "I'm ready."

But he didn't look ready. He looked as nervous as Cam felt. All of Light Squad did. Cam had seen it during tonight's supper when they had shared a final meal. There had been a frenzied edge to their conversation and laughter, and it had only heightened when folks like Victory, Charity, and Merit had stopped by to give them their best and voice rueful complaints about how they wished they were going, too.

Cam hadn't believed them. Despite what Card said about how he and other nobles would be grateful for a chance to lance a boil, that claim had never rang true. And it turned out Cam was right to distrust that statement. The relief that Charity, Victory, and Merit felt about the fact that they *weren't* going had been as obvious as creepy on a spider.

Not that Cam could blame the nobles for feeling that way.

Truthfully, he wished Light Squad wasn't going either. The boil in Surelend had been dangerous enough, but now they'd be facing off against one defended by Sages and Crowns. Cam's lips tightened at the

567

notion. Even the dullest person could calculate what that meant. There would be a whole lot more rakshasas at this boil, and there would be plenty of deaths on both sides.

Sure, Master Winder didn't intend on them taking part in the actual battle. He wanted them in a supporting role. But based on everything Cam had read on military history and the mock-combat games Professor Grey had them play, plans went out the window once the first sword was swung. All of it meant that Light Squad wasn't going to be safe. As Novices, they would almost certainly be the weakest of anyone on the battlefield—be they rakshasas or Ephemeral Masters.

Cam glanced outside then, able to see past the windows since the main room in their quarters was darkened. The night-covered campus looked like a gentle dream; the paths lit by Ephemeral lanterns, the azaleas in bloom—the rhododendrons as well—and the trees with their leafy foliage. A wind stirred, likely holding a perfumed, floral scent.

It was so peaceful out there, and Cam wondered if he'd ever again see this place that had healed him in ways he'd never known he'd been injured. Who would he have been if he'd never come here? If nothing else, it was a reason to be grateful to Master Winder, grateful to the Ephemeral Academy itself.

Which was why his greatest regret was possibly not getting to come back. It was a fear he felt for everyone. Not just Light Squad, but all the Ephemeral Masters who'd be battling at the boil. He'd not met a single one of them, but he also believed that every one of them deserved a chance to live free and pursue happiness.

"We should get some sleep," Pan suggested.

Although Cam wasn't tired, he knew Pan was right. Master Winder would arrive early in the morning. Still, though. It was dark outside, but the night was young. Maybe it would be fine to stay awake a little longer?

A knock on the door interrupted Cam's thoughts, and he went to answer, already figuring on who it would be.

He was right. Avia and Jade stood beyond the threshold, and he stepped aside to let them enter.

"Y'all nervous about tomorrow?" Cam asked, once they settled on the sofa.

"I'm scared," Pan said.

His words got Cam fixing his gaze on him. The last time they'd been challenged with a lancing—Surelend—Pan had never made mention of any kind of fear. He'd been excited and glad. So had Avia and Jade. So Pan saying he was scared likely meant he finally had a clearer understanding on what they were fixing to face.

Jade chuckled low. "I doubt I'll be able to sleep more than a few winks."

"Which is why we're here," Avia said. "It's going to be a long night, no matter how short it is."

Cam smiled. "That doesn't really make any sense, but I know what you mean."

"Then it does make sense," Avia countered. "After all, you said you understood it."

"Or maybe *I* don't make sense."

Avia rolled her eyes.

"Where's Card and Weld?" Pan asked. "I wish they'd stopped by, too. We're a team."

The unhappy expression worn by Jade told Cam that Weld was likely off drinking and carousing. He scowled. Jackhole. He needed rest if he was going to be of any use tomorrow.

Jade's words, though, robbed him of his anger. "Weld is in his quarters. We checked on him. So is Card. We asked them to come, but they both said they wanted to rest."

"That's not what Weld said," Avia said with a smirk. "He asked Jade if she wanted to spend the night with him. She said no, and *that's* when he said he wanted to get some sleep."

"You turned him down?" Cam didn't know why it surprised him, nor why he was proud of Jade for doing so.

"Let's talk about something else," she said.

Cam shrugged. He might every once in a while think about Jade's relationship with Weld, but it wasn't his place to say anything about it. "Everyone pack enough food to last a week?" Cam said. "Hardtack and dried meat?"

"We have it," Avia said in a tone of exasperation. "Even though Master Winder will anchor line us to the site."

"But the village—Dander—should have food," Jade said, arguing a point Cam had thought settled.

"We can't count on that," Pan replied. "The villagers will take whatever they have for the road."

"And they can't leave us any?" Jade pressed.

"Maybe they can. Maybe they can't," Cam said. "And if they can, then we'll have extra supplies. If they can't, we'll be thankful for our foresight."

They spoke some more about what they might face and need, their fears and hopes, but eventually the conversation wound down.

"We're off to sleep," Avia said, glancing at Jade. "I'll make sure we go straight back to our quarters and not stop anywhere else. Especially anywhere distracting."

Jade scowled. "I don't need a minder."

"Yes, you do," Avia said, propelling her out the door. They left, still arguing.

Cam shook his head. "Those two… And Jade and Weld." Another shake of his head.

"Weld is too stupid to see what he could have if he could only not be—"

"Arrogant? Self-centered? Conceited?"

Pan grinned, gesturing with a stalk of bamboo. "All that and more."

A moment later, Cam sighed. "I hope whoever we end up with, we're worthy of them, and they're worthy of us."

"I hope so, too." There was a longing note in Pan's voice.

Cam could guess why. "Avia was especially pretty tonight, wouldn't you say?"

Pan's munching paused a moment. "Oh? I didn't notice."

Cam laughed. "Really? Somehow, I doubt that."

Pan deflated. "It doesn't matter anyway. Avia and I are of different lineages. She's an orca. I'm a panda."

"A panda-person," Cam corrected.

"Right. A panda-person." Pan flashed a grin. "And she's a fish."

"Not a fish," Cam replied with an answering grin.

Pan's humor left him with a heavy exhalation. "I'll only have a chance with her when I'm a Glory and take on a near-human form."

"Avia already has a near-human form."

"You see what I mean? And Avia isn't interested in furry folk."

Cam laughed. "Then we're going to have to help lance this damn boil, Advance, and Advance a couple more times so you aren't so furry."

"I like my fur," Pan said, sounding wounded.

"You like it enough to never have a chance with Avia?"

"I see your point."

The next day, Master Winder arrived in the middle of the morning just like he'd promised. The air hung still, and fog wafted off the dew-laden grass of the Kinesthia field. A cold snap had come along, and last night's rain made the morning feel like fall. Cam was glad he had made sure everyone had packed some cold-weather gear. They might need it since Dander was well north of Nexus and in the foothills of the Diamond Mountains. It would be at elevation, which meant it would likely also be cooler.

Master Winder's eyes flicked approvingly over the pack-laden mules standing next to each member of Light Squad. "I'm glad you had the foresight to bring supplies. You never know how these things play out."

"How many rakshasas are there?" Pan asked. They'd never found out when Master Winder had first told them about the boil, and Saira hadn't learned either.

"From our latest calculations, more than a hundred," Master Winder replied.

"Then we might have to dig in for a siege?" Cam asked.

Master Winder snorted. "I hope not. That's the last thing I want."

A siege might be the last thing Master Winder wanted—Cam didn't want one either—but he also had other concerns. "If the battle lasts longer than expected, can we bring in extra support? Can they?"

"Yes. And yes."

"Can we deny them their support or ambush it when they arrive?"

Master Winder wavered. "It's difficult, but maybe."

Cam nodded acceptance. "If we can, we should do both."

"We'll do our best," Master Winder said. "But it's not a discussion for now. It's time to go." He gestured, and a black line split the air, rotating and exposing a doorway into infinity. Within swirled a rainbow bridge. The anchor line.

Saira and Professor Shivein were the first ones through, and afterward, Master Winder halted Cam a moment. He had his head cocked like he was listening to a message. Apparently satisfied, he nodded, and Cam stepped toward the anchor line, tugging his mule after him. Before entering, he took a final breath to quiet his butterflies. Then it was time.

Cam stepped onto the anchor line.

His body stretched. A screaming sensation filled his ears, and the rainbow bridge extended beyond his sight. A twirling motion, sweeping through a helical curve curdled his stomach. Then he was out as freezing cold bit bone deep. The mule was on his heels, braying his unhappiness.

Cam empathized. His stomach heaved, and he worked to contain his gorge.

"Move," Saira barked from directly behind him. "Someone else is likely to exit any moment."

Startled out of his temporary misery, Cam quickly got himself and the mule hustling out of the way. He glanced back, and seconds later Card stepped out of the anchor line, green faced and shivering. His jaw was clenched, and his eyes were closed. Cam knew why. Card was trying not to vomit.

Saira repeated her admonishment, and Card hastily made his way over to Cam.

"That was my third time traveling by anchor line," Card admitted.

"How was it?"

"Not so fun."

Cam chuckled. Had Card just attempted humor? If so, it was a first.

The rest of Light Squad was exiting the anchor line, and while they did, Cam turned his attention to the area around them.

Light Squad stood in the midst of chaos. Dozens of people were charging about, shouting, gesticulating, and carrying on like their houses were on fire, which they were in a roundabout sort of way.

Cam scowled. These folks should have gotten gone days ago instead of waiting until the last minute. Their presence made a tough situation even more difficult.

A moment later, Master Winder stepped through the anchor line, letting it close behind him, glowering the instant he stepped foot in Dander. He spoke to Cam. "You see my problem. These morons should have left days ago." He indicated the motley band of villagers. "What a mess."

Cam shared Master Winder's frustration, but as had been the case in the other situations in which battle loomed, a calmness settled his nerves. "We can see them on their way," he told Master Winder. "Just tell us who we should look for, and we'll get them hustling off in whichever direction they should be going."

Master Winder threw him a grateful look. "Thank you. More than anything else, this is what I need from you and Light Squad. Follow me, and I'll fill you in. Afterward, a few miles east of town on Brewery Road, you'll come across our encampment. Come find me or if I'm not around, Perit Line. He's a Crown and the commander of the unit here, Sidewinder Company. He'll spell out what else I might want you to do."

Master Winder left Cam and Light Squad once he'd introduced them to Gard Singer, the mayor, who was a portly Acolyte—orange-eyed, bald-headed, and of middle-years. He struck Cam as being a bit flighty, but his heart seemed to be in the right place. He had stayed in Dander, sending his family to safety while he tried to convince the fools who had insisted on remaining behind on the need to evacuate.

It was too bad so many of the townsfolk hadn't bothered listening to him. Cam's job would have been a sight easier if they had. But then again, some people were just so sure they knew better than everyone else. In this case, they didn't. This battle might not pass them by, but it was only now, with time inching away, that they finally recognized the disaster they faced.

Cam followed Mayor Singer toward the largest inn—the mayor's home and business—within Dander. As they walked, he glanced around at the tumult, wishing wisdom could be beaten into a person. Light Squad trailed after him, likely also sharing those same wishes.

They entered the inn's main room, a place where folks would usually have a drink and dinner, but it currently rested lonely and empty. The bar on the right-hand wall stood unoccupied, and whatever liquor it might have once held was now removed, likely transported with Gard's family to wherever they had gone. In addition, given the stillness hovering over the room, the lack of occupancy, the space felt melancholy and dim, even with the bright illumination from chandeliers of Ephemeral lights.

Just then, a strange sensation distracted Cam, a tugging from the north. It faded after a few seconds, and he shrugged it off. *Probably nothing.*

"I don't know what we're going to do," Mayor Singer said, running his hands over his bald head. "The others will be here soon. Maybe you can talk some sense into them." His hands wouldn't stop moving, fluttering now to pat his portly belly.

Minutes later, a man entered the room, throwing open the front door like he owned the inn. He was reed thin, short, and wearing a proud sneer. Cam mentally sighed, already knowing how this would go. It didn't matter that the man had the orange Haunted-eyes of an Acolyte. He was an idiot, and an arrogant one at that.

"I am Regim Baid, the man said. "The assistant mayor."

"Assistant to the mayor," Mayor Singer corrected.

Cam didn't care what Regim's title was. He stood, staring down at the smaller man. "Are you the leader of those who chose to stay?"

Regim drew himself up, a proud expression on his features. "Yes, I am."

"No, you're not," Cam said, having sized up the situation. "You're the dumbass the others are hoping will take the blame for their stupidity. Tell me who sent you, and we'll settle this."

The man gaped in anger and upset. Cam didn't care. He had a job to do, and if there were some hurt feelings, so be it. As long as the people here got to leaving for safety.

"It would likely be Gob and Nona Felt," Mayor Singer said to Cam before turning to address Regim. "Where are they?"

Regim shot a quick glance toward the front door. "I speak for—"

Cam had heard enough. "They're outside, waiting on his report. Let's go." Sooner they got this done, the quicker Light Squad would be able to see where the real battle was to take place.

Cam shoved a squawking Regim out of the way and exited the inn. As expected, standing around the corner was a couple—a thickly built man with a beard hanging down to his belly and a woman of similar stature but less hirsute. They started when Cam sighted them. He paced their way, Light Squad at his back.

"I didn't tell them nothing," Regim shouted.

"He didn't have to," Cam said. "You two Gob and Nona Felt?" They shared a reluctant nod. "Good. What's it going to take to get this mess of people on the road in the next couple hours? I'm told you two hold some sway with them."

The man jutted his chin. "This is our home, boy. We want assurances that it'll still be standing when we come back."

Cam narrowed his eyes. He could understand the man's fears—empathized with them even—but it didn't mean he agreed any. "I can't make those kinds of assurances, but I can tell you that Light Squad"— he indicated the others standing behind him—"will give our all to see your town and homes protected." Before Gob could say anything else, he continued on. "Have you seen the boil? The rakshasas? Seen what a Sage can do if they're having a bad day?" Head shakes met his question. "I have. I was five. It was a battle between Master Winder and Borile Defent, the Silver Sage of Weeping. They wrecked a forest and flattened a mountain."

"I heard tell about that battle," Nona said. "They raged all up and down the duchy, tearing it apart."

Cam gave a nod. "Good. Then you know what can happen here, and why I can't give any assurances. I can't even assure you that I won't die when we face the rakshasas."

"We ain't stupid," Gob muttered.

Cam wasn't so certain about that. "Then you know what you have to do. Gather all the wagons you can find. If possible, one for each family still in Dander. If you don't have enough, then folks will have to share. Get them loaded with all the food you can muster." Cam glanced up and down the dusty street where people were still rushing about; pots, pans, clothes, and even a few paintings clutched in their hands. They ran into each other at times, tumbling to the ground and fixing to fight. Adding to the madness were unattended children, crying while their parents shouted.

"Sort them out," Cam said. "There have to be some others the people will listen to. Get them organized however you can." He glanced at the sun, which was still early in the sky. "Tell them that anyone still here by tomorrow will likely be dead by noon. Let them know Master Winder said so."

Mayor Singer went white. "Master Winder said that?"

Cam didn't like lying, but if he had no other choice to help the folks of Dander move along, then so be it. "He did."

"He never said that before," Gob said, sounding suspicious. "The boil is miles away from town. He said he figured the battle wouldn't even touch our walls."

"Have you been to the boil lately?" Cam asked.

"No," Gob said, looking like he hated giving the answer.

"Then you best understand this. There are three enemy Sages over there and over a hundred rakshasas. Miles away, sure. But with a battle among so many, and them wielding that kind of power, you want to wager that you'll be safe behind your walls?"

"But—"

"Time's burning," Cam interrupted. "I want those wagons filled full of people before noon, and I want this town emptied an hour later. Get it done." For some reason, maybe it was his tone or the gravity of the situation, but Gob, Nona, and Regim snapped to it, rushing off and calling for folk to give them their attention.

Mayor Singer made to follow, but he paused. "What happens when we leave? What if the rakshasas attack us on the road?"

"I don't know, but I can ask Master Winder to send a Crown to provide overflight and protect you and yours."

"I'm grateful for your help then," Mayor Singer said. "And I'm especially glad Gob and Nona listened to you." He frowned. "I'm not sure why they wouldn't listen to me."

Cam offered a crooked smile. "Imminent death tends to focus the mind."

The mayor laughed. "I have to tell you something. When Master Winder told me who would help with the evacuation, I had my doubts."

"Oh?"

Mayor Singer nodded. "I heard of a person with your name."

Cam tried not to stiffen.

"A merchant mentioned a tale about a Novice and some wolves," the mayor continued. He said the people of a town out west—Travis or Traverse—had nothing good to say about him." He licked his lips then, appearing nervous. "They say that he's a worthless drunk and that he lets his friends die. That he's a curse."

Cam was dumbfounded, appalled by what he was hearing. An instant later, fury took the place of shock. It had to be the "fine folk" of Traverse—Mayor Stump, the Benefields, and the other wealthy families, like the Echos and Lords—spreading such rumors about him. They'd sent their falsehoods journeying all this way, probably even farther. And while their lies had been spreading, the truth hadn't even roused out of bed.

Pan moved to stand next to him. "You're telling a tale you thought might be real, but tales don't always tell whole story. Would someone like the man you described have earned Master Winder's sponsorship at the Ephemeral Academy?"

The mayor hesitated. "I suppose not."

"No, he wouldn't," Cam said, rallying to his own defense. "Rumors are just rumors. Sometimes they contain a nugget of truth, but that truth is often covered in layers of fabrications and obfuscations so deep, a body can't tell what's real. But I promise you this. I ain't a curse, and I've never murdered no one."

"But you're a drunk and useless?"

"I was one of those things, but not now. Not for long while." Cam shrugged. "As to the useless part, you'll have to decide that for yourself."

The mayor appeared to size him up. "I think I already have. And I'm glad you're with us."

Cam smiled. "See to your people."

50

The people of Dander exited the town only an hour later than Cam had wanted, but the fact that they were gone was itself a relief. The dust kicked up by their passage still lingered in the air, settling to the ground at around the same time that their raucous calls and the rumble of their wagon train dimmed with distance to a whisper before fading away altogether.

Cam glanced at Light Squad. They stood close at hand, and having worked hard in organizing the people of Dander, dirt and sweat-streaked lines covered their faces and necks. They looked bedraggled and tired, but there wasn't time enough for getting clean or catching some rest. Not with a battle to fight.

And like it was a bitter harbinger of things to come, a cold wind blew just then. It lofted the dust, tossing it in the air and obscuring the sun, which stood an hour past noon. An unkindness of ravens winged overhead, cawing shrilly.

"What next?" Card asked, breaking into Cam's thoughts.

"Now, we go find the commander of Master Winder's forces and make ourselves useful," Cam said. "Get your weapons and gear."

Light Squad exited Dander's gates, heading in the direction that the Wilde Sage had told them his forces would be gathered. An hour's walk later, along a lonely stretch of Brewery Highway and among fields still fallow with trees yet to bud, they ran across them. It was a cluster of tents housing Sidewinder Company—Master Winder's strongest unit, which consisted of eleven Novices, five Acolytes, four Adepts, two Glories, and two Crowns.

Before Light Squad could proceed into the camp, though, they were confronted by an Adept, a tall and gangly fellow with a streak of gray at his temples and yellow-Haunted eyes that indicated his Stage of Awareness. He also appeared a gloomy gus. Saturnine—a word Cam had learned the other day—was the best way to describe him. "Who are you?" the Adept demanded.

"Light Squad, from the Ephemeral Academy," Cam replied.

The Adept's sad demeanor changed in an instant, becoming a welcoming smile. "Glad to have you then. I'm Sholl Singer—no relation to the mayor here, though I was born a few miles north of these parts. Let me take you to our commander, Crown Perit Line. Just don't go naming him Parrot. He hates that. His name is Perit; not Parrot. Doesn't rhyme with carrot. Got it?"

Cam couldn't hear the difference.

The Adept rambled on about all sorts of matters as they walked through the field of tents, pointing out the names of other Ephemeral Masters, mountains in the distance, and even a squirrel he said had become friendly enough to take nuts from his hand. "I'm hoping I can Awaken her. It's a passion of mine. To help normal beasts achieve sentience."

On he talked, and Cam shared a wide-eyed stare with Pan and the others. He had never met a person like Sholl. Not just because his personality had transformed so rapidly—one moment, sad and the next, happy—but his energy. Where did it come from? And did he ever stop talking?

Thankfully, he trailed off when they approached a large tent, taller than Cam by several feet and broad and deep enough to contain a full bedroom.

Sholl passed inside after announcing himself. "These are the students from the academy," he said to a man standing within, likely the commander, Perit Line.

Much like the Wilde Sage, the man was of medium height and build. He had a drooping mustache, and his most remarkable features were his intense eyes that burned with the indigo Haunt of a Crown. The commander stood before a table, peering at a map and not bothering to glance up when Light Squad entered. "You are the Novices from the academy?"

"Yes, sir," Cam replied.

"You may leave, Sholl," the Crown ordered, waiting until the Adept was gone. "I've been given information about you, including all your names, so introductions aren't necessary. I am Perit Line. You may call me Perit." He finally lifted his eyes, resting them on Card. "I knew your mother. We've fought alongside one another more than once. How is she?"

Card tensed at hearing the question, heightening Cam's interest. *What's going on there?*

"She is well," Card said.

"Give her my best next time you see her," Perit said.

Card flushed—definitely something going on—but was unable to reply since the commander was speaking once more.

"Are the people of Dander on the road?" Perit asked.

"They left about an hour ago."

Perit nodded. "Good. I'll have someone watch out for them. One of Duke Shun's Crowns. This is their duchy and their people." He muttered the last, frowning. Seconds later, he was shaking off whatever had him unhappy. "We face a hard battle. Outnumbered one hundred fifteen to thirty-two, including you lot. Wouldn't want to have too easy a time of it, would we?" He snorted sourly. "At any rate, the rakshasas have three Sages to our one. Master Winder will have his hands full. There are also eight Crowns, which means *I'll* have my hands full as well."

"And our role?" Cam asked, already seeing how this might go sideways.

"You'll be defending a rough trail, well back of where the main battle should take place. A valley floor we've already lined with traps and deadfalls." He indicated places on the map, detailing what kind and where the ambushes had been laid. "There really shouldn't be much more than a light skirmishing force that you'll face."

"And we're simply to observe?" Cam asked.

"And kill them if you can," Perit said. "But if it's a stronger force, I'll want you to fall back. Don't be a hero. Those are Master Winder's exact orders. We have signaling arrows. You know the kind?"

Cam nodded. They'd covered it at the academy.

"Good. Use them if you need to. I'll have one of my Glories watching for them. If you need extraction, we'll see it done."

"How many enemy Novices are there?" Weld asked, taking on a cocky pose, which Cam wished we wouldn't. "If we kill them, won't that take a load of pressure off Sidewinder?"

"Yes, it would," Perit replied. "But there are seventy-five Novices."

Cam jerked his gaze to the commander. *Seventy-five?*

Perit flashed a mirthless smile. "You sure you can kill that many?"

"Are there no other Masters we can call upon?" Jade said, sounding as appalled as Cam was feeling.

Perit sighed. "This boil also houses fourteen Acolytes, ten Adepts, five Glories, and the aforementioned eight Crowns, and three Sages. Beyond that, four more rakshasa Sages and their assorted Crowns, Adepts, Acolytes, and Novices are harrying this duchy. It's a major offensive, larger than any in decades, and the other Sage-Dukes are still organizing their own Ephemeral Masters. They'll join in but by then, our part in the battle will be over." He pinched the bridge of his nose. "So in answer to your questions. No, there are no other Masters available. We're it."

"Where is this trail?" Cam asked.

"Here. Near this ridge." Perit pointed to a place on the map. All of Light Squad pressed forward to study the area in question. "You'll have the high ground. Keep watch, and if any of the rakshasa reserves sally forth—I expect no more than twenty—and you can take them, then take them. If not, fall back." He stared about the tent, meeting the gaze of each member of Light Squad. "No heroics. I mean it. You won't have even an Adept with you. Stay safe."

"If they do sally out from that trail, they'll have lots of cover," Jade noted, pointing out markers for trees and stones.

"So they will," Perit agreed. "But as I said, we've set traps all along the valley floor. Plus, I'm told you're all solid archers. If it's only Novices and Acolytes, you should be able to hold them there."

It was a good enough plan. Light Squad would see some action, but they should be well out of the danger of facing off against Glories and higher-Staged rakshasas. Perit explained further about the deployment of his company.

"And Sidewinder's Novices?" Cam asked. "Where will they be?"

"Battling alongside our Acolytes and Adepts. They'll fight from the rear. Distract the rakshasas while we kill them."

Fighting from the rear was fine, but it was still a much more dangerous situation for Sidewinder's Novices. Plus, there were holes in Perit's plan. "Why don't we have ballistae and any other Neophyte archers set up in the rear? Having them fire in volleys could distract or even kill the rakshasas better than just a handful of Novices."

"Ballistae are too easy for even an Adept to destroy," Perit explained. "And the destruction usually kills their crews. As for Neophyte archers, it's a notion, but as slow as they are, they're usually killed after that first volley." He tilted his head. "Have you not seen how slowly they move compared to even a Novice with Kinesthia?"

Cam had never paid it any attention in Traverse, but on thinking about it now, he could understand the commander's point. He grunted. "Then we better get in position."

"Good hunting," the commander replied.

They exited Perit's tent, and on their way out of Sidewinder's camp, they ran across a familiar figure striding toward them. *Saira*.

Cam's mood lifted, and he might have smiled until Jade elbowed him in the side.

"She's our professor," she reminded him in a whisper before raising her voice and speaking loudly to the rest of Light Squad. "We'll meet you at the ridge. I'm sure Professor Maharani has further instructions for you."

Light Squad departed, greeting Saira on the way out, but Cam didn't miss the knowing expression Pan aimed his way. Avia even winked.

"Cam," Saira said. "Walk with me. We need to talk."

She sounded upset, and Cam's rising mood drooped. What was going on now? He might have asked, but Saira's posture told him that she wanted his silence. Instead, he quietly followed in her wake as she led him past the tents and along the road back to Dander.

At an empty clearing, she halted, staring into the woods, arms folded across her chest. "We may not win this battle."

"Why do you say that?"

"The numbers are concerning," Saira said, still staring outwardly. "I fear for you and Light Squad. Master Winder shouldn't have brought you here. It's too dangerous, but I can get you to safety if you wish."

Cam frowned. That most certainly wasn't what he wished. He had been given his orders, and he'd carry them out.

Saira must have seen the refusal on his face. "It was merely an offer. What will you do?"

Cam continued to frown, upset that Saira had even suggested such a thing. It was a coward's ploy, and he wondered and worried if that's how she saw him. He eventually gave a mental shrug, letting go of his upset. "We'll study the terrain. Figure a way to help if we can."

"If anyone can, it's you." She stepped closer, and he grew aware of how alone they were.

Sidewinder's camp wasn't visible. No voices reached them, and Cam's heart pounded. Butterflies filled his stomach, and his mouth went dry. He wouldn't have been able to talk even if his britches were on fire and he had to yell for help.

"I see something in you, Cam" Saira said, peering up at him, her brows furrowed. "You have to live. Light Squad must live. Your unit can do great things together."

A flare of confusion flashed through him. For a second, he'd thought… Well, it didn't matter what he thought. "I'll do my best."

"You always have," she replied. "And I know you think of yourself as just a Novice, but you'll Advance soon. You'll be an Acolyte, and after that, you'll Advance to Adept. But in every Stage, you have it in you to make a difference. To change the world for the better." She peered intently at him. "Live to see it happen."

Unexpected courage had Cam speaking a question that had been on his mind for a long time. Truthfully, since the moment he met Saira. "When I become an Adept, what will happen then? To us?"

"Us?" Saira quirked a brow. "In what sense? As colleagues? You know my plans on regressing, so who knows? Maybe we'll be Adepts together." She smiled. "I'd like that."

Cam's heart swelled, his prior agitation with Saira gone. What she had said wasn't much, but it was something. And something was a whole lot better than nothing.

Cam arrived at the ridge overlooking the site from where some of the rakshasa reserves might eventually sally. Light Squad was already there, on their bellies, staring into the base of a wooded valley fifty feet below. Cam got low, crawling forward until he was alongside them. He had a spyglass in his gear, a better choice to view the area down below than waste a True Bond.

Too bad only Pan and Avia had also thought along those lines.

"Drop the True Bonds," Cam ordered. "You don't need it for this. Use your spyglasses."

"We'll be in cooldown," Weld reminded him.

"No, you won't," Cam said to Weld, peering about as he studied the valley. "You'll have whatever is left of your current Bond, three more uses, and then the longer cooldown. If we get the longer cooldown out of the way now, you'll have four full uses again."

Weld grumbled something Cam didn't catch, but he did as he was told and let go his True Bond. So did Card and Jade. They all should have known better, though.

Cam set aside his unhappiness with them. He'd talk about it later. Right now, he needed a better way of dealing with the rakshasas.

"There is a small ravine," Pan said, sidling alongside him and pointing out what he meant. "It exits into this broader valley. We've seen a few Awakened Beasts journey from there to here. Acolytes given the orange glow around them when they moved."

"Scouts?"

"Almost certainly," Pan replied.

"Where does that ravine lead?" Cam asked.

"The boil," Pan answered.

"And this valley itself?"

"Likely south of where Sidewinder is encamped," Card said. "A set of woods. It should give the rakshasas cover for when they attack Master Winder's forces."

"Have we scouted that area?"

"No, sir," Card replied.

Cam pondered the problem. If a large force *did* come through here, Light Squad couldn't hold the valley. That much was obvious. The best they could do was thin the rakshasa numbers, and even then, only the Novices. But what about where the valley opened into those woods? If the enemy could use it for cover to attack Sidewinder, couldn't Master Winder's company also use it to ambush the rakshasas?

"Hold position," Cam ordered Light Squad. "Jade. You're with me. We're going to see where the valley ends."

"Yes, sir."

They followed the ridge overlooking the valley, running low so they remained unseen from any rakshasas down below, hunching when necessary. Ten minutes later, they reached their destination: the end of the valley, which was a natural chokepoint, several yards wide and formed by two opposite-facing, steeply pitched ridges coming together in a pincer.

Cam got on his belly, crawling forward, careful to remain quiet. The spyglass came out again, and through it, he searched the valley floor for any sign of the enemy. *Nothing.* Cam breathed a prayer of gratitude and took his time then to study the area.

The ridge he and Jade had followed was now only twenty feet above the valley floor with the space around the chokepoint clear of trees and shrubs and the walls made of a mix of solid stone and scree. It would be difficult for the enemy Novices to attack Light Squad while they held the heights. From what Cam could reckon, it would be far better to defend here than at the ravine.

He kept on studying, angling the spyglass so he could search past the chokepoint, toward Sidewinder. There, the land fell away in a tumble of stone and heavy boulders that abutted a set of conifer woods. Plenty of cover along that rocky slope and within those trees. Perit had a small detachment within those woods. They could kill the enemy as they descended, and from there, retreat and lure the enemy into a set of ambushes when they entered the forest.

Cam wished he could talk to Saira about it, but that wasn't his mission. His was to observe, kill the enemy if he could, and otherwise retreat. In the process, he'd keep Light Squad alive. That above all else.

Still, if the enemy *did* come in force, there might be some means for Light Squad to thin the herd, so to speak. Cam had some notions on how to get it done, but first, he wanted Jade's opinion. Other than him, she was the best in their unit at tactics.

"You don't have to say it," Jade said before he voiced any questions.

"Don't have to say what?"

"About how we messed up forming a True Bond back there," Jade answered. "It was a mistake. You don't have to tell me."

Cam nodded. "Glad to hear it. Now, what do you think about what we're facing?"

Jade considered a moment before answering. "I think we should defend that chokepoint," she said, gesturing with her chin. "The area around the ravine is too wide. If the rakshasas came in force, we'd be overwhelmed in seconds. Here, we could do some damage."

"What kind of damage?"

"If we position Light Squad on opposite sides of the ridge, we could catch them in a crossfire of arrows."

Cam nodded. It was a good idea, fixing in the same direction as his own thoughts. But there was also plenty more they could do than just shoot some arrows.

Jade must have sensed his caginess. "What do *you* have in mind?"

"I'm thinking we should create some new traps for when the rakshasas exit the ravine, however many there are. They've likely marked the ones Sidewinder already planted, but some new ones might-could kill a few. At least before the more Advanced rakshasas disarm them, but a few is better than none."

"It'll also put them on their guard."

"True," Cam agreed. "Which is why we'll keep on hitting them from the heights. Take potshots and run."

"If we did that and they have even a single Crown or Glory, we're all going to die."

Cam offered a crooked grin. "If they have a single Crown or Glory among those we face, we're all going to die—even if we just ran from the battle at a dead sprint. We have to pray that doesn't happen. As for our plan, it will either work or it won't. It doesn't matter in the end, though, so long as we're true to our dharma."

Jade faced him with a confused frown. "What?"

"Nothing," Cam muttered, embarrassed. "It's just something Professor Grey told me once." And the first time Cam had heard the advice, he'd thought it was… well, stupid. Only useful for a monk. But sometimes it seemed like maybe it *was* useful, which was a whole lot of unexpected. "Anyway, we take potshots at the rakshasas, but really, it's just to distract them. The whole time, we're running for this place."

Jade was nodding excitedly. "And then we'll ambush them."

"Not the way you think," Cam cautioned. "We'll attack, if they are enough of them to push through and they're using shields—"

"Which they will be."

"—we won't be able to do much."

"Then what do you suggest?" Jade asked.

Cam pointed. "See them rocks?"

Jade frowned, studying what he had pointed out. Seconds later, she slowly grinned. "Did I ever tell you I like the way you think?"

Cam chuckled. "No, but I don't mind hearing it if you feel like saying it." He nudged her shoulder. "Come on. Let's tell the others what we have in mind."

It was early the next day, the sun shining through a cloudless sky, when Light Squad got the last of the rocks levered in place. They'd worked all day yesterday, into the night, and got back to it as soon as dawn broke. Cam didn't know why the rakshasas hadn't attacked yet, but he was grateful for the hours of extra time Light Squad had to prepare.

They'd now be able to give the enemy a proper welcome. He only wished the strange sensation urging him to head north would go away. It perked up now and then, and he didn't know what it meant.

A rushing sound from the woods downslope caught Cam's attention. A Sidewinder Glory approached, and Cam straightened from where he'd been helping Card and Avia—the only two members of Light Squad here at the chokepoint. The others were waiting by the ravine, and the three of them would join the rest as soon as the work here was done.

But first there was the Glory to deal with. He was a tall, lanky man who might have a decade or a century on Cam. A person could never tell at that level of Awareness.

The Glory didn't give Cam a chance to offer welcome. "What are you doing here?" he snapped, his breath fogging in the cold morning air. "You're supposed to be at the ravine. This area is too close to the battle for unprotected Novices."

Cam did his best to suppress his anger. Light Squad had been working tirelessly to get ready for whenever the rakshasas attacked and were only doing their duty. "No, sir," Cam replied. "We were instructed to hold the rakshasas in this valley. Thin their numbers if we can. That's what we've been doing."

"Tell me what you have planned."

Cam explained, and the Glory's irritation quickly faded. "That's actually a good idea. How much longer until you're ready?"

"We're ready now."

"Then get back to the ravine. I'll keep an eye out for you. Use your arrows if it's too dangerous." His words spoken, the Glory left in a swirl of wind.

"Good to know someone's watching out for us," Card said.

It was, and Cam felt a mild relief at knowing Light Squad wasn't alone. A part of him had worried over it. "We need to hustle and get back to the others."

The three of them rushed back to where the ravine opened into the valley. From its depths came the faint tramping sound of marching feet. Cam's eyes went to the opposite ridge, picking out Jade, Weld, and Pan. No rakshasa had yet exited the ravine, and Cam signaled Jade on the other side of the valley, indicating what he wanted.

All of Light Squad quickly had arrows on the rest of their bows. The noise within the ravine echoed louder. The rakshasas didn't seem to care that anyone could hear them coming. They were either reckless, bold, or astoundingly sure of themselves.

The first rakshasa to exit the ravine was a large man, taller than Cam and every bit as heavily muscled. He held a shield in place, but given his yellow-Haunted eyes, it seemed unnecessary. Three arrows slammed into the invisible barrier protecting the Adept. The rakshasa barked an order, and dozens more rakshasas followed after him, a mix of Novices and Acolytes with an interspersing of Adepts.

Cam's mouth went dry. This wasn't a light skirmishing force like Perit had expected. This was a much larger one. Sidewinder's initial tally of the enemy rakshasas seemed to be wildly inaccurate. Heroics or not, Light Squad would have to hold here.

On the rakshasas marched, emptying out of the ravine, and Cam counted their numbers, recording them in his mind—thirty Novices, four Acolytes and four Adepts.

"Oh, shit," Card whispered.

"Focus," Cam ordered. He signaled for the whistling arrows to let Sidewinder know what was going on.

"Shouldn't we retreat?" Avia asked.

"If we don't help, Sidewinder's going to get mauled," Cam said. "That small force in the woods won't do them any good. Now get to work."

Cam set to firing off arrow after arrow. And while he shared Avia and Card's terror, Light Squad had a mission to accomplish. A total of five Novices went down beneath that initial barrage.

"Time to go." He signaled and Light Squad ran along the ridge, stopping now and then to take shots of convenience at the advancing rakshasas. A few more went down, still all of them Novices.

A half hour of what felt like a game of cat-and-mouse passed. Cam's heart pounded his terror. For once, the calm of battle eluded him, but it didn't slow him down any. He kept his eyes on the enemy. They had to stay clear of the Adepts. If they realized they were only battling Novices, and five of them at that, they would likely scale the walls of the ravine and kill Light Squad in a matter of moments.

Cam reached a stand of pine where he stopped, hidden in the foliage. He sighted down an arrow, a Novice beaver as his target. The creature darted in and out among the woods of the valley floor. Cam loosed the arrow. It whistled, thunking into the meat of the beaver's thigh. The creature howled, hopping on one leg before the buck-toothed rascal set to chewing the arrow out of his leg.

Good enough.

Cam signaled Jade, and Light Squad raced onward, pulling far ahead of the rakshasas. They quickly neared the chokepoint. This was where Cam's plan might see them do some real wreckage—or see them all dead.

51

Cam observed the advancing rakshasas, silently urging them on-ward. *Come on. Run.* There was no reason to slow them down anymore. As far as he figured the situation, it was better to see the rakshasas hurry on so Light Squad could see to the next part of their plan. It was also the one where they'd be in the greatest danger. And while their odds might not be as good as Cam wanted, it was better than the alternative.

He formed a True Bond, telling the others to do so as well.

"I wish we didn't have to do this," Avia said as they descended down the slope to the valley floor.

"It's a good plan," Card said in disagreement. "You won't hear any complaints from me about it."

Cam nodded appreciation at Card, glad to have his support. But soon enough, there was no further time for reckoning or measuring out other ideas. Light Squad was in position, and the rakshasas were charging hard, only a few hundred yards distant.

Cam stood at the point of a wedge. Everything depended on the en-emy seeing Light Squad as a sacrifice. The knowledge had to have been passed down among the rakshasas at large by now. How the Wilde Sage and Sidewinder Company were using their weakest members as bait.

But seeing them alone, this time the rakshasas slowed, stepping carefully, likely sniffing a trap or an ambush. There were both, but not in the way the enemy probably calculated.

The Adepts in charge of the rakshasas—a man, woman, and two cougars—paced a few feet ahead of the rest of their formation. On seeing no further attacks coming, they pointed at Light Squad, roaring as one and urging the rakshasas forward.

Cam hunkered behind his shield, spear at the ready, like he was willing to take the charge. But only for a moment.

He and Light Squad threw aside their weapons and shields, pretending panic. They sprinted away from the rakshasas as fast as they could.

And here was where the danger lay. They had no defense against the Adepts, and if the rakshasas attacked from a distance, Light Squad was as good as gone.

Cam kept the fear away. His team needed him calm. He watched, waited, planned. The rakshasas were closing fast. Light Squad reached the chokepoint. Were through it. The ground dropped away, the downward slope briefly hiding them from the enemy.

At a marker, Cam immediately broke to the left, back upslope. Card and Avia with him, both already to the top of the ridge. On the opposite side, Jade and the rest did the same. Just in time. The Adepts were yards from the chokepoint. Card tugged down on a lever set underneath a boulder. It rumbled down the short incline.

The Adepts saw it coming. They sprinted to get through before a small rockslide caught them. The rest of the rakshasas followed after, but a good score pulled up short.

One of the Adept cougars leaped upward, high enough to clear the ridge. Cam, re-equipped with a shield and spear, raced to intercept. He rolled under a line of fire aimed by the rakshasa. A stab of his spear caught the creature mid-flight. And while Cam couldn't puncture the rakshasa's protective barrier, the spear did arrest the cougar's ascent. The creature fell backward, buried under a wave of stones.

The other Adepts and another half-dozen or so rakshasas, made it through. They immediately faced around, preparing to leap toward the ridge. They were too late. Jade and Avia sent another rockslide toward them. The rakshasas halted an instant, horrified by the tide of rocks and boulders rumbling their way. As one, they turned and fled down slope. The Adepts looked likely to stay ahead of the rockslide, but the others probably wouldn't make it.

They also weren't Light Squad's problem any longer. Cam faced the remaining rakshasas. "Attack!"

With a hail of arrows, Light Squad put down five of the enemy before the rest wised up enough to get their shields raised. The rakshasas didn't bother counterattacking either. They'd been broken. They threw down their weapons and ran, looking to do nothing but escape.

No chance of that happening.

Cam charged down the ridge's slope. "Form up," he ordered. Light Squad drifted into a wedge. Card, their most powerful warrior, was at the head. They raced after the remaining rakshasas, intent on putting them down.

The creatures ran pell-mell, no thought of fighting. One of them glanced back. Did he just grin? Cam studied the rakshasas. They ran in a bunch. None of them had raced away into the wooded parts of the valley.

"Hold!" Cam shouted. Light Squad responded without question.

"What are you doing?" Weld asked, hopping about. "We've got them on the run. Let's finish them."

Cam scanned the rakshasas. The creatures had slowed, staring back at Light Squad, taunting them. They wanted Cam's unit to chase them. *An ambush.* Just like the one Light Squad had enacted. Cam kept his eyes on the enemy but was distracted by motion in the sky. Far in the distance and high above, a line split the heavens.

Cam's heart dropped. "Seek cover!" A rakshasa Sage was about to enter the valley.

Light Squad raced into the woods, running flat out. No thought for anything but getting as deep into the trees as possible.

A thundercrack shook the valley. Lightning sizzled, chasing after Light Squad. Dirt blasted upward, launched in plumes. Echoes of explosions rippled. Cam was bringing up the rear, and he saw and felt it all. His hair stood on end, and a burning smell filled his nostrils. Dirt and stones rattled around him like rain.

"You cannot have them," a voice roared, loud enough to reverberate through the heavens. *Master Winder.*

"Try and stop me," another voice mocked.

Don't stop. Keep running. Those were the words Cam told himself. Jade lagged, looking back at him. He shoved her hard, not letting her slow down on his account.

Another lance of lightning blazed, striking like a storm of spears. It punctured the ground. More dirt was hurled heavenward. The world exploded. Cam found himself flung end over end. He landed on his back, rolled head over heels, and slammed into a tree. His ears rang, and the taste of metal filled his mouth. He'd bitten his tongue.

He struggled to his feet. Shaking his head to clear his vision. His eyes wouldn't focus. The world was a blur, but it didn't matter. The enemy Sage was coming.

Someone scooped him up and they were off. Cam blinked, unable to figure on what was happening.

"Down!" someone screamed, sounding like they were shouting from a mile away.

Cam was abruptly dropped. He stared at the blue sky, so pleasant and peaceful. A score or more of uprooted trees raced across his sight, like some strange flock of birds. They trailed dirt, only ten feet off the ground, spiraling end over end before crashing into the forest in the distance.

Once again, Cam was lifted. His ears still rang, but some semblance of thinking was slowly returning. He remembered ambushing the rakshasas, chasing the Novices. A Sage had arrived and then…

Nothing.

But his body was working again, even though his ears still rang and his head felt like he'd bashed it straight into a brick wall. "Put me down," Cam ordered.

"They're moving on," Pan said.

"What do we do?" Weld asked.

"Put me down," Cam repeated. It was only then that he realized it was Jade who was carrying him. He stumbled a bit when she did as he ordered.

"Are you alright?" she asked, worry in her voice.

"Just give me a moment," Cam answered. He closed his eyes, focused on the pain throbbing through his head. It was… He bent over, vomiting, not prepared for it. On it went, feeling like forever until it was over. Cam straightened, feeling around for his canteen. He nodded thanks when Pan handed him his. A couple of swishes and spits, and he was feeling a mite better. "What happened?"

"A rakshasa Sage arrived," Jade answered, still peering at him like she was worried he might fall over and die at any moment. "Then Master Winder came. He and the other Sage are fighting."

"What about the enemy Novices?" Cam asked.

"We don't know," Pan said. "Once you told us to run, and we saw why, we ran and never slowed down."

Cam glanced about their current location, which was devastated. Trees, broken and uprooted, had been tossed about like kindling. Gouges in the earth, deep and wide enough to sink a house, pockmarked the land. A strange smell flooded the air, pungent yet clean. Cam faced the center of the valley, where more destruction met his gaze. He wasn't sure if anything could have survived out there, but it was Light Squad's job to find out. And if an enemy lived, they'd kill it.

He was about to call out orders when a screaming sound from overhead drew his attention. What now?

Perit landed in a swirl of debris.

Cam had to turn aside, coughing.

"Report," Perit ordered.

Cam's mind wasn't quite yet moving at full speed, and he had trouble answering. He found Perit studying him.

"You're injured. Here." Before Cam could move, the Crown grasped his head. Cool waves seemed to flow from Perit's hands. They brought soothing relief to Cam's aching head.

"Thank you," Cam said when Perit released him. ""We set off the rockslide like we planned." He grinned. "It worked like a charm."

Perit chuckled. "I saw your handiwork. Well done. You crushed the enemy. Those rakshasas you killed were their reserve. They could have pincered us. As it was, we ended up destroying most of the ones we faced. We have them on the run."

"What about Master Winder?" Cam asked.

"He can take care of himself," Perit said. "And I still need you. There were a number of rakshasas who escaped. Track them down and kill them. I'll send Saira to help." With that, the Crown was gone, ascending skyward.

"What now?" Card asked.

Cam didn't respond at once. He shook out his limbs, rotated his head, checking to make sure everything was working right. Once satisfied, he answered Card. "Now, we're going back to the valley floor. That's where the rakshasas are likely to be. And I aim to deal them some death."

"Fragging hell," Card intoned. "Now that's a plan."

But Weld didn't seem pleased. "And if we run into Acolytes or greater?"

"We have Saira to handle them," Cam replied, glancing around. "Anyone have a shield and spear they can spare?" Jade passed him a set, and he indicated his thanks. "Head out. Card, you have point. Avia, Jade, and Weld cover his back. Pan, you're with me."

They struggled to make it through the devastation, picking their way across the rubbled and ravaged landscape. Minutes later, Saira arrived in a rush.

"Stay close," she said without preamble, eyes flicking around. "Rakshasas fled the battle. Many of their Crowns are dead. Same with their Glories."

They reached the valley floor, where the ruination continued. From here, Cam could see that the ridges on both sides had been destroyed, carved and shattered like some titanic child had thrown a tantrum. Boulders the size of buildings littered the valley floor, and water gushed from an underground stream exposed to the air. Light Squad pressed on, coming abreast of the ravine, which had been ripped apart like old clothes.

Another screaming in the air caused Cam to tense.

"It's Master Winder," Saira said.

The Wilde Sage alighted. "Thank Devesh, you're all still alive." He sounded and appeared relieved. An anchor line opened close at hand, and Cam tensed. "Relax," Master Winder said. "It's a friend."

From the anchor line emerged Sage-Duke Zin Shun of Charn. Or at least that's who Cam figured it had to be based on his appearance. He was slight of build, of middle years and frail in appearance. Rumor said he had yet to fully heal following the war with Bastion.

"I can't stay," Duke Zin said. "The other rakshasa Sages are attacking throughout my duchy." He grimaced. "I've had to call Josie for assistance. You know how well that pleases me." He must have meant Duchess Josie Salin of Bastion, his near-mortal enemy.

Master Winder appeared unsurprised, merely nodding. "Go. We'll handle this boil."

"I'll leave you to it then." With that Duke Zin stepped through his still open anchor line.

"I have to go as well," Master Winder said. "Sidewinder remains engaged with the enemy. I just wanted to ensure you were safe."

Saira quirked a smile. "I'm sure my mother appreciates it as much as I do."

"I meant all of you were safe," Master Winder said with a hearty laugh. "But yes, your mother would flay me alive if anything were to happen to you." He then rose into the air, departing even more rapidly than Perit had.

Cam gazed north, through the ravine. There came the strange sensation again, pulling at him.

"What is it?" Saira asked, peering at him, apparently noticing his concern.

"I don't know," Cam said. "I keep feeling something. A tugging. From over there." His eyes widened with remembrance. "The last time I felt something like that was with the Pathway in the woods. With Honor."

Saira's Glory-heavy focus landed on him, and Cam had to lock his knees in order to stay upright. "You're certain?" she asked.

Cam nodded.

The pressure eased as Saira's gaze swept north. "Rainen wasn't sure, but he thought the rakshasas were waiting on something to finalize. An Aware Pathway to help them Advance."

"What's an Aware Pathway?" Weld asked.

"It's a Pathway that is somehow aware of those who enter, becoming what they most need. It has no limits, and it only lasts for a day at most. Within it, nearly any Advancement is possible. Adepts to Glories; Glories to Crowns; and Crowns to Sages."

"What about the questions?" Cam asked as Saira led them at a run into the ravine. "The ones you have to answer in order to Advance."

"For rakshasas, every answer to every question of Advancement is the same: gain Ephemera, by any means necessary."

Saira could have raced ahead, moving at a Glory's speed, but she remained with Light Squad while they chased into the ravine. Cam, no longer the slowest, ran in the middle of the pack, arms and legs pumping under the power of a True Bond.

In spite of his heightened senses, at the speed they were running, the world was a blur, the center of it shadowed. The sky overhead— still sunny and with a scattering of clouds—was nothing but a thin slit as the ravine's walls narrowed. The air grew cooler in the darkness, enough to raise goosebumps, and there was no sound but the percussion of Light Squad's boots as they pounded along on the stony soil.

That and their heavy breathing as they ran at speed.

Cam dug deep, keeping up with the others. The sensation was increasing by the moment. Whatever Saira feared would happen at that Aware Pathway, Light Squad needed to reach it sooner rather than later.

"We're almost there," Saira said, just as the walls of the ravine began to open.

The early afternoon sun peered down, brightening their way and bringing some warmth. Tufts of grass appeared. The clumps grew together, transforming into a meadow when the ravine's walls fell away. A set of low rises cupped the far side of the field, while to the left was a small pond. Clear, calm, and mirrored, it reflected the blue sky. Cattails bobbed along its peaceful shores, mingled with other tall grasses. Most days it was likely a good place to spend a lazy summer afternoon.

But not this day.

The sensation came from under the water, and Cam pointed it out.

"I was afraid you would say that," Saira said. "We'll have to swim."

"I should go," Avia said. "I was born in the water."

"You can't," Saira said. "If I'm right, there will be rakshasas of significant Advancement within the Pathway already."

"You shouldn't go alone," Cam protested. "We can help. There might be Novices or Acolytes. We can keep them off of you."

Saira sighed. "Perhaps so, but—"

"Perhaps nothing," Cam replied. "We're going."

"Cam's right. We're coming with you," Card said, stripping off his armor and his weapons.

"All of us are," Jade added, doing the same as Card.

Saira took a deep inhalation. "So be it."

Once their heavy gear was removed, they entered the water. Cam took the lead, Saira and Avia swimming next to him. They dove deeper, startling some fish. The sunlight grew hazy and dim, but Cam didn't need the illumination. He could feel the Pathway. It pulled on his Source, showing him where he needed to go.

Seconds later, they arrived. The Pathway was a shimmering portal, having a different watery appearance than the rest of the pond and glowing with an iridescent shimmer.

Saira gestured, indicating she was to go first. Cam nodded, getting Light Squad's attention so they knew the order of who would enter after her. He treaded water while Saira approached the Pathway. This was only the second time he'd seen someone enter one.

Saira swam forward, and the moment she touched the portal, it was as if she was sucked inside. She was gone in an instant

Then it was Cam's turn.

Cam touched the portal, drawn inward and immediately expelled. He was falling. A moment of panic consumed him before he got himself under control. He spun in the air, landing on his shoulders and hips with a grunt. Thankfully, the floor had only been a few feet below.

He grimaced, rising to his feet and staring about to take stock of his situation. A dimly lit tunnel that was otherwise empty met his gaze. He turned in a circle, frowning. Where was Saira? She should have been here. Had she decided to leave Light Squad behind? Cam shook his head. She'd never do something like that. There had to be some other issue going on, and until he could figure it out, he'd be best off waiting for Light Squad.

Cam stepped away from the place where he'd entered the Pathway, a stone wall, smooth and white like stucco, expecting the rest of his team to arrive at any moment. Minutes passed, though, and no one else entered the tunnel. Cam's frown deepened, impatience and worry bubbling. Where were they? Had they been attacked or decided not to come?

He paused a moment, considering his situation. Saira should have been here, and yet, she wasn't. Light Squad, too. So what did that mean? He studied on the answer, reckoning in the end that the most likely possibility was that everyone had entered their own personal Pathway. After all, this wasn't the usual kind. This was supposed to be an Aware

Pathway, one that could allow anyone to Advance in Awareness, be they Novice or Crown. It made sense then that it would also be individualized to whoever entered.

Having no other choice, Cam faced the other direction and began walking. The tunnel, initially dim, was formed of curved, white walls that arched around him, glowing from within, lighting the passage to steadily increasing illumination until it was bright as day.

His footsteps echoed along the lonely corridor, and he lost all sense of time. Minutes or hours might have passed as he continued pacing through the unchanging tunnel.

Cam halted, an involuntary hiss expelling when a moaning echoed down the passage. His heart thudded, and he swallowed heavily as fear gripped him. He knew that sound. He'd heard it before, recollected it from his nightmares. The moan was the same as what he'd heard in the first Pathway he had ever dived. The one where Tern died.

He swallowed again, controlling his fear, steeling himself to get moving. His eyes peered, ears listened, every sense on alert. He could have formed a True Bond but figured it was better to save it for when it was really needed.

On he went, seemingly for miles and hours with nothing but his footsteps and thoughts to keep him company. The tunnel walls were smooth and unmarred, and it was impossible to gauge distance. Worse, Cam couldn't tell if he was making any headway as he trudged onward. His echoing footsteps sounded like a musician tapping out a beat, and the only variance to the tune was the ongoing intermittent moaning that reminded him of loss.

Cam's thoughts spiraled around what he might find in this place. He could Advance here, but only if he could answer the question that every Ephemeral Master had to solve for themselves. *Understand the difference between selfishness versus selflessness.* He pondered the question, wondering if it might have something to do with how he'd lived his life so far. Or was it related to the problems he'd set for himself?

Lost in his thinking, bored with the walking, he stumbled when he realized the tunnel had ended. It branched here, and Cam had a choice. Just like the very first Pathway, there was a way right and one to the left. The last time, right had led him to Saira, so right was the choice he made again.

Maybe hours more of walking proceeded, of solitude that felt like it lasted for days, and bored again, Cam almost missed the barred doorway to his right. He initially passed it by, halting only when his mind finally caught up with his eyes. He reversed course, hope cresting. Was Saira in there? He peered within, finding a woman lying on a cot that was pressed against the far wall. Her back was to him, and her long dark hair was draped over her shoulders. "Saira?"

The woman chuckled, throaty and cruel, sitting up, still facing away from him. "I am not she, but we know each other well, don't we, boy?" Her torso turned, but only her torso—not her legs and hips—until she twisted about to face him.

The crone from his dream. He remembered it now.

"It wasn't a dream," the woman said, as if she could read his thoughts.

Cam stumbled away from the door.

"Why are you running?" The crone asked, cackling. "When you were so eager to see me." Her hips and legs moved like worms until her entire body was facing him, and she rose to her feet, stretching her arms luxuriantly over her head. The entire time, she smiled a lurid grin, just like she had in the dream. She tsked. "I told you. It wasn't a dream."

Cam stared at her, frozen in terror, unable to move until something slammed him away from the door.

Saira.

"Run," Saira said, hauling him to his feet. "If she catches us, we're dead."

The spell of fear broken, Cam Delved his Source and forged a True Bond. Time stretched. The world grew crisper, and his body hummed with energy. He raced after Saira, catching her when she slowed for him. "Who was that?"

"She isn't anyone," Saira said. "At least not anyone real. She's a sending from the Merciless Deceiver, Shimala. Rather a portion of her."

Shimala. The Merciless Deceiver. One of the Great Rakshasas. Fresh fear clogged Cam's throat, and questions tumbled through his mind. "Can we fight her?" It was the last thing Cam wanted to do, but he had to ask.

"There is no fighting Shimala, even a sending. There's only escape. Her sending has the power of a Sage. She can kill us both without any effort."

The rattling of bars chased them. "Wait for me, sweet child," Shimala crooned. "It's not kind to leave an old woman all alone."

"She's bound for now, but if the sending receives more power, she could break free."

"Not could, little slave. Will," Shimala said with a laugh, apparently able to hear their conversation. "But run all you want. I'll be along shortly."

A flash to his left told Cam they'd rushed past the branching point of the initial passageway guiding him here. He dug deeper into his Bond, forcing everything to improve his mind and body. For a moment, he pulled ahead of Saira.

She caught him quickly. "Stay with me," she urged.

"I'll do my best," Cam said. "But you're a Glory. If you can escape on your own, then you should."

"I won't leave you."

Cam wished she would, but he could tell there was no changing her mind.

As they ran, he realized the moaning was growing louder. The corridor they followed had become dimmer, the stones rough-hewn rather than smooth. In the distance was a bright light. He prayed—to Devesh, to Rukh, to Jessira—that it was the exit from the tunnel and the escape from this Pathway.

Brighter grew the light.

Cam and Saira exploded out of the passageway, and a welcome sight greeted them. There was no ocean surging. No cliff to climb. Only a meadow surrounded by a towering forest. That, and a small pond, glinting and reflective of the sun and clouds high overhead. The exit to the Pathway was within the water, just like the entrance.

The moaning sounded out, mixed with the clangor of iron, reaching them just as they were about to enter the pond.

"She's coming," Saira gasped. "Go. Swim. I'll slow her down."

No matter the panic in his heart and the desire to escape, Cam wouldn't leave Saira. Not now. Not ever. A moaning came from the woods, and the trees shook.

"How kind of you to wait for me," Shimala said, stepping into the meadow.

52

She was here. Shimala. The Merciless Deceiver. Her dark hair hung loose about her face, masking her eyes and a ragged dress exposed knobby knees and muddy feet. She grinned, toothy and malicious. "Stop me if you've heard this before. A so-called Glory and a Novice walk into a Pathway."

Saira stepped in front of Cam. "What do you want from us?"

Shimala offered a hearty chuckle. "I want nothing from you. Not anymore. It is him who holds my interest." She pointed at Cam. "He and I have history. Don't we boy?"

Cam pushed past his terror, past the voice that told him to run, and moved to stand next to Saira. He refused to hide behind her courage.

"The boy is brave," Shimala said with a chortle.

The moaning sounded again. It had to be from an Ephemeral Wind, and Cam flicked a glance to the woods. Among the trees flowed a frayed cloud. It was white with a tinge of violet, diaphanous, moving in eddies and flows, as if in time to someone's breathing.

There might be a way…

Cam stepped in front of Saira, holding an arm out to keep her from

606

moving forward. "What do you want from me?"

"Want? You mistake my interest for want," Shimala said. "My interest is in what I can give."

"And what is that?" Cam asked, risking another glance at the wind. It was silent now, but still shifting forward in shifts and starts.

"Her life," Shimala said. "I'll let that one live if…" She let the word hang.

Cam waited for her to finish her sentence, but she didn't. "If what?" he asked.

"If you serve me."

"Serve you how?" Cam asked, anything to keep her talking.

"There have only been a rare few Plasminian Ephemeral Masters of your standing. None who were rakshasas. I would see that change. See what you might mean for me."

The wind, silent now, had crept out of the woods, but no one else seemed to notice.

Cam made sure to turn his gaze elsewhere, to focus his thoughts on his conversation with Shimala, so she couldn't pierce his plan with her ability to read his mind. "You want me to become a rakshasa?"

Shimala smiled, cheerless and deadly. "Exactly." She glided forward, feet unmoving. "And I am not a villain; nor am I an idiot. I know what you seek." She glanced at the woods, to where his gaze had gone. "You think I don't know of the Ephemeral Wind within this Pathway? I've heard it since you first entered my web."

Cam kept his mind blank, attention on an empty area of the forest, feigning fear that the Ephemeral Wind was coming apart. "Your web?"

Shimala glanced again at the woods, this time to where Cam wanted her to look. "The Ephemeral Wind is coming apart? So sad." She faced him again. "And yes, my web. I placed the Pathway here. To Advance my children or bring you into my lair. You see, everything that has occurred is by my design."

Cam forced thoughts of Pan, Jade, and Light Squad to the forefront of his mind… anything but what he truly wanted. And Saira couldn't be here if it was to work. He pushed that thought toward the crone as well.

"You want that one's safety so much?" Shimala asked.

"I do," Cam said, stepping toward the Great Rakshasa. "Let Saira leave, and I'll do what you want."

"I can't let you sacrifice yourself," Saira said.

Cam tried to grab her, but she rushed past him. From her hands bloomed a wall of icy arrows. They hammered into Shimala, who held still, uncaring as concussive waves blasted into her. The shockwave from the impacts blew outward. The meadow flattened and trees bent under the force of Saira's attack. Cam struggled to retain his footing as well.

The Ephemeral Wind shifted then, heading toward Saira.

Cam sprinted, his plan in shambles. But there was still a way.

Through it all, the crone cocked her head. "Is that your best, slave? Can you not control your Spirairia with finer dexterity? Control is the key to everything, and I find yours lacking. It has always been the case. Let me show you how it is done."

Cam was nearly upon the crone, but with a gesture, she held him in place. "Your Ephemeral Wind, your last hope, is spent. Your Glory will die. And you will soon call me mistress."

The Wind shifted direction again, moaning. Shimala darted a gaze toward the sound, eyes fearful. "You—"

She wasn't able to get out another word. The Wind was on her, howling now as it wrapped around Shimala. She screamed. Her skin frayed, torn apart, exposing muscle and viscera.

Cam would have exulted, but a finger of the Wind drifted and touched him. Fire filled his veins. His vision blanked to white, and his ears filled with thunder. Power poured into his bones, swelling them. And into his Source poured a waterfall of energy, enough to rupture his very being.

A hard yank pulled Cam free of the worst of the torment, but he was still suffering, still feeling as though his body was immolating.

A voice crashed through the thunder in his ears. "You have to Advance." *Saira.* Terror filled her voice. "It's your only hope. Do it now!"

Cam struggled to comprehend what she was saying. Pain consumed him, but inch by inch, he recognized what was needed. He'd already saved Saira, and now he had to save himself.

Selfishness versus selflessness... All the hours spent considering what it might mean for him. Reviewing his life's choices. The possible ways one might be better than the other.

But actions, while they spoke louder than words or thoughts, did stem from them. For Cam, clarity cleared the fog of confusion when he recognized a single notion; one that inspired what he wished for his future. His answer—all along it had been his answer was simple. Selflessness in all ways; to do what was needed for those who couldn't.

A waterfall of energy drowned Cam's Source, causing it to pulse, to expand and contract in time to his heartbeat. Suffused every layer of his being and all of his Tangs, beginning with Plasminia, traveling in a steady tide, down and up, down and up, washing Cam clean with every circuit.

It would have been wondrous, but the endless energy never ceased. On it poured, and his Source took it in, pulsing still in synchronicity with his heart. But it contracted less than it expanded, bloating like a balloon. Distended and misshapen.

Cam's head felt like it was about to split open, pain unlike anything he'd ever experienced. His eyes burned as if he'd shoved glowing embers into them. And every muscle contracted, threatening to break his bones. But he wouldn't surrender. Cam clenched his teeth, holding himself together by sheer will. This wouldn't be his end. His Source wouldn't rupture. He wouldn't allow it.

The Ephemera continued to flood into him, and while Cam endured the pain, he fixed his attention on his Source. Willing the walls to strengthen. Forcing them to condense and regain a rounder shape.

An endless time later, the flow of Ephemera finally ebbed, and Cam got ahead of it. He worked, focused and determined, and his Source, dense and full, constricted in slow measures.

His Tangs flashed—all of them—and their ruddy tinges lightened, transforming to red-orange, orange, and then finally, resolving to a Haunt that was in between orange and yellow. Every Tang had Advanced to Acolyte, and his Source, while still enlarged, had the proper shape of a globe.

The Ephemeral flow ended with a jarring suddenness, and the pain relaxed by drips, lessening until Cam could unclench his jaw. He stopped grinding his teeth, unlocked his fisted hands and took a deep, fulfilling breath. His head no longer threatened to split open, and the inferno in his eyes receded.

Cam realized that Saira was holding him in her lap, stroking his brow, whispering encouragement. He opened his eyes, noticing a smell, pungent and malodorous. Biles, phlegm, and serum had been excreted from his body. It reeked, but Cam was just happy to be alive. It was far better than the alternative.

"You Advanced," Saira said, beaming down at him. "Are you ready to leave?"

"Absolutely," Cam said, groaning as he sat up.

"Then we need to be quick. The Pathway will close at any moment."

Cam took Saira's hand as he rose fully to his feet. He grimaced on standing. While the pain was gone, there was a great deal of lingering stiffness and soreness. Cam rolled his neck, arched his back, and loosened his limbs. *Better.* Even if it still felt like he'd been simultaneously drowned and run over by an avalanche.

"We'll still have a battle to fight. Light Squad must not have entered the Pathway," Cam said, glancing to where he'd last sighted Shimala.

Saira must have figured on what he was wondering. "Shimala was destroyed by the Ephemeral Wind."

Thank Devesh. Cam never wanted to see that crone ever again.

They re-entered the pond, diving deep. The water washed away some of the sediment from Cam's skin and the act of swimming relieved the last of his soreness. They shortly reached a watery doorway, white in color this time.

Once again, Saira was the first one through. Cam followed directly after, arriving in the original pond—he could tell—but there were differences. The sun had been brightly shining in the sky above the water when they had left. Now, it was dim, which meant they had been gone for hours.

Cam saw Saira swimming for the surface, and together, they breached the water.

It was early evening, and a cacophony of sound reached him. Shouts of encouragement. Cries of efforts. And the echoing roar of thunderous explosions. The world seemed to rumble and shake. Cam spun about, trying to make sense of what was happening.

He created a True Bond, which made it worse. A cascade of sensations hit him like a hammer. He closed his eyes, took several deep breaths, and centered himself, focusing inward.

A moment later, he opened his eyes. This time, the sensations didn't overwhelm him. His mind was swift enough to decipher the information, and he immediately noticed a difference in his thoughts, his body, and his awareness of creation and Ephemera. It was like someone had removed a fog muffling every aspect of his being. He could see, hear, smell, taste, and feel like never before. His body burned with power. The world was suffused with Ephemera, and it wasn't only white but spanned every hue Cam could imagine.

"Come on," Saira said, swimming to shore.

Cam followed, surveying what was around him. In the nearby hills, a number of rakshasas, only a dozen or so, battled Sidewinder. But where was Light Squad? Cam reached the shore, searching for his team, his friends.

A Glory streaked to their side, and this time Cam could follow his motions. It was the same one from right before the beginning of the battle. "Where have you been?" he snarled at Saira.

"What happened?" Saira asked. "And where are we needed?"

"Disaster is what happened," the Glory answered. "And we needed you hours ago. Both of you. Why did you run?"

He thought they had fled? Cam took an aggressive step forward. "We didn't run from anything."

"Then where were you?" The Glory glared at Cam.

Cam glared right back.

Saira stepped between them, the only one keeping her cool. "What disaster?"

The other Glory gave Cam a final glare before replying to Saira's demand. "We have the most powerful remaining rakshasas holed up." He pointed to a distant cavern in the hills.

The rakshasas had formed a line around it, trembling the earth, launching ice bolts, and raining fire. And just like at Surelend, Cam noticed twisting lines of what he reckoned to be Ephemera pouring out of that cave, maybe connecting to each rakshasa. It was clearer this time, although the image still disappeared every now and then.

"But we've lost too many to attack frontally," the Glory continued. "We're down to Perit as our only Crown. Misha's out of the fight."

"And Light Squad?" Cam asked.

"I'll take you to them," the Glory said, seeming a bit less peeved.

He led them toward the rear of battle, slowing for Cam, who still felt himself moving fast enough to outrun an arrow. They arrived shortly, to where Light Squad was laid out, all of them injured.

Pan was either asleep or unconscious. Weld groaned now and then, and blood soaked a bandage around his chest. Avia slumped on her side, leg in a splint and out of it. Card had his eyes closed with burns all over his body, but it looked like he'd already been given some healing. As for Jade, she lay on the ground, her face swollen and heavily bruised and an arm in a sling, obviously broken.

"Where were you?" Jade growled on seeing him, levering herself upright. "We needed you. Both of you."

"We were in the Pathway," Cam said, guilt roiling his stomach. He'd Advanced while his friends had nearly died. "What happened here?"

"Right after you went into the Pathway, rakshasas arrived. They attacked and nearly did us in." She gestured to rest of Light Squad. "They drove us away from the Pathway, and Sidewinder did the same to them. We've been in the rear ever since."

Cam bent down, squeezing Jade's uninjured shoulder, wishing he could have done more. "I'm sorry we weren't there. I'm sorry y'all got hurt. I'm—"

"The battle's not going well," Saira said, interrupting their conversation.

Jade sounded a note of shock, staring at Cam. "You Advanced."

Cam nodded. "I'll tell you about it after we lance the boil." A final squeeze to her shoulder. "Stay safe. We'll see you in a bit." He and Saira weren't injured. They should be in the battle.

"How do you plan on doing that?" Saira said as they left Light Squad. "Lance the boil, I mean."

"The rakshasas dug deep to hide the core," Cam said. "So deep that it's likely only a few feet from the back end of the hill."

"How can you tell?" Saira asked, staring at him in confusion.

Cam wasn't sure how to explain. "I can see these twisting spirals of Ephemera—different than the woven world. Not all the time, but I see it enough. I think it's how the core supports the rakshasas."

"Can you see it through the stones?"

Cam vacillated. "I don't know. We'll be on the other side of the hill, and…" He shrugged, not knowing what to say.

"Get some gear," Saira said, gesturing to Cam's lack of armor and weapons. "We'll try your plan first."

"It's not much of a plan," Cam said, scavenging armor and weapons—a spear, bow, and a quiver of arrows. Minutes later, fully kitted, he raced after Saira, his True Bond heightening every aspect of his being.

Now to find a core from the back side of a hill.

A stuttering run, ducking low and full of mad sprints, got Cam and Saira around the wooded hills. Even still, as an Acolyte—and he had yet to fully embrace the wonder of Advancing—he could run so much faster than he'd ever managed as a Novice.

Of course, Saira said it would only be a temporary increase. That his use of a True Bond would eventually lasso him back to his abilities as a

Novice. But for now, he felt like anything was possible.

As a result, Cam ran wide open over broken stones, rugged terrain, and along the borders of streambeds. But it wasn't a quick or simple charge. It took a lot longer than Cam would have liked to get around the hills. Their run lasted for a half hour maybe, and by then, the sun was dipping to twilight. Shadows stretched, darkening the woods in which Cam and Saira raced. But with the senses of an Acolyte, he could see as clearly as if it was full sun.

At last, with his fourth and final True Bond in place, they reached the opposite side of the hills. Luck was with them because a pair of rakshasas—a man and a woman—stood guard outside a narrow passage. There were two entrances then. Cam wouldn't have noticed them except a flickering line of white escaping a darkened corridor behind the rakshasas. It trailed in a paired helical twist attaching to the enemy. *The Ephemera from the core.*

Cam placed a hand on Saira's shoulder, causing her to halt. He whispered in her ear, telling what he saw, and she peered in the direction he pointed, nodding understanding.

"They're Acolytes," Saira whispered to him. "I can take them. But we'll want to get close. Kill them before anyone inside hears."

"I'll be right behind you," Cam whispered back.

Saira darted off like a silent arrow, no sound to betray her. Cam chose to remain in place, unable to move as quietly. Instead, he watched the rakshasas. They stood unmoving, giving no sense they knew of Saira's approach.

Seconds later, first the man and then the woman jerked upward before collapsing to the ground. The paired helical lines of Ephemera cut off.

Cam rushed to where Saira waited just beyond a jagged, narrow passage.

"Follow," she ordered.

Cam paced behind Saira as she led them inward. The sounds of battle became evident, distant with exhortations, cracking thunder, and booming explosions. The noises would hopefully keep the rakshasas from hearing them close in on the core. Cam sensed it like he did the Pathway, an itch in his mind.

The tunnel twisted right, straightened, before curving left. Just a little further to go. Over Saira's shoulder, Cam could see the passage open. A single rakshasa—a fox—stood next to an altar upon which rested a violet globe. *The core.* Many more threads extended from it.

Saira spared a hungry look toward the core before speeding forward, killing the fox. Cam was on her heels. He reached the core, lifting it off the altar. Cries of alarm reached him. Saira raced off to slow the incoming rakshasas. It was up to Cam now. He held the core, peering intently. Spirairia allowed him to see how it was held together, and he searched for a place of weakness.

There!

Cam focused on the area he had found. An extension of his will expanded the point of weakness into a crack. Enlarged it until, with the tinkling of breaking glass, the core was lanced, and a surge of Ephemera poured from it.

The rakshasas shouted in alarm. Their voices were quickly silenced as Saira tore through them.

Cam pocketed the core. Time to get back into the fight. He stepped past the altar and entered a broad corridor. The noise of battle pulled him on as he rushed past scattered corpses of men and Awakened Beasts—rakshasas all. *Saira's work.* Seconds later, the corridor branched.

To the left, sounds of conflict arose. Cam raced in that direction. A couple more corpses. The hall opened into a wide space shaped like an atrium. There, Saira battled a pair of Glories, the wispy blue outlines of Ephemera around all three. A couple of Novices harried her as well. Cam unlimbered his bow. He fired an arrow. Followed with another. Kept on until the Novices were dead.

The Glories continued to press Saira. She leaped a line of water powerful enough to carve stone, then she evaded a screaming red-hot beam that melted a boulder.

Cam fired an arrow at the Glory closest to Saira. It distracted the rakshasa allowing her to elbow him aside. Cam shot another arrow. It hit an invisible shield, and the other Glory glared his way. Diverted in his awareness, he never saw Saira's attack. She ended him with a bolt of fire, spun and decapitated the final Glory.

The way out was clear, and Cam hurried after Saira. They peered beyond the bounds of the boil, relaxing a moment later. Sidewinder was finishing off the last of the rakshasas. His sense of respite ended when he looked to the skies above.

As if from a great remove, he watched and lurked. Shimala's Sages couldn't know of his presence. He pressed himself deeper, hiding in shadows where no one could ever find him, not even Her whom he had deceived thus far. But eventually, he would emerge. And vengeance would be his.

Nailing and another Sage faced off against Master Winder. All of them bore injuries. Nailing was missing a hand and one of his horns had been ripped off. The other rakshasa clutched his stomach where blood seeped from a wound, and one of his legs appeared shattered. As for Master Winder, this was the first time Cam had ever seen him injured. Dried blood crusted one side of his bruised and battered face. His nose was broken, his robes rent, and a spear protruded from his ribs. If it hurt him any, Cam couldn't tell. The Wilde Sage's features were impassive as he stared down Nailing and the other Sage.

They spoke, their voices carrying.

"You have the day," Nailing said, a scowl twisting his bullish face. "But the war is far from over."

Energy crackled along Master Winder's form, and when it passed, his face was healed and his robes repaired. The spear remained, though. "The war is far from over," he agreed, "but stay here, and you'll find your part in it ended."

Nailing smiled. "Threats are unbecoming of you, Wilde Sage. Especially since luck played a large part in your victory today. You know of what I speak." The Sage of Warring Thunder glanced down.

Cam bristled with alarm when Nailing's eyes landed on him.

"We will leave," Nailing added, "but you should have protected your secrets. We are aware of them now." With that, Nailing gestured, and an anchor line formed. He and the other Sage exited the battlefield, leaving it quiet.

The silence was ruined an instant later by Sidewinder's celebration. Looking at them—only two-thirds of their numbers remained—Cam wondered how they could count this as a victory.

Then again, they were alive, and the enemy was dead. And all of Light Squad lived. Cam's heart swelled. The battle had been difficult, but, yes, it *was* a victory.

53

Some of Cam's jubilation ebbed when Master Winder sagged and a heavy wince passed over his face. The Sage pulled the spear from his side and dropped it, following the weapon to the ground. He looked done for in ways Cam had never expected to see from him.

Sidewinder Company silenced their own cheering, watching as Perit approached Master Winder. The Sage placed a hand on the Crown's shoulder, squeezing it, empathy on his face, and with a wave of his hand, Perit was healed of his wounds. It looked like a dislocated shoulder, heavy bruising to his face, and a foot pointed the wrong way. Perit breathed deep in obvious relief, saying some final words to Master Winder before turning away to address Sidewinder.

Cam wanted to see to Light Squad, but Saira fixed her gaze on him, silently telling him to remain. He held in a sigh when he saw why. The Wilde Sage was heading toward them.

"You did well," Master Winder said, offering a proud smile. "I can't tell you how relieved I am that you discovered the core. If not for that, we might not have won."

"It's mostly Cam you should be thanking," Saira said, gesturing his way. "He's the one who discovered the core's location. If not for him, this battle could have been a catastrophe."

Master Winder's face went tight. Cam didn't know why, but he didn't seem happy. "Keep that information to yourself," he whispered to Saira. "Nailing has noticed Light Squad. He has also noticed Cam. That's not the kind of attention any Novice needs."

"He's not the only one who knows of Light Squad," Saira said. "We entered the Pathway when it became Aware. A sending of Shimala was waiting for us. Specifically, for Cam."

Master Winder's eyes widened in shock, and his stare locked on Cam. "No one else can learn about this." His eyes locked tight on Cam's. "Will you let me place a compulsion on you?"

Cam viewed Master Winder with uncertainty. He had a vague sense of what a compulsion might entail. It wouldn't harm him, but just as importantly, he also didn't like the notion of someone tampering with his mind.

Master Winder must have noticed his reluctance and gave an impatient exhalation. "I don't mean to place one on you for no reason. But if you tell anyone you love about Shimala, they'll almost certainly be in the same danger as you are."

Fair enough. Cam wouldn't want anyone's lives risked on his account, but he still didn't like the idea of his thoughts being locked away from his ability to express them, no matter the noble-sounding reason. "Will I ever be able to speak on it?"

"In time," Master Winder said. "When you're stronger and more prepared to defend those you love." He gazed at Cam. "Do I have your permission?"

Cam considered the request a mite longer. It wasn't that he distrusted Master Winder—the man had given him a life he'd never have dreamed of having—but this was a monumental matter the Wilde Sage was asking of him. Cam looked to Saira, seeking her advice. She gave a faint nod. That was good enough for him. "Do it," he told Master Winder.

The Wilde Sage stared into his eyes. "You will not speak on the matter of Shimala, except with me and your direct instructors at the academy," he said, his voice reverberating.

The world was altered, and Cam felt the change within him, felt the compulsion take hold. The Sage had done something to his mind. A way to prevent him from ever telling what had happened in the Pathway.

"Did Shimala indicate why she was interested in you?" Master Winder asked after it was done.

"Because I'm a Plasminian, and no Plasminian has ever reached my level of Awareness."

"You've Advanced," Master Winder breathed, finally noticing the color change to Cam's eyes. The Sage appeared stunned or awed. "Not only that, you escaped Shimala and lanced the enemy's core. Well done, indeed."

Cam might have wanted to preen under Master Winder's praise, but there was a more important situation he wanted to see addressed. "Light Squad could use some healing. Some of us took a battering at the Pathway."

Master Winder gave a brisk nod. "Let's see to them then."

Saira conversed with the Wilde Sage while they walked. Mostly she went over her part in the battle as they passed by the injured members of Sidewinder Company. Perit was seeing to another Crown while the surviving Glories were healing Adepts. Those then sought out the Acolytes and Novices. In Sidewinder Company, the weakest were apparently healed last.

Master Winder glanced back, apparently noticing Cam's irritation. "Do the math. Think it through. If two people are equally injured, why heal the strongest Ephemeral Master first?"

The answer arrived quickly, and Cam ducked his head in embarrassment. It was so obvious when he wasn't thinking on it with the blinders of outrage. "Because then there will be two stronger Ephemeral Masters able to heal the injured."

Master Winder wasn't yet ready to let the matter go. "We don't use up our youth. And if you ever follow that path, or think to follow that path, you might as well call yourself a rakshasa."

Cam flushed, embarrassed further. He'd never think like what Master Winder was saying. "Yes, sir."

Their conversation trailed off, and shortly thereafter, they came upon Light Squad, all of whom remained where Cam had last seen them. Jade sat up as Master Winder approached. The Wilde Sage crouched down, resting a hand on her shoulder. A pulse of violet traveled down his arm and into her, causing her to cry out in pain as the bones of her broken arm were set. But an instant later, the cry became a sigh of relief, and she slumped over, asleep.

Master Winder moved on to Weld. Another touch and pulse of violet, and Weld's groans relaxed as he, too, fell asleep, snoring softly. Next was Card. Then Avia and Pan. Master Winder saw to all of them, and when finished, he stood. "I've done what I can, but a Sage's power is generally too great for any Novice. A Glory would do better at finalizing their healing. We will talk later."

He readied to move off, but Cam held him back, a notion occurring to him. "What about the villagers? Shouldn't we tell the people of Dander that they can return to their homes?"

"I'll see to it," Master Winder said with a smile. "But I'm leaving their organization to you." His smile became a chuckle. "You seemed to have a way of getting them to do what's needed."

Cam groaned. Having to deal with Gob and Nona… he shuddered at the notion.

It took days of recovery before Light Squad was ready to return to the academy. During that time, Cam trained, getting a better sense of what he could do as an Acolyte, which at first had been quite a lot.

In that initial day, it wasn't just his mind and body that seemed to work many times faster and better, but his insight into the world around him as well. His connection to it. Cam couldn't say for sure how much of a difference there was, but through will alone, he had been able to lift a wagon and move it down the road. In comparison, as a Novice, shifting a large stone a mere five feet would have proven taxing.

And his awareness of emotion had been heightened just as much. He had been able to sense Pan's feelings from a dozen yards away. He even got strange tinglings that Saira explained might one day allow him to talk to others with his thoughts. She had the same abilities, but it was apparently considered rude if the other person couldn't answer in the same way. There had been other abilities as well, such as the use of elemental forces and the ability to create a shield.

But none of it remained with him, and it was all because of the True Bond. Within days, Cam was reduced back to his abilities as a Novice. Nevertheless, he couldn't wait for the rest of Light Squad to join him as an Acolyte. Even if they'd only have the improvements for a short time. And all they had to do was figure what they wanted to be in life when it came to selfishness or selflessness.

For that, Cam might have a solution.

Professor Grey had been right when she'd once said that it all boiled down to three ways of looking at the answer. Selflessness in most everything, like Cam had done. Pure selfishness like a rakshasa. Or a pragmatic approach—a mix of the two with no shame felt for being selfish sometimes, which is what most folks chose.

Cam hoped Light Squad would listen and learn from him because in the end, the question wasn't so difficult to answer.

His thoughts lingering on Advancing, he stood with the rest of his unit on the early evening of their leave-taking from Dander. There were a bunch of folks to see them off, including Mayor Singer, Regim Baid, and Gob and Nona Felt. A number of those gathered even insisted on saying words, which Cam found embarrassing. They made it seem like Light Squad bore the brilliance of the Holy Servants.

Thankfully, Master Winder cut their speechifying short, stating he had to create the anchor line and attend to other business. The villagers muttered and complained but gave way to the Wilde Sage's will, falling into an awed silence when an anchor line split the world.

Seconds later, Light Squad was back at Nexus. It was several hours later in the day, nearing twilight, but the sun remained high enough to kiss the aquamarine waters, making it glisten like a million stars while a warm spring breeze idled about the island. Gossamer clouds paraded across a lush blue sky. The familiar smells of fish, brine, and a thousand types of spices perfumed the air along with the calls of merchants and the laughter of friends.

Cam was happy to be home, and after Master Winder left, Saira and Shivein—who Cam had barely seen during the battle—led them back to the academy. During their short journey, he stared about in fresh appreciation at every sight that met his gaze. Soon enough, they reached the school and Saira and Shivein left them there to their own devices.

"I missed this place," Pan said, striding at his side when they marched up to the Secondary Level.

"We all did," Jade said, sounding content. Cam hoped her good mood would continue. She'd acted disgruntled ever since the battle's end, and he had no idea why.

"I still can't believe we survived," Card said.

Cam smiled at him. "You'll get used to it."

"Devesh, I hope not," Card said with feeling.

"Devesh, I hope so," Weld disagreed. "If we get used to it, that means we're always surviving."

"And we're always winning," Jade added. "That's almost as important."

"I had no doubts about us winning or surviving," Pan said, nudging Cam with a hip.

Cam tossed an arm around his friend's broad shoulders and kissed him on the forehead. "So long as we have each other, we'll be alright."

"I heard from my father," Avia said, addressing Cam. "I told him what happened. He wants to talk to you."

"I bet every Sage-Duke will want to," Jade said with a laugh. "They'll want to talk to all of us. How many Novice squads can say they lanced two boils inside of six months? One of them solo and the other one we had no business being a part of." She scowled, dropping her voice as she spoke to Cam, Pan, and Weld. "I don't trust your patron."

"This wasn't his fault," Cam said, feeling a need to defend the Wilde Sage. He'd had a chance to talk to his mentor during their two days in Dander. "He honestly thought this was a mission Sidewinder could have handled. We weren't supposed to be as involved as we ended up being."

"Really?" Jade's brow lifted in apparent disbelief. "Because the way I see it, he put us in danger twice when he said we wouldn't be."

The same notion had already occurred to Cam. "We'll talk about it later," he groused, not wanting to discuss it in public. "Let's get settled first. We deserve some time to relax a bit."

"Well, look at that? Squad Screwup survived," a voice called out.

Cam pulled to a halt, finding a grinning Victory, Charity, and Merit walking over to them. He smiled back. "Well, look at that, yourself. These days, I guess they'll let anyone into this academy. Even rich, idle folk who are still Novices."

The nobles shared a frown of confusion, but when they drew close, their jaws dropped. They spoke over one another, shouting and carrying on, all of them wanting details on what had happened.

Cam laughed, raising his hands for quiet. "Gather anyone who's free. We'll tell all y'all about it in the cafeteria."

Victory chuckled. "All y'all. Love it."

"You actually said it right that time," Cam said, pretending to be impressed.

"Really?" Victory exclaimed in excitement. "I've been practicing—"

"No, you didn't say it right." Cam grinned. "But you're getting there."

Victory laughed again, sounding not a single note of annoyance, and Cam realized the man always seemed to be genuinely happy. A part of Cam wished he could be like that.

"We'll see *y'all* later," Victory said. "In about an hour?"

"Sounds good," Cam answered.

Light Squad split then, everyone heading to the dorm or other places. Cam watched them go, surprised to see Pan and Avia walking in lockstep.

Jade remained with him, and she smiled. "Those two. Who would have ever guessed?"

Cam watched her askance, noticing her eyes shift over to Weld as he and Card returned to the dorm. She shuffled her feet, something on her mind. Cam kept quiet, waiting for her to say her piece. He prayed it wouldn't be about her feelings for Weld. He'd done enough thinking on that, and frankly, it was tiresome and none of his business.

"Did you know the rakshasas were coming to the glade?" Jade spoke the words in a rush, like they were burning her tongue. "Did you go into the Aware Pathway after Saira and use us to slow them down?"

Cam gaped. "Is that what's had you acting a like a beehive bothered by a bear?" He was abruptly furious, wanting to shout at her, but at the last second, he lowered his voice. "Does everyone else think this?" he hissed.

Jade shook her head. "Not that I can tell. All of them—even Card—are just grateful that you were there to lead us."

"Then why would you think I'd leave you like that?" Cam asked, struggling to contain his hurt.

"Because it's how a lot of nobles would have treated us. Saira is Master Winder's favorite. You're *her* favorite. It only makes sense."

"Well you better kick that evil notion straight out of your head. I won't have anyone thinking on me like that. Besides which, Master Winder and Saira aren't like those nobles you're talking about."

"So, you didn't do it?"

Cam threw his arms in the air. "I just said so, didn't I?"

Jade's lips quirked. "In point of fact, you didn't."

Cam considered what he'd just said and realized she was right. "Then let me be clear. I didn't leave you behind as a sacrifice or anything. I had no idea the rakshasas were that close."

Jade finally smiled. "Thank you. And for what it's worth, I think you're a much better person and commander than we deserve." The smile slipped. "There's one other thing. It's about Weld."

Cam groaned. "Before you say anything, let me say my piece on that matter. I. Don't. Care."

"You should," Jade said, her voice soft as a whisper. "The reason I got hurt was because I took a blow meant for him."

Cam narrowed his eyes. "Why?" And the reason had better be a good one. Otherwise, Light Squad had a serious problem.

"Because I'm a fool. When you look at Weld, you think he's a lazy jackhole. And he is that. I know. But when I look at him, I also see someone worth saving."

"Some people can't be saved," Cam growled. "They are who they are, and they have to save themselves."

"You only say that because you don't like him."

"I say that because I was once like him. But that's not why I might dislike Weld. It's more about disrespecting the choices he's made."

"He can make better ones," Jade said, a desperate plea in her voice. "He's worth saving."

"Is that your role? To save him? Is this your answer to your question of selfishness versus selflessness?" Cam prayed it wasn't so.

"Not everyone can be perfect like you," Jade replied, scuffing the ground.

Cam laughed in her face. "I'm lots of things, but I'm definitely not perfect. If you met me back in Traverse, you'd probably think I was also a bad young man in need of saving."

"And I'd have wanted to," Jade said, meeting his gaze.

"Save yourself first."

Jade stared at him, a frown creasing her brow, but in the end a thoughtful expression settled over her face. "Maybe I will," she said after a moment. "I'll see you in the cafeteria."

Cam shook his head, watching her walk off. He prayed on her behalf. Of everyone in Light Squad, she seemed to need it the most.

"You really killed that many Acolytes and Adepts," Kahreen asked, her normal sneer not as… Cam wasn't sure what the right word was, but she wasn't sneering as much. In fact, she might have even sounded a little bit impressed.

He was glad for it. The last thing Cam wanted was to suffer through the raven-cawing unkindness of Kahreen's insults. But she'd surprised him, listening quietly as he'd explained what had happened at Dander.

The entire crowd of Novices had done so, too. And Cam was honestly surprised so many people had come to the cafeteria to hear Light Squad's account. As nobles, scions of high houses and such, surely they must have heard many similar tales while growing up?

And yet, here they were, nearly a hundred of them, almost all of the Novices currently at the academy. They filled the cafeteria, some of them seated on the tables themselves. Cam viewed the room. Some of the people here he knew, but none of them did he know well, and the vast majority, he only recognized. But everyone seemed to know about him and Light Squad, listening close like Cam's unit were prophets come down the mountain.

"We really did kill that many," Card said, answering Kahreen's question. His response seemed to settle the matter, which only made sense.

Card was a noble, like everyone else here, and more importantly, he was considered one of their best. Learning he'd changed affiliations to Light Squad meant something to these folks. And hearing him agree with Cam's report of what Light Squad had endured also meant something.

"But it wasn't like we were actually directly fighting against Adepts and Acolytes," Card continued. "Cam is being too modest, but his plan saved Light Squad *and* Sidewinder. We destroyed the rakshasa reserves. There were more than was expected, and if we hadn't done as we had, the battle would have been lost."

Charity was shaking her head, seated next to Cam, shoved up close. She gazed at him with amazement and respect on her face, along with the unsettling intensity he'd come to expect. "It is a wise commander who destroys their enemy without ever lifting a finger."

"We lifted plenty of fingers," Weld said with a guffaw. "Setting those boulders in place… they didn't move themselves."

A few chuckles met his statement, but Charity flashed him a look of irritation. "You know what I mean. And if you don't, then it's a good thing Cam is your leader and not you."

The gathered Novices responded to her words with laughter, some of it jeering.

Weld flushed, embarrassed and angry. Jade's hand twitched, her features empathetic like she wanted to console him. Cam was glad to see her do neither. If Weld said something stupid, then he should face the consequences when someone called him out on it.

"And how did you Advance?" Victory asked. "You never explained."

"I'm not sure what happened," Cam replied, unable to tell more since Master Winder's compulsion still locked his lips and didn't allow him to speak on the matter. "All I can say is that I was lying on the ground and Professor Maharani said if I didn't Advance, I'd die." He shrugged. "So I did. Then I woke up."

"What a sight to wake up to," a woman in the front row said with an appreciative sigh.

"You didn't receive a puzzle box?" Merit asked. "That's supposed to be the gift of completing an Acolyte Stage Pathway."

"But this was an Aware Pathway," Pan explained. "From what I read about them—" When did he have time to read about them? "—they don't give out any gifts."

"It's too bad you didn't get a gift," Charity said, nudging Cam's shoulder with her own. "You might have gained enough Ephemera to Advance to Adept."

"I'd have to understand how I view giving versus receiving," Cam said.

"I think you'd have figured it out." She nudged his thigh with her own.

Cam shifted in discomfort when he noticed the cat-wanting-to-play-with-a-mouse expression on her face.

"Well, congratulations on being the first in our class to Advance," Victory said, ending his considerations. "There's a tradition at the Ephemeral Academy when that happens." He gestured, and a couple of Novices brought out a round, brown thing several fingers tall. A single candle with an orange flame burned atop it.

Cam had no idea what he was looking at.

Upon seeing his confusion, Kahreen pealed mocking laughter.

Ah! There it was. The woman Cam had come to know and dislike.

"It's a chocolate cake," Kahreen said. "It was Jessira's favorite dessert."

Cam didn't let Kahreen's response harshen his mellow mood. And on taking his first bite of the chocolate cake, he could readily understand why the great and gracious Servant had loved the dessert.

54

The next morning, Saira sent a notice to Light Squad, asking them to meet her in her quarters. Cam had an inkling as to what the meeting was about, but when Pan asked him, he could only reply that they'd all find out soon enough.

"You truly don't know?" Pan repeated as they headed down to Primary Level.

"I might, but not for certain," Cam said. He withdrew a stalk of bamboo from his backpack, passing it to his friend. "Here you go."

Pan stared at him, looking somewhat offended. He then stared at the bamboo, stared at Cam again, and finally took the bamboo. "By giving me this, I think what you're really saying is you want me to munch on the bamboo and stop talking."

"Now, you're getting it."

"What I don't understand is why," Pan said.

They passed some Novices heading to Secondary Level and nodded acknowledgement to them. Cam spoke once they were out of earshot. "It's a surprise, and I'd hate to ruin it."

Pan grunted, sounding dissatisfied, but nevertheless went ahead and chewed on the bamboo. "This is quite tasty," he said after a moment, bumping his forehead against Cam's. "Thank you."

Cam smiled at his friend. "Any time."

They soon reached Saira's quarters, and inside, discovered the rest of Light Squad.

"Thank you for coming," Saira said. "The reason you're here instead of at Kinesthia is because your other professors and I feel like you need a few more days to recover. There's also another reason." She glanced around the room then, as if weighing Light Squad's worth. "How many of you think you comprehend your personal understanding of selflessness and selfishness?"

So, it was what Cam suspected. Saira didn't want her Ephemera to go to waste when she regressed. She wanted to make sure at least some members of Light Squad were prepared to Advance.

After a period of time, Pan diffidently raised his hand. "I do."

Cam smiled in encouragement at his friend, having already spoken to him and the others regarding the very question Saira had posed. Thankfully, they had listened, agreeing that it was actually pretty simple, especially when considered through the lens of Professor Grey's explanation.

Next to raise a hand was Avia, and after a few seconds of thought where Cam found Card staring at him, the other man did so, too.

Only Jade and Weld didn't lift their hands.

"I'm last again, I guess," Weld said with a rueful chuckle, while Jade stared at the ground, flushed with embarrassment.

Saira smiled encouragingly at the two of them. "You'll get there," she said before addressing the room at large. "The reason I ask is because in order to Advance, you need an answer to the question posed, but in order to *maximize* your Advancement, you also need a large source of Ephemera. Master Winder and your sponsors can provide you with the latter, through special fruits and tonics, but so can I. I plan on regressing."

Unsurprised mutters met her declaration.

"As to why I'm regressing, I have my reasons," Saira continued. "The main one being that I want to form a Plasminia Tang, and the only way I can is by regressing to an Adept. At Glory, it's denied to me. I'm too Advanced."

"You really think that's a good idea?" Card asked.

Saira nodded. "I do. I've spoken to Professor Grey. From what we've observed with Light Squad and some material I've read, my choice seems like the correct one."

"What about Master Winder?" Pan asked.

"He would disagree, but it's also not his decision."

Which sounded like Saira hadn't told him. The whole *"better to ask forgiveness than permission"* way of approaching problems.

"You're certain?" Card pressed. "About the importance of forming a Plasminia Tang?"

"Yes, I'm certain," Saira said, a note of exasperation in her voice.

Card grinned. "Then I'm glad I joined Light Squad. I wasn't sure at first about the way you lot approach the Way into Divinity, but if both you *and* Professor Grey feel like a Plasminia Tang is that important, then I guess I should get to it, too."

"You're lucky we let you join," Weld said.

"Luck had nothing to do with it," Card countered.

Cam spoke up, cutting off a brewing argument. "What happens next?" he asked Saira.

"What happens is that when I regress, I can grant my Ephemera to anyone willing to accept it. I was once a Crown, and I still have that knowledge and dexterity in using my Ephemera."

Cam recalled Shimala stating Saira's control wasn't very good, and he'd wondered on it ever since hearing it. Was it a lie from the Great Rakshasa? Or was it the truth and there was simply that vast a gulf between Shimala's abilities and those of even a Crown?

"What I possess," Saira continued, interrupting Cam's thoughts, "is enough for everyone in this room to Advance their Primary and Plasminia Tangs to Acolyte."

"Except me," Weld said, scowling.

"And me," Jade whispered, humiliation clear on her face.

"And me," Card added. "I still need a Plasminia Tang."

Cam wished she wouldn't feel that way. There was plenty of time for her to Advance. And as for Weld, he should scowl. He was probably the reason Jade didn't know how to answer what wasn't all that tough a question.

"Prepare an answer," Saira said to Weld, "and there will be enough for you as well." She clapped her hands, calling an end to that aspect of the conversation. "Who wants to go first?"

Pan rose to his feet from where he'd been seated on the ground. He offered his toothiest, most infectious smile to the room at large. "If no one else minds, I'd like to."

"Step forward," Saira said to Pan when no one disagreed with him.

Cam was glad to see he wasn't the only one unable to say no to Pan when he was grinning like that and looking so cute.

"Take my hands," Saira continued, "and Delve your Source. As deep as possible. I'll release my Ephemera to you. It will naturally go into your Primary Tang at first. Once you have Advanced, send the next portion to Plasminia. If Professor Grey is correct, that is the key to eventually Advancing your other Tangs. Do you understand?"

"I do," Pan said, shivering like he was cold, but more likely, it was nerves. Pan didn't like folks staring at him, and right now, everyone was. He was also probably worried about failing at this, which was reasonable. Pan was trying to Advance by taking in someone else's Ephemera. It just wasn't done since only idiots regressed.

Well, Saira wasn't an idiot, but this was still an unusual situation for most everyone here. They'd never been trained for this.

"We're about to begin," Saira said. "I'll send a small amount of Ephemera at first. Let's see how you handle it. And if you lose some, don't worry. The more important thing is to prevent the Ephemera from warping your Source. If that happens..." She hesitated. "You understand, this is dangerous. You might die. Are you ready?"

Pan licked his lips. "Yes, ma'am."

All is Ephemera and Ephemera is All. Cam imagined the phrase reaching Pan, sending him positive thoughts and prayers. *Please let him do this.*

Saira closed her eyes, and Pan followed suit. Moments later, he grimaced, and Cam could reckon why. It was the pressure of Saira's Glory-Stage Awareness pressing into him. Cam remembered the anvil-like weight of Honor's Ephemera when she had given it to him.

Pan seemed to figure out a way to adapt to the heaviness, though, and his grimace resolved.

On seeing Pan's relief, Cam relaxed, realizing only then that he'd been gritting his teeth with worry.

Saira opened her eyes, smiling. "Well done. You accepted almost everything I sent."

Pan grinned. "I'm an Awakened Beast. Accreting and Imbibing Ephemera is our one advantage over humans."

"Then let's try some more," Saira said.

On they went, for a couple more hours until a moment arrived when Pan opened his eyes, and they had the orange Haunt of an Acolyte. He knew it as well, grinning wide, more cute than usual.

But even then, they didn't stop, not until Pan stated that he had Plasminia Advanced, too. He grinned again, proud of himself, which was only right. It wasn't easy what he'd just done. For Cam it had been torture, but it had been worth it. He wouldn't have the life he did now without enduring the pain.

"How you feeling?" Cam asked when Pan dropped next to him, both of them on the ground.

"Tired," Pan said. "I could use a nap."

Cam chuckled. "Nap away. I'll tell you if you miss anything."

Pan rested his head on his shoulder, slipping into a peaceful sleep while Avia worked on Advancing. Cam didn't have to stay. He didn't have to be here at all, but he also couldn't see himself leaving. It was only right for him to remain and support his people.

"What happens next?" Pan asked.

Cam glanced at his friend. "You mean what happens when you Advance your other Tangs and Enhance them all?"

"Enhancing shouldn't be too hard," Card said. He was walking with them, the trio making their way toward their first class in Synapsia since returning from Dander a week ago.

They strode along the walkways of the academy, and Cam was happy to finally get back to a normal classwork routine. Kinesthia had been fun, being able to go harder and faster with his True Bond. It wasn't what a normal Acolyte could manage, but it was a far sight more than what he had been able to do as a Novice. It was also to be expected, though. Light Squad had the bodies of Acolytes, if not the abilities.

Their work had even earned a grunt of approval from Professor Shivein.

But then had come Spirairia, and Cam's earlier optimism faded. That's when he recognized just how far below a standard Acolyte they really were. Light Squad could impact the world—be it moving objects, controlling the elements, or even the basics of empathy and telepathy—but at less than a quarter what others of their same Stage of Awareness could manage. Cam didn't like it; none of them did.

But for now, it was a limitation they'd have to accept.

Following that had been a quick snack in the cafeteria, and now it was time for Synapsia.

Clouds had rolled in sometime during the morning, and the smell of rain was in the air. A brisk wind blew, swaying the trees and setting their leaves to rustling like a thousand rattles. Students nodded their way since Light Squad was recognized after that night in the cafeteria when Cam had explained what they'd done at Dander.

"Enhancing shouldn't be too hard," Cam agreed in response to Card's comment. "But don't forget how bad it stinks."

"You don't have to tell me," Pan said. "You'll reek even worse this time."

Cam grimaced, figuring as much. There would be more yellow bile since there was more Ephemera to Enhance, and he'd also be able to purify more of his body.

"You're going to be late," Jade called from well ahead of them as she, Avia, and Weld hustled on into the classroom building.

Cam cursed, realizing she was right. Professor Grey wouldn't be happy. He set off at a sprint, Pan and Card staying with him. They raced up the stairs, through the hallway, dodging other students, and rumbled into the classroom. Jade, Avia, and Weld were only now taking their seats, and Professor Grey merely raised a single eyebrow upon their entrance. Thankfully, she didn't say anything about tardiness and waited on them to settle into their chairs.

"Now that everyone is here," she began, "we can discuss what you've learned during your adventures."

"Does learning how to hurt count?" Weld asked in a joking fashion.

"Of course it does," Professor Grey replied. "Learning to overcome pain is an important aspect of both martial training and martial prowess."

"There's a difference?" Cam asked. An instant later, he wanted to plant his face in his palm. "Of course, there is. Some are good on the practice field but don't show when it matters."

Professor Grey smiled. "Exactly. You'll learn more in my husband's teachings. Next year, he'll be your instructor for Kinesthia."

"What about Professors Maharini and Shivein," Weld asked.

"As Adepts, they are not allowed to teach you." She held up her hands, shutting off any discussion. "And I know Professor Shivein is still a Glory, but as you're aware, he plans on regressing. In fact, I would imagine that if they wanted to, the two of them could actually join some of your classes."

It was a strange notion—sharing a class with Saira. Almost like they were equals. Cam quickly shut down the avenues where such a thought might lead.

"And you?" Avia asked. "You'll still teach us Synapsia?"

Professor Grey shook her head. "Sadly, that won't be the case. My contract was for only one year, and I must move on."

"What's your husband like?" Weld asked.

Cam unconsciously leaned forward, curious as to the answer.

Professor Grey smiled. "My husband is… unique." Her expression grew wistful, full of a hopeless longing.

Cam wondered. What kind of man would inspire that kind of expression from a woman like Professor Grey?

"I hope he's good at what he does," Weld said with a cocky grin. "Because as soon as I'm an Acolyte, I aim on being the best. Even better than… What did you say your husband's name was?"

"I didn't," Professor Grey said, still smiling. "But he calls himself Cinder. And you'll see what I mean about his unique qualities when you meet him." Her face firmed, a sign that the discussion was at an end. "Now, while you still have me, let's review what you learned. Other than how to endure pain."

"You're really going to Enhance all your Tangs in one night?" Card asked.

In the weeks following Light Squad's return to the academy, he'd come to accompanying Cam and Pan back to their quarters after their library study session. Currently, he sat at the dining room table alongside Cam while Pan—who for once *wasn't* chewing on a stalk of bamboo—sat at his usual spot on the floor.

"Not all of them," Cam said. "But definitely Plasminia and one other."

"He will reek," Pan said, waving a hand, like he could already smell the stench.

Cam glared at his friend, feigning anger.

"It's true," Pan exclaimed. "And you better stay on the balcony until you're done. Otherwise, our apartment will be unlivable."

Cam glanced outside.

It wasn't as late as normal and with summer ascending, it was barely past sunset. The lamp posts hadn't yet come on, and there were still plenty of students out enjoying the weather; playing with their spinning, flying disks or sitting around enjoying the weather, conversing and laughing. Cam figured that although he'd be able to hear more of the goings-on when he went out on the balcony, he'd have his attention focused on the more important issue of Enhancement.

His gaze then went to Card. Why had he taken to spending so much time with the rest of Light Squad, especially him and Pan? None of them could say they knew the man well—Card wasn't exactly talkative—but Cam liked what his presence might mean.

Card had originally joined Light Squad to gain an advantage, to access secrets that allowed Light Squad to do so much better than the nobles. But then had come Dander, and Card had gone with them there, fought and bled alongside them. That was when the changes had started, when he began spending more time with them after hours, socializing even. He had become a true member of their team.

"You didn't say much in classes today," Cam noted to Card. It was the norm for him, but he generally had at least a few worthwhile comments. Today, there had been nothing but silence.

"I had some decisions to make," Card said. "Primarily, if I should remain in Light Squad."

Cam gave him a hard stare. And here he'd just gotten to thinking Card had already made that decision.

"I've been feeling pressure from my family," Card began. "To return to Squad Chalk. They made some good points. With what I've learned while in Light Squad, I can continue to Advance to Adept and possibly beyond and not have to risk myself like I did at Dander."

Cam frowned, not bothering to hide his disappointment, although he understood Card's reticence. What Light Squad had suffered and survived at Dander wasn't something any person of intelligence would want to repeat.

Card never noticed Cam's unhappiness since he was busy staring at the ground and fidgeting his fingers. "There's also Weld and Jade. They're still Novices, which I don't get. Have they always lagged like that?"

Cam could have answered truthfully, but he was learning that as the leader of Light Squad, it was best if he didn't speak badly about any of them to anyone but their instructors.

Pan, however, didn't have the same limitations. "Weld started the year as the strongest of us, but he's lazy. He also lacks courage, and if he doesn't change, he'll fall too far behind to keep up."

Card grunted, scowling some. "Jade thinks she needs to save him."

"She told you that?" Cam said, surprised Jade would tell such a personal piece of information to Card, a person who was still a mystery and a stranger.

"She didn't have to," Card replied. "I figured it out on my own. She's an idiot, and I wasn't sure I should remain in a squad with two damaged people like that."

Cam didn't have a means to erase Card's concerns. The truth was, he shared them.

"Then it sounds like you made your choice," Pan said, speaking in that diffident way he had when bringing up something uncomfortable.

Card nodded. "I'm staying. We have a strong unit, even with Jade and Weld—assuming they Advance. Plus, I like the two of you and Avia. We fought together, and none of you quit and cowered. That's worth a lot in my book. I'm not ready to see that end."

Cam breathed out in relief. "In that case, let's stop talking about Jade and Weld." he suggested. Gossip and him went together like bread and butter, but he wanted to change that part of himself.

Card grunted in agreement.

"I learned something interesting in the library," Pan said. "Professor Grey was right about Klevonia Tangs. We can form them."

"She's always right," Card said, with an approving nod.

Cam hid a smirk. As far as Card was concerned, Professor Grey had hung the sun, the moon, and the stars.

"Anyway," Pan continued. "What I learned was that with a Klevonia Tang, the rakshasas can create a channel that leads from their Sources directly to the surface of their skins. It usually ends in their mouths. So instead of slowly Accreting Ephemera like we do, they Imbibe what they want like they were drinking it. It only takes them hours to do what it might take us days or weeks."

Cam recalled the Awakened wolf standing over Lilia, feeding off of her. It was a memory that haunted him still, and he wished he could somehow unsee it. Thinking on it also reminded him of Shimala. He had trouble erasing her from his mind. Too often, his nights were interrupted with terrors about her, what he'd seen in the Pathway, and the promise she had made. She knew him, which was more frightening than any nightmare.

Cam did his best to shove his worries to the back of his mind, though. Now wasn't the time to ponder them.

"Is that what they do when they're feeding?" Card asked Pan.

"It seems like it," Pan said. "They're feeding, but it's not of the flesh."

"Maybe we should do the same," Card said.

"I don't know," Pan said. "Their way is faster, but depending on how much they Imbibe, they can be weaker in their Awareness by an entire Stage for weeks afterward."

Card countered. "But if we ever lance another core, and we all had this channel, we could capture every bit of Ephemera it still contained. We could maximize how much we hold, and possibly even Advance our other Tangs."

It was actually a good idea, and Cam nodded. "We'll want to discuss it with Professor Grey," he said. "Until then, we're better off Enhancing whatever Acolyte Tangs we have to Crystal."

Card smiled. "Which is another reason for me to stay in Light Squad. I have a solid chance of reaching Acolyte Prime. It's common enough, having two Tangs at Crystal as an Acolyte, but four? That's unheard of."

"I'm glad we've been of benefit," Cam said, faking a scowl.

Card exhaled heavily, like he was being put upon. "I know I can seem mercenary, but I also said a lot of good things about you and Pan just then."

"You did, and I was joking," Cam replied. "It's what friends do."

"We ain't friends yet."

"Well look at you," Cam said. "Using proper country diction and all." He glanced outside, to where the sun was setting and darkness falling. "Time to Enhance my Tangs."

"Does the stench penetrate the windows?" Card asked.

"It does," Pan said, sounding mournful.

"Then that's my cue," Card said, rising to his feet. "Show me what you can do tomorrow?"

"Of course," Cam replied. He waited on Card to leave before taking off his clothes. "You know, as painful and difficult as it is for me to Enhance, I'll probably want a drink when I'm done. A shot of whiskey would go nice."

The moment the words left his mouth, an urge swept over him. An urge for a drink. He wanted it so bad. All he had to do was get dressed, walk into Nexus, and find a bar. Any would do.

"Cam!"

Cam opened his eyes on hearing Pan's shout. Only then did he realize he'd put on his pants.

His heart suddenly raced, pounding out his fear. He'd come close to breaking just then; all on account of a joke. Professor Grey had said karma wasn't what he'd always assumed, but just now, it sure felt like it was. Just now, karma had nearly paid him back good and hard for making a joke that he should have never made. If Pan hadn't been around…

Cam shuddered. He had hoped that siren song was gone, but clearly not. "I shouldn't have said that."

Pan gave a grave nod. "No. You shouldn't have."

"I'm going to go Enhance," Cam said, quickly removing his pants. Mostly he just wanted to escape Pan's gaze, which felt accusing instead of sympathetic.

Card wandered back to his rooms, knowing his life might never again be the same. He'd just told Cam and Pan that he intended on remaining with Light Squad. It made sense. Through the help of Professors Grey and Maharani, he'd managed to add a Plasminia Tang.

He winced at the painful memory. In truth, it had taken everything he had and then some, and in the end, Professor Grey might have actually had to carry him across the finish line. Without her, Card might have died.

Which meant even if other young nobles wanted to do as he'd done, it wouldn't be easy. Not unless they had someone like Professor Grey to help them. Regardless, by using his Plasminia, he was later on able to Enhance all his Tangs to Crystal. It was amazing when he considered it, impossible really.

But his mother didn't care.

She'd sent him a missive, indicating that he was to return to Squad Chalk. By choosing otherwise, she might go so far as to cut off his support. He doubted it would come to that, and even if it did, Sage-Duke Arta, Victory's father, had an obvious interest in Light Squad, especially Cam.

Then again, who didn't. Cam was one of a kind, and every Sage-Duke on Golden was probably figuring on how to steal him away from Master Winder. If so—and Card felt sure about the politics of the situation—then staying close to Cam would be, not just in his own best interests, but that of his Sage-Duke's as well.

As for his mother… Card scowled. He might have respected her more if she wasn't so selfish. She had innumerable lovers, and for all Card knew, the Crown in charge of Sidewinder, Perit Line, might even be his father. He had no way of knowing, especially since he looked nothing like the man who had raised him.

The jokes and japes Card had endured throughout his life could have been forgivable, except his mother was the kind of person who gave no love or time to anyone, and yet, expected everyone to heed her every need. This included her children, and that *was* unforgivable.

Card's scowl deepened. A mother shouldn't withhold love from her children.

55

The next morning, Jade surprised them outside the cafeteria by showing up with the orange eyes of an Acolyte.

"When did this happen?" Cam exclaimed, holding Jade's shoulders so he could make sure he was seeing right.

She grinned, content and peaceful like he'd never seen from her. "Last night. When I found my truth."

Cam hugged her, glad to see her happy. "I'm so proud of you."

"You don't have to be," Jade said. "It's the easiest step in the Way into Divinity."

"Nevertheless, I'm proud of you, too," Pan said, also hugging her. "So proud that I'll even let you have my bamboo." He offered her a stalk. "You can have the whole length."

Cam guffawed while Jade wrinkled her nose and laughed. "No, thanks. And you might want to think on how that sounds."

Pan tilted his head, replaying his words. He flushed, which caused Cam to laugh even louder.

"What changed?" Cam asked, leading them toward the cafeteria's entrance and out of the morning sun.

It promised to be a hot one today with no wind to stir the oppressive humidity. Cam swore it felt like wading through water. But inside was blessed coolness with the lovely scents of dosa, idli, and sambar. Cam scoped around and saw bacon, eggs, and fried potatoes as well.

"A talk with Avia is what changed," Jade said as they got in line. "She gave me some words of wisdom."

Cam eyed her in question, waiting on a further explanation. Jade didn't answer, though, and he didn't pester her. She'd tell him or she wouldn't.

They collected their food and drinks—orange juice for everyone else and a mango lassi for Cam—and grabbed a table. Cam noted when Avia, Weld, and Card entered the cafeteria, and he waved at them, getting their attention.

Jade stared at Weld, and her jaw might have tightened a moment before she faced everyone at the table. "I want to apologize," she said. "I haven't been wise in my feelings."

Cam reckoned where this was going. "You don't have to say anything," he told her, not wanting her to feel awkward.

"I do have to say it," Jade said. "The reason I Advanced is because of what you told me. What Pan told me." She laughed, sounding disgusted with herself. "What even Card told me. All of you said the same thing. That I have to save myself. Not young men of questionable morals. It took the battle at Dander for me to really think it through. And last night, Avia said the same thing."

"That's it?" Cam said, somewhat stunned and disheartened. Why hadn't everyone's advice penetrated Jade's thick skull until last night?

"It wasn't only that," Jade said. "It was also what Weld said yesterday. About how he wants to be the best." She laughed in disbelief. "His arrogance when he's still a Novice, and not a particularly skilled one at that."

"You mean about Professor Grey's husband?" Cam asked.

"It was rather stupid," Pan said in agreement.

"That's putting it mildly," Jade replied, still laughing. Cam couldn't tell if she was laughing at Weld's claim—which was laughable since the man didn't have it in him to achieve greatness—or at herself for pining after him for so long.

Just then, Victory, Charity, and Merit showed up, carrying their trays. They took one look at Jade and halted, appearing stunned.

"All of you are Acolytes?" Charity exclaimed. "How?"

"Weld isn't," Pan said.

"He doesn't count," Victory scoffed. "I can't believe all y'all"—he checked with Cam on the pronunciation. It was actually spot on, and Cam gave Victory a thumbs-up—"I can't believe all y'all managed to Advance. Half my squad still hasn't."

"Oh, stop showing off," Charity said, "I'm the only one in my unit who has."

"They better hurry up then," Cam said. "The year ends in a month."

"We'll get them there," Victory said. "And if not, they'll have six months grace back home to succeed."

"And they're not ever offered second chances?" Cam asked.

"This is their best chance to Advance," Merit said. "If they can't make it to Acolyte with all the treasures of Ephemera they've been given, they likely never will. But, no. If they do Advance a year from now or even however many years, there's always the chance their Sage-Duke might sponsor them. More likely, they'll simply remain home and receive instruction at a local school."

Merit's answer raised a question Cam had often wondered about. "Why even send you lot to the academy?" he asked. "Your instructors are from your duchy, and the tests here could all be done just as easily back home. So why here?"

"You assume learning is the only reason to attend the academy," Merit said.

"What other reason is there?" Pan asked.

Merit offered a mocking smile. "Fishing for new blood. Marriage. All these nobles. Tossed together. What better place for the younger generation to get to know one another. And for our families to plan our futures."

"That's not the only reason," Victory objected. "There's also the shared learning. There is no finer library than the one here. Plus, while our primary instructors are from home, we also rotate with those from the other duchies. It's the best way to learn what the others know in terms of how they train their young Ephemeral Masters."

"We never rotated," Cam pointed out.

"That's because you're Light Squad," Charity replied. "You don't get the same perks." She winked at Cam. "Unless you want them."

Cam blinked, not knowing how to respond.

Victory tsked. "You're incorrigible," he said to Charity, drawing her away. "We'll see you later," he called over his shoulder.

"That woman is impossible," Jade said. "I can't tell if she's honestly interested in you, or if she just likes teasing you."

"The latter," Cam said, irritated at so often being the focus of Charity's teasing. "You heard Merit. The nobles are here to find spouses."

"Unless she just wants a fling," Jade replied.

"Who wants a fling?" Avia asked.

"Charity. With Cam," Pan answered.

Avia grunted. "Makes sense." She faced Cam. "Are you going to take her up on it?"

First, there was nothing to take up. Second, Cam had his heart on someone else. And third, he desperately didn't want to discuss this right now. Or ever. He sought out any means to change the conversation, latching onto an earlier topic. "So that's what opened your mind?" he said to Jade. "What Weld said about Professor Grey's husband. That's what got you seeing him in a proper light?" Why couldn't she have come to that conclusion about Weld on all the other times he'd acted like a fool?

Jade shrugged, clearly self-conscious. "There were other times I should have seen him for who he really is, but whatever reason, this time it stuck. It made sense. You know? I mean, think about it. Any man who Professor Grey chooses as her husband must be someone amazing. She wouldn't settle for anything less. And for Weld to say he aims on being better than him is one of the stupidest things he could have ever said."

"His name is Cinder," Avia said. "I wonder what he's like."

"Wonder what who's like?" Weld said, plopping his tray down and scooting in next to Cam.

"Professor Grey's husband," Avia replied.

"He's probably amazing at everything," Card said, arriving just then and sounding bitter for some reason.

"He better be," Weld said with a grin, staring at Jade. "You heard what I said yesterday, right? I meant every word."

Card snorted, not bothering to hide his derision.

Weld scowled at him. "Why's that so funny?"

"Because it's Professor Grey's husband, stupid," Card replied. "You think she'd marry just anyone? Cinder whateverhisnameis is probably just like her. Scary smart and deadly as they come."

"What makes you think Professor Grey is deadly?" Weld asked.

Cam rolled his eyes. Weld had said a lot of idiotic things, but every day, he pushed into a new realm.

Card seemed to think so, too. He stared at Weld in disbelief, while Avia and Pan coughed into their hands, hiding their amusement. Even Jade fought a smile.

Weld glared at them before fixing his gaze on Jade. "We've never seen her fight," he said in a mulish tone.

"We don't need to. Not to know she's deadly," Pan said.

"I need to know," Weld declared.

"Then what about the respect the other instructors give her?" Cam asked. "Not just ours, but Victory's? You think they'd do that if all she had was book learning?"

Weld was about to answer, but Card broke in, addressing Jade. "You Advanced!" He appeared genuinely happy for her. "Congratulations! When did this happen?"

Jade gave a vague explanation about how she had finally listened to lessons given to her by her friends. Her eyes never went to Weld.

Card nodded. "It's a good thing to have friends."

"To have a friend, you have to be a friend," Pan said to Card. "Do you have friends then? I'd like to believe that you do."

Card smiled—a rare occurrence. "I have friends. I even like some. A plump panda for one."

"I'm not plump," Pan squawked.

"And he's a panda-person," Cam corrected.

"Whatever," Card said. "But with all those bamboos he eats, he's definitely plump." He reached over and poked Pan's belly. "Plump."

"I'm not plump. I'm furry," Pan said, swatting Card's hand away when he tried to poke him again.

"His fur is soft," Avia said. "I like it."

Cam watched it all with a grin. It was good to see Light Squad coming together. He viewed Weld askance. Well, most of them.

"Why do you tease Cam like that?" Victory asked.

Charity looked to Light Squad's table, shrugging away the question after a moment's consideration. "Why do you care?" she asked, facing Victory with a knowing smirk. "You're not jealous, are you?"

Victory rolled his eyes. "Our parents are interested in a marriage between the two of us, but we both know that neither of us share that desire."

Charity feigned a hurt expression, batting her eyelashes. "How can you say that to me? After all we've been through together."

Victory didn't take the bait, sighing heavily. "Can you be serious?"

"I can be." Charity grinned. "But it's funner to not be serious."

"You're avoiding the question," Victory said. "If I didn't know better—

"If you didn't know better, you'd know next to nothing."

Victory gave her a flat look of disapproval.

"Fine," Charity said with an exaggerated huff of annoyance. "It's probably because it is funny, seeing such a large, powerful man seize up in terror whenever I just look his way."

Victory raised his brow. "Powerful?"

"Isn't he?"

Merit, quiet until now, spoke. "I think you like him."

Charity scoffed. *Her like Cam Folde? Ridiculous.* Merit was probably just trying to get a rise out of her. How typical. "A yokel from nowhere," she said. "And you think I like him?" Charity shook her head in feigned pity.

Cam flopped to the ground, chugging water. It was the afternoon class in Kinesthia, and Devesh was it hot. He exhaled heavily, wiping the sweat pouring down his face, fanning his shirt, and wishing for winter. Even autumn would be better than this scorching heat and blistering summer sun. The muggy weather reminded him of a kitchen fogged by a pot of boiling water.

And thinking on *that* reminded him of cooking meals with Pharis back home and spending time with his kinfolk. He needed to send them all letters. It had been awhile. Even better if he could go see them, both family and friends, especially Jordil and Master Bennett. Just thinking on it, an intense longing rose within him, and he wondered if he ever would.

Maybe eventually, but not anytime soon.

All Novices at the Ephemeral Academy were given a couple months off after their first year, and most were fortunate enough to have their sponsoring Sage-Dukes anchor line them home. For Cam, Pan, and Weld, though, there would be no such luck.

Master Winder would be too busy—likely lancing a boil, fighting a powerful rakshasa, or seeing to whatever important issues the Wilde Sage figured was the best use of his time. Cam didn't think sending his students to their disparate homes counted as important.

"It's hot enough to melt my granny's teeth fillings," Weld said, dropping to the ground and sucking down water like a man about to die of thirst. His Acolyte-orange eyes—he'd earned them a week ago—went distant. "They're made of lead, which makes her *very* interesting when she starts drinking." He chuckled, apparently thinking on his granny.

"Granny's a wonderful lady."

"I thought you lot Advanced to Acolyte?" Professor Shivein said, standing over them. "Where's your stamina? Your strength? Your speed?" He scoffed, shaking his head. "Absolutely lazy. You're barely better than you were as Novices."

Some of what Professor Shivein said was true, but there was a reason for it, and it had nothing to do with Light Squad being lazy. It was their True Bonds, and Professor Shivein knew it.

"I sometimes wonder if we made a mistake choosing those True Bonds," Card said, seated close at hand.

Cam didn't share those doubts, and just as importantly, he was patient. "The past is the past," he said, rising to his feet. He offered a hand to Pan, drawing him up. "It's better to let it go and stop fretting."

"I'm not fretting," Card said. "And who says a word like fretting, anyway?"

"Folks from the country," Cam answered with a smirk. "We're right smart in how we talk."

Card snorted in good-natured humor, rising to his feet. "I can't believe I'm led by a yokel."

Cam laughed, even as he helped Jade stand. "Come on. It's time to work. Embrace the grind, and we'll kick some ass."

Avia groaned in mock-weariness as Pan helped her up.

"What about me?" Weld said, raising a hand for someone to draw him up. Cam offered him a hand, tugging hard.

"What fresh devilry do you suppose they'll have us doing?" Pan said.

Cam did a double-take at the odd turn of phrase, he but didn't have a chance to ask about it as Saira shouted for their attention. "We're going again. You'll learn how to fight without a shield even if it kills you."

"Wouldn't that ruin the whole point of fighting?" Cam asked. "If we're dead, then we can't really learn."

Saira smiled, and it wasn't friendly. "For your smart comment, Mr. Folde, you get to spar with me."

Good-natured laughter met her proclamation, while Cam groaned in genuine upset. Sparring against Saira when she wasn't feeling too charitable was going to leave some bruises.

"Prepare yourself," Saira said.

Cam scooped up his shoke, a wooden training blade that legend claimed had once been able to perfectly mimic the pain of an injury without leaving any lasting harm. The Servants were supposed to have invented it, but nowadays, a shoke was just a piece of wood; a single-edged, wooden blade stained a dark purple. A hand-and-a-half hilt and a wide cross-guard completed the weapon.

Cam rolled his shoulders and crouched in the position Saira and Professor Shivein had taught Light Squad over the past week. A True Bond brought his body and the world to full life. Ephemera flitted about, never still. His muscles prepared to surge. His senses heightened, and his mind raced, picking out the smallest details. A bead of perspiration on Saira's cheek. Her tongue wetting her upper lip. Her eyes narrowed, making her loveliness appear deadly.

Cam shook off the distraction of noticing Saira's beauty. "Ready."

Saira came in slow, sending out testing slashes and thrusts. Cam didn't have any trouble defending. He focused harder when she increased the pace. A feint got him off balance, and only his True Bond-enhanced reflexes let him reset.

If Saira had wanted, she could have laid him out just then.

Cam hunkered lower, settling into his defense. Another feint. He didn't bite. A thrust, and he twisted away. He gave ground, struggling to recall the lessons taught.

"Form a shield," Saira snapped.

Cam cursed under his breath. It wasn't that he'd forgotten, but it wasn't exactly easy to both hold a shield and defend against her. Still, he should ingrain proper habits now rather than work on fixing bad habits later. He focused on his Source, reached out with Spirairia and formed a shield. Only he could see it, although Ephemeral Masters of higher Awareness could sense it.

"Better," Saira said, her Glory-blue eyes flashing approval.

Here she came at him again, harder, faster.

Cam parried a horizontal slash. Gave ground to a follow-up elbow. Blocked a thrust. Three powerful blows, and Saira hadn't pulled any of them. Cam grinned to himself at his success.

In the next instant his breath exploded from his lungs. He'd hardly seen Saira move. It was a front kick plastering into his stomach. His shield barely slowed the blow, and he lay on the ground, heaving.

"You lost focus," Saira said. "You lose focus, and you die. It can't happen as an Acolyte. At your Stage, you're finally starting to become dangerous."

"Yes, ma'am," Cam wheezed when he could breathe again.

"We're going again."

Cam nodded, rising to his feet. He set himself, focused on her shoke, her hips, and her shoulders. He wouldn't go down like he'd just done. Three strikes it'd taken for her to defeat him. She'd have to work harder for it next time.

He parried a horizontal slash. Gave ground to a follow-up elbow. Blocked a thrust. Twisted aside from a front kick. Reset. It was the exact same moves as before. Saira repeated them, even faster. Cam defended, losing form but not focus. Again, but this time, Saira altered her approach. Her elbow became a feint. The thrust nearly got him, but Cam got his shoke up in time to block. He twisted from the front kick he knew was coming.

… And got caught by a horizontal slash as once again, his shield did nothing. He groaned, closing his eyes.

When he opened them, Saira stood over him, smiling. "Much better." She offered a hand, hauling him to his feet.

They went back to it, pausing briefly when Cam's True Bond went into cooldown. Sweat dripped down Cam's face like a river. His shirt clung to him, and he'd taken more than a few bruises from Saira. The only good part of the classwork was the way her shirt clung to her.

He just didn't have time to appreciate it. His attention had to stay on her shoke, on her fists, elbows, knees, and feet. Finally, though, Saira called a break, and Cam dropped his arms. His shoulders ached from keeping them up so long, and his thighs wanted to cramp from crouching low as long as he had.

"Take a break," Saira said. "You earned it."

Cam made sure not to look too much when she fanned her shirt. Instead, he hobbled over to where Pan was on the ground, looking done for. He lay flat on his back, mouth agape as he panted. If the perspiration was uncomfortable for Cam, he could only imagine how bad it was for his friend.

"Saira worked you pretty good," Jade said, seated next to Pan and passing Cam a jug of water.

"You don't know the half of it," Cam said, making a solid effort of draining the water. "I think you'll have to carry me back to the dorms. I'm bruised all over."

"You'll survive," Jade said with a chuckle, sobering a moment later. "I have to tell you, I'm pretty disappointed with what we can do as Acolytes. We're so weak. So slow. And our shields are barely worth the name."

"We all knew this would happen," Cam said. "We'll just have to get to Glory faster than everyone else so we're not the weak striplings that get our backsides handed to us."

"Will Shivein really regress?" Jade asked.

"That's the plan. He'll pass off most of his Ephemera to Saira so she can form a Plasminia Tang and maybe Advance some of her others. Anything left, goes to us."

"I wish I could just take it in one go like Pan and Avia," Jade said. She snorted a moment later. "I shouldn't complain. Without Plasminia, none of this would be possible anyway. Having a chance to Advance all our Tangs."

Avia dropped down next to them. "Professor Shivein killed me," she moaned. "Avenge my death."

"You'll have to avenge mine first," Pan said. "This weather is a villain. My great enemy. One of you must Advance to Divine and never let a poor panda suffer in such heat."

"That's a great idea," Jade enthused, speaking to Avia. "You always talk about how you need to Advance to Crown so your family will accept you. Just imagine what they'll do if you reach Divine."

"I have a feeling they'll accept me no matter what I manage," Avia said, looking off into the distance and smiling faintly.

"I'm glad to hear it," Cam said, happy to see Avia content with her life. They all could use some of that good feeling.

Another week passed, and soon would come the months-long break anticipated by those Novices who had Advanced to Acolyte. For others, though, that break meant the end of their time at the academy. Sure, they had a six-month grace to Advance while at home, but most knew it unlikely, and their sorrow was palpable.

It wasn't all sad news for them, though. After all, they were nobles and would likely land on their feet. Such were Cam's thoughts as he approached Saira's quarters. She'd asked to meet with him tonight, after he'd finished studying at the library.

The academy was quiet this evening, and the pathways wandering among buildings and fields, peaceful. The heavens shone as bright as ever, like some luminous blanket of lights, especially with the moon being new. Crickets chirped, and a kind wind kissed Cam's face while bushes rustled softly, like the breeze was trying to put a baby to sleep.

"Thank you for coming," Saira said, when he knocked on her door. She stepped outside, joining him there. "Let's walk."

Cam shrugged. If she'd wanted to walk, he could have just walked back with her from the library. After all, she'd been there tonight, same as he.

"How are the others doing with their Tangs?" Saira asked.

It was an unexpected question, and Cam shot her a look. He'd figured she would have already known the answer. "Pan Enhanced his Primary and Plasminia. Same as Avia and Jade. The other two aren't there yet, although Card is close."

"I'm glad to hear how well they're coming along," Saira said. Her Glory eyes were still blue but a pale, dull Haunt compared to the beginning of the year. "But once I fully regress, it'll be up to Shivein to help them."

"You mean if there's anything left from him when you create a Plasminia Tang."

"There will be," Saira said, flashing him a smile.

She didn't say anything more, and their conversation fell silent as they walked along narrow paths, side-by-side with jasmine and honeysuckle perfuming the air. It smelled good, but the whole time, Cam was wondering what Saira wanted to tell him. As much as he might have wished for it, they weren't out here on a romantic stroll.

A moment later, Saira spoke. "I'm barely a Glory anymore, and Rainen was livid over what I've done."

"What did he say?" Cam asked, genuinely curious. He never had a good sense of Saira's relationship with the Wilde Sage. It didn't seem like it was what he'd have expected for a teacher and a student.

"He ranted and railed, but in the end, there's not much he can do about it," Saira said. "He owes much to my mother, and if he fails to see me safe..." She smiled humorlessly. "Let's just say that even a Wilde Sage should tread carefully around the Sages of Sinane."

It was good to know that Saira didn't have to rely on Master Winder, but it still left a larger question unanswered. "So, what does this have to do with Light Squad?"

"Possibly everything," Saira said. "I'll need Shivein to form a Plasminia Tang, but we also have to find a way for him to create one, too. And since Rainen didn't leave us with a core, we have a dilemma. It's why I wanted to talk to you tonight," Saira continued. "I wanted to know your thoughts on your future."

Cam scowled. Not getting to keep the core that he and Saira had lanced still burned him, but Master Winder had been adamant that it would go with Sidewinder. As for the future... what did Cam think about it? The question was vast and terrifying, the answers changing day-by-day. He wanted to work hard, Advance, become the best student at the academy. Save those who needed saving and protect those who needed protecting. What else was there? He said as much.

Saira nodded. "I want much the same," she said. "But the question is how do we achieve it? As far as I can tell, it centers on lancing boils and destroying any rakshasas that refuse to set aside their evil ways."

"Isn't that the same as what Master Winder wants to do?" Cam asked.

"It is," Saira allowed. "But the difference is that Rainen's plans too often rely on using those who are young and only starting out on their Way into Divinity like tinder. He burns through them when they are worth so much more. *We're* worth so much more, and I include myself and Shivein since we'll both be Adepts again."

Cam shifted uncomfortably. That wasn't how he saw Master Winder. The Wilde Sage made mistakes—plenty of them—but Cam never thought he saw young Ephemeral Masters as tools to be used. In fact, Master Winder had gone out of his way to demonstrate in both words and deeds how he *didn't* view young Masters like that. If anything, he seemed to treasure them.

"I'm not sure what to say," Cam said. "Where does that leave you then? Where does that leave us?"

Saira didn't respond at once, clearly picking through on what to say. "I'm thinking about leaving Rainen's service, and I want you to come with me. But not now. Not yet. Not until you've Advanced to an Adept's Awareness."

Cam nearly halted. Leave Master Winder's service? It felt like a betrayal, leaving the service of someone who had done so much for him. "What about the rest of the squad? Shivein?"

"It depends. Jade, Avia, and Card have their own sponsors. For them, it isn't a simple matter of leaving the academy, not like it is for you, me, and Pan."

"And Weld?" He hadn't missed his exclusion.

"We'll see about him," she evaded, which was answer enough.

"Where will we go?"

"I haven't decided," Saira said, coming to a halt. They'd circled back to the area near her quarters. "I want you at Glory or even Crown as quickly as possible, and the way they do things in the Ephemeral

Academy is too slow. The traditional way is safe, but harder work and a little more risk allows for quicker Advancement for those who already know the answers to the questions of Awareness."

"Isn't that what Winder wants?"

Saira shook her head in negation. "Rainen wants you to fight boils, with Advancing as a mere side effect. I want you to seek out areas rich in Ephemera. Ponds thick with it, fields of flowers, natural Winds, un-claimed boils... any place where Ephemera collects. It can be a more dangerous method than what's taught at the academy, but it's also much faster."

"Is that how you learned in Sinane?"

"It is," Saira said. "And I think it is how you should learn as well. You have so much talent you haven't even yet touched. You could become someone of note. But not if you die battling rakshasas you have no business fighting."

Cam didn't reply at once. "Can I think about it?"

"Of course."

A young couple strode past them just then, both of them looking their way in curiosity. Cam watched them leave, smiling faintly as a notion crossed his mind. "And you're not worried about the two of us out alone like this? Your reputation and all."

Saira chuckled. "You think it might set too many tongues to wagging?"

"Set too many tongues to wagging," Cam mimicked. "Now you're talking like me."

"It must be your bad influence," Saira said, still smiling when they arrived back at her quarters. "I'll see you tomorrow."

Cam wished her farewell before meandering back toward his dorm, considering his options. A slow, steady Advance at the academy or a more dangerous but quicker approach? And the latter had the benefit of traveling with Saira. She could guide him through that which she'd already accomplished.

Then there was the rest of Light Squad. What would they choose? Would they want slow but safe or quick and dangerous? For most of them, he figured it would be the latter. He hoped so, especially for Pan since Cam couldn't see himself ever being separated from his closest friend. Not for anything.

Cam halted then, gazing at the stars while still considering the situation, growing lost in heaven's majesty. For a moment, he felt himself rise to join something vast and majestic.

Creation occasionally requires destruction.

He wondered what it was he might have to destroy in order to create.

THE END

A FINAL NOTE

Thank you for taking this journey with me. Without folks taking an interest in what I write, I would have no chance to do what I'm doing. I am humbled and gratified beyond measure that there are so many of you who are willing to give my words and worlds a chance.

I'd also be grateful if you decided to add a review for the book. Those social proofs are pretty much the lifeblood of an author. In addition, if you're really feeling ambitious, please consider **signing up for my newsletter**. It includes all of latest news, and while there's usually not a lot to tell, hey, at least you'll be up to date with what I'm doing.

In addition, I also have a Patreon account. If you subscribe, you'll receive an early look at whatever work I have in progress as it's happening. You get to let me know what's working and not working and potentially have a voice in the final outcome. It won't matter if it's the sequel to *Blood of a Novice* or the next book in *Instrument of Omens* or something completely different. Whatever the work, you'll get to see it first.

Davis

GLOSSARY

Alset: A Divine who achieved her Awareness through deep thinking and study.

Avia Koravail: An Awakened orca, who is the adopted daughter of Sage- Duke Kelse Vail of Saban.

Barth Lord: Young man from Traverse. He is a friend Pivot Stump.

Borile Defent: The Silver Sage of Weeping. Presumed to have been killed by Rainen Winder.

Braver Highway: Leads from the duchy capital of Charn along Bastion Lake and from there, down to the duchy capital of Codent.

Brewery Highway: A north-south road that runs from south of Traverse, curls south of the Diamond Mountains, and ends at Coal Pass.

Cam Folde: A Plasminian from the town of Traverse.

Card Wolver: A young nobleman from the duchy of Chalk. He comes from a long line of accomplished Ephemeral Masters.

Chandra: One of the only two emperors the continent of Golden has ever had. He is the great-grandson to the other emperor, Guptash.

Charity Kazar: A young noblewoman who is the daughter of Sage-Duke Ahktav Kazar of Maviro.

Coal Pass: Cuts through the southwestern Diamond Mountains and leads to Vivid Pass.

Corona: The Sage of the Fiery Sun. She was once an instructor to Shivein.

Cougrail: The Sage of the Bloody Claw. Allied to Nailing at Surelend.

Dander: Town-village where Cam and Pan originally Advance their Tangs as Novices. Later on it is the sight of a large battle where Cam Advances to Acolyte.

Darik Fold: Cam's brother. He's following in their father's footsteps at drunkenness.

Einton: A Divine who achieved his Awareness through deep thinking and study.

Ephemera: Mystical and mysterious particle that permeates all aspects of Creation.

Ephemeral Academy, the: The finest school in the continent of Golden on the instruction of Ephemera.

Ephemeral Master: General term for those on the Way into Divinity.
Eveangel Grey: A Glory and an instructor at the Ephemeral Academy. She teaches Synapsia.

Farmer Sigmon: Kind-hearted farmer in Traverse.
Fetch Devile: Plasminian from a wealthy family in M
oviro. Cam heals himself based on the instructions in Fetch's autobi-

ography.

Gob and Nona Felt: Husband and wife in Dander.

Golden: A continent in the world of Salvation. It is where the Nine Duchies are located.

Gordeon the Crown: A historical figure. He was a Crown who was killed shortly after Advancing to Sage.

Gorn Higin: A short, stocky nobleman from Valkin, a place near the city of Chalk.

Great Rakshasas, the: The first rakshasas. Their Stage of Awareness is presumed to be Divine
- **Coruscant**
- **Simmer**
- **Shimala:** Also called The Merciless Deceiver, Mother of Lies, and Corruptor of Innocence. She is seen as an old crone and might be the greatest of the rakshasas.

Guptash: One of the only two emperors the continent of Golden has ever had. He is the great-grandfather to the other emperor, Chandra.

Haunt: The color of an Ephemeral Master's sclerae. It denotes their Stage of Awareness.

Honor: An Awakened squirrel who have Cam a tremendous gift.

Ingold Brest: A young woman from Traverse. She is a friend to Maria Benefield.

Jade Mare: A noblewoman and daughter of a fallen house from the duchy of Bastion.

Jordil Oil: A Novice from the town of Traverse. Married to Lilia Oil and childhood friend of Cam Folde.

Kahreen Sala: A young noblewoman from an exceptionally wealthy family in the duchy of Bastion.

Light Squad: It is the squad in the Ephemeral Academy in which the members are sponsored by someone other than a Sage-Duke. Also known as Squad Screwup.

Lilia Oil née Fair: A Novice from the town of Traverse. Married to Jordil Oil and childhood friend of Cam Folde.

Lord Font Queriam: A Crown and currently the current Dean of the Ephemeral Academy.

Maria Benefield: A beautiful young woman in Traverse with a heart of coal. Her family is wealthy.

Marigold Spenser: Old midwife and healer in Traverse.

Marta Lightwell: The daughter of Surelend's mayor. Master Bennett: An Adept and teacher of Novices. Master Carlson: The town farrier of Traverse.

Master Moltin: An Adept and general teacher in Traverse.

Mayor Amale Lightwell: The mayor of Surelend.
Mayor Gard Singer: The mayor of Dander.

Mayor Long Stump: The mayor of Traverse.

Merit Thens: A young nobleman and the son of Sage-Duchess Marsula Thens of Santh.

Nageena: The Sage of Whispering Scales. Allied to Nailing at Surelend.

Nailing: The Sage of Warring Thunder.

Orthosial Shivein: A Glory and Awakened turtle. Once a rakshasa and saved by Sage-Duke Kelse Vail. He is now an instructor at the Ephemeral Academy. He teaches Kinesthia.

Pan Shun: An Awakened panda from the Diamond Mountains. He is the focus of a centuries-long prophecy.

Pathway to Grace: Strange locations or emanations where entire worlds can be found an Ephemeral Master can quickly gain Ephemera and Advance.

Perit Line: A Crown and commander or Sidewinder Company.

Pharis Fold: Cam's sister, and the oldest of the siblings. Widowed to a husband named Jared.

Pivot Stump: The son of Traverse's mayor. He is engaged to Suse Marline.
Placido Werm: A Glory and an instructor at the Ephemeral Academy. He teaches Spirairia.

Prahlass: A historical saint who prayed so devoutly that he achieved an Awareness beyond Sage, becoming a Divine.

Purien Fold: Cam's father. He's known as Traverse's town drunk.

Rainen Winder: A Sage without attachment to a city. He is the sponsor of Light Squad. He is also known as the Wilde Sage.

Regim Baid: An assistant to the Mayor Gard Singer of Dander.
Rizfam: The flute master who taught Pan.

Sage-Dukes, the: There are nine of them and they rule the nine great cities on Golden.
- **Sage-Duke Ahktav Kazar:** Duke of Maviro.
- **Sage-Duke Dorieus Arta:** The Duke of Chalk.
- **Sage-Duchess Josie Salin:** Duchess of Bastion.
- **Sage-Duchess Karmin Berjeak:** Duchess of Corona.
- **Sage-Duke Kelse Vail:** The Duke of Saban.
- **Sage-Duke Knarl Pune:** The Duke of Codent.
- **Sage-Duchess Marsula Thens:** The Duchess of Santh.
- **Sage-Duchess Shah Pharin:** The Duchess of Twine.
- **Sage-Duke Zin Shun:** Duke of Charn.

Saira Maharani: Once a Crown but regressed in Awareness. From the nation of Sinane. Also an instructor at the Ephemeral Academy. She teaches Kinesthia.

Salvation: The world of *The Eternal Ephemera*.

Sholl Singer: An Adept and member of Sidewinder Company.

Sidewinder Company: A powerful unit of Ephemeral Masters who are under the control of Rainen Winder. They range in Awareness from Novice to Crown.

Stages of Awareness: The Awareness of the Stage is seen in the sclera, and this is also called a person's Haunt.
- **Neophyte:** Not really considered a Stage, and sclerae are white.
- **Novice:** First Stage and sclerae are red.
- **Acolyte:** Second Stage and sclerae are orange.
- **Adept:** Third Stage and sclerae are yellow.
- **Glory:** Fourth Stage and sclerae are blue.
- **Crown:** Fifth Stage and sclerae are indigo.
- **Sage:** Sixth Stage and sclerae are violet.
- **Divine:** Seventh Stage and sclerae are diamond.

Surelend: Village nearly the size of Traverse southeast of Corona, and it is where Light Squad destroy their first boil.

Suse Marline: A young woman from Traverse. She is engaged to Pivot Stump, the mayor's son. She is a friend to Maria Benefield.

Tern Shorn: A young boy from Traverse. He died while diving a Pathway to Grace.

Tormick Echo: A young man from Traverse who is reputed to have a way with women.

Victory Arta: A young nobleman and the son of Sage-Duke Dorieus Arta of Chalk.

Vivid Pass: Final north-south pass that eventually ends at the small city of Game along the Charn River.

Warren: Village on the southern coast of Lake Nexus where Light Squad disembarked while journeying to Surelend in *Blood of a Novice.*

Way into Divinity: General term for those who wish to Advance their Awareness of Ephemera.

Weld Plain: A young Ephemeral Master, who thinks very highly of him- self.

ABOUT THE AUTHOR

Davis Ashura is a bestselling author, a full-time practicing physician, and a one-time woodworker. His motto has generally been, 'Try it. The worst you can do is fail.' It usually works out—except when jumping out of airplanes. Davis is best known for his *Castes and the OutCastes* trilogy, which is part of the Anchored Worlds universe, a set of linked epic fantasy series.

His books are hopeful in nature. He likes to write about heroes who see themselves as servants first. Heroes who fall in love and become partners and make time for family, friendship, and fellowship. His characters are folk with whom it would be fun to have drinks and dinner, but who could also handle any trouble that might crop up.

Davis is married and shares a house with his wonderful wife who somehow overlooked his eccentricities and married him anyway. Living with them are their two sons, both of whom have at various times helped turn Davis' once lustrous, raven-black hair prematurely white. And of course, there are the obligatory strange, stray cats (all authors have cats—it's required by the union). They are fluffy and black with ter- ribly bad breath. Additionally, there is the rescue dog—gnarly-toothed, beady-eyed, and utterly sweet.

Visit him at **www.DavisAshura.com** and sign up for his newsletter to learn the latest information on his books or simply follow him on Facebook, Instagram, or Twitter.